PRAISE FOR *BLOODWINTER*

"Once again, Tom Deitz has proven himself a master of the fantasy genre. He has created a detailed, realistic world, characters who are both engaging and believable, and a compelling, fast-moving story that draws the reader in from the first page. I hope that the author will continue to explore this fascinating new world and its inhabitants in future books."
—John Maddox Roberts

"Deitz has always been a superb fantasist, but he's outdone himself in this richly developed, character-driven story!"
—Josepha Sherman

BLOODWINTER

A TALE OF ERON

TOM DEITZ

BANTAM BOOKS
NEW YORK TORONTO LONDON SYDNEY AUCKLAND

BLOODWINTER

A Bantam Spectra Book / April 1999

Library of Congress Cataloging-in-Publication Data

Deitz, Tom.
Bloodwinter : a tale of Eron / by Tom Deitz.
p.   cm. — (A Bantam spectra book)
ISBN 0-553-37863-5
I. Title.
PS3554.E425B58   1999
813'.54—dc21   98-39999
CIP

Published simultaneously in the United States and Canada

PRINTED IN THE UNITED STATES OF AMERICA

FFG   10   9   8   7   6   5   4   3   2   1

for
Tom and Linda Jean:
you *can* go home again

ACKNOWLEDGMENTS

Stephen Andersen

Juliet Combes

Tom Dupree

Anne Groell

Kate Hengerer

Linda Jean Jeffery

Tom Jeffery

Buck Marchinton

Deena McKinney

Howard Morhaim

Lindsay Sagnette

Anita Wilson

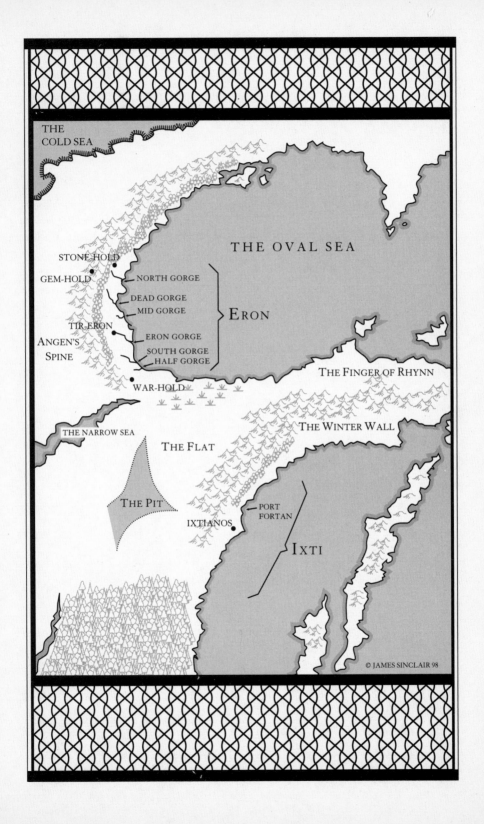

PRELUDE: A SCENT OF BURNING

(ERON: APPROACHING GOLD STAR GAP – DEEP WINTER – DAY LXXXVIII)

~~~~~~~~~~~~~~~~

Spring, Amalian concluded, had arrived not an instant too early.

It had snowed as late as yester morn: thick, heavy flakes that had come wafting out of the northwest, as though the mountains in Angen's Spine were airing out their linens for the Light. Which, she supposed, made her and the trek she mastered among the larger, more recalcitrant motes of accumulated detritus. If The Eight dwelt in those gloomy peaks behind her, which she doubted—or if the rocks themselves were subtly alive, which some of Common Clan averred—they'd have to rise early indeed to loathe the cold season as much as she.

Oh, it had been beautiful enough in Stone-Hold-Winter, where the Fateing had sent her last Dark Half. The head-high drifts had made a fabulous backdrop for the statuary in the forecourt: warriors this rotation, carved in ruddy catlinite that contrasted nicely with the dark green hollies. Still, the cliffs and crags so prevalent thereabouts were harsh, naked rock that had as its primary virtue its many grades and colors, most of which were good for carving—which Amalian had spent all winter doing, and which was another thing she wouldn't miss with the turning of the year.

At least she hadn't been cold. Some of the winter holds were absolutely frigid, in spite of the steam-springs with which they were heated. Besides, Gory had been posted with her, and he was furry enough to keep several people warm—even through those wild solstice storms when three strong sets of walls and doors between living quarters and the cold without failed to stave off winter's fingers.

But she'd missed *people*, curse it! People in all their variety—*any* people beyond the same double-hundred-odd she'd seen day in and day out at the hold. And over half of those were her kin, whom she saw most of the year anyway.

Which was why, when Stone-Hold's weather-witch predicted an early spring and the Ekkon River broke through its ice a whole eight-day sooner than expected, she'd determined to take the risk.

So far it had been worth it, with far more color in the first-blooms than usual. Why, the gold stars that named this place almost glowed, and the ferns and bracken were particularly bright and frothy in the hollows among the pines. And the skies! Clear for days (yester morn notwithstanding) and so blue she wanted to reach up and chip away a chunk to carve into something precious.

Something for the twins, perhaps. Carmil and Egin: girl and boy. Thirteen now, and poised on the chisel blade between the children they'd been last Sundeath, when the journey north had begun, and the adults they were fast becoming. Both were a hand taller than when they'd left the lowlands, and Carmil had breasts and a woman's bleeding. Egin's voice was shifting so that his singing, which had been so sweet, was now rather more like croaking. And Gory, who'd seen him daily in the baths, had confided that their little boy now had hair in all men's places—matching that on his head, which was the same red-lit black as his sire's. Carmil's mirrored Amalian's own rare tawny gold.

She wondered where they were now. Riding ahead with Gory, perhaps? Or back swapping tales with the braver folk from Oak, who'd swelled their ranks that morning? She envied them—the children their freedom, the Oak folk their proximity to the northmost of the gorges where the bulk of clan, craft, and kin spent Eron's too-brief summers. It was to that cleft in the coastal plateau that Amalian led the trek now, through melting drifts of knee-deep snow. If luck rode with them, some of them would sleep in their own beds tonight, which would be change enough from the crowded chaos of the way stations that marked the nights between holds, halls, and gorges.

Sighing, she reached back to flip up her cloak's fur-lined hood. A breeze had come whipping out of the gap ahead, and she wondered if the twinge troubling her knees as she resettled them was merely token of a winter's inaction or the first insidious gnawings of old age.

Not the latter, she prayed. She wasn't far past thirty, and the sixty more years she expected to attain would be no great joy if her joints chose to ache through most of them.

And then the wind shifted, riding in from the south, bringing with it a hint of warmth that stirred her heart out of all proportion to its intensity.

But it brought other things as well: the scent of death, and, so faint as to be barely discernible, the scent of burning.

. . .

"I smell death," Amalian informed her husband, reining back the team: golds from Arsten, which had been part of her wedding dower from Gory's clan, who bred them.

Gory slapped his fractious gray gelding and nodded, his breath making blizzards in the air, riming the beard that framed his narrow, blue-eyed face. His cloak twitched in the wind. "Sheep," he grunted, as though that explained everything.

Amalian raised a brow. Gory was a fine man and an excellent mate—and said about ten words an eighth, as though he'd been born with a fixed allotment and treasured them like his clan treasured wagon-cattle.

"Which I presume belong to somebody," Amalian sighed, thinking that perhaps she might get a better account from the spindly pines that flanked the road to the left, or the rough-shelved slate cliffs slanting up to the right.

Gory grimaced. "Haven't been dead long, and there's only two. Margil's spent some time with the sheep folk and says the clan clips on their ears mark them as belonging to a small sept-hall on the south rim of North Gorge."

"A good day's ride from here."

Gory nodded.

"Wolves, then? Or birkits? Or—" She refused to name the other, because there was supposed to *be* no other. Wisdom said it was too cold for geens—man-sized lizard-things that walked on their hind legs—north of South Gorge. But Amalian wondered. Wisdom also said they were stupid as snakes, and she *knew* that was a lie.

Gory shrugged. "Just dead. A little rotten, no sign of violence."

"How long?"

Another shrug. "Thawed maybe two days. Beyond that, the only way of knowing is if we had a female, to check the unborn. They tend to conceive close to the same time."

"Lucky for us—if we had one," Amalian snorted. "Still, livestock escapes. And escaped livestock often dies."

"Aye," was Gory's sole reply.

By midday they'd crested Gold Star Gap and were on the last long winding slope before the road poured them out on the plains southeast below them: a patchwork of waving sheep grass and lingering snow, framed by the tips of the flanking pines. By midafternoon North Gorge should be in sight. By sunfall, they should be well on their way to Tir-Mil at the bottom.

But somehow she was uneasy. Not one person in the hundred had offered anything useful about the dead sheep, and they'd seen fifteen now. Speculation over them had been curtailed when they'd found the dead man.

It had been Gory (again) who'd discovered him—poor Gory, whose draw it had been to lead the day's outriders. The man had been dead at least eight days, and scavengers had been at him, so that it was hard to tell much save that he'd sheltered at Sharp Stone Station to bathe in the waters there and succumbed—naked—on the deep pool's stony marge. Heart freeze was possible. Heat could do that, and it was a *very* hot spring (and one Amalian had looked forward to sampling before their final approach). As best they could tell, the man had been in his early twenties. And, by the clothing flung about and ravaged—likely by the same beasts that had gnawed away his insides— he'd come from a prosperous clan. Beyond that, he'd been unremarkable. Black-haired, lightly bearded, fairly hairy, fit, and of the middle height and slim build typical of the Eronese. His clan tattoo, which would have revealed much, had been devoured along with most of his shoulder. Or scratched away, for the bulk of the man's intact skin was covered with long, deep furrows. He'd hacked off his hair, too, and not neatly, though men often did that near the end of the Dark.

It was another mystery. Amalian had ordered his body wrapped in oiled canvas and stored in the rearmost wagon. Burning would come later, when they'd determined his identity.

Four sun-hands later, they'd found a dozen more sheep, dead exactly as the others, but clipped to a different clan. And while that disturbed Amalian, it didn't truly concern her. By nightfall they'd be in Tir-Mil, where'd there'd be people whose duty it was to attend such things. She was merely the messenger.

What *did* disturb her was the fact that they could *see* the gorge now: a dark slash on the horizon, with the perpetual veil of steam rising out of it. But that steam was laced with darker vapors, which could only be the smoke of copious burning.

She smelled it, too, as she had that morning. But now it held a sharp, sweet tang she didn't like. If she didn't know better—if such things hadn't been rendered impossible by unshakable oaths between clan and craft— she'd have sworn war ravaged the gorge.

But that was absurd.

Besides, the road was flattening, the pines falling away to either side, and there was more waving grass ahead than melting snow, and *that* made her heart sing and fly.

The children sang as well—when they deigned to ride beside her: Carmil in her usual clear soprano, Egin in a cracky, pretentious boy-bass. It was a new song, too, one someone at Oak had contrived over the Deep, and seemed to involve a drunken man trying to sleep with women who were not always women. So much for her children's innocence. Egin fairly glowed. She wondered if that spotty glitter along his jaw was the first outpost of stubble.

Three hands later, they crested a rise and saw the guard station sprawling across the road ahead, maybe a shot from the gorge's northeast rim. Like most such structures built in High King Kryss's time, it was utterly unadorned and of the prescribed configuration: a single square tower five levels high, with smooth, trapezoidal sides and a flat roof. Each side fronted a square, walled courtyard marked by a two-story gatehouse, and the whole complex was enclosed by a lower wall to form a square within a cross within a square when viewed from above. The walls were thick, the stonework set with such impeccable skill as to show only hair-fine joins, so that neither foe nor winter could claim a hold. With shots of open country around, the former was unlikely; the latter a foregone conclusion.

Usually, though, such places were alive with people going about their tasks like ants upon a hill. And while Amalian knew that she'd come upon them days before expected, that offered no explanation for the air of decrepitude that informed the place.

And then the wind brought smoke from the gorge, which set her choking and folding her hood across her nose, while Carmil made disgusted faces and Egin scowled.

Gory came flying back with the other two outriders close behind, all wide-eyed and harried-looking. "Come!" Gory called tersely. "Ride with me. Only . . . come."

Amalian hesitated, then tossed the reins to Egin as the boy switched deftly from saddle to wagon seat. She mounted nigh as easily, flinging a leg across Skipstone's back with relaxed familiarity. An instant later they were galloping.

"I could explain," Gory muttered. "It'd be simpler if the guard did."

Amalian started to remind him that there was a time for silence and a time for speech, and then she *saw* the guard.

It was a woman, no older than herself and possibly younger. She wasn't in the tower, nor even atop the gatehouse that barred entrance to the forecourt; rather, she slumped like a door page just inside the gatehouse's portcullised entry arch, as though her duty no longer mattered.

She was dressed appropriately, in North Gorge heraldry—cloak of black and deep green slashed with silver, over the blood red tunic of War-Hold—but the cloak was dark with stains that mirrored the shadows beneath what should've been remarkably pretty gray eyes. A naked sword with War-Hold's plain barred hilt rested across her mail-clad thighs, but Amalian doubted she had the strength to use it—not that she would ever have had much need. Eron, after all, was civilized.

Wordlessly, Amalian dismounted and strode to within the armspan politeness proscribed. "Greetings," she said formally. "I am Amalian of Clan Eemon of Stonecraft, out of Stone-Hold-Winter. I hope the Dark has favored you and that the Light favors you twice and thrice again."

The guardswoman stared at her unblinking, as though she barely heard. *Sickness,* Amalian thought—*or bone-tired weariness*. Which, now that she looked, seemed more likely.

"Greetings . . . Amalian, or whatever you said," the woman mumbled in a raspy whisper. "If you seek Tir-Mil, you seek that which will please you little to find. Which some of you, by law of its council, are forbidden to enter."

Amalian's brow furrowed in a mix of anger and concern. She folded her arms across her breast, letting her cloak fall free to frame what could be, when she chose, an impressive figure. "It would be best if you spoke plainly."

"Plainly, then," the guardswoman gritted. "Plague."

Amalian flinched back a step. A people who lived so close together so much of the year must fear such things indeed. "Plague," she echoed numbly.

The woman nodded. "A new plague, the cure for which no one can discover. It arrived from the south, with the last trek before the Deep. Beyond that, we know little for certain. The winter holds—we pray—have been spared. But communication has all but collapsed. I have heard nothing from Tir-Mil for four days—and yet I dare not return."

Amalian felt heartsick, not only for her dashed hopes—though surely there'd be some way to risk the gorge—but also for the despair on this woman's face, which she knew was reflected a thousandfold elsewhere.

To her surprise, Gory spoke. "We found a dead man—"

"It begins as an itch in the ears, nose, and privates," the guard broke in tonelessly, "more often in men than women. The itch grows worse, and no potion or balm can cure it. In time it grows strong enough to drive men mad. Often, they attack each other or carve out their own ears and noses— and other things. I've heard more than one say that their brains were being eaten from within."

"And . . . women?" Amalian breathed.

The guard wouldn't meet her stare. "It . . . attacks the female parts and womb. We bleed uncontrollably. Those with child miscarry—or worse. It's feared those who survive will conceive no more."

Amalian shuddered. "And how many *do* survive?"

The woman shrugged. "A few. We don't know why, though the healers have tried everything. When I came here, it had taken one in three of the men, and maybe one in nine of the women. Mostly younger women."

Amalian's eyes narrowed. "Men—or *males?*"

"Men," the guardswoman answered. "Children are rarely afflicted. The weavers, however—"

Amalian looked troubled. "Weavers . . ."

Gory scowled at her. "What are you thinking?"

Amalian shook her head uncertainly. "That there might be a connection. Weavers to wool to sheep to those dead sheep we saw."

Gory stroked his chin. "And sheep are driven north with the season, so that the cold may thicken their coats."

"And this plague began in the south."

The guard plucked at her cloak, which, Amalian noted, was thrice-woven sylk, not the wool she'd have expected. "That much we do know, but little more. No one is allowed to wear wool—and *that* was only decided four days ago. Since then, I've had neither word nor relief."

Amalian scowled. "So what you are telling us is that we advance at our own risk. Surely you know some of us will dare the gorge. Many have family there."

The guard didn't move. "The Law I am given is this: Women may enter at their peril. Men may not until the plague runs its course."

"Damn!" Amalian spat, spinning 'round to glare at Gory as though it were all his fault. His face, too, was hard and grim. Then again, he had kin in Tir-Mil; she didn't.

"You lead the trek," he said simply. "You don't lead the people. You've brought them where they need to go and that's sufficient. What they do as concerns this plague is their decision."

The glare softened not a whit. "And you, husband?"

"I value my life. And I'd prefer that my children have a father."

"Well," Amalian sighed, "I'll alert the trek."

Egin loved a mystery. Close behind that, he had what his mother had always called a reckless fascination with danger. It was therefore inevitable that he'd catch wind of this plague and the fact that entire halls were being systematically closed up and torched down in North Gorge, not to mention the people who dwelt in them—once they'd died. And that, he decided, embraced both elements. There was the puzzle of what had brought this contagion, how it was spread, why some survived once it had run its course, and the greater enigma of why it singled out men. And there was the thrill of the forbidden.

The guard had said men were banned, period (as though she'd strength to enforce such a thing alone), and that women went of their peril.

Nothing, precisely, had been said about boys. And while he wasn't exactly a boy anymore—not in height, hairiness, or (as he'd happily discovered one cold winter night back in Stone) the ability (in theory) to beget children— still, he was not so far along that rather-too-responsible road that anyone actually expected to find him there. Which meant he'd get away with as much as he could for as long as he could, and damned be the consequences.

So it was that shortly after first-moon, he left his bedroll beneath his parents' caravan and ambled off in the direction of the livestock picket, officially to add his excreta to what was already stinking there. Happily, that stench had resulted in the packhorses and wagon-cattle being billeted downwind—which was to say between the camp, with its circled wagons and toobright fires, and the gorge. And more happily, the fact that they were first trek down this season meant that the grass hereabouts hadn't been grazed to stubble; indeed, was waist high on him and afforded excellent cover. Add a dull tan cloak and hair still spiky from sleep, and one had a recipe for stealth.

Except that his sister seemed to have heard him (he could tell it was her by the whistle in her breath when she panted) and tagged along. And since he knew from experience that she *would* demand to accompany him and would raise an Eight's-awful cry if denied, he held his tongue when that tawny-topped shape burst through the grass beside him, clad in riding leathers, and with a face that far too closely mirrored his mother's when anger sat upon her like a mountain gathering thunder.

"You're a *fool*!" Carmil hissed. "People are *dying* down there!"

He tried not to show his fear as he paused for her. "I'm only going to the edge—no farther down than I have to in order to see—"

"What?"

"Buildings burning. People . . . dying. I dunno. Excitement! Anything besides Mother and Father and this wretched trek!"

"You're a man, Egin. Men are forbidden."

He laughed at her. "Last night you told me I was a boy. You can't have it both ways."

"Neither can you! I bleed; you squirt. That's what adults say marks the line."

"But they don't *see* those things; therefore they don't think about them; therefore they don't act on them. Besides, I say it's responsibility makes the difference, which is the same as accepting risk."

Carmil started to reply, then clearly thought better of it. "If you die, I'm not going to cry!"

"Wouldn't want you to," Egin sniffed, and strode off through the grass toward the gorge.

They took pains to avoid the trek road, which terminated in another tower, poised right on North Gorge's rim, where the river road came in from the south. It was deserted, which was both odd and frightening. But there were always more ways down than one, and it took barely another finger's scouting to locate a trail that snaked along the cliff to the floor of the gorge, a shot below.

Trouble was, it didn't give much of a view of Tir-Mil, North Gorge's only true city. It did, however, reveal the burning. What looked like boats—ships, even—had been set alight and left to float down the river that divided the fourshot-wide gash in the land. Maybe there was a better view lower down. As best Egin could tell, the trail ran among boulders, scraggly trees, and what might be a ruin, tending always west. This had the sense of a place that had once been important but fallen out of use.

"Egin, no!" Carmil warned as he made to descend. At least the pavement was still solid: plain flat stones set without mortar, but decent work all the same.

And sure enough, a wall jagged across the trail, with evidence of crenellations along its top, while a whole shattered tower clung to the cliff on the right. More interesting was the empty archway that spanned the trail— though even Egin hesitated upon entering. It was *really* dark in there.

"Egin!" Carmil snapped.

"Just through here and I'll stop," Egin retorted. And though he had actually been considering a retreat, there was no way he'd not dare the barrier now.

Steeling himself, he took a deep breath. And had not gone two steps into the blackness—not far enough for his eyes to adjust—when he tripped over something soft. He screamed. The cry cracked halfway through, in a mostunmanly fashion, yet he screamed again when his hand brushed another hand—and *not* Carmil's.

"Cold!" he yelped, even as he scrambled backward toward the arch.

Abruptly, he was up and running, grabbing Carmil on the way, and not stopping until they'd regained the rim.

"See anything?" his sister challenged when he paused there, winded from that long, mad scramble. She was barely panting.

"Dark!" Egin gasped. "And a . . . dead man."

Carmil's eyes narrowed, exactly like their mother's. "Dead of what? And how long?"

"I don't know! He was still soft. And he didn't smell."

Carmil glared at him, and most especially at his nice wool cloak. "Leave that here," she commanded. "We'll have to ask Mother what to do about it."

"I'll freeze!" Egin protested, hugging himself. But he unclasped the garment and let it fall.

"The price of disobedience," Carmil snorted. "But I'll let you off easy. You can tell Mother—or I will."

"In the morning."

A reluctant nod.

Egin rehearsed that telling all the way back to the camp. And he was still rehearsing when he crept back into his bedroll and snugged the blankets under his chin. A layer of padded fabric lay between him and the trampled sheep grass around the caravan; even so, the broken stems tickled his ear. He scratched it, then the other, which had decided to protest in sympathy. And sneezed—likely from the grass pollen that was already scenting the wind.

He awoke to find his head in agony and his ears filled with an insidious tickle. In fact, he itched pretty much everywhere—his scalp, his armpits, his groin, even inside his nose.

By midday he'd clawed himself raw and Amalian had dismissed the rest of the trek under command of her second, with one blood-chilling word.

Plague.

Egin had the plague.

By sunset, he was babbling incoherently, and they'd had to tie his hands.

Two days later, while the year's final dusting of snowflakes drifted down upon breakfast, he died.

Nor was he the last.

Prologue: Violation

(Eron: Tir-Eron – High Summer – Day XXI)

~~~~~~~~~~

Strynn squinted at the sun, then at the hiltless dagger in her hand, and scowled. It might do; then again, it might not. She shifted the blade experimentally—as long as her forearm, elegantly tapered as a willow leaf, and folded the requisite three-hundred-and-sixty times, so that the grain flowed like sylk and gleamed like moonlit fire: delicate as mist, yet so strong and flexible it would never dull or lose its temper. It all but glowed in the afternoon glare, sunlight waking glittering embers where iron and certain alloys known but to bladesmiths merged and danced and mingled.

But was it good enough?

She'd come to the water garden behind Smith-Hold-Main to find out—and for two related reasons.

The first was the light. What might look smooth as ice by candlelight could look pocked as an old man's face by harsher midday rays, and different again by mornlight, glowlight, or moonlight. This work must be perfect in all of them.

The second reason was that she couldn't focus her attention amid chaos, and chaos reigned in the hold behind her, where masters of the various smithcrafts (most of them born to that calling) labored to pass on their skills to the next generation. Never mind the students from other clans and crafts who were obliged to spend a quarter at each hold in turn, so as to acquire a minimal working knowledge of, for instance, forging, if only the making of nails. Trouble was, those people talked too much—even her *peers* talked too much—which was why she was seeking solitude and silence.

"Honing is partly a function of sound," Tyrill, the ancient crone of a Craft-Chief, had confided. Sometimes you could tell something was perfectly sharp by the sound it made when you flipped it with a fingernail. Strynn tapped the blade experimentally, smiling at the ensuing "ping."

Sunlight, silence, and water. Things best had here, in the complex of glades, gardens, and retreats between Smith-Hold's north arcade and the face of Eron Gorge, where two hundred years of plantwrights had twined nature and artifice into a series of environments each utterly unique, yet complementary. A test of another kind—for them.

It was time for *her* test to begin.

A pause for a yawn, and she rose from the sandstone bench against which she'd been lounging and threaded between an overgrown hedge and a carefully placed sheep-sized boulder to where a trained stream no more than a foot wide swept into a shallow pool rimmed with irregular white stones. She knelt where the water entered and set the blade aside long enough to reach up and pluck a single long black hair from her head. That accomplished, she retrieved the dagger, set it point down in the water facing upstream, then released the strand so that the current would carry it toward one gleaming edge. If a blade cut hair in running water with no other force behind it, that was indeed a blade. And since this one was intended as a gift to her bond-sister and best friend, Merryn san Argen-a, she wanted it to be absolutely perfect—a blade such as one heard of only in legends.

Closer . . . closer . . .

The hair drifted sideways, away from the edge. She shifted the dagger to meet it.

Closer . . .

Now!

The hair met the edge at an oblique angle, stopped for the barest instant, then moved on—in two pieces.

Strynn laughed and withdrew the weapon, drying it first on the hem of her robe, then on special cloths made for that purpose. It gleamed in the sun. Bright as the sun, in fact, for at this angle all grain vanished, replaced with the mirror sheen that reflected her face perfectly.

She frowned at that, as she locked the dagger away in the box she'd made for it.

She hated mirrors.

Not of themselves, of course. Glass, silver, and well-wrought wood, iron, or bronze were innocuous enough. Except when they reminded her of the curse most of her friends—her *female* friends, she amended—would've given a winter's crafting to endure.

Beauty.

Oh, it was fine enough, in theory. She was Eronese, after all, and her countrymen prized beauty—*any* kind—above all things. But it was different to value a thing because it was well designed, lovingly made, and elegantly finished, than to prize a person simply because the chance meeting of a man's seed and a woman's had contrived a certain set of proportions.

She wasn't even *that* remarkable. She was no taller than average—exactly as tall as Merryn, in fact. Nor was she notably slim or fat, but few of her countrymen were, save the aged and infirm, when inaction might render them a trifle stout. She had black hair, but so did nine in ten of the clans and every single person in her adopted craft. And she had dark blue eyes beneath arching black brows, but most women could claim the same. Smooth skin, too, she had, and full rosy lips and an elegantly arching nose, and cheekbones that neither hid nor announced themselves.

Yet somehow the combination "achieved some finer synthesis" (to use her mother's phrase), so that she'd found herself, at the summer fair two years back, proclaimed the most beautiful woman of her time.

Which had become a curse, because she'd somehow managed to shift from a slightly gawky girl everyone liked to a symbol of unreachable desire. Which utterly discounted her smithwork (which was what *really* mattered, especially as she hadn't been born to that craft) and scholarship (which wasn't far behind), both of which had once been universally lauded.

Had it only been last autumn when she found herself catching more compliments on her smile than on the swords she'd spent whole eighths beating and folding? And discovered to her dismay that young men seemed more interested in what lay between her legs than within her skull?

And that was another curse: that she'd been born in these particular times. It had been eighteen years since the plague. Eighteen years since one in six of her countrymen had died, and three men to one woman at that. It had played havoc with clan and craft alike, upsetting balances that had always been precarious if the winter holds were to be properly staffed. The upshot was that while no one had forced her mother either to wed or reproduce, every woman of Strynn's generation was under intense pressure indeed to bear at least three children, and men competed for brides like rabid wolves. Why, even the few conceived by the unwed—the *unfathered*, as they were called—were now granted a place within their birth-clan, in a desperate push to bolster Eron's population before Ixti realized how vulnerable her northern rival truly was.

She, Strynn san Ferr, the most beautiful woman of her time, was therefore a prize indeed. And while it would be her choice whom she wed, it seemed unlikely that she'd have much say as to when some wedding occurred, other than fairly soon.

"Oh Eight!" she muttered. Here came one of the principal claimants now, thrusting through the far gate which led down to Clan Argen's gaming fields, and striding for the near one, a mere three spans away.

She prayed he wouldn't see her—and since her summer robe was the same green as the surrounding grass, and her hair dark as the evergreen shadows behind her, that was a reasonable aspiration. If she looked down so that her hair veiled her face, drew her hands into her sleeves, and didn't move, perhaps Eddyn would miss her entirely.

He *seemed* fairly intent—and not happy, to judge by the scowl that showed even through an unruly fall of sweat-sodden hair worn too long for the season. And the way he was walking: long, hard steps that all but set the ground to shaking, with his hands curled into fists around his ball-sticks as though he would strangle them . . . And no sign of either shirt or shoes, which was a breach of decorum— Well, it was plain to see that Eddyn syn Argen-yr was furious.

Probably at losing a game of orney, to judge by the sticks and the short, baggy breeches he wore above muscular legs. Eddyn didn't like to lose, and for that reason tended to seek the company of those similarly inclined—in sports, arms, and craft alike. Even when he did yield to defeat, there was always an excuse; often (Strynn conceded) a good one. He disliked weakness in others, too, and pushed himself harder in compensation, as though to set a standard.

Certainly the body revealed as he drew near was pleasant to look upon, with its hard, spare muscles, sharp definition, and the smooth waxed skin that had been enforced since the plague, lest body hair harbor the tiny mites that infested wool and hair alike, and whose larvae (it had finally been determined) thrived on mucus membranes and earwax.

Still, by the look on his face, she pitied anyone who got in his way.

Including herself, if he saw her. He hadn't been shy about pressing his suit of late—not that he had a chance—and certainly not after the boast she'd overheard: that she, Strynn, was saving herself for the best.

That was a laugh! Eddyn was no more the best than she was (though she *was* very good at certain things, in which she took justifiable pride). Rather, he sought her for two reasons alone: her beauty and the power of her clan. Her mind— Well, it would've been beneath him to wed someone stupid. And her craft—that might in truth be a problem. He was accounted one of the best smiths of his generation, yet even so was no more than her equal, and she doubted Eddyn could endure a mate as accomplished as he— especially one who'd been born to another craft and clan.

Poor man. It wasn't even his fault, really. He'd no more asked to be principal protégé to the daunting old Chief of Smith-Hold than Strynn had asked to be born beautiful. The best thing that could happen would be if the

Fateing posted him far away next Deep Winter, which would give her time to make up her mind about whom to marry, since she doubted her clan would grant her much more grace. A Dark at most, she suspected. Three quarters, then figurative doom.

Which realization lit an explosion of frustration, so that before she could stop herself, she slapped her hand against the pool's surround.

In the silence—and perfect acoustics—of the garden, the sound carried. Eddyn froze in mid-stride and mid-glower, spun ferociously, and looked straight at her, eyes narrowed as they sought to pierce the shadowy gloom.

For a moment she thought he would ignore her and continue on. The Eight knew she'd been avoiding him like the Cold of late, for his eyes went places they shouldn't, and his hands often twitched as though they'd like to follow, and there was nothing Strynn could imagine more repellent than Eddyn's hands upon her body.

Instead, he marched straight toward her. She looked up at him, giving him no welcome with her eyes; rather challenging with a hardening of her jaw, a lifting of her chin. If the man had any sense . . .

"Greetings, lady of the cool and the shade," he called civilly enough as he came within the requisite span for speech. "You make quite the picture there, though the blue of your eyes would shame the sky reflected beside you."

"Mine are dark, the sky is pale—or are you blind as well as rude?"

"Blinded by beauty," Eddyn chuckled, sounding a little giddy.

"I take it you lost?" Strynn replied flatly, in no mood for frivolity. She was angry with herself, for letting this casual encounter spoil what had heretofore been a fairly productive day. And now angrier still for letting that much weakness show.

Eddyn flung his ball-sticks to the ground with a flourish and flopped down beside her without asking leave, shaking the hair from his eyes. "It wouldn't hurt you," he said roughly, "to speak kindly to a defeated man."

He smelled of sweat and—faintly—of imphor wood, which he'd likely been chewing to dull the pain of injuries suffered during the game. Unfortunately, it dulled judgment as well. She'd have to watch her tongue.

"Truth isn't always kind," she replied carefully. "You could've had a bad day—they can't *all* be perfect. Or the other team could've had an especially good one. Maybe The Eight simply decided to see how one who so often claims their favor would act if that favor deserted him."

"No one will ever curse you for lack of wit," Eddyn muttered, reaching down to scoop up a handful of water, which he splashed into his face. He dumped a second over his head and a third across his bare chest, which he proceeded to rub with exaggerated relish.

Strynn refused to be distracted. There were scores of men in Tir-Eron as handsome as Eddyn. Some were even as accomplished—and better company. And if he was taller than most, what of it? Height merely meant you could see farther, that low-ceilinged rooms gave you grief—and that it took more fabric to clothe you. Only one of which was any advantage, though Eddyn seemed to think otherwise.

"No one will ever curse you for lack of vanity," Strynn retorted, impulse giving voice to hostility she'd heretofore kept restrained.

A fourth time the hand flashed down—but this time Eddyn flipped the water in her face. "Cool your fire, woman; I've done nothing to harm you."

"Only made my days miserable," Strynn snapped, wiping her brow. "Pressing your suit when you know I've no use for you save as a childhood acquaintance, which is thin steel on which to hammer. I'm no fool, man; I know what you want. Not me, but my—Eight forgive my pride when I say it—my beauty. And my connections and clan. An award, not a wife."

"You could do worse," Eddyn purred. "You have to wed soon; you've no choice. Clan and craft both must have heirs, and the King himself has ordained it: three children, regardless of sire. You can't avoid that, unless a healer says otherwise. But you can choose who begets them. And if you must choose, it makes most sense for you to choose the best."

"What makes you think that's you?"

Eddyn's eyes sparked with fury; his face took on the stormy flush it only wore when he was very angry indeed. Strynn's blood turned to ice. Now she'd done it! Had awakened the birkit in his lair. She reached for the box that held the dagger.

"Eddyn," she managed, forcing her voice to calm. "Go. Now. You're out of sorts, and so am I. And you've been chewing wood—"

It was the wrong thing and the wrong time, and one taunt—one *failure*—too many. Anger beyond anger boiled up in Eddyn—at himself or the woman wasn't clear, nor did it matter. With one deft swirl of motion, he knocked the box away and flung himself upon her. He'd show her! Put fear in her anyway; teach her that whatever he was, he was not a man to be trifled with! Sure, she was a woman—but she was also Clan Ferr, which ruled War-Hold. She could fend him off—or not. Women often meant the opposite of their words.

No, you fool! another part of him raged, a part that hadn't been seduced into abeyance by imphor.

He ignored it—his body did. Instinct was riding him now, and instinct had one goal. Survival—of the self (which imphor aided on the orney field, in the form of resistance to pain and enhanced reflexes alike). And survival of the kind.

Which was raging through his loins like fire in oil, awakened by the feel of that warm, beautiful body beneath him. Already he was fumbling at his waist ties with one hand, while pinning Strynn to the ground with the other. "I lost once today," he heard himself growl, "but there's one thing that can only *be* won once."

She gasped, face gone odd and distant, as though viewed from far off. He closed his eyes to shut it out and rocked back to straddle her thighs. Fists beat at his bare legs; nails raked them, as she tried to buck him off. The pain fed the fury, which drank of the imphor, which released the beast he at the best of times could not always control. With one swipe of his free hand, he grasped the suede-leather girdle that closed her robe and tore it open. It parted with a harsh snap. He opened his eyes, and for the first time in his life saw Strynn's naked breasts. White, like mountains, tipped with pink-brown stone.

"Fool!" rationality screamed again, but his hands were already upon her. On her mouth—not his preference, but he had to stop her resisting, had to smother her into panicked quiescence. She bucked again, beat at him, waking more pain and more anger, and shattering what little restraint remained. His mouth replaced his hands on her mouth, as much to ensure silence as to placate lust. He felt her shudder as she fought to inhale, while his hands went everywhere they could reach that was soft and sleek and female. Sweat soaked him, blood ran in rivulets down his back where her nails continued to rake. Once she caught his ears and twisted. He slapped her, leaving her half-senseless, no longer caring what he did. This was for all the slights she'd visited upon him. And for all the other women who'd treated him the same. And most of all, it was for Tyrill, his father's father's mother, who was also his Craft-Chief, who always and forever drove him onward, never praising him, though he did his best, never satisfied with anything he did. Trying to make him be *her*.

Well, he'd satisfy her now! Strynn had to wed. And if he got her with child, she'd *have* to marry him, which would mean he would be the one to bring this prize among prizes into Argen-yr: his and Tyrill's sept of the clan.

Maybe then the old bitch of a two-mother would be satisfied. In the meanwhile, he was going, for once, to please himself.

The thing Strynn remembered afterward was the wetness: Eddyn's slobbering and his sweat-soaked skin that made it hard to fight him, even when she tried every hold her War Mistress had taught her, and dug into every part of him she could reach with her nails. And finally that awful burning pain between her legs when he finally got her skirts up and his breeches down, and pushed his manhood into what had heretofore been inviolate, moistened by nothing but her blood.

She felt nothing when he squirted, the event marked solely by quickening grunts. Then stared with dreadful fascination down the white length of her naked breast and belly as Eddyn raised that perfect sculpted torso and with deliberate nonchalance withdrew his ornament, red around its root with blood that was not his own.

"Well, there you have it," he gasped, as he splashed himself clean with water from the pool, rose languidly, and secured the waist tie of his breeches. "The Law says you will wed," he continued, glassy-eyed, "and that no child will be born unfathered. You live by the Law; therefore you will name me. The next time—our wedding night—will be better. The Eight know, lady, that I don't hate you."

"The Law," she raged behind him, as she sat up, fumbling for her girdle, "will see you exiled!"

He turned to grin at her. "Not with healthy men at seller's price. Nor do you reckon with Two-mother."

Strynn watched him go—wide-eyed and dumb-mouthed. He'd done it. Had actually done it! An eternal instant on the grass. A confused mingling of pain she'd expected and humiliation she'd hated, and the world forever changed.

But Eddyn wasn't as smart as he thought—certainly not on an imphor high. Nor was he the only one well connected.

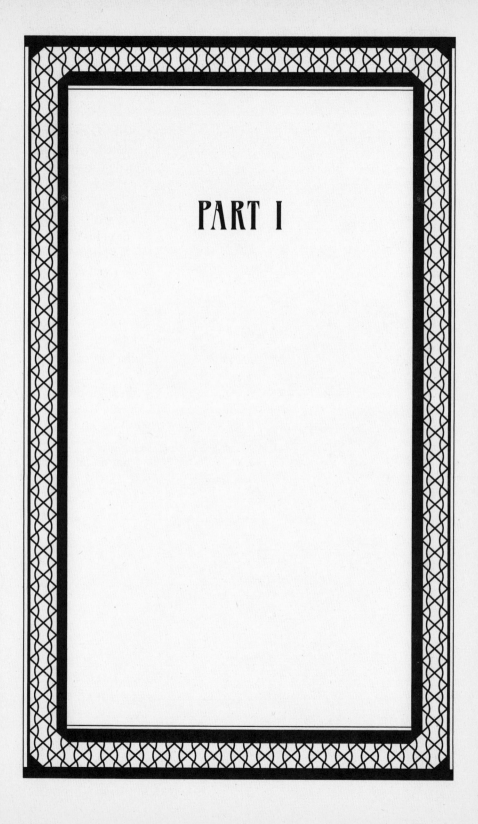

PART I

CHAPTER 1:

THE PROVING

(Eron: Tir-Eron—Sundeath: Day 1: King's Day—dawn)

The first row of the second level of the cold limestone octagon called the Hall of Clans was not where Avall syn Argen-a would've preferred to spend the first morning of the eight-day festival called Sundeath, which walled the year's dark half from the light. First and most pragmatically, it was a waste of precious mornlight, which was absolutely the best possible illumination to reveal certain imperfections in a particular kind of filigree work he'd been perfecting for two eighths now. Noonlight wouldn't suffice, for noonlight flattened. Afterlight was too harsh for anything subtle. As for torchlight, candlelight, or even precious glowlight—none were fit for more than basic cutting, filing, or fitting.

Which, now he considered it, was what was in a sense about to occur here, in the most ill-shaped public space in all Eron.

Certainly the place offended every sensibility that saw it. But instead of leveling the chamber to the rock from which it was carved, the elite of the kingdom's artisans had spent generations disguising flawed proportions beneath a gloss of technical virtuosity in every High-Clan craft his people practiced. So it was, then, that each of the twenty-four inset sigils beneath Sarnon's famous (and well-shaped) dome was carved or gilded, inlaid or veneered, reliefed or tapestried, frescoed or sculpted or mosaicked into a conflicting assemblage of styles, from the understated elegance of Emlyn san Garn's porcelain medallion, to Varynin syn Starkk's carved amber diorama.

The dome itself was another matter entirely: eight plain stone ribs separating curved triangles of blue mosaic set in subtle knotwork patterns that danced and twisted as the light from the octet of windows at its base altered with the progress of the day.

Avall was glad he couldn't see his own clan's insignia. The double-span-long slab of rough-cast iron beneath Argen's witness-box was rusty with age and dented from a fall suffered during last year's quake. Had it not been the final work of the renowned Mygin, it would long since have been rendered down to ingots. As it was, those flaking smelters, smiths, and founders survived mostly as writhing knobs, and only in perfect light could one gain any sense of their genders. Still, as his twin sister, Merryn, had observed, he'd be fortunate indeed to look that good when he was nine hundred years old, had survived a dozen quakes and three fires, spent almost a hundred years as booty taken in Ixti's sole significant raid, and had endured Council debates in the interim.

It was just such public display and his clan's obligation to attend same that had brought him here before sunrise, barely a day after his return to Tir-Eron from visiting his surviving uncle in Half Gorge. Chance—drawn lot (no surprise there; everything in Eron was determined that way)—had named him among Argen's Witnesses at the Proving of the King, and he supposed he ought to show some interest, given that it was his first attendance at that solemn rite, courtesy of having turned twenty during the previous eighth. He *was* interested, too, in a way. And it really was an honor to wear the maroon robe and hood and sit with a random selection of the adults of Argen-Hall and Smith-Hold overlooking the floor, where the Council of Chiefs alternated clan and craft around the proving dais.

They all looked hungry now, though he couldn't see the chiefs of his own factions—Eellon syn Argen-a, Clan-Chief of Argen-Hall; and Tyrill san Argen-yr, Craft-Chief of Smith-Hold—because they were sitting directly beneath the box, facing inward toward the dais. Or more properly, toward the knee-high, fractured-basalt prism of the Stone, which centered it. They had faces *like* stone, too, he imagined. The pair detested each other.

Avall shifted in his seat, watching the progress of a beam of focused sunlight sliding around the file of span-high windows beneath the dome. As if sensing that attention, the light caught a certain prism at a precise angle at a particular time, and daughter beams split and raced around the hall, aided by strategically placed mirrors and slabs of semireflective glass, so that in half a breath a cone of brilliant light flared down from dome to Stone in token (so Priest-Clan claimed) of The Eight's approval.

Whereupon the plain, driftwood door to the east opened, and without fanfare or herald, Gynn syn Argen-el, High King of all Eron, strode in.

Alone, barefoot, and robed in white, without insignia or ornament, he looked no more regal than anyone else in the room, if younger than the bulk. Avall knew for a fact that he had just turned forty, though a casual observer might've guessed him at most five year's Avall's senior. Nor did the similarity end there. Both were a bit shorter than average and lightly built. Both had shoulder-length black hair, sharp-cut features, and piercing, dark blue eyes; not unreasonable, given that they were kin. Eellon must surely be gloating now. After all, it was *his* outmaneuvering of his old rival, Tyrill, that had put Gynn on the Stone two years back. Avall supposed he ought to be proud of his two-father's political acumen. He wondered, though, as he always did at the breakings of the year, how his father or one-father would've dealt with all this conniving had they not succumbed to the plague. Merryn said that he should consider the Proving merely another exercise in making. He wrought toy kings of fine-cast gold; it was time he watched kings being forged of baser metal. After all (she also said) nothing short of premature death would prevent his being Craft-Chief someday. It was a reward—*the* reward, allegedly—for being the acknowledged master of all skills in one's particular craft. Avall didn't consider responsibility any reward at all.

Nor was Kingship much to be desired today.

Gynn looked less stern than grim as he halted before the Stone. Nor did he look any happier when the Priests of The Eight advanced down the mosaic-paved aisles that bisected the facets and circled him on the dais, each in the robe and mask of the particular aspect of The Eight-in-One he or she served. Blank-masked Grivvon of Law, who had officiated during the last Proving, alone carried any sign of office, and that merely a hand-sized eight-sided die, each face graven with one mask of The Eight. Wordlessly, he approached the Stone, shook the die eight times, and cast it there. It came up Fate, which was no good omen.

Nor was Fate's Priest any friend of Gynn's, though neither his movements nor vertically divided black-and-white mask betrayed that as he joined Grivvon in flanking the King over whose approval he would now officiate. For his part, Gynn reached to the cincture at his waist, unbound it, then parted his robe and let it fall. Backlit by the cone of light, he stood naked before the assembled chiefs.

From where Avall sat eight spans away, the King looked fit and healthy, if pale from a summer spent indoors administering a kingdom's worth of affairs. Certainly no obvious flaws marred his smooth, clean-muscled flesh. Which was fortunate, since this whole embarrassing display was mounted so that the Priests of The Eight could inspect him for any imperfection that might render him an unfit receptacle when he donned the Masks, drank from the Wells, and for a hand became the avatar of each of The Eight in turn. Fortunately, Law seemed satisfied, and Fate likewise nodded approval as he paced around the silent, immobile King. When he returned to where Fate's sigil was inset on the dais, the remaining Priests mounted their own inspections, in order, from the east. None complained.

All this was conducted in silence. *Boring* silence. Though technically any of the chiefs sitting on the floor could likewise claim an inspection, in practice none ever did. Avall relaxed, leaning back in his seat and helping himself to a sip of ritual wine from a plain golden cup set in the limestone arm. He liked Gynn as far as he knew him, which wasn't far, though the King spoke to him on sight. And hated to see a good man poked and prodded as though he were some prize ram.

Avall was on the verge of risking some inane, harmless comment to the bland-faced female cousin to his right, when he heard her sharp intake of breath and joined her in straining forward to stare over the rail. A hush filled the hall, followed by a rumbling murmur like an avalanche rolling down a mountain. Someone had risen—from Smith-Hold's ranks, Avall realized with stunned surprise—and was making a slow, halting progress to the dais. *Tyrill!* He recognized the gait even before the silver-velvet Craft-Chief's tabard she wore above her parti-color robe of clan maroon and craft gold. With her hood up, her face was invisible, which was probably just as well.

What could *she* possibly want? What could she reasonably hope to gain by asserting her ancient right to inspection—and protest? It was too much to hope that she merely wanted a close look at a handsome piece of manflesh. She need not have left home for that, what with Avall's troublesome cousin Eddyn ever ready to pose in his skin for one of the old bitch's countless studies for bronzes she never cast.

Still, she'd been vehemently opposed to Gynn's raising (or to Eellon's support of him, which amounted to the same), and the webs of Tyrill, the Spider-Chief, were not to be trod upon if one hoped to emerge undrained.

She'd reached the dais now, and stepped with practiced ease upon its rim, as though she, not Gynn, were sovereign of Eron. To his credit, the King remained immobile, though Avall knew from reliable sources that if Gynn feared anyone, it was this harsh, outspoken old woman twice his age. The plague had hollowed out her soul, it was said—much as it had scoured the womb of her lone one-daughter in its early stages, then returned three quarters later to slay her only one-son two years to the day after the birth of Eddyn, the son Fate never allowed him to see. Gynn was the first fruit of a niece's womb that had escaped that awful, parasitic mauling to produce five more after him, but Tyrill had never forgiven her sister's daughter that fruitfulness. Then again, Tyrill never forgave anything—including Eddyn's failings.

He doubted she'd forgive the King, should he prove wanting. Wordlessly she stalked around him, inspecting him minutely from toe to head, peering blatantly at every curve, bulge, and hollow. She looked hard at his ears, stared (glared rather) into his eyes, then, in an insult no monarch should have to suffer, reached up and squeezed his jaw until his mouth popped open. Throughout it all, Gynn maintained the requisite silence, though his eyes spoke eloquently.

And Tyrill— The old hag was actually prying at the High King's lips as though he were a prize stallion! "Ah-ha!" she crowed, as she slowly turned around. "He lacks a tooth!" Even on the first tier, Avall caught the gleam of triumph in her eyes.

"Hold!" someone called from directly below. Avall caught but the briefest glimpse of his two-father's face as he rose and advanced on his rival, yet even that showed gray eyes flashing like light on waves, set in a face worn and angular as mountain rock. Of course Avall expected no less from the High King's major partisan, for all he was nearly ninety. "He lacks *part* of a tooth," Eellon corrected calmly, as he joined Tyrill—likely so he could look down on her. "He took a blow to the mouth last War Day, as well you know. The root remains, and the rest he had made into a stud which he wears in his ear—when he is not naked beneath the gaze of old women. So no, he is not perfect, but he is intact. And be reminded, Craft-Chief, that Fate showed him *Victory's* face at that contesting."

"Still," Tyrill challenged, "he is no longer perfect."

"Men wear out," Eellon retorted. "The Law allows for that, else Kings would never be able to trim their nails, cut their hair, or wax their bodies. And we must crown a new sovereign every time an eyelash fell or a cut deigned to bleed."

"I demand a vote," Tyrill replied stiffly.

"A waste of time," Eellon snapped back.

"Nevertheless, I demand it."

Eellon sighed. His face was like building thunder. At a sign from Fate, every member of the Council except the contending parties drew from contrasting pouches at his or her waist a black marble and a white one. Without further commentary, each selected one and let it fall through a hole in the arm of his or her seat. From there a complex system of gears and scales tallied them. The result was displayed by the bronze statue of Choice that stood in an alcove in the north facet: a half-clad, half-nude gearwork hermaphrodite that slowly moved the sword it held in its two hands so that the weapon pointed . . . downward. Which meant Tyrill's assertion had been defeated— by how much, no one would ever know.

"If you would house The Eight in that which is less than ideal," the old woman hissed, as she stepped down from the dais, "be that insult on all your heads!" And with that she limped back to her seat. Eellon followed, conspicuously ignoring her presence.

"The Eight," Fate intoned, voice amplified through his mask, "through Their mouths and Their eyes, have accepted the High King's shell as a fit receptacle for Their Power. Now must his mind likewise be proved agreeable."

Twenty-four questions—one per craft; next year it would be one per clan—and the King must answer them all to the chiefs' satisfaction. Again, Chance had determined who would speak and in what order. When Fate and Law had helped the King back into his robe, it was Tryffon syn Ferr, of War, who rose: a hard-faced man of forty-one, with short, iron-colored hair, wide shoulders, and a close-clipped black beard he wore in defiance of convention. He spared Tyrill a long appraising glare before he spoke, hatred almost palpable in his eyes.

"It has been eighteen years since the plague; eighteen years in which Eron has stood shaken and weak with a powerful neighbor to the south which has long cast covetous eyes upon her. My question then, is this: Why has Ixti waited? A foe on the ground naked and wounded is more easily overcome than a healthy foe on horse in full war gear."

Gynn gnawed his lip, which generally meant he knew the answer but it might not be one War liked. "It is easy to forget," he began at last, "that events that occur unseen occur at all. We suffered plague—most of us in this room saw sons and brothers and husbands and fathers die. And sisters and daughters and wives and mothers. We forget that Ixti likewise endured that contagion, though not to our extent. We forget this because we did not see it. We forget that Ixti's warriors wore beards, which harbored the mites that bore the plague. We forget that where we lost a third of our men, they lost over half their army, if reports we hear are true, and a land whose army is weak does not seek attention. Nor should we forget that it was your own War-Hold that was least troubled by the plague, so that where Ixti was weakest, we were strongest, and the other way around.

"Still," he went on, "it might also be said that while it takes far less time to beget new citizens than it does to train new warriors, those warriors become functional *as* warriors far sooner than children become viable citizens. Therefore one might consider the disposition of Ixti's population. North and west of Rhynn's Finger lie the Flat, the Fen, and nameless moorland neither of us is fool enough to claim. South and east of it, in the ancient heart of Ixti, lies even less arable land than we possess, which must yet support the bulk of Ixti's people. Their *best* land, however—and the bulk of their resources—lies south of that, still somewhat confined by the Flat and the sea. These factors together would make for complex logistics should Ixti contrive to wage . . ."

Avall stopped listening. This would surely take until noon, if all twenty-four claimed their right to question. Then would come the debate. It would be midafternoon before this was concluded, the King fully Proven, and Sundeath officially begun. And while he knew he would learn a great deal if he remained here, information that might be useful if he indeed became Craft-Chief one day, he was increasingly and uncomfortably aware of a certain other person with whom he shared Argen's box.

Namely his cousin Eddyn, two seats over (though he shouldn't be; his sept, Argen-yr, was properly ranked one row back)—who was whipping glares his way as often as he observed the proceedings. Like Tyrill, Eddyn didn't like to lose. And Tyrill's defeat just now had surely soured her two-son's mood. Especially as he'd recently suffered a rather more personal upset.

That was how *Eddyn* chose to regard the rape Strynn had made short work of reporting. But where most men in Eddyn's boots would've shown their faces no more than required to salve the Law, been desperately glad to escape exile or unclanning—and to have connections in the Council powerful enough to advocate before the King (and then nerve enough to challenge that King's sovereignty two eighths later)—it was oh-so-typical of Eddyn to ignore all that in favor of the fact that Avall, not Eddyn himself, had . . . acquired the prize-above-prizes, Strynn.

And if Eddyn was furious that Strynn had evaded him, Avall wasn't certain he was happy about the alternative himself, for all he was about to wed her. True, he'd known her since birth, and all but grown up with her, seeing as she was his twin's bond-sister. She was certainly attractive, and he'd spent more than one night since his body changed imagining what it would be like to possess her, and had no doubt whatever that he'd be able to perform his marital duty as often and enthusiastically as either of them desired.

But likely without true passion.

Strynn was like a *sister* to him, dammit, their impending marriage less a love match than a lifelong favor to a treasured friend. And while it was doubtful he'd ever find a woman he liked better or who was more his match in attitude, interest, or accomplishment, it was equally unlikely he'd ever find a person of either sex—friend *or* lover—who could win him away from his first true love, which was making.

So it was that while he didn't *mind* being married to Strynn—since he was legally obliged to wed and add his three to the population—it was something he'd neither desired nor actively encouraged.

And, of course, she also carried Eddyn's child, and he'd never cared for Eddyn, even . . . before (though the child was blameless in any case). But when Strynn had come to him and asked him to be the child's father—well, it had surprised him and scared him, but eventually it had simply seemed right. Besides, Eellon wanted it, though less for Avall's sake than for the sake of his sept of the clan, representing as it did yet another victory over Tyrill. Advanced age notwithstanding, as far as *that* rivalry was concerned, those two elderly chiefs could easily have been children of eleven.

As for Eddyn—Avall didn't quite know what to think. At the deepest level, he hated him for what he'd done to an old and treasured friend, imphor high notwithstanding. The man was also arrogant, self-centered, and reckless—which were not reckoned virtues in *his* sept of the clan. But they were also much of an age, shared a fair bit of history, and were both, in far too real a sense, pawns of their powerful two-parents.

Finally, it simply didn't seem real. Women like Strynn didn't get raped. Men like Eddyn didn't *commit* rape. And so his emotions were dulled. The hate had become an abstraction that had little real bearing on the man glowering to his left.

As if realizing he was the subject of his rival's musing, Eddyn eased over to claim the empty seat beside Avall. "You seem . . . distracted," he muttered amiably, though his eyes all but dripped with malice. "Surely someone with as much wit as you would be pleased to see his mentor plying *his* wit so publicly—especially in support of a King with whom you have *so* much in common."

Avall wanted to ignore him, but to do so would be to acknowledge that the taunt had worked its intent. "Gynn and I?" he replied instead, with forced nonchalance. "We're no more alike than he and you. Besides," he went on, "comparisons generally lead to—"

"—jealousy?" Eddyn supplied, with calculated rancor. "I've heard that word too much of late, from people who know nothing about either of our . . . situations."

Avall almost laughed in spite of himself. *That* was true enough. Everyone in Eron knew their two-parents couldn't stand each other, but not one in a hundred knew why. (As it happened, Eellon had bested Tyrill the year they mounted their master's competition and had become Craft-Chief. Tyrill had been forced to wait sixty years for him to become Clan-Chief—the oldest mentally competent member of the clan—before she could claim that longsought title. Never mind that it could've gone to someone half her age, or less. That was the balance. Age versus skill. Knowledge versus ability. Theory versus practice.)

"Of course everyone *does* know," Eddyn went on in a confidential tone, "that you no more love Strynn than you love that robe. It's attractive, comfortable, and conveys the requisite symbolism, just like this marriage of yours will—but you don't love her. Nor do you deserve her."

Avall wondered what had gotten into the usually taciturn Eddyn to make him air all his anger—all his *weakness*—to the one person least likely to be sympathetic. "No one *deserves* her," he gave back because he had to, or seem the gutless dreamer too many already styled him. "No one *deserves* anyone. And she certainly didn't deserve . . . what you did."

There. He'd said it: what he'd wanted to *shout* ever since word had reached him of a hard-eyed Strynn storming into Argen-Hall demanding to see Eellon and have him lay her case before the King, or else she would. It was just as well he and Merryn had been studying at Glass-Hold at the time, or his sister would surely have challenged Eddyn then and there for insult to a friend. As Avall had also been tempted to do: for that, and for staining the honor of the clan. As it was, they'd returned to find the matter settled. No exile for Eddyn because his lineage and skill were too valuable to lose. Massive payment made by Argen-yr to Ferr for insult conferred. A vow to seek no wife of that clan, ever; and no wife of any clan for five years. And any children he did sire were to be given to Ferr to atone for the insult, with additional payment made to the clan thereby deprived, should the mother prefer to have named a father from another clan than Argen-yr. That Strynn had insulted Eddyn almost as badly by refusing to name him the father of her child had gone unnoticed in the furor. That Eddyn dared show his face in public now was as much testament to favors owed his two-mother in the Council of Chiefs as it was to his own reputation as one of his generation's premier artisans.

Avall wished he'd found some other time and place (better yet, *no* time and place) to bring up this latest source of contention. Indeed, for a moment he thought Eddyn was about to strike him, which would certainly give the gossips something to discuss besides Tyrill's brashness and Gynn's missing tooth. But Eddyn simply shrugged and looked away—straight toward the rail. "You'll never have any good of her," he gritted. "Sooner or later she'll want more than you can give—love, passion, lust, whatever you want to call it—and I'll be waiting."

"Marry the man who raped her for gain?" Avall snorted, "You *are* mad!"

"Hush, both of you!" an elder aunt hissed behind them. "Or I'll grab you by your arrogant young ears and drag you out of here like the overgrown apprentices you are!"

Eddyn grunted. Avall said nothing at all, but was desperately glad when, two questions later, one of the hall pages slipped him a summons to the corridor that ringed the boxes. He followed the boy up the shallow steps to the marble-walled passage—and was more than a little shocked to find Lykkon, the senior clan page, lolling in a blind arcade, discreetly posed and smug-faced. "What?" Avall rasped, as he joined his year-younger cousin.

"Your mother needs you," Lykkon informed him with a grin.

"Mother!" Avall groaned, rolling his eyes in exasperation. "Why?"

"I wasn't told."

"I have to witness."

Lykkon raised an expressive brow. "If I wore that robe, no one would know the difference."

"You're not of age."

"By less than a year, and I've heard history and seen naked men. Besides," Lykkon added, "I actually *want* to be here."

"You have a point," Avall agreed, glancing furtively around the empty corridor. "Very well," he continued recklessly, "if you'll promise to tell me everything that happens."

An enthusiastic nod. "Done!"

A side corridor provided sufficient cover for the transfer: civilian cloak for ceremonial robe and hood, leaving Avall in maroon hose, boots, and short-tunic. With the hood up, they did look uncannily alike. But then again, so did most of the clan. Tall rangy Eddyn was a rather obvious exception to Argen's elegantly trim norm.

"Beware of Eddyn," Avall cautioned, as his cousin secured the cincture around his waist. "If he finds out, I'll never hear the end of it; never mind what Tyrill might make of it if she caught wind. She'd probably make poor Gynn Prove himself all over."

"Probably," Lykkon acknowledged. "But I'll be careful. Besides, this will be useful for a treatise I'm writing on 'Clan Politics and the Succession.' "

"I'll trust you on that," Avall replied wryly. And would. Quick-witted young Lykkon looked set to challenge for a seat in Lore, though he'd remain a member of Clan Argen. He was Avall's sept, too: Argen-a; not -yr, like Tyrill and Eddyn; or -el, like the High King.

Avall spared his cousin a final good-luck wink and turned away, trying not to let his relief at escaping show. *What in the world could have possessed his mother to summon him from witnessing at a state occasion?* He was still trying to puzzle out a viable probability when a final turn of the stairs spat him out into the hall's austere entrance foyer, whence he passed through the only ever-open doors in all Eron into the stone-paved sweep of the combination street, plaza, and riverwalk that constituted Tir-Eron's main thoroughfare. The bulk of the Citadel rose to the right, its carefully altered spire of wind-shaped stone joined to the hall by walled gardens that ran right up to the cliffs, into which the bulk of the Citadel was hewn. Straight ahead lay the Ri-Eron, its waters veiled as usual by steam from the springs down on South Bank, save where the Isle of The Eight rose from the center. In any event, South Bank was invisible here, masked by a screen of trees. Nor did he venture there often, it being mostly the province of the unclanned, clanless, or Common Clan who comprised over half of Eron's population.

This bank—North Bank—was where his steps took him: through the artfully contrived maze of clan halls and craft holds that climbed the low rolling slopes at the feet of Eron Gorge's sheer northern wall, each carefully situated to evoke the illusion of rural privacy within the city. His own hall lay two shots to the east, nor did he note any form of conveyance to transport him there, which made him suspect both messenger and message.

Nor were his suspicions allayed when, a short while later, he turned left through a rough stone archway and entered the precincts of Clan Argen proper—for years uncounted the controlling clan of Smithcraft and site of Smith-Hold-Master. The spacious forecourt before the low limestone sprawl of trapezoidal towers and round-arched arcades was utterly empty—no surprise. But he was taken aback when the young door page stared blankly at him when he inquired where his mother might be.

"Safely away consulting the Gods," his sister laughed, easing out from the foyer behind the page, where she'd obviously been lurking, unsuspected by the panicked-looking lad. He yipped and danced aside. She laughed louder and reached out to snare Avall in what was half embrace, half wrestling hold. Years of experience at such assaults made him relax against her; and years of reading his mood kept her from pressing that advantage, save verbally.

"What's the matter?" she chided. "I assumed you'd be grateful to someone who'd rescued you from—"

"Don't say it!" Avall yelped, glancing anxiously at the far-too-attentive page.

Merryn merely snorted and drew him none-too-gently past the boy and down the corridor to the right. She was clad, as she usually was around the hall, in the loose, belted short-tunic and skintight house-hose that were more commonly the province of men. Not for the first time did Avall question Fate's sense of humor, which had made him the sensitive artist and his female twin the dangerously competent almost-warrior. At least she loved him. And at least she had compassion enough to protect his dignity until they were away from the page.

"You!" he growled, when they'd turned into a sunlit arcade fronting a water garden. "Mother didn't send that message!"

"Mother doesn't think of such things," Merryn retorted easily, with the bright, if wicked, smile she managed so effortlessly—and which he'd always envied. Not the least because her face, save her more delicately pointed chin and thinner brows, had always been such an eerie mirror of his own. With her similar build and identical height, she'd more than once passed as him on this or that misadventure.

"You owe me," she continued flatly. "It just happens that I saw Eddyn strutting out of -yr's sept-gate in full regalia not long after you left, and given the circumstances, I figured there was only one possible place he could be going. And since I doubted anyone in -yr would warn you, and I knew you wouldn't dare leave if he appeared, lest you lose face, the only way to spare you half a day of misery was to concoct a ruse. Besides, Mother really did want you two hands ago, though it wasn't important. Anyway, Lykkon likes you, adores me, and is too sweet-tempered for Eddyn to harass without looking a worse bully than he does already. You owe Lyk a favor, by the way."

Avall glared at her askance. "I could've handled Eddyn."

Merryn shook her head. "You've got enough on your mind without adding him."

"Such as?"

She folded her arms and regarded him warily. "Be honest, brother. To-morrow night you'll be bedding someone you like but don't love, who's with child by someone neither of you can stand. Who's had sex—if you can call it that—exactly once, and never made love. Not that you have either. It's not supposed to be like that. You and Strynn can't really be friends anymore, yet you can't be proper lovers. It's—"

"You know," Avall growled, "I appreciate your concern, but what I really want to do right now is to hit something. Preferably something shaped like a certain tall wretch from Argen-yr."

The wicked smile returned. "Meet you in the war court in half a hand."

He grinned back, already tugging at the ties of his tunic. "Make that a quarter!"

Avall's suite was one level up and two corridors away, but he was there before he knew it. By the time he strode through the door, he'd shed his short-tunic, doffed the house-shirt beneath, and startled the floor steward out of her mind. Sparing no time for even a drink, he re-dressed in plain black house-hose, yard boots, and a skintight armoring coat. As an after-thought he tied his hair back in a stubby tail, and so arrayed rejoined his sister. She was dressed exactly like him and was just retrieving his practice padding from a carved wooden cabinet when he arrived. Half a finger later their torsos, hips, forearms, and thighs were clad in quilted leather.

"Blood or bruises?" she asked casually, as she opened the pierced-wood door of the weapon cabinet that took up one whole wall.

"Bruises, if you'll avoid my face," he replied, shouldering her roughly aside to begin his own inspection. "Not from vanity," he added. "Stitched lips are more likely to cause a man trouble on his wedding night than sore-salve."

Merryn lifted a brow. "I could always hit you in a particular place and spare you that anxiety."

"You do, and it *will* be to the blood," Avall retorted. "It's my head that's concerned about marriage; my other parts have no trouble with the notion."

Merryn tested a dagger meaningfully. "I could see that a certain part *never* troubled you. Think how much more sharply you'd be able to focus on your craft if half your blood didn't desert you every time a pretty face ambled by."

"I hadn't noticed that you'd been struck blind either," Avall shot back archly. "Besides, you have to dress like a lady tonight, and laces and stitches aren't compatible either."

Merryn sighed exaggerated regret and returned the dagger to the rack from which she'd retrieved it, then reached for the one above it, which held practice staves: arm-long shafts of springy wood hilted with light metal cages to protect craftsmen's precious hands.

"Let's see," Avall mused, as they strode from beneath the surrounding arcade into the sand-paved square that comprised Argen-Hall's war court. "When was the last time I beat you?"

"When we were three," Merryn informed him instantly. "Now, which will it be? Strict rules or none? No, wait: You chose goal, which means style's mine."

"Which means . . . ?"

"None!" Merryn cried, as she favored him with a whirling kick that sent him sprawling to the ground. Avall raised his stave to parry the ensuing blow. Wood smacked smartly against wood. The impact made his hand hurt.

"Think Eddyn," Merryn advised, as she deftly danced away from Avall's follow-through.

"Better not," he panted as he rolled back to his feet. "I don't think Mother would be happy if I killed you."

"Nor would Strynn," Merryn breathed—lunging forward.

Avall stepped aside at the last moment. Then *did* think of Eddyn, and proceeded to fight much better. In fact, for the second time in ten years, he bested his sister. "Remind me," she gasped, as she lay on the ground with him crouching atop her, the stave pressed against her throat, "not to mention Eddyn if I want to win."

"Better yet," Avall spat, as he released her, "don't mention him at all—ever."

CHAPTER II:

MEETINGS

(ERON:TIR-ERON—SUNDEATH: DAY I: KING'S DAY—MIDAFTERNOON)

Eellon heard the rising rumble of acclamation that greeted Gynn syn Argen-el when the multitudes gathered below the Hall of Clans saw him recrowned High King by the Priest of Fate.

Heard it, but heard more clearly the slap of his own feet against cold marble as he strode with a force and speed that would've tested a man half his age to the retiring room where the chiefs and Priests met for refreshments after the Proving and before swearing formal homage. Tyrill was behind him, but he hadn't waited for her. All *his* courtesy had been exhausted not flaying her alive with words on the floor of the hall. Those words still seethed in him, too. Indeed, he was rehearsing them now so vehemently they overshadowed the shout that signaled the official start of Sundeath.

He *wasn't* expecting ambush when he thrust through the heavy oak door.

"You fool," Law hissed, seizing him by the arm to draw him aside before he could do more than note that the low, domed chamber was barely half-full and that none of the Priests had unmasked, which meant they still served in their official capacities. Eellon flipped his hood up, signifying that he did, too.

"And in what way, Lord Law, am I a fool?" Eellon rasped, in no mood to be called to task by someone who, by his hands, had been playing with toys when Eellon first sat the hall as Craft-Chief.

"By letting Tyrill try those little power games! Surely you know that she—"

"I know that if I'd called her down too soon there'd have been a minor scandal with who knows what kind of repercussions. I know that by letting her have her way Gynn gains sympathy he could use and Tyrill looks a fool, which benefits me—*and* Gynn. Excuse me, the *King*."

Law didn't reply, though World looked at them sharply, and Craft rolled her eyes behind her intricate mask of gold, mother-of-pearl, and inlaid wood. Eellon used that silence to seal the initiative. "Lord Law," he continued bluntly, "let's not fool ourselves. This isn't about me, Tyrill, and the High King's teeth. It's about me, Tyrill, and that randy two-son of hers."

"Who happened to be a Witness today."

"Whom *Fate* made a Witness, just as it did Avall."

"Who vanished halfway through the Proving, though he thinks nobody noticed—and I hope to Cold Tyrill didn't, or there'll be Winter to pay. All we need is to have both your craft's rising stars acting like irresponsible children."

"As though they had no precedent," World put in smoothly. "I hadn't noticed that age has tempered either of their two-sires."

Eellon glared at her. "I trust you'll inform her of your . . . displeasure with the same dispatch with which you informed me. Keep in mind that I'm generally reasonable; you can't count on Tyrill to be."

"To be *what*?" Tyrill snapped from the door, where she'd paused, white hair a flame of light against the gloom behind her. Her eyes flamed, too, as she dismissed the two hall pages who'd escorted her with a disgusted shrug. Eellon marked that as well: The irony of Tyrill's demands for perfection in others contrasted with her own frailties. He wondered how much longer she'd be able to get around on her own, and how that would impact her standing in the craft—and the Council.

"Reasonable," Eellon told her flatly, in no mood to feign even ritual politeness.

"*Reasonable?*" Tyrill flared. "Is it reasonable to allow that . . . *boy* to remain on the Stone when there are far more competent alternatives?"

"In some areas," Eellon corrected, snaring a goblet of sun-wine from among those arrayed on the central table and passing it to her with a flourish. "But none as competent overall. It was Balance The Eight said was needed when the auguries were read before Gynn's Raising. He was most balanced."

"And will remain so for at least another year," World finished. She tapped her mask pointedly. "You might want to raise your hood, Craft-Chief. We would speak to you of craft matters."

"And clan matters," Law inserted.

Tyrill glared at him as she raised her hood. "*We?*"

"Priest-Clan."

Eellon caught her eye before she could look away and shot her a wink.

Surely she'd noted his own raised hood—and troubled expression. Nor did he look forward to what he suspected was coming. Having Tyrill suffer with him would make the unpleasantness marginally more endurable.

It was Weather who spoke, his tones eerily formal and given added volume by his mask. "The Eight speak in riddles when They convey Their will unto us. But we, Their voices, perforce must sometimes be blunt, and blunt I will be. We are . . . displeased, my fellow Priests and I, about a certain matter involving your clan, your craft—and a certain young man." He paused. "Ferr needs to be here, too; could someone get him?"

"He swore on the Stone never to be in the same room with Tyrill unless it be the King's direct command, save at the Proving," Fate supplied, as though he'd heard everything, and not just arrived from the Acclamation. "There's no point in seeking him. And a summons he'll ignore, unless Gynn gives it."

Weather huffed his disgust. "Very well. It is this bargain you two have lately concluded."

"After an eighth's debate," Eellon retorted. "It was no easy accord, I assure you."

"Nor should it have been," Fate conceded. "But—"

"To speak plainly," Weather broke in, "we feel that by arranging this agreement amongst yourselves, you assumed prerogatives normally assigned to Priest-Clan—or the Council itself. I'm not at all certain this . . . amnesty for young Eddyn is either desirable or legal."

"Gynn approved it," Tyrill shot back icily. "Even the parts I loathed."

"Gynn? Or the King?"

"What difference does it make?"

"The difference between man and god."

"Or Balance," Eellon observed carefully, easily as aware as Tyrill that neither of them was entirely in the right in the matter of the deal. "Balance said it was better a child be born than not, given *this* child's lineage, and recalling that the Law says no child will be born unfathered. Balance said that it was better Strynn wed someone she cared for than someone she loathed. Balance said insult should be compensated."

"It said that ability such as my two-son displays is more important than any minor insult he might have propagated," Tyrill finished.

"Strynn can't reclaim her virginity," World spat.

"Which she'd have lost anyway," Tyrill gave back. "But if we'd exiled Eddyn, we'd have lost sixty years of crafting unlikely to be equaled, and it was my duty as Craft-Chief to consider that."

"And not as his two-mother? Or member of his sept?"

"As Craft-Chief," Tyrill repeated. "Even Eellon agrees with that."

Eellon shot her a scathing glare. "I . . . agree that it would be a waste for

Eddyn to be exiled. I disagree when the Craft-Chief says his crafting is un-likely to be equaled, when Avall is more than Eddyn's match, and Strynn herself not far behind."

"So you say!" Tyrill snapped.

"So says the craft," Eellon retorted. "In that I had one vote, like the rest."

World cleared her throat. "It is not of that we are concerned. It is the way this deal was contrived, without recourse to Law or the will of The Eight."

"I imagine," Eellon replied drolly, "that The Eight will make Their opin-ions known soon enough. I suggest we see where They stand on this matter."

"Cold!" Tyrill all but shouted. "It matters not what They say! The matter is resolved, as the Clan-Chief says, by Balance. Strynn lost her virginity and her dignity but gains a child for her bond-clan and a husband suited to her temper. Avall loses his freedom of choice about a matter which doesn't deeply concern him, and gains a wife he claims he can enjoy, though I sus-pect he'll find himself enduring her instead. And Eddyn . . . loses his child, loses his dignity, costs his sept a completely unreasonable sum paid to Ferr, loses any real chance of marriage before he's too old to enjoy it—and main-tains his freedom to do what he does best. You think Strynn has suffered? She suffered once, and that's something that would have occurred anyway, in kind. Eddyn will suffer every time he walks the street. Every person he meets will look at him and say 'there goes one who should have been un-clanned.' Balance, my lords, *is* achieved."

"As you define it," Law snorted, turning away. "But I think Lord Argen is correct. We should defer any action until we see how The Eight and the Fateing rule upon it."

"And *then?*" Tyrill demanded.

"And then," Law replied, "we decide if it will become necessary for us to balance . . . *you.*"

"Both of you," Fate concluded with a mirthless laugh. *"Both* of you."

Merryn had to force herself to knock before entering her quarters, for all it was simple courtesy. Strynn was sharing them with her for the nonce—until the marriage, so the rite prescribed—and that gave her certain prerogatives. It felt odd, too, Merryn reckoned, to be on the threshold of admitting an-other to that formalized closeness they'd sworn not long after their first bleeding.

Relinquishing it, rather say, to someone she loved as much: her brother.

Just as it felt odd to be standing on her own threshold waiting for some-one she suspected was asleep to open the door.

But Strynn hadn't been sleeping, to judge by her face when she cracked the portal to peer out, even if her eyes did display a certain redness. Not from tears, however. Not after decision made and action taken. Not over *that*, at any rate. Strynn cried almost as rarely as Merryn did. The difference was that any man who raped Merryn would never have lived long enough for Law to intervene.

No, Strynn had the look of a child caught prowling through adult property—which, on a beautiful grown woman was amusing, winsome, and a little sad. As Merryn stood there trying to choose between sympathy and sarcasm, Strynn stuffed something deeper into the pocket of the leather smith apron she wore over a sleeveless house-tunic and loose-woven trousers of Ixtian cotton.

Making, Merryn determined. And given the circumstances, either a wedding gift for Avall or Merryn herself, who would stand as Strynn's Shadow in the ceremony. "Am I . . . interrupting?" she inquired with deliberately ironic finesse.

Strynn smiled nervously—her friend *was* a bit high-strung; too much to have prospered in her birth-craft. The arts of war demanded cold, quick, accurate judgments, not reflective flightiness. Not for the first time did Merryn wonder if perhaps she and Strynn had been switched at birth. Except of course she and Avall had been joined by skin at the hip and had the scars to prove it.

"Nothing that won't keep," Strynn smiled, stepping back for Merryn to enter. The suite beyond was typical of most in this wing of Argen-Hall: big, low-ceilinged rooms; inward-sloping walls; tapering faceted pilasters. The sharp edges and massively severe stonework contrasted with softly blowing curtains of semitransparent sylk. Oddly, for the hold of such storied craftsmen, there was little metal ornament.

It was also typical of Merryn in that there was no furniture beyond the bed pad, a quartet of chairs, and a round table exactly large enough to support a light meal for four, which is how she used it. A rack of weapons gleamed along the nearer wall, behind the wooden mannequin that wore her helm and mail. The rest of the red-tiled floor was bare, to better accommodate the exercises, with sword or dagger, shield or hand, that were her joy—and the reason she'd dared defy Eellon to apprentice with War.

"You look tired," they burst out together, punctuating that spontaneity with a round of laughter that was dangerously close to girlish giggles.

"Secret," Strynn admitted smugly. "Eye-tired, mostly."

"Keeping my brother sane," Merryn retorted, sliding a sleeve up to display the handsome bruise that bejeweled her forearm.

A brow lifted. "Fighting keeps Avall sane? I'll have to remember that."

"It keeps him from killing people he doesn't like. *Wanting* to kill them, anyway."

"What did Eddyn do now?"

It was Merryn's turn to lift a brow, which she did while filling an earthen mug from the pitcher cooling in the wall. She drank the contents—tart, sweet wine—at one draught. "Actually, it wasn't much. They both wound up as Witnesses today—Fate be cursed—and Eddyn couldn't resist making remarks."

Strynn looked puzzled. "Such as?"

"That Avall doesn't deserve you; that he'll never have any good of you."

"People don't *deserve* other people!" Strynn growled, filling a mug for herself, then refilling Merryn's.

Merryn laughed. "That's what Avall said—exactly. Still—"

"What?"

A deep breath. "I—I, uh, know we've talked about this before, but I have to ask again, because the two people I love most in the world are about to undertake one of the most serious things in the world. Strynn, *do* you love him? Do you love my brother? Or is this just convenience? If it is . . . I don't know how I'd feel. I don't think I'd hate you because I know why you did it. But if—" A pause, then: "Dammit, I'm scared Avall will be hurt, and I know you wouldn't do that deliberately, but—"

"Stop," Strynn interrupted. "Nothing's changed since the last time we discussed this. I *do* love Avall. At least I love him as much as it's possible to love someone you don't love absolutely. I love him as much as I can love someone who doesn't love me more than anything else, and let's face it, Merryn, I'll always run second to whatever it is he's making. And you know what? That doesn't bother me. It's certainly better to wed someone who'll place you first among people if not above things, than it is to wed someone who treats you *like* a thing. And even if he doesn't place me first among people—there's you, for instance, and Rann—I'll still be pretty damned important. So . . . no, I won't hurt your brother deliberately, and not only because he's your brother. Because I'll look at him and see the boy who was so crazy in love with me when we first changed that he wrote me a poem every day for six eighths. It still kills me that I had to break his heart."

"And now you're giving him yours."

"Not my heart, but everything else, and without guilt, fear, or shame. I'll give him as much of me as he'll ever want."

"Will that be enough for you, though?" Merryn wondered, staring intently at her mug.

"It'll have to be," Strynn sighed. "The rest I had to give—and I'm not talking about my maidenhead—doesn't exist anymore."

"You're too young to be bitter," Merryn snorted. "Watch out, or you'll start sounding like Tyrill."

"She had everything she wanted, too, but one thing—and she got that—when she was eighty."

Silence, for a while, as both drank, drowsed in their chairs, and let the simple comfort of friendship engulf them.

"If I have to marry," Strynn offered at last, "there is no one in the world I would rather wed than Avall."

"If you have to die," Merryn whispered back, "a quick death is better than a slow one."

"Where'd you hear that?" Strynn replied carefully, a spark of anger in her eyes that Merryn both regretted and was glad to see, because it meant Strynn hadn't lost her passion.

"I heard it," Merryn admitted, "from your father."

Eddyn laid down the silversteel calipers with which he'd been measuring the dagger resting before him on supports of padded velvet, and glared first at the instrument, then at the weapon, and finally to the manuscript spread across the table.

And swore silently. He'd had it: the absolute perfect ratio between length and width of blade, and length of blade to hilt that had been spelled out in Wylin's treatise on that topic, which was still, after three hundred years, the standard reference. Had it, then lost it somewhere in that last filing. And while he still knew that the slim length of thousand-folded steel and hand-cast gilded bronze was more than proficient enough to see him elevated from apprentice smith to master and therefore to adulthood, he was not at all certain it would suffice to pass one final, and more important, muster.

Not his own—and he *was* proud of the weapon, and had no qualms about it being fit for the ritual gifting to the King—but his two-mother's.

He glared at the calipers as though they were gleaming spies that might tell tales on him. They were accurate to a tenth part of the width of a fine hair, but it was said that Tyrill, even now, could discern variations twice that fine, and Eellon (whom Eddyn avoided like death itself) that much, and half again finer. It was his curse, he reckoned, to be born in such demanding times. Eellon and Tyrill were accounted the best to have practiced since Wylin's own epoch—and here *he* had to meet their so-exacting standards. That Fate had also delivered him into one of the few eras which could excuse his reckless rape of Strynn was no comfort. That was a thing for another time and place. This—making—was what he truly was: the thing most intrinsically *him*, done absolutely right, with no quarter asked or given between himself and the great god, perfection.

If it wasn't for that last pass with the next-smallest file, which had removed just a breath too much from one side and destroyed the fragile symmetry. Nor did he dare shave a matching amount off the other. That would upset the proportions, and from there the whole piece would tumble down to mediocrity: sufficient to ensure his Raising, but no more.

"You seem to be . . . concerned about something, two-son," a far-too-familiar voice rasped far too close behind him. Eddyn started—couldn't help it—even as he wondered how in the world someone as rough-gaited as Tyrill could possibly sneak up on anyone—especially when he thought he'd locked the door to preclude this kind of intrusion. He rolled his eyes in despair.

Unfortunately, the blade was a near-perfect mirror, and Tyrill saw his reaction exactly as he saw *her* scowl reflected there. She still wore Council robe and tabard. Which meant, should she now raise her hood, that anything she said carried the force of Law. Blessedly the hood stayed down.

"Good work," Tyrill said flatly—this was the first time she'd seen his incipient masterwork, and indeed custom, if not Law, said she should *not* see it, though as Craft-Chief she only voted to break ties.

"Good sources," she continued, folding her arms, but otherwise not moving. "And good equipment: good materials."

"Thank you, Two—Craft-Chief," he corrected lamely.

"Good," she repeated. "Excellent. But not good enough."

Eddyn's heart skipped a beat as the weight of those words sank in.

"Good enough to secure your mastership and maybe a subchieftainship," she went on sharply. "But not good enough to best Avall."

"I am sick," Eddyn gritted, "of being compared to him."

"Prepare to ail a long time, then," Tyrill snapped. "Or do what it takes to best him."

Eddyn twisted around to stare the old woman hard in the eye, meeting her face-to-face as few of his years dared. Clan-bond, he supposed, was good for something. "Two people in the world will know the difference," he growled. "Three, if you count me. You can't vote and won't talk. And Eellon doesn't like to fight and has already ground me into the dirt enough to satisfy even his self-righteous arrogance for a while. The rest don't matter."

Tyrill shook her head. "Avall will know. He won't mention it unless you do, and he'll be excruciatingly polite and sincerely lavish in his praise. But he'll know you took—what? Two swipes too many with a number nine file, where one with a ten would've assured perfection."

"What's Avall making?" Eddyn dared, to break the building tension.

"Something better than that," Tyrill snorted, and swept from the room.

Eddyn watched her go. Then, for as long as it took to melt the offending file in a sun-fired brazier, he wept.

King's Day always concluded with a feast in the Citadel's Hall of Greeting, which adjoined the Hall of Clans. The great bronze doors opened on a vast, lozenge-shaped plaza called the Court of Rites and were hauled back precisely at sunset. They closed one hand later, at which time no one save the King himself, should he be late, was admitted. Half the seats in that high, square-arched space were reserved for those with birth-claim or worth-claim there: Clan-Chiefs and their sept-chiefs and Craft-Chiefs and their subchiefs, and spouses, and other notables of their houses. Avall was included because he was in the direct line to the chieftainship of Clan Argen, though myriad dour uncles, aunts, one-uncles and one-aunts lurked between. He was also there because Eellon had asked that he be, rising adult as he was, and because, so Eellon said, Gynn liked him—though on what the High King based that opinion, he had no idea. Gynn was some variety of cousin, one degree more closely related to Eellon than to Tyrill, through something involving marriages generations back. Still, being the focus of the High King's eye, even briefly, alarmed him. How Eellon and the others dealt with the sovereign on a regular basis was a mystery past understanding.

Sure, Gynn was also a man, and as of that morning Avall knew precisely how much of one. But that aura of stoic vulnerability evinced at his Proving had lasted exactly as long as it had taken him to reclaim his physical crown, and with it all the power—and distance—that were his by Law to command.

Fortunately, there were a number of folks about that Avall knew and liked. Like Merryn, for instance, though anything that included him and didn't depend on Fate by rights had to include her. She seemed to be enjoying herself more than he, however, if the way she was dancing about the hall was any indication. Few in attendance had claimed their seats, and she resembled some bright insect darting from flower to flower. An insect with a sting, of course. He'd felt that barb that afternoon and had a bruise too close to *there* to prove it. If only he didn't like his sister so much, he could cheerfully have hated her for that. Naturally she'd done it just to prove she could.

Eddyn was there, too, of course, lurking in the corners and for once trying to be unobtrusive. He'd found a batch of his orney teammates to regale, and that seemed to satisfy him. He was also keeping as far away from Tyrill as possible.

Tyrill had found her place—in the angle where the high table turned a corner to form one side of an enormous "U"—and was holding court at a furious pace, mostly to a bevy of anxious-faced subchiefs, who seemed to have been drafted as bodyguards, to judge by the way they tensed when anyone from Ferr happened by.

Tryffon of Ferr was *not* present, true to his vow, but Strynn was—Avall had just bidden her a genuinely fond farewell as she went in quest of a pair of cousins she hadn't seen in over a year, who'd barely arrived in time.

As for the other to whom he felt any connection: Eellon was playing the same game as Tyrill, claiming territory, staying by it, and letting the world come to him. The only difference Avall could discern was that he was standing and she wasn't. Which was surely designed to contrast his relative vigor against her obvious frailty. Avall hoped he wasn't that petty when he got old. Not for the first time that night did he wish that Rann, his bond-brother, was there. Unfortunately, someone had to man the winter holds even during Sundeath, and Rann's had been the bad luck of the draw. Avall might see him again in the next year or not. It depended on how he fared in the Fateing, and on whether Rann chose to return home in the eighth before the next one or remain where he was, at Gem-Hold-Winter.

And speaking of Fate—the side doors were opening now, to admit those whose clan or craft conferred no claim on royal largesse, but who sought it anyway: those chosen by Fate to swell the ranks within, and which could include everything from brave children determined to observe ceremony firsthand to a small but representative smattering of clanless, unclanned, and Common Clan. They poured into the room in a disorderly tide, slowing instinctively as they reached the largely empty space in the middle of the hall. Avall was amazed all over again at the extremes reflected in their faces, which were in marked contrast to the attractive, if boring, sameness of most High Clans and Crafts. Sometimes, he realized, it was nice to see someone with scars, or rough-cut hair, or who was a bit on the stout side, or had a broken nose, or was tall.

Well, except Eddyn, on the latter.

He was spared further speculation when a flourish of trumpets signaled that the High King himself had entered the hall. Gynn paused at the top of the stairs directly opposite the main doors and behind the center of the high table, and watched in neutral silence as the hall erupted into a mad scurry for seats. Avall found Strynn (or she him), and then Merryn, and they all three located Evvion san Criff, Avall's mouse-quiet mother, and joined her, one twin to a side. They sat just down from Eellon, which was close enough to see Eddyn and Tyrill, but not so close they'd be expected to converse.

His guests having claimed their places, the King walked calmly down the stairs, unescorted, for he had no consort but Eron itself while he reigned. He wore white again, but velvet this time, and gold-velvet shoes and gloves accented his crown. He also wore his cloak of state: eight panels in the colors of The Eight-in-One, each marked with its respective mask in a sweep of embroidered gold across the shoulders. The whole was bordered in alternating tassels and herald-bells bearing the colors and insignia of every single sept and division of clan and craft alike. The bells jingled softly as he walked, and the effect was oddly soothing. Avall felt himself relaxing.

The King paused as he eased in front of his throne, then cleared his throat. "The sun has set!" he cried. "It dies the death undying, yet already it dreams of its rising, and with that, of rebirth. The sun rises tomorrow," he went on.

"Not the sun we have known for this half year, however, but its shadow, its reflection in the mirror of the sky. The sun is strong and must strive forever against the night. But the sun must sleep, to rebuild its strength, and so it leaves its shadow. Lords, Ladies, Chieftains all: I bid you remember the sun as we enter the year's dark half. And I bid you think on . . . rebirth!"

And with that short speech—which was half ritual and half improvisation, and the cosmology of which not one person in ten assembled there believed—High King Gynn of Eron, in the north of Angen, sat down and began to eat.

The first dish was sunblood. Actually, it was a thin, sweet cake, surrounded by stubby spikes meant to represent solar rays, and sprinkled with genuine gold dust. Gold: the blood of the sun and therefore its life, of which everyone present was entitled, in equal parts, to partake.

Avall ate his with the rest. But in spite of the fact that his bride-to-be sat glittering like the sun itself on his left hand, he couldn't make any of the complex tableaux of food and entertainment seem remotely real. He didn't like crowds, and so he withdrew a little, and watched and waited.

For somehow—and he had no idea where he'd acquired the notion—*something* was about to change.

Eellon was trying hard not to be angry at Avall, who'd done nothing to deserve it. Actually, he was angry in general, and targeting his most accomplished two-son was brutally inappropriate. Not that he'd have objected to the boy actually *displaying* some of the brilliance that lurked in his hands and brain—and tongue when his attention was focused. Eddyn had him there, he conceded: Eddyn had . . . charisma. Eddyn commanded loyalty and built cadre after cadre of followers—most of whom abandoned him once they realized the depth of his superficiality. Whereas people like Avall in spite of himself, and liked him forever once they did. He wondered if Avall knew that. Or Tyrill, or even Eddyn himself: how much of Eddyn's anger could be abated if the boy could manage to acquire—and keep—even one true, heart-deep friend. Certainly he had no bond-brother, though one youth had dissolved such a bond.

If only he didn't cause so much Cold-cursed grief!

And here came more—if the page marching toward him was any indication. Eellon had just seen him and a twin receiving murmured orders from the King. Well, Gynn had certainly witnessed his lame defense during Council, and would've received word of what transpired after, but the King wasn't quite clever enough—or was too involved with his own agenda—to see that anything that made Tyrill look foolish played into his hands. Which was the trouble with Kings who were elected, not born to command.

Eellon scowled at the page, though the message was a simple one: "When His Majesty rises, you are to retire to his withdrawing room."

He nodded, noting with sour pleasure how Tyrill had clearly received similar instructions. She saw him looking and glared at him, and for a moment they both locked gazes, neither daring to be the first to look away. *"Now,"* the page prompted, and departed—as an explosion of smoke in the center of the "U" signaled the beginning of another entertainment. The crowd gasped happy alarm, and Eellon used the excuse to break eye contact, exactly as Tyrill did, feigning smoke in her eyes.

The King *had* risen, too, but beckoned the assembly to remain in their seats and enjoy the festivities. By walking very rapidly indeed, Eellon was able to reach the appointed chamber a pair of strides ahead of Tyrill, to whom he smugly offered his arm, as was his duty as her Clan-Chief. She frowned but accepted, abandoning the two weary-looking pages who'd all but supported her.

The King paid no heed to her infirmity, nor did he offer them seats when he joined them. Instead, he claimed the middle of the octagonal room and studied them speculatively, arms folded. He'd shed his cloak, but that meant nothing. Eellon dropped Tyrill's arm and folded his arms in turn: master to apprentice, but that apprentice was still, for at least the next year, his sovereign.

"Fate crowned me today," Gynn said without preamble. "But I saw far more of His dark aspect, Contention—and have heard of even more—and I don't like it. Your clan, your craft, are strong. I won't deny that. You suffered less than most from the plague and so retained enough power and position that you elected one of your own to rule you. But I am, so The Eight say, the King of Balance. And I see Balance skewed. I see those who should work together at each other's throats. I see—there's no sense in lying about what we all know—a throne rendered less than stable by the squabblings of competitors who should be on the same side. How long must this continue? Both of you are old. You may soon be dead. What happens then? Schism within your clan? Energy, material, talent—maybe even lives—wasted?

"No!" he went on before either could reply. "This I cannot allow. I cannot make you friends, but I *will* remind you that your duty, if not to my self, *is* to my crown. Therefore, I lay a—let us call it a request—upon you. The Dark Half is upon us. Deep Winter draws nigh. Your protégés, Eddyn— *whom I name first because he is firstborn and thus first in protocol, lest Lord Eellon take insult where none is given*—and Avall, this Sundeath will enter their first Fateing. During the quarter that comes after, it would be wise of the two of you—and profitable for the two of them—to turn their genius to the service of the crown. In view of that, I cannot help observing that the present royal regalia has not been renewed since my predecessor's time and no longer represents the best our people can achieve. And"—he eyed Tyrill appraisingly—"if I must embody perfection, so should my regalia. There-fore I *ask* that Eddyn and Avall—and Strynn, if she will—spend Deep Win-ter, wherever Fate places them, constructing the following items for their King, which commissions I will reveal to them in my own good time.

"A sword. A helmet. And a shield."

Silence, though Tyrill opened her mouth.

Gynn stifled her with a glare. "Craft-Chief," he observed with a chuckle. "I am content with my *present* crown."

Balance! Eellon mused with a grimace as he swept from the room with Tyrill on his arm. *That was a laugh.* Balance, Gynn might have said, but what he sought was more contention. Argen—and Smithcraft, which it warded—was the only clan strong enough to raise him. It was therefore the only one strong enough to break him as well—as Tyrill that day had not-so-subtly sought to do. And such power, from Gynn's point of view, meant the Coun-cil of Chiefs itself was out of balance, which wouldn't do. It was thus in his best interest to set the competing septs of clan and craft at each other's throats in the guise of cooperation.

At which point he heard Tyrill muttering under her breath. "Balance," she snorted. "Indeed!"

CHAPTER III:

DEATH IN IXTI

(IXTI—IXTIANOS—YEAR BIRTH: DAY ONE—SUNSET)

~~~~~~~~~~

The year was all but dead.

It was getting dark.

It was supposed to, of course, but the effect was still chilling. So thought Prince Kraxxi of Ixti, who waited, silver-chased bowl in hand, at the northern point of the flame-filled pit that centered his father's Fire Hall, watching the Year of Sand expire. Sky shimmered above, like a canopy of blue-purple sylk, framed by the square soul-vent that mirrored the pit in shape and size. Smoke bound the two in fading spirals that smudged stars less bright than the jewels in King Barrax's domed crown.

His Majesty of Ixti stood in the west, where the sun had so lately descended in the same garish shades as his robe. Karvanni, his consort, balanced him in the east, a slender, half-veiled shape in gleaming sunrise brocades that set off her trim physique and made her eyes glow with more than reflected light. Between them, Azzli, Kraxxi's only brother, occupied the south: whip-thin, black-haired, and restless—and trying not to grin in a short-robe of red-and-gold stripes that made him look younger than the year that divided them. Together, those three superficially similar but very different men embodied House Fortan, the ruling house of Ixti: twentieth generation of the fourth dynasty. Kraxxi would be twenty years old in four days. He wondered if that was significant.

In any case, it had nothing to do with the dark; nothing to do with the

ritual his house was bound to execute. Restless, he shifted his weight, letting
his gaze dance through the forest of columns around them. Mosaics glittered
among those sandstone pillars like the stars above, their colors ten times
brighter. Torches flared there as well, but fewer every instant as, in descending precedence from the walls, the lords and ladies of Ixti's Landing Houses
extinguished their mother-lamps in silver bowls of seawater Barrax's servants had placed at their well-shod feet. Women sang, their veil-softened
voices ghostly as the night winds murmuring beyond Ixtianos's crenellated
walls. Cymbals jingled. Flutes twined melodies with those voices as the year
dissolved.

Less light now, and less again: a bare twinkling among the pillars. The
Mother-Fire was dying, too, in the pit. Eyes watched it, lit with waning
flame, as jewels winked and metal threads in rare brocades sought vainly to
hoard illumination.

Ten lamps remained, then five, then none. The Mother-Fire began to
fade and flicker as an unseen movement of Barrax's foot upon a hidden lever
flooded the pit with water diverted from the narrow rills that tinkled across
the hall's marble floor beneath bronze gratings. Steam hissed up like those
phantom, chanting shades made manifest, and mated with the smoke. Four
fires alone remained: stubborn flickering sparks more ember than incarnate
light.

A nod from Barrax, and Azzli stepped forward to empty his water bowl
atop one of those stubborn flames. It spat and died. Steam rose. Barrax
smiled his approval.

Another nod, and Kraxxi copied his brother, upending his bowl over what
were mostly sparks. They, too, vanished. Barrax did *not* smile, however—
which surprised Kraxxi not at all.

A third nod, and Karvanni, likewise, emptied her bowl. Again, no smile.

Only one flame remained: that at the feet of the king. The hall was a
thicket of pillared gloom. What sky glow survived was masked by clouds
that had blown in from the north—which *might* be an omen, Kraxxi reckoned. He wondered what the Eronese were doing tonight, for they also cele-
brated the autumnal equinox.

Kraxxi heard Barrax's sharp intake of breath as he inverted the final bowl.

Steam fogged the air, and darkness reigned. The singing soughed away to
a single whisper, one brave voice chanting lonely in the night.

Then silence indeed. Kraxxi prayed his stomach wouldn't growl. They'd
been fasting for eight days.

Silence . . .

"The year ends!" Barrax intoned ominously.

"The year *sleeps*!" Karvanni gave back the ritual correction. Her voice
rang, as though she relished that challenge. And with that she folded herself

down, in the east, where the sun rose, feet—now bare—tucked neatly before her. Azzli and Kraxxi followed her example. After the briefest of pauses, so did the king. *He doesn't like this,* Kraxxi mused. *Even for this, he hates relinquishing power. Even to his consort. Even to my mother.*

Silence again, as with calm deliberation Karvanni removed four objects from the folds of her robe: a plank of cedar wood with a finger-sized concavity bored into its center, a packet of dried moss, a straight stick of harder wood, and, finally, a curved twig bound at the ends with bark-twine to form a small bow as long as her forearm. A deft series of movements, and she wrapped the bow around the stick and placed it vertically in the hollow in the plank she had set between her feet, then began to saw back and forth. Her hands became a jewel-ringed blur.

It took excruciatingly long, and Kraxxi became anxious. Not because of the time, but because he feared his mother would fail to execute one of the few rites that were her province alone. Men destroyed; women made. His father proclaimed the end of the year; his mother its renewal. His father ordered the death of the Mother-Fire from which all other fires were born. His mother's duty was to produce new fire—Maiden-Fire—and by this archaic, cumbersome means, so that even House Fortan might not forget those days when Ixtians went naked and lived in tents of untanned hide.

And if she failed? Well, there were others among the court who could conjure fire this way. And surely, somewhere in the palace, someone had defied law and preserved some well-banked coal, in case.

Still, it would be very bad. Barrax would fly into one of his all-too-frequent rages. And Kraxxi's mother (but not Azzli's) would be disgraced, which would do neither of them any good.

But was that a spark he saw? A glimmer of man-made light? He held his breath. *Yes!* Flame glittered! His mother was feeding it web-moss and shavings, as her ancestors had done two thousand years ago. Unfortunately, the wind had shifted, and for a long, sick moment, Kraxxi thought the flame would fail—until another shift added the world's breath to his mother's. The glow promptly grew brighter. Fire sprang up healthy and true. She scooted back, adding more kindling in larger pieces. Her face showed clear as a moon, soft contours further smoothed by a waxing glow from beneath that flattened them into bas-relief. A glimmer of sweat sheened her brow. But she was smiling, lips curved in the thin line that was all she dared when Barrax's authority was in question, as though she was pleased by her success, yet knew that her husband had, in some part, wished her to fail.

Kraxxi knew *that* feeling too well.

A low, impatient cough, and Barrax made a sign. Servants appeared, bearing a shallow golden tray onto which the fledgling flame was shifted, to be set once more into the fire pit (which another hidden lever had drained).

"The year *is* alive!" Karvanni announced, rising.

The brothers and the king followed her example. But Barrax alone snatched two staves of red mountain cedar from a servant and thrust one into the fresh new blaze. Thick with resin, the wood caught at once. Night whirled away. Dark pillars regained their colors. Mosaics sparkled. Women began to sing again. Held breaths released as careful sighs. Taut muscles eased to softness.

Twenty breaths later, the new Mother-Flame was as bright as it had been throughout the year before. Barrax grimaced, but did his duty, lighting a second torch from the pit, with which he rekindled the household's Father-Flame. Lynnz, his brother-in-law, and the second most powerful man in the kingdom, approached in turn and lit his own mother-lamp. A parade of nobles followed—Lord Yaran, Lord Morvill, Lady Min, and so on—each relighting a personal household brand. By dawn, every fire in Ixtianos would be renewed, as couriers plied the nighted avenues with coals, embers, and torches of their own. Eight days from now every hearth, forge, and candle in the realm would have been extinguished and replaced.

Kraxxi risked a pair of fleeting smiles, first at his brother, then his mother, angling his head so his father wouldn't see.

"The year lives," Barrax acknowledged eventually, his face and voice wooden. "Let the feast begin!"

The Mother-Fire was covered by a brazen grate above a pierced-iron shell and would be tended for the rest of the year by a pair of trusted servants with no other duty. The surrounding hall was empty. Soot was black snow upon the mosaics.

Barrax's Feast Hall, across the adjoining courtyard, was *not* empty.

Though identical in size and shape to the Fire Hall, with the same forest of pillars centering an open square, it differed by being roofed with a raised sheet of stone supported by delicate, pierced-marble panels that let in light and air. This season, this far south, there was no need for heat; not with the press of well-dressed bodies, more than two hundred strong.

The king and consort reclined in the north, two steps above the central square, where a fabulous mosaic wrought by Eronese artisans (or slaves, it was hard to tell), showed the making of wine in intricate detail. There was method to Barrax's location, too. Eron lay to the north, beyond the dry desolation of the Flat and the forbidding heights of the Winter Wall, and by placing himself so, the king was deliberately turning his broad, strong, well-muscled back on that oft-stated, never-invaded, foe.

Kraxxi, seated by his brother in the south, wondered about that, as he wondered about most things to which he was denied more than cursory access. "The mysteries of adulthood"—yet they were no mysteries at all, but information, skills, *experiences* a person ought to acquire when he would. Why, many were merely things the common people knew as a matter of course. Barrax said he was too young. Too immature. Too lightly built to travel far afield. (Ignoring the fact that he was a skilled bowman, decent with a sword, and truly loved to hunt, though he'd long been denied his most desired—and dreaded—prey).

Not for much longer, however! In four days he'd be an adult and able to demand entry to his father's councils, to have his signature affixed beneath his sire's on royal decrees, and to claim full access to every book, document, and scroll in the royal library.

He also knew what Barrax feared. That he would impart whatever he learned to Azzli and thereby free the boy to think for himself, instead of simply be adored.

It was too late for that already.

Kraxxi fingered the dagger at his waist, and pondered how he would replace the wire-wound gold with a more appropriate hilt, then washed down the notion with a sip of syrupy wine and a morsel of skewered beef dipped in a nutty sauce. Azzli was watching him. He winked. Azzli winked back. His brother was enjoying himself, flashing that easy, white-toothed smile; maintaining a steady, witty repartee with the pretty daughter of Barrax's Master-of-Fleets without making Kraxxi feel in any way excluded. Which was his genius. Everyone loved Azzli—with cause. Kraxxi worshiped him in a way rare among sons of different mothers.

Just once, though, Kraxxi wished *that* particular knowledge would forsake him long enough to let him enjoy something. Like a truly sumptuous feast to welcome the new year after eight days' abstinence, like good company, like entertainment that had widened his eyes more than once in awe. But none of that changed the fact that Kraxxi was Barrax's son by an arranged marriage to a woman he didn't love, but who, like Kraxxi, tried to make the best of her situation.

Azzli, however, was the son of Barrax's sole legal concubine, and therefore a child of love. And when a brief flare-up of the plague five years back had taken Azzli's mother in spite of Karvanni's tireless nursing and a phalanx of Eronese healers, Barrax had salved his grief by wrapping both Kraxxi and his mother in a shroud of indifference that bordered close on hate.

An elbow in the ribs jostled him from his reverie. "You're supposed to be having fun!" Azzli teased. "If not, at least have some of this." He passed Kraxxi a plate of fried crustaceans of a type he'd never seen. "Caught without their shells and tenderer that way, but still crisp," Azzli advised. "Try them with sauce and without."

Kraxxi's face broke into a grin at the subtle, salty-sweet taste. "They're wonderful!"

"They're new. Fresh from a fleet that went far south and just returned."

"Hmm. Maybe Father will send for more."

Azzli regarded him gravely. "And you'd go, wouldn't you? Your eyes are full of wishes."

Kraxxi glanced around furtively, fearing to be overheard. Cushions rustled as he shifted closer to his brother. "I have to get away from here soon or I'll go mad. I know you're sick of hearing this, but I can't stand this incessant disapproval. Most of the common folk like me. The Master-of-Fleets likes me a lot—he was my sword master for a year, remember? It's only Father who—"

"Don't start!" Azzli warned. "You won't tell me anything I don't know."

Kraxxi sighed and looked away, wishing he could find heart to hate his brother. He couldn't; Azzli wouldn't let him. He was too good, too honest, too sincere. Too much the child of Kraxxi's own mother, who had all but raised him.

He started to speak, but Barrax was rising, motioning to a servant, who fled at a run, to return with a flat box of carved wood as long as his arm. This the servant placed on a low table between Barrax's cushions and Karvanni's, leaving the lid closed.

Barrax cleared his throat. The room mumbled into silence.

"Lords and Ladies," the king began. "The year has died. The year has been reborn. And four days hence, my elder son, Kraxxi, will reach the age at which he will be called a man—"

Kraxxi started at that: at the mention of himself, *and* at the subtle wording which carried implicit sly doubts about his worthiness to be so styled.

"—a man," Barrax repeated. "Now we all know that it is customary at Year Birth to give gifts; also that it is customary to bestow gifts to recall a child's birth, and other gifts on rising to adulthood—which would mean three gifts for my son in four days. I have thought long upon this and determined to dispense all three gifts at once. Kraxxi, would you come here?"

Kraxxi covered his surprise with a cough as he rose, smoothing the stiff green folds of his robe and stilling his face to neutrality lest the confused joy he felt be short-lived. He hadn't expected anything beyond the customary Year Birth gift, and even that was often delivered by servants. Still, the auguries had run strange of late; perhaps his luck was about to alter. He barely breathed as he crossed the glittering mosaic and knelt upon the single step one tier beneath that on which his parents reclined. His mother looked at him bright-eyed and smiling. Barrax's face was blank.

"You asked for books," the king intoned. "Books you shall have in good time, but for now, I give you this." And with that, he opened the box and brought out a circlet of golden metal two fingers wide, set with four enormous rubies. *A crown!* Kraxxi realized with a gasp. *Symbol of adulthood.* Eronese work, if he'd ever seen it, and surely among the finest. Which meant it could have come from a pillaged tomb along the border.

"Law does not permit you to wear this for four days," Barrax cautioned. "But you shall see it now."

When people can watch him bestow it and thus know his wealth and how much he cares for his son! "I thank you most humbly," Kraxxi replied clearly. "I—"

"The raising gift is the crown itself," Barrax interrupted. "The birth gift is the stones within it. The year gift is the gold of which it is wrought."

Fair enough on the stones. But the gold? Surely Barrax wouldn't announce that he'd been tomb-raiding. "Again, sir, I thank you most humbly."

Barrax's expression betrayed nothing as he raised the crown high, then lowered it to a hand's width above Kraxxi's head. To place it on him now would be very bad fortune indeed. Blessedly, Barrax didn't. Instead, he raised the crown higher, so that all could see, and addressed the assembled court. "This is Eronese work," he rumbled. "Let that be a challenge to all of you: that nowhere in Ixti are artisans born who can shape gold as well as this, for all our years of trying. The design is ours, in part, but even there the proportions were set by Eronese formulae. The gold came"—his voice broke, as real tears started into his eyes—"the gold came from the dowry of my former concubine."

Kraxxi's breath caught. *So that was it! Give him what he wanted—what he deserved—then taint it with a permanent reminder of that other. It wasn't as if his mother hadn't had her own dowry, and a rich one at that: enough to make that crown a hundred times over.*

Barrax was glaring at him, Kraxxi realized. "Return to your seat, Prince Kraxxi," the king said. "You may reclaim this at the proper time. For now," he continued, "I have also to bestow a gift on my *younger* son."

Kraxxi performed the requisite three short bows of formal obeisance and departed. Azzli was rising as he resumed his seat, looking bewildered. Kraxxi settled himself among the cushions to watch. It was another box like the first. But surely . . . surely, Azzli had a year and more to go before he could claim adulthood.

Yet Kraxxi watched shock-faced as Barrax brought out another crown, identical to his own save that it bore emeralds, sign of a second son. Otherwise . . . *there was no difference!* Though Azzli was by rights due only a Year Birth gift, Barrax had overfavored him again in the most blatant way possible, as though to say, "Kraxxi is my son, but this, his brother, is his equal in all things, save my heart, in which he has first place."

Kraxxi found something crisp to eat and let the crunching drown out most of Barrax's speech about "beloved younger son" and "revered and much-missed mother" and "gifted with glory before her time."

At least he didn't crown the boy, though he might as well have, and sure as the sun rose, a year from Azzli's true birthday, there'd be another crown, even more elaborate than this.

It wasn't Azzli's fault. Both brothers knew that, and Azzli had apologized more times than he could count for the fact that their father favored him. Happily, the king had stopped speaking, and Azzli was turning to face the assembled court, blushing like a girl at the rumble of applause Kraxxi knew was intended for both of them, but which Barrax had contrived for Azzli alone.

Even his gifts hurt, Kraxxi thought sullenly, quaffing the last of his wine and holding out his goblet to be refilled while he awaited his brother's return. Azzli flashed him a resigned grin as he reclaimed his nest among the cushions, but his eyes, unlike his face, were grim.

Fortunately, the bestowing of gifts signaled the end of the feast, so that Kraxxi was soon able to abandon the Feast Hall for the sanity of his own quarters, in the southwest quadrant of the palace's low, meandering sprawl. He considered waiting for Azzli, so as to assure the boy that he harbored no ill will regardless of their sire's intent, but the lad had been snared by the bright eyes and quick wit of the Fleet Master's daughter, and had lingered. Kraxxi had caught the words "escort you to your chambers," and that decided him. It made no sense to await his brother now, though Azzli wouldn't be so foolish as to sleep there. Young as he was, he knew well enough what would befall should he sire a royal heir outside marriage. And since marriage would be arranged for him, as for Kraxxi, and probably soon, he doubted Azzli would do anything to upset whatever negotiations were in process. Granted, the Master's daughter would be a prize, but Azzli had long ago confessed that he disliked casual couplings. "I have to love the person," he'd admitted simply. "And I can't love someone in an evening." For reasons not entirely clear even to himself, Kraxxi prayed his brother would maintain his resolve.

Since the palace was well guarded both within and without, Kraxxi refused escort to his quarters. The corridors grew progressively plainer as he strode away from the formal areas in the north. Fresh torches glittered in bronze cressets set in the walls, each with its own stone cupola in the roof to vent the smoke. The walls were tawny stone, the floor the same with a carpeted wool runner set into a groove to soften the tread. As he often did, Kraxxi paused in transit to remove his shoes and continued in bare feet. A pair of turns, skirting an open court, and he reached his room, already pulling at his robe's closures, as an evening's lavish food and drink on top of a fast made him eager to find his bed. A moment later, he fell naked atop the thick sylk pad that covered the knee-high bed-slab along the southern wall. Windows gaped to the right, giving onto his private sun court. The other walls were mostly hidden beneath a series of rough-woven tapestries that depicted the hunting of geens with bow and arrow, spear and lance, which were interspersed with Kraxxi's weapons, and the waist-high series of shelves beneath them, overflowing with books and scrolls. Hunting and books. The two things Kraxxi most enjoyed.

He wished he had something to read now; he'd read everything in those shelves twice over, which was why he'd requested books for Year Birth. He certainly hadn't desired a crown he'd wear once a season at most, and which would give him far less joy than his father took in flaunting it.

No! He was doing it again. Thinking about his father and the slight he'd delivered tonight in the guise of honor, and he's spent too many nights pondering that kind of thing already. Better to drink himself to oblivion and spend tomorrow like the rest of court: too hungover to rise.

But he didn't *feel* like getting drunk, and his last overindulgence was recent enough to dissuade him from a repeat encounter. Which left him alert (too much kaf with the wine at the feast), and with nothing to do but lie awake and fume, then get angry at himself for that feeling.

What he needed was someone to talk to, but he had few friends of equal rank and none inside the palace, yet travel outside was forbidden this time of night. Which, much as he hated it, left Azzli.

Sighing, he rose, shrugged on a loose white night robe, belted it carelessly, and strode for the door. No one was without save the hall guard, who wouldn't tell on him. And so he bent his path to Azzli's quarters, which lay (by law) in the next quadrant, so that no one assassin could slay both heirs with ease. He had just turned down the final corridor when someone rounded the far corner coming his way.

Azzli.

The boy's face lit up immediately. By the time they met outside Azzli's door, the lad's grin was so wide Kraxxi expected the top of his head to slide down his back. "I assume there's a story here," Kraxxi chuckled, as Azzli popped the latch and steered him deftly inside.

Azzli leaned against the carved wooden slab. "Two things. One is that rumor has it Father's planning to betroth me to Amna—the girl I was sitting with tonight. The other is that I actually think I like her well enough to—"

Kraxxi smirked. "Assuming she'll let you!"

"I . . . think she will. She's no fool, though, so maybe . . . oh, Gods, Kraxxi, I don't know! I—" Clearly exasperated, he began tugging at his robe, quickly removing it, then the underrobe, the trousers and shoes, halting at his skimpy underbreeches. Kraxxi watched absently, there being nothing else to observe. Bare, they looked even more alike: slim, spare-muscled, narrow-faced, dark-eyed.

"What don't you know?" Kraxxi prompted.

Azzli rounded on him, but not angrily. "Just that I've always held off because I'm a romantic, while women pursued me constantly—and now that I've found one I actually want, I may not be able to have her!"

Kraxxi found a low, stuffed chair and sank down in it. "You have any wine?"

Azzli blinked at him in consternation, then padded to an enameled chest near his bed. He returned with a carafe of green liquor and two small ceramic cups. "We both have troubles," Azzli sighed, as he curled up in the twin chair to Kraxxi's, with a wedge-shaped table between. The brothers looked not at each other, but at the opposite wall, where a fantastic landscape done in fresco dominated the room. They'd made up countless stories about that strange place when they were younger. Kraxxi's imagined-self had hunted every fantastic creature there, with every sort of weapon.

"You weren't just out for a walk, were you?" Azzli ventured at last.

Kraxxi sipped his drink and shook his head. "Couldn't sleep. Didn't really try, actually. Just needed to talk."

Azzli studied him anxiously, all traces of his earlier ebullience fled. Which was another good thing about him. He'd always listen. Always care. Whoever got him would get a good man indeed. "I'm sorry," he said, without the question being posed. "I had nothing to do with it. You know that."

Kraxxi nodded in turn. "I know. It still hurts."

"Hurts me, too," Azzli murmured. "Your mother's more popular than mine ever was, and that makes some people hate me right there. Favoring me in spite of it makes them hate me more. Father doesn't see that. He's a decent king—everyone says so—but in that one area he's blind. He doesn't realize that by bending the law for me like he did with that crown fiasco, he's causing trouble in the long run."

Kraxxi closed his eyes. "Father hates the bond between us; we can't let him destroy it. And he wants to, and that's a fact. Tonight was a hammerblow."

"I noticed."

"Ever wish we could just go away and forget it all?"

"Every breath."

"I'd hoped to go to sea this season. I'd wanted to see the south."

"Not while you're heir!" Azzli snorted. "And not because Father loves you so much. He's afraid that if anything happens to you—even something legitimate that goes wrong—people would blame him, whether or not he was at fault."

Kraxxi didn't reply. The lad was right, his argument concisely stated and well reasoned, utterly without vanity.

Azzli drained his cup and refilled it. "Know what *I* want?"

An eyelid slitted open. "What?"

"I want to get out of here, out of the city. Away from all this protection, all this partisanship, all these demands. All these *secrets*. I want just the two of us to go away and sleep out under the stars and—"

"And what?"

Azzli took a deep breath. "You're going to think I'm using you, that I'm playing to your weaknesses. I swear to you, I'm not. But . . . I want to go hunting."

"Hunting?"

"Geens."

"Geens!" Kraxxi all but shrieked, stifling an urge to cuff some sense into his brother. The things were deadly. Cunning, fast, and deadly. Why even *he* was wary of them. And he couldn't wait to hunt one.

"No, think," Azzli went on desperately, obviously repeating words he'd rehearsed. "I have to do it eventually. So do you. That's one thing Father dares not change. He can give all the crowns he wants, but without the geen's claw, birthday or no, crown or no, we're still not men."

Kraxxi rolled his eyes. "You think I don't know that? I've been anticipating that for years. I'm more than decent with a bow and can use a sword as well as most city boys. I've read every word on the topic I can find, studied the ones in the royal menagerie—"

"Scared you, too, didn't they?" Azzli broke in. "I've been doing the same thing."

"But why? You've got two years before the pressure really begins. I've got one."

Azzli quaffed his liquor in one draught, refilled the cup, and drank half of it. Which meant he was recklessly angry. Or scared. "Look, Krax. I *hate* the way Father dotes on me. It may look wonderful from the outside, but it's absolute misery. He watches me constantly. I can't relax. I have to be perfect. If I do well, I get praised more than anyone else who does as well, and that makes people hate me. If I do badly, he doesn't have me punished like he should; he makes up excuses—and I don't know why! No, I do: It's the love he still has for Mother. But I'm not her, Krax. I can't be. But because I look a little like her, he expects me to be her. Any day I expect him to get drunk and drag me to bed."

Kraxxi guffawed. "He'd get a surprise, too!"

"More than he knows. Men are fine—they're safe. Incest is another matter!"

"We were talking," Kraxxi observed, "about hunting."

Azzli set down his cup. "I want to go hunting, Krax! I want to go as soon as we possibly can. I want to do something reckless that might get me killed. Not because I want to die, but so Father will know he can't control me. And I want to hunt geens because I'm tired of him treating me like this precious fragile object. I want him to see that I'm a . . . man."

"Even though you aren't?"

"You'd want exactly the same, in my place!"

Kraxxi puffed his cheeks. The liquor made his head spin. "I could use a night outside, and that's a fact. But he'd never let us go."

"Then we won't ask!"

"We'd have to sneak. And whether you like it or not, we'd have to take some guards. Not even seasoned warriors hunt geens alone."

Azzli gnawed his lip. "Anyone you'd trust?"

Kraxxi regarded him warily. "Maybe. I know some guards. But I'd have to bribe them, and Father still might hear."

Azzli grinned again. "Not if we go tomorrow. He's leaving in the morning to inspect the port. He'll be gone six days. That's more than enough time."

"To escape maybe, not to find geens. They don't come this close to cities."

"Don't they?"

"You've been investigating?"

Azzli nodded sheepishly. "Let's say I've heard rumors that they're coming closer and acting oddly. Let's say we decided to check out those rumors. Let's say that if I accidentally killed one, it would still fulfill the law."

"And you'd be the youngest man in Ixtianos to have a geen-claw dagger. Which would make you special again."

Azzli glared at him. "That wasn't worthy of you."

Kraxxi sighed. "You know," he conceded, "I'm a fool for saying this, but you're right. Let me talk to some people, and I'll see what happens. But we can't do anything until tomorrow night."

"Tomorrow," Azzli smiled, reaching over to hug his brother, "it is."

For reasons entirely unclear, given the preposterous thing to which he'd just agreed, Prince Kraxxi of Ixti slept very well that night.

CHAPTER IV:

A JOINING AND A WARNING

(ERON: TIR-ERON—SUNDEATH: DAY II: BONDING DAY—NOON)

According to Ilfon, Chief of Lore, whose task it was to know such things, it was an especially good omen when the sun and all three moons stood in the sky together for Day II of Sundeath, which was called Bonding Day. It was called that because that was when all contracts proposed during the past year were assessed, approved, and solemnized—including betrothals. The astronomical manifestations were desirable because sun and moons were ancient symbols of man, woman, boy-child, and girl-child; therefore their appearance on the day when a season's worth of wedding bonds were proclaimed, blessed, and ratified could only be auspicious.

Avall wasn't so sure that was actually the case, though he was angry at himself for the thought, as he stood beside a radiant, ritually silent Strynn amid most of Eron's incipient newlyweds in the great plaza below the Citadel. Once the bonding would've been done on the Isle of The Eight. And briefly, following the plague, those seeking marriage had been so few that the custom was reinstated. Now, however, with childbearing encouraged, which required token service to wedlock, the numbers had swelled to fill the entire plaza. There were maybe two thousand couples in all, at least a quarter of them High Clan. Indeed, the place was packed solid with bodies when one factored in brides, grooms, and their Shadows. Merryn stood Shadow for Strynn, for instance, and Eellon himself was surrogate for Avall's bond-brother, Rann, whom the Fateing had banished elsewhere. The

worn cobbles were warm underfoot, but hard, and Avall had trouble avoiding the white and black ropes which lay athwart those stones and ran up to
the Citadel, where they disappeared through the mouths of man-sized sun
and moon disks made of pure gold and set up to either side of the Citadel's
Prow. At least the traditional dress, which dated from Eron's antiquity, was
comfortable: loose cotton robes for the women, knee-length wraparound
kilts of the same material for the men; white for first-bonders; black for
those seeking final confirmation. It was the most bare skin the bulk of them
would expose outdoors until spring. Just as well, given the occasional gust of
cold autumn wind, though the press of bodies and the steam pipes that
warmed the pavement made even that endurable.

Avall was having more trouble enduring the waiting. Not that he wasn't
looking forward to this; it was just that he'd found his brain locked in the
grip of a pair of contradictions.

He was in a crowd, and he hated crowds because they made him feel unreal. Indeed, he barely sensed himself as a conscious entity at the moment,
with his hands and feet half-numb from standing in one place for over a
hand. But he was also desperately excited because, while part of him had
misgivings about this whole affair, another aspect knew that tonight, when
all this unreality faded, he would be alone with Strynn, and she would be his
forever, and nothing would be the same after.

Assuming they renewed today's bonding a year from now. One usually
did unless there was good reason otherwise, which neither he nor Strynn
had been able to imagine. Besides, they'd have the baby, and The Eight
knew there'd be Cold to pay if they didn't continue. Avall favored it anyway;
if for no other reason than to protect Strynn from Eddyn's attentions.
Banned from marriage his rival might be, but that wouldn't stop him courting or casting his eye about.

A soft "ah" spread through the throng, rousing Avall from reverie. He
blinked as light caught his attention. A certain crystal on the Prow had begun to glow, which meant the sun's rays had found it at the correct angle to
indicate noon on this particular day. And at that exact instant, the doors to
the Citadel opened and two people marched out.

One was High King Gynn, dressed as a groom, save that he wore his
most ancient crown: the Crown of Oak, of which hardy wood it was made.
To his right came the Chief of Priest-Clan—a woman, as it happened:
World by her mask, though she was otherwise dressed in bride's guise—as
would've been the case regardless of her sex. Both carried unlit torches, one
in either hand.

Neither spoke—typical of Eronese rites—as, with well-rehearsed precision, they halted side by side flanking the gleaming crystal. It was getting

brighter, too, becoming difficult to look at. Avall could feel the heat pulsing off it even in the crowd.

"As light and heat are the pledge of sun to earth," the Priest intoned abruptly, touching her torch to the glow, which caused it to burst into flame, "so let this fire be the pledge of The Eight to the King . . ."

And with that the Priest brought her torch to one of Gynn's, which blazed up as brightly in turn.

"As fire is the pledge of the Priest to the King," Gynn responded, touching his unlit torch to the crystal, "so let this fire be the pledge of authority to worth."

So saying, he touched his new flame to the Priest's other torch, which likewise flared.

"As the sun gave us fire," they cried together, in an eerie singsong cadence, "and fire sealed the pledge of authority and worth; so let sacred fire seal your pledges one to another."

As if on cue, the jewel went out. A gong sounded in the Citadel, and at that signal everyone in the plaza reached down to retrieve one of the black or white ropes. Strynn found theirs before Avall did, and smiled as she slipped it into his hand ahead of hers: a white one, symbol of first-bonding. The strands were oddly slick, and covered with a damp, grainy substance that was rather unpleasant to touch. Eellon closed his hand on the rope ahead of Avall, and Merryn clamped hers onto it behind Strynn, and thus bracketed by their Shadows, they waited.

Not for long, however, for the gong sounded again. As the last notes thrummed across the plaza, Priest and King lowered all four torches and set the ends of those black and white ropes alight.

Fire awoke, bright as lightning, and swept down the twisted filaments faster than eye could follow: *too* fast to inflame even the flimsiest wedding garb. Avall saw one coursing his way and tensed, even as Eellon muttered an amused, "relax"—and then the flame hit Eellon's hand and disappeared. Avall felt the jolt—painful, but less like fire than like the tiny sparks that jumped from finger to metal in dry weather, and as quickly gone. He heard Strynn gasp and Merryn grunt, but when he opened his hand, only dark dust remained. The rope itself had vanished.

A mere breath it had taken for that bonding of man to woman by fire to run its course. And then it was over.

Over in Tir-Eron. The bonding fires would be preserved and sent by couriers to the other gorges where similar rites would be enacted by the subpriests and Gorge-Chiefs, all using torches lit from the primal source. There wouldn't be many; most who wed at all chose to wed in Tir-Eron.

And then Avall glimpsed Strynn out of the corner of his eye and embraced her. And for that time and place, in spite of the multitude around them, there was no other.

There was feasting that night in Argen-Hall, but it was not a lavish celebration. Those occurred at other stages in a courtship, most often at the concluding of the initial contract, at the final bonding—the black bonding, it was sometimes inauspiciously called—or upon the birth of the couple's first viable child.

Which didn't prevent Eellon's private dining room from being crowded. Besides Avall and Strynn, who held place of honor in the wide, low-ceilinged chamber overlooking Clan Argen's Judgment Hall—and Merryn, of course—there was Eellon himself. And Avall's mother, Evvion—who as usual had little to say, as had been the case since the plague had carried away her husband the same day it had devoured an unborn child in her womb—and Gynill, sept-chief of Argen-el. There was also Strynn's father and mother, and both sets of one-parents, not to mention Tryffon, Craft-Chief of War and his wife, Morginn, and testy old Preedor, Chief of Ferr itself. (Most of Strynn's direct line had been isolated in one of the most remote holds by a late-season storm and hadn't made it down to the gorges until Sunbirth, by which time the plague had largely run its course.) There were also assorted friends and more distant relatives, but few, beyond Lykkon, to whom Avall felt any closeness. Again, he wished Rann were here. Rann, who had no expectations of him, with whom he could be himself without artifice. He almost had that with Merryn, and would have, had she been male. He hoped he could have that same relaxed closeness with Strynn, because he'd *had* it with her once, when they were barely into their teens. Now— Well, they'd acquired titles to define their relationship, and that, for some reason, rendered them almost strangers. It would've been easier to bed Strynn, Avall concluded, if they'd simply decided one day to couple (as they nearly had when they were fourteen), instead of when ritual proscribed.

Still, he managed to enjoy himself (the excellent food didn't hurt; especially the fish chowder), and so was fairly relaxed when the midnight gong sounded at the Citadel, which was the signal for him and Strynn (and other doubtless more eager couples elsewhere in Tir-Eron) to seek their wedding beds.

It was a short walk from Eellon's dining room to Avall's quarters, as distances in the sprawling maze of Argen-Hall were measured, but for Avall it seemed to take forever. Never mind that by the time he and Strynn actually arrived, his wine-born sense of calm had dissipated, leaving him scared to death. He tried to hide it as he fumbled the key from a waist-pouch and passed it to his new wife. "First decent thing I ever made," he mumbled, blushing like a boy with his first unclanned courtesan. "After I became an apprentice, I mean. Lock, key, and bolt, all three."

She smiled, almost a grin. "I gave you the idea, as I recall."

The blush deepened. Trust the wine and . . . nerves to make him forget so important an episode. Even so, it had been six years. A lot could happen in that time. He cleared his throat awkwardly and began the speech he'd prepared. "With this key I give you access to all that I am. All that I own. All that I think. All that I feel. All that I know."

She took it and kissed him softly on the lips before inserting it into the lock, with the barest trace of a blush of her own. Good. She'd caught the symbolism. Someday he'd tell her how he'd determined the length of the key. It was no longer accurate anyway.

The small stone foyer beyond the steel-bound door looked familiar yet subtly strange, until Avall realized that a pair of Strynn's clothing chests had been left discreetly by the nearer of the two doors that gave on study and bedchamber in turn. There was also a bath and a tiny, seldom-used kitchen, but neither was accessible from here. Nor was the cluttered sprawl of his workroom.

"Five years," Strynn mused, as he held the door for her. "Five years since I was last here."

Avall started to say that was hardly his fault—and not even that, for asking—but decided that such a reminder would awaken memories best left undisturbed. Instead, he eased past Strynn to the bedroom door, pushed through, kicked off his shoes, and gestured for her to enter.

"I like this!" she cried, gazing around with clear appreciation that told him she approved of the way he'd arranged the spacious chamber, even if the basic layout hadn't altered. Inward-sloping stone walls were braced by tapering square pilasters, while a bank of windows set in arches to the left looked down on the Winter Garden. A fireplace gaped to the right, and straight ahead his bed—their bed now—rose a step above the floor, draped in the maroon velvet of his clan. A table and four chairs identical to those in Merryn's suite occupied the corner between the windows and the nearer wall. A carafe of wine chilled atop it, behind two silver goblets Avall had made just for tonight. "Wine, first? Or—?"

He glanced uncertainly at the bed.

"Wine," Strynn acknowledged, no more talkative than he. Which was just as well. Like him, she'd sensed the solemnity of the occasion, and more to the point, how circumstances darkened what should be unmitigated joy. Eddyn was an unseen presence for both of them. And though Avall's manhood had been reminding him since sunrise of how much he'd anticipated this moment, now that it was upon him, all he could think of was how Strynn would recall her violation every instant along the way. She would recall it when he touched her (even now she tensed a little), when he undressed, when he saw her bare, when they lay down, and drew together, and—

"Where are you, Avall?" she laughed, offering him a brimming goblet he'd neither seen her pour nor heard filled. He blinked and opened his mouth, but she shushed him with a finger. "Don't fret, my love. Nothing has to happen."

He nodded clumsily, took the wine, and quaffed more than was good for him. "I'm sorry," he sighed. "I've been playing roles all day and I'm just tired of acting. I— It's hard for me to deal with this confound ritualizing of things that should be spontaneous. It's like the Law's telling us we have to make love *right* now, but that may not be what we . . . want."

"I do," Strynn replied, reaching up to stroke his hair. "And I mean that. I need to touch someone I care about."

"I hope so," Avall mumbled, wishing to Cold he didn't sound so inept, yet desperately glad that Strynn wouldn't laugh at him even then.

"We don't have to, though," Strynn stressed. "I'm not even sure it would be comfortable, though I'm only showing a little. My breasts are . . . a little tender."

"Showing," Avall mused. "*That* might be a good place to start." Abandoning his wine, he reached for the cincture that bound the loose, blood red velvet of Strynn's bonding robe. Red for Warcraft, and Clan Ferr that ruled it. Red for the blood that most violent craft conjured in its season. She reached for his as well—they weren't cut all that different save that his was shorter and only wrapped around at the waist beneath the tie, where hers was also bound at the throat by a complex knot called a love-bow. Her bond-sister was supposed to tie that for her. Avall couldn't imagine Merryn doing such a thing.

Only an instant it took for two sets of deft fingers to loose those closures. Avall let his hands fall to his side when she got his cincture undone. She inhaled sharply, not quite looking him in the eye as he likewise took a deep breath, opened his robe, and in one graceful shrug let it fall, a puddle of maroon velvet on the limestone floor. And so, for the first time, Strynn, his childhood friend, object of his adolescent longings—and now his bride— saw him bare. *All* of him: what only one woman had seen since his Change. "You're beautiful," she whispered. "I always knew you would be."

He stood frozen, trying not to think of High King Gynn standing naked for another, less pleasant, inspection. And then Strynn reached for her bonding knot. He couldn't resist helping her ease the thick fabric away from her shoulders, nor could he help but echo her words as he saw her as she really was, not idealized by juvenile lust. And then he closed his arms around her and for a very long time they stood there, newly wed, naked, beautiful—and afraid. Eventually, the wine forgotten, Avall drew Strynn to the bed. Fire filled him: youth and joy and vigor, and his hands danced across her as hers did over him. Smooth flesh tensed and shivered. Laughter tumbled from oft-kissed lips. Chests were licked and breasts tasted. And the fire in Avall banked hotter and hotter—except in one crucial place. His manhood was dead as winter.

"I'm sorry," he choked at last, sliding off her and turning away so she wouldn't see his tears.

"I know," she whispered through tears of her own as she snuggled against his back and eased her arms around him. "I know."

His hands folded across hers on his belly, above that part he would most, at the moment, like to curse. "I'm sorry," he repeated.

Strynn's hand moved up to his lips to block further apology. "I know," she echoed. "Truly, Avall, I know."

It was his spontaneous triumphant snort that undid Eddyn. One moment he was lounging against the wall that divided Avall's bedchamber from the unused suite he'd co-opted, and was alternately appreciating Strynn's naked body and assessing his rival's nuptial nonperformance, courtesy of a small hole he'd drilled in the complex knotwork mosaic above Avall's bed—and the next a latch was rattling. The door to the corridor outside flew open, and he was face-to-face with a furiously glowering Merryn.

Though no larger than most Eronese women, Merryn blocked Eddyn's sole means of escape with her presence alone. Nor did he fail to note that the nice gray cloak she wore over sparring leathers was contrived to heighten that effect. Merryn wasn't hiding anything. Not her displeasure, and not the sword she was rather too conspicuously caressing with one elegantly tapered hand as she stood her ground, watching, but otherwise—save that dratted hand—unmoving.

Bolting was both unmanly and futile, so Eddyn did the only thing he could. He straightened with great dignity, flopped against the wall, and folded his arms languidly across his chest.

She crooked a finger at him—which angered him beyond belief. Before he could so much as reach for a dagger with which to defend himself, she was on him. One hand grabbed the neck of his tunic, the other replaced the sword with a wickedly pointed dagger, all in a blur of motion—and he was hauled into the corridor, well out of earshot of Avall's chamber.

"I assume," Merryn hissed, as she shook him to a stop against the opposite wall, "that there's a reason you're spying on my brother?"

"Curiosity," Eddyn rasped, making no move to twist away, which would only feed Merryn's vanity. Trouble was, the woman *was* good, and they both knew it.

"Curiosity?"

"I thought I might acquire some . . . pointers."

"Not with every woman in Tir-Eron desperate to wear your balls as earrings for what you did to Strynn! You think any woman will let you near enough to *need* pointers?"

Silence.

Merryn never wavered, but her gaze darted to the telltale wall. The room was long unused (and forgotten to the nonobservant; the corridor outside Avall's suite ended, it appeared, in a dead end), so Eddyn had made no effort to hide his handiwork. Even at this distance, the hole was obvious, as was the wooden plug he'd fashioned lest some random ray of light betray his clandestine endeavors.

"Spying!" she spat. "You *slime*!"

Eddyn didn't reply.

She shook him roughly and prodded him with the dagger so hard he feared she'd draw blood—which a lesser warsmith than Merryn would have.

"Silence is the safest response you could give," she growled. "You open your mouth, I may have your tongue for breakfast. But right now I have two things to say. One is that tomorrow morning as soon as Avall leaves his rooms, you and I are going to come up here and you're going to fill that hole. I'm not going to mention this to Avall or Eellon—and probably not to Tyrill. Not because they shouldn't know, but because I don't want tonight to be anything but wonderful for my brother. And because the others are more likely to show you mercy than I am."

She paused for another shake, then went on. "The other thing is that if I *ever* hear, or suspect I might hear, of you doing anything like this again, I *will* unman you. I may anyway, if Fate chooses us as opponents on War Day. I could do it then—legally. A slip at the wrong time, or a misjudged shot— and no one would ever know."

"They'd suspect," Eddyn blurted out, in spite of himself.

"But not *know*," Merryn snapped back in disgust. "Now, you and I are going . . . away. You are going to give me whatever key you used to get in here from *wherever* you entered, and you are leaving this level *now*. And I *will* be guarding Avall's door, per tradition."

Eddyn colored to his hairline and wished desperately he had access to *something* that would dispatch Merryn here and now without leaving any sign of foul play—or implicating him. Eight, but he was a fool! It was no comfort that Tyrill would've chastised him as much for getting caught as for spying. Not for the first time, as he fumbled through his belt-pouch, did he curse the whole sorry lot of them. Women: men's desire and men's bane. His whole life was circumscribed by women.

Soon enough, he found the key. Merryn snatched it away from him in stony silence, eyes blazing. Not until he'd turned the corner at the end of the corridor did his back stop itching in anticipation of a knife being bedded there. Clan-kin or no, Merryn would be seeking excuses to punish him further. Legal and legitimate ones.

Damn her!

And Tyrill.

And Strynn.

Eddyn went straight back to his quarters in Argen-yr, in the opposite end of Argen-Hall. He drank half a bottle of wine at one draught, undressed, and lay down, amusing himself with thoughts of Strynn. And would have drained the bottle, had he not feared Merryn's smugness if she saw him hungover. She'd know the cause to the letter.

Another triumph for Argen-a was more than he could ponder.

Blessedly, The Eight seemed neutral that night, and in spite of himself, Eddyn drifted off to slumber.

CHAPTER V:

INVASIONS AND EVASIONS

(IXTI–IXTIANOS–YEAR BIRTH: DAY TWO–LATE AFTERNOON)

~~~~~~~~~~

Kraxxi was sitting on the red-rugged floor in Azzli's quarters trying to fold his tawny-tan sand cloak into the smallest possible bundle while his brother pruned his collection of bowstrings and blowguns when the door, which was supposed to be locked, burst open and three armed men in unmarked livery tromped in.

Training asserted. Kraxxi flung the cloak at the nearest as he leapt to his feet, gaze questing frantically for his house dagger (out of reach on the bed, where he'd tossed it upon entering). The last invader parried the garment with an absent sweep of a mail-clad arm and joined his fellows, who'd fanned out to either side, black surcoats flaring ominously beneath mouth-masks and half helms that revealed only dark, angry eyes. Gloved hands moved as one to sword hilts.

"Going somewhere?" the nearest drawled in a woman's voice, as she casually kicked the door closed with a high-booted foot.

Impulse balanced between sarcasm and bolting, and had gape-mouthed Azzli not been dithering between Kraxxi and the garden vestibule, Kraxxi might have attempted the latter. At least that way he could make his assailants work for their blood money.

But intellect caught up with instinct and he froze in mid-twist and cocked his head. "Olrix?" he dared uncertainly.

The middle figure raised a slim hand to slide down the mouth-mask, and grinned, white teeth flashing wickedly from between full, pretty lips. "Wrong!" she snapped, relaxing out of aggressive attention to flop against the wall. "Or maybe she *is* Olrix. I can't remember which is which today."

The third clutched his crotch pointedly. "At least I know who I am." Male voice, which meant—

"Tozri!" Azzli yelped, having recognized his favorite of the three. Still shaken, Kraxxi sat down abruptly on the corner of the bed pad. Friends or not, this could still be bad, depending on whose orders had precipitated this invasion. "Where do you *think* I'm going?" he asked carefully. "More to the point, what are the terror triplets doing here? I thought you were enduring endless sunny days on the coast in the guise of guarding North Point."

Tozri folded himself into a neat black bundle that conveniently blocked the door. His sisters spread out on the floor to either side, removing helms and masks, to reveal matching crops of short black hair. "Hard to guard without a guard station," he began. "And as of that last blower, there is none—which I'd assume you'd have heard by now if I didn't know your father."

"Right," Olrix agreed brightly. "It was important, and we all know how eager he is to inform you of everything important."

Kraxxi rolled his eyes. "North Point," he prompted, ominously.

"Well," Elvix began, "it started getting dark in the east. Clouds so thick they looked solid and black as squid ink. It began to rain. The rain got harder. Wind began to blow and lightning to crash. We moved to the lower level. *Not* a good idea: We met the ocean coming up and spent the worst night of our lives cowering while the place came down around us. Being as how we three were closest to fulfilling our duty time, we were dispatched here to report. We have done so. We doubt we'll be returning anytime soon. Barrax would be a fool to send soldiers before he's sent an architect."

"As though Eron were likely to attack with winter coming on. An eighth from now they won't be *moving* up there."

"Stupid," Azzli echoed. "Not like they'd attack by sea anyway."

"Not like they'd attack, period," Elvix huffed, rising and starting to pace. "No one thinks they're enemies but those with a stake in keeping their commissions."

"Objective, aren't you?" Kraxxi chuckled. "One wouldn't think you had any Eronese blood at all."

Elvix's eyes flashed; her hand was back on her sword hilt faster than Kraxxi could follow. "You wouldn't, by any chance, be questioning our loyalty, would you? Not what I'd call wise for a lad on the verge of breaking every Denial in the Kings' Book, never mind the actual laws derived from them."

"Which brings us back to our original question: Where do you think you're going?"

Kraxxi took a deep breath. "To the Water Palace. It's been hot here. We thought it'd be cooler."

A brow quirked up. "And then?"

Kraxxi tried to look blank, which was stupid with Azzli looking so guilty.

"One does not," Olrix observed archly, "typically take a sand cloak on a pleasure outing. Nor blowguns. And especially not bows."

Elvix had found wine and cups and passed them about, patently ignoring Kraxxi and Azzli.

Kraxxi glared first at one triplet, then the next. *"Usually,"* he stressed.

"About time you loosened your locks a little," Tozri advised. "You don't need to lie."

"We're hurt, though," Olrix teased, sampling her drink and wincing.

"That you'd consider such an undertaking without your trusted advisers."

"Never mind your trusted guards."

"I think," Kraxxi growled, "we need to start this conversation over."

"How would *you* begin?" Olrix inquired, fixing him with impossibly in-nocent brown eyes.

Kraxxi drew himself up very straight. "I would recall, first of all, that I am a prince of the house of Fortan and order you three hellions to rise."

"*Is* that an order?"

"It is now!"

The three grimaced but stood. "We await your pleasure, Your Highness," Elvix, who was firstborn, intoned formally.

Kraxxi grinned. "My orders, then, are for the three of you to stay where you are, so I can give you an official welcome and then . . . *hug you!*"

All decorum dissolved as Kraxxi embraced each old friend in turn, with Azzli right behind. For good measure, he hugged his brother. Levity reigned. Though not heirs to a Landing House because of their Eronese blood, Elvix, Olrix, and Tozri were nonetheless the three best friends the royal princes had. Two years and a bit older than Kraxxi, they'd known each other since six-year-old Kraxxi was fostered in their father's household. Lord Aroni mar Sheer had been a ranking officer in the army and had sired the three on an Eronese healer he'd managed to entice south to tend a dying wife and with whom he'd then fallen in love, much to the chagrin of the rest of his house. Kraxxi had liked them instantly, and been so despondent at the notion of los-ing them when his fosterage concluded that Barrax, in his more indulgent days, had brought them to court and had them educated as well as any royal scion. With adulthood, he'd found them positions in the army, when they weren't serving as Kraxxi's personal guard.

They made a fine set, too: exactly of a height, and lithe rather than lean, with narrow faces and angular jaws and chins that looked better on Tozri; and full lips and dark, flashing eyes that looked better on the women. Their noses were identical: middle-length and slightly pointed. Their hair was the usual black and clipped short, as befitted soldiers, though the women's was perhaps a finger's width longer than their brother's.

"Well," Elvix announced, flopping down in a chair, as Azzli supplied them with more wine and a collection of odd-lot snacks, while the others found lounging places on bed, cushions, or floor, "now that we've all been introduced, I feel it my duty to repeat my question a second time: Where do you think you're going?"

"I repeat, a second time," Kraxxi retorted. "To the Water Palace."

"Both of you?"

Kraxxi shot Azzli a warning glance, then nodded.

"There's rumor to the contrary."

Kraxxi's heart skipped a beat, not wanting to contemplate what the punishment for such an unauthorized expedition as he and Azzli had been planning might entail. "What *kind* of rumor?"

Olrix grinned. "That you and someone who is very close kin might be embarking on an impromptu on-site inspection of some outlying holds to the northwest, where there's been trouble with the local wildlife."

"Who told you this?"

"Someone you can trust, who won't tell your father, and who assures me no one else will either, but who trusts us even more than you do."

Kraxxi drank silently, still uncertain whether to continue with the plan or abort it.

"What *is* your plan?" Tozri asked eventually. "Or did you actually have one?"

"The plan," Kraxxi conceded with a scowl, "was for Azzli and me to leave just past sunset with a small escort of trusted men-at-arms—destination, as I've said twice, the Water Palace. Once there, we'd have a light repast, swim, and when the household went to bed, we'd sneak out and head northwest, where we'd hunt for a day without supervision—which means we might actually *get* to hunt, as opposed to simply targeting terrified animals someone else runs to us. We'd spend one night in the wild and return the following day. People would see us come and go. But not Father—who's supposed to be gone by now anyway."

Olrix eyed Azzli speculatively. "And since the golden child here would be party to all this, there's some chance the king might keep his temper—and let those poor men-at-arms keep their heads."

"I'm hoping," Azzli said solemnly, "that I'll give him reason to be proud of me."

Olrix's eyes narrowed. "Oh?"

Kraxxi cleared his throat. "We didn't tell you what we were planning to hunt."

"Doesn't take a scholar to figure it out," Elvix replied, nodding at her sister.

Azzli's voice was barely a whisper. "Geens."

Tozri fingered the dagger that hung at his waist. Gold filigree crusted the sheath, but the guard and handle were visible, the latter a hand-long curve of dark material roughly two fingers wide at the base, tapering to what would've been a dangerous point, had it not been capped by a ball of more filigree. "I'd argue with you, were it not for the fact that I got this one when I was Azzli's age."

"I know," Azzli observed dryly. "That's where I got the idea."

Elvix and Olrix glared at their brother. "You were whipped for it, too."

"Still got the claw."

"It *would* be good," Kraxxi inserted, "to have experienced geen hunters along."

It was Tozri's turn to raise a brow. "*Along?* To what does this foolish prince refer, sisters?"

Matched shoulders shrugged as one.

Tozri feigned surprise. "Oh, I see! He thinks we will accompany him on this fool's errand. He thinks we wish our backs laid open with the lash when he is found out."

"He thinks," Kraxxi broke in, "that there's been talk enough. We're leaving for the Water Palace in"—he glanced at the complex time counter on the wall—"two hands. I'd love to have you three as company, never doubt it. But do *not* think to stop us."

"Wouldn't dream of it," Tozri grinned. "We're already packed."

Two hands later, five figures, all of whom now wore the livery of the princes' guard, ambled into the golden stone splendor of the royal stables, which lay between the palace proper and the Sunset Gate, in the western wall of Ixtianos.

A quarter hand after that, the same five, with an additional five in slightly less ornate regalia, rode smartly out from beneath the stable's low but impressive vaulting and onto the Sunset Road. The sun *was* setting, too: a dull red orb on the southern flanks of the Winter Wall. The sky was clear. Two moons showed, one full, one crescent. Hooves raised little dust on the soft stone pavement as Kraxxi urged Noowa, his lithe black stallion, ahead. He felt as good as he had in ages. He felt . . . *young*, and only then realized how long it had been since he'd truly let himself go, and consequences be damned. That, and the thrill of the forbidden that lurked beneath it, made him want to dance and sing and jump off his steed, rip off his clothes, and run naked through the surrounding fields, where wheat and rice and cotton alternated, increasingly, with patches of lifeless salt-sand.

He resisted. Three hands later, with all three moons bathing the sand with three subtly different lights, they crested a rise and saw the Water Palace ahead, a splendor of delicate white amid its lush green oasis, with the river Oblink running by on its way to link with the Morhab, which bisected Ixtianos itself. Half a hand after that, Kraxxi did strip bare and dive into the bathing pool, with Azzli and Tozri close behind. Elvix and Olrix chose not to indulge (though they'd been known to), and instead made a show of seeing the horses stabled and stowing gear so it could be accessed quickly.

Kraxxi made a note to reward them when he got the chance.

By midnight, they were dry again, well fed on a minimal meal the household servants had supplied, and had all grabbed brief naps. By the set of the first moon, all ten were riding again: northwest, through more fertile country. If they were lucky, they'd come to hunting land by dawn, could hunt a little, then sleep through the hottest part of the day.

For the first time in ages, Kraxxi was happy.

CHAPTER VI:

BY THE RIVERSIDE

(IXTI: MYRRLL DISTRICT—YEAR BIRTH: DAY THREE—BEFORE DAWN)

～～～～～

Kraxxi yawned lavishly, savoring the taste of the predawn air. His weariness didn't embarrass him as much as it might have, because Azzli had been yawning constantly for the last hand—not unreasonable, given both had been riding since shortly past midnight, along with the rest of their band. Elgwyn-yl, the last town of any size in this direction, was itself more than three hands behind, and they'd long since exchanged seemingly endless fields of irrigated cotton for a mix of rolling grassland, scattered woods, and desolate salt pans framed by distant rock outcrops that were not quite mountains. The *real* mountains, the Winter Wall, rose beyond. Their nominal goal was Sprinet, which was the center of the wool trade in this part of the country. Wool meant sheep, and sheep were easy picking for pack carnivores like geens. Lately there'd been an increase in attacks, mostly on outlying farms, and it was Kraxxi's intent to rationalize this trip as firsthand investigation. He was legitimately interested, too. These were his folk, after all; their welfare was his own. And if the rumors he'd heard were true, royal troops might soon be needed to patrol the more remote farms. There'd been a garrison in Elgwyn-yl, but it had been withdrawn during the plague and never reinstated.

"How much longer?" Azzli wondered, edging Wanoo, his sand-colored mare, closer.

Kraxxi squinted into the moonlit gloom, amused that his brother might actually consider him the leader of the expedition instead of a foolish, head-strong prince who was being indulged by three friends who were also royal guards, and a host of men-at-arms, any of whom would have no compunction about throwing him over the saddle should he prove recalcitrant or rash.

Not daring to press his luck so far as to risk this venture alone, he'd tried to pick kindred spirits: four men and one woman who professed more loyalty to him than to his sire, none of whom were so old their own youthful misadventures were more than a hand of years behind them. One of them, a wiry young man named Lynzil, had been a sometime playmate since youth, denied closer attachment because of his common birth. The others consisted of a slight, pretty woman named Dazz, who might or might not be Lynzil's lover; a pair of short, sturdy brothers named Sarx and Mazil, whose humor was even more subtle and dry than the triplets'; and the somewhat older Lord Yaran, whom Kraxxi suspected was the source of the rumors. Still, Lynzil, who'd recommended him, swore he was worth the risk, for his knowledge of geography, geens, and outdoor living.

"How much farther?" Azzli persisted, swiping at dust that had given him a mustache his bloodline might otherwise deny.

"A hand and half to Sprinet," Kraxxi replied, "but we won't be going there." He pointed left, where a finger's gallop away a long thread of trees between the rolling, grassy hills hinted of water. "This may be your trip," he continued, "but if we go to town first there's no way we'll be able to do this unobtrusively. We'd have to meet the ra-lord; we'd be feasted. You know the rote; first thing we know, half the day's gone, and with it, the best hunting."

Azzli grimaced.

Yaran trotted up to join them. "Your brother's right. Geens hunt just past dawn and right before dusk, because that's when their traditional prey are most active. But we'd be fools to seek active geens while we're sleep-dull, so I'd suggest we rest by that river there, nap who can, but with a guard— though I've never heard any reported on this bank—and be fresh when the geens are."

Azzli swallowed hard. "But do we *want* them to be fresh? Most sources say its wiser to come on them unaware."

Tozri squared their number with a loud snort that indicated he'd caught the tail of their conversation. "Doesn't really help," he opined. "They just look like reptiles; their blood's as hot as ours. They move as fast. Might be almost as smart. Probably *are* as smart as some of us, given what we're doing."

Azzli studied him warily—a little alarmed, Kraxxi suspected. "What our friend is saying," Yaran inserted, "is that they're *never* sluggish. They're active and *very* active. Nor do they all sleep at once; they always leave one per pack awake, and there's usually four in a pack because they're born that way. But you did have one thing right: It's better to face them in the daylight than in the dark—because they can also see better at night than we can."

Azzli scowled. Tozri grinned at him. "Getting worried, are you? Suddenly realized that this isn't just shooting targets somebody finds for you that happen to be alive? Geens have their *own* agenda."

The scowl became a pouty glare. "So why'd you let us come? You could've told Father."

"He doesn't know everything. You needed to do it for all manner of reasons, and so does Kraxxi. You're never going to be kings of real people and real things if you don't meet real people and real things. Barrax has forgotten that."

Kraxxi cleared his throat, noting that the copse had grown closer as they'd conversed. And yawned again. "You're right, a nap would be good. Azzli and I will sleep, you three can if you like, and the rest will guard since they're only here to keep us from harm."

Tozri rolled his eyes—and kicked his horse to a slow gallop. Kraxxi paced him; so, after a moment, did Olrix. Lynzil rode up beside them as Yaran fell back, his rust-colored sand cloak at odds with the others' tan. He grinned at them. "Race?"

Kraxxi's reply was to dig his heels into Noowa's sides. An instant later they were tearing across the plain, through grass that brushed their feet, with Yaran shouting unheeded warnings in their wake. It was wonderful to be so wild and reckless even for this brief time. Still, Lynzil managed to find the only thornbush around and swore vividly as finger-long spines savaged his leather leggings. His mount screamed, too, and Lynzil reined in the stallion immediately, all frivolity vanished. Kraxxi, in the lead, ignored the incident and continued to grin like a maniac as they arrowed toward rest and sleep and dawn.

The grove proved more thickly grown than expected, but was almost as pleasant as the deliberately wild gardens at the Water Palace. Indeed, had the wide, slow river been bordered with paving stones instead of a beach of coarse sand—and had the place not sported nature-wrought walls of overgrown hedge in lieu of carved surrogates—it would've been easy to proclaim the site civilized, though it was actually as far into the wild as Kraxxi had ever gone so lightly attended.

Lynzil arrived while they were setting up their temporary camp, leading his horse, which had not only caught a thorn in his side, but one in his hoof as well, which the youth immediately began tending, ignoring his own bleeding leg. The stallion and other mounts were picketed upslope from the river on a narrow bit of greensward between the sand and a thicket of chest-high laurels, beyond which skimpy, flat-topped trees gradually gave way to grassy savanna. Yaran had words with Lynzil about misuse of horseflesh (which wasn't fair; the youth clearly loved horses better than people), and the upshot was that he got stuck rubbing down the mounts, with Dazz helping. Kraxxi volunteered as well, but Tozri shook his head and told him to get some sleep. It had been a cool night, for all the day's fierce heat, and the beasts were neither particularly tired nor lathered.

Satisfied that affairs were in reasonable order, Kraxxi followed Tozri's advice and stretched out in the sand beside Azzli, with Olrix (who'd had too much to drink at the Water Palace and was complaining of a headache) at his back, and Elvix behind her. Tozri sat upright at their feet, professing, as always, no need for sleep. Yaran and Mazil made the other two points of the guard-triangle. Sarx relieved Dazz on the horses, while Lynzil worried at his mount's tender hoof. Azzli was asleep immediately, but Kraxxi had a hard time relaxing, in spite of having found a depression in the sand that needed only slight reshaping to accommodate his hips and shoulders. Once padded with his cloak, he had a snug little nest indeed, almost flush with the ground. With his hood flipped over his face, he was all but invisible—even to the sleep he needed.

Still, he managed to doze, slipping into a light, drifty lethargy full of dreams of sparkling water.

A horse screamed.

Pain awoke him: an explosion of agony across his thighs, coupled with an impossible pressure as some vast, shifting weight sought to drive him deeper into the sand. Sharp points dug into his flesh. Horses whinnied; people yelled: male and female alike. The air clogged with the stench of blood and a sweet, dry muskiness he recognized as geen.

One of which was standing right atop him! Dazed, he opened his eyes, only to close them at once as a scaled foot as long as his forearm stamped down a handwidth from his nose. Nor could he reach his sword because the same three-toed talon that pinned his legs prisoned the weapon. In any event, he had sense enough to know that holding still was his best defense, though it all but killed him to lie there while pain ebbed and flowed along his thigh and at least two horses died screaming. A man-at-arms was screaming, too, long and piteously, then cut off by a swish-rip-gurgle that made Kraxxi's gorge rise. Blood splattered his head from above. By the clamor of voices, he knew that Tozri and one of his sisters lived. Otherwise . . .

More pressure and worse pain, as the geen dug in. He almost cried out as another shift of weight let him twist onto his side. And then the pressure resumed, immobilizing him. Steeling himself, he opened his eyes—to see Azzli peering out of the other depression, absolutely terrified. Their choice of beds had saved them—for the nonce. That, and the sand-colored cloaks. But the geen's head was directly above the boy; Kraxxi could see its shadow dancing there, dim in the predawn light. Worse, he caught occasional glimpses of the small but effectively clawed forelimbs, and the dagger-toothed lower jaw.

Someone was fighting it, too—black boots: Yaran and Mazil—feinting at the beast with spears, trying without success to lure it forward.

Azzli's face was white, and he was clearly about to scream, but Kraxxi shook his head frantically and bit his lips, hoping to silence him. If the geen didn't notice them, they *might* live. They mostly smelled like sand and leather, not blood. (And he bet it was the blood from that wounded horse that had drawn them here, farther east than he'd ever heard them reported.) Given that the horses had sounded the alarm, the geens must have attacked from the south, which was upwind (though he hoped they weren't smart enough to know that). They'd gone for the horses first because they smelled most like prey animals and one was bloodied. The horse guards had attacked—and likely been killed for their trouble.

A supposition confirmed an instant later when the geen stepped back, then sideways, which let Kraxxi slide far enough up the hollow to see a second man-sized fury of tan-yellow scales, snapping jaws, flashing claws, and whiplash tail assailing the terrified horses, two of which were dead, while another ought to be, as its entrails were tangling on the grass. Dazz was also down and minus an arm. Lynzil had been disemboweled. Sarx was holding his own—barely. And then he wasn't, as a feint from the geen drew his aim left while teeth went right. Blood spurted as the geen bit into the juncture of neck and shoulder, but he managed to wound it as he died, thrusting his sword into the abdomen and ripping down. The geen screeched. Blood spurted. "Brother!" Mazil yelled in despair, shifting Kraxxi's attention back to the battle above him.

He had to get out! Not only from fear of being trampled to death where he lay trapped like a rabbit in a cage, but because people he cared about were fighting for their lives around him and he could do nothing to aid them. And his brother was right *there*: as helpless as he, more terrified—and more rash.

"Draw it off!" Tozri yelled, and Kraxxi saw his friend ease into view from the left, using—he was disgusted to note—Dazz's severed arm to lure the geen above him and Azzli away. That worked where mere feints had failed, and the weight left Kraxxi's legs—to be replaced with a wash of pain so intense he wondered if bones were broken or, worse, major arteries ripped. Winded, he lay there, half-frozen by shock, as the battle moved toward the water, providing a glimpse of the largest geen he'd ever seen snapping and pawing at Mazil, Yaran, and Tozri, who held it off with spears and sword respectively.

Finally free to act, Kraxxi scrambled to his feet and had just drawn his sword when a random sweep of the leathery tail flung sand into his face. He pawed at eyes suddenly thick with grit and burning with tears. And then arms swept around him from behind and he was hauled backward to the shelter of a low bank on the north side of the copse. By Olrix, from the distinctive smell of the soap she always used. A similar tan-gold shadow was Elvix dashing past to wrest Azzli from his hole and drag him back to join them.

"Let me go!" Azzli shouted, sounding far less a prince two years shy of adulthood, than a boy half that age.

"No!" Elvix gave back sharply.

"*You! Stay!*" Kraxxi added, as he finally regained sufficient command of himself to wrench free of Olrix. He swabbed frantically at his face with a wad of cloak. Vision slowly cleared.

"There ought to be more!" Olrix hissed. "One down, one attacking—where are the others?"

"Waiting," Elvix muttered ominously. "Letting their friends do the work so they can come in and pick up the rest. The horses aren't going anywhere."

"Because half of them are dead," Olrix snapped. She eyed Kraxxi dubiously. "You hurt?"

He shook his head. "Can't half see—but I'll live. They *won't* if we don't help."

She gnawed her lip as though deciding which of the available options best fulfilled her obligation to protect the heirs.

"If Toz dies," Kraxxi told her, "you lose a brother, and I lose a friend I love like one."

Olrix stared at him an instant longer, then nodded. "Hold him whatever you do," she told her sister, indicating Azzli. "Give him a bow if he wants to play hero. But keep him out of the fight—and watch your back! There's enough blood around that you two ought to be safe if you stay still, but one never knows with geens."

She didn't give her sister time to respond. With a shout that was clearly intended to distract the geen attacking her brother, she leapt forward, flapping her cloak behind her as she'd taught Kraxxi to do: increasing apparent mass to cow would-be assailants.

Kraxxi followed her example, not daring to think. That way lay fear, and with it disaster. He was angry. He was afraid. He had no feelings at all save a blind desire for all this to end—and for that, geens had to die.

Olrix had reached the big geen now, and severed a third of its tail with a casual sweep of her blade—just as it knocked the spear from Mazil's hands. A swipe of that same clawed limb took most of the man's face along with his helm. He fell, flailing at the rent in his neck from which his life spewed red upon the sand. "Spread out!" Tozri cried, moving away from those jaws as the surviving man-at-arms danced across his comrade's body. Olrix eased toward her brother, leaving Kraxxi to complete the square, wishing he had something longer than a sword. One normally hunted geens with a bow: from a distance.

"Look out!" Elvix yelled behind them. "Kraxxi—!"

He spun around barely in time to parry a claw that would've beheaded him, then ducked, spun again, and came up under the belly of a third geen, no taller than he. He managed to open its stomach as he ducked once more to avoid the lashes of matching tails. It vented a liquid screech, staring down with an oddly human expression at the widening line along its belly. And then a fourth leapt into the fray from behind the shiny-leafed bushes whence they'd all come. It hesitated, gazing around as though assessing the situation, then attacked the horses—in an unbelievable fury of teeth and claws. Kraxxi saw two go down at once. A third was blinded; a fourth, lamed. But a fifth—his own Noowa—managed to free himself sufficiently to lash out with hooves. One came down on a scaled skull—a grazing blow, it nevertheless knocked that geen to the ground. Noowa reared again and stomped the reptile's legs. One snapped with a sickening pop, the other scythed out and laid open Noowa's leg from knee to fetlock. He screamed and collapsed—which put him in range of the downed geen's jaws.

Kraxxi dared not watch, for the geen he'd wounded took one absent swipe at him, then dived into the mass of dying flesh. Blood fountained. Kraxxi glimpsed two sets of reptilian jaws tearing at his mount before instinct sent him diving to earth again as the big geen's stump of tail narrowly missed him. The beast spun around, slamming hard into Olrix, who had no way to leap aside. She "oofed" and fell heavily onto her left arm. Tried to rise and grimaced, even as she shifted her sword to her right hand.

Kraxxi picked himself up, half-dazed, deciding while vision cleared that geens feasting were less a threat than geens assailing his comrades, and joined Tozri. Olrix rose, too, grim-faced, left arm hanging useless at her side, though that didn't stop her from slashing at the geen's freely bleeding tail as it swished by. Its balance was off, Kraxxi noted, a result of that caudal amputation, but that only made it angrier. Were it not for Yaran's expert spearwork, it would surely have breached their guard. "Hold it off!" Tozri cried grimly. "Just for a breath!"

Yaran nodded, not taking his eyes from the beast, as Tozri scooted behind him to retrieve Mazil's spear. Kraxxi moved to fill the gap, feeling no fear at all as he stared across a shard of metal at a head as big as his torso with teeth as long as his hand.

Why wasn't it jumping? That was how they usually attacked: jumping and slashing out with those enormous toe-claws that made such fine dagger hilts. But then he saw: A long, puckering scar down one fowl-like leg effectively crippled it.

As though it mattered when he was staring up at its leathery chin with only a pair of spears between himself and death. And then not even that, as it batted Tozri's spear aside and bore down upon him.

"Azzli, no!" Elvix shrieked. Footsteps pounded—two sets—but Kraxxi dared not turn. His fool of a brother had managed to free himself from his nominal warden. But then it didn't matter because Azzli was beside him—with Elvix—covering Olrix's unguarded side with sword and spear alike. The beast lunged toward them. Jaws snapped. Claws flailed. Yaran stabbed a muscular haunch with a spear, but the beast twisted around like a metal spring and snapped at him, wrenching the spear from his hands as it advanced. Tozri jabbed at its neck as the head flashed by. It coiled around to snap at him, missing his arm by fingers and catching a handful of cloak that refused to tear. Still, the maneuver would've given Yaran time to roll away had the tail not caught him solidly in the head.

Tozri was in trouble. The geen threw its head back, and Tozri, caught by the cloak, rose with it. A flip, and fabric ripped, sending the guard flying toward the river, where he landed in a heap and did not rise.

Kraxxi's heart skipped a beat, but his blood was hot as he narrowed his eyes. Elvix chose that moment to stab the beast in the chest with a spear, but it was Kraxxi's sword that found the jugular.

"Krax!" Azzli shrilled behind him, voice so full of panic Kraxxi knew he was under attack from that quarter. Reflexively, he spun, letting the momentum of the blade carry him around—and stared in horror as his sword found purchase not in another geen, but in his brother's throat.

"That hurt!" Azzli yelped, eyes going ever wider, as blood drowned the ensuing panicked scream.

Elvix screamed, too—and Olrix. "Sweet Gods!" the latter choked as Azzli crumpled. Kraxxi could only stare numbly, not even caring that the geen lay twitching-dead behind him. So did the others—evidently. He didn't care about them either. He cared about nothing save his brother—his *dead* brother, he feared, as he collapsed to his knees beside the boy, pressing his hands to the smooth tan throat awash in pumping blood. "No!" he breathed. "No! No! No!"

"Not your—" Azzli managed through a mouth clogged with gore. He smiled—and then his eyes glazed over and he stared up at the mauve-blue sky of a sunrise he would never see.

Kraxxi sat back with a thud, sick beyond nausea as his gorge fought him more fiercely than any geen. He couldn't move. Absolutely could not move, though his hand grew stickier as the last of Azzli's heart blood subsided.

It had taken no longer than required for Elvix and Olrix to join him, their faces white beneath their tans. Olrix had lost her helm and her hair was like a slick black helmet. Elvix removed hers and with it her cloak, and swept them across the boy. Her cheeks were wet. Her eyes were wide and staring. "It was an accident!" Kraxxi breathed. "You know it was!"

Olrix nodded. "But, oh Kraxxi, it was still your sword. And we're bound to repeat what we saw if we come before the king."

"Then don't!" Kraxxi countered recklessly, rounding on her. "Don't ever go back. I'm not—I can't. Not now!"

"You must," came another voice, harsh with anger. Yaran, who'd finally made his way there. He, too, had lost his helm, and the side of his face was bruised black where it had caught the brunt of the dying geen's tail. "You slew your brother. You're bound to report that death to the king. If you won't, I am so bound!"

Olrix was on her feet at once and would've engaged the man right there had her arm not been useless. "You know it was an accident!"

Yaran shrugged in a nonchalant manner that made Kraxxi's blood grow cold. "He knew his brother was nearby. He could've stayed his hand. He didn't."

Elvix joined her sister on her feet, and Kraxxi would have as well, had that not meant leaving Azzli, and he couldn't bear the thought of abandoning him. "You can't possibly be saying," Elvix hissed, "that Prince Kraxxi killed his brother deliberately!"

Yaran raised a brow and backed away ever so slightly—toward the river. Which was also, Kraxxi noted with a frown, where the single remaining intact horse was now grazing. "It is well-known," Yaran replied carefully, "that Prince Kraxxi *hates* his brother."

"I do not!" Kraxxi flared, finally making it to his feet to stand with fisted hands before the older man—who outmassed him by half. "I love him more than anything!"

"More than your crown?"

"Fuck crowns!" Kraxxi raged. "I want no crown! I want my brother back!"

"You won't have him," Yaran retorted, taking another step back. "Nor will you have your crown when your father hears of this. He will pronounce anathema on you."

"Why are you doing this?" Kraxxi choked.

Yaran regarded him levelly. "Because I serve the king. Because the king asked me to watch over Azzli no matter what."

"But why not tell the truth?" Elvix challenged.

"Which truth?" Yaran gave back. "Mine, or yours?"

Olrix glared at him. "You'll never leave here alive!"

He met her glare with a wicked grin. "You'll still have a dead prince to explain. You have honor—one of you must. You won't lie. Kraxxi did slay his brother. That's kin-death. Which is punishable by death, no matter what. The law was made to prevent exactly this sort of thing."

"You," Elvix gritted, "are a dead man."

"No," he corrected, "I'm the king's man, always and forever." And with that he flung the sand he'd concealed in his clenched fists straight into their faces—and bolted. The women tried to pursue him but, half-blinded, tripped over the body of the big geen, and by the time they'd managed to untangle themselves, Yaran had reached the horse—his own, as it happened—and was spurring to a gallop down the beach, toward the shelter of the trees. Kraxxi simply stood numbly, only then realizing he still held the blood-stained sword, with which he could have slain the traitor.

If traitor Yaran was.

Kraxxi cursed himself for a fool. For having trusted Yaran in the first place, when he'd had misgivings; for not having killed him just now; and for the simple fact that the man was right: He had committed fratricide, which was a death offense without recourse. Azzli's body *was* here. Soon enough Yaran would return with men to take him captive. The only option then would be to lie: to say that Yaran had killed his brother, or one of the dead men had; that this so-called expert had lured them into an ambush.

His breath caught. Yaran had directed this hunt all along, subtly, but surely. Suppose, though, that it hadn't been Azzli's death that was intended, but his own? The rumor of the hunt *had* gotten out. Maybe it was all a cleverly contrived ruse, beginning with Barrax's gift of the crown, which would make Kraxxi angry, which—

He kicked at the sand and tried not to look at his brother, and by looking elsewhere, saw Tozri, and was sick all over again.

"Elvix," he said numbly, "we need to see to him."

"And anyone else who may have survived," Olrix added, sounding as dead inside as he. She'd loved Azzli, too. As much as Kraxxi had, perhaps. In any event, Tozri was stirring, which he supposed was a good sign.

His eyes slitted open when they reached him. Blood trickled from his mouth where he'd bit his tongue. His sisters sat down beside him, but Kraxxi held back, gaze flicking constantly to his brother's still form. "Geens," he began. "They do only hunt in fours, correct?"

"Usually," Elvix assured him. "If there are others—right now, I doubt I'd fight them. The whole future's changed."

"To what?" Tozri managed thickly, wincing as he tried to lean up on his shoulder. The three of them had four good shoulders among them, Kraxxi realized.

Elvix told him.

"You couldn't stop Yaran?" he demanded when she'd finished.

"Not with him having the only remaining horse."

"Have you checked?"

Elvix looked sheepish. "No."

"You ought to. You ought to search the other men, too, and secure whatever weapons you can. And those claws we've ruined our lives for," he added, indicating the dead geens.

"And then what?" Kraxxi managed.

"Disappear. I've never trusted Yaran, and I don't trust him now. He knows we're yours and will speak against him if he tries to make what you said more than an accident. He knows that we're well liked. He knows that if he's proved forsworn before the king, his life, too, is forfeit."

"He's playing a dangerous game," Elvix agreed.

"So," Tozri observed, as he rose—wincing again and grabbing at his shoulder, "are we."

Olrix nodded glumly and started back up the beach, then paused and studied them all in turn. "Claws," she told Elvix. "Because you've got two good arms. I'll check bodies. Toz, if by chance any horses still live, you know what to do."

"And me?" Kraxxi wondered, swallowing hard, suddenly aware of exactly how much pain he was in, mostly from bruised thighs, though blood also oozed from assorted puncture wounds.

Elvix regarded him sadly. "You mourn."

• • •

"How long do you think we have?" Kraxxi asked a short while later. The sun had cleared the horizon, washing the clearing with light the color of bloody sand. Kraxxi had shed his filthy tunic and used the clean lining to wash the blood from Azzli's face and neck before arranging him more gracefully atop one cloak, with another over him. He was covered now, and Kraxxi doubted he'd ever see his brother's face again. Not if things went as they might.

The triplets sat around him, not threatening, not judging, simply coping with their grief, their wounds, in their own way. As they'd feared, no one else had survived, though Lynzil hadn't actually breathed his last until Elvix found him. His final words had been of Dazz. The men-at-arms were laid in neat rows just above the high-water mark, covered with more cloaks. All the horses were dead—now—though an appalling three had required dispatch. In any case, none would have supported even one rider to give chase to Yaran. The only good thing, Kraxxi reflected, was that they had a fine collection of geen claws—for barter if things went as he feared. He'd been awarded two; the big geen had been his legitimate kill. And he'd make sure that one claw burned with Azzli. Which raised another question.

Too *many* questions.

Tozri looked at the sky, wincing as that simple movement wrenched his damaged shoulder. And scowled. "You say Yaran rode south?"

Olrix nodded. "Along the river, though that could've been good sense. We couldn't chase him, and there was too much cover that way for bows."

"Nearest town's still a hand to the north and the wrong way, if his duty's to the king, as he says. More like he'll ride to Elgwyn-yl and send word on to Ixtianos from there, then return here with whatever forces his royal writ can muster."

"To take us prisoner," Kraxxi sighed.

Tozri shrugged. "He's a practical man. He knows that we're snared in a quandary. Either we remain where we are and await justice, or we flee and are outlawed."

Kraxxi looked at him sharply. "*We?* You've done no wrong. It was my sword, my impatience, my carelessness—"

"Don't!" Elvix warned. "We're as guilty as you are because we sanctioned this, and don't forget that we're Azzli's guards as much as yours, for all we've known you longer. What we *should* be doing is following Yaran as fast as we can to tender our resignations."

"We're guarding the body," Olrix growled. "That's also part of our duty."

"Which raises a question," Tozri mused. "If there's no body, there's no proof. And we've geens aplenty. We could—I hate to say it, but we could savage Azzli's body with their teeth and claws—"

"No!" Kraxxi snapped. "He's been savaged as much as he's going to be."

"There's time to cremate him," Elvix observed. "If we're being thorough here."

"Or we could give him to the river."

"*No!*" Kraxxi repeated. "It's the fire or nothing. The only question is, where will the fire be? Here, or in Ixtianos?"

Tozri's brown eyes were very sad. "You're his family, my prince. There's only one person who can say you nay, and he's not here. Nothing you do will affect the outcome at all."

Kraxxi was already glancing about in search of firewood. "Make a fire," he commanded. "If you don't mind. This is for me."

Tozri nodded but didn't rise. "There's still time, my prince. There're still things to discuss."

Kraxxi looked at him, eyes suddenly a-brim. "I don't know," he burst out. "I don't know what I ought to do! I don't know what's really ethical. I don't know what . . . a prince would do. Nor an heir."

Elvix took his hand. "Yes, you do. The law is clear on this. Fratricide is punishable by death. If you return to Ixtianos, you'll die. You won't lie about this, nor will we. Nor, I think, would you want us to. Your father might show mercy, but I doubt it—not until it is too late. You've seen his rages. He might well cut you down where you stood. Still, your options are twofold. One we've just discussed, the other is that *you* could take your life. There would be honor in that. Or, you could pronounce your own exile."

Kraxxi gnawed his lip. "But what about the succession?"

Olrix spoke up. "Azzli's death and yours leave the land without a direct heir. Your father is young enough to sire others, but that could produce a regency. He has sisters who have children."

"One of whom," Elvix observed slyly, "is promised to Yaran's brother."

Tozri frowned. "This suddenly becomes *much* more complex."

"There's another possibility," Elvix went on. "Even if you were under death sentence, there'd be some flexibility about when it was carried out. Your father could marry you off, see you sired a child, *then* have you executed. And have you watched at all times to ensure you did your . . . duty."

"What about you three?" Kraxxi wondered. "I've got you into this. It's for me to get you out."

Olrix shook her head. "We could've said no. We could've reported your plot to the king. We're guilty by association. We"—she eyed her siblings warily—"I, at least, *would* lie for you if you asked. You're my friend, and that fact overrides blood for me. You can choose your friends, and you chose us. Kin are catch-as-may."

Kraxxi's frown deepened. "Well, then. Since we're inspecting options, let's look at *yours*. You give yourself up and are, at minimum, disgraced. Or you fight to keep Yaran's men from taking me; but two of you are injured, and *can't* fight, so that gives you an honorable death. Only I won't let you do that, and that *is* a command. Or you could go into exile."

"With you or alone," Tozri added, "to keep all options open."

"Assuming *I* go into exile," Kraxxi countered.

"You've been wanting to see Eron," Olrix supplied helpfully. "We've Eronese blood—and, frankly, I can think of no reason to stay in Ixti."

"I would never ask that of you," Kraxxi protested. "Much less command such a thing."

"We're half-Eronese," Olrix retorted. "Once there, we're under their law."

"I'll have to think about this," Kraxxi sighed. "But right now, I have to do something much more mundane." He indicated the river meaningfully.

Tozri squeezed the prince's shoulder with his good hand. "You think. We'll make that bier."

Kraxxi rose stiffly, snared his cloak, a fresh tunic, and his pack, and limped—courtesy of his injured leg—down to the riverside. Just out of sight of the carnage, he concluded his business, then paused before returning. He'd brought the clothes because he had some notion that a prince ought to greet his captors in good array, and indeed, that was still his intent as he washed himself thoroughly, then changed from the skin out, saving only the brother-ring Tozri had given him when he'd entered his service, which glittered like dark fire on his left forefinger.

Yet as he stood staring at his murky reflection in the water, something occurred to him that split the difference between honor and desire for life. He had three choices: execution, suicide, or flight, in decreasing degree of prestige. But Olrix was right: Ixtian law held force only in Ixti. And his people, almost as much as the Eronese, worshiped Fate, which manifested most strongly at crucial junctures in one's life. So suppose he resigned himself to Fate? Suppose he let the Gods decide?

As for his friends . . . He loved them, but their lives and therefore their choices were their own. He dared not twine their lives with his, nor drag them down to his own private dark.

So it was that without really thinking about it (or perhaps it was delayed shock manifesting), he waded out into the river until it lapped against his chin. Taking a deep breath, he leaned back—and let the water take him. If the Gods ordained his death, this would effect it. It was a form of suicide, and in that, too, he was doing the honorable thing. And if the Gods delivered him to shore before he drowned, he'd take that as a sign he should live and—

What?

Head north, he supposed. Into exile. Into Eron.

There were deserts and mountains between here and there; and suicide, he concluded, as coolness wrapped him, didn't have to be a sudden undertaking. The water dragged at him, but he spread his arms and, for a long time, floated.

CHAPTER VII:

JUSTICE IN THE RAIN

(ERON: TIR-ERON—SUNDEATH: DAY III: SUNDERING—DAWN)

~~~~~~~~~~

Avall awoke to find rosy dawnlight replacing the candles that had gut-tered down to puddles in the night.

A night in which he'd slept better than expected but still not well, and not because, for the first time in his life, he'd shared his bed with a woman. A woman and a friend. Strynn.

He wondered how many young men in Tir-Eron—how many in this very hall, where she was as constant a sight as in her own native War-Hold—had gone to sleep envying him last night? How many would've laughed them-selves silly if they'd known how that night fared? How many—

She moved. Nestled comfortably against the small of his back. Yawned, by the sound of it. He yawned, too, spontaneously—and rolled over, to see the curve of her shoulder silhouetted against the lozenged mullions of the window. Stone showed across the courtyard beyond: crenulations painted warm pink-gold by incipient sunrise.

The dawn gong sounded in the Citadel. The sun had cleared the rim of the sea.

Avall considered rising, bathing, preparing to greet the day—but it was nice simply to lie there all warm, cozy, and secure, beside a woman he'd al-ways . . . idolized, he supposed, more than loved. And with that notion pil-lowing his mind, he dozed.

When he awoke again into brighter light beyond the window, Strynn was looking at him. She lay on her side, head propped on her left arm, black hair tumbled across her brow so that her eyes were shrouded. Her face was serious. Calm. Contemplative.

He blinked, then caught himself and smiled. She smiled back: woman to girl in an instant's time. All at once words welled up in him. He started to speak, but she preempted him with a finger to her lips. "Don't say it," she warned.

"What?" he dared, in spite of her.

"That you're sorry. You're going to say you're sorry again, and you don't have to be. We both know what we were trying not to think last night, and thinking anyway."

Avall flopped back on his pillow, arms folded behind his head, staring at the dark oak ceiling and the carved-knotwork panels set into the coffers there. The sheet had slipped below his waist, and his body felt cool and flushed at once. Had he been alone, he'd have pulled up the cover. But he'd denied Strynn so much already, he wouldn't deny her access to his body. "Perhaps," he replied, with an honest chuckle, "I was merely going to say, 'Good morning Strynn, my new and very lovely wife.' "

She laid her hand on his chest above his heart and stroked the smooth skin there. "Good morning, Avall, my new and very beautiful—and honest, and unjustly sad—husband."

And then came the gong signaling that an eighth of the time had passed until noon. And since ritual called again—the traditional wedding breakfast with the groom's clan—Avall put away the notion that had begun to awaken in his groin now that he was comfortable and relaxed. With great regret, he kissed Strynn lightly and slid out of bed. He could feel her eyes on him, but that gaze was like a caress: soft spring winds on bare skin. He ambled toward the bath, then noticed last night's wine, still mostly chilled and largely untasted. He filled his goblet and Strynn's and brought them to her in bed, sitting on the edge as they clicked the silver together and drank each other's health.

They bathed together, in Avall's deep mosaicked tub. They also toweled each other dry, and brushed their hair together, and helped each other dress—he in hose, short velvet tunic, and suede house-boots all in the requisite clan maroon; she in her first gown of the same, tight-sleeved and quartered with her own clan red, and both in black tabards in honor of the solemnity of Sundering Day, or as it was more commonly called: Death Day. When they went down to breakfast, Avall was already anticipating their return to his quarters. Tonight, he was certain, would be nothing like the previous one.

. . .

Noon found the elite of Clan Argen and the twenty-three others gathered before the Citadel in the Court of Rites. The Court was lozenge-shaped, one point terminating in the doors of the Citadel itself, the opposite comprising the Prow, from which the Binding had been performed. The sides angled out from those two foci, those closest to the Citadel (and thus the walls of the gorge) sculpted into stone benches behind a waist-high railing; the other two forming the sides of the Prow. The benches were occupied now by a solemn company required by Law to attend and witness (if not enjoy) the two primary ceremonies that were heart of the Sundering. Avall and Strynn were there, attending their first public function as man and wife, which would've been ironic had there not been many another set of newlyweds scattered among the throng. Merryn was present, too, and Lykkon, officially as Eellon's body page, but actually because he'd begged. Tyrill was in attendance as well, as Craft-Chief, in the company of Norvvon, sept-chief of Argen-yr, who'd only that day recovered sufficiently from a forging accident to attend any functions at all. Eddyn was also there: distant, stiff, and white-faced—and as far from Avall as decorum allowed. He was glowering at the world in general.

But perhaps that was appropriate, since anger was associated with Sundering and its ultimate expression, Death. And so they stood there: clan robes and craft robes shrouded by black tabards, black cloaks, and black hoods—raised now, to signify that their wearers functioned in official capacity as Witnesses. The King, too, sat black-clad upon a simple throne on the steps of the Citadel, facing the Chief of Priest-Clan on a plain chair in the Prow.

Between them, centering the lozenge, rose a temporary dais of the same shape and proportion as the Court, atop which stood the Priests of the day: Law, Fate, Man, and Life, each appropriately robed and masked. They were chanting in ritual singsong the names of everyone clanned or crafted who'd died during the previous year in all of Tir-Eron. Their subpriests and subchiefs did the same in the other gorges. Avall felt an eerie thrill at the notion of all those names entering the air, floating on the winds, then . . . *gone*; as the smokes of their burning had entered those winds in their own times and seasons. At least it didn't last as long as it could have. Once—the year of the plague—it had taken a day and a night to invoke the names and stations of the dead: one in six adults in Eron at large, and one in four in Tir-Eron, where it had begun soonest and longest lingered.

One in four. Himself. Strynn. Merryn. Eddyn. One of them would've died.

One in three men, too: Himself. Eddyn. Rann.

One in three, for a fact: His father, and Merryn's. Eddyn's father. Lyk-kon's. Rann's.

Eron was a nation of elders and adolescents. Almost nowhere, as he gazed around, did he see a healthy, middle-aged man. But perhaps his children might.

Which reminded him of Strynn's child, which reminded him of Eddyn, which put him out of sorts again.

It began to rain, a ghostly sprinkle that slid off hoods and masks alike, to cover the Court with a sheen like a sylken shroud. A hand later, under thunderous skies, the sentencing began.

The same Priests presided as before, one at each point of the central dais, but now they were joined by a phalanx of men in the livery and masks of Law augmented by two of its aspects, Justice and Mercy. It was from those two that executioners came. *Not* torturers. Eronese justice was firm; always final—and quick.

Grivvon, Priest of Law, who faced the King, cleared his throat, then spoke, his voice ringing across the paving stones. "Of the crime of treason against the Kingdom of Eron, the King of Eron, or the people of Eron, committed by those of foreign birth, it pleases me, Your Majesty, to announce that there are none.

"Of the crime of desecration against the Kingdom of Eron, the King of Eron, or the people of Eron, committed by those of foreign birth, it dismays me, Your Majesty, to announce that there is one."

The King's face was grim. "Let that one be brought forward and his crime be stated," he commanded. Nor had he any choice; treason and High Clan matters required display of protocol, but the number of cases would increase as the Priests worked their way through lesser crimes and lower clans. Still, some crimes were granted all the time they required. Like crimes against the State, the King, and the people. Like treason or desecration.

Avall held his breath as two guardsmen trod up the stairwell set into the paving between the Prow and the Citadel, with a man in soft-chains between.

Even had Avall not heard the facts of this case expounded numerous times across the eighths since the man's arrest, he would've known the prisoner was from Ixti. He had the same tall, angular build; the same severely barbered jet-black hair; the same sun-darkened skin. And he'd been granted the clothes he'd worn: ankle-length merchants' robes and expensive ones. No surprise there; most Ixtians in Eron were merchants—or spies. Even so, Eron still sought to honor a man above his deeds, and so the merchant hadn't been stripped or deprived of his extravagance of golden jewelry; and had been fed and given the comforts his station would've afforded him, save that he'd been imprisoned in the dungeons beneath the Court.

Again Law cleared his throat. "There stands before you, Majesty, Chiefs, clansmen, and craftsmen, one Rylixxor, merchant of Ixti, in this land by the free leave of High King Gynn, to whom he presented proper tokens; and now convicted of the crime of desecration."

The King rose—a variation of the usual form. "My Lord Law," he intoned, "rare is the crime of which this man is guilty, and of which he freely confessed, and rarer yet the fact that its perpetrator is a foreigner. Therefore, it might be instructive if the particulars were proclaimed and relayed to those who wait without."

Law paused the barest moment, then nodded. "Know then," he thundered, "all you assembled, that by ancient Law the charge of desecration will be invoked for the willful defacing or desecration of any work of man or nature deemed by the masters of any craft to constitute a masterwork, or determined at later date to constitute a Treasure of the Realm. Said act to be considered as heinous as murder or any other crime which results in damage that cannot be precisely recompensed in kind."

A pause for breath, then: "So says the Law."

"And this man's crime?" the King inquired.

"That on the fifteenth day of Sunbirth this man did seek to carve his sigil in the statue of Choice at the Shrine of Southgate."

The King nodded. "I have heard it said," he remarked casually, for all he wore his crown and thus his word was Law, "that some in Ixti do this thing on a dare—certainly others have carved their marks there. I would have thought, however, that this man was of age and dignity not to assay such a thing."

Silence.

The King looked at the motionless, tight-mouthed merchant. "Have you anything to say?" he demanded.

"I was drunk, Majesty," the man replied carefully, in clear, if accented, Eronese. Politely, too, which was just as well, considering the time he'd had in which to ponder his fate. "I was not thinking. I meant no disrespect."

"Nor would I to you if I killed your horse unknowing," the King retorted. "But I would still know it was not my horse and try to recompense the owner."

"I have offered all I have!" the merchant pleaded.

"The Shrine will never be as it was, for all your offering; for all your King has to offer, for that matter. It will always and forever be less."

The merchant bowed his head. "I can say nothing to that."

"Nor should you," Gynn gave back. "It is to educate those who hear that I repeat the facts of this case. Know then my judgment, made in consultation with the Priests of Law, the Chief of Clan Eemon, and the Craft-Chief of Stone-Hold, whom you have in particular offended." Another pause, then: "The sentence imposed upon you is fourfold. You are exiled from this land never to return. Because you say you were drunk when you committed this offense, you are to lose one half your tongue so that you may think on that whenever you taste strong drink again. And because you say you were not thinking, you will lose one eyelid so that you may always be thinking of the value of what you see. Finally, because you sought to carve your name in a part of my land, my name shall be carved into the flesh of your head so that bone shows through."

The man blanched, tensed as though to bolt, but was held firm by the guards to either side.

"So has the King proclaimed," Law announced, as Gynn resumed his seat. "So let his justice be done."

And with that, the man was escorted below.

Avall breathed a relieved sigh, as did Strynn. "Good," he murmured. "I was afraid we'd have to watch."

"Not for so complicated a procedure," Eellon confided, having overheard him. "Only the results will be displayed: first here, then to those who wait without. If there were fewer cases, it might've been done before us all, but Gynn has sense, and time is one thing he'll *never* desecrate."

"I think," Avall muttered, scratching an itch that had appeared between his shoulder blades, where he couldn't reach, "this is going to be a very long day."

"Get used to it," Eellon informed him. "It's the price you pay to be what you are. I—"

He broke off, for the Priest had moved on from crimes against the State to crimes of people against their equals.

"Of the crime of murder without cause, regret, or compensation, committed by those of High Clan against High Clan, it pleases me, Your Majesty, to say that there are none.

"Of the crime of murder with cause, or in defense, committed by those of High Clan against High Clan, it pleases me, Your Majesty, to say that there are none.

"Of the crime of murder by accident or neglect, committed by those of High Clan against High Clan, it pleases me, Your Majesty, to say that there are none.

"Of the crime of assault with permanent injury, committed by those of High Clan against High Clan"—there followed a slight but very deliberate pause—"it pleases me, Your Majesty, to say there are . . . none."

Avall noted those pauses, too, and was among many who turned their gazes—discreetly or not—toward Eddyn. Rape fell into the greater category of assault with permanent injury. Had Tyrill not interceded, Eddyn would've been standing out there now: brought to bow before the Priest of Law, stripped of the colors and robes of clan and craft, and escorted by two royal guards to the gorge's rim, thence to go where he would so long as he set no foot in Tir-Eron or any holding of Argen or its septs, or Smithcraft and its divisions.

Eddyn wasn't reacting, but Avall was sure his hood was pulled farther forward than heretofore, and that there was a guilty stiffness in his bearing. Tyrill reached over to clasp his hand in one of her bony claws.

"Of the crime of assault without permanent injury . . ." the Priest went on.

And so on, through all crimes that could be committed by those of High Clan, in descending order of severity. Destruction of goods without compensation. Destruction of goods with compensation. Theft. Breach of contract. Oathbreaking.

On and on ran the tally of crimes of which those of High Clan might be accused. Blessedly, there were none; nor were there usually. What passed for Eronese nobility had sense enough to respect the Law and stand clear of it. Or knew how to manipulate it.

At the end, the King rose once again. "Of crimes announced and executions undertaken, of High Clan against themselves or lower, I stand here as Witness and Judge, well pleased that my trusted friends, clansmen, and advisers so well respect the Laws of Eron."

The ceremony—if one could call it that—lasted the rest of the day. Crimes committed by High Clan were followed by those committed by Common Clan—those people of good character or family, who by Law, inclination, or circumstance had either drifted from the official ranks of the High Clans or never held that status (though some, in fact, lived as well)—and then the few unclanned (most of whom did not). Inevitably, too, as rank decreased, crime increased, though Avall suspected that Tyrill wasn't the only one guilty of clandestine maneuvering. Eventually, there were actual executions, performed with numb precision around the dais. For murder, uncontested and before witnesses: death by beheading. For murder by accident: servitude of various duration to the offended party's clan. For murder in defense: exile for a year to a nonclan winter hold. For theft: loss of fingers determined by value of object, plus the value of the object itself. For breach of contract: the sign for "distrust" branded into the offender's forehead. And so on. Of rape—officially assault with permanent injury— there was little. One man was exiled. One, a repeat offender, unmanned. A woman who'd used two young boys against their will became the servant of their clan.

Avall was yawning before it was over. Lykkon, who'd replaced Merryn beside him, elbowed him in the ribs good-naturedly. "Long night?" he murmured. "Or not long enough?"

Avall wished he'd had time to set the lad straight about the facts of the previous evening. Nor would Lyk have teased him even slightly had he known the truth, for he was a good-hearted, if impetuous and opportunistic, youth at heart. As it was, he was acting under his best guess—and galling Avall beyond belief without meaning to. Nor did his next question improve matters.

"So . . . what did you think?" Lykkon asked, as the last offender, a man guilty of slander, had a hot nail laid on his tongue.

"I think," Avall snorted, "that I'll be careful never to run afoul of the Law—and I'm glad I've managed to avoid this until now."

"Not to your good," the ever-vigilant Eellon inserted over Lykkon's head. "Nor Eddyn's, else he might have thought twice about a certain indiscretion."

Avall tried not to look at his rival—who'd seemed too intent on the events in the Court for Avall's liking. "Much as I hate to admit it, that's probably true. I've never understood why Law grants *all* Common and unclanned the right to observe whatever punishments are relevant to them, but denies it to High until we're of age—excepting body pages."

"Which you could've been," Eellon noted dryly.

"I've been researching that," Lykkon volunteered. "The Law, I mean."

Eellon rolled his eyes. "Is anyone in our entire clan *or* craft going to remain in it? I'm tired of our best defecting." He eyed Merryn pointedly.

"You choose to forget," she replied tartly, "that even if Avall hadn't married her you'd still have got Strynn."

"Now if I can only get Lore to ante up a smith, balance will be maintained," Eellon sighed. "But sooner ask those stones to speak."

The skies spoke instead. The rain that had threatened all afternoon arrived in force as the Sundering concluded. Avall tried not to watch as the Court's white paving stones were brocaded with swirling blood beneath a veil of cauterizing smoke.

Unfortunately, he stepped on a severed finger upon passing through the gate—and was promptly sick. And while he crouched there, clutching his stomach and gasping, with Merryn and Strynn to either side, he heard Eddyn, who'd followed close behind in the exit procession, laugh.

The rain escorted Avall and Strynn back to Argen-Hall. Law said that everyone in good health who attended that solemn rite had to return to their home halls afoot. The intent was that they take that time to ponder Justice, Law, and the Power of The Eight and of the King.

Avall needed no such inducements, nor did Strynn. Actual executions witnessed firsthand had been enough for both of them, and had left Avall thoroughly shaken. There was a vast difference, he discovered, between the theory of justice and the act. Nor did the fact that Eddyn's indiscretion had brought the whole matter uncomfortably close to both him and Strynn help.

He shuddered, and not from the cold. Reflexively, he looked around. The sodden mob was slowly dispersing. Merryn and Lykkon were helping Eellon, who was determined to walk in spite of their protestations about his age. Tyrill had already departed by horse cart and was probably warm and dry by now.

Avall shuddered again, and this time Strynn saw him. She started to speak, but he shook his head. "I'll be all right," he murmured. But he wasn't sure he meant it.

"Too much death," Avall admitted when they'd finally made their way to his quarters. He was sitting by the window, a mug of hot wine cooling in his hand, watching the rain slide patterns onto the glass. Trouble was, those runnels looked too much like blood, when backed by sunset light.

Their cloaks had been left at the hall door. Their ceremonial black steamed by the fire. In maroon and red they were once more merely Avall and Strynn. The room was lapsing into a comfortable, sleepy, gray-tinged gloom.

Strynn joined him opposite. Silent. Face serious and even more pensive than was her wont. Water trickled down Avall's neck, joining more slithering down his spine. Water: the life of the world, as blood was the life of a man. The only difference was that one was cold and one hot. Color didn't matter. Water could be tinted red.

"Too much death," Strynn agreed eventually, stirring her wine with a finger.

Avall looked up at her and smiled—because he loved her. Cared about her anyway. She was trying to assuage his pain. Or reveal her own.

He reached over and touched her face. One finger to her cheek, seeking, in part, to smooth a random lock of damp black hair away from her brow.

She caught the hand as he made to withdraw it, and clutched it fiercely, then let her grip soften as she drew it to her lips.

"Too much death," she repeated, into the sunset gloom. Her voice was barely a whisper.

Avall closed his eyes and tried not to think, not even to move; simply to stay where he was and enjoy the *now* of that simple touch, that gentle, loving gesture. And as he did, warmth awoke in him. In his head and his heart and another place he hadn't expected. He opened his eyes and smiled at her, even as he rose from his chair. "I think," he murmured, "I know a way we can both feel more alive."

And this time, in the soft part of the day, with no anticipation or expectations, and only the pattering rain to witness, Avall proved that was no lie.

CHAPTER VIII:

RITUAL AND REUNION

(NORTHWESTERN IXTI—YEAR BIRTH: DAY THREE—SUNSET)

The trouble had begun with Fire, Kraxxi concluded, as he fed more twigs to the tiny flame he'd coaxed into marginal stability in the rocky hollow a dozen head-heights above the nameless river that had coughed him up that morning. Up until Year's End, when Fire died at his father's hand to be reborn at his mother's, affairs at home had been normal. As normal as they could be, anyway. Which meant avoiding Barrax when possible and being slighted by him otherwise; comforting the perpetually sad Karvanni; wishing the triplets were in the palace instead of indulging Barrax's notion that Eron posed sufficient threat to warrant impressing every nonroyal into Ixti's army for two years after adulthood; studying under a variety of masters, none of them remarkably competent; and enduring daily drills in weaponry and horsemanship. Not to omit feasting to excess more often than was good for him. Lovers he'd had none, because Landing Lords' bastards were trouble in general, *royal* bastards posed incredible complications as far as the succession went, and Barrax wanted Kraxxi's claim (or Azzli's, more likely) to be unambiguous.

Which didn't mean he was celibate, only that he sought physical gratification in ways that didn't risk procreation: generally with other Lords' sons in similar straits, or sporadic oral love with the palace *ouris*. Intercourse with women came *after* marriage for the Landing class; in his case, an arranged marriage to someone he likely wouldn't love. Only when he was wed could he claim a concubine purely from affection.

Azzli wouldn't have to worry about those things, now.

Azzli was so much smoke and greasy ash. Azzli no longer had blood and bone and heart and mind—and fine brown eyes, thick dark hair, a lithe body, a heart-shaped mole just to the right of his navel, and a toe that never lay straight because Kraxxi had broken it for him in a wrestling match two summers back.

But he still, so said the priests, had a ghost that needed tying—soothing it at first, then sustaining it until it could be reborn in proper body and station—lest its fear force it to infuse the first newborn that came along. And since Fate had shown Kraxxi favor once that day, by saving him when he could've drowned, it was wise to retain that favor. Which meant playing by the priests' rules as far as tying went.

Which was why he was here: alone in the sunset wilderness (for so Azzli's ghost would be), with only Fire for company. Fire: the messenger to the Shadow World.

He'd found the place by accident, while climbing a barren, sandstone ridge in hopes of determining where, exactly, he was. Now, he was halfway up a steep slope more rock than earth, with a series of rain-smoothed projections rising waist high around him to cup the aerie like protective hands. A stone eagle had nested here—until the shadow-rabbits on which it preyed had departed, following the particular grass they relished, which grew only at the edge of forests. Forests that were themselves receding as burgeoning cities leveled them to fuel their fires. Still, the nest had made fine tinder for the Fire he'd made by the same means his mother had employed at Year's End. Azzli would like that, because Azzli had adored the outdoors and its lore, and had often said that he would like to die while hunting.

A breath, and only a thin bright edge of sun survived above a horizon that was all but level. Wasteland. Almost desert. Empty, because nothing existed there that couldn't be better had to east or south. The north was rather more evocative, since that way lay the jagged, deep purple sweep of the Winter Wall, as his folk called the enormous mountain range that separated Ixti from the flat, the Cold Sea, and Eron. Closer lay plains, scraggly new-growth forest, and odd eruptions of rock. What civilization existed this far north and west was masked by the ridge glowering behind him.

A final breath, and the sun set.

It was time.

Azzli had entered the world naked. Kraxxi would therefore perform the tying rite the same way. Most of his clothes were still drying anyway, so he had only to remove the cloak that blanketed his shoulders, his leather hunting breeches, and his loin guard, to stand exposed and shivering in the first breeze of evening. Still, it was far from unpleasant, the way those gusts stirred his hair around his ears and brushed insubstantial fingers along parts of his body not normally exposed to land and wind and sky.

Too, it provided another chance to inspect the damage the geen had done to his legs: massive bruises along his right hip, thigh, and calf; more across the front of both limbs; and puncture marks in his hips where talons had dug in. Those still seeped blood and made moving an increasing trial, but he'd see to them later. For now he had more pressing matters to attend.

Closing his eyes lest he be distracted and forget the ritual words, he turned to face the east, whence came rebirth, and intoned one simple phrase. *"Azzli min Barrax min Fortan, I call you here to witness that I do what is required to see you once more among your kin."*

And the same again, to south, west, and north, with the ritual repeated one final time at the east.

And was it his imagination, or did the breeze intensify at those words? He only knew that he was supposed to stand motionless while his heart beat one hundred times beneath the hand he'd placed on his chest. It seemed to take forever.

The second part was both more pleasant and more disconcerting, for it required that he offer up the seed of his body, which carried the plan of how a man should be built. It was difficult to achieve the desired result, however, perhaps because he sprawled against unyielding rocks—never mind that he was consumed with guilt and fear. Nor would he have been reduced to this had they planned more carefully. Normally one used a phial of the deceased's seed (or menstrual blood, for women) decanted at leisure and renewed at need, so as to assure an accurate duplication of its former body for the reborn soul. But Azzli's phial was either back in Ixtianos or at the camp, and in either case unavailable.

Still, he managed what was needed, wiped it on a leaf, and laid it atop the Fire, rising once again to address the quarters. *"Azzli min Barrax min Fortan,"* he repeated, *"breathe the wind, taste the smoke, and know that as man is seed of the earth, so do men make seed. Take this seed, of your blood if not your body, and let it grow in you so that you may once more walk among us."*

Now came the bad part. He had Azzli's attention. He'd given him a pattern by which he could be remade. It remained to provide fuel for that making.

Steeling himself, Kraxxi folded himself down atop his cloak and removed his hunting knife from his pack. It was a plain, if keen-edged, weapon: good for declawing geens. A still-bloody claw from the one he'd slain fell out with it: fibrous-hard and green as a nighted emerald.

Most appropriate—as he scooted around to face the surrounding rocky rampart—for it was while pursuing geens that Azzli had lost his life. He stared at the rock, then at the knife, then back to the rock. And squared his shoulders. This was where the living of House Fortan gave of themselves to its dead, thereby anchoring the royal soul to its proper rank in the tangible world. And with it, too, came a reenactment of the pain and fear that rode vanguard to death.

Still, there was no way to end it but to begin. And with that, he spread his left hand against the rock, took the knife in his right, and with meticulous care, pressed the gleaming blade of Eronese steel down on the end joint of the third finger of his left hand. Had he lost a sister, he'd have assailed the little finger. A mother meant middle finger; a father, index. A child past puberty, the thumb. He smiled at that: He'd cost Barrax something after all. One sacrifice per family per death was all that was required, but Barrax wouldn't know what Kraxxi did here and would want to be careful—and, of course, make an appropriate show of grief.

"Hear me, Azzli min Barrax min Fortan," he called, staring fixedly at the brother-ring on his forefinger. Red lights danced there—reflected flame, or some internal fire. *"Hear me: Kraxxi min Barrax min Fortan, your brother. I summon you to witness, to taste my blood, to bond to my bone, to inhabit my flesh, to feel with my nerves, all that which I am about to give you."*

And with that, he closed his eyes and pressed down with the knife. The joint popped, which surprised him more than the extravagant pain. Yet at that, the pain was no worse than what he felt already: that Azzli was truly *gone*. They'd never converse again, nor roll their eyes in dismay at their father's efforts to sunder them, nor study together, nor practice archery together, nor swim in the cool clear pools at the Water Palace.

Never.

The blade grated against stone. Kraxxi opened his eyes, felt the pain more as a pulse than a steady flare, but saw he had succeeded. The fingertip slid down the stone. Setting his jaw, he retrieved a second dagger from the Fire and pressed it against the bleeding stump. And bit back a scream in truth.

Still, pain was part of atonement. Gritting his teeth against agony that grew stronger as the shock that had shielded him wore away, he reached out his good hand, picked up the fragment of smooth, tanned flesh, and dropped it into the Fire, adding more fuel in its wake to coax the flames hotter and higher.

For pursuit to see, he realized stupidly. Or maybe not, against the sunset glow. Too, he was most of a day away from that fateful copse; surely the king's men wouldn't be searching here yet.

But *someone* was approaching. He could hear the crunch of boots against loose stone, the rasp of fabric against fabric, and the increasingly loud breaths of more than one person scrambling up the slope below him. Panicked, he flung himself flat on the rocks and eased forward to peer over the aerie's open side. It was dark down there, and he could only make out shapes. *Moving* shapes. Metal gleamed. Whoever approached was armed. But he still had the dagger, and there seemed to be only three of them . . .

Three . . . ?

His heart leapt.

Still, caution could save his life, and so he pressed against the rock, unmoving, hand throbbing abominably, until the topmost figure drew close enough to make out features.

"Elvix?" he hissed, before he could catch himself.

"Kraxxi?" the shadow-shape gave back. "Gods bless us! It *is* you!"

"Aye!"

"Alone?"

"Of course!" Kraxxi started to rise, then recalled that he was naked and dived for his clothes. He'd just secured his breeches when a breathless Elvix clambered over the edge.

His friend's face was wet with the sweat of exertion and begrimed with more than that. Blood still speckled her tunic sleeves and cloak. She smelled of smoke and river water. "Give me a hand," she barked, moving back to the cleft up which she'd come.

Kraxxi started to oblige, but then her eyes narrowed as she noted the Fire, his state of dishabille, the knife—and the mutilated finger. "Sorry. But we could use whatever assistance you can manage. The others—"

"Injured," Kraxxi acknowledged. "I'll do what I can."

He did, oblivious to the pain it cost him, so that a short while later, the aerie was packed with four damp, dirty, weary-eyed people.

"We found you," Tozri sighed through a tired grin, as he stripped to the waist for Elvix's inspection. Kraxxi gasped at the extent of the injury: a swollen shoulder bearing a bruise easily the size of Kraxxi's own. It didn't hurt precisely, but Tozri couldn't move it beyond a certain range, nor could it bear much weight. Damage to the rotating socket at the top, Olrix opined. He'd suffered no permanent impairment but would be useless on that side for a while. He'd completed the climb one-handed.

Olrix had a fractured left forearm which had been reset and bound, but which she managed better than her brother. At least they all had good legs. And more tenacity than Kraxxi could imagine, to have found him at all, much less dared the climb to his makeshift camp. He didn't want to think what that must have cost them.

Out of respect for the dead (once the reason for Kraxxi's Fire had been explained), they'd postponed discussion until the flames burned out and another, for warmth and cooking, could be contrived, which Elvix did with flint and steel. Not until they'd all drunk wine from the common cup and consumed mouthfuls of salty way-meat softened by boiling, did they wrap themselves in cloaks and settle themselves for the night. Olrix gave Kraxxi imphor bark to chew and rub on his finger, which made the pain bearable. Her siblings refused the same offer.

"There are two stories here, my prince," Tozri announced at last. "Ours and yours. Which would you have first?"

Kraxxi shook his head. "No prince any longer. Merely a man who doesn't deserve friends as loyal as you."

"You liked us when no one else did," Olrix shot back. "That's enough. But that's not what we need to talk about now."

Kraxxi nodded toward the river. "What about pursuit? That should be our main concern."

"Assuming you don't want to give yourself up," Elvix countered dryly. "Which it doesn't appear you do."

Olrix took a sip of broth and leaned back on her stretch of boulder. It loomed above her: illusionary security, at best. "*No* pursuit—for a while. Longer than we thought."

Kraxxi poked at the fire. Sparks raced up to meet the stars. "Why not?"

A deep breath. "Geens. More geens than you've ever seen—three fours, maybe. The pyre had just started to burn down when we heard noises—of the sort we *didn't* hear before, which meant the geens were careless. Which is *very* disturbing, since it implies that they think well enough to know there was a banquet there for the taking, and that we posed no threat. It was like . . . they could tell we were tired and defeated and they could pick us off when they wanted."

"Like rowdies in an inn," Tozri inserted.

"In any event," Olrix went on, "we dowsed Azzli's body with oil, flung what was left on the others, snared what gear we could, and fled under cover of smoke. I doubt enough of him remained for geens to bother with if they had freshly dead horse."

"The upshot," Elvix concluded, "was that we made for the river. Toz had seen you wade out and knew right off what you were about. He also knew it was your decision, and that he couldn't stop you. But with geens everywhere, we had to leave or die."

"Not a hard choice," Tozri snorted. "We waded out as far as we could, and half swam, half floated just like you did, until we reached the other bank. We hid there, watched, and waited. The geens ate until they were sated. They also destroyed a lot of evidence—conveniently. And about when you'd expect, Yaran and a band of horses came riding up—twenty or so. Well, the men—you could tell he'd gathered them in a hurry and they didn't want to be there—took one look at the geens and half of them bolted. The rest stayed to fight—cowed by Yaran, likely—which was stupid, since sated geens wouldn't have bothered them if they hadn't been attacked. Most died, including that bastard, Yaran."

Kraxxi couldn't help but grin. "Serves him right."

"The point is," Tozri finished, "that no real pursuit can begin until tomorrow, because the survivors will take a while to get back to Elgwyn-yl, and then they'll have to decide what to do, and then send word to . . . whomever. And somewhere in there whoever Yaran sent on to Ixtianos will arrive, but there'll be more muddle because there's no chain of command."

"Which means we have a day's start, if we're lucky."

"And if we're luckier, no one will think to look on this bank at first, and certainly not south. They'll expect the three of us to head north because we're half-Eronese. And there's always a chance they might think we're all dead, from the torn, bloody clothes lying around."

"Chance," Kraxxi murmured softly. "I gave myself to Fate, and Fate delivered me. Fate favored you, too. It made your decision for you: Flee or die. Flee toward *me* or die. I think"—he swallowed hard—"I think things were supposed to work this way."

"Perhaps," Elvix agreed, looking at the sky, where stars shone brighter than Kraxxi had ever seen them.

Kraxxi wrapped his cloak more closely around him, leaning against Tozri for comfort. "So how did you find me?"

Elvix looked at Olrix who looked at Tozri. "Family secret."

Olrix shook her head. "He has no family now, nor we either—south of the Wall."

Tozri gnawed his lip. "We're all family now, I think. We have to be."

Elvix shrugged. "I'll say nothing if you tell him."

Olrix scowled in turn. "Very well," she began. "You know our mother was a healer from Eron. But before she came here, she did as all folk of that land do and spent time at the various holds studying all the arts of that people. One of those holds is devoted to mining gems, and while working in these mines, our mother found a gem somewhat like an opal. She tried to cut it, but it broke. While seeking to rejoin the pieces, she discovered that it acted like a lodestone save that it only was attracted to itself. A curiosity, she decided. So she took it with her, and thought no more about it."

A pause for another draught, and Olrix went on. "In due time, she came here to Ixti and brought the gem with her. For no particular reason, she began to study it and learned that, unlike a lodestone, the attraction didn't diminish with distance. Wherever one part was placed, the other would point toward it. Anyway, we were children then, and tended to run wild, which vexed her, so she hit upon the idea of splitting the stone again and setting the fragments into four rings, one for each of us, and one for her. That way, should we stray, she could hang hers from a string and in due time it would point toward us."

Kraxxi nodded incredulously, looking sideways at Tozri. "Which is how she found us when we were lost that time! We thought it was luck."

Tozri shook his head. "Not luck. Love, maybe. She didn't tell *us* she could find us that way until we were adults. I suppose because she feared we'd remove the rings."

Kraxxi stared at his hand, where an opalescent stone still gleamed, two up from the mangled finger. "And this—"

Tozri smiled weakly. "Elvix's stone was destroyed by accident, but we were almost grown by then, so Mother gave us hers. What better way to look after two inseparable princes than to be able to find them at any time? But the brotherhood I felt when I gave you that was real."

Olrix poked the fire so that it blazed up half again as bright, setting knife edges of shadow along her cheekbones. "In any event," she said into the sudden awkward lull, "we found you. We must now have your story."

Kraxxi drained the last of his broth, wishing there was ale, and wondering if he were up for a trek to the river for water. "Luck," he murmured. "Or Fate, if you will. I decided that if the Gods wanted me dead, *they* could choose. They'd let me survive attack by geens. That seemed proof that I was favored. They'd let my three best friends survive. More proof. They'd rendered my principal foe unable to take me as I stood. They'd cost me a brother I love, and that seemed to be their price. But I lived. I therefore thought that they might let me live longer.

"And so they did. I should've drowned from the weight of my wet clothing and the bag I carried. But I wore hunting leathers, and they held enough air between them and my skin to buoy me. I swam a little, always on my back, or just kicked myself along. Once I was sucked under and saw the waiting Dark, and thought I heard Azzli telling me to leave. Or maybe not, but my body did what my mind resisted and brought me back to the surface. A floating log nudged me—more Fate. I held it and floated—I don't know how long. But then I felt sand beneath my feet and knew I'd come aground—on the opposite bank from where I'd started, at the place where two rivers joined in a V with cliffs above them. I could see a town at a distance. I didn't want to see a town. I therefore turned north along the unknown river. I found berries and ate. I found this place. The rest you know."

Elvix scratched her nose. "What we *need* to know is where we go from here."

Kraxxi rolled his eyes. "No chance of escaping you, is there?"

Olrix raised a brow in warning. "None."

"The *question*," Tozri said, "is do we continue as we were considering—

return to Ixtianos, dance to the law's tune, and die when none of us did wrong? Or do we go into exile, and if so, how far? We could live off the land for a while. And there's always Eron."

"Eron," Kraxxi mused dreamily. "It seems so far."

"An eighth or less," Olrix gave back. "Straight line from Ixtianos. In good weather."

"In *good* weather," Elvix emphasized. "Winter walks toward us from those tall mountains. Would we be wise to walk toward winter in turn? And you know what's said of winter in Eron: Nothing moves outside save in the gorges. We'd have to be outside—in the mountains."

"Their *southern* mountains," Kraxxi gave back. "It would be warm there longest."

Tozri probed his injured shoulder and flinched. "There're villages along the north foot of the Winter Wall. We've geen claws. We could buy horses and supplies with them."

Kraxxi shuddered. "And cross the Flat?"

"Shortest route," Elvix snorted. "The safer but much longer option, if we want to avoid detection, is to cross the Wall, then make for the coast. But that's mostly salt marsh and outright swamp. The land's subsiding, and there's nothing but reeds, mud, disease, and death. Still, anyone going to Eron from here has either to brave the desert, the marsh, or try to find that scrap of unclaimed no-man's-land between—which is wildly out of the way."

Olrix eyed them all in turn. "Fate favors us," she said slowly. "Suicide doesn't have to be sudden, and if we die in the effort, the Gods will be appeased."

"And if we die," Kraxxi sighed, "which I don't intend, I'll die with friends. And Barrax won't get to see it."

"Well, then," Olrix concluded, snugging her cloak closer to her chin, "I say we should sleep half the night, and when third moon rises, head north along the river."

"Toward Eron," Kraxxi agreed. Elvix merely grunted her assent. Tozri didn't—because he was snoring.

CHAPTER IX:

REWARDS AND TRIALS

(ERON: TIR-ERON—SUNDEATH: DAY IV: CONTESTING)

~~~~~~~~~~

(SMITH-HOLD-MAIN—MIDMORNING)

In spite of a breakfast of meat pies and mulled wine, followed by a hot bath and a massage from an obliging Lykkon, Avall was as nervous as he'd ever been as he waited with the other candidates for mastership—and thus adulthood—in the windowless anteroom of Smith-Hold's Proving Hall. The stone-lined chamber was large enough to accommodate twice as many apprentices as were present, and was deliberately austere to heighten the effect when one entered the adjoining room. Certainly, Avall felt far too conspicuous as he straightened his short-tunic yet again and tried not to let his gaze drift to the opposite wall, where Eddyn leaned glowering against the pale granite, half a head taller than everyone else, and half again more accomplished than all save Avall himself and one other. Though the two weren't competing in their respective subcrafts, ironmongery and gold-smithing; they would be contending for the overall prize now being judged next door by the assorted Craft-Chiefs, subcraft-chiefs, and other established masters. Avall knew that not a few bets had been laid on whether he or Eddyn would emerge with the grand prize and see his work moved to the Citadel for display before being locked away forever in the Hall of Master-works a year later.

At least Strynn was with him, holding his hand in the silence they were once more obliged to endure. And wouldn't it be a treat if she, a weapon-wright like Eddyn, managed to defeat the man who'd defiled her! If there was justice, that would occur. Then again, this was a trial of skill, and against Eddyn, Strynn stood little chance, for all she was acclaimed best in her division.

The silence stretched and lingered, and the room, which had no direct access to fresh air, became hot and sticky. Sweat beaded Avall's forehead. And still they waited; far longer than typical—which hinted of contention among the judges. Fyllyn, the sturdy cousin to his right, sighed plaintively and rolled his eyes. Eddyn's latest partisans looked as though they'd take the weapons they were so fond of forging and carve their way through the door if progress weren't forthcoming.

Avall tried not to worry about the petty concerns that had consumed him since arising. Would the Priest who'd arrived at dawn to retrieve his master-work and the plain, black-wood cubicle in which it would be displayed handle it so that no fingerprints marred a surface he'd spent most of the previous night polishing? Would they display it at the precise angle needed to highlight the delicate calligraphy engraved below the rim? Would the box be positioned so as to capture optimum light?

Would? Would? Would?

Avall had no more cause for speculation, for a gong sounded and the vestibule echoed with the rustling hiss of young men and women taking deep breaths, scrubbing sweating faces, and adjusting gowns or tunics one last time. "Luck," Fyllyn muttered beside him, which wasn't allowed, though the Priests haunting the corners didn't seem to notice.

Another gong, and the doors—each twice his height and half that wide—parted along an unseen seam and swung inward. Avall found himself cursing yet another formality that commanded them to enter in order of birth from oldest to youngest—which put him past the middle. He endured the slow, shuffling steps as he approached the opening. The massive jamb brushed his shoulder—

—and then space exploded around him.

The Proving Hall was a long, high-ceilinged room, pierced with windows in round-topped arches, beneath which the boxes containing the masterpieces were arrayed in an order determined by Fate. None were identified, so that they might be judged by worth alone. Still, those to the left gleamed with the gray-silver of steel and other ferrous metals suitable for ironmongery. Eddyn was already moving that way, as apprentices abandoned decorum to seek out their entries.

Ahead, barely visible, was the warmer glint of brass and bronze—mostly medium-sized sculptures, complex machines, and assorted household utensils too beautiful and well wrought ever to be used as such.

To the right . . . The very air glittered there, for that was the province of Avall's craft, goldsmithing. Granted, the objects were smaller, but each was a wonder of perfection: goblets, bowls, plates, minute statues, necklaces of links too fine to see, bracelets thick with filigree, circlets, a miracle of layered metals. Especially impressive was a wall plaque made of overlapping sheets of pierced silver, copper, gold, blued steel, and verdigrised bronze that comprised a hunting scene that actually moved as one turned first one knob upon the rim and then another. But when Avall bent to inspect it more closely, he saw file marks everywhere, and overcuts, and the unsure curves of some of the smaller windows. It was a masterwork, sure enough. It would earn its creator—who turned out to be a friend of his named Nyall—adulthood. But it was nothing to his own contribution—which he hadn't located.

Ah! There it was. He should've known by the crowd gathering halfway along the wall. Should've known, but hadn't. For while everyone claimed he was the best his craft had seen in generations, he refused to believe it. However easy it was to spot the imperfections in others' work, it was twice as easy to find deficiencies in his own.

Steeling himself, he maneuvered through the throng, some of whom recognized him and gave way with a reverence that unnerved him. Until suddenly there was no one before him, and he once more confronted that which had consumed virtually every free moment since Fate had defined his commission at Sunbirth half a year gone by. It didn't look like that much of his life. But it didn't look like the final key to adulthood, either.

A chalice. A drinking vessel for the Well of World; that much was spelled out on the lot he'd drawn. He could use any design, any materials as long as they were metal and over half the content by volume was gold. Beyond that, he'd been free. And so he'd shaped it carefully: sturdy base, short stem, wide cup, two handles. But the proportions had been perfect—and the finishing, and the polishing. And then had come the embellishment: plain segments juxtaposed with strips of knotwork so complex he couldn't believe he'd wrought them himself. For some sections he'd been forced to work only in sunlight, for others by candleglow, since each showed different textures, grains, or flaws.

The result was precisely what he'd envisioned. Except that the handles were a tad too thick, and if you looked *very* closely, one of the cast-gold cartouches was a hair's width out of round.

"Nice work," Fyllyn breathed beside him, slapping him on the back. He started at that, blushed, blinked stupidly, even as he responded with a muttered "thanks."

"Congratulations," someone else crowed at his other hand.

"For what?" But then he saw what his own anxiety had caused him to miss: the narrow golden circlet of adulthood that lay before the chalice, which meant he'd passed his master's competition. But beside the plain, finger-wide band all rising adults received gleamed a quartet of gems to be inset later. There was an amethyst for best functional vessel; a sapphire for best ecclesiastical work; a topaz for best goldsmithing—and a ruby the size of the end of his thumb for best overall smithwork.

He had won! Of the scores of talented craftsmen assembled in this room, who were the best his craft could muster, those who had passed before him had judged him best. And though his friends had told him to expect as much, the reality overwhelmed him. All at once he was mumbling inanities at the flurry of well-wishers, slapping backs, accepting hugs and kisses. But all he could think of, as joy flooded him, was Strynn. Somehow he freed himself and made his way toward the opposite side. Another clump as large as his own massed there, and he could see Eddyn's head above it, enjoying similar praise. He veered close enough to hear the phrase "first in iron, second overall," then angled for the third largest group, assembling around his wife.

True to convention, she'd completed her masterwork in private, allowing no one to observe its progress save the relevant subchief, one trusted adviser, and Tyrill. Not even Avall had seen her submission.

Though weaponwork was her skill-of-record, it wasn't a weapon at all but a piece of armor. A gauntlet: blued steel accented with hardened bronze, leafed with copper. The workmanship was perfect—of course. He knew Strynn well enough to expect no less, and had seen enough of her earlier work to assure it. And the design was excellent. But what struck him was the cleverness of the engineering. Surely those tiny hinges couldn't bend two ways at once as it appeared they could. And surely they didn't also stretch in the process, yet they did. For Strynn had defied custom and was modeling it on her hand.

And then she saw Avall and grinned. He eased forward, knelt at her feet, took the steel-cased hand in his own, and kissed it. When he rose, he saw her award stones. Second in ironmongery, second in weaponwork, first in armor. Which confirmed that iron's winner had been Eddyn.

Strynn, however, was stunned.

"I won!" she enthused, as though she still couldn't believe it. "Avall, I won! Best armor!"

His reply was to hug her. "I won, too! Everything. And," he added, "I suppose the civil thing to do is congratulate Eddyn."

At first he thought Strynn would refuse. Certainly she stiffened. But then she squared her shoulders, and together they made their way across the hall. Eddyn greeted them both with wary smiles, grunting in surprise when

Avall—who admired good work regardless—gave him the ritual hug. Strynn contented herself with a gracious "congratulations," and he in turn complimented her close placement. It was the first time they'd spoken since . . . *then*.

At which point someone raised the question of whether Avall or Eddyn had been deemed worthy not only of adulthood, but of a subcraft-chieftainship, which prompted blank stares from both, then quick denial. Neither circlet had borne points, which would've been the sign. "Politics," someone muttered as Avall broke away from Eddyn to join Strynn in contemplating the other pieces.

Soon enough the doors opened again, and the room was flooded with the remaining masters and most of the staff of Argen-Hall, clan and craft alike. Merryn wasn't present, being busy with affairs of her own apprenticed craft over at War-Hold, but Eellon was. He did not look happy.

"What's wrong?" Avall inquired, when the two found a moment alone.

Eellon shook his head. "Sometimes I lose," he grumbled. "The vote was tied to raise you to subcraft-chief of gold. Tyrill wouldn't give it."

Avall felt a twitch in his stomach: a mingling of relief and disappointment that settled on the former. "No surprise," he managed before distress became obvious. "She doesn't like me."

Eellon studied him keenly. "That shouldn't matter—she's usually objective about such things. But maybe it really was my fault."

"Why?"

"Because one more vote would've made a tie to raise Eddyn to subcraft-chief in iron, and I wouldn't give it, and not because of politics, though she won't believe me. The proportions were off, and I said as much. She had to agree with me."

"Mine were, too," Avall confided.

"I know. And I marked you down for it. You were actually off as much as Eddyn, but over less distance; therefore, it wasn't so crucial an error. But a subcraft-chief can make *no* errors."

Strynn snorted. Eellon's face betrayed nothing, but his eyes were twinkling. "And you," he sighed, "need to learn to rivet."

"I think," Strynn sniffed defiantly, "we need to look for Merryn."

(WAR-HOLD-MAIN—LATE AFTERNOON)

. . . a pause for breath as his opponent slowly rose, sword in hand . . .

Eddyn's gaze flicked sideways through steel-rimmed eyeslots and caught it all as image fragments, like the world viewed through a faceted lens . . .

. . . an eight-sided stone arena paved with hard-packed sand and rimmed at the lowest level with archways alternating with blind arcades, all wrought of gray limestone . . .

. . . two thirds of the population of Tir-Eron occupying tier upon tier of benches, all of them in livery, and most having placed bets . . .

. . . combatants on the adjoining field in helms, gauntlets, and practice leathers, in the colors of clan and craft . . .

. . . marshals from War-Hold noting every move, turn, and block with the eyes of the masters they were . . .

. . . heralds from War-Hold and Lore marking every salient point and announcing them through enormous horns that amplified their voices . . .

. . . High King Gynn himself in the lowest box at the western end, looking by turns interested and bored as the sun lowered behind him . . .

A final twist of Eddyn's wrist drew a line as elegant as the blade that had made him an adult along his opponent's forearm, signaling victory. Impulsively, he exerted more force, so that the guarded tip slit not only leather and padding but the skin beneath, prompting a startled, irate yip from his opponent: a young man from Clan Byrrch of Weaver-Hold.

"Sorry," Eddyn muttered, whipping his sword into his belt before reaching over to touch hands with his opponent, oblivious to the blood trickling down the man's blue-green gauntlet.

The weaver's eyes flashed within his helm. He snatched his hand away. "You had the victory!" he spat. "Why mark me as well?"

"Sorry," Eddyn repeated. He removed the light helmet he wore above sparring armor. Air found him, and he reveled in that coolness: in breezes that didn't smell of sweat, hot metal, and oiled leather. It also allowed him to hear the buzz of the spectators and his name proclaimed by the heralds. *"Victory by advantage,"* that distant voice intoned, having read the signals the marshal sent him via an elaborate system of flags and hand signs. "Victory by advantage," that voice repeated, "Eddyn syn Argen-yr!"

A pause, then the gruff rumble of Tryffon, Craft-Chief of War: "By this victory War-Hold proclaims Eddyn syn Argen-yr to be victor among the challenger clans. By this victory he advances to the final round."

Eddyn grinned smugly, not bothering to hide his glee. He'd done it! Had beaten every other challenger in the afternoon's competition in war arts save those from War-Hold itself, or its apprentices. Which meant he was, in theory, the best swordsman outside War-Hold this year. And he'd had the pleasure of hearing Tryffon, who hated him, confirm it.

War-Hold had been engaged in its own systematic weeding, beginning at sunrise. How that weeding had progressed, he had no idea. Such matters were not revealed until combats were announced, exactly as combats among the other crafts were kept secret so that the fighters could focus on their present foes alone.

He wondered, as he waited the obligatory ten breaths for his victory ovation to subside, how Merryn had fared. Well, likely. Damn her.

The ovation ended. Eddyn spared one final wave for the crowd, a second for his clan and craft (wishing Avall had contested within one or the other—which he *might* have been good enough to win—so Eddyn could've humbled him), and a third for High King Gynn, who ought to have been fighting, too—and might yet, since he had that option *and* War-Hold connections.

By the time he'd passed under Victor's Arch, a hall page, acting as squire, had taken his helm, blade, and gauntlets. A second offered him a cool drink from Contention's Well, while a third passed him an ice-cold towel with which to wipe everything he could reach without removing armor. "Thanks," he murmured politely, trying to atone for his earlier temper—or arrogance. No reply being needed, he strode through the vestibule to the larger chamber, where a number of the previous combatants were still removing armor, and up the stairs to the marshal's paddock, in case someone had challenged him. Convention, nothing more.

But the red-tabarded woman who faced him there looked both amused and grim, as she handed Eddyn a slip of folded parchment. "Challenge has been given. Do you answer or abstain?"

"I answer!" Eddyn snapped, even as he realized who that opponent might be. Holding his breath, he opened the note, saw the name within, and flung it to the floor. "Accepted!" he growled again, and turned to vest for one more combat than expected. One of the Argen-yr pages retrieved the slip and inspected it, frowning at the name. "She can't do that!" he protested. "She's War-Hold. They've already chosen their champion!"

Eddyn glared at the boy. "She's also Argen and Smith, and has the option of fighting for either."

The page looked puzzled, "But I thought . . ."

"She's *apprenticed* to War," Eddyn told him, wondering why he bothered. "The fact that she's in a position to challenge means she's *not* their champion. That means I won't have to fight her in the finals."

"But if she beats you, she's got a second chance for an overall win."

"I doubt," Eddyn gritted, "that her agenda has anything to do with victory." And with that, he strode back downstairs to rest the quarter hand to which he was entitled.

Merryn took the drink her squire—the ever-obliging Lykkon—offered, and wiped her mouth with a hand. She was panting lightly, a little winded from the null bout she'd been obliged to fight so as to assure a level of fatigue equivalent to Eddyn's, whom she was about to face. It hadn't been her idea, though she would never admit that. Nor had it been Strynn's, or Eellon's, or Eight forbid, Avall's. No, the request that she challenge had come from the Clan-Chief of Ferr himself: Preedor, Strynn's two-father.

He'd promised nothing, threatened nothing. Had simply smiled that honest, old man's smile, and said, "If Eddyn were taught a lesson, I would not complain."

That had been sufficient. A chance misstep had cost her victory among the War-Hold women—a victory everyone had assumed she'd achieve. The woman—Cyryne—had been good, if overcautious; but the misstep had been avoidable: rank carelessness for which she'd failed to compensate. Not that it would cost her mastership; that had been assured already, and a sub-subchieftainship as well. Still, it angered her, and that anger needed an outlet. Eddyn provided one within the rules of the games. Never mind that it also forced him into a corner. Refuse, and he looked a coward and would forfeit the final match besides. Fight and win, he looked a bully for defeating a woman and the bond-sister of one he'd wronged. Fight and lose, he looked less a man. She couldn't contain her glee.

"If you keep on grinning like that," Lykkon muttered through his teeth, "your jaw'll stick and we won't be able to get your helm on."

She elbowed him smartly in the ribs, snatched the proffered helmet—a Sunbirth present from Avall the previous year—and slipped it on, raising her chin for Lykkon to snug the strap. Another pause ensued while he brushed dust from her gambeson and returned her sword, and she watched the herald at Challenger's Gate for a sign. The woman raised a finger, then turned and moved her mouth to the brazen announcing horn.

"Your Majesty, Chieftains, masters, apprentices, and laborers for clan and craft, before the final combat, there will be another. Challenge has been given to Eddyn syn Argen-yr, and that challenge has been accepted. Hear now the name of she who challenges in the name of Clan Argen-a: Merryn san Argen-a"—she paused, gave the parchment she held a startled glance, which proved she hadn't read it—*"nic Strynn na Avall."*

Bond-sister of Strynn, blood-sister of Avall, Merryn thought. *Let everyone know what I do, and let Eddyn, in particular, cogitate on that. Let him wonder how extreme my vengeance will be as he faces me.*

"Go!" Lykkon hissed, and shoved her toward the archway.

The glare hit her squarely, for she faced the sun. Eddyn stood opposite, dark against the white of Victor's Gate, fifty strides away. He advanced as she did, clad as she in Argen's maroon, but differenced by the silver bar across his chest that marked his sept. Might as well be lace filigree, Merryn concluded. Webbing for the Spider-Chief.

The marshals advanced in their tabards of parti-color white and black, both chosen by lot from War-Hold by the Priests of Contention, who cosponsored this event.

They halted when all four were a span apart, facing each other across the iron disk of the Victory Boss in the center of the arena. "My lady, my lord," the marshal informed them, "you know the rules: A wound to the face through the eyeslots, or to the hands that impairs permanently, will result in exile. How many blows do you propose?"

Three was typical for women, four for men, though any number could be ordained so long as combat ended before sunset.

"Eddyn," the marshal prompted, "you were challenged; you proclaim."

A pause, then, with a wicked glint in his eye. "Four."

The marshal looked at Merryn. "How say you, lady?"

Merryn took a deep breath. "Five."

Eddyn's eyes widened, but he covered well and nodded. "Five it is."

The marshals studied them carefully, then nodded in turn and made special effort to check the tips of their swords, which bore guards that would prevent most penetration deep enough to kill. The idea was to cut the leather sufficiently to expose the red padding, symbolic of raw flesh, not to maim or worse. One blow wounding real flesh, intentional or not, was victory. It was also risky enough not to be sought capriciously.

"My lady, my lord, make ready," the marshal commanded.

"Aye," they replied as one, whereupon Merryn reached to the small of her back and locked her left hand into the ring set there lest reflex tempt her to use that arm as a shield. Shields were used in other combats but this was sword-on-sword alone.

"Very well," the marshal to Merryn's right murmured, backing away. "My lady, my lord, for honor and glory—lay on!"

And with that he and his fellow stepped away.

Gazes touched and challenged: identical shades of blue. Swords clanged above their heads as blows were met and parried without either moving otherwise, and without their gazes breaking. The blow shook Merryn, unused as she was to fighting someone as large as Eddyn in this form.

She balanced, braced, and stepped back—twice—luring him in. Heard the hiss of his blade past her helm, then a different hiss as its blunted edge raked the padding on her shoulder. If stuffing showed, a marshal would call hold. None did. She noted that and shifted to attack, catching Eddyn's sword with hers on his follow-through, spinning around as he unbalanced, then sweeping on around to slice at his middle as he recovered. Red showed along his lower ribs.

"First blood!" the marshal cried.

Wordlessly, they regrouped. Eddyn's eyes were cold blue ice, utterly devoid of emotion. Merryn grinned, knowing the lines would show.

"Lay on!"

Eddyn's attack was like twin strokes of lightning: an incredibly complex set of feints, and then something that shouldn't have been possible with his wrist, that got under her guard and raked her armpit. She heard the rip of parting padding, the harsh grate of the edge against the denser underlayer, and felt a twinge of pain from the force of the blow.

"Blood!" the marshal called. *"Hold!"*

A third time they faced off, but this time Merryn was ready. She was willing to go the whole five rounds, but the longer they fought, the better Eddyn would appear. And since her goal was humiliation, it was best to get on with it.

She went cold. Her blademaster had told her to do that: to forget anything but that which kept her alive, which lived cold and dark in the center of her brain. Which made snakes, spiders, and geens so deadly. The reflex of life and death.

She let Eddyn press her; let him push her back, using his greater mass to the advantage he intended. She met his blows accurately but with less force than he might expect, as though she were tiring. More than once she felt his blade touch her but not cut, nor did the marshals call hold. She feigned attack but turned her blows deliberately, seeking the proper opening.

Eddyn's eyes blazed with victory, the way they might've blazed when he pressed himself on Strynn. Which almost made her quicken her strokes, strengthen the force of her blows. But not yet . . .

Get his sword high—higher—*too* high to block in time. She met him, lured him on, as he followed guilelessly.

She moved. A twist—another—while her arm darted out and back with viper's speed, the blade a silver blur slashing along the crease where leg met abdomen, down to the crotch. Leather parted. Blood red padding showed, but another redness glistened there as well. Eddyn hissed his pain, and the marshals called *"Blood!"* then *"Hold!"*

One ran fingers along the new cut, raised them to show the other. Blood shimmered. *"True blood,"* he called—and made a sign at the herald.

"True Blood!" The herald proclaimed. *"Victor by blooding! Merryn san Argen-a nic Strynn na Avall!"*

"Bitch!" Eddyn spat, as he clamped his hand on his leg and let the churgeon lead him from the field.

Merryn followed, ignoring the acclamation exploding around her. She wrenched off her helm. "Bitch I may be," she told him. "But we both know that it was only by *my* grace that you won't be called eunuch!"

Eddyn ignored her, and a word from the nearer marshal advised her that she really should heed the accolades. She strode back to the Victor's Boss and raised her sword above her head. The crowd went wild. It scarcely mattered that the final combat of the day, which was no longer between Eddyn and Dorvvyn syn Ferr-mor of War-Hold, but between Dorvvyn and Merryn, gave the former a hard-earned and much-deserved victory—after a matched pair of slashes on fourth blood required a fifth. He raised her hand with his, and it was impossible to tell who grinned more. But Merryn gloried for a different reason. She doubted she'd fight better in her life.

War-Hold's churgeon was just setting the last stitch in Eddyn's groin with his wickedly curved needle when Tyrill came storming into the clean, white-tiled room off the main vesting chamber, scattering squires, pages, and half-dressed young men like storm wrack. Clad in clan maroon, she looked like an ambulatory blood clot save for her bone-white face. The churgeon ignored her, intent as he was on tending a wound that had come less than a finger from diminishing Eddyn's assets, if not unmanning him outright. Not until he'd wrapped Eddyn from navel to knee in thin cotton did he look up. Nor did Eddyn remove the bar of imphor wood from his jaws, given that the juices numbed pain, while the vapors induced a pleasant, drifty stupor—which was the best way to endure Tyrill in high dudgeon. That he was also (save the bandage) as naked as the day he was born didn't concern him. Tyrill had seen him bare countless times since he'd peed in her face when two days old, and he'd posed for her ever since.

The churgeon, however, was more concerned, and flung a towel across Eddyn's privates as he tried to reclaim the stick of wood. Tyrill snatched the stave from him and waved it in his face. "Go. Now. All of you! He won't die, though I intend to make him wish he might!"

The churgeon's mouth rounded into an O, but he did as commanded and followed his panicked assistants into the vesting room.

Never in his life had Eddyn felt so vulnerable.

"Sit up, boy!" Tyrill barked. "You're not as drugged as all that!"

Eddyn tried twice before he managed the maneuver. His head was spinning abominably as he lurched to an uneasy slump on the churgeon's table, fumbling absently for the towel.

"I presume there's a story here?"

He gazed at her blankly.

"Or did someone as subtle and clever as Merryn simply take it on herself to challenge you? No, don't answer—yet. Just think: No matter what you did, she had you. One way you were a coward, another a bully, the third a second-rate swordsman. Now I know you're none of those things, and most of Eron knows the same—objectively. But you let them see what they wanted to see—you failing—when of those choices, the only one that would've done you any good, was to beat her. The world already thinks you a bully; a bully who's also decent with a sword is marginally more acceptable."

Eddyn closed his eyes.

Tyrill slapped him—hard. His eyes snapped open again. "I repeat," she gritted, "there has to be more to this than appears. If it was simply the Strynn affair, Merryn could've called you out when it occurred. But she was fighting for her new sister *and* her brother—so what was that about?"

Another blink. "I—"

"Have you been up to something, Eddyn? Something you'd rather I didn't know? Something beneath you?"

Eddyn's head spun.

Tyrill slammed the stick against the table hard enough to break it. The room filled with heady vapors. She thrust the stub under his nose. He couldn't help but inhale, the stuff smelled so good.

"Tell me!" Tyrill demanded. "Tell me, Eddyn, and do not lie!"

Unable to control himself, Eddyn blurted out the whole shameful tale of his spying.

Tyrill's face was still when he finished. "Twice," she said at last. "Twice today you've disappointed me. You're so good at so many things, Eddyn, so close to being truly good, truly talented, truly accomplished, and you let tiny things destroy you! If you were to hone your charm as often as you hone your arrogance and pride . . ."

"I'm sorry," Eddyn mumbled.

"It's well the Fateing is upon you," Tyrill replied stonily. "Else I might slay you myself before Deep Winter."

Eddyn's blood went cold, but the part of him released by the imphor wood blundered on. "Do I still have to go to the Raising? Injured as I am, it'll—"

"What?"

"Hurt?" he whispered meekly.

She stared at him. "You will go," she said. "You will not discuss today's events. You will be raised to manhood with the rest. And when you receive your circlet, you will not limp."

And with that, she departed.

Eddyn stared numbly at her shadow. When the churgeon returned with squires bearing fresh clothes, he was crying.

(FERR-HALL-PRIME—EVENING)

Strynn was tired of waiting. Clad in War-Hold crimson, she sat among her age-peers in the Apprentice's Eighth of the Clan Sanctuary—whose architectural nuances she'd already analyzed several times. There was nothing else to *do*, dammit, there in the vast eight-sided chamber used for Ferr's most private rites. Except indulge in reflection.

She missed Avall, and that surprised her. Not because she didn't love him—

care about him, anyway—but because her feelings toward him seemed to have altered unawares, so that she no longer felt complete without him nearby. It was partly the chaos of the season, of course: Sundeath was confusing enough without the added stress of impending adulthood. In the past it had simply been rituals, festivals, or events she'd been deemed too young to attend. This year there'd been the masterwork competitions, her first viewing of the executions; the first combats in which anyone she cared about had participated—and now her Raising was upon her. Any one of which would've been enough without adding pregnancy and marriage.

Avall had been her stability throughout. Withdrawn and reflective by nature, he hadn't spoken with her a great deal, but he'd always been around. Now she was alone again, and that felt strange.

Perhaps marriage was no bad thing after all.

Perhaps after the chaos of the next half eighth subsided, she and Avall would be able to relax in each other's company as they had when they were children. Perhaps then, they'd become the lovers they both desired to be, instead of merely friends.

But probably not for a while. There was the rest of Sundeath to endure, and with it the Fateing, which would determine where they'd spend the Dark Season. At least *she* no longer had to make that decision; as a new wife, she would share Avall's Fate. And who knew what could transpire in another eighth?

Four eighths ago, she'd been a virgin, centered mostly on her friendship with Merryn and on her masterwork, with Avall an attractive ornament flitting in and out of her life. Now, in a very real way, he *was* her life. Until the child came and everything changed again.

And so she waited, feeling the stone grow hard beneath her and a stirring in her stomach that *might* be more than nerves.

More waiting, then a door opened in the eastern facet, and her two-father, who was also Clan-Chief of Ferr, strode into the otherwise empty wedge of chamber.

Preedor syn Ferr was ninety, but moved like a man half that age, with hard, spare muscles and a head of spun-silver hair tied back in a tail beneath the raised hood of the crimson robe he wore as token of his official function. Gold showed there, too, and gems: the circlet of his rank and awards. The other adults followed him, in order of their septs' creation. Slowly the eight wedges of inward-facing seats filled with the folk of Ferr, until all empty ones were occupied. Strynn shifted expectantly. A gong sounded in a screened alcove behind her chief. The deep tones echoed off the stone walls and ceiling and the unadorned floor, until drowned in flesh and fabric. And with that, Preedor spoke.

"Balance," he said. "You, who would claim full rights and responsibilities of Clan Ferr have stood on the scales of Balance. You have placed your knowledge and your skills in the Balance and been found worthy to join the ranks of those who have gone before you, those who stand with you, those who will join you in future times. Clan Ferr welcomes you. Be joyful."

And with that, two women, chiefs of the second most tenured septs in protocol, rose from Preedor's sides and marched toward the low altar that centered the room. A chalice stood atop it, simply shaped of unglazed porcelain. Wine glimmered within, red as blood. A matching ewer showed behind.

"You stand on the past," one said, raising the chalice. "This chalice represents the past. It is ground to dust every year and that dust mixed with the ashes of the oldest of those of our clan who lie in the crypts beneath this place. At the end of this rite, it will be ground to dust again."

She passed the chalice to her companion. "The wine within this chalice represents the past and the present commingled: the blood of the grape for the blood of men. But within that wine there *is* blood: one drop from the chief of each sept of the clan. And with it, too, are the ground bones of those who have gone before. Drink it, and know that of which you are part."

Strynn watched breathless, feeling the slightest stirrings of nausea. Still, she managed to stay calm as the two sept-chiefs stepped down to flank the front row of the wedge of Rising adults and passed the chalice to the first one to her left. Strynn, midway along the third row, took it boldly when it arrived, noting how the slightly porous texture made it both oddly soothing and vaguely warm to the touch. The wine was sweet, with a subtle grittiness (not surprising), and she had no trouble swallowing, even knowing what it contained. A long draught, and she passed it on. Soon enough it was over, the chalice returned to the altar, and the chiefs to their posts.

"Balance," Preedor stressed again. "You have been balanced and found of good quality; but you also stand on the knife edge of Balance: between childhood and adulthood, between knowing and doing. Between what you were, and what you will become. And with that knowledge comes pain. As we suffered pain to fill that cup of which you have tasted, we now require pain of you."

At that, thirty-four adults rose from the ranks behind the chief and advanced toward the rows of inductees. Each chose one, seemingly at random, raised that person to his or her feet, and escorted the inductee to one of the doors in the north or south facets. Strynn followed the woman who'd chosen her to the one on the south, which opened onto a long corridor flanked with arched doorways along either side, where she was ushered through the first open door on the left. That proved to be a plain cubicle marked only by a square stone seat and a shelf bearing a shallow bowl of bone clay, a jar of the same material, and a fist-sized object with a flattened disk at one end and a shiny black string protruding from the other.

Wordlessly, the woman poured dark liquid from the jar into the bowl, swished it around to mix it, then set it back on the shelf. "Bare your torso," she commanded.

Strynn had expected something like this, and her hands barely trembled as she released the top three clasps of her loose velvet robe and slid the garment back over her shoulders to pool around her waist. It was cold in the stone-walled space beneath the clan hall, and she shivered. Her nipples tensed. The woman smiled as she took the disk, stared at it a moment, then set it against the skin of Strynn's left shoulder. It was cold as ice.

"This will hurt," the woman cautioned. "Try not to flinch. And remember that it will hurt you no more than it has hurt anyone in Clan Ferr."

Strynn took a deep breath and watched the woman set a candle to the string. It sputtered with the same quick-fire that had bonded her to Avall.

White pain burst against her shoulder and she all but cried out as an array of tiny needles were driven into her flesh. The woman removed the disk at once, but the pain did not diminish. Blood gleamed on its face. More trickled hot down her arm.

Meanwhile, the woman had taken the bowl of black liquid and a small brush, and swabbed the liquid atop the freely bleeding pattern. Strynn did gasp then, for it hurt worse than the initial piercing. But she could feel an odd puckering, too, and knew that for good or ill, the pigment in that bowl was now part of her, and that she would forever bear the tattooed sigil of Clan Ferr: a circle surrounding a human arm, bent at the elbow, and flourishing a sword.

A final pause to wipe away the blood and ink with a crimson towel, and the woman nodded approval. "Cover yourself and come with me. And may that be the worst pain you ever endure."

It was pain enough, Strynn thought, trying not to rub the throbbing flesh as she accompanied the woman back to the Sanctuary, which was roughly half-full by now. She found her old seat and waited while the others returned by ones and twos, some pale-faced, a few showing bright eyes or cheeks wet with tears. Dark stains on several robes hinted at bleeding not yet abated.

When the thirty-four had reclaimed their places, the Clan-Chief spoke again. "Balance," he intoned a third time. "You balance on a point, like an upright dagger. Your life, like that dagger, could fall any way—into our craft, or into another. But know that Clan Ferr claims you now and forever. Yet as you must claim your own future, the last part of this rite you must perform yourself. As you have tasted pain, now taste the pleasure of pride. Touch the clan insignia on the floor before your seat and remove what you find there."

Strynn blinked in mild confusion, but reached forward with the rest to press the emblem carved into the stone between her feet, which she'd thought one with that paving. It slid back soundlessly, revealing a shallow recess in which something metallic gleamed. Something she recognized—as she withdrew the circlet she'd seen that morning in Smith-Hold.

"That circlet has no front, back, or sides," Preedor recited. "It has no beginning and no end. You are like that circlet: a simple thing yet complex. But know that you are *always* Clan Ferr. Know that. Remember that. Be proud of that. We have made you what you are, but you will make yourselves what you become. Crown yourself now with the circlet of adulthood."

Strynn stared briefly at the gleaming metal, then did as instructed.

No more was said, and with a flourish Preedor turned and strode back through the door by which he'd come. The rest followed, and when all had exited, Strynn and her clan brothers and sisters likewise departed—through the same door, which they'd never passed through before, and through which, from here on, they would always enter.

A feast waited in the reception hall beyond, and with it the company of family and friends, all of Clan Ferr, wardens of War-Hold. Congratulations danced around the room like music, and faces that heretofore had been solemn were flushed and merry. Only two things were missing: Merryn and Avall.

When Strynn returned to Avall's chambers that night, he was there before her, sitting at the table, drinking wine, and waiting. He wore househose but no tunic, and on his shoulder—his right, because he was a man—a circular tattoo trickled blood. He grinned. She smiled back.

"I've missed you," he murmured, offering her a chilled goblet. "More than you'll ever know."

"Ah, but I do know," she replied. "Believe me, Avall, I do!"

CHAPTER X:

SEEDS OF DREAD

(ERON: TIR-ERON—SUNDEATH: DAY V: GODS' DAY—LATE AFTERNOON)

~~~~~~~~~~

It had been a windy day, and the prophecy the High King had just pronounced on the Hill of Weather far too strange to dwell on. Rrath syn Garnill was having a hard time *not* dwelling on it, however. He shifted his weight and straightened the folds of the white Priest-Clan robe he wore beneath Weather's formal tabard: gray, striped with stormy blue, the latter a match for his eyes (so Esshill, his bond-brother, had told him), and the former not far off his stone-toned hair. And tried to think of more imminent matters.

Fate's temple lay before him, across a flagstone plaza that encircled the waist-high, unadorned cylinder that comprised Fate's Well. It was an unremarkable structure—no more than two spans wide, the same high, and twice that long—though singularly appropriate in construction, being made of enormous undressed stones piled without mortar to reflect the fact that while Fate determined what transpired when Man interacted with Spirit, the results were like to be rough, unexpected, and strange.

Rrath studied the sky apprehensively, waiting for the sun to enter the final eighth of its arc, which would signal the last of the day's eight rites.

Closer . . .

Now!

Without fanfare, the undressed birkit skin that formed the temple's door swept aside and High King Gynn stepped out. He, too, sported fur: a strip of birkit hide wrapped around his loins and tied with leather thong in token of the fact that Fate was oldest of man's adversaries and should therefore be addressed in the garb of man's most ancient forebears. As Mask, Gynn wore the bleached skull of a dolphin, the wisest beast on Angen, and which had already been present when men arrived on its cold, wind-blasted shores. The Mask hid Gynn's face entirely; only his eyes showed as an occasional glitter within the sunken orbits. The toothy snout gouged marks of red across the King's smooth white chest, wounds he patently ignored as he strode forward, flanked by two Priests clad like himself without the Mask. Neat bare feet slapped loudly on the pavement as he approached the Well, his tread a trifle uncertain—likely because of the incessant fasting he'd had to endure since his Confirmation Feast, so as to empty his mind for its eight-fold refilling by the Eightfold God.

Rrath held his breath as Gynn approached, craning his neck to see around the taller man ahead, whose still-bleeding shoulder told Rrath he'd likewise been Raised the previous night. He jostled another someone who grunted irritably and frowned at him, but by then Rrath had settled.

Gynn had reached the Well and was resting his hands on the rough-stone curb. Rrath wondered what he'd use as a vessel. As a newly Raised adult, this was the first time he'd been allowed to witness these rites (of which adults were forbidden to speak save among themselves), so each temple, vestment, and mask he'd seen here on the Isle of The Eight had evoked a new thrill of wonder. And likewise each new vessel.

But instead of a goblet, chalice, or flagon, Gynn bent far over and thrust both hands into the pristine water, cupping them and raising them to his lips beneath the Mask. Rrath had no idea how he'd managed to open his mouth with that thing over his head, much less swallow, yet he caught the pulse of movement in the King's throat, the trickle of water across his bloody chest, and knew the last sacred draught had been consumed.

A long hush ensued, broken by anxious breathing, the rustle of the surrounding grove (holly here: evergreen, as Fate was ever-watching; and sharp-pointed, as Fate was ever painful to encounter), and the distant clatter of voices on the nearer shore.

And still Gynn remained silent, though his muscles went taut as tumbler's cords—surely a sign that the God had possessed him again.

The crowd stirred restlessly—then gasped as, against all tradition, the King reached forward and claimed another handful from the Well.

More water coursed down his chest, reddened by rivulets of blood that stained the pure white fur around his hips.

Another breath. Gynn tensed even more, then flung himself forward to brace against the Well. His back arched upward like a cat's, then sagged— and the High King collapsed to his knees.

And spoke.

"I have been called the King of Balance," he announced, voice thin and reedy within the Mask. *"But Balance may soon be a stranger to us all. A change is coming that will upset all balances, both for good and ill. Nor will this unbalancing end quickly."*

He slapped his hand into the Well, sending water everywhere. *"As this water splashes outward, so shall the people of Eron splash outward. As ripples stretch and twine and mingle, so from this day will Fate set our lives rippling, twining, and mingling in new and unexpected ways. This time next year, we will know a world different from that we now take for granted."*

A chill shivered across Rrath that had nothing to do with weather. A King had uttered a similar prophecy the year of the plague, and the ripples from that had not even remotely subsided.

"I see ice!" the King went on. *"I see our Fate forever bound with ice. I see stones like ice, and hearts like ice, and fear a dagger of ice in the hearts of every man and woman in Eron. I see ice that holds World in the hands of Death. I see ice that may be Death, if it be not forestalled.*

"But that is not yet," he continued. *"That is for our children's children a thousand times sired to face. What we face is that which may, in time, come to burn that ice. Yet as ice is water and water also air; so we must be prepared to change yet remain as we are."*

"Balance has ended!" Gynn rasped at last. *"Chance and Choice are hopelessly entwined. But know, people of Eron, that we are about to enter what shall someday be called the Winter of Blood.*

And with that, Gynn fell senseless to the ground. Rrath started, more from excitement than alarm. After all, who *wouldn't* faint when the God departed him, leaving him merely another human?

The assisting Priests knelt beside the High King, then raised him to his feet to escort him back to Fate's Fane.

The witnesses waited politely until all three had vanished behind the skin, whereupon the entire grove erupted with astonishment as opinions on this last utterance spread. Rrath was beyond puzzled—who wouldn't be, at such an odd mix of real and irrational? At least his duties were over for the day. He'd seen, learned, and witnessed. It remained to reflect and digest—which he'd do tonight, and for many to come, in Priest-Hold.

A moment later, in the vanguard of the grim-faced folk flooding across the bridge from the Isle of The Eight to the southern shore, he was already looking forward to beginning that debate.

As the most holy and ancient of all the twenty-four, Priestcraft's principal hold (it alone had no separate controlling clan) occupied the second most prestigious location in Eron Gorge. No other hold lay so near the Citadel, for all that the Ri-Eron and a handsome sprawl of gardens separated that imposing pile of hewn stone from the arcade of rough-shaped boulders that bridged the entrance to the narrow splinter gorge that housed Priestcraft's sacred precincts.

No buildings showed beyond, as Rrath turned his steps that way, only gardens designed to appear as though they'd grown in calculated disarray. Of actual structures there was no sign, but the gorge's walls were pocked and fissured with openings and slits that were proof of habitations carved into the rock. Other holds did that as well, of course, and winter holds had to of necessity. But only here was there no outward display, for Priesthood must come from within.

By the time Rrath reached the smooth-stone path that twisted toward the arcade, he was walking very fast indeed. By the time he passed beneath the startled eyes of the gate-warden, youth had set him running. Anticipation—raw excitement—welled up in him, as the Power of the God had welled up within the King for most of the day.

What must that be like? he wondered, as his shoes smacked against the paving stones. To have one Face of the God after another take up residence within your mind and body? Would it be pleasant? Awful? Both? Or neither? Would it (blasphemous notion) be for the King as it was for the un-clanned women who sold their bodies across the river, who let one man after another fill them in the course of an evening's work, one tender and considerate, another taking them with brutal force?

He didn't know, for all he'd certainly felt *something* at his own Raising last night, when he'd tasted of Weather's Well. Something else to debate with Esshill, he supposed—assuming he could find him.

Too bad his friend wasn't a year older, so that he could've seen all these things firsthand—some of which Rrath was forbidden to detail. At least the prophecies themselves, as gifts from the God to the people, would be written down and distributed to every hall and hold, so that by dawn tomorrow everyone in Tir-Eron who had an interest in such things would have seen the entire text of this year's utterances. A quarter eighth more (Weather willing) and the remotest holds would know—*and* the king of Ixti, though he prayed Barrax wouldn't take all that talk of change as an excuse to begin the war everyone had feared for two generations.

Rrath found Esshill—not unexpectedly, given the time of day, his friend's schedule, and his sensual predisposition—in the baths. Actually, they were a series of hot springs that were the envy of the other crafts, so much so that Priest-Clan derived a nice additional income from selling access at certain times of day.

This wasn't one of them. Esshill was lounging alone in the pool-of-middle-heat in the Priests' private section of the spring, tactfully screened from the coldest women's pool by a sturdy, head-high hedge. The tinkle of water masked the sounds of Rrath's approach even as it soothed him—as it was supposed to do. Esshill was either asleep or drowsing heavily—until Rrath splashed water in his face, then folded himself down beside his bond-brother on the pool's limestone border.

Esshill flailed, sputtered, and eventually got his eyes sufficiently clear to identify his assailant and raise a quizzical brow. "And?" was all he said.

Rrath sighed. "Would you like the formal or informal version?"

"I want *every* version, but give me the gist, first off."

Rrath sighed. "Figured you'd say that. Okay, then, in order—" And with that he proceeded to repeat with perfect wording and inflection every single prophecy Gynn had made since dawn, when he'd strode from the Temple of World to say only that "the World is about to honor us with something new, which will be both a gift and a curse to our kind," through the utterances at the Wells of Man, Life, Craft, Strength, Law, Weather, and Fate.

Esshill listened patiently as Rrath expounded, his bland, smooth face by turns enthused, puzzled, and troubled by the High King's words. "About what I expected," he confirmed at last. "Affairs as normal in the short term. No unexpected disasters, no terrible winter, no drought, no plague. No war with Ixti—yet. Lots of recurring images."

Rrath nodded. "Gems—that's one, though it's hard to tell if that simply meant that Gem-Hold would strike a new vein, or something else. Increased contention—which is no surprise, given how the clans like to vie with each other. Remember last year when he said the Smiths would go to War, and then War would go to the Smiths? We couldn't figure that out until that business with Avall and Eddyn and Strynn came up."

Esshill scowled. "And damn Avall for it, too, lucky—"

"You barely know Avall," Rrath hissed. "I *barely* know him, and he and I were roommates at Weaver-Hold when we started our cycle. I liked him and admired him, but that's about it."

Esshill shrugged. "Whatever. Back to where we were: We've got gems, we've got Change and Contention. We've got . . . ice?"

Rrath nodded. "That was strange, too, because when *don't* we have ice? Except that it's supposed to be a *milder* winter than usual, so Weather says. But that was ice in the future—the very far future—which is odd of itself, since The Eight don't usually hint at things more than a year ahead."

"Didn't hint of the plague at all."

Rrath shook his head. "Actually, They did. Fate's words that year were 'Beware of what you cannot see, that you yet smell and hear.' "

Another snort. "The Eight should make Themselves clearer."

Rrath grinned. "They're Gods—*a* God, anyway. They do what They want. If you ask me, They're bored."

Esshill sighed, closed his eyes, and leaned back against the spring's stony rim. The waters farther out belched and hissed—and vented a dozen bubbles of rotten-smelling steam, as they did at intervals.

The air thickened. Rrath (who detested the stench as much as he liked bathing) coughed and sneezed, then rose wearily. "Wish I had some of that ice right now, to cool my brow. But I'll leave you to think about it."

"You're going?"

A nod. "Have to. More duties to attend—fortunately interesting ones."

"Dinner?"

Another nod. "But not mine."

"Oh," Esshill replied knowingly, "I see!"

It was a duty Rrath had stumbled into, by virtue of having said at the wrong time that he was from tiny, southern Half Gorge, which had raised certain questions about the local wildlife. He'd been rather too quick—and truthful—to reply.

The upshot was that Rrath had been assigned his present task, which first required that he climb a precipitous trail to the last of the dead-end splinter gorges that branched off Priest-Clan's larger one. It was a wild place of towering cliffs, narrow ledges, and extravagantly weathered stone—which suited its function perfectly. He'd turned the last corner now, and that removed any sign of man's dominion save the path itself and the strong iron fence up ahead that completely blocked the canyon's mouth and rose three spans above his head. A key opened an inset gate there, which he shut behind him to face another fence a span away. That barrier was similar to the first, save that the bars were thicker and barbed along their far sides with hand-long spikes of knife-edged steel, some of which showed blood along their edges. Those bars fringed the top of a cliff maybe four times his height. He paused there, peering down to where roughly a square shot was enclosed by a continuation of the bars, the barrier kinked sharply inward at the top to make more than certain that within didn't escape. Nothing moved in there that he could see, and squinting into the dusk revealed only tawny boulders, clumps of waist-high shrubs, and the distant line of waterfall that slid out of the gorge's wall to feed a stream at the right.

But sight-seeing wasn't his task. He sighed, steeled himself—in spite of the pride he took in this office, it frightened him beyond telling—and moved left, to where a square iron plate as long and wide as his arm was set in the ground. Beyond it, a short tunnel gaped. Passage through that darkness brought him to a third gate, through which daylight showed. This gave onto another dead-end canyon, but hardly an empty one. Goats herded there, most free, but always a few—the eldest or most infirm—housed in pens. He unlocked the gate and steered his way among them, wrinkling his nose at their musky stench, then selected a sturdy old nanny with one blind eye and a bad leg. She bleated trustingly and nipped at the edge of his tabard as he freed her from her prison, but he didn't loose the chain around her neck. "Well, lady," he murmured wistfully, patting her on the head. "Allow me to invite you to dinner." A moment later, he was leading her through the tunnel to the strip between the fences. Halfway there, the nanny began to shrink back against the chain, and by the time they'd reached open air again, it was all Rrath could do to keep her in check, bad leg or no. Once she butted him (fortunately, she'd been polled). Once she tugged so hard the chains tore his flesh. Still, he outmassed her two to one, and in the end, he got her back into daylight.

Fixing her chain to a post set up for that purpose, he freed the bolts that held the trapdoor closed. Holding his breath—this part scared him most—he hauled it back. It moved easily on counterweighted hinges. Darkness gaped beneath: a smooth-sided shaft that sloped steeply down to the enclosure below. A final deep breath, and he returned to the goat, having first secured himself to the post by way of a second chain in case he, too, should fall. Bracing himself, he corralled the wretched, struggling animal, and dragged her toward the opening. She teetered on the edge, bleating plaintively, then toppled inside. He didn't hear her land because he was already throwing the trap back down and securing the bolts that latched it.

Done. He waited—always did, it was part of his duties—to watch as the poor crippled animal dragged herself into view at the bottom of the cliff, bleating at the top of her lungs. Plants stirred. Wind whisked down the gorge—and in the fading light, Rrath saw something come skipping toward the goat. Something a little taller than he, but naked, scaled, with a long tail held straight out behind for balance, and a mouthful of evil-looking teeth. A geen: one of a pair Priest-Clan maintained for reasons not to be revealed outside their craft. There were only two others in Tir-Eron, so far as he knew, both in the royal menagerie behind the Citadel. He wondered what the rest of the city would think if they knew such dangerous beasts were kept, even under tight security, this close to their homes and kin. But knowledge was knowledge, after all, and Priest-Clan had long maintained a second, breeding population of the dreaded reptiles at their summer hold on the heights south of the gorge, so that they could be thoroughly watched, their habits closely noted.

Rrath knew what *he* thought already, but he watched anyway, spellbound, as this rather small example of the most dangerous beast in Eron slowed its odd eager dance and began to pace warily around the goat, eyeing it with careful interest. Its leathery nostrils dilated as it sniffed, tongue slipping in and out as it tasted air. Its skin gleamed: the most beautiful and expensive leather there was. The line of knobby, hand-sized plates down its back shone like ruddy jewels. It looked at the goat, then up at him, then back at the goat, nostrils flaring again, as if in disdain. For a moment he caught its eyes—forward-facing, as was right for a predator—orange around gold, and glimmering with feral knowledge if not outright intelligence. Almost it grinned at him, mockingly, as though to say, "Someday, little human, it will be you who falls down the chute—or perhaps I will find a way to climb up and feast on *you*!"

Rrath backed away reflexively. Just as the geen—perhaps from fury, perhaps as a show of arrogance and strength—leapt straight up, arms no bigger than Rrath's catching the lowest bars on the fence neatly between the barbs. Which put its head half a span from his feet. He uttered an unmanly yip and jumped away. The geen's maw gaped: mottled black and red. It hissed at him, then uttered what had to be an angry cry, released its hold, and vanished. Thrashing sounds issued from below, along with another round of bleating—suddenly cut off. He had to force himself to look down again. There were two of them now: The female had taken advantage of her mate's posturing to stake her claim to food, which she'd already half devoured. He was fighting for it with nips of jaws and slashes of front claws, but the dreadful back claws remained fixed on the earth. It was like watching humans squabble. Common Clan, yes: but he'd seen husbands and wives go at it like that, with curses and slaps but no true violence to leave the other dead. Not often. And like as not, love came after.

The female snarled again, ripped a haunch off the carcass, and, to Rrath's amazement, held it out to her mate, hissing all the time.

The male took it, growled in turn, and bounded away to eat. Rrath made a note to write the whole episode down as soon as he got back to his quarters. This was conduct he'd heard of but never seen. They had one more documented case now.

He was just resecuring the hold-side gate when he saw Nyllol, who had charge of the menagerie, trudging up the hill, his bald head gleaming like a melon in the westering sun.

"Just curious," Nyllol panted as he joined Rrath, too out of breath for someone who claimed to be healthy.

"About what?" Rrath wondered.

Nyllol gestured toward the geens' enclosure. "About them. About the day. About how it feels to be an adult."

"The day's a day," Rrath replied carelessly, which Nyllol wouldn't have suffered had they not been alone. "I haven't decided about the other. But the geen . . . I think you're right. More than ever I do."

Nyllol's eyes narrowed warily. "What makes you think so?"

Rrath told him.

Nyllol listened patiently, not interrupting until Rrath had finished. His brow furrowed—whether with anger or thought, Rrath didn't know. "Damn," the old man spat at last. "One more stick on the pyre of our ignorance."

Rrath looked at him. "But only *one* more stick."

A sigh. "Enough sticks make a fire that will consume us all. Think of what you've been taught. Man is intelligent, and it is his soul that makes him so. No other beast can make that claim save perhaps the dolphins— and we've granted them a God against that possibility. Too, dolphins are friendly; geens aren't. But suppose geens *are* intelligent; it therefore follows, by all the theology we've hoarded and kept holy, that they have souls."

Rrath shrugged like the boy he almost still was. "That means we can no longer kill them without reason, or hunt them without penalty due."

Nyllol shook his head. "It means much more than that. It means, when you start taking it apart, that every definition we have, of soul, intelligence, and human must be reassessed."

Rrath snorted derisively. "For geens."

Nyllol glared at him. "If they have souls, it means The Eight have regard for them, which means we may have been in sin since the Arrival. You're no fool, Rrath, surely this is clear to you."

Rrath shook his head, as thoughts piled up inside his mind. "It is, yet it isn't. I have to . . . to unthink. It's hard."

"It always is. But consider what happens if those outside our craft learn that we even suspect geens might be as smart as we, but lack our ethics."

"That would make them demons in some eyes."

"There are no demons. We all know that."

"We all *hope* we know that," Rrath corrected.

Nyllol chuckled. "What I was suggesting was that such knowledge could fuel the first of many debates that might then prove that many of our beliefs are built on sand."

Rrath shook his head. "But the prophecies: They're real. They come true."

"But do they come from The Eight, from inside the King himself, or from the water in the Wells? We all know of substances that make us hallucinate, that alter our perceptions, that shift our sense of time."

Rrath stared at him aghast. "No one told me these things before."

"You weren't an adult before. But surely you've questioned?"

"I . . . have," Rrath conceded. "But I then questioned my questioning. I didn't want to believe things were other than they seemed."

"They may *be* as they seem," Nyllol retorted. "Then again, they may not. You will spend the rest of your life learning to tell the difference. And still not know."

Rrath gnawed his lip. "Well," he sighed at last, "I doubt we have to worry too much about losing our source of geen leather, even if they are intelligent."

Nyllol regarded him curiously. "How so?"

Rrath grinned. "If they're deemed intelligent, they'd come under human law, wouldn't they? Any geen that killed a man would therefore be termed a murderer and be condemned to death."

"Which raises another argument," Nyllol advised. "The Law is clear on this. The act of murder forfeits the murderer's humanity. That's why we're allowed to execute them. Were they fully human, we couldn't—save as you've explained."

Rrath shook his head again. "I must think on these things. And I must write down what I've seen in the log."

"Write carefully," Nyllol cautioned. "You have no idea whose eyes may see what you set down there."

"No," Rrath murmured. "But I'd like to. Maybe someday I'll find out."

"Maybe you will," Nyllol agreed. "But I doubt you'll like it if you do."

Silence. Neither of them moved, but Rrath sensed an agitation in his mentor, as though he had something more to say and couldn't decide if the time was right. "Is . . . something bothering you?" he dared at last.

Nyllol shot him a sharp glance. "I never know about you, Rrath. I never know if you're as smart as you seem or simply have a good eye and a good memory. I also never know if you're as naive as you sometimes appear, or if that's only a clever ploy to make people underestimate you."

"Would it make a difference?"

"It might."

"How? About . . . what?"

Nyllol exhaled deeply and sat down on a rock where he had full view of anyone approaching up the trail. He motioned Rrath down beside him. Rrath acceded. "Are you loyal to the craft, Rrath?" the old man asked flatly.

Rrath started. "I am, sir. That is, I hope I am. The craft has given me everything; otherwise, I'd be herding goats among the clanless down in Half Gorge."

"Instead of herding goats here, but I understand what you mean. You've come far—in some ways. But I ask you now: How far would you go?"

"How far would I need to go?"

"Would you put loyalty to craft above loyalty to King?"

"I would need good reason."

"Suppose you were given reason."

Rrath's eyes narrowed suspiciously. "I don't want to commit treason."

"There is treason, boy," Nyllol informed him, "and there is treason."

"I need more information."

Nyllol stared at him a long, still moment, blue eyes probing Rrath's face as though his soul were a pelt stretched on his forehead that perhaps Nyllol might buy. Finally he spoke. "What I have to tell you could be construed as treason," he said. "To reveal it—any of it—could well bring down the craft. To act upon it, could . . . take you very far indeed. You must choose: ignorance and security. Or knowledge and uncertainty—but with that uncertainty, a great potential for power."

"Power," Rrath mused with a wily grin. "I've never really thought what it might be to actually have power."

"Well," Nyllol informed him briskly, "hark to what I say, and you might."

CHAPTER XI:

RUMBLINGS IN IXTI

(IXTI: PORT FORTAN—YEAR BIRTH: DAY FIVE—EVENING)

~~~~~~~~~~

Barrax wished he were one of his ancestors. Not to be dead, but so that he might possess the power that remote progenitor was reputed to possess to burn men where they stood with the fierceness of his gaze.

Certainly if he had that power now, Lord Nyleez wouldn't be sitting there trying to look smug, when in fact he looked vacuous. Unfortunately, Nyleez was also married to Barrax's most vocal sister, so incinerating him in place would not be a good idea. Maybe a fall down the stairs . . .

Nor did Nyleez have sense enough to read Barrax's scowl as other than confusion—confusion over a situation Barrax comprehended perfectly well.

"My king, is there something you don't understand?" Nyleez asked innocently, his eyes round and guileless as his face, which was as round and guileless as the rest of him.

Barrax took a long draught of wine, not bothering to hide his frustration. "I was wondering," he growled through gritted teeth, "why my intelligence officer has nothing more specific to report regarding the situation in Eron. If we are to attack them this spring—which is, after all, why we are sitting here rather than enjoying our beach palaces before winter sends us indoors—we need to know particulars. We don't need to know that cotton production was up and wool down. We need to know by how many bales in each case and why. Was the weather bad, so that the shearing wasn't finished? Was there too little forage, too much predation from geens? Were the

Clan-Chief and Craft-Chief at each other's throats again? Were there quotas to make the merchants happy? Was there a vogue for woolen bed hangings so that surpluses were exhausted?"

He polished off the goblet, then flung it at the wide-eyed Nyleez. "*That* is what I need to know—for every craft.

"You are new at this," he went on. "I will forgive you this—*once*. But next year—if we still sit here next year, which isn't guaranteed, as I have ten other counselors to hear from tonight—*next* year, I expect you to have a spy in every hall and hold. They should already be in place. If your predecessor didn't leave records, there should still be those who know these things. If you don't wish to follow your predecessor into oblivion, you will do these things, and you will do them now. You will keep records, you will keep me advised. You will appoint a successor known and approved by me, and that successor will be kept well apprised. Then, should accident befall you"—he glared at Nyleez—"there will but be a tear, a breath, and a heartbeat, and the office shall continue as before. Do you understand? There will be precision. Absolute precision."

Nyleez exhaled—finally—but didn't move. Around him in Port Fortan's Hall of Strategy, the rest of the council relaxed by ones and twos, carefully shifting to more comfortable positions. It was a small, high-ceilinged room, lit from above by a raised cupola that encouraged the sort of relaxed intimacy suitable for plotting, though none were relaxing now.

"Now," Barrax continued, "does anyone have anything to add to Nyleez's very inadequate report?"

Silence, for a long strained moment, then a thin woman on the back row rose. Lady Maab, senior member of the council, and old enough to have seen Barrax in birth windings. "Lady Maab," Barrax acknowledged.

Maab nodded curtly. "My lord king," she began, "if we are to speak of Eron, we must speak of the prophecies of King as God. They should have been pronounced today. Has any word reached us yet?"

Barrax tried not to glare at her as yet another flaw in his governing system stood revealed. He masked that displeasure with an acid smile. "Does everyone on my council expect me to do my own advising?" he snapped. "Does everyone have to remind me of what this kingdom is not? We are here to rebuild, but every time we seek to firm up our foundations, we only find more damage."

"My lord . . ." Maab ventured, white-faced.

"A generation ago there would've been couriers and signalers all along the Flat Road," Barrax continued. "Word of the first prophecy would've reached us as the last was being made, which is to say *now*. At this very moment we *should* be debating what those prophecies mean to us and how the

Eronese might interpret them. We would have our experts here discussing those auguries and casting auguries of our own to confirm their validity."

"My lord," Maab dared. "You know the reason for this. Most of our spies in Eron were born there and raised to that trade, in positions we worked generations to render invisible. But many of them died of the plague, and one doesn't bribe an Eronese easily. They don't induct us into their mysteries. They marry carefully and rarely from outside. Links broke. Our own codemaster died. Folk from the way-garrisons were recalled to replace the dead in the cities. When one is starving, new clothes seem unimportant."

"Unless one dies of exposure before starvation," Barrax retorted. "Very well, we will speak of this again. In the meantime"—he stared at her relentlessly—"you will take those rubies on that necklace you wear, and you will sell them, and you will use that money to rebuild and restaff the nearest way station on the Flat Road. You will report to me when this is accomplished, with the name of the merchant, the amount paid, and those you have hired— none of whom are to be kin. An eighth from now, another of you will do the same with the next-nearer, an eighth after that another. I mean to have those stations up and running. If we go to war—*if* we go to war—we will need that communication. But don't let the Eronese know we're doing this. Let them think the stations are still ruined or deserted. Build new ones just out of sight; construct secret rooms in the old ones—I care not. But this time next year I want to know the prophecies as soon as the folk in North Gorge do."

"Or sooner," someone purred. Barrax didn't need to look around to locate the speaker.

"Lord Tixx," he sighed. "Do you have something to add?"

Lord Tixx nodded, rising from his corner like an emaciated stork. "I was only suggesting, Your Majesty, that you might well be there yourself—next year. You might even be uttering those prophecies."

"I don't wish to become their priest," Barrax informed him.

Tixx regarded him coldly. "You don't *wish*!" he thundered, oblivious to Barrax's rank. "Rather say you don't *think*. You berate your counselors for ineptitude, and yet you don't think yourself! Have you considered, lord king, what you will do if you conquer Eron? I know why you think you need it—we all do—though I will state it again for the scribe so that there will be no ambiguity in this meeting. We desire war with Eron because we desire Eron's food and timber. Simple as that. We have no natural heat sources such as they have; therefore we burn wood. Burning wood destroys forests. Forests gone destroys the land because we can't reclaim it before the winds and waters do. We have to send farther every year for fuel. We have to send farther every year for meat. We have to work harder to raise the same crops on the same weak soil. Eron not only lacks these problems, it knows how to prevent these problems—as we were advised to do a century ago. If you were to take only every fourth tree from the mountains—"

"The mountains stay," Barrax boomed. "Do you not recall the command we were given when first we made landfall here? 'Keep it as you see it. Do what you will with the rest, but keep this as you see it.' "

Tixx nodded. "Which was interpreted to mean that whatever forests were visible from Point Down were to remain forever unharvested."

"Would you go against the Gods?" Barrax challenged.

"Sooner than against a starving mob," Tixx gave back easily. "The Gods *might* blast you; the mob *would* eat you alive."

"We aren't so far gone as that," Barrax replied. "The silos and warehouses are full."

"But for the first time in history we've built no new ones," Tixx retorted. "As for this war, we have resources to fight for one year. That's all. If we do this thing, we had better make it count. And whether or not we do this thing, we need to tend to our own land. The first thing I would do would be to invite some Eronese landsmiths down here. Pay them whatever it costs and tell them that an Ixti well fed is less likely to be an armed beggar on Eron's porch than an Ixti hungry. Tell them—"

He broke off, for a knock had sounded on the great bronze doors at the south end of the room. Echoes reverberated around the chamber, setting wine to tingling in brazen goblets, and making Barrax's hair rise up on end. He rounded on the door furiously. No one was supposed to interrupt the council while in session. Not unless Ixti was under attack, or there'd been—

Barrax's hair prickled again, and he leaned on the table for support, for he'd just had a premonition.

The door warden—Lord Benelez, who was also on the council—looked at him for permission. He nodded assent and managed to compose himself as Benelez opened the heavy portal. The young man who entered was clad in guardsman's livery—and sweaty, tired-looking, and dirty, yet still managed a proper salute as he took the requisite two steps into the chamber and froze. "My lord king," he began, bowing. "I have . . . news."

Barrax steeled himself. This was no time to display caprice or temper. "Someone get this man a drink—and then we'll have his story."

The guard accepted the goblet Maab handed him, and drank deeply of it before going down on one knee. "My lord king," he said again. "I have grave news. The prince—your son—Azzli is dead."

The room erupted into furor, but Barrax heard none of it. Only those same words, over and over, echoing in his head like the tolling on the doors. *"Azzli is dead . . . is dead . . . is dead . . ."*

"How?" someone ventured. Barrax realized with a start it was himself, still playing king, though his soul wanted to run and hide and pretend it had never heard those words. *Dead dead dead dead dead* . . .

The soldier cleared his throat. "Geens, Majesty. He was hunting geens. All who were with him were slain, but not before report was sent by Captain Yaran—who is likewise dead of his wounds. Yaran was one of a band that went hunting . . ."

"Who gave them permission?" Barrax roared.

The soldier turned white. "No one, Majesty. Rumor has it they wanted to spend some time alone, away from court. Time to—"

"Who is *they*?"

"Azzli, and Kraxxi, and the honor guard, Olrix, and Elvix and—"

"I know who they are!" Barrax yelled. "And I'll know who they are even better when I see their heads on my trophy shelf. Now: What happened?"

"As Yaran reported it," the soldier managed, "they were attacked by geens and during the attack, Kraxxi found an opportunity to kill Azzli and . . . did."

"We have proof of this?"

"Yaran witnessed it. But Yaran is dead. He had no choice but to flee or be slain, so he fled, returning when he could with more men. They, too, were attacked by geens. They were all killed, too. Or . . . fled."

"And so a half a day passed between my son's death and Yaran's? And yet I learn of both at once?" He glared at Maab again.

"There was . . . confusion, sir. The death of princes is no light matter. Yaran's words were unclear. We wanted confirmation. We wanted to report things *correctly*. And you were moving away from us as we moved toward you."

Barrax contained himself—barely. "And you're certain it was Azzli?"

The soldier stared at the mosaic floor. "There was no body—not much. Apparently they burned it."

"Again, *they*! Who is *they*?"

"Kraxxi survived. The triplets as well, Yaran said. I would assume it was their doing."

"It would've been Kraxxi's right," Maab noted dryly. "He may have done right by that as well. For to leave Azzli dead where geens have attacked— would you rather have your son eaten or burned?"

"I would rather have him here to my hand!" Barrax growled. "Barring that, I would have Kraxxi's head."

"Your own son's?"

"If he slew his brother, he's no son of mine. You know the law for fratricides."

"I know he wouldn't have slain Azzli deliberately. They loved each other."

"Then why endanger him?"

"Danger to himself as well!"

Barrax shifted his attention to the guard. "And if Yaran went for help, returned, and was slain . . . that implies certain things. So I will ask you: Where is Kraxxi now?"

"That isn't known," the soldier replied carefully. "There were two attacks. The first, in which Azzli was killed, with most of the guard save Yaran and the three. And a second—the geens were likely lured there by the scent of blood. That one a few survived. There could've been another between the two, however. Kraxxi and the trio could've been killed as well—they found Kraxxi's bloody clothes by the river, but no tracks nearby. That means little, though, since geens don't fear water."

"But you think he's fled?" Barrax demanded.

The guard nodded. "We think so."

"Or killed himself," Maab noted. "He would've known his choices. Death by your choosing or by his."

"What are you saying, Maab?"

"That you held no love for the boy. That he knew that. That the fact of that would inform his decisions—don't look at me like that, lord king. I tell you nothing that isn't known to this council. I merely put a name to it."

"And if you continue, I may name you traitor, Maab!" Barrax spat.

"You may name me what you like," Maab gave back haughtily. "I am old. I care not. But you won't get your way station that way. You'd be wise," she continued as softly as her voice had previously been hard, "to remember that your son has died and act in a way that honors his memory. As for Kraxxi, either he lives or he doesn't. If he lives, he'll still be your heir."

"And the law will still be the law," Barrax finished for her. "And Kraxxi is still a fratricide." He looked straight at the soldier. "I hereby lay a bounty on the head of my son. Alive, or dead, he is to be returned here as soon as can be. His actions have proclaimed his guilt. And with him, I pronounce sentence of death on Olrix, Elvix, and Tozri, his guard. And now, if you will excuse me, this council is ended."

And with tears welling in his eyes, Barrax, King of Ixti, turned, and strode from the dais, exiting though the north door. Outside, atypically, it began to rain.

CHAPTER XII:

THE HAND OF GOD AND MAN

(ERON: TIR-ERON–SUNDEATH: DAY VI: FATEING DAY–MORNING)

~~~~~~~~~~

Avall woke to rain, weariness, and anticipation.

The rain was obvious. Heavy, harsh sheets of it raged against the windows like sloppy scythes harvesting a late-autumn gale. It rendered the outdoors a blur, as though the dyes that defined the tapestry of reality had run or faded into a gray-white gloom that made him glad he'd no call to go abroad before afternoon. He could see nothing from the bed save the crenellated roofs of the wing across the court, and that but sporadically. Land and sky had merged. He was sorry for the messengers who would throng the streets today with the results of the Fateing.

The Fateing . . .

That which would define where he spent most of the next three eighths.

The only given that hadn't been a given a year ago was that he'd spend this Dark Half with Strynn.

He looked down at her beside him, clad in a night shift, face at peace, but with a smear of darkness beneath her eyes. She mostly slept on her back, and usually with her lips slightly parted, which he found most beguiling.

She'd earned the smudges, too: victim of a restless night, courtesy of a tattoo that didn't seem to be healing right, which had pained her—and also, she confided, of a certain other discomfort she thought might be the first stirrings of her child. He'd laid his hand on her stomach in the wee hours but had been unable to detect what she swore were occasional twitches. Or perhaps he didn't want to. He'd witnessed none of it—the rape, the ensuing furor—and hadn't even been an active partner in most of the marriage negotiations. Strynn barely showed—yet. Therefore there was no child— yet—tender breasts and morning sickness notwithstanding. He dreaded the day it all became real. And hated himself for that dreading.

So he'd spent half the night worrying about his wife, another fraction tending his own selectively oozing tattoo, and the rest wondering what daylight would bring. In the meantime . . . Strynn showed no sign of waking, and he intended to let her rest as long as possible. Himself— He rose, dressed in a room-robe, and padded barefoot to the archway that let onto the balcony, where he pushed open the door, amazed at the force needed to overcome the wind—and bit back a dismayed shiver. Not only was the rain actually rattling the thick panes, but the temperature had dropped sharply in the night (as the weather-witches had suggested it might), and the air held a tang of winter it shouldn't possess for another eighth. He wouldn't have been surprised to hear sporadic sleet merging with the slanting downpour.

He shut the thick-paned doors with more force than intended, wincing lest he awaken Strynn. There was bread, wine, and cheese on the table, but it was cold, and a little stale; he wanted something hot, thick, and sticky.

No, he corrected, what he wanted was for Strynn to wake up (of her own will) so he wouldn't have to think about the Fateing.

Again.

He'd listed four choices where he would like to spend Deep Winter. Argen-Hall-Prime was his first—reasonably enough; it was where he lived, and it had easy access to Smith-Hold-Main, where he expected to spend most of his time. But since more folks were likely to choose Smith-Hold than Argen-Hall, choosing the latter effectively gave him two choices in one.

Not that he'd actually *get* it. First priority would go to those in the last of their rotation: those who'd entered the Fateing four cycles ago, given their four choices, then seen them reduced to three, then two, then one. The ones would have guaranteed positions. And then they'd start over with a different set of choices.

His second choice had been almost as easy: Smith-Hold-Winter. The nice little fastness tucked back in the mountains between Tir-Eron and Dead Gorge. Hard work but necessary, as the mines there never shut down, and everyone was expected to spend time producing raw material as well as perfecting it. Few people would choose it, however, and his logic was that he'd get the heavy labor a tour there entailed over and done. It was also close enough to Tir-Eron that Strynn could return if her condition warranted—at the cost of repeating a cycle there when she recovered.

Gold-Hold-Winter was his third. It was his major area, which was one appeal. But he'd done so much goldsmithing of late that he'd welcome the change the other choices entailed. Not that he'd mind spending all winter in company with the masters of his craft. Surely he could learn *something*, like that new granulation technique Anorin had so dazzled folks with last Sundeath. It was also, as it happened, the closest hold that interested him to War-Hold, which was where Merryn would be going if she had her way. With her luck, she would. She always got what she wanted.

Last choice? Gem-Hold-Winter. Remote, beautiful, location; hard trek to get there (bad for pregnant women); interesting work that would augment his craft, since he knew next to nothing about either the mining or cutting of the gems he used in his projects.

And Rann was there.

His bond-brother. His best friend since childhood. Enough older than he that he'd entered the Fateing the previous eighth. Avall hoped he elected to remain at the hold an extra eighth so the two of them could leave together. Not that he expected it. Winter-hold duty in Deep Winter was something one did because one had to, not because one desired it. Staying an extra turn in one got you advantages later.

It had been a quarter since Avall had seen Rann, and then but briefly. More times than he could count he'd wished Rann were here: to advise him about the wedding (tease him unmercifully, more like), to calm him when he got too anxious, to drink with him when he needed to relax, to spar with him on the field when Merryn was too aggressive, to knead the kinks from his shoulders when he got too tired. To listen to him, and be listened to in turn. Rann's gift was to make even bad times seem pleasant. And while these were not exactly bad times (being married to the most beautiful woman of her generation and almost winning a subcraft-chieftainship first time out were not things of which one normally complained), still . . .

He needed to escape, to be a boy again (as Rann was perfectly able to be), instead of the man he was being forced, against his will, to become.

A soft sigh behind him was Strynn stirring; a more forceful one, a yawn. He saw her start to roll over, then hesitate, one arm flung across her body. Another, and she stilled.

He wouldn't wake her yet. Instead, he poured a goblet of wine and stared out at the rain, knowing that somewhere on South Bank two subcrafts of Lore (Ciphering and Records) had, since the first of Sundeath, been meeting with the Priests of Fate's aspect, Chance, to determine the outcome of the Fateing. It wasn't as random as intended; there were too many factors to consider for that—balancing personal choice and the needs of the winter holds was never easy.

But what was the alternative? Winter holds need full staffing. They needed healers even at Lore-Hold; needed smiths even at Glass—and weavers at Leather, and stonemasons at War. Not many, sometimes, but all those things were required. And if no one asked— Well, there were ways to fill the gaps.

It wouldn't be long before he'd know for certain. He'd seen Eellon last night, checking the need lists for Smithcraft and its facets against Tyrill's proposals for the same. They'd mostly concurred. A few too many fourth-cyclers had listed Iron-Hold, but that had been anticipated and extra work found for them: making nails for the shipwrights. The rest— For once, Tyrill and Eellon were in agreement.

He wondered where Eddyn would be posted. For that matter, he wondered what he'd requested. Eddyn was being uncharacteristically circumspect, and that gave Avall pause. Still, he'd know by noon. That was when the heralds would arrive with the postings for each hall and hold.

Sighing, he filled his goblet again, drained it, and went off to bathe—alone.

There was a leak in the mosaic ceiling over the garderobe. He hoped Eellon got a *good* stonemason this time around.

Noon arrived, but no messenger—a fact Eellon blamed on the rain and Tyrill, who was waiting with him in the no-man's-land of the vestibule where craft hold and clan hall met, laid on Teneem, the aging subcraft-chief of Records, who really was in her dotage and ought to be replaced soon. Avall ignored them, as he tried to ignore everyone else—save Merryn and Strynn.

Merryn was her usual casually confident self, and seemed not one whit troubled by the fact that she'd defected from her birth-craft. She'd challenged him to a drinking match later—offering to spot him one if she got anything other than War. She was wearing Argen livery, though, and women's clothing in the bargain, and looked magnificent in both. Avall felt a pang of regret when he considered how unlikely it was that he'd ever see his sister in clan maroon again.

Strynn looked less peaceful awake than asleep, and more worn. Indeed, she had a touch of fever, which Tyrill advised might prompt a call for a healer if it persisted. Merryn didn't think so—and Merryn knew Strynn's vagaries as well as anyone. Avall wished he did. She'd been withdrawn and distant all morning. He could think of any number of explanations, too; but the most persistent was that she'd figured out, as he had earlier, that she was on the edge of something about which she had no choice. Later she *would* be able to state her own preferences in the Fateing. But in this one area the

Fateing was firm. Newlyweds spent their first cycle together in the husband's hold. And couples were always posted together the cycle they had a child—normally at the mother's choice, but this was a special case, with wedding and birth so close together.

Avall hated it, as he hated all this ritual. Better to be in Ixti, where one did what one wanted, and if chaos ensued and affairs began to fray around the edges, still, beyond the royal family, every thought, breath, and deed wasn't bound up with some kind of rite. It would be nice, every now and then, to do something stupid and spontaneous and . . . *free*.

A rumble in the assembled ranks signaled a new arrival—far more folk than he were getting restless with anticipation. He craned his neck with the rest, but should've known.

Eddyn. Tired-looking and disheveled—and walking with the limp that had plagued him for two days. Was this a calculated appearance, Avall wondered, or accident? Eddyn rarely missed a chance to play to an audience, but would he get sympathy for his wound (which even some in Argen-a thought unfairly bestowed), or approbation for so blatantly emphasizing it?

In any event, Eddyn seemed as anxious as anyone and promptly melted into as much anonymity as his height allowed. Tyrill glared at him for no reason Avall could determine. Not that she needed one. For good measure, she glared at him, too. He rolled his eyes and looked away.

More waiting.

"This is ridiculous," Tyrill spat, a finger after noon, which was supposed to be the appointed time. And with that she strode toward the door—to be all-but-knocked-down by the hall page bursting breathlessly through to announce (as protocol required) that a messenger had just arrived from the Temple of Fate with news for Lord Eellon of Argen and Lady Tyrill of Smith.

"Admit this messenger," Eellon and Tyrill chorused.

A bow from the page, a hasty (and rather inelegant) retreat, and the door opened again to admit a handsome young man in Chance's black and white, so thoroughly soaked and splattered it looked more like Fate's gray. His hair hung in his eyes, dripping, and in serious need of cutting. The waxed-leather cases he carried resisted water, however, and he managed to twitch his face into suitable solemnity when he presented one each to Tyrill and Eellon. Each accepted with equally formal bows, and promptly swept to the opposite sides of the vestibule. Eellon glared at those who crowded too close, and Merryn used her elbows with careful dispatch to maneuver the worst offenders away. So it was that Eellon had relative freedom in which to uncap the leather tube and remove the parchment scroll inside. He broke the seal, located the top edge, and fixed it to the appropriate bracket beside the door to the hold. A final tap unrolled it—to the floor and beyond. (Tyrill thought the scribes should use smaller lines, so as to avoid that awkwardness.)

Eellon barely had time to back away before, with an appalling lack of decorum, clan and craft descended upon the scrolls. There were two per side. The first listed positions available at hall or hold during the winter, and who had been chosen from the other crafts and clans to fill them. The second listed everyone *in* Argen-Hall who'd entered this term's Fateing. Avall found his name with no trouble—it was near the top of the list—but had trouble tracing it to his destination because so many people were jostling the rest of it. Finally, he resorted to being rude: putting both hands upon it, while leaning into the wall, effectively blocking all other views.

Yes, here it was: Avall syn Argen-a . . .

His heart sank.

"Gem-Hold-Winter," he blurted, backing away, already searching for Strynn. "Gem-Hold-Winter," he repeated, when he found her, trying to smile, though he was far more disappointed than expected, for all Rann was at Gem-Hold, too. It was just that he was used to winning. And if he hadn't precisely lost the Fateing, he certainly hadn't won.

Merryn had. No need to see her face; the yip she uttered bounced around the room like light striking mirrors. "War-Hold!" she crowed, dancing over to hug first Avall, then Strynn. Eventually she saw his face and hers likewise fell. "Not what you wanted?"

"What I can live with," he replied. "I have to remember it's fourth out of a hundred-odd, not last out of four."

"Good way to see it," Merryn grinned. "Rann'll be eager as a puppy to see you."

Avall strained on tiptoes. "Wonder how Eddyn did."

Merryn scowled. "I doubt he listed the Not-World, though that's what he deserves. But we'll find out soon enough."

Too soon, as it evolved, for Lykkon (who'd once again invited himself to a function he was legally too young to attend), came ambling over by way of Eddyn and informed them all quietly that The Tall One had also been posted to Gem-Hold-Winter. Avall's heart sank indeed, and Merryn's face went hard as granite, while Strynn blanched. "Chance, my ass!" Avall spat. "No way this doesn't represent meddling. Someone with a very poor sense of humor!"

"I think," Eellon broke in unexpectedly from behind them, "we'll find out more this evening."

Avall glanced around for Tyrill to try to gauge her reaction, but the Craft-Chief was already gone.

Avall looked at Merryn warily, then took Strynn's hand. "My sister has promised to drink with me," he murmured. "I'd say it's time we began."

"Yes," Strynn agreed with unexpected venom. "I agree."

In spite of his intention, but in common with a good portion of the population of Tir-Eron, Avall spent the first part of the afternoon seeking out this friend or that in order to determine who'd been posted where. Though duty—drudgery, even—lay at the end for most of Avall's contemporaries, it was a new thing, and new things were to be savored. It was something adults did, after all, and he was eager to embrace those newfound rights. That responsibilities came with them was overlooked for the nonce. Already he had plans for his tenure at the winter hold.

A quarter of his time would be given to the hold itself—mining, specifically: dirty, tiring work moderated by the fact that one kept a tithe of what one found, never mind that one also got more exercise than most holds provided and could enjoy the hold's famous hot springs in the bargain. A quarter ought to be consigned to his craft. A quarter he would sleep. The rest he was free—to play hermit with Strynn and Rann if he so choose. Free to be alone with two of the three people he cared most about in the world.

He spent the rest of the afternoon in Merryn's suite, drinking (as they'd vowed), while Strynn kept tally and was excused from half the draughts because she was with child. Lykkon joined in unasked and kept trying to skew the results by surreptitiously adding to Merryn's portion when he thought she wasn't looking. She tolerated him through four attempts, but as the bottle dipped low on the fifth, a dagger appeared in her hand and summarily pinned Lykkon's sleeve to the table before he could withdraw. Fabric ripped. He yipped, and they all laughed like fools except Lykkon, who was made to down an entire full goblet of strong brandy at one pull.

"He doesn't need to be anywhere tonight," Merryn noted philosophically, as the youth's eyes went out of focus. "We can leave him on the bed until we return."

Strynn grinned wickedly. "There're any number of things we could do to him in the meantime . . ."

Merryn's brow shot up. "Such as?"

"Well, we could look for that birthmark he's always talking about. The one that changes shape when he's—"

Avall's brows shot up.

Merryn grinned at him. "Something wrong?"

"You mean besides protecting the modesty of a very good friend? Not really. I've *seen* the birthmark. It won't impress you."

"Says you!" Merryn giggled.

"I think," Avall replied dryly, "he'd prefer to enjoy the experience."

"I think," Lykkon slurred, "you're right."

"Oh, Eight!" Merryn groaned. "He's going to—"

Avall got him to the garderobe before he did. But had to take one more bath that day than planned. Lykkon, Avall decided grimly, owed him for this.

There was another banquet that night—the last of the season. Avall was certain his waist was at least two fingers thicker than it had been at the start of Sundeath, though he'd likely work it off—and more—pedaling the drills up at Gem.

Once again, the feast was held in the Court of Rites, and was intended to honor those who'd be setting out into the world at the end of Sundeath. Since a good portion of Eron's population was roughly Avall's age, the Court was packed. Blessedly the rains held off, though massive pavilions had been erected just in case. Drink was on the crown to a limit of four (tokens were provided and could be traded), but food was courtesy of the clans and crafts. By ancient custom, their cooks had sent over two meats, bread, two vegetables, a fruit, and a sweet sufficient to feed one's own hall or hold for one night. The food had been accepted at the gate and whisked inside to be distributed at random among the endless tables. At sunset, the gates opened and the crowd poured in: young people alone this time. Avall was jostled unmercifully, but was more concerned for Strynn, though Merryn was striding through the mob like the soldier she almost was, making way for both of them. One more good thing about winter in Gem-Hold, Avall decided: The exercise of mining might make him, for once, stronger than his twin. Caught in mid-crowd as they were, Merryn aimed them to the right, where the rain would be unlikely to blow in should it return. Avall followed dutifully, occasionally having to switch his robe out of pools of standing water.

It was almost dark when he, Merryn, and Strynn found a seat on one of the long benches set up alongside trestle tables around the Court. The crowd was thinner there, and both Avall and Merryn were nursing headaches, courtesy of the afternoon's indulgence. Strynn, who by contrast was much recovered, was enjoying their misery immensely. Still, the food was excellent. Avall had venison medallions, two kinds of fish, a handful of prawns, and enough spiced rice to balance it, along with a tangy fruit salad. He was halfway through the second fish and wondering if he ought to dare the mob in search of more herb bread when he felt, rather than saw, someone at his shoulder. "May I . . . ?" a soft voice murmured. Avall looked around to see a slight, sharp-faced young man in Priest-Clan livery peering down at him from beneath a nonofficial hood. Perhaps because of that, it took Avall a moment to recognize him. "Rrath!" he cried at last, motioning the youth down beside him. "I haven't seen you since—"

"—we were at Weaver. I dyed, you spun, and all that."

Avall nudged Strynn with his elbow, so that she—and Merryn, to whom she'd been speaking—twisted their heads like geese to peer past Avall at his new companion. "Strynn, Merryn: Wife and sister, allow me to present Rrath of . . ." He hesitated. "Priest-Clan, right? Blue and gray: that would be . . . Weather?"

Rrath nodded, obviously pleased at being recognized at all, never mind at meeting the fabled Strynn. Avall supposed he ought to get used to that. He'd seen Strynn every day for years; enough, almost, to make him forget that she was a famous beauty. Clearly that beauty wasn't lost on all who saw her. Rrath had been fairly randy, if memory served. Talked it, anyway.

Rrath nodded greeting—there was too much noise to speak now that the pipes had begun to play. Strynn nodded back, leaving Avall to shout into the ear of his former roommate. "You were Raised, too?"

Another nod. "Quite an adventure, I must say. But I suppose the question of the night is where you've been posted."

Avall rolled his eyes. He was tired of answering that, because he always had to explain how someone as accomplished as he allegedly was had wanted to go somewhere as remote as Gem-Hold-Winter. Still, Rrath was looking at him with eager earnestness—a trick he'd used at Weaver, if Avall wasn't mistaken. "Gem-Hold-Winter," he replied at last. "Don't ask."

Rrath's face lit up like the bonfires now being set at the north end of the Court. "You jest!" he laughed. "Back in the Spine, cold as a flounder's heart?"

"You know the place?"

Rrath shook his head. "Never been there—but I'll know soon enough, because I've been posted there, too!"

Avall grinned, though not entirely sincerely. "Great!" he replied, slapping Rrath on the back. "One more familiar face."

He didn't add that since Rrath was rather shy and tended to attach himself to anyone who liked him, he feared he'd just acquired a shadow. On the other hand, Gem-Hold was reputed to be a veritable warren. It would be easy to lose a shadow there.

And in any event, Rrath wasn't a bad-intentioned person, and was quite bright besides. Avall therefore spent the next quarter hand quizzing him about the royal prophecies, most of which he hadn't bothered to read when the messengers had arrived yesterday with their postings. He was relieved by predictions of a fairly mild winter—especially in light of where he was going to spend it. On the other hand, the weather-witches were also predicting an *early* winter, with the first snow due any day. For that reason there was serious talk at that very moment of having the treks leave as early as tomorrow morning.

"Want some dessert? Or cauf?" Avall asked Strynn when he'd tired of discussing snow.

"Cauf," she replied, intent on her conversation with Merryn—which sounded remarkably like women's gossip.

In the process of disentangling himself from the bench, Avall nearly bumped into a royal page who came bustling up, ignoring Rrath altogether. "You and your lady are summoned," the boy blurted out, "to an audience with High King Gynn."

Avall felt the pressure of eyes upon him as he and Strynn threaded their way through the crowd to the Citadel. They didn't enter the main doors, however, but angled right, to one of the towers in the wall that embraced the Court. A door stood open at the bottom, a twist around a turnpike stair took them up a level, to a plain but elegant room that overlooked the feast on one side and the gorge on the other. A low table occupied the center, while two more doors gave onto the wall-walk on one side and a wing of the palace on the other. Five chairs faced the table in a semicircle. A sixth stood opposite. A choice of liquors and cloisonné cups glittered on the polished wood. "Drink what you will," the page informed them, indicating the two most distant chairs. "His Majesty will join you anon."

Strynn and Avall had no time to discuss what the High King could possibly want with them before the door by which they'd entered opened again, and another page scurried in—with Eddyn. Eddyn was given the seat farthest from them, which showed excellent foresight on someone's part. He was also offered the delights on the table.

The page departed.

Avall looked at Eddyn and shrugged. "I have no idea."

Eddyn shrugged in turn. "Nor I."

"Would it be polite to drink now, or should we wait?"

"I doubt the King cares," Eddyn retorted. "He's not one to suck knucklebones when he's got beef to chew."

Avall grunted grim agreement. Whatever had brought them here was unlikely to be pleasant, which in part explained their cautious courtesy. How serious it was depended on who occupied the remaining seats.

"I'll pour if you will," Avall offered. "Walnut or almond? Which was it you preferred?"

"Almond," Eddyn murmured. "Good memory. You like walnut, if I recall? And Strynn, it would be blueberry?"

"Please," Strynn acknowledged. Avall served her, then he and Eddyn each other. In the face of a greater unknown, there was comfort even in drinking with the enemy.

They had just raised their cups when the door opened a third time, and Eellon and Tyrill were ushered in. Eellon was a model of calm control—though he was wearing full clan regalia. Avall poured him a cup of the same walnut liquor he was drinking, which happened to be his favorite. Tyrill looked like day-old thunder, having clearly been roused from her bed. Eddyn gave her a cup of melon brandy. *Someone* certainly knew their business; this was not mere random hospitality. Then again, Gynn *was* Argen-el.

Drinks and greetings exchanged, the five sat—with Eellon and Tyrill next to their respective protégés. Eellon proposed a toast to Change, since that seemed to be in the wind, which was duly accepted.

They'd just put down their cups when, without page or protocol, the palace-side door opened and High King Gynn walked in. He wore a simple circlet and a plain black house-robe, ennobled by the embroidered black velvet around collar, cuffs, and hem. All five made to rise but he motioned them back to their seats. "I'm sick of ritual," he said. "I'm half your age," he added to Tyrill and Eellon. "I don't know how you've stood it all this time."

"If I were impolite," Tyrill shot back acidly, as though she spoke to a boy, "I would observe that you could remove a large part of it from your life by yielding your throne."

"Not for another year, at least," Gynn answered through a grin that showed a great many very white teeth. "Besides," he added, "The Eight outrank even you."

Dismissing her by looking away, he turned his gaze first to Eddyn, then to Avall, and finally to Strynn.

"You are all intelligent people," he began bluntly. "It would take far less wit than the least of you possesses to conclude what bond the five of you share. It would take scarcely more wit for you to have wondered at the outcome of today's Fateing. Chance, you might be tempted to say, may have tossed loaded dice. To that, I can only reply that The Eight spoke through me yesterday and not all They said was for every ear. Avall, Eddyn, and Strynn, you should be advised that I am fully aware that posting you three together represents an . . . uncomfortable situation. I also know that it would be less than desirable for Strynn to be in the heart of any city when her child arrives for fear of reviving old grievances. For the same reason, I think it wise that Eddyn be out of the common eye until that child has come. Therefore you have all been posted to Gem-Hold-Winter. One of you would have been anyway, by the roll of the dice.

"But be that as it may," he continued, "I don't intend that your tenure there be spent idly. It hasn't escaped my notice that the three most troublesome young people of this age are also the three most accomplished. I intend to use that talent to the good of the crown and perhaps focus some of that jealousy and anger you hold toward one another to a higher end. You, Avall and Eddyn, have competed—been *forced* to compete, I should say"—he eyed Tyrill and Eddyn unflinchingly—"as long as you've been alive. I intend one more competition, if you wish to call it that."

A pause for breath, then: "Your . . . mentors already know of this, but I've brought them here to hear again. What I propose is this: During your term in Gem-Hold-Winter, you shall each fashion an object for the royal regalia—your work is already of that quality, as surely you know. Avall, you shall make me a war helm of iron and gold. Eddyn, you shall construct a shield of the same. And Strynn, you shall make a sword. Specifications will be given to you. Materials will be provided without stint. I ask only that this work be begun after you arrive at your destination and finished before you return a half year hence. That, and I also ask you that you incorporate into each item one gem that you yourself have mined. Are there any questions?"

Silence, then, inevitably, from Tyrill: "As I told you before," she said, more calmly than was her want, "these are properly Craftmaster tasks."

The King regarded her coldly. "And we both know all three have the makings of Craftmasters in them. We also know that two of them would at any other time have been made subcraft-chiefs two days ago. The reasons they weren't are known to me."

"You saw their work," Tyrill challenged. "You're enough of the craft to know why they were found wanting."

"Compared to an absolute standard," the King gave back. "But in relation to the rest of those who were Raised, never mind the present masters . . . no. You, perhaps could do better, given time and many tries. They almost eclipsed both of you, at a quarter your age."

Tyrill's mouth popped open, but she didn't reply. She had sense, Avall knew—if only she'd occasionally use it.

"You honor us," Eellon said into the ensuing lull. "You honor *all* of us."

Avall looked at the King, as he was usually too shy to do. For the first time he saw there someone who was no more his own man than he was himself. Someone who'd been maneuvered by clan, craft, and Fate into a position to which he might be suited, but had not, in his heart, desired. "My Lord King," he said clearly. "To make this helm would be an honor."

"My Lord King," Eddyn echoed at once, so that his reply had the form of ritual, not reaction. "To make this shield would honor me as well."

"My Lord King," Strynn repeated last. "To make this sword would likewise be an honor."

Gynn smiled. "You honor me by being born in my time. You may take the cups—and the drinks—in memory of this evening." And with that, he strode from the room.

"Well," Eellon breathed, offering his arm to Tyrill, "it would seem that we've all been honored. But," he added with a grin, "while the young folks get to spend Deep Winter making wonderful things, Tyrill and I get to spend it placating the rest of the hold. I don't know a single subcraft-chief who'll be happy to hear this."

"Nor," Tyrill agreed sourly, rising and taking his arm, "do I."

CHAPTER XIII:

ON THE WINTER WALL

(IXTI: THE WINTER WALL—YEAR BIRTH: DAY SEVEN—JUST BEFORE DAWN)

~~~~~~~~~

K raxxi and his comrades had reached the ruin in total darkness, complicated by a fog that had caught them unawares. The terrain had been terrible on the particular slope of the Wall they'd elected to scale, but the gap had promised level ground and, more importantly, a place to sleep securely, if not in comfort—right at the timberline and therefore too cold for geens. It had been an impromptu decision, one of Olrix's caprices.

They'd not expected to find an abandoned monastery, still roofed and with a sweet well and enough running water to permit sketchy baths. There'd also been a modicum of preserved stores—wheat, cheese, dried meat, wine. Even clothing. A trove from an order of astronomers that had died out during the plague.

Kraxxi watched the sunrise from the south-facing terrace that exactly straddled the gap. The bulk of the building sprawled below him, for they'd sheltered on an upper level. Had it been warmer, they'd have slept on this very pavement. His finger throbbed, but not badly. Or perhaps he'd grown used to it.

Sunrise.

Day birth.

East.

The past.

Ixti spread before him, to the left: the mountains first, and a substantial river they'd spent most of a day crossing. Beyond lay the plains and fields of the heart of the realm and, barely visible, the silver line of the sea. He thought he could make out the gold dome on the grand temple in Ixtianos, the silver one on the palace. Places he'd taken for granted all his life and might never see again.

Before lay more mountains, some forested, but less so the farther south one looked, where ridges out of sight of the capital were denuded and whole mountainsides had been laid waste to warm Ixtiano's palaces, fire its kilns, and stoke its furnaces. It was the same to the north, and every year the blight spread, as more forests were ravaged to feed wood-hungry cities.

The few Eronese they'd consulted as advisers had suggested they replant— which made excellent sense to Kraxxi. But with so much being spent to bring fuel from ever-greater distances, there was little left with which to hire laborers for the drudge work of reforestation. There'd be camps to build, provisions to source, amenities to provide, all in terrain ravaged by the fellers, who moved on as fast as trees were cut, leaving a confusion of stumps and tortured earth that had to be removed before new growth could be planted.

"Next year we will raid Eron," had been the litany for more years than Kraxxi could count. *"Next year there will be gold to spend rebuilding."*

Next year, next year, next year . . .

Kraxxi was worried about tomorrow.

Another glance to Ixti. To forests and fields and, not far off, comfort.

And prison.

Past, with no future he wanted to contemplate.

To the right . . .

The future. Opportunity. Adventure. Life.

As if to reinforce his thoughts, the sun climbed high enough to show the actual landscape there.

The mountain sloped down more gradually to the northwest, and no logging had been done—probably because of the difficult terrain. Nor was the slope as long on this side, for the Winter Wall's north face bordered higher ground than the fertile coastal plain. And the view truly was spectacular. One could see clear across empty space to another dim, red-rimmed ridge of mountains, like a torn edge on the horizon.

The World Spine—Angen's Spine, it was sometimes called—which was the southern terminus of Eron.

And between . . . nothing. The empty, desolate, rock-and-red-sanded reaches of the Flat.

Ixti here. Eron there. And what between?

Death?

Or rebirth into new life.

He was like Azzli, he realized: poised in a not-place between two worlds, two lives, with a perilous journey to be assayed before he reached either end.

A moment longer he stood there, leaning against the crumbling wall, with the plain stone bulk of the monastery behind him. And then he heard the slap of feet. Olrix probably, coming to remind him he'd promised to help with breakfast. Tozri, who'd been restless all night, was off in the storerooms, prowling. Elvix was keeping watch.

Wind found him as he lingered. This high, the wind was cold. It came from the north, too: out of Eron by way of the desert. Lower down—among those dunes and ragged nomad villages—it would be appreciated. Here, it hinted at more trouble than Kraxxi anticipated. For along with that wind had come something more sharply stinging. A single drop of wetness against his cheek. Rain, or sleet, or something he'd seen falling but once in his life.

Snow.

"Is that what you want to face, my son?" came a voice behind him, so soft—or muffled—he couldn't place it. He turned—and started half out of his skin.

A man stood there—a monk, by the short fringe of beard, the robe, and the spangle of enameled ivory icons crisscrossing the chest. The face was shrouded, but there was something familiar about the size and stance—

"Toz," Kraxxi sighed, his voice easing into an irate growl.

Tozri sauntered forward, sweeping his cowl back with a one-handed flourish to reveal a newly shaven head. The beard came off, too: a stiff fringe of animal hair. "I convinced you, didn't I?" he crowed.

"For a moment," Kraxxi hedged.

"That's all it takes, if you're careful," Tozri replied, joining him by the parapet. "People see what they expect to see."

"I expected to see no one."

"But anyone else—what would they expect to see?"

"It wouldn't matter. This place is deserted."

Tozri nodded. "But people may come looking."

Kraxxi regarded him dubiously. "You've been plotting again, haven't you: the three of you?"

Tozri studied the floor. "We have," he admitted. "We've learned some-thing and maybe decided something. The first is that I've been sorting through some of those records we found last night, to learn who was here before us, how they looked, what they believed—the result of which you see."

"And the other?"

"It's as I said: People see what they expect to see. People will be looking for you, and with your face on half the coins in Ixti, people know your profile. I thought about breaking your nose for you, but decided that might be too radical. But if you were to shave off your hair, let your beard grow, and dress as a monk—that might suffice long enough for us to make certain purchases in the villages along the northern rim."

"Monks," Kraxxi mused, gazing again at the northern sky. Clouds had lowered. He could no longer see all the way to Eron.

"We'll have to be careful," Tozri continued. "But it would be good for us all to hole up here a while. I'm injured, so's Olrix. We need time to heal. And for you and me to grow beards."

"That would take me forever," Kraxxi protested, rubbing his chin where the merest trace of stubble showed after three days without a razor.

"They wore false ones," Tozri grinned. "The combination ought to suffice."

"Also," Olrix chimed in from the door as she joined them, "while we're healing, you can take time to think."

"About what? About which very important thing, rather say."

Olrix pointed to the northwest, to where the clouds massed thickest. "About that. It's been known to snow for twenty days straight there, Kraxxi. Enough to clog even the gorges—and drown them when it melts."

"And it's cold," Tozri added. "Deep, hard, bone-numbing cold. Even in the south."

"It's what's saved us, frankly," Olrix agreed. "A country ought to be united, and the cold makes Eron fragment for a quarter of the year—makes it in effect a series of tiny palace-states that can't rely on each other if danger threatens. Nor unite long enough to wage a war, save in summer—which is when they have to farm."

"I know all that," Kraxxi grumbled.

"You've *heard* it," Tozri retorted. "But do you truly *know* it?"

Kraxxi started to reply, but held his tongue. He'd caught a flash of movement down in the fringe of ragged laurels that lapped about the flanks of a collapsing courtyard wall.

Tozri saw it as he did. "We've been fools," he hissed, not moving, "to stand here so exposed."

Kraxxi started to duck down in alarm, but Olrix restrained him. "They'll see what they want to see," she murmured. "If they've seen monks, they'll expect them to act like monks. There *is* movement toward reviving some of these derelict sites." A pause. "How good an actor are you?" she asked her brother.

"Good enough," Tozri muttered, urging her with a glance to return to the building. "Pretend nothing's happened," he continued in a whisper, and spoke no more until they were safely inside.

Elvix met them there, wide-eyed, bow in hand. "Someone's—"

Olrix nodded. "Could you see who?"

"Common soldier in royal baldric, best I could tell. Probably some local farmer conscripted to search."

"Alone?"

"It would seem. There aren't enough people in all the army to do the kind of search that would do any good. Barrax has to know that. It'll be blind luck or blind foolery that catches us in Ixti. After we leave is the problem. It's easy to hide in a crowd. It's nigh impossible in the Flat."

"Come," Tozri motioned, pushing Kraxxi toward the stairs to the lower level. He was already tugging at his robe.

"What?"

"You're the only male with two good arms—which is what they'll be looking for. Quick, change clothes with me."

Kraxxi had no time to protest as Tozri quickly slipped out of his musty-smelling robe and helped Kraxxi into it. The hood went up, covering his hair.

"Beard?"

"No time."

"What am I doing?"

Tozri stuffed his geen-claw dagger into Kraxxi's hand. "If we're lucky," he murmured into Kraxxi's ear, "you're going to fool that man long enough for one of us to kill him."

Kraxxi started to protest and realized there was no time. Besides, if he waited, he would think, and that could be fatal. Composing himself to calm, he arranged his borrowed piety as best he could and made his way down the stairs, careful of his injured legs, which still pained him terrifically. Still, he'd managed a suitably calm stride as he unbarred the single door on the lower level and walked out into the light of what had been an herb garden.

He pretended to be inspecting it for something—assessing what must be done to set it right, perhaps—all the while making his way toward the outer wall, which was the last place he'd seen the spy. Perhaps foolishly, he began to chant in a low singsong. Nonsense syllables.

Closer.

The outer gate lay on the ground, crushed by fallen mortar from the arch that had stood above it. Yawning, stretching, he ambled that way. Pausing to scratch his sides. He halted in the gap, as though regarding the world without.

And watched—as intently as he'd ever done.

He saw the shadow, even as he heard the snap of breaking twigs.

Another, and he glimpsed a man—hunched over, making a frantic dash from bush to bush. Olrix had been right. The man looked like a common freeholder conscripted into search duty. A good man—a family man.

"You!" Kraxxi called genially. "Don't fear. We may look rough, but our ways are not. We've only just reclaimed this place."

The man slowed, then halted. He turned toward him uncertainly. "Who are you?" he called, from behind the screen of bushes.

Kraxxi froze. His own name had rushed to his lips unbidden. And he could think of no other.

"Who *are* you?" the man demanded again, easing forward into the clear space between them. He was five spans away, no more. And he was armed, Kraxxi saw, with what was probably an heirloom sword. But he wore a gold-leather baldric, too: And that meant he carried royal writ.

"Kr-alli!" Kraxxi replied from nowhere. "If you need our help, you have only to ask—"

The man took another step, toward a patch of sunlight that had awakened between him and the laurel. Kraxxi tried to keep his hands away from the dagger. "I carry the king's command," the stranger called back, trying to sound defiant, but with uncertainty in his voice. "Put back your hood so that I can see you."

Kraxxi hesitated, though he raised his hands to either side of the cowl.

"Put it back! Have you no heed for the word of your king?"

Another step, full into the light. A hand brushed the hilt of the sword.

Kraxxi heard the swish of the arrow as it flew by his head to bury itself in the man's chest. Brown eyes went wide as the man slowly toppled.

"Bless you," Kraxxi whispered—as the truth of what had just occurred struck home.

He looked back, to see Elvix on the parapet, bow in hand, and Tozri striding through the ruined garden toward him.

"Well," Tozri said, when he arrived, "now you're not the only one to have committed murder."

Kraxxi nodded toward the dead man. "Will he—?"

"He'll be missed eventually—maybe soon, since he's out here so early, which implies his base is either close by or he's been out all night."

"So our plan . . . ?"

Tozri shrugged. "Maybe some of it can still be salvaged—we may be able to disguise the two of us as monks if we have to. And there should be some things here we can sell or trade. But we can't wait around now to heal and grow beards. I'd say we've got maybe a hand—to dispose of this body in the well, to hide the blood, and to leave down the opposite slope. Olrix is already packing."

"So much for breakfast," Kraxxi sighed.

"Welcome," Tozri chuckled, as he struggled to take the body under the arms one-handed, motioning Kraxxi to take the feet, "to being alive."

*   *   *

According to a map Elvix had found in the ruins, there was a spring-fed pool four shots down the north slope of the mountain, surrounded on three sides by steep cliffs thick with moss, and backed by a shallow shrine-cave. Nor did that map lie. Indeed, they hid there for the rest of the day and the following day, up until the following night, with someone on guard at all times. It wasn't comfortable, for they dared not risk a fire with searchers out. But luck—or Fate—once again was with them, and on the night of the second day, just at sunset, they checked their monks' habits one last time, and Elvix, Olrix, Tozri, and Kraxxi (with newly shaven head) turned their faces north, toward where the lights of a tiny town glimmered on the fringe of the Flat, and with prayers to the Gods but faith only in each other, stepped from what little security remained to them into the unknown.

CHAPTER XIV:

OUT OF THE GORGE

(ERON: TIR-ERON—SUNDEATH: DAY VII: LAND'S DAY—DAWN)

The world was white, tinged with faint pastels where the sun nearly pierced the fog, shading its frailer edges pink like fresh-cut fish, or revealing wisps of sky that balanced between purple, mauve, and blue. The tinkle-slap of water lapping at the clan barge's boards was the loudest sound in all the cool white world; buildings, trees, a few people ghosting by on the banks, the only motion. It was a still time that in turn brought stillness to the soul. A fitting prelude to what could easily be a quarter eighth of confusion.

Avall snuggled more deeply into the fur rug his mother had brought along on this first voyage of his manhood. It felt good, too; yesterday's cold had lingered, imparting a chill to the early air that defied the wakening sun. Beside him, Strynn yawned, covering her mouth with a gloved hand. Those gloves were a wedding present from his mother: the first real acknowledgment that she *had* two daughters now. But Evvion rarely acknowledged anything.

Nor was anyone inclined to speak, not one of the thirty-odd people on this barge, and few on those belonging to the other septs, including Eddyn's. Certainly no voices carried over the water from those vessels; only the plash of oars, where they made their way along the river road to Farewell Island. Only the lap of water against the sides, the sound of breathing, or the occasional chink of cauf cups being filled or set down on the railed tables between the rows of high-backed passenger benches.

Another yawn. This time Merryn picked it up. Avall looked at her and grinned—then surprised himself by yawning as well. He was unaccustomed to being up so early, having been allowed to sleep late most of Sundeath, often after nights spent reveling. There'd be no revelry tonight, however, nor the one after, nor any night, until the trek reached its destination. Which didn't bother him. He'd eaten his fill of rich food, drunk far more strong spirits than needed, made too many stupid jests (the bulk of them last night after the audience with the King, which had left him both giddy and frightened to death).

He wondered about Strynn. She'd always been a quiet person. Nor was he one to pry into motivations. He knew his own self and priorities to a fine degree, and that had always been sufficient. That he might find items of interest in other minds didn't often concern him unless brought to his attention. Strynn wasn't one to do that. Like him, she let her accomplishments pay her way in the world. It would never have occurred to him to inquire if she was content. It would never have occurred to Merryn not to say she wasn't. Neither spoke. Both were as sleepy as he and still somewhat hungover from yet another night's drinking.

Still, it was remarkably pleasant to sprawl amidships and let his mind drift along with the fog and the barge. Strynn and Merryn leaned comfortably against him to either side—mighty solace, that. Eellon sat ahead, so that for once Avall didn't have to conduct his life before his Clan-Chief's scrutiny. Tyrill was on Argen-yr's barge. This sort of weather did terrible things to her joints, too. Nor would she be here if not for her protégé.

Merryn stretched across him to fill another cup: far more cauf than was her want. A nutty pastry joined it. She passed Avall another without asking, and a third to Strynn—and a fourth. "For he who lurks within."

"Or she," Strynn murmured back.

"Or them," Avall finished, rolling his eyes.

The fog parted. A side gorge had intersected the Ri-Eron's main channel and let a breeze from the south sweep the mist away. Avall was startled to realize they'd left the city and were now passing through farmland. The air was warmer, too, for the hot springs were more numerous here, and not all their heat was channeled to greenhouses and livestock barns until Deep Winter. Nor were the fields beside the river deserted. This was Land's Day, the seventh of Sundeath, when every sound-bodied person in Eron left hearth and home, hold and hall, palace and hovel alike to bring in the last of the autumn harvest. It was the great equalizer—one of several—and High King Gynn would be in the fields with the rest, clad as simply, getting as dirty, as tired, as scratched and bloody from plants with thorns or prickles.

But for the weather-witches, Avall would be there as well. But as Rrath had informed him the previous evening, the witches had predicted an early snow and a deep one, though the winter itself was supposed to be relatively mild. The Priests had then conferred with the King and the various chiefs (Eellon had had very late night of it indeed), and it had been decided far too close to dawn that all treks going north would leave a day early and be excused from harvest duty in exchange for an extra day's drudgery during the planting.

Everyone else— Well, Eellon was too old to do more than sit at the edge of fields and sort good fruit from bad. Tyrill was too frail for anything useful, but would do what she always did: plant herself just in hearing of Eellon and bark commands at anyone over whom she had even vague authority. Merryn would work till she collapsed, for War-Hold was a southern hold, and she wouldn't depart until tomorrow. She would head for the fields as soon as her good-byes were said.

Which wouldn't be long now. The fog had returned, thicker than ever, but Avall felt the barge shift as it negotiated the kink in the river that signaled the approach to the island. The river was widening, too, where the gorge's walls swept lowest before rising again to shadow the long road to the sea.

Eellon strained forward eagerly. As if to taunt him, the fog grew denser yet. Avall could barely see the pilot in the bow, clad in stripes of chartreuse, orange, and white so as to be more visible at night, in fog or rain, or at a distance. Torches in either hand told the steersman which way to turn the rudder. The oarsmen—a dozen, chosen from those who would winter in Argen-Hall—adjusted their efforts accordingly.

And then the fog vanished as though severed with a sword. Other barges became visible ahead: a vast file of them, for Argen-Hall was far up the gorge, closest but three to the Citadel, which meant that most other clans had got their barges in transit first, working from some obscure schedule Records had contrived. Most were identical to Argen's vessels save for the clan colors with which they were painted and the sigils emblazoned on their midship pavilions and flags.

The river widened further, more banks swept into view, and the file began to disperse to either side, seeking the clan docks that studded the west end of the island. Before Avall knew it, they were nosing against one, the requisite maroon paint freshly renewed, the banner sagging for lack of wind. Avall rose as Eellon did. When Strynn didn't, he looked down and saw her asleep. Just as well. She'd been sick again last night, though she was making a brave show of it.

She awakened, however, when Argen-el's poorly captained barge jostled them into the dock. Avall reached to brace Eellon, but Lykkon (who'd invited himself along, ostensibly as Eellon's squire) took the brunt of that upset. Strynn uttered a little cry and blinked at Avall wide-eyed. "I've never done that," she yawned. "Gone to sleep all at once. I can't think why—"

"You *know* why," Merryn countered, as Avall helped his wife to her feet. She smiled at him, then scowled, "Before, it wasn't so bad, but lately—"

"Worry makes it worse," Eellon told her offhand, not stingy with advice about what were normally women's affairs. "And change," he added. "And excitement. I hadn't noticed any of those things lacking of late. But after you set out . . . it should improve."

Strynn nodded sagely. "That's what's kept me going. Trekking is boring, but it wears me out, even when I'm not—"

She didn't finish. No surprise there. Though she might refer to the child itself, she never spoke of being *with* child. As though the two were in nowise connected.

Avall hugged her impulsively, not releasing her until the oarsmen had secured the barge to the dock. A portable stair was set down and the little parade assembled—another ritual, for the order of disembarkation was, like everything else, predetermined. Lykkon went first with the clan banner. Eellon followed, then the members of Argen-a in order of age. Avall's mother was there as well, silent as always, but with her head held high.

Avall and Strynn stepped down together. The stair was wide enough for that, and Avall was vastly relieved that the lashings had rendered their departure steady. One moment he was on deck, the next on the quay. His stomach twitched, even as his head spun briefly, for even the glass-smooth river moved constantly when compared to dry land. He paused until the press of people behind him forced him none-too-gently toward shore.

Wood beneath his feet gave way to stone, then sand. The air cleared, bringing warmth from the south and the merest hint of salt from the distant sea. Water birds wheeled and spun above their heads. He glanced back west, saw more barges emerging from a solid bank of fog, but with blue sky above. The grass was green and smelled of freshness. Other odors rode the wind, however: campfires and cooking food, horses and wagon-cattle.

They faced a gentle, grassy rise overrun with men and the trails they'd made up that slope. Two figures were cut into the turf there, ten spans high: a man and a woman, standing back to back, near hands lowered to their sides and clasped, far arms raised and pointing north and south. Simple yet elegant.

Eellon led their party until they reached a place where the clan sigil was carved in low relief in the stone pavement, the colors worked in hard-sand. He turned to face the assembled clan. "Of old your fathers would do this," he intoned. "But too many of you are fatherless now, and so I speak for all of them when I bid you safe journey as you travel beyond these canyon walls.

One world you enter. You will someday leave another. It is up to you to see that it is better, richer, more beautifully made and crafted than that in which you dwell now. Go in peace, joy, and accomplishment, with my blessings."

He lowered his hands and relaxed. Chaos ensued, as they waited for the other barges to arrive and empty themselves. As they paused, Eellon motioned Avall and Strynn aside—with Lykkon, who carried a small, flat box. The lad was grinning like a fool as he presented it to Eellon. Two smaller boxes were arranged within, one with Avall's sigil, one with Strynn's. "I will confer Merryn's tomorrow," the Clan-Chief apologized, "though it seems bad form to break up a set, even if Chance has done exactly that."

So saying, he removed the boxes and passed them to their recipients.

Avall fumbled in his tunic and also brought out packages, which he gave to Merryn, Eellon, and his mother; and suddenly there was much passing around of gifts—not uncommon at this time; others were doing it as well.

Avall found himself possessed of the finest pair of calipers he'd ever seen. Eellon had made them himself, as was required of such things by craft law—which did not, however, prescribe the quality of that making. It was easy to forget that until he'd become Clan-Chief upon the death of Tyrill's older sister, Eellon had been Craft-Chief, and like Avall, the best of his generation. These calipers proved that he'd lost none of his touch. The metal gleamed—silver/blue for the main parts, of an alloy impervious to heat and therefore remarkably precise; fittings of brass plated with gold; other metals here and there at need. Avall gasped at the splendor of the gift and wondered if the one he'd conferred on Eellon was even vaguely worthy.

Certainly, it was nothing so functional, yet a masterwork all the same: a brooch of the antique penannular style Eellon still preferred in defiance of the present small-pin fashion. Solid gold, and cast in one piece, then endlessly refined by mornlight so that the knotwork spirals and twists were perfect in their width and spacing, with the background filled with glass-paste and fired—in Argen maroon.

Eellon grinned like a boy, which was part of his charm. His actions varied with his moods, and he censored none of them. His wrath was legendary, his joy unrestrained. Impulsively, he grabbed Avall and hugged him hard and long. "I'm proud of you," he murmured—and only then released him.

"And I to be kin to you," Avall replied with more reserve.

"And I!" Strynn added, beaming as she displayed the silver bracelet set with rubies Eellon had made for her, the gems alternating dark red and bright in the colors of Argen and Ferr: Smithcraft fire and Warcraft blood.

Avall gave his mother a tiny icon-die marked with the masks of The Eight-in-One, receiving an exquisite ceramic crucible in turn. And then Merryn cleared her throat in anticipation of her own gift-giving. Though not equal to her twin or bond-sister, she was still no mean smith. It was therefore no surprise that the matched daggers she gave the couple were elegantly, if plainly, made. "And would cut air!" Strynn breathed, as she tested the edge against a finger. She'd learned most of what she knew about fining edges from Avall's sister.

From her brother, Merryn received a scabbard for her favorite sword, of leather he'd commissioned, but with fittings he'd wrought himself. She took one look at her old one (she always wore a blade when not expressly forbidden) and passed it to Lykkon with a shudder.

Strynn laughed when she presented her gift, for it was also a dagger. The metal gleamed, the many foldings like water in the waxing light; the hilt plain, because Merryn liked them that way. "It'll cut a hair in water," Strynn confided. "I finished it the day I had my encounter with Eddyn," she continued more darkly. "But try not to think of that."

"Somehow I doubt I'll have time," Merryn murmured. "They work you hard at War."

"We'll all be working hard this winter," Avall chimed in.

"Aye," Eellon nodded, inclining his head toward where Tyrill was finally disembarking. "In more ways than one."

"I think," Avall sighed, "we should seek the Trek-Master."

A final round of good-byes ensued, while Avall and Strynn bade farewell to her mother, who'd joined them, and to Lykkon, and Avall's mother, and the other members of the clan who'd come to see them off. Not many friends, however. A number were already away at postings. A few would be accompanying them—six from Smith-Hold beyond Avall, Strynn, and Eddyn. The rest— It was considered bad form to witness a Leaving without being involved in one. Lykkon was an exception—as he was to many things.

Hand in hand, Avall and Strynn marched up the hill. Neither looked back. Avall felt his eyes misting and glanced at Strynn. Hers were, too. Neither spoke. Avall tried not to think about Eddyn.

Their gear had arrived ahead of them, so Avall and Strynn had little to do but seek the trek that would be going to Gem. It wasn't hard to find. Once they'd crested the hill, a flat plain spread before them, open, save where a copse of ancient hardwoods on the south end housed a number of small shrines, and where a cluster of low buildings set into the ground closer in provided stabling, maintenance, and storage for the treks. A pair of bridges to left and right led to the gorge itself. Avall could see North Road snaking up the steep sandstone walls to the left, still tortuous for all it was the easiest way in and out. Beyond the bridges, docks took over for treks, since the more distant holds to north and south were usually accessed by sailing up the coast, then up the gorge rivers, then trekking inland.

The treks themselves were ranked in a semicircle around a field, with those that would go to South Bank to the right, those to North on the left.

Those intended for the closer holds were nearest; the more distant, farther away. Gem-Hold was farthest of all.

It was an amazing image: the green grass marked with spokes radiating from the wheel-road's outer rim, each spoke the province of from ten to forty wagons, some with canvas tops, but most like small houses cleverly made of wood to be both light and strong, and of a size to be pulled by two to four horses or wagon-cattle. The area was already packed, for the chiefs would've had their people down early, setting things aright. Horses stomped and snuffled. Cattle lowed. Children dashed about. People hailed each other. Some cooked, others drank. The place had a carnival atmosphere far more conducive to enjoyment than even light-duty rituals like the Fateing Feast.

Avall felt more like a boy in search of a picnic site than a man on the verge of his first real service to clan and country as he and Strynn veered left along the north curve of the wheel-road. Their clan-mates joined them—the three from Argen-a, anyway. Eddyn's Argen-yr mates were nowhere in sight—if Eddyn had any mates in that sept. Avall wondered what he'd do without fawning partisans.

The sun was full up by then and warm enough that the short-tunic that had felt so comfortable upon landing began to itch. Avall loosened the throat ties and actually skipped a short way before remembering that he was twenty and too old for such things.

Strynn laughed at him, then rose on tiptoes to scan the area in search of Gem-Hold's banner. The wind brought the smell of horse droppings, fresh hay, and frying fish. Avall inhaled briskly, saw Strynn do the same, and grinned again, holding her hand tighter. She looked good. The outdoors had finally put a healthy flush on her face. Only then did he realize how little time they'd actually spent in daylight since they'd wed. It had all been rituals, feasts, nighttime events. Either that, or it had rained.

Strynn looked radiant. She'd also, he noted, loosened the lower lacings of her suede half bodice.

"Promise me one thing," he muttered.

"What?"

"Promise me you won't have this child on the road."

She regarded him seriously. "If I have it on the road, there'll be more concerns than the child, let me assure you."

He blushed. "It's still hard for me to think of it as real, I guess."

"Me too," she agreed. "So . . . shall we teach him to make jewelry first, or her to make armor?"

"How about *them* to make machines? We haven't had a toolsmith in Argen-a lately."

"Good point."

"There!" Avall announced, having spotted the banner they were seeking:

a field gyronny of eight in white and gold, with eight stars in a ring super-imposed upon it, each a different color to represent a different gem.

And wonder of wonders, the Trek-Master was standing by the banner pole. Carmil: roughly thirty, slim and small, but very quick. Avall recognized her from years ago, when she'd spent a study-cycle at Smith-Hold. She'd been an indifferent student, but had a way with animals and had only missed transferal to Beast-Hold because that particular hold was overrun with applicants during those years. She liked being outdoors—and looked it. She also looked sad most of the time. Merryn (who knew her better) said it was because she'd lost a much-beloved twin brother to the plague. And a father.

Eight knew she wasn't alone in that, but Avall also knew what it would be like should he lose Merryn. Almost he looked back, as though expecting to see her standing there, hands on hips, looking smug. Instead, he saw Eddyn walking toward them at a brisk pace only slightly roughened by the limp. He wondered how long that would last: They'd be riding a lot this trip. Avall doubted that would improve Eddyn's moods.

Eddyn saw him looking, grimaced, then nodded absently. Avall nodded back. Maybe this wouldn't be so bad. Eschewing the Strynn situation and massive vanity, Eddyn wasn't a *bad* person. Selfish, maybe, and impulsive, but not evil. He treated the pages decently. He was generous with his time and talents. He was never drifty and distant, as Avall knew himself to be, so that people took him to be aloof when he was only preoccupied.

Maybe things *would* change once they were away from the pervasive influence of their patrons. Indeed, Avall realized, save for a cycle spent at Wood, he and Eddyn had spent almost no time together without the shadow-presence of Eellon and Tyrill. Perhaps, had they had different two-sires or been less talented themselves, they might even have been friends: sharing triumphs, advising each other of new skills acquired, egging each other to greater and greater achievements.

Not simply younger extensions of Clan-Chief and Craft.

"Dreaming is best done in bed," Strynn teased, tugging at his hand. "Come, I see our horses; they'd probably like to see us as well."

Avall managed a semblance of enthusiasm as he let Strynn drag him to the paddock where a groom in Smith livery quartered with Beast presided over the dozen-odd horses that would carry Smith-Hold's entourage. The groom grinned at Strynn, since she was quite the horsewoman, as well as being beautiful. Strynn danced up to greet the youth—Nyyl was his name—and to fondle equine noses. Nyyl indicated an array of saddles set neatly on appropriate racks.

"Greetings," he said. "I think you'll approve of my choices." Strynn wandered off to confirm, leaving Avall to reacquaint himself with the mount he rode when riding was necessary: a sturdy gelding named Tarnish. They'd never bonded as some beasts and riders did—Avall simply didn't think of them as any more than necessary conveniences—but they respected each other well enough. Avall could expect a smooth, steady gait; Tarnish could expect prompt, if workmanlike, attention and the odd treat—and no outrageous demands. That was enough for both of them.

"Avall!" someone called. He turned to see Carmil herself striding toward him. She wore a Gem-Hold tabard and a Trek-Master's cap, but her clothing was otherwise nondescript: basic browns and tans of thick, serviceable wool; trouser-skirt and leather jerkin above a gold-sylk blouse—warm for the day, but adaptable for the season. She'd abandon the tabard as soon as they were under way.

Avall managed a smile as he greeted her, surprised when she hugged him back. She was distant kin on his mother's side a few generations back. There was a certain roughness to her, too, which both put him off and attracted him. Then again, roughness was common to what were called the Earth Clans, whose trades were unsuited for cities. Stonecraft was an odd lot: part art, but with septs too labor-intensive to deserve that designation. And Carmil had married into Beast, as had her mother, who was now subcraft-chief of Stoneware.

For now, it only mattered that she was friendly, competent—and glad to see him. "I've heard wonderful things about you," she laughed as she released him. "If half of them are true, I'll have to remind you every night of how you spent an entire cycle at Beast and *never* learned to milk. What was it? Half a pail the whole session?"

"Animals don't like me," Avall sighed. "Not big ones, anyway. Cats love me."

"That doesn't surprise me."

"No?"

"You're both unconsciously aloof. You make everything look as though it was orchestrated to precise effect. You look remarkably chagrined when you're clumsy."

"You know me pretty well, don't you?"

"You're not a bad lad," she laughed again. "Just try to *forget* that you aren't, sometimes. I think this trek will be good for you."

"I think it will," Avall agreed, indicating Strynn. "Do you know—?"

"Oh, yes. She could milk very well indeed."

Avall wondered if that was some slightly ribald joke. "Are we set to leave on time?" he asked, to cover.

Another nod. "One more batch to arrive besides your crowd, and it's up and on our way." She scanned the crest of the hill. "Ah, there they are now. I'd suggest you get old Tarnish here saddled. Do you need some help?" she added, with a smirk.

"No," Avall growled. "But if you'll give me that tabard pin when we get to Gem, I'll rebraze it—again."

She colored. The pin had been her sole finished project during her tenure at Smith. Avall had heard the tale of her many failures more than once. "See you," she called, striding toward the new arrivals.

"More than you want," he yelled back, and returned to where Strynn had finished saddling a spirited black filly named Bellows that Merryn had given her as a Bonding gift.

Avall managed to fasten his saddle without disgracing himself; though Strynn insisted on checking his straps and cinches. People were mounting up. Half the Smith-Hold contingent had already. He gave Strynn an assist, then swung up atop Tarnish. The gelding snorted and stamped, but Avall got him soothed. "You make me look good," he whispered in a perky ear, "and I'll do the same for you."

"Attend," Carmil cried abruptly, and without apparent effort the chaos that was the Gem-Hold paddock began to organize, as Carmil arranged her trek to her liking. Then they were moving: Carmil, as Trek-Master, leading Gemcraft's large contingent. Once around the wheel-road they went, waving at the well-wishers who lined the top of the rise but weren't allowed on the Trek Ground, and then they were moving toward North Bridge, and then upon it. Avall felt the change as Tarnish's well-shod hooves came down on stone instead of packed earth. The bridge rang hollowly, and the rush of the river was loud enough to drown out conversation. He caught Strynn's eye, mouthed a silent "luck," and extended his hand. She took it, smiled back, and patted her stomach. Avall rolled his eyes and grinned. Without quite knowing why, he was happy.

He was still happy a quarter morning later, when the trek crested a final slope to emerge on a promontory that permitted a spectacular view of all Eron Gorge. Avall was not alone in slowing to savor it.

The island was directly below, a hundred spans or more. Beyond it, to the south, the cliffs closed in again, funneling the river into dangerous rapids before widening at last for the slow lazy journey to the sea. That end of the gorge was filled with fog—or steam. Around it stretched the plains, framed by distant forests.

West lay the bulk of the inhabited lands and Tir-Eron itself. Avall was always amazed at how little of the city actually showed from here, what with the gardens and stone buildings shaped to complement the landscape. He could see the Citadel plainly, however, and the side gorge that led to Priest-

Hold—which reminded him that Rrath was somewhere in this mass of flesh, and might appreciate being sought out . . . sometime.

He watched a few breaths longer, then let the press behind him steer him toward the West Road. Plains stretched before him, seemingly endless, though bordered with forests beneath whose arms they'd camp. Ahead, barely visible, lay Angen's Spine, dark, though the sun shone full upon those peaks, and somehow forbidding.

It was clouding up, too: gray masses tumbling over those mountains as though they ran some sinister race. The sky above still sparkled—but something cold brushed his cheek. He blinked, saw a random drift like powdered diamonds floating casually through the air.

And shuddered.

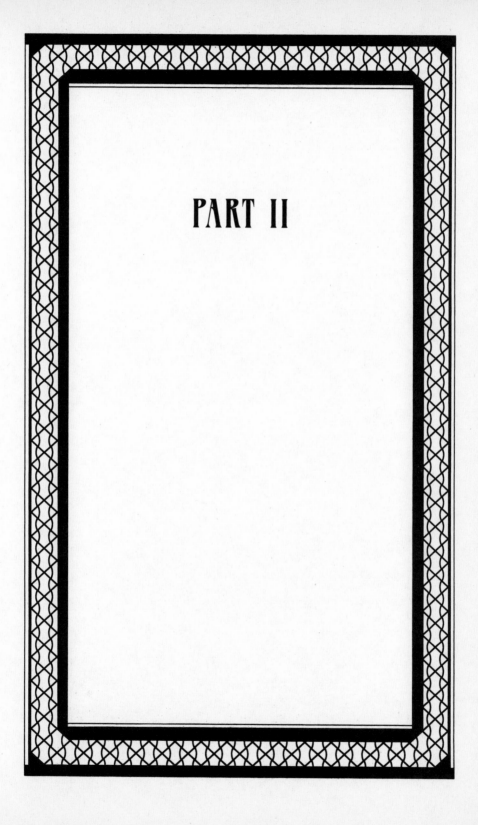

PART II

PART II

CHAPTER XV:

TREKKING

(Eron: Ezhran Vale Station—Near Winter, Day VIII—late morning)

~~~~~~~~

W atch it!" Avall snapped at the rider ahead of him, as the snow-laden cedar limb the man had pushed aside swung back to slap Avall in the face, raking his cheek with the fierce little needles, flipping his hood back, and sending a cascade of snow down his tunic neck. Newly exposed, his ears burned in the icy wind. Too much wind and too early. It was not yet Deep Winter and travel should've been relatively uneventful. Rain, perhaps, and sleet; possibly flurries. But not full-fledged, knee-deep snow. Not nine days out of Tir-Eron, with maybe that many more to go before they reached Gem-Hold-Winter. True, the weather-witches had said early snow and bad ones, and then things would moderate. But Avall wondered.

At least the morning's reconnoiter was almost over. Himself, a lad from Pine, and a pathkeeper from Lore, who could read landscape like Avall read books— and was self-absorbed, thus the ill-used branch—had been the chosen scouts.

Now, scowling when the man didn't reply to his protest, Avall chose to leave his hood down. It wasn't that cold, and only two shots to the way station. Warmth awaited there: warm food, warm clothes, warm fire, warm company. And Strynn. Silent, peaceful (or stoic?) Strynn.

Already they were on the last upslope: a narrow side trail thick with cedars that made the air smell fresh as it was clear. The snow was pristine, too, save where their own beasts had marred it upon departure.

Closer, over the ridge, and he could see the station.

Ezhran Vale was typical of the travelers' rests that had been built along major (and some minor) routes over the years. Chest-high walls fronted a low, stone, U-shaped building big enough to house a hundred or more for several nights. The wing to the right was for livestock, and usually stocked with feed; the one to the left for living quarters and kitchen. The all-important bath was in the center. Typical; though as many were T-shaped, with bath to one side and stables to the other. Not that it mattered. What mattered was whether they'd stay another night or press on. Supplies were getting low, and tempers flaring. And it was all the fault of this Eight-forsaken snow!

They'd reached the courtyard now, which was overflowing with wagons being swept clear in anticipation. Not for the first time in the last two days, either; that was why they'd been reconnoitering.

Eddyn looked up from where he sprawled across a stack of thick wool rugs, rubbing the kinks out of hands that had spent the morning in the rear court splitting wood for the enormous fire that blazed in the hearth to his left. Pots of wine and cider stood around it like acolytes before a Priest, and the crowded room smelled of savory drinks, rich with spices. He'd have one himself, in a moment.

He studied his hands absently: long-fingered but knotty, scoured with a thousand tiny scars where metal had bit him as he fought it into shape. A fine new one still oozed blood from where a splinter had taken him off guard. Too bad about that, though not the labor; he was no better than anyone else in that regard. Everyone who could labored on treks. Even pregnant Strynn was off in the kitchen baking way-bread to leave behind for the next trek through. No, the labor wasn't the problem, but the reason for *doing* it: the damned, too-early, all-pervasive snow that had plagued them off and on since they'd left Tir-Eron. Making them late to reach stations only to find supplies depleted by others who'd had to stay too long and not, for various reasons, replenished when they'd departed.

Eddyn suspected the next trekkers here would be themselves, staying an extra night. They'd find out soon enough.

Right now, in fact—as he heard the outer door open, then, an instant later, the inner. Three figures strode in, flush-faced from the cold, and with snow caught in hair, brows, and what fur showed on winter boots and tunics. Cloaks would've been left in the vestibule. Unconsciously, he searched for Avall—found him: red-faced as the rest and looking tired, if conscientious, as he glanced around, likely in search of Strynn.

Carmil rose from where she'd been shaping a soapstone pipe by one of the narrow, slab-glass windows, and strode toward them, fit, and neat in pant-skirt and tunic-blouse worn double-belted. "Well?" she demanded, as the men made for the fire. Two continued. Avall stopped (just like him: dutiful to a fault). She rolled her eyes, then stepped to the hearth herself and passed him a mug, claiming another in the process. "Well?" she tried again. "Do we go or stay?"

Eddyn popped his fingers one last time and sat up, straining to hear. Nor was he alone. What Avall said affected them all.

For his part, Avall looked uncomfortable, clearly preferring the path-keeper make the report. Seeing Carmil's insistent expression changed that. "It took a bit of time to find the right trail, what with the snow and all. Eventually Wylm found it. We went west till we crested the ridge—maybe twenty shots. It looks better down there. A lot of this, I think, is due to altitude. In any event, it seems to be melting lower down, though there's plenty of standing water—which means we'd have to be careful of getting stuck."

Carmil nodded, then went off to speak with the other trek leaders. Too many voices at once made their discussion hard to follow, especially with the rumbling mumble that had broken out when Avall had held out promise of moving on. A moment later, Carmil uttered a terse, and much louder, "Fine!" and stepped up on the hearth, banging a mug with her dagger hilt to rouse their attention.

"Good folk!" she announced. "What I have to say is this. We've been here for two nights and are well into another day. The policy is always to leave at dawn and arrive at dusk. The policy is also that treks don't travel under threat of bad weather. The weather on *this* trek, however, has been unusual—typical of an eighth from now, in fact. Therefore all policy is up for debate. I ask for debate now. Do we continue on to Gem-Hold, knowing that the way may be harder going than many of you are accustomed to, but knowing as well that the sooner we leave, the sooner we'll reach the security of our destination? And knowing, finally, that Fate is unlikely to throw bad weather at us every day?"

"Or what?" someone challenged.

"Or do we stay here until we know it's safe, and risk winter finding us on the road and pounding us without letup? Or stranding us here, where we'd likely die?"

"A hand of snow for many days, or a span for one? Is that what you're asking?" a woman wondered.

Carmil nodded. "You could say. Our scouts have checked the next day's trek to the west. They say it's passable. Wet and muddy, but passable. Forest for over half of it, which has kept the snow to a minimum. A good stretch of plain that might be mushy, and which we'd have to cross in the dark if we're to make the next station by midnight. The moons should be bright, however. And if it snows again, better to encounter it in open land where you know the surface is fairly level, than in the steeps and the woods."

"Makes sense," another woman replied.

"Aye," Avall agreed.

Eddyn glared at him—couldn't help it. *He* had something to look forward to, dammit! He had Strynn for company, a bond-brother waiting in the form of Rann. But until they arrived, he, Eddyn, would endure pure misery. Misery for many days, or misery for one or two, that was the way Eddyn saw it. But not overeager Avall. Eddyn snorted his disgust and went back to massaging his fingers.

"What?" someone snapped: sharply and close by. Eddyn looked up with a start, surprised to see Avall glaring down at him. He look tired, Eddyn realized in a flash; probably was. Nine days on the road, close quarters, an increasingly uncomfortable wife. Only one of which was Eddyn's doing.

"Which what?" Eddyn replied, from reflex.

"I take it you don't approve?" Avall gritted, running his fingers through snow-dampened hair. His eyes glittered dangerously.

"Given eight days of comfort against seven of comfort and one of misery, I'd take the former," Eddyn gave back.

"You would, would you?"

Eddyn's mouth dropped open. What was going on? Avall had been avoiding him all trek—until now. They'd exchanged maybe a hundred words, mostly vague pleasantries. Nor was it like Avall to provoke confrontation.

"I'm no fool," Eddyn growled. "And no gambler."

"Except when it came to stretching Strynn on the ground last summer!" Avall spat. "You gambled then, didn't you? And lost. You—"

He broke off, looking dumbfounded. But Eddyn no longer cared. He'd had enough living with that indiscretion, which he'd be paying for a very long time indeed. Too many sideways glances. Too many pointed remarks. Too much public scrutiny for too long. And here Avall had dredged it up again.

Before he knew it, he'd reached out a foot, hooked Avall's ankles, and yanked, tumbling him to the flagstone floor. Avall "oofed," but Eddyn was already atop him, wondering stupidly what he could possibly hope to gain from this and not caring now that he had a chance to do what he'd wanted for a very long time, which was to pound a smug and self-righteous someone's face into sausage.

He got in two blows and Avall a halfhearted one (not bad actually, given that he was on the bottom), before strong arms snared his from either side and he was hauled roughly to his feet. He stood there shaking, hot-faced, full of fury at letting something so petty inflame his anger past breaking. And at Avall for provoking it. And at the whole trek, who were looking at him with cold, accusing eyes. He could almost hear their thoughts. *Arrogant. Conceited. Hellion. Rapist. Should've been unclanned.*

"No!" he shouted, shaking free of whoever had restrained him—Carmil herself, as it turned out, and a slim youth from Priest named Rrath, who seemed to have fixed on Avall as an object of adoration.

"No," he repeated, as he found his arms free and watched two of the senior smiths help Avall up. Strynn was in the door to the kitchen, also glaring. "Too many people too close together too long," he muttered to the room at large, not looking at Avall. "Sorry."

Carmil moved around to regard him furiously, then stepped onto a wooden bench and once again tapped her mug with her dagger.

"This settles it," she proclaimed. "We're getting on each other's nerves and it's going to stop! This is the third fight in two days. And while fights are normal on treks, they accomplish nothing. If you're going to fight, see it's against a storm, not someone who may hold your life in his or her hands an eighth from now. Or a year." She paused for a sip of cider. "Pack your things, good folk, this trek leaves at noon!"

Avall's face was still smarting when the sun went down. Strynn said he had a handsome bruise (getting handsomer by the moment, he imagined) on his right cheek, and another on his shoulder, where he'd hit the floor. Both were sore. His lips were sore, too, where he'd cut the inside of one. And the tooth Eddyn's fist had loosened was worrying him something fierce. He kept probing it with his tongue, which was getting sore in turn.

All because he'd been unable to hold that tongue. *Stupid fool!* he told himself, to have provoked that ridiculous fight. Eddyn was supposed to be the bully, not him. Not goody-goody Avall. It was just that he was tired of being watched all the time, tired of being expected to be perfect at everything, when he was in fact very good at one thing in particular.

But analysis was for indoors, when you didn't need to keep your senses alert in order to assure your survival. Storms didn't care if you were smart and talented. Nor did wild beasts. Nor did the ground when you fell off your horse and broke something. The light wouldn't last much longer, and they still hadn't reached the plain.

Shaking his head to clear it, he took fresh stock of his surroundings. They were nearing the open valley—the one where most of the snow had melted. This was the second time he'd approached it today, but the other had been by way of a narrow forest path: straight, but through rough terrain. This was by the road, a longer way, sometimes stone-paved, sometimes not, but the only route the wagons could assay.

It had been touch-and-go for a while, when they'd had to traverse a stretch where the snow had drifted waist deep and no one had any idea whether the actual ground beneath it housed ruts, pits, or fallen trees (all three, actually). That had taken two hands to navigate, and it had been less than a shot. Since then, the going had been easier. It was forest, mostly, pines and firs in lieu of the earlier troublesome cedars. More and more oaks. Less space between than heretofore, however, and more undergrowth: laurel and dwarf holly and rhododendron.

"How far?" Strynn asked beside him, bulky in a dull green traveling cloak lined with short white fir, identical to the one he wore.

Avall shrugged. "Up this rise, through the trees, then maybe another two shots downslope, and the land opens out."

She nodded. "I don't like this. Being closed in."

"Try not to think about it. There's a pass up ahead, between steep banks overhung with trees. That may be bad, but just remember it's only transitory. You can stand anything for that short a time."

She smiled wanly. He smiled back. This was a problem he hadn't anticipated. Strynn was fine indoors. Outside—sometimes she had trouble. The way she'd tried to describe it was that it always felt like the world was watching her. And the closer the trees grew, or the taller the cliffs they rode beside, the worse it got. Conversely, she was fine in high places—places, say, where there were cliffs to one side and nothing but open air to the other.

Which was why he'd suggested they ride at the end of the trek for a while: so she'd feel less enclosed.

One moment they were plodding along in the low, slushy ruts left by the rest of the trek, which had pretty well rid the route of snow, what with over a hundred people and half that many wagons passing that way (and with Rrath, not coincidentally, riding next ahead, looking back as often as he looked forward); the next Avall caught a blur of motion from the corner of his eye—and was promptly hurled from his saddle, with something hot and coarse-furred atop him, growling and clawing at him like fury. He hit hard, in virgin snow, and kept on rolling downslope, which freed him from his attacker.

"*Birkit!*" Strynn screamed—which meant she was still alive. He blinked through snow-filled eyes, even as his gloved fingers fumbled for the dagger at his belt, wishing there was more than murky twilight. The beast was nowhere to be seen.

Not up close.

But there it was! Rushing back upslope. Twice as big as he was, and in form somewhere between bear and cat—muscular as one, sleek and low-slung as the other. Fanged like both together, and easy to see, because the snow had caught it before it had shed its summer coat.

For an instant Avall wondered why this one had attacked so recklessly, beyond the fact that they loved horseflesh above all things—including, he was happy to say, humans. Normally they hunted by stealth, not openly, as this one had done. They also hunted alone—normally.

All Avall knew was that his wife was in danger. As was faithful Tarnish.

Who, however, seemed unwilling to forfeit his life without a fight, not unreasonable, considering he'd been a gift from War-Hold some years back.

Avall was on his feet now, blundering clumsily upslope, dagger in hand, while the birkit crouched low on the bank between him and the rearing, leaping gelding. Meanwhile, a white-faced Strynn eased Bellows back along the trail; and those at the end of the file finally figured out something was amiss and turned first to gawk, then to launch counterattacks.

"Circle him!" someone yelled. "He'll run if you show steel."

"Straight at you!" someone else warned. Avall wished he had his bow, his sword—*something*. But all that was lashed to Tarnish's saddle.

"Look out!" a third voice shouted, and an arrow flashed through the air, narrowly missing the creature, and embedding itself in a nearby oak. Avall recalled that Strynn had a bow. He hoped she had sense enough to use it if the beast went for her. Another arrow. Another miss, but it distracted the birkit enough that it swung around, which gave Tarnish a chance to bring both front hooves down on its shoulder. A glancing blow, but Avall heard bone snap and a soul-rattling scream as the birkit lurched sideways, one foreleg dragging uselessly. Avall moved closer. So did the others. Men were skirting around to both sides to ring the animal. He recognized Eddyn (brave, if nothing else), another lad from Smith, foolish little Rrath, and a pair of sturdy older men and one woman, from Stone, War, and Lore respectively. Two had swords. One had found a spear. There were also bows, but that wasn't a good idea, because they were circling the thing, and a miss could wound a comrade.

Tarnish was actually their best asset, for he'd reared up again, as though he would repeat his earlier success.

The beast had learned something, though, and turned at once, snarling, spitting—clawing with one front paw—and then, when the hooves came down, it ran. Straight at the armed company, before suddenly veering downslope—clumsily, for a leg was clearly broken.

Avall stared dumbly as furred death bore down upon him a second time, and then more dumbly as it skidded around to confront a smaller figure running down the slope waving a sword. Rrath—

Brave? Or a fool?

Avall froze as the birkit slumped toward the youth—who'd suddenly realized he was the only thing between it and escape. "Shoot it!" someone yelled.

"Bushes!" another gave back. "Can't see. Might hit the other one."

The other one. Him. Avall.

Avall had a clear shot—but no weapon save the dagger. The thing wasn't looking at him anyway, though it was scarce three spans off. Rather, it was ambling toward Rrath with deadly purpose. And the boy had managed to get himself blocked. If anyone could save him, it would be Avall, if he dared rush in and stab it. Two breaths that would take. To save Rrath, or end his own life, if he failed—and how many ways could that happen? It could turn on him before he got there. He could miss the vulnerable arteries in the neck. He could—

"Help me!" Rrath shrieked, as the birkit moved closer. Avall swallowed. Fear had iced his heart, his throat. His muscles.

And then movement: up and to the left. A dark shape, and the swish-thud of an arrow released and impacting, and a high-pitched scream, where-upon the birkit slumped to the snow, blood fountaining where an arrow had lodged between rib cage and shoulder.

The world spun. The world cleared. Rrath discovered he knew how to move, as did Avall. The dark shape clarified into . . . Eddyn.

Who'd been best sited to ease around beyond the screen of laurel and get in a shot that risked no one.

Eddyn had saved this day—and Rrath's life.

Avall lowered the hand that still clutched his dagger, and slogged through the snow toward Rrath, who looked amazed to find himself alive. Avall stretched a hand down to him, but the youth glared up at him, refus-ing it. "You didn't help!" he growled. "You'd have let me die!"

"I didn't—" Avall began, and broke off. Perhaps the lad was right. Per-haps he *had* been willing to sacrifice Rrath rather than draw the birkit's ire.

He looked away—had to—from all that hurt accusation. He saw Eddyn, hard-faced and grim. He saw Strynn approaching cautiously back up the track. He saw someone steadying Tarnish.

He saw Rrath again, who, he feared, was no longer a friend.

And he saw a dead birkit where there shouldn't have been one.

A man he knew slightly made his way down the slope, sliding in the knee-deep snow. Tamyn, from Beast-Hold by way of Lore. Wordlessly, he knelt beside the dead predator, rolled it—*her*—over on one side, to feel along the stomach.

"What?" Rrath breathed, as he finally got hold of himself.

"What indeed?" from Carmil, who'd made her way down from wher-ever she'd been to assess the situation. "Eight!" she continued. "A birkit. What's one of those—"

Tamyn rose to look at her. "My guess? The weather. Early snow, and long means no easy hunting; means the deer these things usually feed on are dead or gone to cover. This was a female, still weaning cubs. She had to feed them, but not go far. She was hungry. We were meat on the hoof. And we all know their fondness for horse."

"But not for smith," someone laughed. Avall laughed, too, because he had to. Inside, he felt awful. A fool and a coward and no friend to Rrath. Silently, he made his way past the bloodstained beast to the road. Someone passed him Tarnish's reins. Strynn met him there, on foot and concerned. She stared at him intently, sorrowfully, then drew him to her and hugged him as much for his sake, he suspected, as for hers. "You're fine," she whispered. "And don't worry. I saw it. It was too much risk. There was nothing you could do."

"I could've *tried*!" he gave back savagely, jerking away.

Strynn bit her lip. "You can't do everything perfectly," she sighed. "You'll never be happy if you don't accept that."

"I'll never be happy if I don't *try*," he retorted. Then, to no one: "How's Tarnish? Did he . . . ?"

"Small claw mark on the fetlock, but nothing that'll cause trouble," Tamyn told him. "That's a good horse you've got there."

Avall grinned—better that than stare sullenly. "From War-Hold. Gift."

"Shows," the man replied. "You've got good friends, to give you something like that—and good luck. That thing could've gone for you, and you with only a dagger and Eddyn with no good view."

"Yes," Avall grunted. "But it didn't."

"Cubs," Strynn blurted out. "You say it was a mother . . . with cubs?"

"Aye."

"And . . . what of them?"

Tamyn shrugged. "There'd be two of them, and they'd be back in the den."

"And will they . . . ?"

"They'll die."

Strynn looked stricken, and Avall had a good idea why. Mother spoke to mother across the bloodstained snow.

"Skin it," Tamyn ordered bluntly. "And take the fangs and claws. I'd give the first to Rrath here, because they nearly tasted him. And give the claws to Eddyn."

No one argued. Least of all, Avall.

"How's the ankle?" Eddyn asked Rrath, as he eased up beside the young Priest where he sat staring into the campfire beside his caravan, with a mug of cooling cider in his hand.

Rrath managed a begrudging smile. "How'd you know?"

"Saw you limping." Eddyn reached over to take the mug from his hand and set it by the fire to rewarm.

"Glad somebody did," Rrath muttered.

Eddyn stared at him. "You had a hard day. Not every day you face death like that."

Rrath didn't look up. "No," he replied quietly. "And it's not every day you see your— Well, not your hero, but someone you've always liked and admired and cared about in a funny way . . . for what he really is."

Eddyn eyed him narrowly. "And what might that be?"

"A coward."

Eddyn suppressed an urge to defend Avall. He knew the situation pretty well and doubted he'd have done any different if it had been him standing there with just a dagger. Still, the fellow had a point. Too many people liked Avall already and were willing to confer him grace. Better they saw him as Eddyn did: not a bad person, but overindulged and as flawed as everyone else.

"I think they're intelligent," Rrath murmured, still gazing at the fire.

"What are?"

"Birkits. I think there was more than instinct there, more than blind hunger and maternal drive. I think"—he swallowed, tested the cider, and set it back— "I think that one chose her target very carefully."

Eddyn shrugged. This was out of his area of expertise. Still, Rrath obviously wanted to talk, and a man would be a fool to turn down a chance to build a friendship. "How so?"

Rrath poked the fire. It blazed up, setting the delicate bones of his face in sharp relief. "She waited—that made sense. But she didn't attack Strynn, who was last in line—and who'd have made the best target—most obvious, anyway. Instead, she attacked Avall."

"And you think that makes a difference?"

"I think she knew Strynn was pregnant and ruled her out because of that—don't ask me how. I had people beside me, which ruled me out. Avall was a clear target—and he was all but unarmed. His sword was tied because he wasn't expecting anything. Same for his bow. But his dagger was on the side from which she attacked. I think . . . I think she saw all that and knew he couldn't get to his weapons in time to hurt her, and that the dagger would require him to fight too close in to do damage. And that Strynn probably wouldn't fight at all."

Eddyn nodded slowly, as realization dawned. "And you think she didn't really want to kill him; just make him abandon his horse. Because—why?"

"Because they know we're dangerous, and because they know we'd be more likely to go after her if she killed one of us than a horse. She knew how we think, where our priorities are. She weighed our strengths and weaknesses and settled on Avall."

"Maybe."

"Maybe," Rrath agreed. "But watch. Watch a lot of animals. Watch geens, if you get the chance. We think that because they don't act like us, they're simply beasts. But what if they're not? What if they merely have different priorities than we do? What if clothes and cities and . . . language aren't important to them?"

"Large ifs, there," Eddyn muttered.

"Very large. But watch."

Eddyn's eyes narrowed again. "So why are you so interested in this? You're a Priest, for Eight's sake."

"Because," Rrath retorted, "if they're intelligent, that means they have souls, which means if we kill them, it's murder."

Eddyn grinned at him a little too eagerly. "Maybe Avall knew that, and that's why he hesitated."

Rrath glared at him. "Avall," he spat, "is a coward!"

CHAPTER XVI:

MAKING WAR

(SOUTHERN ERON—NEAR WINTER: DAY XIV—EARLY AFTERNOON)

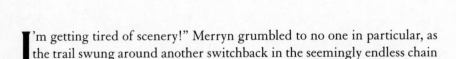

I'm getting tired of scenery!" Merryn grumbled to no one in particular, as the trail swung around another switchback in the seemingly endless chain that carried that narrow, stone-paved trace ever higher up the Stinger—as some nameless trader had long ago christened the last true mountain at the southern terminus of Angen's Spine.

Ingot, her ebony stallion, shivered beneath her as though he'd heard that complaint and agreed. Though a perfectly good trade road shadowed the base of the mountains, they'd left it three days ago, the better to begin hardening themselves for cold, exposure, and altitude. Thus, they followed what was simply called the Hard Trail—because that's what it was. Merryn had long since left off pausing to appreciate the view, though she knew that if she bothered to look at all, she would see—beyond the wisps of her own breath, the tops of increasingly scraggly trees, and ever-more-persistent drifts of clouds—the narrowing green ribbon of the coastal plain, with the vast gray darkness of the sea beyond. A sea that raced the horizon to the north, where it merged into a sheet of slightly cooler gray that gradually became true blue as it rode up the vault of the sky. Most of the nearer part of the green belt was grazing land, for the soil was too salty to support much in the way of useful crops beyond a few odd herbs. What folks lived on the coast in scattered, stilt-raised towns were mostly fisher folk, and mostly unclanned,

Common Clan, or clanless—by choice, so they said. They were Eronese be-cause they spoke the language, looked like Eronese, and were treated as Eronese by the merchants (or raiders) from Ixti who found them the first point of contact. But so far from the seats of power and comfort were they that they might as well have been an independent nation.

Had she looked ahead—east—she'd have seen the greater mass of the mountain starting to tumble down to the vast emptiness of the Flat and the Pit, mostly hidden at present by an outthrust ridge. A little north, though, where the plain petered out, was a wider area of bright green that from a distance looked temptingly lush. It wasn't. It was marsh. The land was sink-ing there (some said because Eron and Ixti were slowly moving apart), and a stretch of coast as long as Eron itself was effectively uninhabitable. Now and then—when the moons lined up a certain way—the sea washed over it en-tirely, to invade the empty sands of the Flat beyond. Once, almost a thousand years ago (it was said), those tides ran so far inland they found the northmost edge of the Pit and flooded in there—until they balanced again. Which ex-plained why people found remnants of ships in that no-man's-land between the realms.

To the right rose the mountain: nothing to see there but naked stone, cracked and flaking where winter wore it away without softness. The only change for two days was which side it was on, and the ever-decreasing cloak of vegetation that had mostly given way to pure rock without even gradated layers to give it character. It was a forbidding place, a cold place. A place she would be spending the winter.

And behind her—

She wouldn't look that way, because that way lay Eron, snuggled between the Spine and the coast—and, to her very great surprise, she'd been beset with homesickness. Clouds massed back there, too, caught on the taller peaks that comprised the bulk of the Spine. *Snow clouds,* which meant trou-ble for Avall, which was another reason she didn't look back: because think-ing of Avall only made the distance greater. They'd been apart before, but never for an entire season, and only twice since their education began rotat-ing them through crafts and clans and holds and halls.

Never mind that Strynn was also back there, and times were fewer yet when she'd had to endure even an eighth without her bond-sister *and* her twin. And while she generally had little trouble making friends, War-Hold's philosophy was that socialization was to be kept to a minimum until after the passing of the Great Dark at the winter solstice. Until then, they'd be embarked on intensive physical training, and the masters had long since learned that people who cared about each other tended to spare each other. For that reason, special effort was made to keep people who had known each other previously from being part of the same cadres. After the Dark, with their skills properly honed, they'd start working together again. Merryn was looking forward to it. Already she was weary of her own company.

Not that she'd be totally isolated. War-Hold had a complete staff the same as any other winter hold. Only one third of her time would be devoted to her craft—and that equally split between perfecting certain weapons skills and basic guard duty. One third would be in general service to the hold, divided between swithwork and cooking, cleaning, maintenance chores. The other third would be her own to do with as she would.

But unlike Avall, she had no loving bond-mate awaiting her. That the Hold-Warden was Strynn's aunt and a lifelong friend was cold comfort. People with that much responsibility dared not be seen playing favorites.

So what did she hope to learn? What did being a weapons-smith entail?

It meant hard physical work—early rising, drills, drills, and more drills. It meant learning ever-more-complex weapons and the ever-more-complex forms that went with them—knife, shortsword, longsword, spear, pike, ax, bows of three sizes, bolas, throwing points, staves—hands, feet, head, even shouts! It meant using every part of them with virtually every part of the body.

To what end?

To guard the Land, to guard the King, to guard the Hall, to guard the Hold, to guard the family, the friend, the lover, and the self: That was the standard litany. It was also the standard priority, though Merryn wasn't certain she'd rank them that way in the unlikely event it ever came to battle.

She shifted in the saddle, moved one leg from the stirrup and flexed it, then the other, then her arms, releasing the reins entirely and twisting at the waist, then the neck, feeling bones click and pop and realign.

Her cloak slipped, and she took a moment to resecure it more to her liking and snug the hood more closely around the cap helm she wore in token of her nominal position as guard-second-alternate. Her sword banged her leg; she moved it, tightening the scabbard belt a notch.

Her breath glittered in the air. The air itself glittered with cold. They'd come much higher without her noticing. It was much colder, too, and she could see clouds of breath puffing out from muffled figures all up and down the line. Ingot's showed as well. She wondered if she ought to put on his winter bardings when she stopped.

Her stomach growled. She slapped it savagely with a gloved hand. It growled again. She fumbled for the flask at her hip, took a long lingering sip of the liquor within: fiery brandy flavored with mint, ginger, and tarragon. It soaked into her mouth, her throat, finally her stomach. Another swallow followed—a big one. She felt blood rushing through her, making her face go warm; could feel that flush Strynn so admired blooming on her cheeks.

Ingot snorted. She patted him smartly. "Sorry, lad, no good for you, though I might let you smell it sometime."

A final sip, a final sniff, and Merryn stored the flask, then straightened and kicked Ingot to a brisker pace, since they'd fallen behind. The swifter gait put her in company with the tail of the first batch of wagons: some folks from Weaver she didn't know, though the tapestry hanging off the back of the bright blue-green wagon was very nice work indeed, if it betokened the abilities of those inside. Perhaps she could have them weave something for Strynn over the winter. Or Avall. Or both.

And then the trail bent around an especially sharp switchback exactly as a wagon *didn't* make the turn, and they spent the rest of the afternoon calming its panicked owners, emptying it of valuables just in case, then pulling it back onto the track.

The Trek-Master took that as a sign and called a rest, with them still four shots out of the hold. Merryn badly wanted to ride on, but convention said no: Treks arrived together. It was part of the ritual, part of the bonding. Part of the show.

Herself . . . Were it not for loyalty to the clan—to a handful of people in it, rather—she would cheerfully slip off some night and not come back. Go exploring. Walk the whole coast, maybe, from the northern ice to whatever lay south of Ixti. Or start out due west one day and never halt until something stopped her. It was a shame for Eron and Ixti both to be so constrained when there were vast, empty, hospitable spaces available to the west. There'd been talk of colonizing the west slope of the Spine around the time of the plague. But there'd been talk of many things then.

And since nothing seemed likely to happen anytime soon, Merryn fed Ingot a sugar treat, removed most of his tack, drew her cloak around her, and set her back against the mountain, looking into the misty air at the featureless sky to the north.

And went to sleep.

She awoke to longer shadows turning what had been a soft landscape harsh and dangerous. There was more red, purple, and black; less gray and green and white.

She rose, stretched, looked around, relieved to find the trek at roughly the same level of preparedness as she. The Trek-Master was making his way up the line, his steps taking him perilously close to the drop from time to time. He'd been born here, she'd heard. That did something to you, made you fearless. Or rash. Or maybe just plain stupid, but she didn't think that over-shouldered young man was stupid, for all he had a broken nose.

"Leave in two fingers," he barked at no one in particular as he passed.

"Look your best." He paused, studied her seriously. "Don't change anything," he told her. "*You* look like you ought. In fact, why don't you come ride with the War Guard?"

And with that he continued on down the trail. Merryn lifted a brow as he departed, noting that he wore no cloak and tighter clothing than most. Before she could stop herself, she was grinning.

Ingot nudged her with his nose, making her stagger. "Jealous bastard!" she muttered, as she sorted through his tack. A moment later, he was ready, as was she—without her cloak, which she'd stashed with the folks ahead.

It took a while to reach the front of the file, where War-Hold's official contingency gathered, most a fair bit older than she, since War-Hold was a choice destination and therefore often claimed by those further in their service. She knew some of these folks, too: a woman from Smith who'd defected as she had. Two men from War: a lanky set of twins with rare blond hair. A slimmer blond man who might be their brother, their cousin, or their friend. The rest . . . she'd know them when she needed.

"Here!" someone called behind her: the Trek-Master. She spun around, extending an arm automatically to snare the mass of red fabric he'd flung her way. It fluttered against the sky, caught in a gust of wind out of the pass beyond. She sorted it expertly, pleased to note it was a tabard in War-Hold crimson—to which she was not yet entitled. She slipped it over her head, arranged the folds as best she could, and found a place in line near the back.

A word, and the file was moving.

It was a slow, uphill ascent, with sheer rock surging up to the left, and sheer rock plunging down to the right. The air had cleared, but the wind had risen, and with it came the scent of smoke as of campfires burning. Merryn sniffed it appreciatively. It was a wilder scent than found in cities, and it suited her mood. That and the scent of horses and wagon grease and clean, but well-used leather.

They cleared the gap soon enough, and the view opened ahead of them: War-Hold on its crag two shots farther on, and half a hundred spans above them.

Unlike most winter holds, Warcraft's citadel didn't snuggle into the land but rose defiantly from it: a lesser peak before a greater that had been smoothed and carved into a formidable fortress indeed. The slope below it was all but sheer, though a skim of snow moss softened it somewhat. The walls themselves were indistinguishable from the dark stone from which they rose, and followed the contours of the land like a coat of ice, save that they were smoothed to a finish like dull glass to three spans' height, so as to allow no invaders purchase. The central mass of buildings was invisible here, but Merryn knew the basic layout: entrance at the far end, so that any attackers had to traverse the full length of the walls to come at the only point of ingress. A narrow forecourt on that side, a mass of building in the middle in the approximate shape of one of the sentry towers up at the gorges, and a wider court at the back, which was used for drills and exercises. Steam emerged here and there, for the mountain on whose knees War-Hold perched was alive and kept its own fire, and sometimes rained it down on the hold, for which reason nothing flammable was suffered to remain outside save flags and banners. Several were visible now: long pennons of crimson sylk and scarlet velvet.

But there was something odd about this approach. She squinted toward the walls, shading her eyes against the westering sun. There was no one *on* those walls—and given that it was a fine day and reasonably warm, there should be a sprinkle of children and young people watching their approach, eager to see what interesting newcomers the trek would bring, and equally eager, some of them, to see proof they would themselves soon be safe away.

There were none. Merryn scowled, wondering if anyone had noticed the same. Surreptitiously, she freed her sword in its scabbard and kneed Ingot closer to the next man up—the slimmer of the mismatched twins. "Notice anything . . . odd?"

He blinked at her from beneath his helm, then followed her gaze toward the wall, which was now very close indeed, its lowest buttresses barely above their heads.

"Nobody's watching," he said flatly, looking uneasily at his twin.

The twin looked, too. "Any number of reasons, though. We're—"

"—Late, not early," the thin twin finished.

"Guard," Merryn muttered. "That's all we can do. If anything happens, we won't be the first to know."

"Unless oil comes down on our heads," the larger twin replied, sounding more and more uneasy.

"Slop from the kitchen, more likely, and I'd doubt that!" the thin twin retorted, with a laugh.

Merryn shrugged and tried to relax. She had little authority here, and in this location, at the tail of the guard and the van of the first of the wagons, there was little she'd be able to do anyway.

In any event, it soon became a moot point, because the trail kinked left, and the narrow blade of the gatehouse thrust itself across the entire trail, tower rising five levels above the dark arch of the gate. Torches flared in there, which was comforting. A herald appeared on the parapet above, looking startled, as though roused from a nap he oughtn't to have indulged in.

Closer, and they were under, and there was light again at the end. She was riding into it—

—and into a clot of confusion as horses and riders bunched up instead of moving on as they should. She looked back—exactly in time to hear the portcullis fall behind her—then up to see men in black surcoats and gleaming armor rise from behind the parapets with bows drawn, and to see others rush from archways to either side, as suddenly the War Guard found itself besieged.

Five to one, she made the odds, as she whisked her sword from her scabbard to hack at a man who appeared from nowhere at her side. He parried expertly, followed by a blow that whizzed between her elbow and her body, parting fabric but sparing flesh. She wheeled Ingot around—or he wheeled himself—and part of her wondered why the archers were doing nothing more than standing there looking ominous, and then she had a target again and aimed another blow. The air filled with shouts, screams, the neighing of horses, the clash of blades as more warriors poured out upon them. Four had laid hold of Ingot in such a way that she couldn't attack them for fear of injuring her mount. Another had expertly removed her foot from a stirrup, upsetting her balance. She felt herself slipping, tried to right herself, and couldn't. She fell—with some help—and found herself flat on her back looking up past a forest of horses' legs and dark-helmed faces at a sky that was incredibly blue, and wondered grimly if it was the last thing she'd ever see that was pretty. And then the face above her grinned and reached back, and she was certain she was about to die.

But instead of steel flashing down, something wet splashed sour/sweet into her mouth and burned into her eyes.

Wine!

They were dousing her with wine.

Laughter, and then more, and she suddenly realized that the sounds of battle were becoming those of mirth, as her erstwhile attackers joined in hauling her to her feet. She resisted, then gave in and let them, wiping muddy grit off her fine new tabard. A glimpse left showed the slighter twin nursing a light wound on his forearm, which his brother was tending with concern. She was spared asking the question that had risen in her mind, however, by the thin young woman beside her, who demanded in the shrillest voice she'd ever heard, "Would someone please tell me what in The Eight is going on?"

The stranger next to her took off his black helm and shook out long brown hair bound back from Eronese features. "A test," he said. "It used to be a tradition, but numbers became too small, and we weren't up to it in quality."

Merryn relaxed, even as she heard someone pounding on the gate inside the tower. The man grinned triumphantly. "Also, lady, you've just met the return of the Night Guard!"

Merryn was too stunned to speak. The Night Guard were the elite of War-Hold. A hundred strong, no more, no less, they hadn't existed since the plague because their numbers had grown too few and those adept at the training too overextended. They were evidently back—with a vengeance.

And had mounted what had seemed a very real attack indeed without injuries. That was their true skill: battle with minimal loss of life. Why, the way they had moved to subdue Ingot while avoiding making targets of themselves . . . !

"Clearly I have much to learn," she grumbled, to the man's back.

He turned and grinned. "Clearly, lady, you do—but not so much as some others."

And then, as fast as they'd appeared, they were gone. Silence filled the forecourt. The Trek-Master looked at them all meaningfully. "A test," he whispered, "and an initiation, and a goal. And you *will* keep silent about it."

Merryn suppressed a shiver. Clearly there was more to War-Hold than she'd thought. More rites, more secrets, more lore. She was going to like it here.

And then she had no more time for deliberation, for the doors to the main keep opened, and the usual welcome poured out in a tide that met those who'd been delayed in the gatehouse. Somewhere in the midst of the chaos, the wide-shouldered Trek-Master found her again and asked her to be his companion for dinner.

The welcoming banquet that night was a wonder, and Merryn actually wore women's attire and enjoyed the Trek-Master's company immensely. His name was Ormyrr, and he was very charming, but Merryn slept alone in a comfortable stone-walled room that was far more opulent than her own quarters in Tir-Eron.

She wondered if Avall was as happy.

CHAPTER XVII:

STORM WRACK

(Eron: Gem-Hold-Winter—Near Winter: Day XVI—midafternoon)

~~~~~~~~~~

Strynn could see Avall ahead of her and that was all. The storm had caught them at noon, blown up out of a sky that had been clear as glass when the trek had set out that morning. There'd been rain at first—it had been warm enough for that—but far too soon, drops had changed to sleet, then to blowing, driving snow. The firs to either side were shadow-shapes, the trail ahead a mushy beige mystery marked only by slush, where old snow mixed with new.

More snow rose to either side, head-high banks that betokened even earlier storms here than those which had delayed them. Seventeen days. Three days longer than anticipated. Snow over half of them, and one blizzard before this. She hadn't seen more than a smear of open ground since they'd camped in the vale the night after the birkit attack.

At least they weren't riding last now, though that was more a function of Carmil's methodical rotation than of any desire to calm their particular nerves. That their present position—between Smith and Leather, roughly in the middle of the long lumbering file—put them in proximity to Eddyn hadn't, so far, been a problem. Eddyn had been on his good behavior lately—as had Avall. There'd been no more fights. But neither had there been more than token conversation. Not with Eddyn, and not with Rrath. That had hurt Avall, too; it was hard to go from being adored to ignored for no good reason. Nor had he spoken about it. Most of their conversation, in fact, had been about the King's commissions. More than one night they'd stayed up far too late sketching, planning, exchanging ideas with each other. Strynn couldn't wait to get back in a forge. Neither could Avall.

Privacy wouldn't be bad, either. Caravans were fine—if one weren't newly married. Not that it would matter if the storm got any worse! The pathkeepers had been out twice and had reported, most recently, that they were no more than four shots out of Gem. But four shots could easily be fifty when the drifts were growing a finger deeper every quarter hand. The lead teams had slowed to a veritable crawl as they sought to push through snow as high as the horses' chests. And that delay allowed more to pile up between the other riders and wagons faster than it dispersed.

Never mind the cold. She had no idea how chill the air itself was, but the bitter wind made it worse, so that she had on everything she owned and Avall's spare hose as well—and still felt ice creeping up her legs, beneath three layers of woolen skirts.

Would that she'd done as Avall had suggested and ridden in the wagon. But that would've meant consigning Bellows to someone else's care, and if she did that, and anything happened, Merryn would never forgive her.

But was the snow lessening a little? Where those actual mountain peaks ahead, blue-gray cutouts against a pale gray sky? And were the trees falling back, as she knew they did on the final approach to their destination?

As sometimes happened, the snow stopped abruptly, as though it had been a diversion before a play. A final few gusts, and blue sky showed. Sunlight stabbed down. Trees found colors. The wagons lost their pastel spirals and became almost garish. "Hold ho!" someone called ahead. A rustle of relief spread down the trek like a snake shedding its skin. Strynn relaxed. Impulsively, she moved up to pace Avall, reached out to pat his leg. He started, half-asleep in the saddle as he'd been, then smiled, blinked, and blinked again as he realized where they were. He took her hand and squeezed. "Finally," he murmured.

And then the trail bent downward and they got a clear glimpse of Gem-Hold-Winter.

In common with most mountain holds, it was built as much into the mountains as on or beside it. According to the tale, Tar-Megon—as the mountain rearing before her in a tumble of bare, blue-purple rock was called—had once possessed a smaller twin that pressed against it like a child at its mother's bosom. That twin had been shaped and reshaped over the generations into what she saw now: a vast building a shot long and a fifth that high, set against the mountain wall, and whose outward-sloping lower reaches rose from the floor of a narrow valley, almost completely windowless for half their height. Buttresses, the occasional ventilation slit, and a long, winding stair on the eastern side gave some relief to what was otherwise unrelieved hewn stone. But higher—there the glory began. Long galleries of thick stone fronted the top third on its three free sides, their contours stepped in or out as the contours of the mountain of which they were carved dictated, so that the whole effect was of a massive upsurge of stone becoming lacier and more intricate as it rose, like foam atop a wave. The top was flat, but even that was terraced, and only the upper few levels were completely free of Tar-Megon behind it.

Mostly it was whitewashed, but here and there banners flew, or a shutter, door, or balcony had been painted. There was steam, too: vented from the hot springs that warmed the place and which in part had determined its location. And there was a glint of glass at intervals, token of the famous greenhouses that fed body and mind alike with lush growth all year round.

Winter came to Gem-Hold. But Gem-Hold, more than many, resisted.

And then the sun broke through in force and painted the lower walls pink and gold, and the higher galleries mauve, maroon, and scarlet. "Beautiful," Strynn breathed. "One could do worse than be born to Stone, if such things are your legacy."

Avall nodded mutely. "*We* make beautiful things, you and I, and those of our craft. But we don't make things for the ages. Not like this. Not that can be seen for shots."

"No," Strynn agreed. "We don't. But we might make replicas out of gold."

Avall grinned at her. "A present for Carmil, perhaps? For tolerating your moods?"

"*Our* moods," Strynn corrected. "I'm the one with child, remember?" Then, "Look!"—she pointed to a spot about a third of the way to the right of the enormous pile—"There's the Smithcraft banner."

Avall found the long gold-and-maroon pennant. And then they both lost the view as the trail twisted sharp left into a narrow defile with rock to the right and a gentler slope to the left. The geography—and the return of trees—had kept most of the snow away, so the going was easier.

And easier again, a hand later, when they once more swung right and found themselves facing the hold's narrow southern side, with only a freshly swept paved forecourt between them and the awesome upward sweep of building.

The place was thick with people, the Hold-Warden and her staff rushing out to meet them, taking horses, handing up ritual mugs of spiced wine and beer and cider, helping tired bodies off horses and down from wagons. Strynn let Avall help her dismount, feeling how stiff she was and how much her back hurt, as a fair young woman in Gem-Hold livery quartered with Beast gently disengaged her hand from Bellows's reins with a firm, "We'll take care of him. You've tended horse enough of late, I imagine. Go inside. Today is to enjoy."

"I like the sound of that," Avall sighed, as he let Tarnish be led toward the centermost of the three massive wooden doors that marked the entrance to the hold's stables. The wagons would join them there, but in the windowless storerooms closer to the mountain. Gem-Hold would tend to the unloading. For now, for the rest of the day, and perhaps tomorrow as well, the new arrivals were guests.

Strynn found herself and Avall being steered toward a smaller door to the right, where the south wall met the longer east wall in a narrow, trapezoidal tower. Torches lit it, alternating with glass brick, as she and Avall made their way up the enclosed stair—five levels, then six, then ten, and her legs were getting sore indeed. And then their guide opened a door, and a rush of cold air hit them. They were outside again, in the corner of the massive lower arcade that completely wrapped the building with a wide expanse of open space, roofed thrice her height above her head, and with enormous stone pillars above waist-high walls giving a spectacular view of the valley.

They didn't linger there, however, for the guide was leading them left, toward the mountain and the intricately carved oak door that exactly centered the wall on that side. They entered it eagerly, for Strynn knew what lay beyond: light and warmth and good food and, for Avall at least, one very good friend.

For a moment, upon entering Gem-Hold's First Hall, Avall didn't feel real. After so long in the wild, with only plains, forests, meadows, and everapproaching mountains on every side, with little actual time spent in the cramped quarters of the caravans and way stations, it was strange once more to be indoors. Only then did he realize how comforting that was. Born in a hold and raised with the protective walls of Eron Gorge to block out the vast empty spaces of the surrounding plain, he'd always felt exposed and vulnerable outside.

Winter it might be, and Eddyn a lurking presence, but he thought their tenure here might be tolerable after all. Especially given that the place tended toward more than reasonable luxury.

Certainly the room around them reflected that: tall, gold-stone pilasters alternated with tapestries of similar width, which in turn alternated with fresco and bas-relief, to depict the history of the hold. The floor was one vast sea of intricately patterned carpet, which Avall hadn't stood on in what seemed like forever. And the place was warm, the air sharp with the scent of evergreens not only from the boughs strewn about, but from actual trees growing in pots in the corners. Furniture was sparse but comfortable.

"No wind—at all!" Strynn noted with a happy sigh as she and Avall drifted away from the press of crowd.

"Better not be," Avall snorted amiably. "What with *four* weather locks between here and the outside, and chinked hallways as well. Winter's going to have to work to find its way in here."

"Trouble is," a voice broke in behind them, "we have to work just as hard to get out!"

Avall spun around joyfully. "*Rann?* Where—?"

Strynn giggled, pointing to what Avall had taken as one of their welcoming crew, some of whom still wore hoods and cloaks because they'd have to return outside.

The "servant" raised slim hands to fumble with a brooch, then let the cloak drop gracelessly to the floor. By which time Avall had enfolded its owner in a hug that could've cracked ribs. The owner hugged back, and it took a pointed cough from Strynn to separate the two.

"Careful," Avall cautioned, as Strynn also embraced his friend. "She's . . ."

"I know," Rann reminded him. "I haven't been gone *that* long."

Avall laughed. Eight, but it was good to see Rann again, even if his bond-brother was standing there grinning a lot and saying nothing. Then again, what did one say to someone you'd known all your life, with whom you'd spent more time than anyone but your sister? To whom you were closer than anyone else and knew that closeness was reciprocated? Too much had happened since Rann had left Tir-Eron at the beginning of the previous eighth. Why, catching him up on the events of Sundeath alone would require several nights. Never mind what Rann had been up to.

Rann syn Eemon hadn't changed much, save that his hair was longer. It was down to mid-shoulder now, though he wore it caught back in a tail that showed matched gold earrings to advantage. For the rest, he was exactly as Avall remembered. Shorter than he by a bit, which made him low-average for Eronese. Black hair (no surprise), and dark blue eyes. Rann's chin was more pointed than Avall's, his nose narrower. He was slimmer, too, though his shoulders were as wide. Indeed, his main facial quirk was a scar beneath his lower lip where Avall had hit him while wrestling and driven a tooth through.

And that infectious smile.

"Missed you," Avall gasped finally.

"Yeah," Rann echoed. "Me too."

Avall glanced at Strynn, embarrassed at having excluded her, though she knew he and Rann had shared far more of . . . *everything* than she and he had ever done. She shrugged, and he smiled back and gathered her close. "I feel complete," he sighed, as he felt their warmth, their solidity, soak into him. "With the two of you, I don't need anyone else."

Strynn raised a brow. "Except Merryn, to keep you humble; but I understand. It was kind of like that when we married. Me and Merryn and you. I felt more whole than I'd ever been."

Rann snorted amiably. "This sounds too serious for me. What do you say I show you to your quarters?"

"Lead on," Avall chuckled, and arm in arm they passed through the door and entered Gem-Hold proper.

Smithcraft's complex was on the other end of the building, so it took a while to get there, but Avall had no objection to wandering through the rooms and passages. A quarter of the way along, the hallway opened onto an arcade that wrapped around one of the hold's two principal garden courts. Avall gasped at the flood of lush greenery thriving in the steam-born heat. The room was easily fifteen spans square and full of growing things, including whole trees that rose up to a double-glass ceiling a dozen spans above his head. Spiral stairs at each corner led down to the ground, which was cleverly wrought into a number of distinct enclaves (rather like the gardens behind Argen-Hall), providing the illusion of more space than was actually present.

And, of course, there was water. Pools, ponds, and man-made waterfalls, and occasional fountains that shot faintly sulfur-smelling spray into the air. All at once Avall was sweating. He unlaced his overtunic.

"One layer's usually enough," Rann informed him. "And wait till you see the new baths!"

The center of Gem-Hold held another wonder: a vast common room glassed over at the top but open the full height of the building. The main level was several levels lower, but, again, stairs led down to any number of cleverly contrived private retreats and conversation areas.

And on again. Another glassed-in garden, with an actual greenhouse to one side, where Avall saw people tending fruits and vegetables, and then a kink left, toward the back of the building, and another hall.

Actually, a small half tower facing a tiny court between the hold and the mountain proper. Many hold-suites had them here, but Smithcraft's was larger than most. There was a fair bit of glass, and the overhanging porches kept off much of the wind and snow. Mostly it was for light, Rann told them. Artists need light. Therefore Gem-Hold was riddled with these openings, and with light wells.

Another turn brought them to a small foyer with the sigil of Smithcraft set in the floor, surrounded by those of the septs of Clan Argen. Like most interior rooms they'd seen, the walls were creamy white (either stone, bleached wood, or whitewash) but there were enough accents of Argen's maroon to give the place a homey flavor.

"Welcome to Argen-in-Exile," Rann cried—and opened a round-topped oak door. "Your rooms await."

"After you," Avall laughed, motioning Strynn in ahead of him.

Rann followed smugly.

For some reason, Avall had expected student quarters, which were always deliberately austere. This was a private suite: stone-paved vestibule opening onto a sitting room, with a decent-sized window at the far end; workroom to the right, bedroom to the left, with bath and another workroom adjoining it. Wood paneling alternating with stone; thick, gold-toned rug. Comfortable chairs. And music.

Harp music! And though he'd heard plenty of music on the trek, it had been mostly ballads and such: material good for singing or playing on simple instruments.

This was hall music!

With no obvious source. Avall raised a brow. "Your doing?"

Rann shrugged. "Consider it a wedding gift—to Strynn."

She raised her brows in turn. "How did you know?"

Another grin. "I have my sources. Mostly I have a friend who shared a rotation with you at music. She said you loved the harp. And that particular song."

Avall blushed and looked at the floor. "I . . . didn't know you liked the harp," he stammered.

"I didn't tell you," Strynn informed him easily. "A woman ought to have some mystery."

"And a man, too," Rann chimed in. "Would you like to meet him?"

"Who wouldn't?" Strynn cried, then paused. "It's no one I know, is it?"

"I don't think so. Though of course he's heard of *you*." Without further comment, Rann strode to a small screen in the back corner of the room and carefully folded it aside.

Avall saw the harp before he saw the harper. A chief-harp it was, called that because it was as tall as a man. Rumor said, as tall as the first Chief of Music-Hold, who'd invented that particular double-strung configuration.

The harper sat behind it, and all Avall could tell was that he was young, very slight, and wore rather foppish-looking velvet that was only viable indoors. And a floppy hat with a feather. Nor did he stop playing when they approached. Not until the song was finished. And not once did he falter, but continued fingering the strings with absolute precision. Ending with a final, delicate, "ping, ping . . . ping."

"Avall syn Argen-a, Strynn san Ferr, allow me to introduce Kylin syn Omyrr."

Omyrr. Music, Avall tallied automatically.

The harper looked up from his stool. His eyes were shadowed by his hat at first, but then Avall saw, and missed half a breath.

Kylin was blind. A black-sylk mask covered his eyes.

"Greetings, good folks," Kylin said cheerily, looking slightly past them, in the manner of most blind men.

"Greetings, oh most accomplished harper," Avall replied. "You honor us with your craft."

"And you me with your work," Kylin smiled. "I haven't seen it, of course, but Rann has let me feel some of your castings and inlay work. Wonderful."

"No more than your playing."

Strynn gnawed her lip, trying not to stare.

Kylin evidently read the pause exactly. "When I was a child," he began, "very small indeed, my mother left me outside on a sunny day. I looked at the sun, trying to see what shape it was within all that light. I burned my eyes. The healer who attended me did the rest. She confused one herb for another. I've been blind since then. Three years and a day after my birth."

"But you remember," Avall said, as though to himself.

"Aye," Kylin murmured. "I remember."

"We met here," Rann broke in. "He's Music, of course, but not bound to the Fateing or the cycles."

"And has ears," Avall drawled. "Or do you always speak of your friends as though they weren't present?"

"Only," Rann said, "when that friend is you." And with that, he wandered over to a large table where chilled wine in goblets and hot cider in mugs awaited. And fresh fried fish and what would otherwise be summer fruit: oranges, tangerines, and limes. And nuts.

Avall scooped up a handful of almonds. "I think I'm going to like it here!"

Strynn wandered over to look at the window. The glass was thick between heavy velvet drapes, but light came in unabated. It gave her face an eerie, almost ghostly glow. Slowly she turned and wandered, as though entranced, toward Kylin, who hadn't moved.

"Do you know," she asked softly, "the song they call 'Starlight's Dance'?"

Without a word Kylin turned back to his harp and began to play.

Avall snared a mug of cider and sat down. Rann sat down beside him, leaning his head on Avall's shoulder. Strynn did the same on the other side.

Avall kicked off his boots, wiggled his feet in the carpet, and for the moment was utterly content.

Eddyn awoke to the sound of tapping at his door. He roused himself sluggishly and considered ignoring it. It had been too long since he'd slept like this. In a real bed. In a room of his own. Without snores and the snortings of beasts and the smells that went with both to disturb his slumbers. Station, ground, or wagon, none were more than minimal comfort. But this—a vast bed, a warm room. Glass in the windows that let in the best possible light for smithing.

And best of all, Avall was two levels down and had to contend with less light than he, though they shared a light well.

Tap, tap, tap . . .

Eddyn sighed and rose, flinging on a robe to cover the casual nakedness that was another luxury. What time was it anyway? The sun was still up, but the shadows looked long outside and he was starting to get hungry. Dinner in an hour, maybe, in the common hall, so he'd been told; so everyone could see each other at once—three staggered cycles of holders.

Tap-tap-tap. Then a voice he knew: "Eddyn?"

He hastened his step for no reason beyond mere curiosity, undid the door latch, and opened it to the sight of a cheery-faced and very clean Rrath. The Priest's eyes darted about like fish in a bowl, settling somewhere between Eddyn's chin and chest. Not unusual, since Eddyn was most of a head taller. "Are you busy?" Rrath asked carefully.

Eddyn tried not to counter with a sharp remark. He liked Rrath—he thought. More than that, he liked the idea of luring away one of Avall's acolytes. On the other hand, the lad—it was impossible to think of him as his own age, though he must be, to have been in the same Fateing—seemed sufficiently unsure of himself that he might need more attention than Eddyn had to give.

Fact. Given where he was and that he had a private room and few friends or other diversions around, his intention was to fulfill his obligations to the hold, which was to say, do his tour in the mines and spend whatever time remained working on his commission for the King. And this time there'd be no doubt whose was the best. This time he would surpass Avall and win for himself a subcraft-chieftainship. Maybe then Tyrill would give him peace.

All of which musing occurred in less than a breath—though still long enough for Rrath to look crestfallen and start to back away. "Is this a bad time?"

"No," Eddyn sighed, and meant it. "They've left a welcome meal. Wine, beer, cheese, bread—but I suppose they left you one, too."

Rrath nodded as he followed Eddyn into the room. "Oh, yes. Fine fare. But you've the better view."

"Better light," Eddyn corrected. "My craft needs it."

"Don't need light to be avatar of Weather," Rrath murmured, flopping down on a low sofa beside the laden table. He chose a goblet, looked at it curiously, and finally shrugged and filled it with what Eddyn knew to be the least savory wine. Lack of taste? Or consideration?

"Have you been down to the mines?" Rrath asked abruptly.

Eddyn paused in the act of filling a goblet for himself. "When I was here before, as a boy. One cycle." He paused, peered at Rrath intently. "I take it you haven't?"

Rrath shook his head. "I was ill that cycle. I never made it up. I've always regretted it."

Eddyn chuckled. "Regretted digging and pedaling those digging machines? You're a fool if you regret that."

Rrath looked crestfallen.

"I didn't say *you* were a fool," Eddyn went on. "If you'd like to go . . ."

Rrath's face lit up. "I know the hold has folks who'd be glad to show me, but I thought it'd be more fun to have someone I knew."

"You're the only one here from Weather, correct?"

"Besides the weather-witch, and he doesn't like me."

"You going to be one?"

"What?"

"A weather-witch."

Rrath shifted uncomfortably. "My training's been geared that way, but actually, I'm thinking of challenging for a seat in Beast if I can find a sponsor."

A brow went up. "The birkit thing?"

A nod. "And geens. I think they're intelligent. If I prove they are, there won't be much of a place for me in my clan."

"I see your point."

Rrath nodded again, but didn't speak.

Eddyn rose. "If you want to go, we could probably get there and back in time to eat. I'll see if I can find some clothes."

Without waiting for reply, Eddyn padded to the upright cupboard where his sparse travel wardrobe had been stored and chose a pair of black hose, a black tunic, and black house-slippers. No Argen maroon this time. Simple, serviceable wear. Anonymous wear, if truth were told.

Not bothering to duck into the adjoining bath for modesty's sake (he was used to being admired and frankly expected to be looked at), he dressed quickly, belting the tunic with a sash instead of the usual link-belt. "Shall we?" he inquired when he'd finished. Rrath drained his wine in one gulp and rose, eager as a puppy. Eddyn tried to recall that this was, in fact, a good deed.

It took a while to reach the mines. The entrance was on a level lower than that by which they'd entered the hold. It was also in the oldest part of the structure, down where the rock of the mountain met the building proper—except that didn't really describe it either, because parts of the hold had been hollowed into the mountain itself. Whole vast rooms, in fact: enormous chambers that would've held half of Tir-Eron without crowding, and all supported by massive pillars of stone, in some of which matrixed jewels sparkled. To reach that level, one had to descend whichever of the many stairs one chose, then thread through narrower passages than those above, often lit with torches instead of glow-globes, then tend toward the center of the building—directly under the vast, glassed-over court, in fact.

"Smells like dirt," Rrath observed, long before they arrived.

"Rock," Eddyn corrected. "Crushed rock—and running water. They have these pedal-powered machines called trods that drive hammers and screws that cut the rock. You'll get used to that; it'll put muscle on those skinny legs."

Rrath scowled. "They don't use horses?"

"In places. But in the tightest places, horses won't fit. That's where we come in. In fact, small as you are, they'll *love* you."

Rrath snorted.

They walked on in silence, down plain corridors of dark stone. The place felt musty in spite of what Eddyn knew were ongoing efforts to dispel the sense of being underground. It was warmer, too—almost too warm. He wondered if that was proximity to the springs or the fact that the farther one went underground, the more the temperature rose. Or maybe it was residual heat from the machines.

A door loomed ahead: standard weather lock. Eddyn opened it and ushered Rrath into a large, plain common room, to either side of which more rooms opened. He chose the right-hand one, which proved to be a combination changing room and bath of the serviceable sort men used who were too filthy to go as they were to their quarters. The room was mostly white, but like the outer room, there was a griminess to it. Probably it was impossible to keep clean, so far underground, with indifferent light, and with dust constantly wafting in from the mines themselves.

A dozen men were showering as they passed. One grunted an acknowledgment: someone Eddyn recognized from when the man had spent a cycle at Smith. Eddyn raised a hand, yelled, "Giving this man a tour," and strode on.

Another changing room and a stair, and they entered the mines proper. Eddyn had forgotten how noisy they were, but remembered when he found himself having to shout to be heard. It wasn't so much specific noise as a dull roar of constant machinery, amplified through the earth itself and rendered louder yet by echoes. Mostly it was metal on stone, but sometimes, too, it was metal on metal, and sometimes men breathing heavily or singing songs. "We'll each have a vein to tap," he explained. "But not until we've settled in. Expect them to start you the day after tomorrow."

Rrath rolled his eyes—which he did a little too often.

"If I recall," Eddyn went on, "Smith's working off right vein this year."

"Right vein?"

"There're five main ones: right, left, center, top, and bottom. Simple as that. Right's a particularly deep one. Not much comes out, but what does is very good quality."

"Sapphires?"

"Rubies. Emeralds. A few diamonds. The odd topaz."

"I'd have thought there'd be more diamonds."

"Why?"

"Because they tend to occur near hot springs, so I've heard."

"You're full of that kind of thing, aren't you? Maybe you should forget Beast and try for Lore."

"I might," Rrath said seriously.

"You should," Eddyn replied, and continued on.

They didn't go far, though it was enough for the noise to abate as they followed a single opening that branched off two others. Just far enough for the air to smell of something besides stone dust. Like sweat, like the grease used to lubricate the trods, like mildew and rotting wood and smoke from too many torches.

"Hard to breathe," Rrath ventured.

"You get used to it."

They turned another corner and confronted the machine.

Set against the far wall, it was three spans long and resembled nothing so much as a landlocked galley, save that the body of the vessel was a complex frame of metal. And instead of oarsmen, it housed a file of men and women, most wearing no more than short breeches, who were pedaling rhythmically atop a complex of gears and pulleys that drove a massive screw half a span across into the mountain itself. Dirt fell from the bottom of that point, to be collected on a thick fabric belt powered by more cogs and gears. The belt ran to a point to their left, where its contents were deposited in large wooden vats, perpetually sprayed with water. The stuff was more dirt than actual rock, so it dispersed easily, occasionally revealing a gleam of red—or green, or blue, or white. More people—mostly women, because their eyes were sharper— observed the mix as it passed by, and picked out the desirable stones.

Slave labor, Eddyn thought—except that it was no worse than any other routine activity, and in any event, no one had to do it more than half a year—and only three or four times in the course of one's life.

"I don't like this," Rrath said abruptly.

"The work? It's good for you, and you're compensated. You get to keep one tenth of whatever you find, by blind lot."

Rrath shook his head. "No," he whispered. "I don't like being underground. It's too far from the weather."

CHAPTER XVIII:

BARBED THREATS

(THE FLAT–YEAR BIRTH: DAY TWENTY-EIGHT–SUNSET)

~~~~~~~~~

K raxxi wrapped his hand in a swath of cloth cut from the same cheap bolt of raw sylk he'd bought in Vingalinxx to swathe his face, and snared his right boot carefully. His left hand held his sharpest dagger— raised apprehensively. His shadow fell long on the sand: black upon gold, like expensive brocade. He lifted the boot. Upended it. Waited.

Nothing fell out.

He exhaled his relief.

Now the other. What were the odds Tozri had quoted? One in four? Something like that?

Good odds or not, depending.

Higher . . .

Still nothing.

Relief again.

No, wait: He'd heard something thump. He shook the boot more vigorously, felt a dull impact inside. A final shake, and it fell out . . .

A scorpion with a body the size of his hand, black as night and with a pattern of stars glittering on its horny carapace. Its tail was as long as its body, its pincers roughly the same. Enormous. And deadly. The stinger arched over its back. Tiny eyes sparkled in the waning light.

Kraxxi stabbed down expertly, piercing the thorax exactly where he'd planned. He jerked his hand away—almost too slowly. The scorpion thrashed, beat at the gleaming metal with its stinger at full extension—which was closer to where Kraxxi's hand had rested on the hilt than he liked. Claws clashed on the steel. Ichor oozed from around the blade. Poison made a green stream down silver-gray. Kraxxi watched entranced.

It wasn't the first scorpion he'd encountered here in the Flat—searching clothes, shoes, and packs for them had become a tiresomely necessary ritual, since human sweat was one of the things they craved—but it was by far the largest.

It continued to struggle, but more weakly. Kraxxi wished there was some easy way to dispatch it but could think of none that was viable. Behind him, the Morrah—the evening breeze—whistled through the windflute Elvix had hung from one of the tent poles: a soft sound, but urgent, like the ghosts of the scorpion's countless kin come to sing it home.

A shadow fell on him. He twisted around in place, watching his hose-clad feet carefully lest the scorpion have family buried in the sand. Olrix was striding toward him, still a fair way off, but it was nearly sunset, so her shadow stretched even here. It was almost time to travel.

She paused in place, a thin, sand-colored statue clad in loose-fitting desert robes, scanning the horizon. Kraxxi scanned it with her as he waited for the scorpion to die.

Not much to see: flat horizon to north and south. The barest line of mountains to the southeast that marked the Winter Wall's tallest summits, which they'd left eleven days back. Northwest: another line, deceptively far off because of the way the land dipped ever downward toward the Pit, and because the air was so clear here, like the best Eronese glass.

The tent was back there, too: a low, sand-colored wedge angled away from the wind. It was only the third time they'd used it; their other rests had been spent in the squat domed cubes of the shelters. A risk, that, but they traveled at night when most honest folks slept; therefore it was reasonable to assume that shelters found empty at dawn would remain that way until dusk. Just to be safe, however, someone always sat guard on the roof, usually Tozri because he was best at sleeping in the saddle of one of the four sturdy horses the buttons from Kraxxi's robe had bought back in the same town that had rendered up the sylk—and the tent, sleeping rolls, water bags, cooking gear, and as much dry desert bread and meat as they could carry without drawing too much attention to what were, overtly, monks.

It had taken a while, too. Three towns, with at least a day between, and two of them per town had dared the markets in monk's disguise, made purchases, then returned. The monks' robes were gone now, along with the false beards—too many people had voiced unfavorable opinion of their particular sect—but Kraxxi and Tozri still sported shaven heads—which had already started to itch before they noticed the sunburn blisters.

Still, Kraxxi thought they'd succeeded in contriving anonymity, but Olrix evidently wasn't so certain, for she continued to scan the horizon. Tozri was back on the sun side of the tent, checking the food that should've been cooking all day in the brass sun oven he'd buried, save the top, in the sand.

Elvix was seeing to the horses, offering them as much as she dared of the oats they'd bought in Ingtrix, and more than she ought of the precious water she'd pumped from the faltering well at the last shelter. They'd all but drained it upon their arrival, seeing to the horses first, then a meager ration for themselves, saving the way-water they'd brought for real emergencies. How long it would last, Kraxxi had no idea. Long enough, he hoped.

A dry, raspy scrape was the scorpion finally succumbing, but Kraxxi didn't remove his dagger. As though hearing the creature's death throes, Olrix continued her approach. "You've caught breakfast," she opined, looming over him before squatting to his right, to probe the scorpion's flaccid body with her own dagger. The robe flapped around her; the sylk across her face by turns revealed and obscured her features. She batted it absently.

Kraxxi regarded her skeptically. "You're not really going to eat—"

"The tail's a delicacy—if you can find one big enough to taste. And the claws. The rest—no."

She indicated his dagger, now thoroughly sheened with poison. "That'll make breakfast, too—of another kind."

"I'm in no mood for games."

She cuffed him. "Not enough sleep?"

"Never enough. But what about the stinger?"

Olrix sat back on the sand. "We'll remove it—carefully—when we get ready to cook the tail. We soak it in water while we ride, to leach out the poison. We also wipe down your knife and soak the fabric in the same water. We do this with gloves on, and if you've a cut on your hand, you don't do it even then. We discard the stinger, and we discard the fabric—unless you want to murder somebody. We pour the steeping water into something glass and seal it. We discard the previous container. What we've got left? One of the most potent poisons there is. Great for tipping arrows or darts for hunting—and many other interesting effects."

Kraxxi exhaled reflexively. "You didn't tell me that before."

A shrug. "Small scorpions before. This one's big enough to matter."

"And my dagger? If the stuff's that strong, what about the residue on it?"

"Well, if you scratch somebody with it for, oh, the next five days or so, I wouldn't count on seeing 'em again. If you want to purify it, soak it in oil and set it on fire—just don't breathe the fumes."

Kraxxi scowled sourly. "Clearly my education has been lacking."

"Not your education, Krax, your experience. You were too precious to risk, and there were things they thought you ought to know—like all that family history—that won't keep you alive outside the palace. Poverty has its advantages."

"You weren't poor."

"Not rich either. But maybe . . . balanced."

"What about our black friend here?"

"Leave him for Toz. He's got the right equipment—and he's the best cook. Just don't think about it when you eat it."

Kraxxi rose wearily, careful to avoid the dagger. He retrieved his boots. Shook them again at least ten times apiece for good measure, then started back inside the tent.

"Kraxxi!" Olrix called softly, reaching out to stay him. "Not yet."

"What?"

"We have to talk."

"You and I? Or all of us?"

"The rest of us already did—while you kept watch."

"Thanks for telling me."

"We're not against you, but we wanted to have our arguments in order before we talked to you again."

He gnawed his lip. "About going on?"

"Or going back."

He looked at her, dark eyes probing for hidden priorities, but saw nothing save the honesty he'd always seen there. "I thought we'd had this discussion— several times."

"It wasn't real then. It is now. Every time before we could've gone back to where we were, in the physical sense. We could've hidden in the mountains and hunted, or gone back to that monastery after the search moved on and holed up for a very long time indeed. We could've lost ourselves in some town and pretended not to be who we are. But always we had enough supplies to take us back." She paused. "If we go on from here— You knew how we thought there was another station ahead when we pitched camp? Well, Elvix rode on a ways—she gets restless sometimes. As it turns out she rode half the day, and she found nothing. *Nothing!* No station—which means we miscounted or simply missed one. Which means we've already passed the last shelter and didn't know it *was* the last."

Kraxxi nodded uncertainly. "I *thought* it was. I thought I kept count. I—" He paused, as anger welled up in him. "And you didn't wake me for this?"

"We—I—wanted you to decide whatever you decide with a clear head."

"Thanks a lot!" He frowned, tapped the dagger to see if the scorpion responded. He knew how it felt: pinned down with nowhere to go it truly wanted to—except to freedom that now seemed impossibly far away.

"What you're saying," he continued, "is that if we go on, you *think* we've got enough supplies to see us to Eron. But if we travel another night and then decide to turn back, we won't have enough to take us anywhere we can disappear?"

She nodded. "We could get to the last station, maybe, but we couldn't even be sure there'd be usable water there, and we really need to avoid the roads. You can bet that any caravan going to Eron would be on the lookout for us."

"But there's no certainty there'd be any this late in the year. They're coming up on what they call Deep Winter up there: the quarter year either side of Midwinter's Day, when nothing moves outside. Not even in the southern parts. I've not been, of course, but everyone's heard the stories."

Kraxxi certainly had. Horror tales of snow deep as houses, of trees buried, of plains of featureless white beneath which nothing showed and little lived. Of a whole nation of brilliant artisans locked away together for an entire season with nothing to do but make wonderful things and dream. He wondered if that was the source of the rift between them and Ixti: the fact that Ixtians had more choice about how they spent their time. And their resources. Trapped between the sea and the mountains and shadowed by the cold, with only their spring-heated gorges to see them through, the Eronese had to be careful, controlled. Was it any wonder, then, that the mind and hands alone were unfettered?

He shook himself, realized that he'd fallen into a reverie that had little to do with their situation. "It's not an adventure any longer, is it?"

Olrix shook her head solemnly. "No, my friend, it's real. Two nights, I think, to the edge of the Pit, where there *might* be water, and then we get to decide whether to cross it, which is shorter, or go around the northern point. And then—seven more to the base of the mountains that most consider the border of Eron."

"Forget loyalty," Kraxxi murmured. "Forget friendship. Forget obligation. If I weren't here but everything else was the same—that you knew death awaited you back home—what would you do?"

Silence.

"Olrix?"

She grinned, but he wasn't certain if it was in levity or resignation. "The choice is one of something to look forward to, or nothing. The choice is fear for the rest of my life or a new beginning. The risk is death, but that's a risk for only a finite time and I know the odds." She pointed at the scorpion. "If I could find one of those a day, I could eat like a king until I died. And as of a finger ago, we have the means to give all of us painless, quick deaths, if we want."

Kraxxi shuddered. "And back home—back in Ixti, I need to start saying—you'd always be under risk of death anytime you were found out."

She nodded.

More silence. Kraxxi studied the horizon, the bare glimmer of mountains there, turning dark as night crept in. One of those mountains smoked a little. Fire and ice. That was Eron. Extremes. But of extremes like that were passions made, and Kraxxi, after years of living in the palace and having his every move dictated, was finally getting to live with passion. "We go on," he murmured.

Olrix sighed. "Two more things I should've mentioned. One is that the wind has favored us, so far. It's blown steadily. It likely has covered our tracks. We'd be difficult to trail that way."

Kraxxi tensed. "And the other?"

"I lied about my ring being destroyed."

Kraxxi nodded, as a jolt of alarm spread through him. "But—"

"My mother has it. No one knows but the three of us—I hope. But through it, she could learn which way we've gone. If the king should find out . . ."

"Is there reason to think he might?"

"I think he suspects. He suspects everything."

Kraxxi turned on her in a rage. "And only now do you tell me this?"

Her eyes were as angry as his. "It's not a thing one *tells*! I love my mother, I wouldn't have her hurt. But people need to control their own lives. The fact that she could know where we were gave her a little power and comfort."

"Would she betray us?"

"Not by choice, but a body under torture doesn't always have a choice. Besides," Olrix concluded, "it's only a possibility."

Kraxxi shuddered. "Distance should make one more secure than that."

"Distance isn't always the same. Remember the proverb? 'Whoever controls distance controls the world.'"

"I'll remember that," Kraxxi muttered—and rose.

Tozri dressed the scorpion, hacking off the claws and tail, discarding the body, setting the sting to steep in a glass phial, the poison from Kraxxi's sylk in another, all carefully wrapped and put away. The tail was put away, too—inside them; a few moments in the residual heat of the sun oven with butter and herbs, and each took two of the now bright red segments. Tozri showed them how to open the slit on the underside and turn out the tender, succulent meat. It was more like lobster than anything else—and sweeter. Kraxxi couldn't believe that he, child of a royal court, had never tasted this before. Then again, Barrax's court was more austere than opulent. By the time they'd finished their impromptu feast, augmented with watered wine and

212 ~ TOM DEITZ

dried meat steamed in the oven, the sky was dark blue, the stars sparkling, and it was more than time to travel. Elvix, as usual, readied the horses. Olrix and Kraxxi folded and packed the tent.

But for some reason everyone hesitated. Perhaps the finality *had* sunk in. Another night, and there was no going back. No one discussed it, but Kraxxi's gaze kept returning to the mountains behind him, still edged with sunset red on their peaks. As if to mirror their anticipation, the wind whipped up: a nervous breeze from the south—where before winds had come from the north.

Kraxxi frowned even as he raised his sylk mask. That breeze had carried the bite of blowing sand.

And then he saw it, even as Olrix uttered a terse, "Oh great Gods!"

A dark cloud hung on the southwest horizon, where before there'd been only the vague line between land and sky. Already stars were vanishing.

"Sandstorm," Elvix spat. "We go now. If we ride for all we're worth, we may outrun it!"

Kraxxi squinted at the rising gloom. "In the dark?"

"In the light of at least two moons," she retorted. "But come. The wind blows northeast and we go northwest. It should hide our tracks. If any follow us, it'll delay them—if we can avoid it ourselves, or stay on its fringe."

Tozri mounted up beside him. "*If,* my sister says. Brave words."

She glared at him. "Chance. Or Fate. The Gods of the Eronese. They make it so we can't go back—after we've decided as much. They seal one door, but they open another. I think we should take it."

Kraxxi set his jaw. And then, without really intending to, he kicked his mount and galloped off across the moonlit sands. The others followed. If there was protest, it was lost in the howl of rising wind.

CHAPTER XIX:

CONFESSIONS

(ERON: GEM-HOLD-WINTER—NEAR WINTER: DAY XXXIV—MIDMORNING)

~~~~~~~~~~~~~~~~~~

Snow, Avall thought, *Eight-damned snow!* More snow and then more snow again! Was there no end to the wretched stuff? Twenty years old, he was; twenty years of enduring Deep Winter, and four of them in other winter holds. But never one like this!

Drifts lay against the sides of Gem-Hold like sleeping giants, the glittering white slopes already twice a man's height, save at the forecourt, which was kept clear—barely. Icicles hung from the cliffs of Tar-Megon, where the steam that made the hold endurable froze against the stone. The wind howled around the deserted arcades, and half the walls were cased in frozen runoff from the heated porches. Fire and ice—heat and cold. Nowhere had Avall seen that battle waged as viciously as here.

He stared out the bedroom window at the heavy flakes drifting down the light well. He hated it. Why, he could barely see the opposite wall—and it was no more than six spans away! Never mind those to right and left, where candles burned even during the day in spite of whole walls made of mirrors in the workrooms, so as to capture all available light.

A mild winter, the weather-witches said? Not hardly!

Frustrated, he started pacing. Back and forth along the window wall, running his hands along the stone sill. Watching his breath freeze and melt on the thick glass panes. Yet even so, the artist in him was thinking. Frost patterns were actually quite attractive; ordered, yet chaotic. Perhaps if he took some of these patterns and worked with them a bit, they'd provide the cata-lyst he needed to become truly excited about the helm the High King had de-manded he make. He had the shape worked out. Strynn had helped there, and had even had two excellent books on the theory of armor cached among her gear—books good for determining how much space one needed to leave for eyeslots, for breathing, and so on. What he'd lacked was a unifying visual motif to at once glorify the King and Kingdom, challenge his craft, yet make the thing uniquely his own. Perhaps he had it now.

About time, too. He was nearly half an eighth late getting started and his nerves were starting to fray, never mind Eddyn's incessant lurking about, which made everything more complicated. Try as he would to avoid his ri-val, it never seemed to work—not that he thought Eddyn was seeking him, either. Still, they'd wound up in the same breakfast rotation, and for the first three days had had mining duty together—until a legitimately sprained muscle had got Eddyn excused for one day, then put back on a different shift. But they were constantly running into each other on the main staircase that linked Smithcraft's various apartments, and he was often in the craft common room playing board games with Rrath, who seemed to be spending as much time there as in his own suite.

At least Strynn had an excuse to remain in theirs. She was in the middle stages of her pregnancy now, and it was finally beginning to manifest—both visually and in attitude. Given how nontraumatic the first stages had been it was easy to forget all the changes going on inside her. Now, however, they were upon her with a vengeance, so that she kept to her bed most mornings. She hated it, too—not only how she felt, but how it made her irritable—a situation exacerbated by their relatively close quarters. And made worse again by the fact that she rarely felt like working on her own commission.

At least she was spared duty in the mines—hard duty, anyway; though even she sorted pulverized stone in search of chips of color. She'd already found—and been able to keep—one remarkable ruby. And two sapphires.

Poor girl.

Eddyn, however—

Avall pounded the wall beside the window in frustration. If only he could escape the man for just a day! He'd hoped to get away with Rann that morn-ing, for a hunt. He had a free day coming, after five in the mines, and Rann had promised to show him an ice-lynx run, which would've involved an overnight stay at a small half station. Which would've done him more good than he could imagine: just him and his best friend, the thrill of the hunt, and no expectations.

But the snow—*this* snow—had ruined it. *Nobody* was going out today for any reason, the Hold-Warden had ordained. And certainly not for anything as frivolous as hunting something no one could eat. Not even the promise of a wrought-silver circlet lined with lynx fur had prevailed against Crim san Myrk, Gem-Hold's tough old mistress.

Another round of pacing, and Avall breathed on the window again, staring absently as his breath fogged the glass, froze, then melted once more in a gust of warmth from the heat vents below it. The ice-crystal idea wasn't bad. He'd just step into the workroom and get some paper and a pen . . .

Quickly, before that particularly interesting array in the lower right corner vanished. He was almost running when he made the sitting room—and almost knocked Strynn down as he swung through the door. She grunted and staggered back, clutching her stomach more as a defensive gesture than from actual pain. "Careful," she snapped. "Is haste worth what you risk?"

He skidded to a halt and glared back at her—as angry at her as he'd ever been. "Since you don't know what I risk," he retorted, "that's not a very good question."

Her gaze would've melted metal. "I'm sorry," she gritted, without conviction.

He scowled, biting his lip, already regretting what he'd said—what he'd almost done. "Beauty is sometimes transitory."

"So," she spat to his departing back, as she snared a bottle of wine from the table by the bedroom door, "is love."

Avall chose not to hear that last. If he thought about it, it would only make him angrier—at Eddyn, at the winter, at himself for hurting someone he cared about, and who had done him no harm. Better not to think about it now; better to focus what was not an infinite amount of time on the one thing he knew with absolute conviction he could do right.

Strynn was trying hard not to cry as she made her way along the arcade around the enormous central common chamber on the way to her one source of solace, which lay all the way on the hold's other end. She hadn't cried when Eddyn raped her. She hadn't cried when her pregnancy had been confirmed. And she hadn't cried when she'd left Tir-Eron and most of those she loved. So why was she fighting tears now? Avall had things on his mind—legitimate things, some of which concerned her, too. And when they were making together, *talking* about making, or even *planning* making (for they'd already chosen the material they'd use for their various projects, and she'd arranged for forge time), it was a wonder. Their nights were much improved as well, now that they'd had time to adjust to each other's presence—and to unfamiliar bodies constructed in unfamiliar ways. Avall had a nice body, and now that they'd finally been able to share fully with each other, it was—or had been—one more release for both of them.

Until now, when he'd hurt her by being thoughtless, selfish, and unconcerned, which, if not much like Avall, was a great deal like men in general. Which made her wonder which was the actual him?

Which was why she was going where she was. To seek someone who, though himself male, seemed to have no thought but to please.

A pause to see if Eddyn were about, so as to plan her route accordingly, and she moved on again: down another corridor until she turned a corner and saw a certain sigil worked in marble in the floor. Another right, then a left, and she knocked four times on a particular door. Twice, then twice again: a signature code to the inhabitant that she was exercising the grace he'd granted her to enter of her own free will.

Hearing no reply, she tried the handle. No resistance, which meant he was home. A deep breath, a pause to wipe away tears he wouldn't see anyway, and Strynn eased into the room.

Kylin sat, as he always seemed to, on the sofa behind his harp. Rann had moved it to her and Avall's quarters just for them, but now it was back where it belonged. Kylin also, as he always did, smiled radiantly as she entered—and called her name.

"Even without the knock, I would know you," he murmured. "You breathe a certain way, from a certain height, and you wear that perfume."

"That your sister showed me how to make at Scent," she sighed. "Before I knew she was your sister."

"You sound sad."

She nodded, then realized how stupid that was.

"I can hear you nod. Fabric makes a certain noise. It's not hard, if you make a point of noticing such things. Now—sit. Talk to me. Tell me of the snow. And then I'll play a song for you, to show you how snow sounds to me, and ice making patterns on the windows."

"And then perhaps a song to warm my soul?" she dared, as she helped herself to her accustomed seat across from him. Hot cider steamed on a side table. His rooms weren't far from the kitchens, and Kylin was very much loved. She helped herself to a mug; he'd pour his own when he desired.

"Is your soul cold?" he wondered. If he could see, she somehow knew, he'd be regarding her intently from beneath his mask.

"Sometimes." She looked past him to the narrow window that gave onto his light well. He could tell dark from light, but that was all.

"Sometimes," she repeated. "We've known each other forever, Avall and I. Sometimes he's seemed oldest, sometimes I have. We know many of the same people, have many of the same friends. I'm bond-sister with his twin. I know Rann almost as well as he does because for two years you never saw one without the other, and Fate was always throwing the three of us together."

"Are you jealous?"

She bit her lip. "It existed before he and I existed—before we were wed. You can't not take pleasure in seeing that much unconditional love. But I've had Avall to myself through a very hard time. I've started thinking of him as mine above all others. I'm not used to sharing him anymore."

"But your soul is cold."

Another nod. "I married him because I had to wed or there'd have been disaster that would've hurt many many people I loved—including Avall. He's smart, he's talented, he's nice to look at. He's considerate most of the time. He's amazing when his passions are aroused—his passion for work, I mean. I think it's going to be a long time—at least until after I have this child—before he'll truly let himself go otherwise, and that's probably just as well."

"Fine," Kylin broke in. "But why did he marry you?"

Another deep breath. "Because it was the right thing to do. Granted, I was the one who asked him—I had to name a father, so I really had no choice—but he handled it very well, once he thought about it, and Merryn didn't say a word, though Eellon did. He's sworn to me that I'll always be the first person in his life, and I'm sure he'll try to make that so. But I'll never be the first *thing* in his life. That's always and forever going to be making. 'Gold never has bad days,' he used to say, when he'd first started getting really good at working with the stuff. 'It's always bright. You can make it into almost anything. It never bites you like steel. If you ruin it utterly, you can always melt it down and start over. It never cries.'"

Kylin eased sideways to sit behind the harp. He touched a string absently: one perfect note that precisely reflected Strynn's unfocused anguish and drew it to crystal focus.

"You wish, though, that just one time, he'd put you first?"

She shook her head. "I . . . I don't think I'd want to change him. I think we both know that strange as our pairing is, neither of us could do better. I had to wed, and he'd have been reviled if he didn't pass on his extraordinary gifts. He's told me more than once that he'd never find a better match than me." A deep breath. "I told him, I thought he meant a better match that actually was alive . . . and he laughed and said I was likely right. And I knew I'd never find a better match than him either, because I know he actually does care for *me* and not for the symbol I've, much against my will, become."

"Which is why you come here? Because you know I can't see?"

She smiled. "Because you see better than anyone else."

He smiled back. "Sit, pretty lady," he whispered. "And I'll play you a song about summer."

And for the next half hour Strynn cried—not from sadness, but from the sheer joy of Kylin's music.

. . .

"You're stiff as rusty iron," Rann informed Avall, from behind him. "Drawing all day's not supposed to make you stiff!" He punctuated the remark
with an especially hard squeeze on Avall's bare shoulders. He'd been knead-
ing them—and most of the rest of Avall's head, neck, and torso, for the last
half hand.

Avall reached up to wipe steam-sweat off his face, thinking he'd need to
get a haircut soon. And tried to relax. Rann, sitting in the hot-pool behind
him, shifted forward to accommodate as Avall leaned back into his chest.
The steam felt heavenly. And the heat. And Rann's fingers. Not to mention
just having his bond-brother nearby again. "It makes you squint," Avall
muttered at last, having finally realized his friend expected an answer. "The
light wasn't good when I was drawing, but I had to do it then, because I
knew if I waited I'd lose the pattern. Something new would grow over it, or
whatever. And then some even better ones appeared, but it was getting late.
And I *was* straining forward."

"More than I need to know," Rann told him roughly, shifting his attention
from Avall's uncooperative shoulders to the area just below the collarbones.

Avall sighed. "You have no idea how long I've needed this." He let his
eyes slide closed, shutting out the candlelit dimness of this section of the
baths—all but deserted now, not that it mattered. Closeness was nothing to
be ashamed of, and Rann was his bond-brother: one level less close than actual family and the same as a spouse before Law, if not by convention. He
was more concerned with what was heard when naked men fresh from the
mines occasionally ambled along the paved stone around him. They'd see
nothing they hadn't seen before; nothing he hadn't seen in turn. True intimacy was for other places. Not that this didn't feel good. And not that Rann
wasn't enjoying it, too. It wasn't *entirely* innocent.

"Something's bothering you," Rann whispered.

"I . . . I think I hurt Strynn."

"Did she say you had?"

"Didn't need to. She snapped at me—with reason. But it wasn't anger, it
was hurt. I don't like to hurt people, but there's no way you can live, it seems
to me, without hurting somebody practically every day. Anytime three people are together and you choose to talk to one over the other or to answer one
question first, you're hurting someone at some level."

Rann freed a hand to bat one ear gently. "You think too much. You've
strained your brain as much as your eyes, and I can't reach in there and
loosen that."

"You'd try, though, wouldn't you?"

"If I could. You'd do the same."

Another sigh, as they both relaxed backward, half-floating, one head above the other, Rann's hands folded on Avall's chest. "I really was too young to marry. But there truly was no choice."

Rann snorted. "Most people would've killed to have so little 'choice'—the most beautiful woman in the world."

"And still human. And still incredibly sweet and smart and talented. Why can't I love her more?"

"Because she's not what you want just now. She's like good advice. When you get it, you resent it. It's years later, sometimes, that you realize it even *was* good."

Avall tried to twist around to look at him but failed. "What's made you so wise, all of a sudden? You're barely an eighth older than me."

"I'm not wise. I'm simply less . . . preoccupied."

"What do you mean by that?"

"That because I'm decently competent at a lot of things but not exceptional at anything—"

"—except being my friend—"

"—except that, I've been left to find my own level. Nobody's ever goaded me like they have you or, Eight forbid, poor Eddyn, who never gets *any* rest at all. At least Eellon lets you know he cares about you. You never know with the Spider-Chief."

"All of which means?"

"That I've had time to watch and think instead of do, do, do. You've spent so much of your life living up to others' expectations you've never had time to figure out what *you* want."

"Making. That's it."

"And a good thing you love it, too. But we don't all do that like you do. I think—I'm sorry if this hurts you, but I think you've made that your God because that was the one safe thing. You always knew that no matter how badly you failed otherwise, you could knock out a gold belt buckle one night and have them praising you to the skies the next day. There's—I guess there's such a thing as being too good."

Avall patted the hands to stillness. "So you're saying that I need to give my . . . soul some work?"

"I'm saying you should think about it. I'm saying Strynn would kill to have this kind of closeness."

"We've done this, she and I."

"But not so freely, I bet; not without doubt or barriers, no matter how you try. You know perfectly well that if you'd said to me what you said to her, even casually, I'd have knocked you down and sat on you until you apologized."

"She's pregnant, for Eight's sake!"

"And also from War-Hold. She could've taken you down if she wanted."

"She didn't take down Eddyn!"

"He caught her completely off guard. No woman expects that from someone she knows. They're too conditioned. So are we. Do you know even one man who's forced himself on a woman? Besides Eddyn?"

"No."

"There you have it. These aren't normal times. You, Strynn, Eddyn—you're the kind of folks you hear about a hundred years later. Trust me, I know."

"What about you?"

"I'm the one who tells the stories."

Avall smiled, knowing Rann could sense it even from the back by the way his cheeks moved. "I envy the woman who gets you."

Silence, for a moment, save for the pad of feet passing the privacy curtain, the drip of steam condensing off the ceiling. And slow, languid breathing.

"Does it bother you?" Avall asked softly, "that there's no good reason she couldn't have married you? That you'd have been better for her than I am?"

More silence. Then: "She knew that if she married you, she'd only have to share you with your art. She knew that if she married me, she'd have to share me with you. Sharing with a God is always easier than sharing with a man."

For a long time after, they simply sprawled there in the soothing water. Not speaking, barely moving, thinking only in their hearts.

Strynn was asleep when a very clean and relaxed Avall returned to the suite far later than anticipated. He moved silently around the bedroom, making no more noise than the wind and the settling of the building as he slowly undressed. She'd left a light on: a candle on the stone chest next to the bed. Its glow pooled around her, where she lay on her back, facing away. She looked peaceful. Beautiful. Her left hand was raised beside her cheek, palm out, fingers folded like the petals of a flower. Something about the light drew his eye, as the ice had that morning. Now that he'd noticed those patterns, there were similar patterns everywhere, and here they were again: creases and valleys on the palms of Strynn's hands, whorls within whorls upon her fingers. Suppose he took some of that design . . .

He stared at his own hands. He had the same, of course: different, but the same, and these hands would never leave him, would be with him whenever he needed them. He could draw the patterns there anytime.

But, he suddenly realized, he needed to draw Strynn's. If he could incorporate some of her into his work—not her advice, but some of her *self,* something he took from her all unknowing and gave back, and didn't reveal until the work was complete—maybe then she'd know how much he cared. That was all he could do. He could do that deeply and passionately—or with as much passion as he ever *could* feel.

He eased to the workroom and retrieved his pad. And he drew Strynn's hands and fingers and what he could make out of the whorls on those delicate fingertips until the candle guttered and his eyes would focus no longer. And without knowing it, he also drew part of his soul.

(ERON: WAR-HOLD-WINTER—NEAR WINTER: DAY XXXIV: MIDNIGHT)

Merryn had been sitting in her window seat for maybe a finger. She was clad in a loose velvet night robe, with her knees drawn up, her back to the stone wall, and her hair hanging free across her shoulder, still damp from a much-needed end-of-the-day bath. She'd been toying with it absently, waiting for it to dry before rebinding in into her warrior's tail. Her feet were bare on the leather-and-velvet cushion, and the room was dark, save for a single candle in a glow-globe by the door in the opposite wall. It was barely enough light to see by, but still plagued her with reflections, as she'd stared through the thick glazing toward the starlit north and thought about her brother and her bond-sister and how they fared up at Gem, and wondered how much snow they'd had yet and how much Strynn was showing and how she was coping now that Avall had the company of his bond-brother again. She remained there maybe another finger, then got up to check the wine she'd left mulling as a sleep posset—not that she needed one, as hard as she'd been working lately—as hard as she'd ever worked in her life, in fact.

Ten steps, from window to adjoining wall, then back again.

When she returned, someone was sitting in the window seat perfectly mirroring the pose she'd previously affected.

Someone in dead black, utterly glossless, helm and body armor. A black surcoat covered the body, of some equally dull fabric she didn't recognize.

To her credit she didn't falter as she froze in place, but her grip tightened on the goblet. It might do for a weapon until she could reach others.

The figure rose slowly, deliberately, as she held her ground. She didn't speak. That would betray too much. That was for this impossible visitor to initiate. If speech was what it intended, for its hand rested on the hilt of a long black sword.

"The Night Guard," it said, in a voice so utterly neutral it could have belonged to either sex, "has its eye on you."

Merryn swallowed—and regretted it at once. The Night Guard, was it?

They'd impressed her upon arrival, and that was a fact. And she had been making (she thought) discreet inquiries about them. She steeled herself to speak.

The figure preempted her. "Some of the Hundred will leave with the coming of spring, but there must always be a hundred here, in fact, or in training. It may be that you will become one of that number."

And without further word, the figure strode past her, to her door, which she was certain she remembered bolting. It paused there and turned once more to face her. "The key," it said, "will take you to the door."

"What key?" she almost demanded, but thought better of it. And in any event, in the instant it took her to decide as much, the figure opened the door and was gone.

She stared after it for a moment, then drained her wine, and returned to her window and her reverie—might as well, for she knew with absolute conviction that if she'd rushed to the door and peered down the hall she would've seen nothing. And when she went to bed, she found something hard under her pillow that hadn't been there when she'd made the bed that morning.

A simple, utterly glossless, black key.

Somewhere in War-Hold, she reckoned, there must therefore also be a simple, utterly glossless, black door.

CHAPTER XX:

DOUBTS AND SHADOWS

(ERON: ANGEN'S SPINE—YEAR BIRTH: DAY XLIII—LATE AFTERNOON)

~~~~~~~~~~

*O*h no!"
          Words.
          Muttered.

Falling into the frigid air like drops of sleet. Hard as the naked stone beneath thin-gloved hands. Empty of hope as the leaden sky.

Five days ago, back on the Flat, when their problems had been heat, scorpions, and the illusion of pursuit, Kraxxi might have felt something when he heard Elvix utter that phrase. At least he might've felt a fragment of despair. He had nothing to spare for such things now.

Nor for the hope that had fled with those awful words he'd dreaded since they'd begun that climb just past noon.

Not even for anger—at himself, for setting all this absurd flight in motion, or at the triplets who should've known better and let him forge ahead to his own doom.

"What?" he called mechanically. And it was as if somebody else spoke, as if that was no real person half-sprawled, half-kneeling across the bare icy rock a span above him, clad in leather and wool—everything she owned: both her hunting togs (stripped of all insignia now) and the desert clothing they'd bought since setting out. She looked like a clump of lichen: the sand-colored cloak caked with dirt cemented there by ice that melted in the scanty heat of the tent back down the mountain, then refroze when she ventured outside. The wind whipping out of the northwest plastered her clothes to her in contorted shapes, but no more contorted than the black, twisted rocks beneath them, where patches of ice and obsidian that looked like ice but cut like razors lurked in unexpected places.

"You'll have to come up," Elvix called. "I don't want the blame when we tell the others."

Kraxxi would've asked, "Tell them what?" had he any energy, which he hadn't. Moving took most of it—fighting gravity, fighting the wind, fighting footing that had no regard for balance. Breathing required the rest.

Elvix looked around, all but her eyes hidden behind a wrap of wool. Her eyelids were reddened, but not the color of frostbite. She gestured irritably.

Somehow Kraxxi found strength to scramble up beside her. Wind bit at him as he approached, slapping at him sharply from over the ridge, making his eyes tear, so that he had to wipe them before he could truly see.

More cursed mountains.

Another ridge and higher, rising above a slight declivity that had been masked by the slope they'd just ascended. They'd thought this might be the top—*a* top, anyway. They'd thought it might be downhill from here. They'd thought there might be some sign of something they could eat.

There was nothing. The peak taunted them: two shots away, and higher. Barer, colder. More forbidding. He wondered if those were clouds or mountain-smokes farther on, and almost hoped the latter. At least if the mountain belched fire, as some did hereabouts, he might possibly die warm—though he was no longer certain he remembered what warm was.

"Well," Elvix sighed, as she caught sight of his expression. "I know it doesn't help, but I'm sorry."

Kraxxi wanted to hit her. "Not your fault," he managed instead. "Not *your* fault," repeated, louder, addressing the mountain as much as anything, as long-suppressed fury rose up in him. Or perhaps, this high, he was addressing the Gods, though whether his or The Eight of Eron, he had no idea. *"Not your fault!"* he screamed. "Not your fault that sandstorm got us lost! Not your fault I thought it would be shorter to go over than around. Not your fault the horse with all the food drowned. Not your fault I wanted to do this in the first place. Not your fault I got Azzli killed."

"I'm *sorry!*" Elvix repeated.

Kraxxi hit her. It was his arm that snapped out, at any rate, his half-numb fist that impacted her face at the angle of her jaw. His heart that fell deeper into a pit of despair whose bottom he already thought he'd plumbed.

His eyes that widened in horror as she lost what hadn't been the most secure of balances and tumbled back down the slope they'd spent the last two hands scaling. "Elvix!" he screamed, flailing for her, even as another part yelled, *"Gods damn it! I only wanted one thing to go right today. I only wanted you not to defy me!"*

Something so stupid. Overreaction—and he might have spoiled what little remained intact of this trip, their desires, maybe even—now—their friendship.

He scrambled after her, angling down the slope on all fours while she kept on sliding and his brain kept making up excuses and arguments, telling him to go on over the ridge and not come back: that his friends didn't need a friend like him and back in Ixti they could probably gain forgiveness if they told where he had gone. Telling him that no words existed that would satisfy Olrix and Tozri, waiting back in the tent down at the timberline, where the two of them watched horses that could go no higher, and waited for word of their fate.

He wondered if they'd kill him if he asked them to.

Not with his luck. Not if Elvix wouldn't heed so small a request as not to apologize. He was bleeding, he realized; blood bloomed through his glove.

Elvix had finally stopped rolling a dozen spans below him, where she'd fetched up against one of the hard ridges that corrugated the mountainside. He heard her "oof" even here, the sound fighting a sudden new surge of wind that whipped over the ridge behind him, bringing an even more stinging cold: the prickly stabbings of sleet. Four shots from the tent, and sleet. No food to take back to assuage their raging bellies. Another debate on whether to retreat or forge ahead—he was starting to favor the former. On whether to kill one of the horses for food and rely a few days longer on Fate to see them somewhere they could maybe, just possibly, survive.

"Are you . . . ?" he shouted, as the slope turned treacherous and sent him sliding on his back down what proved to be ice over obsidian. He braced for impact, wondering if there was any give left in his frozen legs. Hit. Managed to absorb some of the weight by flexing, and slipped left to where Elvix lay blinking, gasping for breath that wouldn't come, that he prayed was simply the wind knocked from her and not a broken rib or punctured lung.

She glared at him. "If you don't say it, I won't." The words were calm, but her eyes looked colder than the ice.

"I'll explain an eighth from now."

She almost grinned. "I hope I'm alive to listen."

He eased in beside her, suppressing an urge to reach out and touch her bruised cheek, wondering how much of the blood there was his doing, how much the mountain's work. "Anything hurt more than it ought?"

She felt at her left wrist, flexed it experimentally, wincing as she moved it a certain way. "I'll tell you when I thaw. Right now—I think I can walk. Wouldn't want to count on this, though."

He pondered their location—farther down the mountain than the place they'd started upslope, which might actually give them an easier way back to the ridge they'd followed here.

"Peace," he gasped. "Or truce." He held out his hand. She took it with her good one and let him pull her up, though she weighed almost as much as he. His anger fled—melted away by fear—all he could think now was to hug her, but he didn't dare, not with what he'd almost done. Which she had also to be thinking. "I—" he began, then stopped, for the wind had shifted again and the sleet had turned to snow. The sky that had been gray was white. The ridge above them was fading from clarity behind the tiny flakes swirling there.

"I hate wind!" he spat because he had to vent some anger or explode.

"The lower we go, the less cold—maybe," Elvix said, and shoved him toward what passed for a trail. "We don't dare hesitate."

To Kraxxi's relief, his body proved to have more sense than his mind and already had set itself moving. Two hands later, the only remaining landmarks were the darkness to the right, which was the slope of the mountain they were traversing, and the deeper dark below them, which was the last of the woods and also their goal. Black, white, and gray: That defined the world. Moving from a lighter gray toward a dark. No real color at all save the blood on his glove and even that faded in the blowing snow unless he held it close to his eyes.

His feet were numb. His legs worked because they had to. His arms moved in theory, but mostly he clamped them around himself as he stumped ever onward, with Elvix plodding grimly along behind, setting the rhythm of his feet with her steadier tread.

He wondered if anyone back at court would know him now, with over an eighth in the wild having worn most of the softness off his already slender body. He knew his face had changed: burned by the sun, peeled off, burned again, and then assaulted by snow. Never mind his scruffy, halfhearted beard and stubbly hair. It itched, it caught snow, but it warmed a little. It was also a comfort Elvix and Olrix lacked, and he felt guilty for that.

He tripped, stumbled, started, jerked himself back to alertness, realizing to his alarm that the world had started tunneling, that gray and white and black were beginning to spin together, that his body was farther from his *self* than it had ever been.

"Th-here," Elvix called behind him, her voice barely distinguishable from her chattering teeth. Kraxxi squinted, blinking into a spiraling gray nothing swept with a paler gray. At first he didn't see it, but then he did: a darkness that wasn't black stone but green boughs cut and dragged, then flung across the tent when they'd made camp. And closer, as the trail shifted around to give better view, the most welcome sight Kraxxi had ever seen: a tiny spark of flame battling bravely against the sleet and wind. Hope flared there, brighter than that fire, even as he recalled with new regret the fact that it would have to stay outside, warming the endless night because they dared not bring open flame inside so small a shelter.

Closer and he was running, but then the wind caught him and flung him faster than he wanted, and the fire flickered and to his utter dismay went out, leaving him wondering if he was even alive.

"Kraxxi!" someone cried. He groped that way as much as turned, almost stumbling over the tent before he found the entrance, noting how heavy the boughs already were with snow. A glance back up the mountains showed a soft-edged blur resolving from a glare of white. A pink that might have been a face, dark spots of eyes.

"Here," he called, as he stood aside for Elvix to scramble into the tent before him. A single squat candle in a globed lamp burned there, just beside the door, but it was like summer after winter, or day after night. The beige of the tent walls was the brightest of colors. The dull-toned wools and leathers shone like jewels after the bleached tints without.

"One of the horses died," the humped shape that was Olrix volunteered from the far right corner. "I'll butcher it in the morning if the storm subsides. In the meantime . . . I've saved some of the blood." She held out a cup full of something dark and red, that stank yet smelled tantalizing. Elvix took it before Kraxxi could react. "No food." He blurted out. "No way down."

"No hope?" Olrix dared.

Elvix wiped blood from her lips and handed the cup to Kraxxi, who let the person who was mostly his outside-self drink without tasting or thinking, while the other, inner him tried to make sense of their situation.

Silence.

Olrix pried the cup from his fingers and resettled it at the edge of the tent, which had just enough floor for four people to sleep close by each other if none were very tall. "I didn't kill the horse," she said. "I swear. If you don't like it, I'm—"

"No," Elvix warned. "Don't say it."

"Tomorrow I'll cook," Tozri muttered dreamily, as he snuggled down in his blankets with Elvix next to him, Olrix on her other side, and Kraxxi on the edge, by the wall. The tent was warmer than outdoors, and there was less wind; he didn't need to worry about it blowing away. And he assumed (because she'd told him as much over and over the last few days) that Olrix knew enough about horses not to let one die of exposure unless there was no alternative.

There being nothing else to do, and he being bone-tired from the climb, he extinguished the candle and slept.

When he awoke, night had fallen, but wind or no wind, storm or no storm, his bladder demanded relief. Swearing under his breath, he wriggled out of his warm nest and stumbled out of the tent.

The light that enfolded him was that eerie blue-whiteness that can only arise when moonlight shines on perfect snow. And so it was: The whole world beyond the front of the tent was a solid sheet of frosty, glittering white. The sky was dark blue, and a moon gleamed there. It was beautiful—and eerie—and dreamlike. And he knew it might kill them very soon.

The next time Kraxxi awoke was to sudden alarm. He blinked, squinting into a glare that was neither the sun nor firelight. A noisy thrashing to his right was Olrix preceding him into wakefulness—and thence into full alert, to judge by the way she was fumbling around for whatever weapons came to hand. Her fingers reached for her sword just as other fingers folded firmly over them and pried it from her grip. Words flew about the tent: muttered imprecations, their various names, and the word "attack." And other words in unfamiliar voices—and worse, an unfamiliar tongue.

He'd managed to lever himself upright, and to feel for his own sword (though how he'd use it in here, he had no idea), when he finally got a good look at the figure—the woman—who'd planted herself neatly in the door slit with a drawn sword on her lap and two faces, both male, peering in over shoulders clad in a bloodred cloak of heavy wool. Kraxxi's first impulse was to tell her that they were letting out the heat, his second to wonder what time—or day—it was; his third to speculate whether the odd words the woman was peppering them with were Eronese spoken properly—as, for instance, by a native. And his final one, when the woman raised a hand and let her snow-veil fall so that she might make her words clearer, was that she was a damned fine-looking woman indeed.

Strong jaw, but softer-featured overall than Olrix or Elvix. Eyes dark blue where theirs were brown; black hair—what showed beneath a coif and cap helm; short, straight nose, full lips, firm chin. And fair, fair skin that showed no mark of the cold. Nor was she much older than he, if any. She was also looking very perplexed. He glanced around at his companions, taking his cues from them. Olrix was merely observing. Tozri looked guarded and had his hand on his dagger hilt, but was doing nothing overtly confrontational—which was wise. Elvix looked hissing angry, like a cornered cat, but likewise held her ground.

The woman spoke.

It *was* Eronese (there really was nothing else it could be, save some obscure monastic cants); but Kraxxi couldn't get the syntax straight from the scanty bit he knew. Eventually the woman looked exasperated and gestured toward herself. "Merryn," she said slowly and clearly. Likely her name.

They blinked at her neutrally. Kraxxi couldn't decide whether to be scared to death or vastly relieved that someone had come upon them. He hoped they had their story straight, the one they'd debated for so long. That they were part of the last trade caravan out of Ixti, and had been attacked by geens in the desert. They'd fled, then been caught in a sandstorm and decided the odds of finding food were better in the mountains than on the Flat. Their names were to be their own, but shorter. Krax; Ole, Elv, and Toz.

Merryn, if that was in fact her name, looked even more exasperated than before and turned briefly to call to someone outside, though her eyes remained on them. More talk followed, in Eronese, and Merryn backed up, her hand never leaving her sword, but gesturing with the other for them to come outside.

Kraxxi exchanged glances with his companions. "You understand any of that?" he whispered to Olrix, who spoke the language, courtesy of her mother. Her less scholarly siblings had never bothered.

She nodded tersely.

A shrug. "If they wanted to kill us, they would have by now. If they want to fight, it's better done outside than here."

"I don't think they want to fight," Tozri muttered. "This looks like a military band, not a raider's. Patrol, I'd say. Given that we're close to the border, that would make sense."

Kraxxi gnawed his lip. "If they speak, feign ignorance," he told Olrix. "But listen. If you feel we can trust them, I'll trust *you* to decide when and how to reply."

He got no more time for instruction, for Merryn had obviously reached the end of her patience and had seized Elvix with one hand, while holding her at sword's point with the other. Elvix glared at her and slowly removed her hand from her dagger, then as deliberately pushed the hand from her arm, pointed toward the entrance, and crawled that way. Kraxxi saw her boots depart, then waited for Olrix to follow. Tozri was next, and he went last.

The light was the pink glow of early morning, and Kraxxi found himself staring at the snow-smoothed glade, the blue sky, the dark trees in a semicircle around them; at the four remaining horses puffing clouds of breath into the air while two men in those red cloaks tended them.

And at two more men and the woman facing them, their faces grim and stern but not truly threatening, though they all held drawn swords as they effectively moved to block escape. Kraxxi's main impression was of how impossibly red those cloaks were against the snow. He tried to think what he'd heard about Eronese clans and the crafts they controlled. Each had an insignia color. But which was red? War-Hold? Was that it? Red for blood, which made sense. And War-Hold was in the south, somewhere in Angen's Spine.

Maybe this *was* a patrol. Maybe they *had* been rescued. Or taken prisoner. The Eronese were humane. But he wasn't sure how they regarded spies.

Nor did it matter for the nonce, for the men who'd been tending the horses rejoined their fellows. Words passed, then one held Elvix at sword point while the woman methodically divested her of every weapon she possessed. The same for Olrix, and then the roles were reversed, with the woman covering first Tozri, then Kraxxi while her companions removed their sword belts, daggers, and the second dagger in Tozri's boot, going on to pat them down thoroughly up both legs, around the waist, and down both arms.

Eventually the cold found him, and he shivered, breath ghosting out copiously. He shivered again. The woman scowled, said something, and watched carefully as one of the men ducked into the tent to return with their cloaks. Kraxxi claimed his and waited.

The woman barked a short phrase, obviously a question. Kraxxi looked blank, as did Tozri. Olrix started to, then exhaled abruptly—and spoke back in that same tongue.

The woman's brows shot up, but she seemed to relax minutely. Olrix spoke again: another question, to which the woman responded in turn.

"They asked who we are," Olrix informed them. "I told them our names, that we were from Ixti, about the sandstorm and the horse being lost, and that we'd decided to try our luck in Eron rather than dare the Flat, hoping to reconnect with our caravan."

"Ask them who they are."

Olrix frowned but complied. The reply was quick. "They say they won't harm us but that we must go with them for our own sake. They say they'll leave someone here with the horses and send a party for them. In the meantime, we're to go with them."

"Prisoners?"

"Under guard—which only makes sense."

"Do you see any alternative?"

"I see probably decent people being careful of their borders as politely as circumstances allow."

"Ask them if they have any food. Tell them we'll go with them if they'll show good faith by feeding us now."

Olrix gnawed her lip, then spoke again to the woman, who was evidently leader of the band. More conversation ensued, this time rather protracted. Before it was over, two of the men were laying a small fire. A short while later a pot of frozen stew was thawing. The scent was heavenly. Everyone seemed to relax somewhat, though the Eronese took the precaution of tying the Ixtians' legs loosely together with crimson cord.

Merryn and Olrix spoke some more.

As best Kraxxi could tell from Olrix's sporadic translation, someone on patrol from an unspecified location had spotted him and Elvix by chance yesterday evening. That had been duly reported and a rescue party dispatched, which had only now located them. It wasn't far to their intended destination, but in this weather the horses would have to go by another route and would be at least a day in transit.

By the end of which discussion the food was pronounced done, and Kraxxi found himself staring down at a bowl of dark spicy stew, thick with meat, mushrooms, and tubers. He sampled it with the fine silver spoon they handed him. It was more than wonderful.

The ale wasn't bad either—for an Eronese brew.

And then they could stall no longer. Negotiations with their captors failed to gain them return of their packs, save for a promise that they would be delivered with the horses. Kraxxi prayed they'd been thorough in removing all signs of office or titles and fretted over the visibility of the royal signet ring he'd sewn into the waistband of his breeches, outside one of the grommets that laced them closed.

The woman rose first, motioning the rest of them up. They left the fire for the stoic-looking man who would remain with the horses. Olrix wasn't shy about telling him what she knew of their idiosyncrasies either, so that the sun was halfway to noon before they marched out upon that pristine snow, heading back toward the ridge he and Elvix had climbed the day before. This time, however, they went over.

Kraxxi was panting hard when they eased around the west flank of the peak he and Elvix had seen ahead of them yesterday—the one that had made them turn back in despair, thinking it presented yet another barrier atop the ones they'd already surmounted.

Had they only known. For as they made their way around a road that wasn't really a road nor yet wholly natural, he heard Elvix gasp in astonishment. He slipped around the solid mass of stone, and then he saw.

Air and space opened before him, revealing mountains as far as he could see to the north and west, with a faint gleam of ocean to the right. Before them, the trail became a road in truth, swooping down into a valley in which withered grass occasionally showed through melting snow, up to the southern end of a massive fortress planted firmly on a subsidiary cone of the larger mountain to the left. He knew in an instant—from drawings he'd seen in books, true, but equally well from all he'd heard about Eronese artisans— that they had come to Eron in truth.

The building was beautiful: precisely positioned upon its site; exquisitely proportioned; detailed to perfection; looking at once too forbidding ever to assail, and a place one could spend eighths enjoying.

It was also on fire!

Wasn't it? Certainly, puffs of white smoke rose from those red-tile roofs.

"Fire!" he blurted out.

"Steam," Tozri corrected. "They heat everything with steam from the earth. If they don't have it, they don't bother building."

"Silence," Merryn called from the head of the line in clumsy Ixtian, though her tone was mild. Olrix had explained their situation yet again, and in spite of some doubtful looks, their captors seemed willing to take them at their worth. If nothing else, they were too young, tired, and hungry to be perceived as much of a threat.

At which point Merryn called a halt for lunch, and in the splendor of that view, they ate again: cold bread and cheese this time, with the place warmed by screens of paper coated with what looked like gold leaf, which were set up to catch the sun's rays and send it back upon them. In spite of himself, Kraxxi dozed. When he woke, it was to Elvix kicking his leg (now loosely bound to hers by a length of chain that allowed a free movement but forestalled running). "Olrix talked to their leader," she informed him. "While you were napping amid the enemy."

Kraxxi raised a brow. "And what did that leader say?"

"That she hoped you enjoyed the view because we'd be here for the rest of the winter. We don't know yet whether as guests or prisoners," she added grimly. "But we're to meet their ruling council tomorrow."

Tomorrow, Kraxxi mused, wondering how long it had been since he'd had *anything* to look forward to tomorrow.

Kraxxi awoke warm and comfortable to the familiar sound of Tozri breathing softly in the other bed in the cozy, stone-walled room which had been their quarters—no one was saying cell—since they'd arrived in Eron's War-Hold yesterday afternoon. Nor did the room look like a cell, what with the sparse but comfortable furniture, including a small cabinet stocked with a satisfying ample cache of bread, cheese, cold sausage, wine, water, and ale. Never mind the adjoining garderobe and steam-warmed bath (that had been heavenly) whose thick glass window looked onto the open sky—and a frighteningly sheer drop straight down. There were also three doors of sturdy oak with hidden hinges: one to either side just past the beds; the other between them, opening into a flagstone hallway marked with maybe two dozen other portals, which hinted of a series of residential suites. The place was austere—certainly not as opulent as even court scribes' quarters in Ixtianos—but that very austerity gave it a certain richness because the materials, proportions, and workmanship were all so exactly *right*.

But what, exactly, *was* their status? He shifted up in bed to slump languidly against the wall, feeling the nubby richness of the blanket that covered him, watching Tozri sleep. If Toz slept, there should be no need to worry. Either that, or his friend knew there was no hope. But this didn't feel like a hopeless situation.

Still, there'd been virtually no contact with anyone since they'd been ushered in here yesterday—beyond a quick, hot meal in some kind of guardroom. All three doors were always locked, though they'd been trying them regularly. They could also hear low voices coming from whatever lay to either side. Kraxxi's theory about the neglect was that their captors were waiting for the group sent to retrieve their gear to return. That would be inspected to a fine degree and a great deal told about them thereby, without them saying one word. Like the fact that Tozri had aristocratic connections, else he'd not have sported a geen-claw dagger. Like the fact that they probably *weren't* lost traders, because traders usually traveled in wheeled wagons, where they only had one tent, and it far too new. Like horses that wouldn't have calluses in the right places or the right kind of shoes.

He didn't really care. All that mattered was that he was warm and safe, that his friends had come through this alive, and that he no longer had to worry about Barrax's wrath.

Would he reveal himself? Probably, depending on how his captors seemed inclined to respond to such things. In any event, he intended to take himself to the King's court next spring—Sunbirth, or whatever the Eronese called it—and throw himself on Gynn's mercy.

True, his father might go to war in order to retrieve him—it would certainly give him the excuse he'd long desired—but he didn't think that was likely, given how Barrax was always moaning about how unprepared he was. Besides, if Barrax was smart, he was even now trying to produce another heir. Kraxxi found that notion amusing.

He'd just risen, clad in the gray-green hose and loose tunic they'd given him, intent on snaring another bite of cheese, when a rap sounded on the door, followed by someone calling in accented Ixtian "Make yourselves presentable. We will enter in one finger."

"I'm presentable now!" he called back, smirking as Tozri jerked to groggy consciousness and fumbled for a dagger he no longer had before recalling the situation and fumbling on his tunic instead. They were both sitting attentively—like good little child-scholars—when the lock rattled and a tall man in full house armor, down to helm and hold-cloak, swept in, followed by two men dressed more or less like himself and Tozri, but in red. The tall man carried a naked sword with the calculated nonchalance of someone who knew he had nothing to fear—though he'd chosen to keep his mouth-mask up, likely to preserve his anonymity.

"Your presence is required before the Warden of this place," he intoned in that same flat-voweled Ixtian. "You must make yourselves presentable. You must also allow us to inspect you—*all* of you—for the Warden of War-Hold likes information far more than she does enigmas. We regret if this embarrasses you, but it is necessary."

Kraxxi shot Tozri a resigned glance, and Tozri shot him one in return, adding a subtle shrug of caution. Kraxxi shrugged back and proceeded to slip off his tunic and hose, then, at a gesture, the rest. He folded everything neatly and stood, staring at the wall just to the right of Tozri's head as his companion did the same.

"Brothers?" the warrior asked, still in Ixtian.

One of his companions stared long at Kraxxi's face, then at Tozri's, "I think not," that one replied in the same tongue, clearly for their benefit. "The women are certainly sisters of one birth, and this man"—he indicated Tozri—"more resembles them than does this other," meaning Kraxxi.

"Half brothers?"

"Possibly. They clearly care for each other, but I would say as master to servant, since this one seems to defer to the other, though he appears older."

"This one is a man of substance, then?"

Kraxxi suppressed the urge to tell them to please stop discussing him and Tozri as though they were stock at a breeding fair, even as he wondered why in the world the examiners were also in effect revealing what they learned. Better they should say nothing and let their captives betray themselves.

Then again, this was War-Hold. War including intelligence, the ferreting out of information, even torture at need. That their captors were so careless about their speculations now indicated supreme confidence. Or arrogance. He was, he realized, almost in the heart of their—better say rival than enemy's—power.

Meanwhile, he was being scrutinized with remarkable thoroughness. "Soft feet under superficial calluses," Kraxxi's inspector noted, from the floor. "Likely stays indoors a lot."

"Less so on this one," his companion replied, inspecting the like part of Tozri.

Hands felt his calves, the inside of his thighs. "Rides some but not often; has ridden much more of late—" The hands probed higher. Kraxxi flinched. "Some rawness. Healed puncture wounds on hips and thighs: source unknown."

"Thin, probably from recent poor diet, not long-term deprivation."

Kraxxi's hands were examined. "No real labor, but calluses consistent with sword work. Again, exposure over softness."

Fingers now. "One joint missing, and recently, which means death of a brother. Rings worn but not present, except one"—he studied the bonding-gem cursorily, but made no further comment. "Bow calluses."

The warriors' eyes narrowed. "On how many fingers?"

"Three."

"Only the royal house use those big three-fingered bows . . ."

"Legally," the other retorted. "Few such laws can be enforced, and these folks had clearly been hunting geens. They had uncured claws with them."

"Thus the bows?"

"And the leg wounds? Perhaps."

Kraxxi tried to relax while his forearms were checked, compared with each other, and checked again. "More muscle on the right: swordsman's ridge, but not well developed."

"Which means he's had training but little real experience."

"It would seem."

"Assessment?" the leader asked finally.

"Could be what they say they are, but probably are not."

Kraxxi simply gazed at Tozri in numb, appalled silence, even as another part of him was thinking furiously, trying to determine why this assessment was being performed so openly.

To keep them off-balance? That's what he'd do. Take prisoners, treat them insanely well when they expected to be tortured. Win their confidence, maybe?

Which might already be won. Yet now he was in Eron, Kraxxi suddenly felt far more loyal to Ixti. Suppose they *did* question him? Suppose they wanted to know every single secret of his father's court? Suppose they wouldn't believe him (even if they found him out) when he told him that his father never told him anything useful?

At least he had Tozri for company. For a while.

"Dress," the leader said at last. "We will return for you in one hand."

And with that, they withdrew. Kraxxi heard the lock snap home. Tozri was simply staring. He scratched his head quizzically. "This seems wrong."

Kraxxi flopped down on his bed. He snared his hose but didn't put them on. "It does—but yet it doesn't. They have little to gain by harming us."

"Until they've had their way with us," Tozri shot back, gazing absently at the far-too-sturdy door.

"And then?"

Tozri shrugged. "Perhaps I can get word to my mother's kin."

"Perhaps," Kraxxi sighed—and started to dress.

The lock rattled again. "It is time," the same voice called from without. Kraxxi ran his hands through his hair, wishing he had a mirror but glad Tozri had retained the remnants of a comb. Tozri straightened his tunic and rolled his eyes in resignation—just as the door opened. The warrior who'd supervised their inspection stood there, eyes revealing nothing. He motioned them into the hall. They did as instructed, finding the corridor deserted save for seven more men, dressed precisely as the first, much of a height and all masked—and, by the richness of their clothing, close to an honor guard.

A lot for two men, though.

Or maybe not, for a few strides down the hall they stopped before another door, where a similar ritual was enacted—which produced, to Kraxxi's vast relief, Elvix and Olrix, dressed in gowns of similar cut to the tunics he and Tozri wore, but in dull blue and amber. They looked clean, well fed, and relatively happy, though the cockiness that usually danced in their eyes had been replaced by a careful wariness, and their hands twitched constantly, as if seeking nonexistent hilts. Kraxxi tried not to react to them, beyond a casual nod. And then the party was moving again, the lead warrior in the van, followed by two more, then himself and Tozri side by side, then two more guards, Elvix and Olrix also together, with a final three guards taking up the rear.

Clearly War-Hold was taking no chances. Or had surfeit of under-occupied personnel. *Or* were playing another set of games with them—a supposition reinforced by the fact that the corridors and stairs they assayed as they wound their way through the vastness of this mountain citadel were all but empty. Deliberately so, he assumed, though the plague had ravaged Eron as well, so much so that some holds had been abandoned, while many others, especially the larger ones, were still seriously undermanned.

But probably not this one. For one thing, it experienced better weather than most of Eron in winter, and the excitement of its ruling craft would appeal to the young, along with duties that involved a higher level of physical action than he assumed was the norm for the scholarly, artistically inclined Eronese.

Not that it mattered now, because they wound around one final kink of a wide stair (that nevertheless bent the right way for defense), marched down one more corridor, this one lit with glass-brick windows along one side and beamed with fragrant cedar, made a last tight turn to the right, and were there.

There was a room the size of the Hall of Fire back in Ixtianos, but built of warm gray stone in that same severe, elegant style that pervaded his and Tozri's chamber. Narrow windows on either side let in light, and a larger array opposite the massive oak doors revealed a breathtaking view of mountains, plains, and sea. Clearly they were very high up in this massive pile for so much glass to be used so freely. For the rest: the floor—maybe five spans square—was flanked on all sides by raised platforms, those to left and right supporting padded stone benches—empty, for the nonce. Ahead, an additional tier sported a dais upon which a long stone desk loomed, effectively walling the three people behind it from the rest of the room. Those three were dressed in hooded robes of that special red he now knew as War-Hold crimson, each augmented with a tabard in a different color, which carried some protocol Tozri probably knew but Kraxxi didn't. Two of them were men, one a woman. Four guards stood behind them, one of whom Kraxxi recognized as Merryn. Her eyes scanned them critically as their escort ushered them smartly to four plain stonewood chairs ranged two spans before the dais. Words were spoken in Eronese that Kraxxi thought might simply be, "Hold-Warden, we bring you—" The rest he didn't know, though he'd long since made a note to learn Eronese as soon as possible. The response from the dais included the word "duty" and maybe a name or title, whereupon the presumed Hold-Warden stared at them a long, appraising moment and said, "Sit!" in clipped, precise, Ixtian.

They did, alternating sexes, with Kraxxi and Elvix in the center. The Warden's eyes probed them one by one, casually but intently, like a cat in a room full of mice.

"Who are you?" she asked flatly. Not threatening, but certainly not encouraging.

Kraxxi, tried not to glance at the others for support, for all he was neither the true leader here, nor the best liar. But the Warden was looking at him. He cleared his throat, then rose. "I am Krax mun Ilgyon," he announced, not quite lying, since Ilgyon was his mother's child-name, the one she'd set aside upon marrying.

"That is your mother's house," the woman gave back. "Who is your father?"

"I do not know him," Kraxxi replied instantly, having rehearsed this more than once with the triplets. It was also true, in a way. "He has disowned me."

"These others?"

"They should speak for themselves."

"You may speak for them. Are they friends—or something else?"

"Friends."

"They defer to you."

"My family is wealthier than theirs."

"This family from which you were disowned?"

"Yes."

"They came with you even then?"

"They are my friends."

The Warden leaned back, spoke briefly to the man to her right, then leaned forward again. "Very well, we have names to call you. You shall now have ours: I am Lorvinn, Warden of War-Hold-Winter. These with me are Dormill, Sub–Clan-Chief for Clan Ferr"—she indicated the man to whom she'd just spoken—"and Vorminn, Subcraft-Chief of Spear."

And your brother, Kraxxi thought, noting the resemblance. Likely her twin, in fact.

"These others, you have met," she finished, meaning the guards. "They have given report of you."

Kraxxi didn't reply.

"They say you claim to have been part of a trade caravan out of Ixti beset by geens, then by sandstorms—which forced you to flee into these mountains, though you must surely know that the best way to reunite with your clan would be to follow their base around to where the Flat turns to grass at our border."

"It . . . did not seem viable at the time," Kraxxi replied uncertainly.

The Warden frowned at him. "You are not who you say you are; nor are you particularly good dissemblers. But I do not think you are criminals. I think you have suffered some turn and been forced to flee, probably due to ill luck for which your law would punish you. Three of you clearly have Eronese blood"—she paused and looked at the Master Guardsman who had brought them there. "I am surprised you did not see it, but perhaps your students saw what they expected."

Kraxxi's stomach gave a little twitch.

"*Do* you have Eronese blood?" the Warden asked the triplets, staring at each in turn.

"Aye!" Olrix replied at last. "Our mother—mine and Elv's and Toz's—was a healer from this land."

"Did she leave of her own will, or was she . . . stolen?"

"She was hired. She fell in love. She remained."

"And was conveniently from a clan whose ranks were so decimated by the plague that no one here could nay-say your story," the Warden observed dryly. "But you are not who you say," she repeated. "We have inspected your gear and your horses and yourselves. None of those things show use consistent with what you have told us. You therefore present us with a mystery. I enjoy mysteries. Winters can be boring here, and anything that relieves that boredom is to be cultivated. I do not wish to hold you prisoner, and indeed, such would be foolish, for where would you go? Anyone else in Eron will receive you as I have; therefore you will have gained nothing. The mountains will eat you, and I somehow doubt your own land will grant you the welcome you desire."

A pause, and she went on. "I do not think you are spies, either; you are too inept even to be spies posing as inept; yet I dare not give you freedom of this hold. Still, if you are to remain here, you must support this place with your labor. My judgment upon you is this: When you are in your rooms, the doors will remain locked. At all other times, you will remain in the company of one of these folks at my back and perform whatever duties they are assigned. You will eat with them, work with them, play with them, practice weaponry with them. You will have one eighth of a day of your own, which you may spend how you will as long as you are accompanied. These four have expressed a desire to learn your language. You will learn Eronese. You will all benefit. We will meet again in seven days. I, Lorvinn, Warden of War-Hold-Winter, in the name of Clan Ferr and Warcraft, have spoken."

The man on her right rose. "And I, Dormill Sub–Clan-Chief of Ferr have heard."

And the other: "And I, Vorminn, Subcraft-Chief of Spear, have witnessed."

The Warden turned toward the guards, "I believe," she said casually, "that the time has come for you to choose your shadows."

Kraxxi blinked in surprise as the four eased from behind the stone barrier and trooped onto the floor. In spite of himself, his gaze was fixed on Merryn, who would surely be assigned to either Elvix or Olrix. Instead, she strode straight to him, jerked him smartly to his feet, looked him straight in the eye, for she was barely shorter than he, and said, in perfect Ixtian. "*You* will come with me."

A hand later, stripped to the waist in almost oppressive heat, Kraxxi min Barrax, prince-in-exile of Ixti, was squeezing oranges in the kitchen with the most intriguing woman he'd ever met laboring beside him like a common drudge. Not once had she let off asking the names of things (someone had taught her how to say "What do you call . . . ?" in Ixtian). Barely had he left off telling her, while she supplied the Eronese names for things in turn. But what troubled him was the strange, quirky smile that curled her lips when she looked at him. And even more, the equally odd feeling awakening in his own heart, which made no sense at all.

Merryn's attention was not as focused on mysterious young Ixtian refugees as it would otherwise have been, however mysterious—and attractive—one of those possibly lost souls, in particular, might be. Not that evening, at any rate; not when compared with a more personal mystery she'd been anticipating a whole two days longer, which she hoped would have rather more bearing on her life than nursemaiding a batch of foreigners. Once her duty shift had expired at sunset, she'd deposited Krax in the care of her neighbor on the hall, Krynneth syn Mozz-een, and spent every spare moment since then surveying a good tenth of the hold in search of what she in fact only *assumed* was a glossless black door. In the process, she discovered that there were a great many doors in War-Hold indeed, that no few of them were black and a fair number of others showed no gloss at all, but that every single black one was either enameled that color, or polished to a very high sheen.

And a hand of wandering the halls trying to look as though she had no agenda whatever had proved to be unexpectedly difficult—especially since she actually knew some of the Night Guard by sight, and didn't want her search to be obvious. In fact, their identities weren't secret at all; given the public nature of their reemergence, there was no way they could be. But let any of the noninitiated question them about their qualifications or training, and one might as well speak to stones.

Except that her queries had been noted if not heeded, witness her visitor two nights ago. They wanted her, she was certain, but had no intention of making her way easy. Which didn't surprise her either.

In any event, she'd adopted a systematic approach: starting on one end and working her way up and down the levels. That seemed less obvious than pacing every corridor on any given level. Why that mattered, she didn't know. Except that the Night Guard put a premium on stealth, and she didn't want to disappoint whoever might chance to observe her efforts.

But she was tired, dammit! Patrol all yesterday, and then the rescue of their Ixtian prisoners, and then the audience with Lorvinn that had resulted in her accepting the role of Krax's shadow. One mystery on top of another, which was maybe one too many.

Perhaps there was a simpler way around the matter—such as researching the history of the Night Guard in the library. A group so grounded in tradition might easily have a traditional meeting place, which might have been mentioned. There might even be references to the keys.

So far she'd had no luck. She yawned, stretched, and looked up from the pile of books she'd arrayed before her on one of the library's research tables. And blinked. She was staring at a threadbare tapestry depicting the meeting of the mythical King Kael with The Eightfold God in His avatar as Law. Kael stood on the right, Law on the left, indicating the stone door behind which Kael was supposed to have found Eron's prime collection of rituals.

And that door, of cotton and sylk, wool and linen, was indeed black, with no gloss whatsoever.

Merryn was on her feet in an instant, noting how the tapestry seemed fixed to the wall very securely indeed, without the usual wrinkles or folds. And more importantly that the door was approximately life-size and was complete down to the keyhole.

It was too obvious, but Merryn couldn't resist. Rolling her eyes at her own folly—and insanely grateful she was alone—she touched the mysterious key to the woven keyhole.

And was rewarded with a click. A check showed that the hole was cotton over metal, and a firmer push of the key went straight into the wall—exactly like a key in a lock. More clicking ensued, whereupon a section of shelving to the left of the tapestry moved back, then sideways, to reveal a gaping darkness.

Merryn knew she was supposed to enter, but was still a trifle uneasy as she approached. By the time she'd reached the opening, however, she'd seen that it led to nothing more than a bare stone chamber.

Bare, that is, save for a glossless black pedestal as high as her waist, on top of which lay a neatly folded sheet of black parchment.

Taking no chances, Merryn stepped only far enough into the chamber to sweep the parchment from the pedestal with her sword, which maneuver also knocked it in her direction. She could just reach it without moving from where she stood and decided that might be the best policy, though she had no idea why she'd suddenly become so distrustful.

In any event, she had it now. Good quality material . . .

She opened it.

A date. A time. And a place. Written in silver ink upon the black.

It was also a time she was free. She only hoped it was an invitation.

CHAPTER XXI:

FINDER'S FEE

(Eron: Gem-Hold-Winter—Deep Winter: Day VII—near midnight)

〜〜〜〜〜〜〜

Sweat ran into Avall's eyes, blinding him. He dropped the pick with which he'd been chipping away at a particularly rich seam he'd discovered during his last trip down to the mines and reached up to wipe his face. That accomplished, he settled himself to a more comfortable, if still cramped, sprawl in the narrow tunnel (they called them *crawls* here) in which, for the last two hands, he'd been ensconced.

His efforts were largely ineffectual, however, and he knew the discomfort was in part due to the smoke from the lamp on his helmet, which produced just enough wavering glare to see by. It was time for a break, he decided, as he folded his arms beneath his head and closed his eyes, trying not to think of the weight of mountain above him, before him, and to either side. He felt like a grub in the earth—or perhaps a maggot in the moldering corpse of a whale. He yawned. It wouldn't take much to send him to sleep, though that would be dangerous—not that they wouldn't come looking soon enough, or find him.

Not for the first time did he wonder what had driven him back down here in the wee hours of the night. He'd already done his daily rotation on the trod and a second shift in this vein—which was proving remarkably productive, for all the stone itself was a trifle odd: damp in places, but not in the way that made the Mine-Master fear he was about to dig into some unknown lake and flood the maze of tunnels. No, this was a different damp, hard to describe.

And intriguing. Maybe that was why he'd asked for a volunteer shift. The Night-Warden had shrugged, handed him a pick, and told him that anybody here this late wanting to work that crawl was entitled to anything he found up to three stones. Since most of the vein had yielded more like eight per hand, that seemed fair—especially as this was volunteer work, which meant he could *stop* after three if he wanted.

Which still didn't answer the question.

Well, it was curiosity, for one thing. New strata suggested new, or at least different, contents.

Raw greed? His better instincts denied it, but that probably *was* a factor. He was laying the cornerstones of his own personal fortune here. If Chance favored him, he'd find wealth enough this winter to buy himself a hold of his own, which would free him, finally, from reliance on the Clan's largesse.

To escape more serious matters for a while? That was more like it. When he worked on something as drearily routine as this, his mind was free to roam, to drift into that odd daydream state where solutions to problems lay.

Problem: Eddyn. Simply avoid him a much as possible.

Problem: Strynn. Talk to her more—as they had not in the ten days since their minor exchange of words had lapsed into festering silence exacerbated by conflicting schedules. Be more involved in her work. Try to relax around her.

Problem: Rann. Try *not* to spend most of his free time with his bond-brother, whose schedule meshed with his so nicely.

Problem: the helm. The design work was finally moving along, if slowly because of the minute details he wanted to incorporate. He'd also located a cache of suitable steel for the understructure, had made paper templates for the shape, and had cut out one piece—the nasal. He'd also done tentative sketches for the designs he'd work onto the earpieces—but had shown them neither to Rann nor Strynn—in her case, because they included the patterns he'd taken from her fingers.

Everything else was standing still.

Which he could afford no longer. It really was too late for this kind of foolishness, anyway. And by the time he wormed his way out, passed the trods and the treaders and the checkers, submitted his findings to the Night-Warden for inspection (they were on honor system here, which he almost couldn't believe), then bathed and returned upstairs, it would be closer to dawn than midnight—and he'd need to rise early to catch the mornlight.

What had he been thinking, anyway?

Escape probably. From his conscience. From guilt about how he could never seem to get things right with Strynn.

Sighing, he rose on his elbows again, took the pick, and continued tap-tap-tapping along his chosen seam.

It really was more like earth than rock; indeed, was so crumbly he could almost dig out that pocket ahead with his bare hands. He did so impulsively, feeling what he couldn't truly see: the tiny, pealike hardnesses that were gems. He raked out a whole handful—amazed to see them, though their colors were muted—dull red, faded blue, weary green. Reaching to his belt, he retrieved a fabric pouch, then picked through this latest stash. The best three went into the pouch, the rest into another. But were there more? This was very unusual. By flattening himself as much as possible and holding his head just so, he was able to make out the back of the hole he'd excavated. And scowled, even as his eyes rounded in surprise. The strata had changed in there; most of the soft stone had been chipped away, though it remained in pockets along either side of his principal excavation. The surrounding rock was harder, and there were no more gems.

But one. Even at this distance it glistened. A ruby, it looked like; *something* red, at any rate, and easily the size of the first joint of his thumb. Grimy and dim, but potentially quite remarkable. And a perfect accent to the helm.

He reached back into the hole, felt it stick a little, then come free, like a scab pulled off a skinned knee. But *this* scab could easily buy a small house.

And he'd found it by his own labor, in his own craft's vein, on his own time. It was therefore his! He'd give the Night-Warden all the other trove— or maybe not, since that would be sure to raise comment. But this stone . . .

This stone . . .

Freed of its matrix and seen in better light, it was even more remarkable than he'd thought, for it was the true, dark, blue-tinged red most prized. The color called geen's blood. He spat on it, polished it against his bare arm, and looked at it again. And scowled in perplexity. Something about it didn't seem quite right. No use trying to puzzle that out now, though. Back in his workroom, he'd take another look at this remarkable find.

And tell Strynn. And Rann.

No, better to spring it on them later. No one *had* to know about this. Grinning, he shifted the three choice stones into the pouch with the hold's portion, stashed the new stone in the other, tied it thoroughly, and commenced wriggling backwards out of the crawl.

It took excruciatingly long, and he found himself becoming unaccountably excited, as stronger light probed in around him from the master shaft outside. Closer and closer. His feet waved in air . . .

Hands he didn't expect snared him by the waistband and dragged him down. He flailed for the pad he'd lain upon, and nearly dropped the pick, but allowed his unknown assistant to help him upright. Only then did he realize it was Eddyn.

Eddyn gaped at him whimsically, clearly as surprised as Avall. "Find anything?" he asked casually, to cover his chagrin.

Avall started—and hoped Eddyn didn't notice. He flourished the larger bag of stones and on impulse passed it to his rival. "Nice stash all clumped together, but the node's about tapped out. I emptied the easy one, but there're some side veins that might be worth your while."

Eddyn returned the bag, which he'd only weighed in his hand, and picked up his own body pad. The helm lights made both their faces into shadowed, haunted things, all deep-set eyes and hollow cheeks. "Thanks." A pause. "And I mean that."

Avall nodded back. "You, too, and I mean *that*." And as he strode back through larger and larger tunnels, caves, and corridors, he discovered that he actually *had* meant it—almost.

But with a find like this—he fingered the big ruby in its pouch—he could afford to be generous.

"You can still have two more," the Night-Warden said at the exit gate, where Avall had set his two bags on the assay scales. "I told you three—and you *were* on your own time."

Avall shrugged and removed the bag that held the ruby, which indeed weighed about a tenth as much as the other. The scale shot down with a solid "clunk." He made no move toward the other. "Let's consider the rest a donation to Gem-Hold. A gift from Smith to Stone."

The Night-Warden eyed the smaller bag warily. "That good?"

Avall couldn't resist a smug nod. "That good."

"Want to show me? I *could* demand, you know."

"You could. But I intend to use it as part of a royal commission—and *that* project is supposed to be a secret."

"Oh, *that* good," the Night-Warden sighed.

"Just keep an eye out next time you see the King."

"Luck," the Warden snorted. Avall couldn't tell if the man was wishing him luck, or simply acknowledging the existence of the same. Not for the first time that night (though for no good reason he could think of) did he feel oddly elated, a little reckless, almost high. And fortunate for him, finds of this type were common enough that he doubted the Hold-Warden would seek him out to inspect his prize, though that *was* his prerogative. A big ruby was, after all, a big ruby.

So why did he feel as though he were committing some act of subterfuge?

He didn't know—nor care. Sleepy no longer, he strode back to the mine's entry arcade, then veered left down a ramp to the baths. They were all but deserted, and he wasted no time dumping his mining breeches and the body pad into the soaking vat intended for such things, wondering absently when he'd have to do another turn in the laundry. He *didn't* dump the pouch, however, as he secured a towel and padded into the first steam room. Heat hit him from all sides, and steam so hot he gasped, but it felt wonderful, the heat easing the top layer of soreness from his body, relaxing him at last.

He stayed there as long as impatience let him, then moved on to the showers, where he proceeded to give himself a cursory cleaning before entering the drying room, and finally the vesting chamber where he'd left the clothes he'd worn down here. He was all but grinning as he pranced, black-clad, along the hold's warren of corridors and stairs back to his suite.

And in spite of his impressive find, he had no idea why.

Eddyn surprised no one by spending far less than a hand in Smith's designated crawl. Mining had never been his intention, and certainly not an extended stint of it flat on his belly, picking through Avall's throwaways. Still, he had to have some reason for being down here at this odd time, and this was the obvious one. His real intent, however—*that* was something else entirely, something he'd managed before he'd made his way into the dirty, smelly dark. Certainly before he'd helped his rival out of this very same crawl to which he'd paid but token service for a finger or two.

If Avall only knew!

Eddyn patted one of *his* stash of pouches and thought about what now lay hidden in another in the outer vesting room, where he'd also, by contrived coincidence, happened to find Avall's clothes—and with them the key to his suite, where resided his rival's principal hold over him, namely the High King's helm. He *had* to know how that progressed, because however fabulous it was, his own work had to be better. He'd therefore quickly "borrowed" the key and made a wax impression. Troublesome but necessary. Artisans' suites had unpickable locks so complex their own makers couldn't circumvent them. Nor was there any way he could've picked even a lesser one quickly or without detection. It was completely unethical, in any event, and in some cases highly illegal, depending on intent.

He'd worry about that later. For now he had what he wanted. Not gems, perhaps, but something potentially more important.

To his great surprise, Avall wasn't remotely tired as he slipped back into his suite. Still, he considered going straight to bed—it was incredibly late, after all. On the other hand, he didn't need to rise as early as he did some mornings, and a madness was on him to clean up the ruby at once, then maybe do a bit of work on the helm. Perhaps start the wax master-mold for the nasal appliqué. These fits came on him now and then, and when they arrived— Well, one was a fool to ignore them. "The Eight speak through impulse" was a saying he'd heard more than once. And "When The Eight want you, they want you now!"

Sighing, he unlocked the workroom door and spent the next finger waking every light source he possessed, including a precious glow-globe. That accomplished, he poured water from a ceramic pitcher into a shallow bowl already on the worktable, then eased behind it and sat down, placing a silver-backed reflector candle as close as he dared to both bowl and face.

A deep breath, and he emptied the pouch, then set the ruby in the bowl, swishing the water gently around it. Sometimes stones like this were cracked, and one had to be careful not to damage them further. Happily, no such disaster occurred, though the matrix was proving stubborn. He reached for a soft brush and swabbed at it carefully. More matrix came away. The water grew cloudy. He replaced it, repeated the process. By the third try, most of the grime that had befouled his find had dispersed, revealing two very interesting things.

One was the stone's remarkable color and clarity.

The other was that it was in nowise a ruby.

True, the color was correct—but no ruby showed so many secondary hues. No ruby had this incredible internal glimmer of minor facets—or whatever those motes of color were. Opal then? But no opal was this color, not even the so-called flame opals that came from mines down in Ixti. It was something new and rare. Perhaps unique.

Ethics therefore demanded he present it to the Hold-Warden.

They *didn't* demand he do it right away. Besides, it was also the sort of curiosity that would be presented, in turn, by the Hold to the King. And since he was already working on a royal commission, there was a good chance the thing would be returned to him in due time anyway.

It wouldn't need much work; the surface was remarkably smooth already. He picked it up curiously. One side was almost flat. In fact, had he not dug far into the crawl and pried it loose from the crumbly stone with his fingers, he could've believed it had been planted there for some unfathomable reason.

But that wasn't important now. He scanned the litter on his worktable, finally locating what he sought beneath a sheaf of paper templates for the helm's various elements.

The nasal: a rounded diamond shape, the lower curves convex, the upper ones concave, flaring out into a brow bar which would be brazed and riveted to several other so far nonexistent pieces. He'd cut it out that afternoon: the one real thing he'd accomplished that day. Already he had sketches of how he'd embellish the bronze casting with which he intended to cover the steel foundation, and those sketches suggested a jewel between the eyes . . .

He reached for the fresh-cut metal. And swore as a finger caught a shard of raw steel along an edge he hadn't filed. Reflex thrust the digit into his mouth, even as he set down the gem far more carefully. It hurt like—Well, it hurt a *lot*. And while metal splinters were one of the hazards of his craft (along with burns, from forging and melting metal, and smashed fingers from hammering), still, it was a pain he particularly disliked.

Holding his breath, he withdrew the finger and inspected it anxiously. A silvery shard protruded from his flesh like a lone limb on a blasted tree. Another breath, and as he plucked it out, saw blood ooze up around it. A single drop fell atop the gem. He snared a cleaning cloth, wrapped it around his wounded digit, and used another to wipe the blood off the stone.

He was still bleeding, too. Perhaps he should seek a healer. But that was stupid at this hour, for such a minor wound. What would a healer do? Swab it with strong wine and put a stitch in it? And laugh at him. He could do that himself.

He found wine, poured a mugful, and thrust his finger in, noting the swirls as the blood mixed with the pale liquid. More swirls. Swirls like the ice and Strynn's fingerprints. He'd have to remember that.

The pain abated.

Fine. Back to what he'd intended. He retrieved the nasal—carefully this time—and picked up the gem with his wounded left hand. There was something soothing about that, he realized; something calming about touching the gem's smooth surface. For no good reason; he rubbed it against his injury, then set it where he'd thought to use it, at the juncture of eyes and nose.

And snorted through a frown. *What had he been thinking?* Placed thusly, a stone this color looked like nothing so much as a bleeding canker: an enormous carbuncle that had risen between the High King's eyes. He'd still use it, but somewhere else. Maybe in the forehead, centerpiece of a band of others, so the effect wouldn't be so blatant.

Sighing, he removed the gem, replaced it in the pouch, and stowed the pouch in his topmost drawer. And paused.

Should he tell Strynn about it tomorrow—or surprise her with it later, perhaps in the finished piece? Telling her would be a bond, a secret they shared. But he'd always liked surprises, both receiving them and conferring them. So did she.

In any event, she was asleep; he'd assess her mood tomorrow, then decide.

The odd elation continued.

Nor was he sleepy in the slightest. He *was* very focused, however, yet at the same time strangely calm—likely a result of this sense of extreme well-being that had embraced him since he'd found the gem. Security did that, he supposed. And in any event, there was no point wasting that energy. If he went to bed, he'd only lie awake thinking and planning, and get no sleep at all.

Perhaps it was time to begin the wax masters: the patterns he would cast in bronze and leaf with gold. With that in mind, he secured a slab of beeswax from the supply chest next to the worktable and set it near the candle. (Odd how the flame didn't seem to be flickering as much as usual; perhaps some draft had shifted.) A moment he waited—a long moment, it seemed—then cut off a slab, rolled it thin atop the sheet of glass he used as a work surface, and, when it was maybe a quarter finger thick, laid the nasal atop it and scribed around it with a hot knife. He made fast work of it, surprised at how sure his hand felt. One side done; now the other. This was great! The light held steady, seemed brighter, too. If this was how work went in the stillness of the night, he'd have to do it more often.

With a jeweler's spatula he pried the wax loose from the metal, turned it over, and pressed it down on the slab, smoothing the contours with his fingers. He'd only rough the border in now, the rest as he finished the design, then refine continuously across the winter. The casting itself wouldn't take long.

A brief search produced the paper master he'd been perfecting during the last few days, which he laid atop the wax. A few pricks of a stylus left impressions of crucial lines and junctures. He'd start with the outside curves—freehand initially, but he'd file them down later with tools. No way he'd be able to do them otherwise, not even with his own, very steady hands.

A deep breath, and he made the first pass, felt the stylus slip in precisely, sensed the gentle pressure as he slowly drew it toward him through the wax. Closer and closer: a perfect line, not wavering, and exactly the right distance from the edge.

On around the other side, and he inspected the completed work. Not bad at all for the first stage. He picked up another tool: a scraper used to pare off the shoulders the stylus's passage had made, and followed those initial curves—but slowly, oh so slowly, yet with far more precision than he'd ever before achieved.

What had got into him, he had no idea—nor wanted to. All that mattered was that it continue. So what *else* could he do? He'd assumed the stage he'd just completed would require at least a hand—but the time-candle seemed not to have moved at all, and the other was still holding remarkably steady, though he'd detected a gradual ebb and flow of its light, as though it was flickering at a much slower rate.

Which made no sense.

A shrug, and he retrieved the master again, laid it atop the wax, and sketched in the next set of lines.

The work went flawlessly.

Nor was he even remotely tired, merely very intent. The Eight did this sometimes. Before he knew it, he'd completed another portion.

The master again, and more work. On and on. Not resting, not wavering, perfectly relaxed, even as part of him sat back and wondered and worried about time that never seemed to advance.

Eventually he reached for the pattern and realized to his amazement that he'd done everything he *could* do without completing the final cartoon for the central motif.

What he'd accomplished so far, however— Well, it was easy to see even at this preliminary stage that it was the best work he'd ever done. Fit for the King it was meant to glorify.

He looked up, blinking, saw the time-candle had moved but half a hand—which wasn't possible. More like a hand and a half—or two, which should put it close to dawn. Time sense shifted when one worked; that was a given. But not like this.

Not—

He yawned, suddenly very tired indeed. Another, and he blew out the candles and rose. A breeze found him as he stalked toward the bedroom. Pesky draft must be back, or have shifted again. Maybe he ought to look at the windows tomorrow.

In the meantime, he wanted to look at Strynn. Maybe her hair made patterns that he could use. Perhaps he should call the finished work the Helmet of Strynn.

Silently, he undressed and slipped into bed beside her. Everything was perfect—except for one thing. His finger where he'd caught the metal splinter was throbbing abominably.

(Eron: War-Hold-Winter—Deep Winter: Day VII—just before dawn)

Nine days was an eternity when one spent them waiting. Merryn wasn't the most patient of people at the best of times, and when the note from the Night Guard had specified this day and time, she'd been both elated and frustrated. Why so much delay for something so important? It wasn't as if Deep Winter was actually that long, if one were talking about honing skills to the level the Guard, in her two encounters with them, had displayed.

But another part of her was questioning even that. Patience was itself a skill, and an especially valuable one to a fighting man or woman. More than one person she knew had been gravely injured by letting haste overrule judgment. She was *not* going to let that happen to her.

So here she was, in the stables, closer to dawn than midnight, going through the motions, yet again, of alternately rubbing down Ingot and inspecting the stallion's tack.

And then Ingot snorted in alarm, and by the time Merryn looked up, a slit was opening in the back wall of his stall.

In spite of her excitement, she stored her equipment properly, then strode toward the opening. Even as she did, she was thinking. Probably there was a peephole there, so that the panel wouldn't open with the wrong person or persons present. And then she'd stepped over that threshold and into the unknown.

Into darkness, too, for the panel instantly shut behind her: utterly without noise.

Breathing sounded from somewhere ahead. She froze in place.

"No one looks at stable walls," a muffled voice said. "One looks only at horses. Part of what we are about lies in looking somewhere besides where one is expected to look."

Merryn thought of replying, but did not. This was Night Guard's game. She would instigate no action until she knew more about the ground on which she stood.

"If you prove unacceptable," the voice went on, "we can . . . remove knowledge of this from your mind. It won't be pleasant for either of us, so we would rather that did not become necessary. For now, we have a few things to tell you, after which you may ask one question."

A deep breath, and the voice continued. Merryn had given up trying to identify the speaker, save that she thought it was male. "First, as you have surmised, a Night Guard's greatest virtue is patience, and with that patience, economy of movement. You fight well, Merryn; that is no lie. You are one of the best of your generation. We hope to make you better, but I will tell you now: A Night Guard is not made in a day or an eighth or a season. Those you met have, some of them, been in secret training for four years, which is the time our rites prescribe. Not all this training will be done here in this hold. It will try your patience because the discipline moves at its pace, not yours, and you are already burdened with training. Do you have a question yet, or do you save it?"

Merryn breathed deeply in turn, wondering which of many questions flooding her mind should be singled out for the asking. "Why so mysterious?" she asked abruptly. "Everyone in the hold must surely know you exist, and I myself know some of you on sight."

A low chuckle echoed down the corridor. "To know something exists, but not its powers or limitations or the rules by which it plays—there is power in this we need make no effort to attain. The Night Guard were known of old. Tales are told of them in Ixti. Enough time has passed since our dissolution that those tales have grown in the telling. The fact that we have returned should give Ixti pause without us having to do anything at all. Reputation can itself be a weapon."

"Does the king of Ixti—" Merryn began, then caught herself.

"Not a question because not finished," the voice chuckled again. "Those in this hold know, and those members still in training in others know. The King knows, and the Chiefs of Ferr, and, of course, our instructors. Barrax should not know—yet—for we only revealed ourselves when you saw.

"And now," the voice continued, in a tone that implied the interview's impending conclusion, "we must part. Return the way you came. And learn patience, Merryn. The rewards of that are great. Our next meeting will be in five days. Learn something between now and then."

And that was all. The air stirred. Stone grated, and she knew she was alone again.

The door to the stable opened when she reached it. Obviously there were more peepholes than one.

CHAPTER XXII:

THINGS BIRDS DO

(ERON: WAR-HOLD-WINTER—DEEP WINTER: DAY VIII—MIDAFTERNOON)

~~~~~~~~~~

The point—blunted, Eight be thanked—flashed through an opening so small she'd not bothered to defend it and stabbed Merryn smartly in the armpit. The touch stung her, body and soul—pride, rather—alike. This lad was *good*! Good enough to take her off guard, in fact, so that he managed another blow in like place before she simply dropped her practice sword in disgust. Perhaps Lorvinn had been right; it wasn't wise to spar with real weapons, lest these odd "visitors" from Ixti get the better of their wardens.

It had all been her fault, too—this little practice round in one of the dozen or so sunlit sparring courts high in the hold, where gold-foiled walls and mirrors, and movable glass roof panels kept the worst of the snow and cold at bay. *She'd* been the one who'd thought to try Krax's mettle after he'd made one too many remarks (in increasingly fluent Eronese) about how her folk were too arrogant about their finesse with edges at the expense, he thought, of points.

Which might *be* a point well taken, she'd decided—and determined to find out, fitting him with padding from the seemingly limitless spares the hold possessed, noting that he was somewhat slimmer in the hip than most men she knew, and shallower of chest, but wider through the shoulders. Differences in proportion that might *make* a difference or might not.

"Hold!" she called, backing away and raising her sword crossways for emphasis. Krax looked startled, touched his blade to his forehead, then rested the point on the pavement, at the same time loosening the chin strap on his half helm. "Were those touches? I couldn't tell. These weapons numb like wearing gloves . . ."

"Eight *yes*, they were touches!" Merryn snapped, inspecting her armpit critically, where twin smears of yellow point-paint gleamed blatantly, almost atop each other. "Very fine and excellent touches," she added, then scowled at his blank stare and repeated the phrase more slowly, first in Eronese, into which she'd lapsed, and then into Ixtian, which she was mastering decently well except for the future tense, where the vowel mutations followed no rational order. The basic structures were not that unlike, save where one put the subjects and a certain pickiness about the ordering of adjectives. Nine days it had been since she'd begun shadowing Krax, and they were communicating quite acceptably, in a kind of pidgin of both tongues. He was turning out to be decent company too: an intriguing mix of smart and naive, of bold and shy, of authoritarian and servile. She also thought he liked her. If nothing else, they were learning from each other, and Merryn loved to learn.

"Let's see those arms!" she demanded, thrusting her sword through her belt, and reaching toward his nearer. He looked startled again, having not yet learned how to read her humor. Then again, people who'd known her for years didn't always know how either. In any event, he didn't protest as she snared his sword arm and deftly undid the shoulder laces, removed the padding, then rolled his undersleeve up as far as possible, exposing dark tanned flesh sprinkled with more black hair then she was used to seeing. She felt his muscles critically. Then her own, gnawing her lip as she compared the two.

"What?"

"You're quicker than I am," she said flatly, because there was no reason to lie. "I'm stronger. Your muscles are harder; mine are bigger—size for size."

It took him a moment to puzzle out the construction. "I think so."

She sat down with a thump, motioning him down with her. "Would you say you are typical for your land? In build, I mean? Your friend, Toz, he is— Smoother is not a good word, but is the best I can think of. The curves of his body are more gradual, which would seem to be the legacy of his Eronese blood."

Krax got his helm off and wiped his forehead with the arming cap inside it. His hair (nearly two fingers long now) clung to his skull like a cap of ink, making his dark eyes sparkle. "I am not sure—"

She cuffed him smartly, without malice. Teasing. "You'll not betray your land if you tell me. I'm sure someone here already knows all this. But if I am to teach weapon skills, I need to know how body type affects prowess. You are simply one more example."

"Then why ask if I am typical?"

She grinned. "Because my clan sell thinner swords to Ixtian merchants than to Eronese. We've always wondered if the preference was practical or aesthetic."

He frowned at the last word.

"Pretty," she supplied. "Looks. If the way they looked made more difference."

"Lighter bodies are quicker, so are lighter swords."

Which likely meant that Ixtians tended to drill their soldiers in small groups where finesse mattered more than strength—which reinforced popular rumor, not that she'd ever tell Krax. She wondered if he knew how much he was betraying. Probably not. Or else he didn't care. He seemed a man determined to walk away from his past, yet with honor enough to care about his home country. Which was good. She hated men without honor. And wondered why Krax's honor, in particular, concerned her.

He reached over and tapped her helm. "Off!"

She did, shaking her hair loose. Wiping her face exactly as he had done.

"Easier to make out your words if I can see your lips," he explained with a grin that showed teeth that either *were* whiter than she was used to or seemed that way in contrast to his darker face. His mouth was wider than that of most men she knew, too, but with thinner lips.

"I—" she began, then broke off abruptly, whipping a gaze at a sky entirely bereft of clouds, from which something wet had nevertheless fallen to smite her head. A bird wheeled there: straight above, white and delicate-looking, and utterly uncontrite as it dropped another missile which landed with a liquid yellow splat between her outstretched legs. The air reeked of sulfur.

Krax laughed, then saw the look of outrage on her face and laughed louder. Only then did she recall that she had that *stuff* in her hair. She raked it savagely with her arming cap, even as she rose and made for the shelter of the nearest round-arched arcade. It was colder there without benefit of the sun, but the change felt good on her sweat-soaked body.

Krax joined her because he had little choice. "What was that?" he asked, pointing to the bird, which had been joined by two others.

"Snow swift."

"Ah!"

"The hold's worst nuisance. I once spent a whole day washing their shit off the panels on the Master's Hall."

He looked puzzled.

"They eat lava rocks," she explained patiently. "For their crops—their gizzards. The stuff's full of sulfur and it permeates their excreta. It also eats away the gold foil they use lots of around here—if you don't get it off quickly."

"Why don't you kill them, then? For that matter, there are many small wild birds here. Yet I never see them served at dinner."

"Because we don't have a *way* to kill them easily," Merryn retorted. "Our bows are too big—"

"Make smaller ones, just for birds."

"We've tried, but there is no real interest. It was decided long ago that small birds worth eating ought simply to be raised on farms."

"What about poison?"

"It is impossible to control what tastes it and what does not. We do not kill indiscriminately."

"Nor we," Krax gave back, though he looked as though he wondered if that were entirely true. As if to put her at ease, he grinned.

Merryn looked back at the court. No birds flew above it; no shadows danced across the paving stones. "I think," she said, "we should spar one more hand and call it even."

"Yes!" Krax laughed. "And see if these . . . snow swifts can hit a moving target."

A moment later, they were resecuring helms and padding, and had retrieved their swords. Merryn felt her training settle over her like a cloak of focused intensity. She'd let her guard down earlier and it had cost her—in pride, if nothing else. She would *not* underestimate again. But since they'd discussed finesse, Krax might well think to counter with power, so she'd best anticipate that as well.

—Feint. Stroke. Thrust. And she got under *his* guard, exactly as he'd got under hers. He grunted, snarled furiously, then commenced raining blows on her, seeking to overmass her and drive her back with a combination of speed, skill, and strength she'd not anticipated. He really *was* good. As good as Eddyn, though that was like saying silver was as good as gold; their styles were so fundamentally different. As good as some of the masters in this place, too—who would certainly get word of his prowess if they weren't more discreet about these meetings. And she suddenly didn't want his prowess known. If it was, they might assign him another shadow. She wondered why that mattered.

But not consciously, for it was all her conscious mind (with strong aid from well-honed reflexes) could do to hold her own. Until a shadow swooped across both of them, and he flung himself atop her as though that passing darkness were some threat against which she needed shielding.

She flailed, fell back, wondered for a breath if she'd misread him entirely and this was a serious attack—until she heard the third liquid splat of the day and saw what was running down his helmet. She laughed, he laughed back but didn't move to let her up though he was already apologizing. But why did having him sit astride her like that feel so Eight-cursed good?

"Does this belong to you?" Krynneth inquired loftily as he thrust Krax into Merryn's room ahead of him.

She was sitting in the window seat reading Allegri's *Treatise on Falconry* (she had one of the few apartments in the entire hold with a window that actually opened, which she suspected was gratitude from Ferr to Argen for their aid in the Eddyn affair), but looked up with a start. Not at the fact of the entrance—guards on duty call never locked their doors—but because she had no idea how *he* had wound up with Krax, who was supposed to be napping in his room after their energy-sapping round of swordplay.

Where he clearly *had* been, at least briefly, since he'd obviously bathed and changed since she'd seen him. He was looking mighty sheepish, though: like a child caught with his hand in the sweetmeat jar—when he wasn't trying to stifle another one of his silly grins. Clearly he was up to something. And clearly Krynneth was in on it.

"Lost, strayed, or stolen?" she asked dryly, as she put Allegri down and swung her legs off the padded seat, feeling soreness in her muscles she didn't like, and in her armpit to boot, which seemed to be sporting a bruise.

"Lost in thought," Krynneth gave back, rolling the pale blue eyes that had half the women in the hold moaning after him. "Strayed, but with direction. Stolen—let us say *borrowing* figured in what he's about."

"About?" she echoed, scowling while Krax smirked, looking less threatening and more boyish—and appealing—by the instant; like Avall in his lighter moments. Which might be why she liked him. Men of war were often also men of anger. She liked men with a sense of humor.

"He can tell you better than I," Krynneth replied with a little bow of his golden head, and swept away, leaving Krax (back in house-hose and -tunic of green and rust respectively) standing in the obviously open doorway. "Come!" she commanded, motioning him forward, even as she wondered if she was insulting him by treating him like a pet. Or if he, like most men she knew, reveled in such attention.

He held back, not leaving the door, but not threatening to bolt either. "I brought you something," he said. "I'll get it—but it would be more fun if you closed your eyes. I promise not to run. As your Warden said: Where would I go?"

"Where indeed?" she shot back archly, folding her arms and assuming an exaggerated contraposto made possible by the men's clothing (actually, guards' undergear), she wore. "Only for five breaths," she warned—and complied.

Without taking his eyes from hers, Krax reached into the hallway beside the door, snared something, and hid it behind his back before marching into the room. She heard him approach, counted down, aloud, ". . . two . . . one . . ." And opened her eyes.

She couldn't identify what he was holding out to her, resting lightly across his hands. It seemed a length of straight, gold-toned cane of the sort used in making furniture, and sometimes for practice staves. This piece was maybe half a span long and no thicker than her biggest finger at the root. Nothing remarkable, save its straightness and the fact that it had been split along its length then reglued—with rockclam glue (by the smell), which was fast-setting, strong, and good for filling gaps.

"What?" she blurted out, before recalling she'd intended to leave explanations to him.

"I'll show you." And with that, he reached to a pouch at his side and pulled out a spray of wooden slivers no longer than his hand, each arrow-straight and pointed at one end, the other fletched with what looked like thistledown and bound with embroidery sylk. A suspicion began to form, but she let him have his way. He was enjoying this. So, she admitted, was she.

Wordlessly, he inserted one of the shafts into the end of the tube, then raised it to his lips, pointed it casually toward the cushion on which she'd sat—which was easily four spans across the room—filled his cheeks, and blew a short, focused puff. She barely saw the dart fly, but most certainly saw it strike home: up to the fletching in the leather that faced the sides of the cushion. He'd also centered it neatly in the heart of the tooled squirrel there, which couldn't be an accident.

"Blowgun," he supplied. "My people use them for—"

"Hunting birds!" she exclaimed. "We've never had much need for hunting birds, so we've never perfected that art."

"Hunting most small game," he corrected. "Surely you have seen one before."

She shook her head, though she had heard of them and filed that knowledge away under esoteric weapons to be studied before she died.

"So the brilliant, clever, resourceful Eronese are not so all-knowing after all."

"Knowing and acting on knowledge are two different things," she retorted saucily. "I'll let you know how *good* Eronese wine tastes if you'll show me that again—and let me try."

He fitted another dart, blew almost casually—and pierced another squirrel, this time in the eye.

"Hard on the furniture, aren't you?" she grumbled. "Do that again."

He obligingly inserted a third. But this time he pointed it, for an instant, straight at her left eye, and in that instant, she saw her death.

He then proceeded to place that dart precisely beside the first.

"Where'd you get it?" she asked, because she'd determined not to beg to use it. She was, after all, the person in charge here.

He cleared his throat. "Actually, I *had* a real one, but it was never returned to me . . . after. As for this— Well, Krynneth came to the room to bring me some fresh clothes and I begged a favor from him since I'm not allowed out on my own. He kind of likes you, and I said it was for you, and would tell you he helped. Anyway, the tube came from the furniture shop. Krynneth helped me split it and hollow it out, which is all you have to do. The darts came from the same place, and the fletching came from the herbalist. The tricky part's in laying out the down before you tie it."

She eyed him warily. "And these can kill at what distance?"

"More than you think. And with almost no effort. You could also," he added wickedly, "*poison* them."

"With secret Ixtian poison?"

"As a matter of fact. But that's a tale for another time. You wanted to try?" He held the blowgun out to her.

She took it warily, suddenly distrustful but not wanting to be, given how guileless Krax was. She had to keep reminding herself that he was hiding from something, someone, or some deed, and she had no idea what. "Does it matter which end?"

"Not really, but I used this one, so you can be sure it's not poisoned."

She frowned, blew into the empty chamber experimentally, then held out her hand for a dart. She received it as though it might bite her and inserted it fluff-first, tapping it down until she couldn't feel its point. "That deep enough?"

He regarded her askance. "You want me to put my eye up there and check, so you can kill *me* and say it was an accident?"

It was Eronese, and he hadn't got the inflection right, but she thought he was teasing.

"Never mind." She looked around for a target, settling on the wooden mannequin in the corner that held her armor. She aimed at what she hoped was mid-chest, tried to gauge her breath against his, in force and duration, then puffed her cheeks and blew.

The dart made it through the mail and struck home in the exposed wood behind it, just at the dummy's throat, though she'd aimed at the heart. It *had* gone in, however: wood into wood. Precisely, with almost no effort. She wondered if the darts could be made from steel, the tubes of some light metal. Strynn would know, or Avall.

More to the point, though, why hadn't her people thought of this before?

"How was that?" she asked, not bothering to disguise her pleasure.

He studied her seriously—much as she'd studied him earlier—frowned, and traced a finger along her jaw. She resisted the urge to flinch—or slap him away. Or get him down and sit on him and beat him silly for daring to treat her like that.

"Your jaw—your cheeks. You need to shape them more like this." He demonstrated.

She tried to copy but it was hard without a mirror.

"Just a moment," he sighed, and retreated to the door. And closed it.

She raised a brow.

"This could look silly," he told her. "I don't think either of us likes to look silly."

The brow went down, but her expression remained skeptical. "Do that again."

He did. First by himself, then into the blowgun, then by himself once more.

She followed his example, pursing her lips, relaxing, then pursing them again, over and over. "Is it better to keep your eyes open or shut? After aiming, I mean."

"Try it both ways. See how the . . . focus varies if you take your eyes into account instead of your memory."

She thought about that. It made sense. And she was game. With her eyes very wide-open, she puffed out a lungful of air. And then tried to puff out the same size breath with them closed.

But failed because something had touched her lips.

Krax's, as it evolved: soft and very uncertain. She started to thrust him away, then realized she didn't want to. Instead, she drew him to her and kissed him back. At some point she locked the door. Their lips touched many things in the course of the ensuing afternoon. Was she a fool? she wondered at one point. Was she being used or manipulated? *Possibly,* another aspect replied. But, she discovered, she didn't care. She only prayed Strynn was as lucky with her—Merryn's mind avoided the word, but she forced herself to confront it squarely—her *lover.*

CHAPTER XXIII:

MIND GAMES

(ERON: GEM-HOLD-WINTER—DEEP WINTER: DAY VIII—MIDAFTERNOON)

~~~~~~

It was the most valuable floor in Eron. Yet it was not made of inlaid marble, patterned woods, fired tile, or carved stone overlaid with glass. It was made of cork. More precisely, it was made of felt overlying cork overlying loosely laid wood overlying more cork, over more wood, to make a layer a hand deep with the approximate resiliency of ordinary earth. The expense lay in the material.

Cork didn't grow in Eron. Nor did much of it grow in Ixti; the trees from which this was made had been found in Ixti's southernmost reaches and it had taken twenty years to import enough to finish it—fifty years back. Even so, it required periodic resurfacing, which involved covering the whole expanse with felt, then brushing a kind of rare, gooey sap across it. The result was not unlike short grass—which made it perfect for playing games indoors—which were the only kind one could play, in Gem-Hold in Deep Winter.

Ferr had ordered this floor built when the High King came from that clan. The room that contained it was also the largest room in the building—almost fifteen spans to a side and four high, with glass brick along most of one whitewashed wall and a partial skylight as well. It was officially in Warcraft's precincts, but situated so that it bordered both the public areas and, conveniently enough, Smith's compound.

So it was that Avall and Rann hadn't had far to go to engage in a round of orney practice. They'd been at it for a hand already, shirtless, barefoot, and sweating from the heat that filtered out from three walls—which made Avall linger near the cooler window wall, which weakness Rann ruthlessly exploited. It wasn't an actual game—you needed at least fourteen for that—so much as simply rehearsing the moves. And so they'd mostly been doing drills: picking up the woven-leather ball with their arm-long, cup-ended sticks, then throwing it at the portable goal they'd set up in the center—a hollow pipe of light wood two spans high inserted over a smaller post which was itself portable. They missed more than they hit, which resulted in the ball going every which way—often as not caroming off walls or ceiling—or (once apiece) each other. Avall was nursing a fine bruise on his left collarbone from that. In any event, a miss resulted in a mad scramble to retrieve the ball, and those often turned into wrestling matches, which were generally quite protracted, as Avall was taller and heavier, but Rann was a paragon of wiry, slippery strength—and not above such cheats as tickling, pinching, and planting sloppy licks on Avall's ears. The walls echoed with their grunts, taunts, and cries; the sound of their panting and the pounding of their feet on the padded floor. That floor, in turn, was pocked with the impressions of their feet, knees, elbows, hips, and other body parts. Yet come tomorrow, it would be as smooth as when it was laid—assuming no one dug up the felting with a wayward stick.

"Oh no you don't!" Avall gasped, as he feinted around Rann to knock the ball toward the glass wall. It skittered ahead as he leapt after. Caught off guard, Rann stumbled a few steps the wrong way, which gave Avall clear advantage. If he timed it right, he'd be able to snare the offending object and make a goal-throw before Rann reached him. Focused purely on that, he ran, sticks outstretched before him, reaching down.

And was utterly unprepared when Rann blindsided him. He tumbled forward, landed hard on his right shoulder, and executed a sort of flipping roll to end up on his back with his feet halfway up the glass wall. It didn't hurt, but he was winded something dreadful.

Rann wandered over to look down at him, grinning triumphantly as he dropped the ball unceremoniously atop Avall's chest. Sweat dripped into Avall's face from his friend's hair, in spite of the headband he wore.

Avall squinted, executed a mock scowl, and reached up to grab Rann's legs around the ankles. Rann promptly squatted down in place—which almost put him atop Avall's head—and reached out to assail his friend's bare ribs. Avall retaliated with an attack on Rann's torso, and the next instant they were rolling around on the felt giggling like fools, their careless laughter echoing around the enormous chamber.

"Stop," Avall panted. "No, I mean it, stop! I've got to go. I've used up all the time I can give this today."

Rann dared one final prod, and relaxed, rolling away to lie beside Avall, staring up at the distant beams of the ceiling. "Tomorrow, then? This has been fun."

"If I can."

"What do you mean, 'if you can'? You've nothing else to do this time of day. I checked."

"Except work," Avall retorted. "The only reason I'm not doing it now is because the light got too bad for anything but cutting and I've already done all that."

Rann gaped at him, amazed. "Already?"

Avall nodded—wishing he hadn't said as much as he had, at least not yet. "As of midday. I, uh, woke up feeling really energized this morning, and just . . . kind of cut out the whole thing."

Rann snorted good-naturedly. "You really should remember that *some* of us are mortal."

Avall levered himself up, reaching for his sticks.

"I have to remember that I have a commission for my King for the honor of my clan, and that's why I have to go."

Another snort as Rann got to his feet, giving Avall a comradely arm up. "Bathe with me?"

Avall glanced toward the doors that led to the vesting room, then shook his head. "I've spent too much time already. I don't dare let myself get distracted."

"Work clean," Rann countered. "Isn't that what Eellon always said?"

"There's a bath in my suite," Avall gave back. "Like I said—not *this* time. It's nothing to do with you. Or Strynn," he added.

"Whatever," Rann replied too casually and padded toward the door. Then: "You coming?"

Avall gazed absently at the window wall. "In a moment. I'm doing a study of ice-crystal patterns, and just noticed a new variation. I'll show you the sketches if you'll come by."

"Anytime."

Avall wandered over to inspect the window. The door closed as he reached it, at which point he realized that the pattern wasn't as remarkable as he'd thought. Shrugging, he started to leave, then recalled that Rann had been using a pair of War's sticks instead of his own, one of which had been broken during the match. He'd have to return them to the equipment closet. Grimacing, he located them and padded that way. The space in question was small and paneled with cedar, with more of that fragrant wood making shelves around the sides. He stowed the sticks in the appropriate rack, turned to go, then paused. He'd heard . . . *singing*. Nothing remarkable—except that he'd assumed they were alone. He cocked his head, listening. There it was again: "Winterqueen's Lament." But that wasn't what drew his notice. It was the singer.

Eddyn.

But where?

Steeling himself to quiet, Avall made a slow survey of the room, and realized two things. One was that what he'd assumed to be wood overlying stone behind the main range of storage shelves actually wasn't. The other was something he should've figured out before: The storeroom shared a wall with Eddyn's quarters.

Not only that, but a fairly *flimsy* wall that had apparently been added in the process of making one storeroom into two, probably by boarding over an extant archway without first filling it in with stone. He tapped it experimentally, careful lest Eddyn, who was still singing, overhear him. A check revealed a fallen knothole, which allowed a closely applied eye a view through what proved to be the back wall of the storage closet in Eddyn's workroom, which Eddyn had left open. A closer check showed a fair bit of that room—and Eddyn himself.

He was working on the shield, Avall was pleased to note. And yet not pleased.

Rivals like Eddyn and himself would rather die than let others see their works-in-progress. Avall had let Strynn see the initial sketches for the helm, and had involved her in all crucial functional decisions. He'd also shown the initial sketches to Rann, but that was like showing it to one's reflection. This— It was spying, which his conscience reminded him was not good. On the other hand, as he discovered a moment later, it gave him a chance to see how far his rival had progressed. The Eight knew Avall had been distracted of late, unable to work as hard, often, or diligently as he ought. He blamed it on his discomfort with Strynn, but that was only one factor at most. Otherwise— Well, The Eight were obviously giving him this chance for a reason, because Eddyn had actually risen and was flourishing the shield (which at present consisted of a curved, flat-iron-shaped steel frame crusted with wax) aloft, so that the window light reflected off it.

It was good work. More formal than his but, from what he could see, impeccably rendered. And much further along than the helm. Wonder of wonders, too, Eddyn seemed bent on giving him what amounted to a private showing, because he'd evidently decided that it was time to cease work and store his work-in-progress—in that very closet.

Avall therefore got a very good view indeed—though he flinched back reflexively as his rival approached (still singing, which meant he was pleased with his progress) and hung the shield directly beside the spy hole. Eddyn stared at the wall for an anxious moment, then shrugged and closed the door.

Avall left, too, exiting the game room through the baths, which connected to a second game room devoted to another sport, from which stairs led down in a direction inconvenient for Eddyn to follow should he so choose. A moment later he was back in his quarters—energized anew, because he now had a standard to surpass.

. . .

It wasn't working, Avall conceded half a hand later, as he tried to follow the guidelines he'd sketched on the wax that would eventually form one of the helm's earpieces. His hand was simply too shaky to scribe the lines as crisply as he had last night. *Something* had happened, then; something extraordinary. Intervention by The Eight, perhaps—except that he didn't much believe in The Eight. Still, something had made him focus more tightly than he ever had before, made his vision clearer, his hand steadier.

Now—he tried again, taking a deep breath, flexing his fingers, wiping sweat off the stylus. Another breath, and he closed his eyes, trying to shut out the other sounds in the room, the other odors.

And the light—which was wavering again. *That* might be part of the problem.

He squinted at the inert slab of wax, blinked, then picked up the stylus and began anew. A hair's breadth . . . two . . . three . . . His hand began to shake. Not badly; certainly no worse than at any other time in his life, but enough to mar the intended line. No, not so much mar, as simply require the use of mechanical edges and curves. In any event, it bothered him, because he'd been so good last night, which meant he *could* be that good all the time—and wasn't.

Another breath, a scowl, and he leaned back in his chair. What had been different last night, anyway? The light—but this was daylight, which should be better. He'd worked in the mines then; but he'd exercised just now, so his heart rate and so on should be similar.

He hadn't been drinking either time.

The gem! He'd been fondling the gem, noting how very soothing it was to stroke it. And since he hadn't looked at it this afternoon (though he *had* that morning, before— *Before that marathon cutting bout!*), he opened the drawer where he kept it, retrieved the pouch, and tumbled the stone into his hand.

It gleamed in his palm, a third shade of red compared to last night or this morning. Fierier, perhaps. He probed it experimentally, then let it lie fallow. It was heavier than a ruby that size ought to be. He closed his fingers over it, resting the injured one (which still throbbed now and then) atop it.

And got a shock, as a tiny bright pain awoke in the splinter wound.

From which blood had dripped on the gem.

Which made no sense, except it was the only difference he could think of. In any event, it wouldn't be a hard theory to test. Nor was it difficult to find a means to draw blood. His finger still bore a line of scab, so he took a sharp, keenly pointed knife and pried it away, deepening it in the process. It hurt, but no more than his tattoo. No more than one fall Rann had given him not a hand gone by.

In short order, he had blood.

He hesitated, feeling foolish, before setting his thumb atop the gem. Nothing happened—at first. But then he felt the slightest pulse of energy flow into him from the stone.

The world spun in a way it hadn't the night before, then stabilized. As if to soothe his anxiety, the sun came out, brightening the light outside the window wall.

Not the *sun*, Avall realized an instant later; it was simply the work-candle. Its glare had stabilized again, flickering no longer.

Or maybe it wasn't the candle! He swallowed hard. Maybe it was his *perception* of the candle! Everything seemed slower—except his own movements. He squinted toward the window wall, searching for the dust motes that always drifted there. They still did—very, very slowly.

Which meant—he swallowed again and shuddered—something was throwing off his perception of time! The world around him was moving very slowly indeed. Or else he was moving faster. In any event, he felt, once again, that odd, pleasant, calming elation. And while part of him knew he should be deadly afraid of anything that so affected his senses, brain, and body, another part knew that it also made his work easier and better. Besides, Eddyn was doing very fine work indeed, which he would have to struggle to equal, never mind surpass.

But since the madness was upon him, he supposed he'd best get to work. Grinning unconsciously, he retrieved the wax earpiece mold, smoothed out the recalcitrant line with a finger, picked up a stylus, and started over.

The line formed perfectly. The curve was absolutely smooth, the distance from the edge consistently exact, even without calipers to prove it. His grin widened. It was back! For good or ill, the gem-madness had returned. Or the gem-*blessing*, perhaps he should style it.

Another line drawn, and another. The framework of dense lines he'd fill in with complex ice-crystal shapes was almost done already. So engrossed was he, however, that he didn't hear the outer door open, or the slow drawl of a voice calling his name, or the plodding of approaching steps.

He was therefore surprised to the point of crying out when a shadow fell across his hands. He glanced up and saw Rann, looking very surprised indeed.

"What're you *doing*?" Rann demanded.

That's what Avall *thought* he said, for the words sounded slow and labored, as though someone had stretched them at either end, deepening them in the process.

"What?" he growled back irritably, scowling as he lowered the stylus.

Rann's eyes grew wider. "You moved . . ."

"How?"

Rann stepped back slowly, obviously shaken, to judge by his wide, staring eyes and gaping mouth. "How?" he echoed in that draggy voice.

Avall glared at him. Wasn't it enough that Rann had entered his work-room unannounced and seen the commission? But for him also to be playing this stupid game . . .

Unless it *wasn't* a game. His perceptions were skewed; that was a fact. So maybe Rann was speaking normally but he was hearing him at a faster rate. And if that were the case—"How do I sound?" he asked very slowly.

Rann frowned, still looking scared, but also, now, concerned. "You sounded really strange just then"—the words took forever to form—"like you were talking at your normal speed and also trying to talk slow."

"And before that? When you came in?"

"Very fast. I couldn't understand you."

Avall closed his eyes, wishing he could regain control of his senses—his proper senses—yet also insanely reluctant to relinquish whatever this was that made his work so much better.

His work! Panic ambushed him, and he looked around for the gem, saw it lying where he'd left it, in a cloisonné bowl to the left of the work glass. It glowed like a small fire, lit by its own internal flame, which was really only light reflecting off the myriad irregular facets inside it.

"Avall—" Rann began, easing toward him, eyes fixed inexorably on the stone.

Which he'd intended to keep secret until—

His hand reached out to cover the gem (as though that mattered now), but somehow, in spite of his new speed and precision, in spite of the fact that Rann was moving like an old man in Deep Winter, his friend got his hand on Avall's first, restraining him.

"What *is* that?" Rann demanded—at almost normal pitch, which meant he was talking very fast indeed. "It's a gem. But is it—?"

"More," Avall gave back angrily. And with more anger. "Beyond that, I don't know."

"And you didn't tell me?"

"Tell you what?"

"That you've found something . . . strange. That it's doing things to you."

"Like helping me do the best work I've ever done?"

Rann's eyes flashed fire. "But at what price? How long have you been do-ing this? What drug—?"

"No drug."

Rann's eyes sought the gem. "That?"

"Maybe."

"Let me see."

Avall didn't want him to, and he was suddenly angrier yet. His hand closed on the gem as Rann reached for it, and snatched it away, even as he pushed with his other hand.

Rann's eyes nearly popped out of his head as he staggered backward. Not from the force of Avall's blow, but from the speed. He lost his balance, tripped over a low bench, and fell, by which time Avall was rising. He'd lock the gem away, send Rann packing, and never let him in again when he was at work.

He reached for the drawer, already fumbling with his other hand for the key.

And felt the world turn over as Rann slammed clumsily into him. "Bastard!" he yelled, as Avall felt his feet go out from under him and toppled heavily to the floor, even then noting how the pain of that impact seemed oddly blunted and dulled, as though it took a while to reach his brain.

"What *is* that thing?" Rann shouted.

Avall's senses spun: speeded up, then slowed once more, as Rann's strong hard fingers scrabbled desperately for the gem. He tried to buck him away, but Rann was as angry—or frightened, or concerned—as Avall had ever seen him, and held on for dear life. But Avall couldn't let him have the gem, not even see it. Not until *he* understood it better and was ready to make that revelation. He couldn't free Rann's hand from his, but his friend's elbow was in range. Avall bit down on it. Rann yelped and jerked his hand away to pry at Avall's jaws. Avall released the elbow—and bit the hand hard enough to draw blood.

Rann slapped him. And because he was effectively immobilized, Avall saw it coming but could do nothing to avoid it. The pain jarred him—odd to experience something slowly that usually occurred in the blink of an eye. He could almost feel the pain spreading out from his jaw, through his flesh; feel his teeth cut into the lining of his mouth, and the soft gush of blood.

And then Rann was going for the gem again with his bloody hand. "This isn't you!" he gritted. "Let me have that thing."

"No!" Avall yelled back. "No! No! No! You don't understand!"

"Eight, I don't!" Rann raged—and finally got Avall's hand open. Avall fought back, and somehow they clenched hands with the gem between and Rann's blood spreading all over it from his bitten hand, and Avall's old wound open again.

Their blood met and mingled, and once more Avall felt that odd jolt. But he felt something else as well.

He was still himself—but he was also *looking* at himself. It was the strangest thing he'd ever experienced. For it was as though his boundaries had dissolved and he was both himself and Rann. He could see his own body lying on the floor with Rann's legs straddling him and his hand appearing out of nowhere, as one saw things through one's own eyes. And he could see his own angry, confused expression, and the blood that smeared their conjoined hands.

But more importantly, he could *feel* what Rann was feeling. Could feel his concern at the image that had greeted him when he'd entered that room and found Avall's fingers moving far too quickly, doing far-too-high-quality work. But he could also feel Rann's anger at Avall's reaction, when they'd never had barriers between them before. And beyond that, he could feel Rann's concern and love and waning anger at having his offer of a bath refused. But he also realized that those were things he had no right to feel, no right to know—except that another part of him knew Rann was inside him the same way, feeling the weight of his own body pressing down on himself, and knowing his thoughts and feelings and . . . secrets.

But not all of them. Not yet.

Not about the gem.

And then it didn't matter, because they both relaxed and collapsed into each other, and simply lay there for an unreckonable moment, two discrete bodies but one set of perceptions and one soul.

Avall learned things about Rann he'd never known, and Rann about him. It was a joining, but far more intense and intimate than sex. He/they never wanted it to end, but knew they'd have to, if for no other reason (Rann reminded Avall/himself) that Strynn was due back soon and it would never do for her to find them thus. Not the physical closeness—that would neither surprise nor dismay her. But the rest. The skewed perceptions, the slowed time sense.

And so, with great regret, Avall gently eased Rann away from him (or did Rann simply rise of his own volition, just as Avall moved?) and slid back to brace himself against the table legs, still sitting on the floor. Their eyes met, though there was scarce any need to acknowledge the other's presence. Cautiously, tentatively, Rann loosened his fingers from the gem and from Avall's grasp. Avall felt a mental snap (though not unpleasant) and was himself again. And gasped, for he felt energized, as though he owned more *self* than heretofore; as though Rann had taken part of him, strengthened and refined it, and returned it to him without him knowing it was gone.

"W-what happened?" Rann whispered shakily.

Avall rolled his eyes and shrugged. "You tell me."

Rann grimaced in turn. "I—" He broke off. "You sound normal."

"So do you."

"I wonder how we'd sound to someone else."

"We'll have to check—but not now. For now— What did you feel?"

Rann took a breath. "I felt . . . like I was you. I was still me, but I was also you. I felt what you feel, and I don't mean physically. I felt your emotions. Your anger at being discovered, your regret at having to break off the game, your concern about the gem—but you wouldn't let me hold on to that. I kept . . . slipping off."

"Did you like it?"

Rann shook his head as if confused and buried his face in his hands. "It was wonderful—but it was also scary. I'm not sure I liked losing myself like that."

Avall exhaled heavily. "Me neither. But I can't wait to do it again—assuming we can. It was beyond scary—but beyond wonderful, too."

Rann cleared his throat. "Some things I couldn't find, though—or you wouldn't show me, or I didn't know where to look."

"Like what?"

"Like where you found this thing. What you know about it. What you plan to do."

Avall stared at the gem still in his hand and with great regret rose and replaced it in the bowl. Only then did he speak. "I did that so I wouldn't be tempted to show you. To ask you to . . . to bond with me, or whatever that was, and show you those things you want to know."

Rann's eyes widened. Real fear showed there. "I'd do it again—but not now. For now . . . I need to think. How long does the effect last?"

Another shrug. " I don't know." He glanced at the dust motes, saw them floating at almost their normal rate. A glimpse of the candle confirmed it. "We seem to be moving at our everyday pace again. From that I might guess that physical action burns off the . . . effect fairly quickly. I know that when I first discovered this, it went on for what seemed like hands. But that was low-energy work—high-mental, but low-energy."

Rann closed his eyes, breathing heavily. "I think you'd better tell me everything."

Avall did.

The candle was out when he finished, and sunset light was probing the room. Rann would soon have to leave for duty in the mines. Avall had an appointment with a nap, then with Strynn to listen to Kylin's music. And then bed. He had an early shift in the kitchen.

Rann rose. "So," he asked seriously, "what're you going to do? You can't keep something like that to yourself."

"No, I can't. And to tell the truth, I don't know. My plan was to clean it up and give it to the Hold-Warden, hoping she'd return it for use on the helm. Now . . ."

Rann's brow wrinkled. "Much as I hate to say it, since we're dealing with some fairly radical ethical concepts here, I have to agree. So I'll help you keep your secret—for a while. But you have got to help me, too, by including me. You want to experiment with that thing? Fine. But tell me. I could watch, take notes, observe you from a normal person's point of view. And vice versa."

Avall stared at him strangely, feeling strange indeed, inside himself. "Something tells me," he murmured, "I'll never be normal again."

"No," Rann whispered back, "you won't."

CHAPTER XXIV:

CURIOUS INTERLUDE

(ERON: WAR-HOLD-WINTER—DEEP WINTER: DAY XII—EARLY AFTERNOON)

~~~~~~~~~~

As days progressed and Deep Winter crept ever south to enfold even War-Hold in its grasp, Kraxxi found himself relaxing into its routine. The snowfall was too intense most times for outdoor sparring, which meant that the inner chambers set aside for that purpose were getting far more extensive use. Which was bad, because it meant he had to practice his weaponwork before more witnesses than he liked, and Merryn had advised that wouldn't be wise if he wanted their easy access to each other to continue. And good, because it meant he had more opportunities to encounter Olrix and Elvix when there weren't scores of ears to overhear.

He'd known where they were housed since the first day, of course; the layout of their hall was no secret. His and Tozri's room (probably intended for a servant) joined Merryn's on one side, while Krynneth and another man shared a similar suite on the other, with Olrix and Elvix housed beyond, and a pair of female guards on the other side. There could be free commerce through connecting doors, but in practice there was not. Partly that was because of the staggered schedule the hold demanded their shadows keep—which sometimes had them rising in the middle of the night to bake, or in the middle of the day to clear snow, or tend the laundry, or scour down the stables. It was often close quarters, but reasonably comfortable. Too much ritual, for sure, and too many routines, not enough flexibility, and little room for spontaneity. But there was a certain security in that as well—though the triplets, who were used to going their own way more than he, spent a fair bit of time complaining.

Kraxxi's problem was privacy. Tozri was a good friend and an unobtrusive roommate, and was spending much of his spare time in their room reading everything about Eron he could find in the enormous hold library, which erudition he was passing on to Kraxxi and his sisters.

And Merryn—

He didn't know what to think about Merryn. That they liked each other, there was no doubt, or that they enjoyed each other's company. That she was lonely was also clear—lonelier than he, based on how often she talked about her brother and bond-sister, Avall and Strynn. As best he could tell, she'd invested most of her available affection in those two and didn't care much for anyone else, though she liked people in general well enough. What she saw in him, he had no idea . . . except, again, as Tozri had suggested, he had an innocent streak (courtesy of his protected childhood) that reminded her of her brother.

But why take him to her bed?

That was what Olrix had just asked, as they found themselves miraculously unsupervised at one of the trestle tables scattered behind the arcades that surrounded the second largest indoor sparring ground. Nine skylights lit the place, through which patchy blue sky showed above unthawed snow. If the snow grew worse, people would be up there all night, sweeping the thick glass free and channeling the detritus into a network of drains lest the weight crush even those hefty panes. Merryn, Krynneth, and the other two shadows were out on the ground working up some complicated maneuver that required four people to execute, and Kraxxi took comfort from the fact that they'd been trusted without supervision. Provided with ale, too, which they were quaffing in heroic portions, having just recovered from an intense practice bout themselves—during which they'd all tried to appear inept and clumsy.

"So," Olrix persisted, in Ixtian, leaning forward so as to speak as quietly as she could amid the martial clamor. "Why you? She could have any man in this keep, and most of the women, from what I hear. Surely she doesn't *love* you."

Kraxxi glared at her. "Is there some reason you think she might *not* love me?"

"Either she does or doesn't. Those are the facts. If she does, what are her reasons? If she doesn't, why does she dissemble?"

"The answer to the last is obvious," Elvix opined. "Information."

"All she's learned from me," Kraxxi growled icily, "is that I was often in the palace as a child—and she already knew that the richer merchants sometimes have their children schooled there, and that it's also common to name children after royal newborns."

"Is that all?"

"What I look like naked," he flared. "If one were ignorant, one might say she considers me a novelty—except that she was"—he glanced around furtively, lest they be overheard—"a virgin."

"As were you," Tozri observed dryly.

"Because my title left me no choice," Kraxxi retorted. "You know the constraints there as well as I do."

"We all do," Olrix sighed. "But surely— Don't the people of this country require their women to wed early and give birth often? To rebuild after the plague?"

Kraxxi nodded. "That's common knowledge. I don't know why Merryn had waited, but I know she truly cares about only two people: her brother and her bond-sister. She'd do anything for them."

"What happens if you get her with child?"

"By their law, she would have to name a father—not necessarily who it was, but who would acknowledge it—which would probably be me. If I accepted that, we would be wed for at least a year: long enough for the child to be born. If I were from here, the child would become part of my clan. As it is; I suppose the child would be part of her clan by default."

Tozri drummed the table anxiously. "I've heard strange things about the fertility of Eronese men and women. I've heard that their women bleed less often than our women; perhaps only twice a year. I've heard that their men are more fertile to compensate for that. I know Father said that Mother told him he had to couple with her at a very particular time in order to ensure our conception."

Elvix frowned. "Then she should be *more* free to seek love, not less."

"I . . . think they are less interested other times," Tozri hedged.

Kraxxi fidgeted with his mug. "So you're implying that she lies with me because she wishes to lie with *someone*, being a healthy young woman, but thinks I am less likely to get her with child?"

Tozri regarded him squarely. "Between friends, between brothers, almost: Have you had her? Completely? In the manner of women and men?"

Kraxxi couldn't meet his eye. "She makes me . . . withdraw when it's almost time. But she makes up for it!" he added fiercely.

Olrix cleared her throat, her face gone oddly soft. "We're forgetting something here, brother, sister: We're forgetting to ask our friend the most important question. Are you in love with her?"

Kraxxi rolled his eyes, masking his uncertainty with another quaff of ale. "I have no idea. I know that I've never met anyone like her—except you two. She's so completely herself. Even in this country, where rules and rituals run everything, she finds ways to play the law to her advantage; she knows which rules will bend and which will break. I love that about her. She's beautiful, but in a real way, not like the made-up women back home. Maybe I'm just flattered, I don't know. It's like a house cat and a lynx. Both are lovely, but when a lynx makes friends with you, you feel special. She's smart. She's funny. She's never boring. She doesn't lie. She seems genuine."

Tozri laid an arm across Kraxxi's shoulders, pulling him close, then thumped him on his chest above his heart. "But do you *love* her, Krax? You don't do that in your head, you do it here."

Kraxxi didn't answer. He'd been avoiding that question for days, distracting himself with everything he could find. Working so hard he fell into bed dreamlessly, often as not, *his* bed instead of Merryn's, for that door was sometimes unlocked now, to Tozri's dismay—or frustration. Did he love her? He'd never *been* in love, so he didn't know how it was supposed to feel. But he'd never felt anything like this either. And so, at last, he answered. "Let's just say that I think, if I stay here all winter, the answer will certainly become . . . yes."

And then another group joined them, and the conversation turned, as it did far too often, to the weather.

CHAPTER XXV:

TRIALS

(ERON: GEM-HOLD-WINTER—DEEP WINTER: DAY XIII—JUST PAST NOON)

~~~~~~~~~~~~~~~~~

A vall paused in the doorway of the forge and stared at Strynn. Accustomed as he was to seeing women performing that most demanding of arts, it was still disconcerting to observe the most beautiful woman of her age dressed only in leather trews and a sturdy leather work apron that left her arms and a fair bit of sides bare, with her stomach finally starting to swell with the impending child and with her mass of dark hair bound roughly back. Sweat sheened her face to drip hissing on the hot stone marge. Her arms, most times sleek and slender, were rippled with muscles not normally seen, while the ruddy light transformed her features into a mask of crimson and gold limned with black at brows, nostrils, and eyes—and the fixed, intent line of her mouth.

She hadn't seen him—no one had—and judging from the flames of more than one forge, Strynn wasn't alone.

Avall studied her appreciatively, noting the quick, sure strokes she applied to the length of iron bar she was folding. No secret work here—no way it could be, though Smithcraft controlled access to the forge. Still, all swords looked alike at this stage—though Avall knew that with Strynn making it, it would be far more than a ceremonial blade.

She was almost finished. Certainly she no longer pumped the bellows to rouse the fire to new heights of intensity. One more moment— She still hadn't seen him but had exchanged her hammer for tongs and thrust the arm-long shaft back into the coals until it glowed cherry-red, then stabbed it into a bucket of fish oil. Smelly steam filled the air as she paused a long moment, then withdrew it.

Nodding her satisfaction, she grasped the embryonic tang with one thick-gloved hand, covered the blade with a length of fabric (not the casual choice one might think, either), and marched toward the door against which Avall lounged. She started when she saw him, then smiled uncertainly. "So what brings you here," she inquired cheerily, obviously satisfied with her morning's labor.

Avall shrugged. "You're a smith; I'm a smith. This is a forge . . ."

She poked him in the ribs—carefully—with the shrouded iron. "And when was the last time *you* swung a hammer?"

He paused to puzzle it out. "Last summer. But I was building a box."

She pinched his shoulder playfully. "Wouldn't hurt to start again. You're getting soft."

"Try that a little lower and to the front and I'll show you how soft I am!"

She grinned. "Indeed."

His face went serious. He'd thought long and hard about what he was on the verge of undertaking and still had doubts, had in fact almost fled twice while he stood there watching. But if he waited for an opportunity, none might ever come. He'd therefore made one—while the madness to act was upon him. "Actually," he went on, "if you've got time—which as best I can tell, you do—I'd like to"—he swallowed—"I'd like to show you an even more personal part of me: one that's soft and hard at once."

A brow shot up. "You talk riddles."

"I talk carefully lest we be overheard. This isn't a game, not by implication, though it's hard not to treat it as one."

"You've awakened my curiosity," she chuckled as she paced him down a wide, plain hall toward the first of many flights of stairs that wound their way from the basement workrooms up to their level. On the way they talked of nothing more substantial than Avall's reasonable anxiety about the availability of casting kilns to melt the bronze for the helm's decorations. Not gold, for he wanted the thing to be functional, and cast gold over steel wouldn't stand up to even a minor sword blow. And, of course, about security—how hard it would be to work unobserved.

And then they reached their suite.

Strynn excused herself to her private workroom, then returned, minus the sword—but only as far as the bedroom, where she stripped and padded into the bath. "Are you in a hurry?" she called.

"I want your full attention," Avall called back. He flopped into a cushion-chair, wondering why he always thought of this as *her* room. Perhaps because he usually rose before she did and went to bed after? He filled the time trying to relax, failed, then rose abruptly and strode to his workroom, where he retrieved the gem—which he should've done to start with. That accomplished, he returned to the bedroom, prowled through a cabinet until he found a bottle of tart mint wine and two cups, and proceeded to pour, helping himself to a meaty pastry Kylin (who was a remarkable cook) had sent by earlier.

Avall wondered about that—not that he begrudged Strynn whatever happiness she could seize. *He* certainly wasn't giving her much these days, what with work on the helm and playing with Rann, with whom he was as relaxed as a foot in an old shoe. He wondered about that, too: whether he'd ever achieve that level of closeness with his wife. He doubted it. His bond with Rann was based on mutual attraction at *every* possible level, with no secondary agenda. His bond with Strynn was based in part on convenience and politics. And therein lay the difference.

But some of that difference might be about to erode.

Impulsively—but not quickly, for he could still hear water pattering against marble—he took off his clothes and folded them casually on the chest, then lay down on the bed on the side away from the window, stashed the gem in its bag beneath the pillow, and drank half the wine. Thirst assuaged, he set the cup on the bedside table, folded his arms across his chest, closed his eyes, and waited. And tried not to worry about what was about to occur.

The shower sounds ended, replaced by the soft rasp of fabric against bare flesh. He cracked his eyelids as Strynn reentered the room, hair still tangled and gleaming wetly, a shimmery robe draped around her body hiding little, and even less of what made her female. She looked at him uncertainly. Her lips twitched, as though she were debating whether or not to smile.

"Are you—?"

"Yes, but not what you see. This is . . . maybe an adjunct. A symbolic lowering of barriers."

"Then I'll lower mine," She let the robe slide off her shoulders as she moved toward the other side of the bed.

"I poured you some wine," Avall called as she passed the table. "And . . . don't be alarmed, but bring a knife—unless you've managed to cut yourself at the forge."

She looked at him strangely but took the wine. "No—but I got a blister. What I get for neglecting my craft."

"Did it bleed?"

"You need blood?"

He nodded sheepishly. "A little."

She slid onto the sleeping pad beside him, mirroring his position. It was early afternoon and the light was lazy—which might help. Avall looked at her out of the corner of his eyes, unaccustomed to seeing her bare in this kind of light. Her breasts had grown larger (as his hands already knew), and her belly really was swelling. He tried not to think about that. Rather, he tried to think about some of it, to keep parts of *him* from swelling, which was not what this was about.

And still he hesitated.

"Are you going to tell me?" she asked at last.

A deep breath. "You remember that night I worked late in the mines, when I was up all night? When I was telling you about all that great work I got done, and then did another round of good work the next morning?"

She stared at him above her wine. "Aye."

"I— Well, I know the reason all that was so strange."

"Reason?"

"Aye," he echoed. "That didn't just happen, though let me assure you, I wasn't doing anything to make it happen either. But— Well, basically, I found— Wait a moment." He reached beneath the pillow and fished out the pouch, then tumbled the jewel into his hand and held it out for her. The sunlight turned it to frozen fire. "I found *this*. A legitimate claim, I might add, though I'm going to have to do some fast maneuvering to keep it."

Strynn finally found words with which to speak. "Oh, Avall, it's beautiful! And . . . strange! Where'd you find it?"

"In the clan vein, as it happens, which strengthens my claim—our claim, rather."

She gnawed her lip. "I don't understand."

"No," he agreed, "and you won't unless I show you. It's easier than telling, trust me. Rann and I discovered that five days ago."

She frowned. "You told Rann first?"

He shook his head. "Rann *found out* first—by barging in when he shouldn't."

She shook hers in turn. "I'm sorry. I shouldn't have said that. Rann and you are choice—like me and Merryn. You and I are—necessity."

"But that doesn't have to be bad—and may be about to get better." He swallowed. "All it will cost you—I hope—is a little blood."

She didn't reply, but she looked . . . frightened.

He took a deep breath. "Strynn I promise you—vow to you—swear to you by anything I own that I will not now or ever do anything willfully to hurt you. I don't know if this will work, but . . . please trust me. I'm taking no more risk than you."

She finished her wine decisively. "Fine, then. What do I do?"

"Where's your wound?"

She twisted her arm around so she could see what her palm had concealed: a blister that had formed, popped, and been ignored until it bled. She probed the seeping flesh experimentally.

"Ah!" He picked at the scab on his finger, which he'd managed to enlarge that day. It hurt more than expected, but the reward would be worth it—if he could join with Strynn as he had with Rann.

By the time he'd completed his own churgeoning, Strynn's hand was bleeding freely. "Trust me," he repeated, and placed the gem atop the open cut. He held his breath, fearing that the barely familiar shock wouldn't happen, but it did. "Now clamp your hand over this. Let your blood touch the stone. Close your eyes, if it'll help."

She did, exhaling sharply as she folded her fingers around his with the stone between their two palms. He heard her soft, surprised "Oh" and surmised she'd felt the same jolt he had.

Pain—or something—shot up his arm to his brain, then fled as quickly. And in its wake, his thoughts began draining away. Or maybe spreading out was a better analogy, for they immediately came flooding back, stronger than before—and with them came Strynn's, and all at once they were— Not quite one, not like he and Rann had been, but certainly no longer entirely separate beings. He saw with her eyes and his at once. And he saw how she saw him: much handsomer than he'd imagined, and with an incredible admiration she kept hidden lest he (rightly) become too vain. But he felt hurt, too—an empty listlessness that spoke of independence gone, of dreams unfulfilled—and only then realized how much the wedding had placed limits on her she chafed daily at finding there.

Did she love him? In a way. But it was so tied up with gratitude and relief and clan responsibility it was hard to tell on what stone the core emotion lay.

Merryn? The same comfort he felt with Rann but on a less physical level.

Rann? A bit of jealousy, a bit of relief at not having to concern herself overmuch with Avall's happiness.

Her work?

Contentment, above all other things, and fierce pride in work well made and a certain smugness at being so accomplished in what most considered a man's skill.

Eddyn? He didn't go there, save that there were somehow two Eddyns: the man they saw daily; and another, who existed solely as a naked white torso, leering eyes, and bloody penis rising above her with a sated smirk on his face—while in her loins burned pain that Avall could all but feel.

But she was in him, too, though he had no idea what she read there, as barrier after barrier was assailed and relinquished. At one point, he was aware of her touching some level of himself he didn't know existed and tearing down walls, and of a resulting flood of something—energy, or will, or simply raw *power*—that burst out in him as though he'd been color-blind and then discovered rainbows. Something like that had also occurred with Rann, he realized (and wasn't he thinking faster, too?), but then the tide of emotional back-and-forth evened out, and for a long timeless moment they lay there, sharing.

They drifted. They simply were. Their whole reality focused on what flowed between them through that stony link. But as they relaxed into each other, Avall gradually sensed a third presence—one barely formed and not fully cognizant, but nevertheless aware that its environment was changing.

Her child.

Her—their—son.

Joy leapt into him, even as he recalled that it was Eddyn's son. And with that joy came one final . . . presence.

Rann.

Somehow, still, he was linked with Rann—enough to know that his friend had started from what he'd been reading, to gaze out the window with a scowl and call out a puzzled, "Avall, is that you?"

He sent back a *"no,"* and eased away from that bond, for it made him uncomfortable to spread his *self* so thin. Never mind what it might do to Strynn. Or the baby.

"Open your eyes," Strynn murmured—aloud or in his mind made no matter. "I want to try to see with your eyes."

He obliged, but saw only their two bodies and the dark coverlet on which they lay, and the carved footboard, and the bleached stone walls, and the tapestry, and the thick wooden door.

He closed them again. "My turn," he might have said.

She obliged, and it was the same view, but perhaps more blurred, the colors a trifle different and observed from another angle.

Finally, they slept, and during that slumber, the gem slipped from between their hands. When they awoke, they were separate once more, but neither would be completely alone again—ever.

Strynn wasn't certain when she roused and found Avall gone, but for a very long time she lay there, watching the shadows lengthen as her date with the mines drew near. So much had changed. *So much!* She understood so much more now. About Avall and how his mind worked, and why he was as he was. But with that knowledge had come a whole new round of ignorance, most of it centered on two things. The gem itself, and the exact powers and limits and . . . consequences it conferred. And the larger questions that revolved around what this new discovery meant in the grand cold scheme of life.

One thing was certain, it was too powerful—she knew that already—to remain hidden long. Avall knew about it. Rann knew about it. So did she. But Avall had all but told *Eddyn*, of all people, that he'd found something important. And the Night-Warden knew something as well. The implications were astounding. Already she could see beyond such selfish plans as bonding with Merryn as she'd just bonded with Avall, and he with Rann, to what it could mean in terms of education. That stone—or one like it, for surely where there was one there were more—could turn the system of crafts upside down. One would no longer have to explain lengthy procedures, but simply link with a student through that stone and show them directly, mind to mind.

Or maybe not. Avall and she shared a bond of physical, emotional, and intellectual closeness. So did he and Rann. Could one share that closeness with a stranger? Would it even work? So much to do, so many questions (many of which were also Avall's, or even Rann's). She wanted to do nothing but study the gem. Forget the sword. Forget the commission. Forget the High King's regalia and the honor to her clan. She wanted to *know*!

Where *was* the gem, anyway? No longer in her hand, that was certain. Legally it belonged to Avall, and the only claim she had on it was through him. He'd stored it in his workroom, probably with his tools. She started to rise in anger at being thus denied trust, but her hand brushed something crinkly on the bed. A slip of paper, it evolved: a note from Avall telling her that he'd reserved forge time he had to use, and because the gem was too valuable to leave lying around, even in her hands, he'd locked it away in his tool chest—exactly where she'd assumed it would be.

But she had to see it again! And she had to work with it herself, with or without Avall's permission. Had to experience that transformation it had made in his work firsthand. But she wanted more. She wanted to try something *new*: to increase their store of knowledge on her own.

She knew precisely how, too; though it would require initiating one more person into their cabal. Still, it would be worth it, not only for the knowledge she might thereby gain, but as a favor to a friend.

A moment later she was dressed, had retrieved the gem, and was striding airily down the hall. Someone stared at her curiously as she passed, and she realized that she might still be experiencing the gem-euphoria and moving too quickly for either decorum or the safety of her child. (And wasn't *that* wonderful: the way she'd been able to reach in to him!) Or maybe too quickly period—though her gait felt fine to her. Other folk, however—Their voices seemed to drag, and they all moved with the deliberate slow pace of unclanned drudges.

But she was impatient, dammit! She wanted to know!

She settled for taking back routes and little-used stairs (the hold had a couple of thousand rooms after all), and burned off most of the surge of energy in the process. Even so, she was still more than a little taken aback when she found herself so quickly knocking on Kylin's door.

It was her knock, so he called a come-in. She acquiesced, grateful for once that her friend was blind and could see nothing odd about her.

He was sitting where he often was: between harp and writing desk, his fingers poised around a pen and black with ink from the score he'd been composing, a pair of parallel metal edges keeping the symbols straight. "You're in a hurry," he opined without preamble.

"I am," she conceded, deliberately speaking slow.

"Your voice sounds odd."

"It should. For reasons I hope you'll soon understand."

A brow shot up. "A mystery!" he smiled, one hand fumbling in search of a cloth on which to wipe his fingers while the other stabbed the quill into its well with eerie certainty.

She paused, unsure how to continue, then decided to simply blunder on. Kylin wasn't one to gossip. If any man she'd ever met—make that any*one* she'd ever met—knew how to keep his own counsel, it was this one: calm, quiet, sweet Kylin.

She claimed a chair without asking and scooted it across from him with only the desk between. "Bear with me," she murmured, "this will be very strange."

"But wonderful, I'm sure," he replied dreamily, retrieving a mug of ale from which he drank.

She scowled at that—Kylin drank more than was good for him, though with good reason, given his situation. Still, that might be about to change. To which end, she set about shifting the material on his desk to either side, trying not to mark how he was likewise trying not to look alarmed. "Sorry," she muttered absently.

"That funny voice again."

"You'll understand soon enough."

He watched without watching.

Finally she'd emptied the center of the desk, noting as she'd removed things where the cleaning rag was. She cleared her throat. "How," she began awkwardly, "do you feel about pain?"

The mask twitched across his eyes as though he blinked. "I don't enjoy it, if that's what you mean."

She shook her head, caught herself at it, and felt stupid. "Can you endure for promise of reward?"

He gnawed his lip then nodded. "Depending on the reward. What did you have in mind?"

A deep breath. "I would rather not tell you; that way I won't build false hope."

"Ah!"

In reply she retrieved the small, sharp knife Avall had left on the bedside table. "Do you, by any chance have any wounds on or around your hands?"

He shook his head, extending his hands to show her. Fine, slender hands, soft for a man, and far softer than hers or Merryn's. She took the nearer gently, opened it palm-upward, smoothed it with her fingers. It was pale; rarely saw the sun. She wondered how hard the journey here had been for him—but might know soon enough. In any event, she took the knife in one hand as she held him steady with the other. "I'm going to cut you," she whispered. "Only enough to make you bleed. Not enough for damage. You'll have to trust me."

He shrugged. "If you slash my wrist, I'll die. If I die, I'll see again that much sooner, Eight allow."

The thought made her stomach twitch, but she maintained her resolve as she made a quick gash in the fleshy part of his left hand. He gasped but didn't flinch away, though sweat sprang out on his brow and every muscle in his arm tensed. Another—deeper—brought blood. Just enough. She hoped.

"Hold this," she told him softly, laying the gem on his hand so that it touched the blood oozing from the tiny slit. A small "Oh!" of surprise told her *something* had happened—likely that spark-jolt effect.

Another breath, and she reopened her own fresh wound, closed her eyes, and laid her hand atop the gem, curling her fingers around to rest lightly on his wrist. She could feel his pulse, but slow, oh so slow. For an instant she thought something was wrong, then recalled the altered time sense the gem evoked. Finally, making certain that her eyes were open, she whispered what she already knew was unnecessary: "See, Kylin, see! Use my eyes and *see*!"

He shuddered violently. His free hand made to remove the mask across his ruined eyes—even as she found her own vision veiled. Energies shifted and slid, and she lowered her barriers—or felt them assailed. She saw nothing, not even night—then vague shapes: dark and light. And then she saw Kylin's face—not as she would've expected, but constructed from his own imagination—even as vision that was not her own took in the entire room an item at a time, finding wonder in quill pens, ink blots, and paper. In the texture of stone and the stippled shadows from the tiny light-well. In the nap of the velvet coverlet and the patterns in the carpet on the floor.

"I can see!" he choked. Or perhaps she merely *felt* those words in her head. "I can see, but with my heart as well! But"—he paused, swallowed, and she knew his next sentence before he voiced it—"there's one thing I wish to see but can't, and that's . . . you."

She froze, gazed around frantically, before recalling that she had a small mirror in her pouch. She fished it out one-handed and held it before her face, staring with other eyes at her oh-so-fabled beauty.

"They say you're the most beautiful woman of our time," Kylin murmured.

"And you know I don't care about that," she retorted. "I've told you as much, and now you know, for you've lived within me."

"Not far," he corrected. "I could see you open to me, feel you welcoming me, but I dared not go too far. I don't want to know you as well as this thing allows. I don't think I should. And if I know you that well, I'd also know what you know about Avall and Rann, and that isn't my right. *Tell* me what you would, everything you know. But do *not* grant me the freedom you've given me!"

He was right. It wasn't her choice, nor had he availed himself of the bounty she'd offered. He'd entered the vestibule of her house, but politely declined to prowl. And beyond the front hallway, where his own most vivid feelings were displayed, he'd allowed her no farther into himself.

He was crying, she realized, as she tried to reach inside him and turn off that grief—and met barriers from which her soul—or some part of Kylin's that shared its space—recoiled. "It doesn't matter," she said, because she had to say something. And again: "It doesn't matter."

Slowly, with his free hand, he took the hand she'd laid upon the gem and pried it open, then removed the stone and laid it on the desk. She felt an odd tearing sensation as they broke contact. "Thank you," he said. "For the sharing; for the willingness to share, which you should trust to very few; and for the gift you gave me."

"Your eyes," she blurted numbly.

He shook his head. "Your face. Not the shape of it—though it, I suppose, is fair. But what I saw in your eyes."

She couldn't reply, simply sat there staring. Aching. Not caring when she also began to cry and having no idea why, beyond the glimpse she'd had of the beauty of Kylin's soul.

"You should leave," he told her. "This isn't good for you."

"And you?"

"Ah," he chuckled, reaching over to caress the harp strings. "I have memories now: memories of you!"

She nodded mutely and rose, pausing only to retrieve the gem.

"A dangerous thing," he said as she turned, punctuating the remark with another shimmer of music. "I'd be very careful who else I showed that to."

"Never doubt it." As she found the door.

"I . . . love you," he called abruptly. "I'll never tell you that again."

"I know," she whispered sadly.

And knew both things were true.

CHAPTER XXVI:

ACROSS THE WINTER LAND

(ERON: GEM-HOLD-WINTER—DEEP WINTER: DAY XIII—NIGHT)

The cold night wind off the Spine that was called the Ilmone howled along Gem-Hold's main arcade—the one that circled the entire building save the back. It brought a dusting of ice crystals but no snow, thank The Eight. Those who recorded such things said there were three spans of the stuff piled against the lower shield already. Here—heat in the floor kept the pavement clear, though the runoff made icicles as big as three men where they slid down the wall beyond the parapet. The half walls between the thick pillars were usually scoured clean by the wind, but here and there deposits clung—and froze at juncture of wall and upright. The stone benches ranged beneath them were cleared at need, but few found cause to linger outdoors in a cold that froze one's breath into one's hair and eyebrows if one weren't careful.

Avall fingered his chin speculatively with a twice-gloved hand. Perhaps he should grow whiskers—or try. They'd be useful against the cold, and it might be interesting to look different. Strynn might like it. Or might not. Besides, he doubted he could produce more than a sketchy stubble. Happily for him, given the vogue for such things, his body was by nature almost as smooth as when he'd been a boy, save where dark hair showed in men's places. Now, however— The way the wind was howling around the corner ten spans to the left, he'd have been happy to be furry as a bear—or wolf. Or birkit. Cloaks helped, and fur-lined tunics and trews and boots, but you couldn't cloak everything.

He shook his head and leaned against the parapet, gazing out at the silent, empty night. Stars glittered above, and all three moons, making the shadows dance in odd patterns on the drifting snow. Most of the forecourt was clear—it was kept that way by heated stones and men with torches and mirrors that focused the waning heat of the sun. But Deep Winter lay out there, waiting, grinning down on Gem-Hold through the screen of fir trees, like an ice lynx waiting for a rabbit to leave its den. Black, white, and cold blue— and dull conifer-green. That was the world tonight.

Almost, he was alone. The arcade was empty save for a couple down at the far end talking softly and watching their hot cider freeze.

Alone—but never again, he suspected. Not really. Not after what he'd shared with Rann and Strynn. But what came next? What did he do with the damned gem? He'd planned to use it in the royal regalia—but would that now be wise? Rann thought maybe, Strynn thought not.

Strynn also thought it would be wise to keep an eye on Eddyn, since Avall had casually directed him to the same vein that had produced his stone. No reason Eddyn couldn't have found another—or several. No reason to assume that while they'd be experimenting with each other, he'd not been experimenting with Rrath—or that girl from Glass he'd been, against the ban, pursuing.

A chill shook him that had nothing to do with the frigid wind. This was no minor discovery. He could feel the world changing around him and wished he could better recall what Gynn had prophesied about the winter. The gem was certainly a catalyst, but of what? All he knew was that it was his fortune, his responsibility, and his burden.

And, as Strynn had pointed out at dinner, when she and Rann and he had met in Rann's rooms (so they wouldn't be tempted to fool with the wretched thing again), there were simply too many ways in which it could be used, both for good and ill.

Avall stared out at the snow again, and cursed it, even as he wondered if he might not best use this damned nervous alertness that seemed to have found him by returning to the mines in search of another of the troublesome gems. At least it would be warm down there. At least he'd have time to think.

But thinking did no good. Not now. Why, if not for the snow, if not for the fact that it was Deep Winter and nothing was moving between here and Tir-Eron that wanted to live, he'd simply go to Eellon, drop the thing into his hand, tell him what it did, and be done. Or maybe go straight to the King. Gynn was Smithcraft, after all; that was where his loyalties ought to lie.

Eight, how he wished Merryn were here! She'd roll her eyes and cut to the heart of the matter without preamble. Ruffle his hair and tell him he was a fool, and he'd get mad because she was no older than he, but oh so very much wiser.

Which was like wishing the stars down from the sky. Or maybe not, for a streak of light that moment flashed down from the heavens. A breath later two more followed. Omens? Or simply luck? They weren't things of The Eight, that much he knew, as he knew that Angen spun around the sun, and the moons around Angen herself. Numbers told that, and ancient books in Lore-Hold no one but the Chiefs of Lore and the King were allowed to access anymore.

The wind shifted, harder and colder alike; the ice crystals were as bitter as knives. He heard the lovers down the way protest in dismay, and that decided him.

Shrugging his hood more closely around his face, he turned back toward the hold. The nearest door was ten spans away, and inset in the wall, as were all entrances. On the way, he passed a series of windows shuttered against the cold and the night. He wished he could do the same: shut out the knowledge of the gem and all the attendant unknowing, and simply get on with his life.

He banished that thought by turning his thoughts to Strynn. The way she'd looked in the forge—all grim and strong and forceful. And later in bed, a vision of beauty and fecundity. And then at discussion over dinner with Rann: wisdom personified. She was, he decided, if not actually a goddess herself, at least some incarnate avatar. Himself, he suspected, was mostly a toy of Fate in his guise as Lord of Fools.

And then he reached the door, pulled it open, and slipped inside.

Perhaps he should go out again, Avall decided, two hands and three glasses of wine later. At least there'd be more to look at than four stone walls and a pair of bedposts; more to hear than Strynn's slow, even breathing. More to smell than wine and candle wax. More to taste than the bitterness of concern that filled his mouth.

It wasn't working. He'd thought he'd quieted his concerns out there on the arcade, but he'd been wrong. Dawn was approaching and with it the need to rise early, which wouldn't bode well for the rest of the day if he didn't get some sleep. But how? Not by lying here with his eyes open, not by drinking wine.

The gem? But it made you more alert, not less—though come to it, touching it did have a soothing effect. And in any event, he had little to lose. Scowling into the gloom, he rose and padded to the workshop, where he retrieved the gem. A moment later, he lay down again, this time with that clot of ruby fire centered on his chest above his heart, two fingers of each hand resting lightly on it. He closed his eyes, tried to relax, to think of nothing beyond what his senses told him, and most of all, simply to feel the slickness of the gem—he'd have to come up with a name for it sometime—"the gem" wasn't very descriptive. Maybe—

No! He was starting to think again, when he was supposed simply to be. That's what Merryn, who'd taught him meditation, had told him over and over. Just relax yourself from your feet up. Tense and relax, and breathe. Think of nothing—Merryn said.

Merryn.

What he wouldn't give to talk to her right now.

Merryn, he would begin, *I've made a discovery, but you're not going to believe it, but . . .*

What am I not going to believe?

Avall sat straight up in bed, staring at the wall. "Merryn?" he whispered, before he could stop himself. No, of course not! She hadn't spoken. Couldn't have. She was three gorges and more away to the south. Yet it had sounded like her—and he'd sensed her presence in that uncanny way the two of them shared as twins.

Shaking his head, he closed his eyes, began the ritual anew—

And found himself once more thinking of his sister.

And again it was as though she answered. Yet not exactly as herself. This was more like he was *inside* her and neither precisely awake nor entirely dreaming—rather like the bonding he, Strynn, and Rann had shared, only . . . more distant and tenuous. She sounded angry, too—or tired—or confused: sleep-muddled, as though someone had awakened her from much-needed slumber.

Maybe he had! He closed his eyes, tried to regain the relaxed alertness that had characterized that first contact—if that's what it had been.

Merryn? He tried once more. *Merryn. It's me! Avall.*

Avall?

Aye. I'm . . . I'm in Gem-Hold.

I'm dreaming.

No! As contact began to fade. *Something . . . is letting this happen. Something has tied us together mind to mind. Something I just discovered.*

I'm dreaming.

"*No!*"

The contact wavered. Avall felt for the barest moment as though his *self* was suspended in some high, cold place looking down on all Eron. And then, distantly: *Avall?* As though she cried out for something precious that had gone.

He reached for her again. Felt the link strengthen, then shift in a strange new direction as though she were waking—or gaining a higher level of consciousness.

Avall?

Merryn, are you there? If you are, where are *you? Can you describe—*

The reply came faster than he could formulate his query. Partly it came in words, as though she actually spoke somewhere far off: *in War-Hold . . . in my room . . . in my bed.* But with those words came images as well: a room larger than his and Strynn's, with stone walls and a cozy window seat opposite the door; a bed on a dais in the center (which he doubted she liked); a few comfortable chairs, and a wealth of velvet-and-leather cushions. It was entirely too real. He could even feel the muscles of her mouth working as she answered him—like a dreamer talking in her sleep.

But trapped inside the dream. As though she could only respond while he maintained the link.

Which he knew he ought not do.

He couldn't bear to destroy it, either.

Merryn! If this is really you . . . I have to tell you something. There is . . . I have found something wonderful! A . . . gem that lets me speak to you from afar!

It was as though her face moved with his as he spoke. As though he were inside her (yet still himself) thinking those things, while at the same time Merryn's ears heard her voice say his words, in tones that were in no way her own. It was like speaking in a roomful of echoes, and for a moment Avall fell as silent as was possible when thoughts and words were one, to let the unheard cacophony subside. He felt her response as much as heard it. *Avall?* she cried—mind and mouth alike—and there was panic in her voice, a panic he felt as much as heard.

If this is real, Merryn, tell me what to do? I have found this thing, but Eddyn may know of it as well, and it could fix the fortune of our clan! It could—!

I feel it, too. I know what you know, what you feel without knowing it. It . . . frightens me, Avall. This should not be. We are— I think we are in the Overworld. I think The Eight will hear us."

I thought you did not believe in The Eight!

I do now!

Merryn. Do not speak of this to anyone. Let us try this again—tomorrow. We must know—but I must think . . .

Aye, we must, and you must. But be careful. This frightens me beyond reason! I feel your fear I—

Tell me, briefly. In case we fail.

And *that* was the old Merryn again: capricious; all curiosity and decision. It was also what Avall had needed so desperately, and so he complied—in feelings and images, but mostly in ordinary words because, in spite of the echoes, that seemed easiest.

Merryn?

Not his thought, but another's. A voice, rather: a real one, heard with her ears. A question asked of his sister, full of concern.

And male.

Merryn was asleep, he was certain. But she didn't sleep alone. The way she'd lain, even sharing her body as he had, he hadn't known. He heard a name—*Krax,* perhaps—and with it caught a brief image of a thin, tan face; dark hair; and troubled, sleepy eyes.

And then the link dispersed and could not be recalled.

Avall lay back in bed. He was sweating, even as chills ran over him. Had this been real? Had he in fact contacted his sister across all that sweep of land? Or had that been a wish fulfilled? One thing was certain: The gem that lay on his chest like a gleaming red enigma had played a part. What other parts it might play, he had no idea. Tomorrow—or soon. Whenever he had nerve for it, he'd explain all this to Rann and Strynn and see what they advised.

But why did that notion bother him?

Because talking about it made it real? Made him face the fact that he was going to have to make some hard and impossibly important decisions that might well shake Eron to its roots—especially if he could find more gems? And he'd have to make them alone—except for Strynn and Rann. But if he involved them, they might want him to act in ways he didn't desire—or couldn't easily execute. He needed to share—and dared not.

Suddenly he was tired; as though stretching his *self* across all that territory had worn him out.

He felt himself fading.

Almost as suddenly, he slept.

He didn't dream at all.

CHAPTER XXVII:

EAVESDROPPING

(ERON: WAR-HOLD-WINTER–DEEP WINTER: DAY XIV–PAST MIDNIGHT)

~~~~~~~~~~

*M*erryn . . . ?"

Kraxxi wasn't certain if he'd actually said his lover's name, or if Merryn herself had murmured it, as she'd just uttered so many other things that made no sense at all.

He'd thought he might be dreaming—but it had seemed so real: awakening to hear Merryn mumbling, then feeling her body go stiff as a sword beside him, and then to hear her call her brother's name as though she'd just happened on him unexpectedly in a corridor. That wasn't unusual. She loved him and missed him terribly.

But then the reply! Her voice, but not her intonation, as though some muscles pulled others in subtly different ways than those to which they were accustomed. And the words! Someone speaking *to* her, except that it *was* her, and then that strange dialogue about some gem Avall had discovered, that let him talk to her thus.

It was—he faced it, as he lay in the dark and tried to think things through before waking her—it really was as though she and her brother conversed with each other across all that vast unseen gulf between here and wherever Avall was. Which only made sense if he actually *had* found some odd gem. But no! One like that conversation implied *couldn't* exist. It really was a dream. He'd prove it. He'd stay up *until* he woke again, then he'd know that it hadn't happened.

Sighing, he slid away from Merryn, stepped out of bed, and padded naked to the window. Wine was what he wanted, or ale, but neither would keep him awake. Kaf there was, but cold and thick. He drank it anyway, with as much honey as he could stomach, found his underbreeches, and climbed into the window seat, staring out at the nighted land. Frost rimed the panes in places, and his breath made white patches there. It was a beautiful view—one moon, the largest, was up at the moment, so that the patterns of dark and light were undiluted by other illumination.

And somewhere out there, to the north, the brother of the woman he thought he loved seemed to have spoken to her across all that unseen distance. Which he would've thought impossible had Tozri's mother not managed something similar herself—and with a gem from that place, too. But those findings had been at relatively short distance; this was a hundred times greater.

Still, if it *was* true, if gems existed (for surely there was more than one) that could enable people to converse at far remove, the implications were tremendous. It would be invaluable in . . . in *war* for instance. It would be of vital use to spies. Or a source of quick intelligence. Or a more efficient way to relay orders to commanders in the field.

It was, in fact, the sort of thing that could turn the tide of a battle. And though Kraxxi doubted his father would make good on his long-standing threat to raid Eron, possession of the gem and the art of working it—or simply the knowledge it existed could make a crucial difference in failure or success.

It might even earn him a pardon.

If he could prove it.

If it wasn't a dream.

If Merryn would tell him the truth.

Dared he ask her, though? If he did, and it *was* merely a dream for either of them, or if the facts were other than they seemed, he would look a fool. If, on the other hand, he'd witnessed what he thought, and she also knew it was true, then to admit knowledge of that could severely compromise any further action he might take. It was best, he supposed, to feign ignorance and see what transpired. Maybe ask her exactly the right sort of questions and see how she responded.

If it wasn't all a dream.

He was still sitting there, though more warmly dressed and with a fresh pot of kaf brewing on the tiny oil-cooker, when she finally coughed and stretched languidly, then felt for him and rose unsteadily from the bed, grabbing a robe more for warmth than modesty. Neither had duty for several hands. She looked, he thought, like the aftermath of an all-night drunk. It was also a look, he knew from experience, that discouraged conversation. He filled a cup and held it out to her. "Couldn't sleep," he volunteered.

She glared at him. "Headache. The Eight's own!" And took the cup.

He made room for her on the padded ledge. Their bare feet touched. Hers were cold as ice. He saw a chill run through her.

"Are you . . . ill?" he dared.

The glare intensified, but she caught herself and stared at her cup instead. "Headache. Bad dreams. Troubling dreams, anyway." And was that a touch of hesitation? As though she was lying? He wished he spoke the language better. Nuance was still lost on him.

"I'm cold," she went on. "I feel as though all the heat has been dragged out of me."

"I'd offer to warm you," he replied. "But you look as though—"

"Rub my feet," she yawned. He did. They *were* cold: cold as a corpse, almost. Whatever had occurred had taken something from her, that was clear. How much energy, he wondered, would be needed for a man to make his voice heard across two thousand shots?

"Dreams," he prompted. Carefully.

She tensed—another sign. He tried not to react, tried to act as sleepy as she and prayed she wasn't dissembling now.

"Nothing. I dreamed of my brother. It was very real. That's all."

But it wasn't all. The tone had been too light; the hesitations badly spaced and timed.

So what did he do now?

Watch. Learn more. Consult his friends. Then decide.

And one of the things he'd have to decide was which he loved more: Merryn or his country.

(ERON: WAR-HOLD-WINTER—DEEP WINTER: DAY XIV—MIDAFTERNOON)

"Not now," Merryn repeated emphatically, from the door between her room and Krax's. He'd lingered there after their usual postworkout shower, with one thing obviously in mind. She'd tried to tell him she was busy, but that only produced questions about what this supposed business might be. Which had reduced her to where she was now: thrusting him into his room and locking the door.

So much for patience. She hoped no one was watching.

It was time for her first real session with the Night Guard.

A quarter hand later, clad in armor undergear, she was once again in Ingot's stall. As soon as she arrived, the panel appeared. She stepped into it confidently, nor was she surprised when utter blackness enfolded her. What *did* surprise her was the faint odor of smoke that pervaded the place. And not only smoke, the sinus-draining scent of burning imphor wood.

Which, in the light of the wood's properties, was probably not an accident. She wondered what this portended, even as she backed as far away from that scent as possible and tried to take an absolute minimum of shallow breaths. The stuff speeded up reflexes, so perhaps this was a reflex exercise. It deadened pain when chewed and ingested directly, which conjured less pleasant notions. It could also be used to weaken one's will enough to force the truth.

And, she suddenly realized, she actually *had* some secrets for a change.

One was knowledge of Avall's curious stone—if any of that was actually to be believed, which she wasn't sure of herself. And, of course, one had to know about the gem to ask about it . . .

More likely was a suspicion that was slowly gaining primacy. A suspicion about Krax. Namely that the appearance of a handsome young man named Krax, who just happened to be the same age as the king's son of Ixti, whose name was conveniently enough Kraxxi, might be too much coincidence. Never mind what people kept saying about children being named after royal babies.

Except that she had no clue what such a person would be doing here, unless, as Lorvinn had speculated during one of their reviews, he'd managed to get himself exiled. He *had* lost a brother recently, so the mutilated finger proclaimed. But it hadn't been cauterized or bandaged properly, which implied an operation performed in haste, without proper supervision. Which made sense if that brother had perhaps died under . . . awkward circumstances, leaving Krax to make sure his ghost was laid.

On the other hand, he acted too much like a child trying to curry favor with attentive adults, and Barrax's house was famous for its distant, hard-tempered, aloofness.

Of course he did look remarkably like the profile on the recent Ixtian coins she'd located. Then again, royal Ixtians tended, by minted evidence, to look alike.

In any event, that wasn't something she should be thinking about when dealing with the Night Guard. Except, perhaps, as an aid to achieving patience.

Besides which, she could no longer escape the fact that imphor smoke truly was being introduced into her space, for which there had to be a reason.

Worse was the way another scent had begun to weave its way through it.

And then a voice, from some hidden grille or opening that made it sound deep and hollow for all its whispered tones: "Remove your shoes."

Merryn did so, setting them close by the wall so she could find them easily. She'd given up trying not to breathe the imphor, since there was surely method to its presence. A moment later, she returned to her spot in the approximate center of the space.

"Very good," that voice repeated. "Now feel how it is to stand. Note the way the pavement feels beneath your feet and how you would describe that to someone who truly wanted to know what you are experiencing. Remember *all* your senses. Never stop doing that, but become aware of how your body feels from the feet up: how your bones stack together, how the stresses between your muscles shift and alter. Where you feel your pulse most strongly. *Ask yourself how it feels to balance.*"

Over and over, with increasing degrees of detail and difficulty those instructions repeated. They had a hypnotic quality to them, too, one Merryn wasn't certain if she was supposed to resist or indulge. She chose the latter, and soon felt herself slipping away from herself, caught up as she was in the wonders of her own body, the way muscles tensed and relaxed and made compromises with each other to keep her upright and balanced.

At some point she was asked to describe the space around her in terms of how far the walls, floor, ceiling, and corners were from her. The air could tell her some of these things, even in total darkness. Knowing where everyone was in a fight could also save her life, which she imagined was the purpose of this drill.

She never knew when the scent of imphor began to fade. But she was somewhat surprised to discover that she'd fallen asleep while standing. Her body felt perfectly relaxed, though, and utterly, completely balanced.

And no one had asked her about either Avall or Krax.

CHAPTER XXVIII:

VOWS AND PROMISES

(ERON: WAR-HOLD-WINTER—DEEP WINTER: DAY XIV—LATE AFTERNOON)

~~~~~~~~~~~~~~~~

Are you my man?"

Tozri looked up from where he'd been paging absently through an obtuse treatise on the mechanics of gears and pulleys (at which the Eronese seemed to excel, and which no one born in Ixti, no matter how educated, ever seemed to get right). He was sprawled on the bed, clad only in black house-hose, and the afternoon sunlight filtering through the window in the bath gave his skin a ruddy glow that complemented its natural tan nicely. "What?" he asked, blinking as he refocused. He flicked a lock of hair out of his eyes for emphasis.

Kraxxi nodded toward the door to Merryn's room and raised a wary finger to his lips. Tozri nodded in turn and slipped from the bed to the floor beside it. Kraxxi tiptoed to the bath, where he turned on the water in the sunken stone tub—a luxury he still couldn't quite accept, never mind that even common folk in Eron had access to such things. Merryn's, on the other side of her suite, was nothing short of amazing.

That accomplished, he joined his friend, resting his back against the stone platform that supported his bed. "I asked if you were my man," Kraxxi repeated. "If you are, I need to swear you to silence, then tell you some things."

For a moment Tozri looked as though he might take umbrage at that, but then his expression softened. "You know I'm your man, Kraxxi min Barrax min Fortan," he murmured, using Kraxxi's full name as proof. "I'm that because I serve my prince, but more importantly, because I serve my childhood friend above my king. And because we swore to be brothers when we were small—because I *had* no brother and you pitied me."

Kraxxi's eyes misted. "Then I accept your oath. And now I must ask you to swear to keep what I'm about to tell you to yourself. Do not discuss it with Olrix and Elvix, even—not until I give you leave."

Tozri scowled. "They're my sisters; I don't like to keep things from them."

"They're like my sisters, too, and they're also my friends, by choice and oath alike. But they won't like what I'm about to tell you, and my mind is clear on this."

Tozri's face couldn't mask his eagerness to hear more, but he looked wary, too. Silently, abruptly all guard and shadow, he rose, opened the doors to both adjoining rooms and peered through. Kraxxi saw him relax as he checked Krynneth's chamber, and more when he inspected Merryn's. He closed the doors again.

Kraxxi indicated the latter. "She's off on some nameless secret errand, that probably involves reporting on you and your sisters and me."

Tozri grinned approval. "Suspicious little wretch, aren't you? Much more than you used to be. I like that."

"You may not like this," Kraxxi muttered.

Tozri merely looked at him. "Go on."

Kraxxi did, in as low a voice as he could manage and still make himself heard, and in as much obscure Ixtian dialect as he could contrive.

Tozri listened quietly, as he was schooled to do, but Kraxxi could all but hear him taking mental notes and constructing counterarguments as he relayed his tale. When he'd finished, Tozri snared wine for both of them, then returned to his place across from his friend, their legs stretched past each other, barely touching.

"And you believe that?" Tozri breathed at last. "You truly *believe* that Merryn's brother spoke to her through . . . some kind of magical gem? Surely it was a dream."

"I've had dreams," Kraxxi replied flatly. "And seen dreamers. This was . . . It truly was like two people speaking. Her voice changed in a way I can't describe. It didn't even *sound* like her."

"You may have seen a *few* dreamers," Tozri countered. "I doubt seriously you've awakened beside as many sleepers as I, to know what's normal for them."

"I've awakened in the same room as you many nights, and heard you speak—even cry out. This wasn't like that."

Tozri sipped his wine, then scowled. "Obviously you aren't telling me this purely for my entertainment. So let's assume for the argument that what you say is true. Have you pondered the implications?"

"Every free moment since then. For now— What would you do if presented with this information?"

A long pause. Then: "The *first* thing I'd do is try to amass as much additional information as I could. Because I tell you right now, you do *not* have enough solid facts on which to base any kind of rational action."

"No, but I *feel* a rightness in what I might do. I think it's Fate again, Toz. I think— Well, it seems Fate has been looking after all of us since . . . whenever. I think I'd better trust it now."

Tozri rolled his eyes. "I'm the one with Eronese blood, but you sound—"

"Answer my question! What would you do?"

"I'd amass as much information as I could," Tozri insisted. "I'd try to prove and verify."

"And then?"

"I would consider how this information might best be used, if at all, and then I would act upon it—or not, depending on those uses."

"You're dancing between knives."

"I'm trying to be logical about something I don't halfway understand and certainly don't believe, and which I wouldn't be discussing at all if I didn't like you so much—and if you hadn't invoked my oath."

"Fair enough. So, how would you use that information?"

"I would"—another sip—"I would conclude that such knowledge might upset the people, which would not be good. I would conclude that it might tip the balance in conflict—should such conflict occur. If, for instance, Eronese commanders could get information to each other fast as thought— which you certainly haven't indicated is the case."

"In short—"

Tozri swallowed. "I would go to the king. I would let *him* decide who should know."

"And if you were the king's son, with a banishment laid upon you?"

"I would—" he broke off, glared at Kraxxi, then laid a hand on his thigh as though to restrain him. Kraxxi flinched and gently moved the hand away. "You're not going—? Back to Ixti?"

"That's where your vow comes in, even to your sisters. And the answer is: I might."

"You're basing that on nothing!"

"I hope to have something more convincing . . . soon. I don't plan to act at once, but I *do* plan to act."

"Don't be a fool! It's Deep Winter out there. You'd die!"

"Perhaps, but I have to risk it." He paused, swallowed. "Don't you see?

Eron was a dream: a child's notion of the place where I wouldn't have to worry about . . . about the things I've always been worried about, I guess. But I'm Ixtian-born: blood and bone and breath. I love my country whether or not it loves me, and suddenly all these abstracts are becoming real. Suddenly *war* is real, because if Eron finds they have the advantage they *might* have— Well, now that I see a *real* threat to Ixti, I want to protect her."

"And the fact that this *might* earn you a pardon doesn't factor into this?"

Kraxxi regarded him sadly. "Of course it does. No one wants to be outcast."

"I wish you'd thought that before—"

"I had no choice before! Or choice of death, and that was all. I hadn't anything to bargain with. Now I have."

"Fair enough. Now: What about Merryn?"

"What about her?"

"You love her, don't you? You said you did."

Kraxxi felt a pang of guilt, as though Tozri had finally driven home the dagger he'd toyed with all along. "She's the problem. I hate to lie; you know that. I hate pretending that I don't know what she said—never mind what I saw, or how I've interpreted what she did."

"But you'd leave her?"

"What if I stayed? Who would I be? I have nothing to give her, and I know her kind value marriage. I might give her a child, but a man of Eron certainly would. I would do very well by her, but what have I to offer in return? A crown over which I have no claim. Were I my own man in Ixti, I would shower her with . . . weapons, since she prizes such things above jewels. But I'm not my own man."

"But if Barrax pardons you, you might *become* your own man . . ."

Kraxxi nodded.

"They'd never let you marry her."

"But *they* are not immortal! Suppose I did win pardon, and help my country, and . . . become king someday?"

"She's a warrior," Tozri snorted. "She *will* fight for her land. I see it daily in her eyes. She loves you—I think—but I *know* she loves Eron. If you came to blows on the battlefield and she found she must slay you, she would. She'd regret it, and it would change her life forever, but you *would* die."

"Whatever happens," Kraxxi sighed, "I don't intend to tell her. If she tries to learn anything from you . . . resist. That's why I chose not to try to tell your sisters."

Tozri's eyes widened with awe and anger. "You . . ."

"They might torture you to get the information. You can stand it longer.

Simple as that. If Olrix and Elvix know nothing, there's nothing they can reveal."

Tozri drained his goblet and—almost—slammed it to the floor. "You've used me—somewhat."

"It's my job. It comes with the crown. If things go as they ought, they won't torture you. These folk don't like to hurt people."

"Good, because I don't like being hurt!"

Silence.

"Wait," Tozri said eventually. "You're acting as though you're going to do . . . whatever you do alone."

"I have to," Kraxxi replied. "I think I know a way to escape, but there's no way I can accomplish it with the three of you in tow. Even asking you along on what I plan would rouse suspicions."

A brow went up. "So you do have a plan?"

"I'm not a complete fool. But one thing I will need is for you to locate that scorpion poison."

"You're not going to kill her!"

"I hope not. I *pray* not. But from some things I've read here, that stuff has many uses."

"Like what?"

"I'll leave a note with the source before . . . whatever. I—"

Movement sounded in Krynneth's room. Tozri and Kraxxi froze, staring at each other until the steps moved away—as though Tozri's shadow had started to enter, realized someone was in the bath, and chosen to wait.

Kraxxi took Tozri's hands—both of them—noting the scars of their blood-binding in both palms, ragged twins to his own. "I would have your oath, Tozri," he whispered. "Twice in one day I ask it, where twice in one year I have not."

"What is it you would ask, my prince?" Tozri responded shakily.

"That you reveal nothing of what I have said to Elvix or Olrix, your sisters. That you reveal nothing of it to anyone in this hold. That you will obey my bidding in this as best you can. And—and this is the most important one—that you will not try to prevent me or follow me."

"I don't like this."

"Nor I. But it has to be. I need to be able to trust you. My life—and my kingdom—my home—may depend on it!"

"And you won't tell me what you're planning?"

"I don't *know* what I'm planning—much. I still have a lot to work out. But if one day you hear that I've disappeared, you'll know. I hope you'll be suitably upset."

Tozri glared at him. "I won't have to feign that."

"So give me your oath. And I pray I never have to crave another."

"And on what shall I swear? You're exiled. You're no longer, forgive me, holy."

Kraxxi thought for a moment, then recalled the signet ring he'd sewn into the waistband of his breeches. He'd since relocated it in the same position in the heavy house-hose he normally wore inside. So far no one had noticed. Impulsively, he reached out and took Tozri's hand, thrust his fingers inside the band, let him feel the ring around the grommet. "You know what you touch. Not me, but a sign of the sovereign power of my title and my land, as both exist independent of me. If that isn't enough, I can expose some of the metal."

Tozri's eyes were bright, but he shook his head. His fingers shifted to a more certain grip. "I . . . Tozri min Aroni mar Sheer, do hereby give my oath of service and of silence unto Kraxxi min Barrax min Fortan, whom I love as my friend and a prince of the true blood of Ixti, knowing that if I fail in this oath, my life is forfeit to any who care to claim it, but that it is my own duty to carry out that execution."

Kraxxi laid a hand on Tozri's. "And I, Kraxxi min Barrax min Fortan hear this oath and accept it, and pray that I never have to exact such another."

"By blood," Tozri whispered, and slit his finger with the dagger he'd been playing with, extending it to Kraxxi.

"By blood," Kraxxi echoed, doing the same.

"By brain," Tozri continued, laying his hand on Kraxxi's head.

"By brain," and the gesture repeated.

"And by . . . love," and with that Tozri removed Kraxxi's hand from his head, lowered it to his lips, and kissed the centermost knuckle.

"And by love," Kraxxi said automatically, and reciprocated. And then he rose, strode into the bath, thrust his head underwater, and returned, lest anyone enter and wonder.

They spoke no more of it that day—aloud. But Tozri's troubled eyes spoke silent volumes.

CHAPTER XXIX:

KEYHOLES AND ORANGES

(ERON: GEM-HOLD-WINTER–DEEP WINTER: DAY XX–LATE MORNING)

~~~~~~~~~~~

What had been an impression made in wax was now hard metal, newly cast, rough at the end that held it, but neatly filed and polished where it mattered. Eddyn stared at it speculatively, torn (as he usually was) between doing what he wanted and doing what ethics required.

Ethics said to throw this key away, to take it back down to the forge and drop it into the crucible from which it had lately emerged in fire, heat, and hot metal. Ethics said that no matter what it might help him acquire, the result would make no difference because he and Avall were in no real way competing. Ethics said that if he *were* to do this thing and be discovered, he would travel several steps farther down the road to disgrace he'd assayed too far already. He wasn't a *bad* person, he didn't think, with which assessment Rrath concurred—and Rrath should know, because Rrath was Priest-Clan, in whose province ethics lay. Still, if people wanted to think that he was bad, was that really his concern?

So why hadn't he asked Rrath? Rrath, who'd become the closest thing he had to a friend.

Because he knew what Rrath would say. *Do not do this thing; the risks are too great for the reward.* Which was true. And though Rrath seemed well on his way to exchanging what had been a significant regard for Avall for what was perilously close to hate, he still knew the difference between right and wrong.

As did Eddyn.

The trouble was, he was *curious*, dammit! How was Avall progressing on the helm? What would be its dominant motif? Knowing that would assure that his own work was complementary, which would be sure to please Gynn. It might not please Tyrill, but he'd had enough of pleasing her. Now that he was his own man, he would continue to try to make her proud, but he also had sense enough to realize that there were strengths in both hall and hold beyond hers. That old lady wouldn't last forever.

Nor would opportunity. Or nerve. Avall was in the mines: He'd seen him there half a hand gone by. Strynn was chopping onions in the kitchen. And Rann was out with the torch crew melting away the morning's snow. No one else should be about, and if they were— Well, he was Argen, too, and had a perfect right to be in the clan quarters. If anyone challenged him, it was also widely known that while he and Avall were alleged to hate each other, they still had responsibilities within the clan that at times required contact if not cooperation.

Which challenge he would make his omen. If the common hall outside Avall's suite was occupied, he'd turn back. If it was empty, he'd proceed. Chance and Choice. Let them decide.

A deep breath, and he continued down the stair. Four more twists put him in the main clan vestibule. He entered it nonchalantly, gaze fixed casually on the archway at the far end of the long, low, comfortably furnished chamber that let onto the main light well on this side. Avall occupied the middle suite to the right, which was why more clandestine measures wouldn't have sufficed.

To his uncertain relief, the hall *was* empty, though an array of cups and bottles strewn about hinted at recent revelry. Another breath, and he steered toward a clump of clutter conveniently close to his goal. Anyone finding such things was supposed to tend to it regardless of who left it. He therefore snared a pair of goblets that had escaped from the clan feast hall, and with them clutched awkwardly in one hand, turned to Avall's door with the other.

For a moment he feared he'd filed too much off the key—these complex locks were notoriously recalcitrant, even to competent locksmiths like him. But then metal met metal, slipped and slid—and released. Now came the dangerous part. It would take no more than a dozen breaths for his practiced eye to assess Avall's work. A glimpse at the overriding motif would suffice. Leaving was where the risk lay, which was why he'd donned a hooded cloak similar to one Rann often wore. His height would be a problem, but perhaps if he slumped, no one would mark him. And if not—he could always confess everything. If they didn't find out about his invasion of Avall's workshop, a reprimand would be as much punishment as he'd garner from the Sub–Clan-Chief, and that old man was Argen-yr, same as Eddyn. The Sub-Craft-Chief, who adored Avall, was another matter.

In any event that was for later. A deep breath, and he slipped inside.

The place looked roughly as expected: neither cluttered nor particularly neat. A cloak had been thrown down instead of hung up. Grimy footprints showed on the stone part of the floor. A plate of honeyed apples slowly turned brown on a table. His rival had the better angle on the light well, he noted sourly, easing to the door to the right, which should be Avall's workshop if the place were laid out like his own apartment, two levels up. Strynn's would be to the left, near the bath, because swordsmithing got one dirtier than dainty goldsmith work.

The key worked as well in the inner lock as the outer, and Eddyn pushed the heavy oak panel open. Nothing brightened what lay beyond save what shone through the light-well windows, but even in the relative gloom he'd already seen enough to make him clutch the doorjamb in despair.

The helm was nearly done! It faced him on the stand Gynn had provided in the precise dimensions of his head. All the steelwork was in place: four plates forming the crown, a rim two fingers wide binding them together, nasal, earpieces, hinged avantail. The proportions were absolutely perfect, the joinery and hammerwork without reproach.

Two steps closer showed more: a glimmer of bronze lying on the worktable, which had to be the appliqués that would decorate the underlying steel. A brief assessment was more than sufficient to reveal the audacity of their design; the clever synthesis of geometric and organic shapes that seemed familiar yet were difficult to place precisely.

But the level of craftsmanship was far beyond anything Avall had achieved before, never mind the impossible speed with which it had been accomplished.

No way he could've done something like that so fast and so well! It was all Eddyn could do not to smash the thing right there from sheer frustration. The shield he was making might be fine—and was in fact compatible with what he saw here—but in nowise did it compare with the quality of Avall's commission. True, there was no reason Eddyn couldn't equal this if he tried—in workmanship. But there was no way he could match the speed. Not when Avall had been complaining about having done almost nothing a quarter-eighth ago.

The question *now* was whether Avall would finish before Midwinter, as seemed likely; or would continue to refine until they left with the coming of spring. If the former, Eddyn stood a chance, because it would take that long to finish his own piece.

If the latter, he was—

—not doomed, but certain, once again, to be consigned to *almost.*

Eyes misting with raw outrage, he started to whirl away, then paused, as something caught his notice. One of the appliqués was an intricate band of interlace and gems that was supposed to encircle the helm like a crown. The casting looked complete save for a later application of gold leaf, and Avall had placed a number of gems there unmounted, as if to consider possible combinations. They were impressive, too, but nothing he hadn't seen before. Except one. Or rather where one wasn't, for the central boss, which was obviously made for a somewhat larger stone, was empty.

All at once Eddyn recalled Avall's cryptic comment in the mines: in essence that he'd found something special. Special would work well here.

But where was it?

Not that it mattered. Still, he'd come this far down the road to ruin, what was another shot? Hating himself, even as he acted, he made a quick survey of Avall's workspace before recalling that *he* kept such things under lock but close at hand.

With that in mind, he checked every drawer he could find. None were locked—nor was there need, in one's own quarters. No luck though, and he'd just given it up as bad idea when his gaze fell on Avall's toolbox. Jewels weren't tools, but they needed tools to mount them. Another breath, a twist of a pair of Avall's gouges in the simple lock, and he had it open.

Ah! A pouch.

He snatched it up, loosened it—and gaped at what rolled onto his hand.

A ruby!

No, an opal.

Or . . . a . . . garnet?

In fact, it was none of those things.

He stared at it quizzically, poked it with a finger—and felt a jolt. Not pain as much as . . . sensation.

There was no other way to describe it: the gem . . . hated him.

His head spun, awash with what he could only describe as emotions. Strong dislike for him, coupled with intense regard for Avall.

Which was preposterous!

A gem couldn't pass on its feelings, even assuming it had feeling to pass on.

But Avall couldn't finish a helmet in so short a time, either.

There had to be a connection. The gem was the only thing different— and it *was* different, too. Therefore it was where that connection lay.

Reality spun again. The gem—

He couldn't stand to hold it any longer—and wasted no time returning it whence it had come. Eight, but this was stupid! He'd wasted too much time, and . . . and . . .

Too many things were demanding to be believed that were impossible to credit.

Sick at his stomach, he turned away, setting the lock behind him, leaving no sign of his presence. A pair of paces took him to the outer door. A breath, a prayer to Fate, and he eased out—backward, goblets and wine in hand, hunched over just in case. Blessedly, the common hall was still empty, and he made it to the feast hall with the goblets, where he deposited them for pickup by those on cleaning duty.

And then he fled back up to his suite—where he spent the rest of the morning staring distrustfully at the half-completed wax master of Eron's next royal shield, and thinking how it would look if augmented with a certain preposterous gem.

Avall supposed he should've been grateful this hadn't happened before. He'd heard the tales, of course: how pregnant women could become demanding; how they'd develop odd cravings or strange habits at the most inconvenient times—and apparently thought their husbands were the only people alive qualified to assuage those desires. Strynn had been better than most. Indeed it was easy to forget that she was with child.

Usually.

Tonight, however— He chalked it up to too much forging, which she'd rationalized by saying that it was better to do the hard part while she was fit, than to be down there beating steel and setting fire to her belly. Which made sense. Seven more days with the furnaces, she said, and then refining, refining, refining—which she could do in a chair by the window.

He paused at the entrance to the fruit garden. Oranges at midnight was not a thing he wanted to spend every night pursuing.

He yawned and pushed through the steam gate, wincing at the wash of heat and humidity that gushed out over him. Another gate put him in an antechamber even hotter and more humid than the last, but which opened into the fruit hall itself. Thrusting the sodden panel aside, he entered a lush summer forest by moonlight.

It was otherworldly, this vast square chamber over thirty spans to a side with its roots in the rock of the hold and its ceiling twenty levels higher, double-paned with glass beneath a clear night sky. It was brightened now by all three moons, one of which was directly overhead and gave almost enough light to read by. Tall vertical slits of glass brick in the north and east gleamed as well, and admitted sunlight during the day. Torches glowed at three-span intervals along the walls, but in spite of them it was easy to forget one was indoors, for the whole space was full of vegetation planted to resemble a forest, with paths and trails artfully contrived to wander up and down several levels, so as to provide enclaves for conversations—and the inevitable assignations. All paths led to the central spring, however. Alas, this one was too hot to bathe in—one of the few. Still, it, with the heat of the sun, made it possible to grow oranges in Deep Winter.

From where Avall had entered, a flagstone trail bent uphill, a screen of low bushes to the right bearing tart, sweet ormis berries from Ixti, with the waist-high bank to his left overgrown with decorative ferns. He followed the path to where it kinked sharply left, then took a branch to the right, skirting the spring. It was hot as summer there, so he loosened his tunic. By day it wasn't uncommon to find people lounging on that margin as bare as decorum allowed, though the winds outside would have frozen their bones.

The oranges were around the next turn, but Avall froze abruptly. Someone had entered. No, *two* someones: talking too loud—clearly from drunkenness, their shuffling footfalls punctuated by a yip of surprise atop a muffled, "No! In here!"

Likely a couple seeking privacy for what ought better to be done in a cool room than a steamy simulation of outdoors. Except the expected nervous giggles never materialized. Rather, it was a hasty apology from what sounded suspiciously like Eddyn.

Though Avall had no desire to encounter his nemesis, he couldn't decide if he should remain where he was, lest an unpleasant encounter ensue, continue on his quest, since the straight path to the orange trees branched off just ahead. Or simply go into hiding behind some bit of cover.

But then he had no choice, because Eddyn and his companion were coming up the path he'd just navigated, two turns below. They were drunk, too—one of them was, his voice overloud and slurring. Avall caught the phrase, "It's just not possible to work that fast."

A chill raced up his spine that decided him in favor of eavesdropping even as he leapt behind a low hedge that backed one of the myriad stone benches that studded the garden. Not that he had any guarantee that Eddyn and whoever—it sounded like Rrath, which made sense, given the amount of time the two of them had been spending together—would necessarily choose to occupy it. On the other hand, it was the nearest place to sit, and from where Avall had secreted himself, he doubted he'd need to worry about being heard, since the spring made a low, bubbling background roar, never mind the steady drip-drip of condensation from branches. And the squirrels.

An instant later two figures did indeed stagger into view around the nearest switchback: Eddyn and Rrath, for certain. Eddyn was *very* drunk. Rrath didn't appear to be, given the way he was trying to maneuver the larger man, succeeding well enough to deposit Eddyn on the stone seat. Eddyn sprawled languidly. Rrath looked tired and anxious as he wedged himself into what little space remained. Even in his hiding place, Avall could smell the wine on Eddyn's breath. In spite of his strident tone, however, he didn't sound angry or belligerent, as drunks often did, just miserably unhappy. Rrath was trying to console him.

Avall felt a pang at that: at friendship bestowed and withdrawn for no better reason than a stupid misunderstanding. He'd intended to seek out Rrath long ago, to tell the Priest with brutal honesty that he had no right to treat anyone so, given the accidental nature of his complaint. Not so much to regain him as a friend (he was too needy to be the sort of companion one actively sought), as simply to put conclusion to the matter.

For now, however, Avall listened.

Rrath was beginning to wish he hadn't encountered Eddyn that evening. He'd been on his way from Kylin's quarters, concerned as to the cause of a peculiar, melancholy buoyancy he'd noted lately in the harper's demeanor, and had thought that perhaps Eddyn, who was more world-wise than he, might possibly offer some insights.

Unfortunately, Eddyn had been in the mines for some odd reason, and by the time Rrath had located him—digging in Smith's private vein, which was even odder for someone who normally shirked dirty labor—he'd lost the impetus of curiosity.

Mostly because Eddyn was behaving even more curiously. He acted, Rrath concluded, like a man who'd discovered a terrible secret he dared not reveal, but which he was at the same time desperate to expose. And since one of the goods Priest-Clan traded in was secrets, he had no choice but to avail himself of as much of this one as he could ferret out. Kylin could wait. Eddyn was, after all, more powerful in the great cold scheme of things than a skinny, sun-blind harper.

He'd coaxed Eddyn into a late dinner in Priest-Clan's common hall, but the other clansmen had stared at them so intently they'd retired to Rrath's room, where the austerity proved nonconducive to conversation of the rattly, disjointed kind Eddyn had begun spouting. So they'd snared a bottle of wine and started for Eddyn's quarters.

To his very great surprise, Eddyn had drunk half the bottle in transit, then couldn't find his key and had decided to retrace his steps to the vesting chamber in the mines, where he'd located it in the clothes he'd changed out of, whereupon they were off again, with the rest of the bottle gone and Rrath having had not a taste. Somehow they'd acquired a second bottle and taken to random wandering and had wound up here, on Rrath's notion that heat and steam might possibly get Eddyn sober enough to find his way back to his rooms on his own.

If not—Eddyn wouldn't be the first to wake up here.

Except somewhere around the last antechamber, Eddyn had started rambling about Avall working on some kind of special helmet for the King—which was the first Rrath had heard of it, though such secrecy didn't surprise him. It was also something no one was supposed to see until it was finished. But since Rrath rapidly realized that these were private Smithcraft matters, he concluded that if anyone was going to hear such things it ought to be his own discreet self, and, more to the point, that blithering such things aloud wouldn't go well for Eddyn. Therefore, it was best to get him as far away from people as possible.

Trees didn't talk. Nor ferns, berry bushes, flagstone paths, or granite benches.

Rrath actually thought Eddyn had passed out when he finally got him on the bench. Indeed, he'd started to rise in quest of some fruit that might revive him when Eddyn began pouring out words like the spring vented steam.

"I know it was wrong!" he said (not for the first time). "I don't like Avall, and I know it was really stupid of me to go into his room like that. I risked too much and I don't know why I did it, except that it was the same way I felt when I laid Strynn out that day, which I wish I could take back, but I can't. But it was the same, Rrath, it was the same, my *friend*, 'cause you *are* my friend, aren't you, or you wouldn't put up with me? But anyway, it was the same. I knew what was right, but I did what I wanted to anyway, 'cause so much depended on it; 'cause if I can do enough things right I can be Craft-Chief and not have to be bossed around by *her* again."

Rrath nodded sagely. "Not easy being her protégé, is it?"

Eddyn peered into his empty cup as though more wine might appear there if he wished hard enough.

"I'm scared, Rrath," he went on. "I went in Avall's room and I saw that helm, and . . . I don't know if you can understand this, 'cause you're not a craftsman at the level of Avall and me, but sometimes you can just look at somebody's work and see a change—a whole order of magnitude difference. And that's what I saw, Rrath—and it scared me! It's not possible for someone like Avall to have done as much work of that quality that fast, without something changing. I don't know, Rrath. Maybe it's true; maybe The Eight really do favor him like they play games with me—giving me all these accomplishments and then making it so I get no joy from them."

Rrath stared at him. He sounded sober. The slurring had vanished from his voice, and his thoughts were well articulated. But there was still a wildness in the rate at which those words tumbled out, as though he feared he'd never again have nerve enough to say them. And some of them he shouldn't say—certainly not that business about having been in Avall's quarters without permission.

Rrath started to speak, but Eddyn interrupted. "It can't be normal! It *can't* be. Nobody can do work that good that quickly."

"Could Strynn be helping him?" Rrath dared. "Or Rann?"

"They shouldn't, but they might. Both have some right to, given what they are, wife and bond-brother. But Strynn's got her own commission, and Rann's from Stone, not Smith."

Rrath's eyes narrowed. "There are drugs . . ."

Eddyn shook his head. "Not Avall. Nor me," he added. "We're shown those in training and warned against them."

"Still, it sounds as though he was on some kind of drug . . ."

Silence ensued, but it was a silence in which Rrath's mind filled with all manner of preposterous notions as he sought frantically to construct some order from the chaos his friend was expounding. Which put him in mind of the matter he'd postponed earlier.

Kylin's odd elation. It was a leap from rock to turtle, but was there any chance of connection? Avall was married to Strynn, who was good friends with Kylin.

He thought back to that earlier conversation with the harper, trying, with his trained Priest's mind, to recall what had been said word for word. It had been a casual visit: his turn to take food to someone who easily got lost in the myriad halls and stairways of the hold. They'd talked, mostly politeness, but Kylin had mentioned a visit from Strynn. And he'd said something strange. He'd told Rrath that he'd always heard how beautiful Strynn was, but now he knew. And then gone stark white and closed up immediately, as though he'd said something he oughtn't.

Rrath hadn't pursued it, but *had* noted the name of the tune Kylin had been penning. He was calling it "The Dreaming Jewel."

" 'The Dreaming Jewel,' " he said aloud for no reason but to break the silence.

Eddyn looked up wearily, having swapped from overblown verbosity to sullenness all in a dozen breaths. "What?"

Rrath shook himself. "Just the name of a tune Kylin was composing."

"Interesting," Eddyn muttered, suddenly sounding very sober indeed. "Perhaps we should get hold of this tune—or poem, or whatever."

"It had words," Rrath said carefully, "But why—?"

"Words?" Eddyn went on relentlessly. "Can you remember them? Any of them at all?"

Rrath stared at him. "What does it matter?"

Eddyn reached out to shake him. "Answer me, man!"

Rrath flinched from the fierceness of that touch—or gaze. And because Eddyn was so much bigger than he, he closed his eyes and tried to recall what he'd seen there: upside down, but still accessible to his trained memory.

"The lady bears a jewel of dreams.
It glows with fire. With flames it gleams.
It shows the truth, the soul-born kind;
It shows true beauty to the blind."

"And that's all?" Eddyn hissed when he'd finished.

"I . . . think so. It made no sense then, but I wonder. Kylin did act like a man who'd seen for the first time."

"But," Eddyn noted though a yawn, "we both know there's no such jewel."

Rrath regarded him strangely. "Of course not. Such a thing—"

"We would've heard of it," Eddyn finished. And yawned again, then rose. "I . . . think I'm feeling better now. If you can point me to the right stair I believe I can find my way home."

Rrath started to protest, then shook his head. "If you say so."

"I have," Eddyn replied airily, "a jewel on which I wish to dream."

Avall waited in the bushes until he heard no more voices or footsteps. Until he'd heard the nearest doors slam and the softer closure of the two outer ones. Only then did he rise, feeling altogether sick at his stomach. Eddyn had been in his workroom, seen the helm and the jewel; Eddyn, in effect *knew*. And Kylin knew something as well—because Strynn had told him. He could imagine her doing that, and didn't know whether to be furious at her for playing so carelessly with something that was powerful beyond price, or to be pleased with the compassionate use to which she'd put it.

In any event, they would have to talk about it, and soon.

Like tonight.

He was halfway back to their suite before he recalled that he'd forgotten the oranges.

CHAPTER XXX:

ANGER

(ERON: GEM-HOLD-WINTER—DEEP WINTER: DAY XXI—PAST MIDNIGHT)

~~~~~~~

Avall's footsteps rang loud as hammerfalls as he half strode, half stomped through the mostly empty corridors, absently watching rooms, suites, the central hall, and a pair of garden halls slip by as he tried to get his thoughts into some kind of order.

Thoughts.

Ha!

How was he to think when anger consumed him? When he had no idea whom to be angry at first? He'd started with Eddyn because he was used to being angry at Eddyn—even as he understood in large part what made Eddyn work. What he didn't understand—didn't want to understand, rather—was what had made Eddyn so desperate to spy on him he'd take the risk he had. Why, at this very moment Avall could easily be on his way to the local Craft-Chief with a complaint of invaded privacy. Or to the Hold-Warden, for that matter. Privacy was the law and almost holy. Eddyn had broken it.

But he had, too, though not by intent, when he'd spied on Eddyn's work. Perhaps that option was better not considered.

Rrath? Well, Rrath had simply stumbled onto something and was mostly innocent except for talking more than he ought about Avall's affairs—Strynn's rather—to someone who couldn't be trusted with them.

Kylin? He'd done nothing except make a casual, but potentially deadly, slip.

And Strynn?

There was the problem. Most of this devolved from Strynn. Good intentions notwithstanding, she'd acted capriciously, even recklessly. And more to
the point, had invaded his privacy to do it, even to (evidently) removing the
gem from where he'd locked it away. *That* wasn't like her. And Law made
such matters gray, though she certainly had some claim on his property, if
not his art.

But he didn't *want* to be angry at Strynn! He didn't want to be angry at
anyone. Yet if he weighed his choices, the only person he *could* be angry at was
his wife. He couldn't rail at Eddyn or Rrath, because that would rouse curiosity he wanted to allay. Kylin was innocent. Rann, thank The Eight, not
involved—so he assumed.

Or maybe he ought to censure himself for not being careful.

All at once he was back in Smithcraft's quarters, staring at a not-quite-
deserted common hall. A deep breath—no need to start rumors of agitation,
which could lead to other queries—and he straightened his tunic and strode
in, calling casual greetings to the few folks gathered there. Including, he was
startled to note, Dorv, the local Craft-Chief, who was some sort of elderly female cousin. She looked relieved to see him, though she greeted him pleas-
antly enough, adding, "Rann will be glad you're here."

"Rann?"

"He came by a moment ago looking for you—or so I assumed, since he
asked if I'd seen you go out."

Avall scowled. "Where is he now?"

"Your suite. He knocked. Strynn opened. He hasn't reappeared."

The scowl deepened. He didn't know if this was good or not. With Rann
there, he dared not vent his anger. In any event, to do so might damage affairs with Strynn beyond recall. Rann would, he decided disgustedly, be the
voice of reason he always was. And on Avall's side, but trying to be fair.

Maybe he should go out for a long run in the snow. And if he froze to
death in the process . . . Well, that would solve a whole host of problems.

"Avall?" Dorv queried pointedly.

Avall started, realizing he'd been staring at his door. "Sorry. Long night,"
he managed, found his key, and entered.

Strynn looked up expectantly from the game table where she and Rann
had just begun a round of *Corys*, but her face fell just as quickly.

"No oranges?"

"Too many pickers." He snared a mug from the cupboard and joined
them, filling the mug with mead from a blue-glass jar.

Rann finished his move and looked up as well, his grin fading abruptly as
he saw Avall's troubled expression. "More than that, I'd say," he offered
mildly.

Avall suppressed an urge to rail at him for no more reason than to release his anger. "Let's say *wrong* pickers."

"Eddyn?"

Strynn glared at him—or Avall, it scarcely mattered. "In both kitchens?"

Avall shook his head. "Out. And the fruit garden was occupied by two, shall we say, *very* vocal drunks, one of whom Rann just named."

"The other?"

"Rrath."

Rann toyed with a gaming piece. "I take it you had an unpleasant encounter?"

Again Avall shook his head, draining half his cup, then refilling it. "No encounter, but unpleasant—no, let's say *troublesome*—words overheard."

Strynn leaned forward with genuine and innocent interest. "What words?"

Avall took a deep breath and looked Strynn straight in the eye. "Why did you show the gem to Kylin?"

Her eyes rounded. "I . . . intended to tell you about that when it happened, but you were already so upset, I just couldn't bear to add anything to it. Since then—I guess I was scared. Still, it was a favor to a friend. More than that, it was *grace* to a friend. To someone who's lonely and misses what the rest of us take for granted."

Avall wondered if her words carried more than one sense, if Kylin was not the only one lonely or feeling taken for granted. Fortunately, Rann saved him by drawling, "I seem to be ignorant here. Perhaps I should hear this story. Or would you rather I left?"

"Stay," Avall snapped roughly. "Whether or not you hear the story, you'll still see the consequences. Better we all know."

"Better we all know," Strynn echoed. "But I'll expect a full accounting from you as well."

Avall settled back in his chair as Rann quietly cleared away the board. "It was like this," Strynn began. And for most of a cup of slowly sipped honey wine, she told them.

Avall exhaled when she'd finished. "And Kylin? Can he be trusted?"

Strynn shrugged. "He's Music, but he's out of Lore. They're good at keeping secrets. He'd never do anything to hurt me, of that I'm positive. How did you find out?"

Avall pondered his drink. "In due time. For now I need to digest this: that you and Kylin . . . bonded. That seems to be the best word for that," he added.

Rann cleared his throat. "Actually, I think we need to test that notion more than a bit, if we can find enough people to trust, which may be a problem. We know that the three of us can bond— Well, not me and Strynn; we haven't tried *that* yet. But we need to find out if there's any specific basis for that link. We also know Strynn could bond with Kylin, but again: What's the basis of the link? What're its limitations? Or does it even *have* limitations?"

Avall nodded thoughtfully, intrigued in spite of himself. "Well, for one thing, we're all close. We know each other very, very well. But there's— I guess if we're being honest here, there's something relevant to this I need to tell you. But I'm not sure whether to get to it first, or finish with Eddyn and Rrath."

"You'll have to decide that," Rann sighed.

Avall rolled his eyes. "Fine, then I'll start with what I just heard down in the fruit garden . . ."

"Whew!" Rann gasped when Avall had finished, leaning back in his chair while Strynn simply sat there looking stunned. "Two things come right to mind: The fact that he spied on you—and what he learned there."

Avall nodded. "And the first would be simple, were it not for the fact that I spied on him, too, in a manner of speaking."

Which produced yet another revelation.

"Yours was an accident, though," Strynn observed when he'd completed his confession. "But you're right; you'd better not bring up the privacy charge."

"Which still leaves the fact that he knows there's something weird about the gem, or could've figured it out by now. And that assumes he hasn't found one of his own and drawn the same conclusions."

Rann rose and began pacing, pausing only to snare another bottle of mead from the cupboard, filling all their glasses without comment. Avall feared he might get drunk—were concern and anger not burning so bright just now. As it was, he sat silently, glowering at the game board. Strynn fidgeted constantly, opening her mouth, then closing it again, as though more than once she began to speak and reconsidered.

"Merryn," she sighed at last. "We need Merryn in this. Not Eellon, who'd instantly make it all politics and whose first act would be to see what Tyrill might do."

Avall eyed her curiously. "Funny you should mention that."

Rann sat down abruptly. "That's your 'I've got one more secret' tone."

Avall exhaled wearily, looking sheepishly at Strynn. "This is one I was going to tell *you*!"

She snorted—not with anger as much as exasperation. In spite of himself, Avall chuckled. "We're even now as far as secrets are concerned—or soon will be. But the fact is . . . I think I did contact Merryn."

Rann regarded him levelly. "You jest! War-Hold's—"

"I know exactly where it is," Avall shot back. "Now please listen! Remember how I couldn't sleep, Strynn? I went out to get some air and started thinking about Merryn, and then I came back and went to bed, and fell to pondering pretty much what we're doing now—except I had the gem with me. I thought its touch might be soothing—you know how that is. In any event, I started stroking it and . . . drifted off—and all of sudden I was— I think I was talking to Merryn. It sounded like she was asleep. But the feel— It was like when we bonded, only much, much weaker and less intense."

"Could it have been a dream?"

Avall shrugged. "Not unless you can dream the same thing twice on successive nights, about which more anon. And it sure as Eight didn't feel like one. It didn't last long either—I'm not sure she even knew what was going on, though I told her as much as I could. But someone awakened her, and that may have broken the contact."

Strynn giggled, covering her mouth to hid a slightly lopsided grin. "Merryn not alone?"

"Dark-haired, slim-faced, that's all I know. Probably some lad she met at War."

"Lucky man," Rann and Strynn chorused as one.

Avall rolled his eyes. "The point is, I *did* contact her. I've tried again, and got her once, but my free time since then hasn't coincided with times she'd be resting, and that seems to be a necessary adjunct. Also," he added seriously, "frankly I'm scared. It wasn't much fun, having your *self* stretched across all that distance."

"Oh, my," Rann whistled, eyes going very round. "I begin to see. This is even bigger than . . . sharing between friends. This could . . ."

"Revolutionize everything," Avall finished. "Or destroy it. More to the point, it could upset the power balance between the clans because communication hasn't been our province before, but now we *may* control a significant aspect of it."

"And we haven't the luxury of waiting until spring," Strynn groaned. "Not if Eddyn's onto this as well, and we have no idea what he knows or doesn't."

"Or even if he's acted already," Rann gave back.

Avall cleared his throat again. "I don't think we need to worry about Eddyn—yet. He acted too upset tonight. I'd swear he'd never seen a gem like mine—ours—until now. And he's only starting to figure out that it might have powers."

"He'll work on that until he finds out, though," Rann retorted. "Remember what you said about him wondering how you'd got so good so fast?"

"Final blow," Strynn said. "We have to let someone in Tir-Eron know."

"At whose hall or hold?" Avall shot back. "Mine? Yours? This could affect War, too, if we've stumbled onto some way to effect distant communication."

"*If,*" Rann snorted through a yawn.

Avall poked him the ribs. "You're right: We need to test more. But since we also need to let one of our Clan-Chiefs know, I'd suggest we combine two projects and try to contact Eellon."

Rann nodded. "It might also be useful," he ventured, "if Strynn and I also tried to contact some people. We don't know what allowed you to link with Merryn. Maybe just closeness, but I'll bet it's because you're twins. Or at least that blood kinship's a factor."

Strynn nodded in turn. "Which means we should make a list of combinations. But since we don't know how tiring this is or how risky, I'd say we try our best shot first."

Avall raised a brow. "Which is?"

"You try to contact Eellon. You've used the gem most, so that's in your favor. He's family, so was Merryn: another fact in your favor. He's also physically nearer, in case that makes a difference. And he's the one we most need to get hold of."

"And if not him?" From Strynn.

"Well, *not* my mother," Avall sighed. "Given her religious bent . . ."

"Then who?"

"*My* mother, maybe?" Rann suggested. "I've no closer kin. If that fails, then Lykkon, I suppose, though he's only a cousin."

"Strynn?"

"I'll try my mother, too, since she's also in Tir-Eron. One of my brothers is at Glass, the other at Brewing—which is even farther away than War."

Avall nodded. "And then we should both try Merryn."

A sigh, and Avall left to retrieve the gem. When he returned, Strynn and Rann had rearranged the common room so that three chairs were grouped around the small table. Someone had refilled the mead mugs (for nerves as much as anything), and Strynn had set a wind chime to tinkling near one of the air vents. "To help us relax," she said.

"Good idea," Avall acknowledged. "I could use all the calm anyone's got to spare." And with that, he sat down at the vacant place, with Rann to his right and Strynn to his left. A deep breath, and he set the gem on the table, where it gleamed softly but otherwise seemed unremarkable. Another breath, and he retrieved his dagger. "We need to find some other way to do this," he grumbled. "My fingers are getting sore."

"First things first," Strynn countered briskly, taking the dagger and proceeding to prick her thumb in a businesslike manner before passing it on to a reluctant-looking Rann, who—after a bit of coaching—did the same, then passed it in turn to Avall. He closed his eyes and did likewise, worrying at one of his earlier scabs.

"Tell you what," he suggested when he'd opened one. "Let me try this alone, and then you two join in if I fail. I seem to feel . . . *stronger* when I'm linked. The trick is staying myself while still doing what I want to do. You two might have to relinquish control, though."

"Sounds reasonable," Rann agreed. "But hurry if you can; I doubt this is going to bleed very long."

Avall simply closed his eyes and reached for the stone. He felt its coolness beneath his finger at once, along with that odd drawing sensation, followed by a warming which he suspected was the gem waking to his presence. It was easy to use it that way, actually, for the drawing made him focus on it to the exclusion of all else. He tried to recall how it had worked with Merryn. The first time, he'd simply been thinking about her in a wishful sort of way—or worrying at her or about her, and then suddenly she was there. The second—a more formalized version of the same.

He tried the latter with Eellon. It was late, and the old man would be in bed by now, but likely not asleep. He liked a posset, and he liked to read. Often, too, he would take some small project to file at. (Avall had certainly found shavings in the bedclothes, when he'd been on cleaning duty.) In any event, he'd likely be in a relaxed state, which made sense in terms of his being receptive.

Another breath, and Avall tried to conjure an image of Eellon's face: all sharp angles, rough hollows but still handsome for all that. Nose like a mountain peak whose sides had been scoured away. Valleys in his cheeks, gorges following the plain of his upper lip past his mouth to outline his chin. Tangled forests for brows. Eyes like woodland pools in which knowledge sparkled like new-spawned fish. Hair like the ice caps of the north.

He had it! Tried to keep it, tried to desire it; to want it as badly as he'd wanted to talk to Merryn. Tried to picture the space between, and then that space folded like a taut rope loosened and the ends brought close together.

Another breath, and he tried to want it harder, even as part of him noted that one *couldn't* want something just by wanting to want it.

He had no idea how long he tried, for time had gone strange again, but eventually, he recalled that Rann and Strynn were waiting for him, and so he managed a soft, "Not working," that he hoped they'd hear and understand.

Instantly he felt other fingers join his on the stone, warm and sticky with blood. And then another warmth of shocking intimacy as that which made Strynn and Rann themselves coiled its way into him. Part of him was leaving himself, too; entering them. He let it, tried to think of them as two more rivers of desire joining his own. "Think of Eellon!" he said—or thought. "Picture him. Desire him. Think of something you need his advice about and have never asked."

They tried, he could feel their effort, but to no avail.

Other than their own closeness, their attempt had produced nothing.

Eventually Avall withdrew his hand, likewise easing theirs away. He blinked, feeling time twisting and shivering around him.

"I'll go next," Strynn volunteered abruptly. "I'll try to contact my mother."

And without further ado, she laid her fingers on the gem.

Nothing happened when she dared it alone, and nothing that hadn't occurred before when they joined her and tried it together.

"Rann?" Avall prompted, when they'd given up again.

Rann shook his head. "No, I'm sorry. I can't. I've got a headache all of a sudden that's really making it hard to even think. And I'm . . . cold."

Strynn hugged herself. "So am I, actually. Headache, too."

Avall shivered as well. "That makes three of us—which I guess should tell us something."

"Headaches and heat loss?" Rann opined. "Makes sense to me." He started to rise and staggered. Avall caught him, eased him back down, though he wasn't feeling particularly steady himself. The last thing he remembered clearly was Strynn telling Rann that he was going to sleep with them tonight and herding them both to bed.

They slept dreamlessly.

Eddyn had nightmares of being hated.

Eellon, in Tir-Eron, felt something moving around *inside* his head, but decided it was senility arriving.

And Merryn woke abruptly, called out a startled "Avall?" and lay awake another hand trying to decide if she'd just missed another contact, was engaged in wishful thinking, or was going mad.

CHAPTER XXXI:

HUNTING

(ERON: WAR-HOLD-WINTER—DEEP WINTER: DAY XXII—EARLY MORNING)

~~~~~~~~~~~~~~~~~

A carefully calculated puff of breath—lips pursed *just* so, cheeks exerting exactly *that* much force—and the snow swift, which had been busily pecking deliberately planted seeds on the northwest battlement, uttered a choked half chirp and fell, a thistle-fletched dart through its neck.

Exactly where Krax had told Merryn was best to aim if the meat were to be salvageable.

She lowered the blowgun and grinned at him—for her victory (she'd been practicing on the sly for days)—and for the sheer glory of the morning: the warmest all winter, with snow actually melting instead of falling and the sun so bright that being outside was like walking in a ball of light.

She was also grinning at Krax: at the handsome image he made, there, across the flat rooftop, in pursuit of his own prey. Clad in cloak against cold he claimed bothered him more than her, he looked much an Eron-man, with his lengthening hair and the added muscle life in the hold had given him. Another few days and she might convince him to let her wax his body, the better to assess those curves, planes, and hollows.

"Good one!" he cried, his voice carrying clear in the hard, still air, with barely a trace of accent—which was phenomenal. His Eronese was much better than her Ixtian, though to her credit, Eronese had the less complex grammar, and she'd also been wrestling with the Night Guard's secret cant.

"Thanks!" she called back, trotting over to snare the small bird, feeling how cold it was already as the air leached its warmth away. "One more?"

Krax shook his head, face suddenly all shaded. "You're stalling."

The grin became a scowl. "This is stupid. You'll never find that ring."

"So you said. But I have to try. Like I told you, it's the only link I have to my—what you call clan. If I ever run into any of my folk in Eron, I'd need it to prove who I am."

"You're already in Eron!"

"You know what I mean. The cities. The real place. Holds aren't the real Eron."

She regarded him seriously. "No, you're wrong there. They *are* the real Eron, but distilled to its essence. Organization. Art. Duty, duty, duty."

He gnawed his lip. "I suddenly realized something."

"What?"

"The reason you folk are so obsessed with art. It's because the rest of your lives are so structured it's the only way you can express who *you* are."

She puffed her cheeks in turn. "You may have a point. I still don't know how you'd fit in, though. What your place would be. You're not . . . good for anything."

"That's not what you said last night!"

"You know what I mean."

He grinned, his teeth so white they shamed the snow. Very nice teeth. Perfect teeth. The teeth of an aristocrat. Once again, she wondered. If only he weren't so guileless . . .

He glanced at the sun. "The longer we wait, the less chance—"

"The place was scoured when we found you. You know how thorough our folk are about such things. There's no way we could've missed it."

"In knee-deep snow? With horses milling around? As cold as it was that day, so that people *might* not have been as attentive as they could be? There's been runoff since then. There'll be more. The odds decrease every day."

"I still think it's a waste of time. Next summer I'll get my brother to *make* you one. Tell him what you want; you won't be able to tell the difference. Eight! I could probably make you one. I'm that competent a goldsmith."

"Humor me."

"I'd rather bed you. We've no duty today at all. Why not spend it . . ."

He raised a brow, first at her, then at the blazing sky. "If it stays this warm, perhaps we can find a secluded hollow and—"

A brow lifted in turn. "I *would* like to see you naked outdoors."

"Besides, being practical, this is the only day we've got time to go there and back. That and good weather. Chance is favoring us."

"I don't trust Chance," Merryn grumbled.

"Ah, but didn't you say that Chance gave you your first choice among the holds, which is rare?"

She nodded. "It also made me find you."

"So, then; you're lucky. Maybe that luck will help me find my ring."

She hefted the blowgun experimentally. "Squirrels down there," she muttered. "I've been wanting to try this on something besides birds."

He saluted her with his own, patting the small leather case that held his supply of darts—and a small phial of Krax's scorpion poison they'd finally been able to wheedle out of the resident poisoner, when Merryn explained it was needed for an experiment. She wondered, though, if she were making a mistake entrusting the stuff to Krax, though her lover showed no signs of being other than utterly content to be away from his homeland. What must his life have been like there, to make him so eager to erase it from his memory?

Perhaps she'd find out one day. Perhaps he'd eventually open up and let her prowl through his past. There was so much she didn't know, so much she *wanted* to know. He was such an intriguing mix of experience and naïveté, of knowledge and ignorance. So many things he took for granted were wonders to her; so many made no sense. But so much of War-Hold impressed him, too—like the baths and reliable heat—she wondered how he'd behave if he saw real opulence?

He also wasn't budging on this matter of the ring he'd first broached two days ago. She'd promised to help him find it (he was being very persuasive just then), and now he was holding her to her word.

Still, she supposed she could indulge him just this once. Besides, there was always a chance the gate-warden wouldn't let them out—which would let her practice her powers of persuasion on the one hand, and give her someone else to blame if Krax were disappointed.

A sigh, a glance at the sky. "Half a hand: my room. Warm clothes because the weather can change without warning. I'll bring camping gear just in case, and see if I can find something for a picnic—and, again, just in case."

"I'll be there!" he laughed, as he snared his morning's cache of trophies and marched toward the stairs.

Merryn stared at her one pitiful bird and wondered what in the world she was doing.

"This saddle doesn't suit my backside," Krax grumbled, as Merryn led the way up the long ramp from the belowground stables where the horses were housed for the winter to the daylit glare of mid-court. Hers felt odd, too, perhaps because she hadn't ridden in over ten days. Or maybe because Ingot sensed what she was about and was giddy at the notion of sunshine.

"Get used to it," she called back. "Use your knees more and your thighs less."

"I need a joint I don't have for that!"

She laughed at him, easy in his company, even as she wondered how real it all was. Which was what Avall, the ever-analytical, would wonder as well. Which made her try to stop. Much as she loved her brother, she treasured her time away from him.

And then they passed through the archway at the end of the court, and the warmest sun in days found her face. She could almost feel it start to glow.

Krax urged his sturdy North Wall gelding—Balmor was his name—up beside her. He, too, looked happy, though not as relaxed as she'd like. Then again, he was still officially in custody.

The court was mostly empty as they made their way through, but she waved at a couple of people, surprised to see Krax do the same—she didn't know he'd made so many friends.

The north bastion loomed ahead: ten levels of dark stone that were the heart of the original hold. Their path led through a tunnel at its root, gated at both ends. That put them in the north bailey, where walls swept wide around them: smooth, perfectly laid golden stone. Another tower, and they were in the entrance court, aiming for the gatehouse. If they had trouble, it would be there, though she'd *tried* to clear this escapade with the Sub–Hold-Warden, who, however, could not be found when needed. Still, she was a subcraft-chief herself, which gave her more clout than many, so perhaps it was time to use it. It was a fine day, after all, and she was feeling reckless.

So here they were: approaching north gate, with Krax looking ridiculously expectant, and her hoping her native charm would suffice.

Apparently not, for the gate-warden stepped in front of her as she approached, batting the lever that lowered the portcullis as he did. Polished-steel gridwork slid smoothly down. Soundlessly. Krax would be impressed.

"Hold!" the man boomed. "State your business."

Helmed as he was, and half-masked against the chill, Merryn couldn't see his face but knew his voice. "Meekin! I take it you've received no word?"

"Of what?" All business. As he was supposed to be.

"Krax and I are going on . . . a quest. He lost something important to him down the mountain. We're going to look for it."

"Nothing is that important. Nor have I had word."

"Maybe not," she countered. "But that's not for you to say. Krax says it *is* important. And," she added, in the secret speech of the Night Guard she didn't get much chance to practice, "the Warden says if we *do* find it, it could go far in revealing who he is."

"Is that so important?"

"This close to Ixti, it could be. Now are you going to let us through?

There *is* an order; it just hasn't got here. But we're running on tight time. We don't have all day. And we may not get another."

The guard shifted his weight—which he wasn't supposed to do. Which meant he was considering.

She patted the blowgun in its new leather case at her side. "I'll give you lessons! It's a new thing, too," she added, with a cryptic smile.

"Make me one, and some darts, and you've got a deal. But if that order doesn't come, you owe me."

"I owe you," she replied solemnly. "I do."

A grunt, and the man eased sideways. Another lever sent counterweights moving again. The portcullis rose.

Merryn rode through, with Krax close behind. Another gate lifted, and they were outside walls for the first time in half an eighth. Krax exhaled his relief.

"Don't like walls?" she asked, conversationally, as they paced onto the pavement. The freedom made Ingot fractious, and Merryn had to suppress the urge to let him trot—which would be dangerous on so precipitous a trail. It wasn't far to the first switchback.

"Don't like *high* walls," Krax retorted. "We've walls in the city—low ones—but lots of sprawling courtyards, too, and most rooms are open to the air."

"I knew that," Merryn sighed. "But I didn't think it would affect how you . . . think."

Krax's face was serious. "They're mind barriers, your high walls. They keep you confined. Keep you— Maybe keep you more the same. Keep your mind constrained. I think you folk would be better off without so many walls."

"The Cold thinks so, too," Merryn shot back. "But maybe you have a point. I— Why are you frowning?"

"I talk too much," Krax muttered.

"You've betrayed nothing," she informed him flatly. "As of last spring, we know how high the walls around Ixtianos are, how many towers, and how they're manned. Nor do I betray anything by telling you this."

"Spies?" he dared.

"Casual observation of what is there for anyone to see."

"Ah, but who reported it?"

And then they came to the turn, and Merryn forgot about Krax as she took in yet another amazing view. The mountains down here were more broken and angular than those at home, more a tumble of greater and lesser peaks, many with fractured ridges where ice and cold had honed them sharp as knives. Even snow managed a tenuous grip at best, and the contrasts— blinding white and dark, with the sun washing all with its own gold-red glare—made the landscape seem almost *too* real. The air was amazingly clear. The sea glittered. She wondered if it was frozen over up north, and if so, how thick the ice was.

"I've been thinking," Krax began.

"Dangerous that," she teased, as he shifted his seat on Balmor. She wondered how his backside was faring.

"You raised a good point back there. What *is* my place to be in Eron? When you leave, I mean?"

"What do you want it to be?"

"I was talking"—he swallowed hard—"about you and me."

She felt a little jolt in her soul at that, which surprised her. He'd not mentioned this before. It was one of the issues they always skirted, perhaps because discussing it might make it so, whereas to leave all to Chance freed their options.

"I don't know if I could . . . marry you," she began. "If you got me with child, it would help; because that would be something you could give to the clan."

"Give?"

"A child belongs to its father's clan—its *acknowledged* father, as stated by the mother with the named father's consent. I told you about the situation with my brother: how his wife was with child by one man, but by naming Avall its official father she effectively took a child from one sept of our clan and gave it to another. And, of course, our sept now owes hers a favor."

"But I have no clan."

"And that's a problem, though I suspect Eellon would let you bestow any child you might sire on me to Argen-a. Tyrill would fight it like mad, but Eellon could manage it. The best thing might be for you to become close enough friends with someone—someone here, even, like Krynneth—to have him make you his bond-brother. That gives you secondary status in his clan right there; and, you having no other, it would be almost the same as primary. His folk are Wood, but they've a lot of folks in Lore, where you'd fit just fine."

He took a deep breath. "Would you marry me if I asked?"

Another of those little jolts—the man was full of them today. "I would need to know more of your background. I would need to know everything, without secrets or evasions. In Eron, everything is on record as far as who was where, when, with whom—not in private, but in . . . education and so on. You're a cipher."

"But you'd consider it?"

"There are men I've liked less. And you know you're the only one I've bedded."

"And I know part of why, and it has less to do with me than my, uh, relative fertility."

"That matters less all the time."

"And if I did get you with child?"

"If you would claim it, we *could* contract a short-term alliance until the child was born. And then . . . reconsider."

He nodded.

"It's like I said," she sighed. "You're smart and attractive, but you're not good for anything. You can't make anything except blowguns. I don't understand people who don't make things."

Two hands later, they were still talking—playing the game of one-up, rather. Krax would suggest something he *was* good at, and Merryn would counter with something thrice as involved or accomplished of her own. The man did know a lot, but it was random knowledge. Lore would love him, but he'd give them fits because his information was so disorganized. He'd devour everything they'd feed him there. Maybe when they got back to Tir-Eron she *would* prevail upon Eellon. And she could introduce him to Lykkon. The lad was a bit younger than Krax, but in intellect far older than she. Maybe *they* could become bond-brothers. Lykkon didn't have one, because he could never decide which of his myriad friends he liked best. Krax, being exotic, might break the tie.

The sun was past noon when they finally began to spot landmarks Merryn recalled from her foray to Krax's camp. They'd taken a long route to avoid as much snow as possible, and because it was the only route readily accessible by the horses they had to ride if they were to make this trip in the allotted time. Conversation had lagged, not from lack of topics, but because she and Krax had lapsed into a comfortable languor.

"There! I think," Krax called suddenly. Merryn jerked awake, cursing herself for having—almost—dozed off in the saddle. If Krax had wanted to . . .

He hadn't. He wouldn't. He didn't dare.

"Where?" she asked, from reflex. She could read the signs as well as he.

"There." He steered Balmor to the edge of the woods, which began abruptly, as though to taunt the timberline. A good place for a camp in one sense, because it brought one absolutely as high as possible if one were considering pushing farther into the mountains; and a bad one in another, because in spite of the sheltering trees and laurel, it was still dreadfully exposed.

Clearly impatient, Krax dismounted, leaping into knee-deep snow before tying the gelding to a sturdy tree a good ways off from where the tent had been. She followed his example, pausing to feed the horses from her sketchy stash of oats, before joining Krax, who was already staring at the ground. He had his blowgun, too, she noted, even as she caught the telltale rustle of squirrels in the branches far above, enjoying the fine day as much as she. Maybe they'd have something different for dinner. If something didn't have them.

It was too cold for geens, and too high up. Birkits, however, were another matter.

Krax had ducked beneath the eaves of the forest. The snow was sparser there, courtesy of evergreens with very thick needles. Indeed, where the camp had been, it was scarcely more than ankle deep. Krax produced a broom and began sweeping where the front of the tent had been, exposing bare ground a quarter span at a time, and inspecting it minutely. Which method might work, given how it minimized distractions. "I'll be a while, if you want to hunt," he called. "Aim for the head if you can. And try it with and without poison."

"You going to hunt, too?"

He straightened. "Might load up, just in case."

Merryn scanned treetops for movement and the switch of furry tails. Krax hunkered down, busy on the ground, intense and methodical. Which was another side of him Merryn hadn't seen.

More sounds. Farther off. She followed them, keeping half an eye on Krax, and half an ear on the horses in case— Well, just in case.

She saw a squirrel—a fine big black fellow—and raised the blowgun. It caught the movement and vanished in a sweep of fluff and footprints, leaving the woods silent save for the soft rush-rush of Krax's sweeping, the occasional stomp or whicker from a horse, and the hiss of her own breathing.

"Ah-ha!" Krax cried abruptly, voice strangely loud in the silent woods.

"What?"

"Come look. Better you see."

"Did you find it?" She squinted toward him, saw him standing with something in his hands. A glitter of gold—as sunlight caught a particularly well-polished facet.

"Yes, but come here! I need an opinion."

She sighed and slogged upslope toward him. The sun was in her face and it was hard to see. He'd cleared a fair patch of ground and looked like a happy boy as he stood beaming, flourishing what was, beyond hope, the ring.

"Good job," she said. "Now what?"

He pointed to the tree by which the tent had been raised. Scour marks showed there: vertical slashes chest high on her—which she should've noted. Still, she hadn't exactly been looking. "Is that . . . birkit sign?" he asked anxiously. "We don't have them where I come from."

She bent forward to study the raw curls of wood. They were the right height, but the configuration was wrong. From the corner of her eye she noted Krax scanning the area: alert, likely in search of the same squirrel she'd just heard herself. He raised his blowgun—searching . . . searching . . .

"Joker!" she growled. Krax had *made* those marks, probably with the small knife that was all they allowed him to keep.

He swung around to look at her, pipe still at his lips. And stepped forward—far faster than expected—touched the end to her neck as she was turning to chastise him. And blew.

The pain was no worse than a pinprick, but cold raged out of it like a winter stream. "You've killed me!" she gasped, lunging forward even as he backed away. Already her arms felt heavy. Her legs were going numb. Only her head felt clear—*too* clear—though faced with such betrayal, she wished it might be dull forever.

"I would never do that," Krax said sadly, still backing away. "The poison was old. It will numb you . . . I daren't say how long, but you ought not to die. I pray for you *not* to die, and I tell you flatly this is the worst thing I've ever done of my own free will. But duty calls."

"But . . ." she managed, as numbness curled around her tongue.

"That poison works on muscles, not nerves. It stops the hearts of small animals, but yours is too big. Yours it will only slow. You'll cool. You'll sleep. I need the food and the horses."

He paused, looking as sad as any man she'd ever seen and she had no choice but to believe him: that he'd found himself in the impossible crux between two situations, and had chosen the older, the higher, the one to which he'd been longest loyal.

"I love you," he said, as he removed a bundle of food and a blanket from Ingot. "When I'm safe away, I'll let your horse go free. I wouldn't deprive you of him."

Merryn tried to feel angry, stupid, and betrayed all at once, and found she could feel none of those things. Or felt them all so strongly her emotions had gone numb as her limbs—which supported her barely long enough to let her flop down against a tree.

She hated Krax. Yet she didn't—for she understood duty. But duty to what? A man usually had duty to himself, his lover, his family, his country, and maybe his king. Which was this? Not lover, but what? She glared at him as he paused before her. From where she slumped, his hands were at eye level. He'd put on the ring and it was turned toward her, glittering.

A ring that bore the seal of House Fortan: the royal house of Ixti.

Krax. Kraxxi. Ixti's crown prince.

It was true!

But he couldn't be a spy. He *couldn't*!

What had been real, and what a lie?

More to the point, what had brought him here? And why had he betrayed her?

He, who was now watching her from the saddle, who was crying like a child as he set knee to Balmor, with Ingot in reluctant tow.

"Sweet dreams," he called—as though he'd read her mind. "I do love you, never forget. I hope I can return one day and when that happens, that you'll forgive me."

Merryn hoped that day never came. Because for the first time in her life, she had no idea what she would do.

And then darkness found her and left her, barely breathing, in the snow.

CHAPTER XXXII:

BETWEEN AVALL AND RANN

(ERON: GEM-HOLD-WINTER—DEEP WINTER: DAY XXII—AFTERNOON)

Avall yanked down his mouth-mask, flung back his hood impulsively, and thrust his torso so far beyond the parapet that Rann choked in surprise. Hands clutched at his cloak, restraining him. Avall thought briefly that jumping *wouldn't* be such a bad idea, though it hadn't occurred to him.

The world spun giddily. Cold blue sky above blue-white snow. Trees strident in their greenery. A spot of red where someone's scarf had blown away and not yet been recovered. Ice crystals danced in the air like powdered diamonds. The cold nipped his skin with dangerous familiarity, like a birkit one only *thought* was tame.

"Avall . . ."

Avall let his friend draw him back, raised his hood, and twisted around to sit in one of the opposing benches set into the stonework there; the parapet—and the winter—at shoulder height beside him. Hot cider steamed in a double-jar between his legs. Mugs of the stuff were cooling quickly. Avall took a sip, let the flavor burst through his mouth. His teeth hurt.

Rann was looking at him, troubled. "Don't try to fool me into thinking this is youthful high spirits."

Avall started to reply that he was, in fact, still a youth, and high spirits the prerogative of someone who didn't normally display them, then changed his mind. He'd been stalling long enough, and while this was a topic he ought first to broach with Strynn, Rann would have to be involved eventually.

"What do you think?" he began, nodding toward the silent woods, half-shadowed by the mountain now: purple-gray upon blue-white. "How long could someone survive out there?"

Rann studied him carefully. His breath escaped its muffler, dusting his stubbly upper lip with white. "You know the rote as well as I. In Deep Winter, nothing moves outside that wants to live."

"The cold's no different there than here," Avall gave back. "Clearly we can endure that."

"Because we can escape it. We can stay here till we can't stand it and retreat. Heated rooms, hot baths, steaming food—friends with warm bodies at need."

"Some of which could be made to exist out there. Fire's fire, after all: just as hot wherever. And there are the stations."

"Getting to them's the problem. That snow—it can get— Well, no one knows how deep it can get when it's drifted. A person can't just wade through it, and it's not much better on a horse—or skis. And any of those would burn up four or five times as much effort as ordinary walking, never mind what your body would burn trying to keep warm. And you'd—"

He broke off, mouth agape, eyes wide one instant, furiously shadowed the next. "You're not thinking—!"

Avall tried to still his face to calm neutrality. "I might be. No, I am," he corrected. "I've been thinking. Sometimes people simply assume things are impossible without testing them. Like the gem—"

"That's one thing, and we have no idea how it works, or if we're doing terrible things to ourselves working with it, or what. It's an unknown, but a fairly innocuous one. We think. But the winter's a demon we know. We know it doesn't care; we know it would come in here and freeze our bones if we let it, if the earthfires didn't let us fight it off. But out there, you won't have the earthfire."

"At the stations—"

"Assuming you can get to the stations."

"People do. People have."

"In the best possible weather, with a major commitment of manpower to reach even one. And if you're talking about what I don't want to think you're talking about, you won't have access to that."

Avall smiled at him, still somewhat detached, as though the gem he'd used so often of late had consumed some vital part of him it only returned when he awoke it. "What am I thinking?"

Rann drained his cup, wiping his lip with a gloved hand before the liquid could freeze. His eyebrows were casing in rime.

"Go on, say it," Avall insisted. "Name the thing you fear and make it real—and then kill it."

"Priest-Clan tripe!"

"Maybe. But we now know soul doesn't have to be constrained by body."

"*Soul?* How do you know that was soul? It was consciousness, intellect, maybe desire. But soul?"

"What else could it be?"

"Something Priest doesn't know about?"

"Something Priest will *want* to know about," Avall challenged. "Something they *will* know about if Rrath gets back to them."

"You could always kill him," Rann snorted. "You're talking death anyway, if you—"

"You still haven't named it," Avall persisted, almost teasing, though he, too, feared that thing. "You know I won't kill Rrath. I didn't kill Eddyn, who deserved it more."

"Daring Deep Winter alone!" Rann snarled, leaning forward, face a finger's width from Avall's, hands clamped around his biceps like vises. He was trembling. Avall expected to be shaken and shrank back reflexively. "There. I've named it!" Rann finished. "Are you happy that you've scared me to death? Made me mad at you?"

"If I'm going to die, I'm not sure it would be good for you to love me," Avall whispered.

"I already do—more than anyone else," Rann hissed. "But you're serious, aren't you? You think you might actually do this?"

"The Clan has to know," Avall murmured. "Every hand that gem stays here increases the chance that someone will find out about it—that Eddyn might steal it to give Argen-yr the upper hand. That he might hurt Strynn or you or me to get at it."

"You think he's that desperate?"

"I think he might be. We're talking power, here, brother. We're talking me over Eddyn, Argen-a over Argen-yr, Smith over all the other crafts, Argen over the other clans, Eron over Ixti. And we control it all. *I* control it, in fact. But I dare not let anyone else involve themselves or it all collapses. The Hold-Warden could find out any day—or the Mine-Master. Or the Sub–Clan-Chief. I'd lose it then."

"Why does that matter? You hate responsibility—you've always said that. If one of those—"

"I'd spend the rest of my life being the person who let the ultimate power we know fall into someone else's hands. I'd be as tainted as Eddyn in my own way. And he's another reason I *should* do this: because he's probably figured out some of this himself. He'd make the same connections, draw the same conclusions. He'd try to get it for Argen-yr. And he's got less to lose than I have; he's therefore more likely to do something rash."

"So you're going to do something rash before he does."

Avall blinked at him. "You said 'going to.'"

He looked away. "Words. Accidents." He scanned the frozen horizon. "Winter."

Avall didn't reply.

"I hate you," Rann breathed at last.

"Why?"

"Because if I let you go by yourself, I'll worry myself sick, and if you die out there, I'll never forgive myself. But if I go with you, and I die, I'll hate you for doing that to me."

"And if I don't die?"

"If you don't die, I'll be a . . . hero's friend. Maybe even a hero myself."

"I won't ask you," Avall said quietly. "But I'd love to have you."

Rann snorted derisively. "You just did, you know. Ask me."

More silence.

"Strynn," Rann said at last. "Forget me. You have to think about her and the child."

"And the world that child will live in, which will be one way if I act and another if I don't."

"And one way if you die and another if you don't!"

"There're others who'd make better parents. The child will be in the clan, that's a fact. I'd trust Strynn to raise it—she's as much Smith as War. I'd trust Merryn to guard it with her life. I'd trust you, in spite of being Stone, or even Lykkon—"

"Lykkon!"

"Young but brilliant, with a soft side the child would need that I may not be able to provide. It's not gold. If you don't like how it turns out, you can't melt it down and make something else. And if it winds up looking like Eddyn—"

Rann refilled the mugs—to give his hands something to do, Avall suspected. And so he'd have an excuse not to respond.

"Strynn," Rann repeated, when he'd finished, looking over his cup. "You know what you'd be doing to her, don't you?"

"Besides leaving someone who's been hurt too much already to bear a child she doesn't want alone? What else *could* I do to her?"

"Well, to cover all possible options, she could go along."

Avall shook his head. "No, and that's not me talking. I brought this up with her last night—in the most oblique, neutral, hypothetical way possible, in reference to a day-hunt—and she said flatly that she was going no farther outdoors than this promenade until the child comes. Her back's killing her, and her feet, and— Never mind; I hear enough of *her* talking about it! She's staying."

"Which may be the only thing that comes out right in all of this."

"Except that if I leave, she'll have to take the blame for some of it. She'll be the one who has to face the Clan-Chief—and the Hold-Warden, and who knows who else. The Hold-Priest for one, surely."

"Nothing good for any of us."

Avall quaffed his cider and rose, surprised at how stiff he'd become even in that short while. "All my life I've tried to do the right thing," he sighed. "And for the first time in my life, the right thing may be . . . fatal."

Strynn was sitting on a low sofa on the arcade that overlooked Argen's principal light well on one side, yet still gave a good view of its common hall on the other. She was sketching, Avall saw, as he approached—and probably wishing she could work on the sword out here. She was also probably wondering what he and Rann had been leaving her out of *this* time. He made a mental note to spend an entire day with her as soon as possible.

Which might be a very long time indeed! But he'd made up his mind now, and owed it to her to tell her. Better that than sneak off like a coward. Besides, he'd need her help—assuming she would give it.

"You're leaving," she said mildly, not looking up.

He froze, as though someone had thrust a dagger into his heart. All his arguments and explanations trickled away like ice melt. "How did you know?" he blurted before he could stop himself. And with that, he heard his options halved.

She put down the pad and motioned him to a seat on the floor beside her, like a child or a pet. Avall hadn't the energy to protest. Rann claimed a chair with a good view of the entry stair; it wouldn't do for this to be overheard. "I know you better than you think," she said quietly. "I know what you've said, and—" She paused. "I've been in your head and I know why you said some of it. I didn't know how I knew, but I've been thinking about you a lot lately, and wondering how all this is affecting you, and sometimes . . . *sometimes* when I do that, I find that your thoughts on that topic are lodged in there beside mine. It's scary, actually."

"I don't doubt it," Rann broke in, looking at Avall. "Has the same thing happened to you?"

Avall looked sheepish. "Not so I know—but I've been pretty self-absorbed. I'm afraid I've not been thinking much about Strynn. Not that I'm proud of that," he added.

"I won't be understanding all my life," she said flatly. "Someday I'm going to call you a fool and expect to be believed, or expect to be put first for once. But I knew what I was getting, which was a lot of time to myself. Yet I also know this impossible position we've found ourselves in. I know one of the things that worries you is leaving me. And I'll tell you right now, I won't go because I can't. I could die out there, and while the gem has made me more comfortable about even that, because it gives me reasonable proof that what makes me *me* isn't tied to this body, I have another life to consider, which I find I care about a lot. I want that life to have a life. I'd prefer it had a father, but—"

She broke off. Avall saw to his horror that she was sobbing, softly, but with conviction. Which she almost never did. He reached up to take her hand, feeling completely inadequate.

"You have to go," she sniffed. "Logic says it, and I've been in your thoughts and know how much you don't want it but know it has to be. I know it's not been an easy decision for you."

"No," he breathed, "it hasn't. But these thoughts— Are you saying you're you and . . . me, too?"

"Not always, and only when you're relaxed, or when you're wanting something really badly. Sometimes—"

Avall shifted his gaze to Rann, wishing they'd had time to do more tests with the gem. "Have *you* felt this? With either of us?"

Rann shook his head. "Except that I can tell when you're angry. It's like . . . a push, or something. And when we touch, sometimes I feel a flare of . . . *lik-ing,* or whatever. But I've not been in your mind. If we slept close together— maybe more would happen."

"Part of the mystery," Avall conceded. "We really do need to keep trying to contact other folks." He paused. "I'm hoping that if we go and get in trouble, we'll be able to send for help through you, Strynn. Which is another reason you need to stay here. We haven't tested this thing across distance much, and it seems like distance would make a difference, but I hope that I can at least contact you."

"It would be so much simpler if we had another stone," Strynn sighed.

"There could *be* more," Avall cautioned. "Eddyn—"

"—Isn't acting like someone with a gem," Strynn gave back. "I've been watching him—which kind of has him scared. He doesn't know how to deal with that kind of thing."

"Be careful."

"Always and forever."

Rann cleared his throat. "Speaking of gems," he ventured, "I've been reading through everything I can find in the local Lore hall about gem-stones, and *nothing* sounds like what you found, though someone from Healing did find an odd red stone that acted sort of like a lodestone a few years ago, which no one really studied, and which apparently she kept. I've also been down in the vein and found no sign of anything similar, though I intend to keep looking right up to the last—as should you."

"I'm scheduled there tonight," Avall told him, checking the time-candle in the corner.

"Well," Strynn said decisively, "in that case, we should adjourn to more private quarters. We've got to do some planning."

CHAPTER XXXIII:

OATHS AND THREATS

(ERON: WAR-HOLD-WINTER—DEEP WINTER: DAY XXII—SUNSET)

~~~~~~~~~~

Toz was sprawled facedown across his bed: asleep, clad only in house-hose, one arm curled beneath his head, the other dangling to the floor, when Merryn came storming in.

An instant only it took to assess the situation. An afternoon workout (he usually did that), a meal (scraps of bread and meat on the table above the bed), a bath (wet hair, a damp towel on a stool), and a nap. And then she was flinging herself astride the small of his back, snatching the arm from the floor with one hand, while the opposite elbow went around his throat, ready to pull—break his neck, even.

"Krax!" she spat, as she dragged his head up so that his ear was virtually in her mouth. "Who *is* he?"

The body beneath her tensed. Trained senses inventoried those movements automatically. Toz was a trained fighting man as well, and though little larger than she, was better muscled. Which is why she'd gone for the sudden attack—and pain.

The response was as expected from one surprised asleep. A grunt—an awkward body twist. An ineffectual kicking that connected with nothing, and a scrabbling with the free right hand that managed to grope around to the small of her back where it accomplished no more, courtesy of the furs she'd not bothered to shed upon entering.

The gate-warden was still gaping from the glare she'd bestowed upon him upon returning—alone, on foot, tired, and furious—just as the sun hit the horizon. The Hold-Warden would know by now, but Merryn didn't care; Lorvinn was Strynn's aunt. And hopefully by the time she was summoned, Merryn would have information she could use.

A sudden buck nearly unseated her and forced her to tighten her grip. A grunt, a groan—real pain, then.

"Eight damn it, Toz, *tell me*! I don't like hurting people. But I don't like being left numb as a rock in the snow by someone who was supposed to be my—"

She broke off, not knowing which word to use: friend . . . lover . . . now, perhaps, enemy, or betrayer.

Still silence.

She bit his ear. He screamed a bare instant, then fell silent, but she could hear his teeth grinding, feel the muscles tense along his jaw and throat. She tasted blood. Heard cartilage pop. Tasted more, and felt her teeth meet.

Toz writhed. Sweat sprang out on his body, merging with the snowmelt still dripping off Merryn's furs. The free arm beat at her. She let go his throat and grabbed it. The movement freed him to wrench his head away. The ear tore. He made to scream again, but turned it into a growl of pain. No beaten cur this, but a predator overmatched.

"I *don't want* to hurt you," she gritted through a mouthful of blood and cartilage. Gore trickled down Toz's cheek and neck, staining the blanket. She spat out the fragment. It bounced off his cheek to land beside his nose.

"He's my friend," Toz managed at last.

She moved her arms a certain way.

Toz grunted. "I don't want to hurt him," he added. Then: "Why are you doing this?"

"Because I have to know! Because I suspect you know what he did to me today. Because I think you may have helped."

"What did he do?"

"Escaped!"

"Escaped? In the winter? Then he's outside? Oh, Gods—!"

"He planned it well," Merryn told him matter-of-factly. "Which is why you have to tell me who he is."

"Who he says he is."

"No," Merryn replied with deadly calm, "he is not."

Silence.

"That won't work," she hissed. "And if you think I'm hard on you, remember that there are others who don't know you and don't care that you're a decent person simply being loyal to your friend."

"You won't do that."

"Why not?"

"Because you've pushed the limit, too," Toz managed. "You don't want any more attention drawn to you about this than can be helped. You're the bright and shining star here—and you've made a major mistake."

"By trusting someone I shouldn't? I'll accept that. Now I have to fix it. But in order to do that, I need to find Krax, and to do that, I have to know who he really is. And to determine *that*, I have to do this to you. Let me remind you that you've sisters. They probably know what you know. I could do to them as I've done to you."

A hesitant silence. Then: "I took an oath."

"To Krax? How is it that he can command oaths of you?"

"By friendship. We bound ourselves together as boys. You folk do the same, with more ceremony. You should understand."

Merryn relaxed her hold the merest bit, keenly aware of alternate weapons should Toz interpret her slackening as weakness or lack of attention and retaliate. "I also understand that there are ways around oaths. Words can be our friends."

"I won't repeat it," Toz choked.

"I won't ask you to. But I will ask you again: Who is Krax?"

"That is for him to say."

"He's the king's son of Ixti, isn't he?" Merryn snapped. "That one's name is Kraxxi. He's the right age. Krax seems noble-born. Those are established facts. You didn't reveal them."

There: She'd said it. Deliberately—not that she expected him to agree, but because she wanted to gauge his reaction from the cues his body would provide whether his mind willed or no. A sudden tensing, a brief start, a change in breathing . . .

Toz's head jerked slightly. She wasn't sure that was enough.

"The finger," she sighed. "I know about the finger. It means death of a brother. It was recent, which means that brother died recently. It also means Krax made that sacrifice for him, which means no one else in his clan was free to do so."

"That is not rare knowledge," Toz protested. "It proves nothing."

"I saw the signet ring."

Silence.

"You have another ear."

"Bitch!"

"Not an insult. Not to me."

More silence. Toz's whole body was slick with sweat. She was sweating, too, not only from the weight of the furs. Her eyes were wet, but she dared not let Toz see that.

"Eight damn it, man, why won't you talk to me? I don't have time for this! Every breath we waste the trail grows colder. Can't I get it through to you that somebody we both love is out in the most dangerous weather imaginable? That there's a good chance he'll die and do nobody who loves him any good? Do you *want* his death on your conscience? Would you rather have that than him alive, even if he accused you of oathbreaking?"

"He would hate me."

She shook her head. "I don't think so. I think it would hurt him, but he'd know you did it because I made you."

"He'd never respect me."

"I could give him the same," Merryn growled. "I owe him the same. I could make him sample everything I've given you. He'd understand."

"I thought you loved him."

"I do . . . I think. Right now I hate him, too. I want him to hurt, Toz, but I don't want him out of my life. Is that honest enough for you?"

"Let me up and we'll talk."

She hesitated. "Can I trust you?"

"You have in the past. And, as you say, he's our friend—and may be in trouble."

She slid off him. Her arms remained in place, however, though she shifted her grip to accommodate. "The hall door is locked. The door to Krynneth's room is locked. I'm between you and the door to my room. You can't get out before I catch you. You're almost naked and I'm armed. Now—if I release you, will you promise on . . . on your oath to Krax not to try to escape?"

"Oaths bound with oaths are dangerous," Toz gave back.

"That's why I asked."

"I will give you my terms," he rasped. "That is all I dare."

She let him go, sprang up to stand beside him, blocking the exit with her body. He looked up at her, twisted on his side, raised his hand to his head and rubbed at the blood. She snatched the towel from the stool and tossed it to him. The cream-colored wool bloomed with War-Hold crimson.

"I will hear these terms," she announced, face hard as she could make it, eyes unmoving. Yet even as she spoke, she felt another word ghosting through the back of her mind. *Treason.* Whatever else he was, Toz was in part an enemy and not to be entirely trusted. By treating with him thus, she acted without authority. That could get her in major trouble with the local Wardens, as well as the chiefs of her clan and adopted craft. She felt like Eddyn, she realized, in a moment of sick discovery: Her emotions had utterly overruled good sense.

Toz used one end of the towel to scour the sweat from his torso while holding the other to his tattered ear. The remnant lay unnoticed between his legs as he shifted around to a squat that proclaimed as eloquently as words that he wouldn't try to escape.

"I will . . . tell you what I am able," he whispered, "if you will assist me and my sisters away from this place."

She kept her eyes level. "To what end?"

"To find our friend."

She nodded thoughtfully. "That doesn't surprise me."

"You'll do it?"

"I didn't say that. And I don't think I *can* do that."

"Why not?"

She leaned back, counted on her fingers. "Consider. I was seen leaving with a prisoner. I return alone. Conclusion: Said prisoner has escaped. I do not report directly to the Hold-Warden. Conclusion: I have some agenda in this beyond the good of Craft, Clan, and Country. That gives them no cause to trust me. That means they'll watch me. That means I cannot, under any circumstances, attempt what I did today again."

A deep breath. "It also means that word of Krax's escape will go out if it hasn't already. Given that it's dark now, and that no one here is foolish enough to go outside after dark in this terrain and season, that means it'll be morning before pursuit can be effected. But they *will* pursue him. They'll probably find him. If they do . . . none of us are safe."

"Which is why you should help us escape. We could tell you things, help you find him."

"Which I'm sure he foresaw and bound you against."

Toz's face went white.

She grinned fiendishly. "Ah-ha! So that was the oath: that you wouldn't try to pursue him."

Toz nodded carefully. "But *you* could. If we told you . . . some of what we know, you could pursue him. If he's caught, I'd rather it were you."

"Why?"

"Because you love him and he needs someone to love him."

"Is that the only reason?"

The longest silence yet. Eventually Toz shook his head. "So that if things fall out as they could, he'll have a reason to go on living."

Her eyes widened incredulously. "You think he'd kill himself?"

It was Toz's turn to smile. "What do you think coming here was? As he's fond of saying, suicide can be accomplished slowly."

She shook her head. *That* had taken her completely off guard. And what could make someone like Krax want to risk suicide?

Intuition fit the parts together. "He killed his brother! That gets you death in Ixti. He chose the method of that death—or tried to."

Toz said nothing, but his eyes spoke eloquently.

"Then why go back?"

Toz shrugged in turn. "I love him; I don't claim to understand him."

She gnawed her lip. "Why do you want to escape? You've been well treated here. You've made friends. As you've pointed out, this is your native land—you have a claim here. And there's the vow. You can't follow Krax."

"I didn't say that."

"You don't have to."

Toz took a deep breath. "Let's say I might want to follow my *sisters*."

A sly grin. "Ah!" A frown followed hard on its tread. "But if you're oath-bound, yet are willing to do that—"

He raised a brow.

"It means they're *not* bound. Which means they're free to follow him if they like."

"And that you're free to tell them anything you suppose, true or not, and that they're free to act on it."

She closed her eyes—a reckless move, granted—and sank back against the wall. How had she got herself into this? And what should she do?

She didn't know. She just didn't know. But one thing was certain; any positive resolution required that she find Krax. She also knew she'd find no allies inside the craft. Which meant—

"If you will tell me as much as you can," she heard herself saying, as though other thoughts commanded her, "I will do what I can to get you and your sisters out of here. But whatever is done must be done quickly—before the Hold-Warden catches wind of what has transpired."

"You'll need surety from me for them to trust you," Toz told her. "Tell them—" He hesitated. "Tell them—" He broke off again. "No, there's nothing I can think of to make them believe you. I'm not even sure *I* do, but I want the same thing as you. Still—" He paused a third time, fumbling at his hand. An instant later, he'd tugged off the ring he wore there, mate to the ones Krax and Ole wore. "This means you have as much of my trust as I have to give. Still, you'll have to bring us together. Then we'll talk."

Merryn rose abruptly. "We've no more time to waste." Even as she spoke, she was stripping off furs. "Put on everything you've got and these, too. I'll be back."

Without further word, Merryn returned to her own room, found the most anonymous hooded robe she owned, and departed, wondering why the footsteps that echoed down the hallway seemed to fall in the exact cadence of that coldest, most fearsome of words: *traitor, traitor, traitor* . . .

CHAPTER XXXIV:

LEAVING

(ERON: WAR-HOLD-WINTER—DEEP WINTER:
DAY XXII—EARLY EVENING)

~~~~~~~~~~~~~~~~~

Merryn heard the approaching footsteps before they turned the corner. And almost panicked. Here she was in the middle of the hold, clad in thinly disguised weather gear, with suspicious activities shadowing her like icicles falling after a thaw, and she was about to meet someone. She glanced about instinctively, saw nowhere to hide, and determined to brazen it out, should that become necessary.

Closer . . .

She moved wide to give the other room—then froze, as she found herself face-to-face with a glowering Hold-Warden.

"Lady Warden," she nodded casually, as though nothing untoward were afoot.

"Subchief," Lorvinn acknowledged, not moving.

"You—" Merryn began.

Lorvinn cleared her throat with casual menace. "I think, rather, we should talk about you."

Merryn tried to remain calm and hoped that the sweat on her brow was from her encounter with Toz, or from the heat of the hold itself. "As you will," she breathed with ritual formality.

Lorvinn eyed her up and down. "Your room's closer than mine. And since I was on my way to see you . . ."

She didn't need to finish. That alone spoke volumes. Like the fact that Lorvinn knew something was amiss. Like the fact that she respected Merryn enough to seek clarification via informal contact. Like the fact that this could become a very complex situation very rapidly indeed—one Merryn didn't control. "As you will," Merryn echoed, turning to pace the Hold-Warden back down the corridor from which she'd just come. Another few steps, she reflected, and she'd have been able to reach Elv and Ole. Which wouldn't have changed much if Lorvinn was already onto her.

Neither spoke until they were back in Merryn's room. Merryn indicated a pitcher of ale on the table by the door, surprised when Lorvinn nodded back. She filled two cups, but remained standing as Lorvinn claimed the window seat. "What am I going to do with you, Merryn?" The question startled her. "No one like you should do the things you've done today. But when people who are as reliable as sunrise act against expectations, one usually suspects something's wrong. And when that person also burns as bright as that same sun, one doesn't want to risk that person—for one's own sake, for the sake of the craft, or the sake of the person herself. Which is why I came seeking you, and in this I'm answerable to Preedor and Tryffon both—which I'm sure you appreciate."

Merryn nodded grimly. Both those men liked her a lot. The notion of having them arrayed against her chilled her to the bone.

"Do you want to tell me what's happened, or do I have to wait? In either case, I'll be angry. I'll be angrier in the second."

"What do you know?" Merryn dared.

Lorvinn smiled coldly. "I know you left on horseback with Krax. I know you returned without him and your mounts. I doubt he could've got the better of you by any reasonable means unless you let your guard down. I also know that as a subchief you have a certain amount of leeway in terms of coming and going, which you used to no good end, and about which I haven't yet decided what to do. In the meantime, I'd much rather listen than talk."

Merryn took a deep swallow and wiped her mouth. She walked solemnly toward Lorvinn and when she was close enough, turned her neck toward her, exposing the side of her throat where the dart wound still showed red. "That's how he did it: one of those blowguns he showed me how to work— which you knew about. I never thought he'd use one on me."

"Poisoned?"

"Aye."

"What kind?"

"Scorpion. You probably know about that, too. Apparently it only *numbs* people."

Lorvinn's eyes went hard. "It's far riskier than that. Your . . . shadow might not have wanted to kill you, but he obviously knew there was some chance of that. Why do you still protect him?"

"I *don't* protect him!" Merryn flared. "I want him back here in *chains* if that's what it takes! But I didn't want—" She broke off, suddenly feeling as vulnerable as she had in years. "It was my mistake; I wanted to be the one to rectify it. I knew time was of the essence—it still is. I knew that if I went through you first, it would cost time. I went to the best source of information—who happens to occupy the room next door and is probably listening right now."

"It doesn't matter," Lorvinn snapped. "I intend to speak to him soon enough."

Another swallow. "That's your right," Merryn conceded. "But he didn't swear me to any real secrecy. If you want to know what was said, I'll tell you. I only ask that you consider the urgency of this. Whether we proceed by Law or instinct, the fact is that Krax is getting farther away every instant. Every moment we remain here, the number of places we must search increases."

"I know that," Lorvinn gritted. "Speak your say."

Merryn did.

To her surprise, Lorvinn listened quietly, eyes intent, but betraying neither approval nor disapproval—which Merryn found unnerving, though she knew it was simply another skill she might eventually acquire herself.

"So you've decided that I'm right: that he really is the prince of Ixti?"

Merryn nodded. "Now that I've seen the signet ring I don't have much choice."

Lorvinn sipped her drink thoughtfully. "I suppose I should've investigated him more thoroughly, too. Except that it's such an unlikely notion, in the first place—and that I thought I had time, given that it's *winter*. And I guess"—she paused, looking very, very grim—"I guess I didn't *want* to think it, because the implications of that are too enormous."

"What implications?" Merryn asked, as a chill wracked her.

"You don't suppose Barrax *wants* him here, do you?"

Merryn shook her head. "No, but I've also heard there's little love between king and heir. I don't think Barrax would've exiled him, though, which can only mean he exiled himself. Toz as much as told me that. And there's the finger—"

A nod. "And where were you going when we met?"

"To interview Toz's sisters."

"And then?"

A sigh, and the mug was drained. "I would've decided then. I would've had as much information as I could muster in the available time. I can't tell you how I would've acted because I don't know. I don't know what would've been controlling me then: head or heart, and if the latter, what part? The part that wants revenge for betrayal, or the part that just wants him . . . back." She glared at Lorvinn. "There: I've said it."

Lorvinn rose. "We should leave soon."

Merryn gaped at her—aghast. "We?"

A shrug. "He may not be who we think, but if he is . . . there must be some reason he left when he did. What would you think if you were me?"

Again Merryn's heart skipped a beat. She truly had deluded herself. Truly had seen what she wanted to see and ignored what didn't fit that forging. "He learned what he came for and now he's gone. Back to his father."

Silence.

Merryn clasped her head in her hands as she slumped against the wall, completely drained. "Too many stories," she whispered. "I don't know what's the truth."

"We might be able to find out," Lorvinn gave back cryptically. "Now: You prepare yourself—and Toz. I'll find the others."

"Others?"

"The women, their shadows. I'm not fool enough to dare this alone."

Merryn gaped.

"I risk as much as you. I let a prisoner escape. It is for me to find him, knowing what he may know. I don't want to be the one who unleashes the flood of war. But I'd *prefer* the whole world not know of my failings."

"You don't think Barrax—"

"Barrax *doesn't* think—very often," Lorvinn snorted from the door. "But when he does, he often ponders war."

"One winter here would cure him of that!"

"But he doesn't know that. Krax might. Then again, this has been a mild one."

Merryn shrugged listlessly. She heard the Warden's Lock click behind her, and knew she was there for the duration.

She marched straight to Toz's door, unlocked it, and sauntered in. He was half-dressed, puzzling his way through the unfamiliar fastenings on the various fur garments Merryn had left him. "Things have changed," she announced without preamble. "I didn't change them."

Toz nodded grimly. "I heard. I'm not sure what this means, but I stick by my oath. I have to."

Merryn indicated the rest of the clothing. "Bring that to my room. I have to change, too."

He blinked at her, but had little choice but to follow, still busy with grommets and laces. She made short work of finding her second set of snow gear, and by the time she'd donned it, Lorvinn was back—with a confused-looking Krynneth and Ole. Merryn wondered if this was because Ole was overtly the more biddable of the two. In any event, both were clad in outdoor clothing and lugged backpacks holding more. Lorvinn was dressed as before—in indoor garb—but she also carried a small black box somewhat like a churgeon's field kit. "Merryn, Krynneth," she ordered, "claim your shadows." The reflex of command made Merryn act before thinking. She was behind Toz instantly, gripping his biceps in a Night Guard's hold she'd only just learned. What was Lorvinn doing, anyway? She had to know she was taking a risk, even with Elv as hostage against the others' good conduct. The odds were slightly better than even, but would that be enough?

Lorvinn fixed Ole with a steely glare. "What do you know of Krax's escape?" she barked.

Ole flinched—which told enough. "I didn't know he *had* . . . escaped," she replied carefully.

"He has!" Lorvinn spat. "This morning. We need him back for a number of reasons, some of which I'm sure you understand. Since we know you also care for him, we would rather have your aid of your own free will than from coercion. We need to know what his most likely destination would be, now that he's free. I don't think there's any doubt who he really is."

"What happens if we tell you?" Ole dared, not bothering to look at Toz for any kind of prompt. Which probably meant she'd figured out that he'd revealed . . . something. If she were very clever, she could piece together a lot simply from their clothing. And Ole *was* very clever.

Lorvinn regarded her steadily. "We get him back; things progress as they would have. We return to Tir-Eron in the spring and you all plead your cases before the King. In your case, we try to connect you to your kin."

"And if we don't?"

"He may die. That's the major risk."

"Why should that matter to you?"

"Life is not to be wasted," Lorvinn retorted. "But time's not to be wasted either, and this wastes time." And with that, Lorvinn set the box on the table where the ale had been and opened it, withdrawing two short sticks of pale wood, neither longer than her shortest finger. She chose one and marched up in front of where Krynneth kept a firm grip on Ole. Merryn recognized it at once.

Lorvinn waved the stick under Ole's nose. "You know what this is?"

Ole's face betrayed nothing.

"Your eyes speak what your body will not," Lorvinn replied casually. "This is imphor. I don't need to tell you what it can do, do I?"

Ole didn't move.

"I don't have time for games, woman!" Lorvinn snapped. "Everything you do proclaims a background in Ixti's army. And I know full well it conditions you against imphor—which is why we didn't ply you with it when you arrived. There was no real need, and the risk, as you know, is great."

It was, too. Though essentially an anesthetic often used by athletes, enough of it could break one's will sufficiently to make one speak the truth. But if someone were conditioned to withstand it, by eating or inhaling large quantities of it whole, there was a chance further application would also break the mind. Eronese ethics frowned on that and forbade its use, save by those few from War-Hold who volunteered—including the Night Guard. Which was one of the differences between service in Eron and service in Ixti. In Ixti, one had no choice about such things.

"I don't want to subject you to imphor for a number of reasons, most of which I'm sure you understand. However, we *do* want Krax back, both for his own good, for ours, and for the possible peace between our lands. It would be most expedient if you would simply tell us where he has gone—*now!*"

"You know *who* he is," Ole growled. "He has told you, and we have told you. As to where . . . the world is wide." Her voice was calm, but her eyes betrayed—not fear, but a certain uneasiness. More than once they moved toward Toz.

"I . . . made a bargain," Toz managed hoarsely. "I would prefer to stay by it."

Lorvinn turned to stare at him. "And this bargain was . . . ?"

Toz swallowed hard. *Utterly wretched,* Merryn realized. She didn't blame him.

"That I would urge my sister to reveal . . . what was needed in exchange for Merryn's aid in escaping."

"To what end?"

Toz looked even worse than before. "Krax made me swear not to follow him," he said helplessly. "But I can't leave him out there by himself. Someone has to . . . be with him. That only leaves my sisters and . . . Merryn. They're the only people who care enough for him to make him survive."

"Why did he leave now?" Lorvinn barked.

"I don't know."

"You'd better not be lying!"

Toz didn't reply.

"The deal was for both of us," Ole broke in decisively. "Myself and my sister."

"We need one of you as surety on the other's good conduct."

Silence.

"We waste time," Merryn grumbled. "We'd be away ere now, if—"

Lorvinn glared at her. "If what?"

"We can argue, or we can act!" Merryn shouted, thrusting Toz roughly away, already reaching for her gear.

Another glare from Lorvinn, but it was Toz who spoke. "If you hold my sister for surety, I demand surety in turn. Break my mind if you will, and be that on your soul. But any information I give or ask be given must be exchanged outside with us supplied and mounted. After that . . . I can't . . . search," he concluded miserably. "I can only . . . follow."

Lorvinn cleared her throat. "As Merryn said, time wastes." She strode toward the door. "Blindhood our guests, then gather your gear, whatever weapons you would take, Merryn and Krynneth, and meet in my chambers as soon as you can." And with that, she departed.

Merryn's choice of weapons was formidable but included her sword, an assortment of daggers in odd places, and her blowguns (two now) because she was beginning to appreciate the utility of those weapons. As for camping gear, Lorvinn, as expedition leader, would see to that.

So it was that, sooner than expected, she was ushering a lightly bound and blindhooded Toz up the staircase to Lorvinn's private quarters, which occupied the top of the center tower.

The rooms were plain but luxurious, their main attraction being their extraordinary spaciousness and the fact that they were paneled with wood, not stone, and carpeted with finger-thick wool dyed emerald-green to simulate the spring grass Lorvinn loved.

Lorvinn met them there, dressed in fur like the rest, and looking little different, save that she was older. Krynneth and Ole joined them a moment later—with Elv, minus her shadow, but blindhooded like her sister. Lorvinn's brows shot up in anger—or surprise, it was impossible to determine. "I couldn't find Minyn," Krynneth explained sheepishly. "And she threatened to kill herself if we didn't let her accompany her sister. You were in a hurry, so I chose to risk it."

"Remind me to lecture you another time on risks," Lorvinn sighed. "For now—" She said no more, merely ushered them toward what looked to be a blank wall, paused there, and studied the triplets seriously. "Even blindhooded, I'm trusting you more than I would trust most of my kinsmen. I'm giving you power over me, but I'm also claiming power over you." And with that, she touched a hidden stud and a section of wall slid aside, revealing a narrow archway with stairs leading down, lit by the faint light of tiny glowglobes. "Krynneth, you go first. The triplets go in the middle. Merryn and I will follow."

No one argued. Merryn found herself trailing Toz down a narrow, twisting stair. She had her sword at ready, of course, and every sense was alert for any aberration. Fortunately, no one did anything untoward as they made their way downward. Eventually they halted on a limestone landing fronting a blank wall, though the stairs continued deeper into the earth. Lorvinn touched something else they couldn't see, and the wall slid back, revealing a feed room off the stables.

None of the grooms were about, and Lorvinn wasted no time choosing mounts for all of them. Merryn wished vainly for Ingot, whom she only hoped would show up on his own. In the meantime, she contented herself with a sturdy mare named Mud, since endurance and surefootedness would be more useful for the nonce than speed.

The triplets were still bound, nor were they allowed to unhood, which made for complex logistics, like requiring Merryn, Krynneth, and Lorvinn each to lead two horses toward yet another hidden portal, this one large enough for horses to traverse, giving onto a gradually sloping ramp which terminated, after a fair distance, in a room big enough for the mustering of a considerable mounted unit. A final stud, and a section of wall slid upward, shedding a season's worth of snow and ice as it revealed a moonlit vista of more snow mingled with bare rocks. *Southwest of the hold,* Merryn identified, by the turns they'd made. She wondered how many knew about this exit.

She also wondered what it portended as far as the prisoners were concerned. Lorvinn was either taking a frightful risk giving these curious half-breed foreigners the information she'd just provided, and relying on their perhaps scanty honor to seal their tongues, or else she had other plans, about which Merryn knew nothing. Suddenly the whole affair took a different slant—one Merryn wasn't certain she liked.

But she couldn't deal with that now, because Lorvinn was urging them all outside, still afoot, still leading the horses, the prisoners still blindhooded and stumbling along on a route that was less than a road and more than a trail. Not until they were out of sight of the exit—maybe half a shot—did Lorvinn call a halt.

"You can free them now," she said brusquely, gazing at the sky to gauge the time. Two hands past sunset, which could've been better or worse.

"About time, too!" Elv muttered, as Merryn busied herself with Toz's hood. He blinked at her, scowling angrily, but also looking resigned and several other emotions she could guess without much trouble. His eyes darted about anxiously, counting horses, before settling on his sisters.

"You expect a lot," he told Lorvinn.

"I expect loyalty where loyalty is due," Lorvinn replied calmly. "Right now, what is best for Krax is best for the rest of us. If we find him, I suspect you'll find that things will go better for him than if we don't."

"You know nothing!" Toz snapped—and by his expression, wished he hadn't. His sisters' scowls added credence to that supposition.

Merryn sighed wearily. "Tell them to reveal that thing we bargained for."

Tozri puffed his cheeks, staring at the ground. His shoulders sagged like an old man's. "I'm sorry," he whispered. "I don't want to do this, but . . . I'm . . . *very* afraid for our friend. I swore not to reveal who he is or where he'd go if he was free, but he didn't say that you two couldn't reveal as much. Right now," he continued, "I think it might be in all our interest if we could find a way around our oaths."

Elv glared at him. "His death is his own right."

"We also swore to protect him, and by our law, oaths are honored in the order they are made—"

"Oaths are a curse!" Elv gritted.

"They are," Merryn and Lorvinn agreed as one. "But oaths sworn in Ixti might be construed as having no power here," the Hold-Warden went on, "not if they are based on the powers in Ixti. You might use that as a way around your conscience, if you so choose. We won't think less of you for it."

Silence, for a very long while.

Then, finally, from Ole. "His *brother* is . . . who you think he is. As to why he returns: I truly do not know. It makes no sense."

Lorvinn regarded her sorrowfully. "I will ask no more, and for what you have told us, you may accompany us if you will. You know his habits, his motivations, his desires. We don't." She paused, gazing at Toz. "You said you swore not to follow him. That oath doesn't forbid you following us, since we have no surety we *are* following him."

"The ring will find him," Toz whispered, barely audible.

"Brother!" Elv raged. "What are you thinking?"

Toz's face was grim. "I don't *want* to think right now. I only want . . . an end to this."

"An excellent notion," Lorvinn agreed, eyeing Merryn curiously as she moved toward her gelding. "We all risk much tonight. I suggest we be away before what little trail Krax has left is lost. Merryn, Krynneth: Help our guests into their saddles, but watch them—closely. Merryn and I will ride to fore, you ride at the rear. If you see any suspicious action, you have my permission to act as seems good to you."

And with that, she swung into her saddle. Merryn followed suit. A moment later, they were all riding single file into a cleft in the mountainside, the raw stone walls of which rose thrice as high as their heads. Because of its depth and position, little snow had filtered into it, but Merryn didn't like the place at all—because it was so closed in, and because it was obviously near the hold yet she'd had no idea it existed.

Happily, the way opened up not far ahead, revealing a mountain meadow awash with moonglow. She held her breath in anticipation. Soon enough, the road widened into a sweep of snow-clad mountainside, through which road markers showed at intervals. Lorvinn, in the lead, eased aside and motioned her ahead, then turned to face the cleft, from which no one else had yet emerged. She was doing something Merryn couldn't see for the mass of her bulky cloak and hood.

Merryn smelled quick-fire. And saw, too late, that Lorvinn had set something alight and hurled it directly in front of Toz's mount. The mare started, reared, jostling back into the others. Voices cried out in two languages, horses snorted—and then a small explosion lit the land. The entire cleft filled with thick, pungent smoke that instantly engulfed both mounts and riders like a living thing.

"Away—now!" Lorvinn shouted, kicking her steed to as much speed as was safe on the terrain at night. Merryn hesitated—until she caught the barest trace of the scent that rode the smoke and set heels to Mud's sides with vigor. "Imphor," she spat as Lorvinn raced her toward a steeper slope where they'd have to slow. "You tricked them."

Lorvinn slowed for the turn, which put Merryn slightly ahead. "I never said they couldn't follow, but I never said they could come with us, either. The imphor will knock the horses out for most of the night, and them for roughly a hand. They dare not follow on foot, and Krynneth will—I hope— have sense enough to urge them back to the hold. What happens now, I don't want to know about. They may still follow—afoot—but they'll lose another day. They may decide to go north to seek their kin—I've told Krynneth to encourage them to think in that direction. But right now—"

"What?"

Lorvinn's eyes narrowed as she twisted around to look at Merryn. And then widened again, as Merryn calmly put her mouth to the end of the blowgun she'd hidden beneath her cloak—and blew.

The first dart struck Lorvinn's mare, with what results, Merryn had no idea.

The second, from the second, smaller tube, struck Lorvinn herself in the wrist she'd ungloved to light the quick-fire.

"I'm sorry," Merryn said numbly. "But I don't want *you* to follow me either."

CHAPTER XXXV:

INTO THE NIGHT

(ERON: GEM-HOLD-WINTER—DEEP WINTER: DAY XXIII—AFTERNOON)

~~~~~~~~~~

"I'm going to take this warmth as a sign," Avall announced, deliberately choosing to look at the world beyond the arcade in lieu of Strynn, because it hurt too much to look at her these days. She was beautiful beyond belief, but that sadness she tried to hide and couldn't laid a patina across that perfection that made her seem unreal. Instead, he pondered the landscape. He did that a lot these days. But today, for the first time since he'd come there, it was almost comfortable outside.

The sun was bright. Water ran in rivulets down the sides of the hold. The air rang with the sound of icicles collapsing. And yet it was still only halfway to the solstice—the Dark: the middle of Deep Winter.

"It's never this warm now," he went on, because neither Strynn nor Rann had replied. Perhaps they were like him: too caught up in the moment to comment further.

"It never snows as early as the trek, either," Strynn offered at last.

"Gynn said it would be a year of changes," Rann observed listlessly from Avall's other side. Like his friend, he was bareheaded; the wind gave a healthy ruddiness to his slightly stubby nose.

"*Weather,* said that," Avall corrected. "He was speaking with the voice of the God."

"Who may not exist," Rann snorted. "I've been thinking about that. I know we need The Eight, because everyone wants someone bigger than them to rely on or blame things on. And I know there's good evidence to support the fact that *something's* out there, because too many prophecies come true. But this thing with the gem— You were right, it could turn things over. Priest-Clan's not going to like it."

"One more reason to go through with this," Avall noted.

"Have you decided horses or skis?" Strynn inquired.

Avall sighed. "Not horses. One: We'd have to sign them out. Two: There's no way we could get them out unobtrusively, and if we did, they'd still limit our choice of exits. Three: We'd have to take food for them, because there's basically no forage out there and I don't want to rely on the stations."

Strynn nodded slowly. "So that means skis?"

Avall grimaced. "Not my first choice. Still, with it this warm and the wind not blowing, and the weather-witch saying there'll be no wind or snow for another seven days, maybe we can get through. I'm certain we can make Bend Station by nightfall." He patted his thighs appreciatively. "One good thing about working in the mines: All that pedaling's built up my strength and endurance. I ought to do fine."

Strynn looked past him to Rann. "I assume you think you'll do fine, too?"

Avall studied him as well, seeking to read his face for signs of uncertainty. He saw none. "As fine as I can be. We've got food packed—way-fare, because it's light and can be mixed with water. Firewood won't be a problem, nor will making fire. We've got oiled-leather bags to sleep in, as well as a tent. We'll burrow under the snow if we have to—you can actually stay fairly warm that way. We'll be fine as long as we stay in the woods. My fear is the plains. Four days to cross normally. We're thinking eight, minimum. The big problem will be if we miss the stations. Unfortunately, there *is* no straight way to Tir-Eron—damn the Fateing."

Strynn gnawed her lip. "Without the Fateing you'd never have found the gem. But someone else would have, who might've been less scrupulous."

"Or more," Avall retorted. "I'm not at all sure *I'm* being scrupulous in this matter."

"You're doing the best you can, with little information and inadequate guidance."

"I resent that!" Rann shot back, grinning to show he was teasing.

"Laughter's supposed to keep you warm," Strynn chuckled. "In that case, I'm glad you're going with him."

"It's also supposed to induce childbirth," Rann shot back, eyeing her stomach speculatively. "If you'd like me to try . . ."

"That won't be necessary!" she sniffed. "Though I do think it may come early."

Avall felt a pang at that, as a concern he'd thought safely walled away reasserted. In spite of sharing Strynn's bed, seeing her naked daily, bathing her or bathing with her, making what love they could, the child she carried still seemed unreal. There was no true connection between the bulge in Strynn's belly and Eddyn. Or with the fact that she'd been raped. Those things had happened to different people. He wondered, assuming he survived this, if he'd wind up a different person a quarter hence as well. That was when he was supposed to become a father.

Rann dabbed at a film of melting ice. "Is the plan still the same, then?"

Strynn shook her head. "I'm going to tell the Hold-Warden that the two of you are bedridden with flux and would prefer no one else care for you, and that you're both staying in Rann's rooms because they're warmer and I have to be absent a lot. If she mentions the Hold-Healer, I'm going to tell her that I did an extra session at Herbs and want to try some things myself. There's pox in South Wing, anyway, and that has them busy. I doubt they'll mind me taking things into my own hands. I will ask for some medicines, though, just in case."

Avall took her hand, which was trembling. He clutched it savagely. Not to hurt, but to reassure.

"What about the helm?" Strynn wondered. "We've never really covered that."

"It's almost done," Avall told her. "It won't take that much longer if I use . . . certain influences. But the fact is, this is simply more important. Gynn's a Smith, but he's also a King. He'll understand that we're neglecting one power in favor of a greater."

"If he doesn't read it as a *play* for power," Strynn mused. "He's no fool."

"He created this situation," Avall retorted. "He knows his own responsibility. In any event, I've no choice but to leave the helm here. It contributes nothing to the journey but deadweight, which we can't afford. If for some reason I can return before the end of the Deep, I'll work on it again. In the meantime . . . guard it well. Not with your life, but guard it. It's the best thing I've ever done."

"And if you *don't* come back?"

"Bring it when you return from here, of course. And you and Merryn finish it. Or ask Eellon. Even Tyrill. I wouldn't trust anyone else to have the skill."

Strynn went abruptly silent. Avall feared he'd hurt her feelings. "I'm . . . flattered," she said at last. "And I'll do that, never fear. But . . . Avall, I don't think even you know how good that thing is."

He smiled at her, wiped a tear away with a finger, glad it hadn't frozen. "And you still don't know where I got my inspiration."

She regarded him curiously. For a long time they simply looked into each other's eyes. Avall felt himself drifting out of himself—which made him start in alarm.

Rann coughed. The moment shattered.

"Well," Strynn said decisively, "if you lads are going to leave when you say you are, you'd better get some sleep."

Avall raised a brow quizzically.

Strynn chucked his chin. "Yes, my love, some sleep. I've made a potion. Though there might be a little time before it takes effect . . ."

Avall's reply was a warm and very sunny grin.

Rann simply rolled his eyes and followed the two of them inside.

Like all winter holds, Gem-Hold never truly slept. No matter the time or the season, there were always people about, rotating in or out of tasks, pursuing their own projects at all times of the day and night. The mines never closed (time scarcely existed down there anyway), and the heating apparatus needed constant supervision lest the steam find itself confined and blow the place to flinders. That had happened once—years ago—at Lore, which was why there were gaps in some of the chronicles.

And, of course, there was basic maintenance and cleaning, laundry, cooking, and the all-important duty that *no one* shirked: keeping the environs free of ice.

Still, Avall felt more than a little self-conscious as he, Rann, and a far-too-breathless Strynn made their way down what sketchy observation had determined was probably the hold's least-used stair, roughly two hands before sunrise. It also, conveniently enough, terminated near the hold's least-used exit.

They met no one as they followed the twisting spiral of aging stone and wood, though once or twice they could've wished for more light, since only random slits admitted moonlight to the stairwell. Otherwise, they relied on mining torches. There were even rats—a few—proof that the local cats still had duties to perform. Nor did anyone await them at the bottom, where Avall and Rann had been caching gear—which had required some careful machinations and faster talk, under the guise of assembling equipment for two days' hunting which might require a night spent outside, just in case.

Skis weren't a problem. There were skis beside most doors, and early in his tenure at the hold Avall had been fitted for a pair. Rann already had some, on which he'd painted abstract designs. Avall's were plain; serviceable, and that was all, because he disliked winter as much as he disliked crowds and therefore acknowledged its existence as little as possible.

Which made his present journey, now he was literally on the threshold, seem more than a little . . . stupid.

But they were there now: retrieving food, cover, tents, and cooking gear from the cupboards where they'd been stashed. Checking their own clothing—three pairs of hose apiece under oiled-leather breeches with the fur side turned in, and two more pairs each, for spares. Boots the same, and double-soled, and with a spare set in case those got too wet. Two tight tunics, two loose ones, again under leather vests and overtunics. Short cloaks with armholes and front fasteners. Tight caps, face masks, and hoods.

Glare *might* be a problem. Sunlight on all that snow could be blinding, for which they had gauze face veils—which, however, might not prove sufficient. Much of their route lay through forest, however, where branches would screen out some of the light. The rest . . . they would endure.

And then there was no more time for delay. Avall looked around for one more thing to distract him from what he suddenly found himself dreading as much as anything he'd ever undertaken: saying farewell to Strynn. Rann would miss her, too, of course; he cared far more for her than he ever let on. But Rann was taking his signals from Avall.

Avall coughed awkwardly, then reached out and took Strynn's hand, holding it lightly, as though it were a fragile casting that might break if he squeezed too hard. As this moment might; as their lives might. The next time he saw her, nothing would be the same. He started to speak, but she shook her head, held a finger to his lips, then raised his hand to hers and kissed each knuckle in turn. Their eyes met, looked away. A deep breath, and she reached to her side and unsheathed what had hung there, laying it across Avall's palm. A dagger he'd never seen before, but clearly one she'd made. "I finished this the day all this began," she murmured. "Now I give it to you, I hope, on the day some of this will end."

"Thank you," he mouthed silently, as he fumbled for what he'd brought her. "This is silly," he added, ever more conscious of Rann trying to stay busy, but sneaking glances their way. He laid the object in her hand. A pair of lips: *his* lips, pressed in wax and cast in purest gold. "If I can't kiss you myself," he chuckled, "maybe these can."

Strynn laughed softly, but with genuine pleasure. "People only think you're serious all the time," she told him, folding the token into her hand.

"Only because I have to be," he murmured sadly. "Only because I don't get a chance to be anything else and still do what I must."

"Maybe . . . after."

"I hope."

Rann cleared his throat.

Strynn's face took a firmer set. "It's getting no earlier, lads. If you're going, you'd best be at it."

Avall nodded. He retrieved his gear—it made quite a pile and unbalanced him, though he was grateful for what little skiing he'd done near the hold. Skis and pole in hand, he waited while Strynn opened the door to the inner weather gate.

There were three anterooms to negotiate, each significantly colder than the one before, with the outermost not heated at all. Ice made a slippery skin on the floor, where water had melted earlier in the day and refrozen. Avall tested it, felt his foot slide, reached for some of the sand left in a bin nearby for that purpose, and thought better of it. "Wait," he cautioned Strynn. "This is as far as you go."

He reached out to hug her, but she shrank away. "No, Avall, just go. I love you and I know you're doing the only thing you can do, but I'm— *No, never mind, I can't!*"

And with that she turned away in a cloud of fur and fabric. The door closed—her doing—he saw her small, strong fingers. And then he and Rann were alone at the last weather gate. Readjusting his pack, he motioned his friend toward the portal.

It squeaked, sure sign it wasn't often used, then swung away. Moonlight flooded in. Using his pole for balance, Avall stepped forward—cautiously. Three steps . . . two . . . one . . . and then he was outside, drinking in the clear, frigid air. He dropped his skis, sat down on the vesting bench, and slipped them on. Rann closed the door and joined him. That thick slab of oak was now become a wall—between warmth, security, and love; and the cold, cruel, loveless night.

But all three moons were shining, and in such a way that all three shadows lay together. And with those shadows for company, Avall and Rann poled into Deep Winter.

CHAPTER XXXVI:

IN DARK OF NIGHT

(Eron: Gem-Hold-Winter – Deep Winter: Day XXV – evening)

Eddyn had awakened hungover, paid token obeisance to his condition in terms of cleaning himself up and getting marginally fed, then proceeded to get drunk again. The Avall situation was *not* going to leave him alone otherwise. And along with that rationalization, sometime in the dark time had come the realization that if he was ever going to get any answers, he'd have to get them on his own, either by stealth or coercion. Stealth was preferable, because stealth was less likely to get you caught. But it took time, and even then you might not get whole answers. Meanwhile the thing would continue to gnaw at him, while the unfinished shield merely sat there all but grinning smugly, like a goad.

Which left coercion.

And that was a notion that scared him half to death. The Eight knew the last time he'd tried it—when he'd stretched Strynn on the ground—had all but ruined his life.

But there were people who might be able to tell him *something*. Not Avall, of course, and probably not Rann. Strynn just possibly because she was with child and might not want to risk it, but whatever chanced there, she would tell Avall unless he had some way to keep her quiet. Briefly—*very* briefly—he considered forcing the information from her, murdering her, then contriving circumstances so that it looked as though she'd miscarried and died in childbirth.

That *was* an option, but it was one born of wine, ale, and beer consumed nonstop for three days. But there was one other person who, according to Rrath, seemed to know something about all this *strangeness* that was eating away at him.

A pause to finish his latest mug of cidered wine, and Eddyn rose shakily, found his favorite small dagger, and staggered to the door. No sense acting sober now; he'd save that for when he needed it.

Four times on that trek, he almost turned back. Once when he caught sight of a pair of his sparring partners and had to turn aside lest he either be co-opted into a game for which he had no heart or have his ongoing lack of sobriety challenged; the next when a harried-looking healer literally collided with him on a landing, felt his brow before he could stop her, pronounced him flushed but not ill (either of the pox that was raging in South Wing, or the flux Avall and Rann had contracted), then sniffed his breath, wrinkled her nose, and advised him to go back to bed and sleep it off.

The third time was when he caught a whiff of some foul-smelling vapor from one of the heat vents and nearly hurled his gorge right there, which he thought might be an omen. And the fourth was when, from nowhere, his conscience ambushed him and made him actually confront what he was about.

But by that time the target was in sight. The corridor and the common hall outside were empty (which he also took as an omen), and his legs had developed a mind of their own. If not actually more sober, he also had more control of his body, so his footfalls came firm, direct, and straight, and the fingers that rapped smartly on the door didn't tremble.

No reply—though he heard harp music pause, resume, then break off again, as though someone wasn't certain he'd actually heard a knock.

Another rap, and this time a reply.

"Who is it?"

A deep breath. A quick decision in answer to an obvious question he'd not anticipated.

"Eddyn syn Argen-yr. You don't know me, I don't think, but I've got . . . a message from Rrath."

Another pause, a slight rattle. A string jangled tentatively, then: "Come in."

Eddyn tried the door, found it unlocked, wondered why he'd assumed otherwise, and why he hadn't simply barged in—and then, so suddenly it surprised even him, he *was* barging in. He caught a glimpse of a small, neat sitting room, sparsely furnished but with everything finished in rich textures—which made sense if one was blind. A single candle, a tray of smoking scent-spice—and a slight, pretty young man turning a sylk-masked face toward him, mouth widening into an O of alarm, muscles tensing as he sought to rise from a padded stool behind the most beautiful harp Eddyn had ever seen.

Eddyn caught him by the shoulders and jerked him to his feet, then slung him to the floor, all in one smooth arc. The youth weighed almost nothing. Eddyn heard his heels thud into the carpet as his torso and hips made a harder thump.

"What?" the youth managed. "Who . . . ?"

Eddyn realized he'd made his first blunder. He'd revealed his name to a blind man, which was the height of stupidity. Which only fueled his rising anger, his rising insistence that he *would* learn what he wanted, and learn it right now.

"I don't want to hurt you," Eddyn snapped, fumbling with one hand for his dagger, as he shifted his body over the struggling youth, pinning him firmly in what was an eerie mockery of the pose he'd affected before defiling Strynn. One hand held the boy at arm's length, while the youth alternately flailed at him in panic and pried at the hand at his throat.

Eddyn found the dagger, making sure it rasped as it came out of its case. The boy tensed, relaxed, then began to struggle harder. A raking hand caught the blade by accident, and the boy's face went white, though he had sense enough not to scream—or maybe couldn't. Eddyn loosened the grip on his throat a fraction. "Tell me one thing and I'll let you go. I don't want to hurt you—but this dagger tells you I will!"

The boy's mouth clamped closed, only to pop open again when Eddyn tightened his grip once more, feeling all the while that it was someone else doing that, that he was a man outside himself.

"What?" the boy choked.

"You *are* Kylin?" Eddyn had sense enough to ask, as another potentially lethal mistake made itself known. Not that the hold was likely to have more than one blind harper of that name.

"Y-yes."

"Good. Just tell me one thing. No, two things. Three . . . *three* things, and swear on The Eight to never mention I asked you."

"I swear! I swear! But there's nothing I know that should matter to you."

"Don't be too sure." Eddyn shook him for good measure, heard his head thunk against the floor, noting absently that blood was running down his arm from where the boy had struck the blade. He was bleeding, too, and freely. But not in a life-threatening way.

"Strynn," Eddyn snapped. "She came here. She made you see. How did she do that?"

"I don't know what you're talking about!"

Eddyn pushed harder. Kylin gasped. Eddyn shifted his grip on the knife. "It would be no problem for me to remove a finger, but it might well be a problem for you, should you wish to continue playing that harp."

"Don't!"

"Then tell."

"No."

"It's not worth your death."

"Strynn's my friend."

"Is she? She put you in this situation. Now tell me. You can always say I beat it out of you," he continued recklessly.

"No."

The blade prodded Kylin's neck. Blood blossomed.

The boy's face went white.

"A gem."

"Describe it."

"I'm blind. I don't know the words."

"That's not what I heard. Besides, you can still feel. How big? What texture?"

"Big as . . . my . . . as my eyes, maybe," Kylin blurted out in near panic, as though his mind were at war with itself and one part sought to beat the other to revelation or silence. "Smooth," he went on recklessly, "like a river rock."

"What color?"

"I didn't *see* it."

"Yes you did."

"I—"

"I *know* you did! Someone told me. You were careless what you wrote. Someone saw—maybe many someones. Some of us can add."

Kylin coughed, tried to fight again—until Eddyn grabbed his injured hand. "Fingers. Two, now. At least."

"Red. Multicolors, dancing inside, sparking like flakes of color in glass. Like . . . what I've heard an opal is like."

Eddyn slammed Kylin's head against the floor. "And it let you see? It— How did it do that?"

"Please, I swore! The Eight—"

"The Eight treat us like ants, if they exist. Do you think they care what happens to you?"

"They might!"

"Tell—and you'll be free."

"I'll kill you for this—or have you killed."

"You and who? Strynn? Avall? Rann? *Rrath?*"

"I have other friends!"

"And maybe I know where they sleep. Now answer my question!"

The head hit the floor again. The mask loosened. Eddyn feared that, fearing what he'd see if he actually gazed upon blind eyes.

"I— Strynn used her blood and my blood, and we touched the gem, and suddenly I could see through her eyes. That's all."

"Can you see now?"

"Of course not!"

"Is that a no?"

"Yes— No— I didn't *know*! Please leave me alone."

"Soon, very soon. You saw with her eyes, and then— How long did you see?"

"Only as long as we touched the gem. After that . . . it was like *being* her, and then I was me again. Time felt funny. Now is that enough? I've already betrayed my truest friend!"

Eddyn considered knocking him unconscious, hoping Kylin would indeed forget all this. He considered setting the room on fire and letting accident cover his traces. He considered pouring as much wine as he could stomach down the boy's throat and hoping he thought this all a dream.

In the end, he simply locked him in the windowless darkness of his bath, where three sets of doors hid his screaming.

At which time Eddyn realized he wasn't *nearly* drunk enough, snared a bottle of Kylin's wine, and drank half of it at one gulp. He had sense enough to close the door behind him, and sense enough to seek his next destination by way of the hold's lowest levels, then up a staircase again.

Where will failed him was when he saw Strynn talking to the Hold-Healer in one of the adjunct kitchens. Avall was in Rann's rooms, so rumor said; shifted there for no reason he'd been able to determine. Which meant . . .

Once again, Luck was with him, and he found himself pausing outside Avall's suite, the dagger no longer in his hand, and the bloody tunic abandoned someplace he'd forgotten. This time, however, his hand held the key.

Avall's sitting room was exactly as Eddyn recalled, though there was an odd emptiness about it he couldn't fathom. He didn't bother trying. Time was of the essence, so he made straight for Avall's workroom. A moment only it took to get the door open, and he entered, feeling his heart skip a beat as he stepped into utter darkness: not what he'd expected at all. He had to return to the sitting room for a candle, but even by that fitful light, it was clear that Avall was gone. Every tool was put away, every work surface polished until it shone. The floor was swept clean of filings, the trash hampers emptied. The only sign of use remaining in the room was the helm. Though covered with a pall of black velvet, Eddyn had no doubt what the shape centered precisely in the worktable must be. Impulsively, yet with ingrained reverence for finely crafted objects, he pulled the drape aside.

Gold gleamed: an impossibly complex set of swirled and filigreed panels, alternating with bands of unadorned steel austere in their severity. Eyeslots gaped like caves of accusation. A few appliqués still needed to be set. Eddyn was as drunk as he'd ever been and still remained upright, yet he knew instinctively he looked upon greatness. Slowly, reverently, forgetting the risk he ran, he walked around it. Not touching it, never daring. And then common sense returned and reminded him of his mission, and he set to trying every compartment and drawer in the room.

All were locked. Then unlocked. Then empty.

Abruptly, it sank into him.

Avall wasn't just absent, he was *gone*. He'd taken the gem and fled.

Why?

Because it was too precious to leave here?

Because it was too much temptation to use?

But most of all, because it represented a complete reordering of power? How he knew that, he had no idea. But it was true—it had to be.

Which meant *he* had lost. Utterly and completely. *His* work mattered not at all. Avall would be the hero: the man who'd found the jewel that made blind men see, that let people speak mind to mind. That could do who-knew-what other miraculous things.

Avall.

Eight-cursed Avall had defeated him again!

Anger washed through Eddyn like molten fire, aided by the latest infusion of wine. Ruthlessly he flung out his arm and knocked the helm to the floor. The metal rang like a bell on the naked stone—a signal of alarm: that mayhem was afoot, that Eddyn was out of control and didn't care. He grabbed it before it stopped rolling, seized it in both hands, and slammed it into the floor again. The impact made his hands hurt, but he saw to his satisfaction, that it was dented. Again and again and again. The nasal bent inward. A panel popped out. One of the earpieces tore loose.

Footsteps!

Quick. Alarmed. Too direct and hasty to be Strynn.

All at once the enormity of what he'd done crashed down upon him. Rage had conquered him and doomed him for certain now, for it had made him destroy a Masterwork. Which crime would earn him exile—or worse.

The door rattled. He rolled under a table, quaking, clutching the ruined helm to his chest. Realizing too late that he'd forgotten to quench the candle.

The door opened. A head popped in. Eddyn held his breath.

"Eddyn?" a voice called tentatively. It took a moment before he recognized it.

"Rrath?" he dared.

"Where are—"

"Here," he mumbled, easing out of his hiding place, feeling the world spin and gyre as he sought to stand.

"Oh, Eight!" Rrath groaned, as his gaze fell upon the ruined helm. "You didn't!"

"It's over. It's done. You have to help me, Rrath."

Rrath snatched the helm, secreted it under his robe, then steered Eddyn one-handed toward the door, surprisingly strong for a small man. "We can't take—" Eddyn protested.

"If we leave it, they'll know it was an act of vandalism. If we take it, they won't find out—for a while. And by then . . . we'd best be gone."

Eddyn blinked at him, not comprehending. "Gone?"

"Away. Out. Don't tell me you don't know."

"What?"

"Later. Not here. Not your room, either. Mine—I guess—or the baths. No, there's no time even for that."

Eddyn started to protest and found he couldn't contrive one. Still, he was no longer alone in this awful thing he'd done. He had help. A friend. An accomplice. Someone on whom, perhaps, he could fix the blame.

Or—he realized with a chill—someone who knew *exactly* what he'd done.

Reality whirled away, and for a while he was only aware of Rrath sometimes pushing him, sometimes dragging him, sometimes leading him, through a warren of little-used corridors toward the back of the hold. A staircase led down, but Rrath effectively had to carry him to where it spat them out in a deserted room with a pair of doors to one side. Rrath pushed him through the nearest—into a kind of storeroom—and deposited him unceremoniously on a dusty crate.

"Now," Rrath said icily, "you will listen to me."

Eddyn could think of nothing to say—not with Rrath looking like that: eyes blazing, mouth taut, face grim and hard as a man twice his age. Nothing at all like he'd ever looked before.

"I won't chastise you, because there's no time for it. Maybe this will make sense and maybe it won't. But the fact is, we have to flee."

"Flee?" Eddyn gaped, stupidly.

"Flee. Avall has fled—with Rann and, most likely, the gem. I'm not positive of this, but it makes sense. I've been looking for him, officially to apologize, but in fact to try to learn more about this thing. This place is so huge, he's not really been missed. But one set of people think he's one place and the folks here think he's another. Rann's skis are gone, and they've been claiming outdoor gear, officially to go hunting. But they've not been seen in two days. Strynn's looking lost."

"Lost . . ." Eddyn echoed, barely comprehending. "Lost . . ."

Rrath slapped him. The blow stung but restored some sense. Rrath fished in his pouch for something, then thrust it into Eddyn's mouth. He bit it reflexively. Bitterness flooded across his tongue; vapors crept up his nose, into his eyes, his throat, his lungs, his brain. The confusion of drunkenness began to dissipate.

"Don't ask," Rrath grunted. "But listen like you've never listened before. As I said, Avall's gone. I'd already decided I might have to take what I knew and alert the clan before— Well, just before. They'd have to be prepared, if one considers the implications of this thing, among which, very briefly, is the fact that the soul does *not*, as my clan have taught, need to be tied to the body. Therefore it *could* access The Eight directly. In any event, nothing would be the same. If I die in the effort, so be it. But if I don't *make* the effort, I may as well die, because I'll have no life. I'll have betrayed the clan and will be unclanned for my trouble. I can't accept that. Avall and Rann have at least a day's start on us, but they may not hurry. If we push to the limit, I think we can catch them, but we'll have to risk more than the cold. That which I gave you: I have more. With it, for a while, you can ease pain and forgo sleep, your body will burn until it burns out, but until then— Well, let's just say, I hope to only have to use it for a little while—because I've never been so scared in my life!"

"And me?" Eddyn dared.

"Look's like you're going with me."

"I—"

Rrath cut him off. "Do you see any choice? I found Kylin, Eddyn. I went to see him, and heard him, and figured out what you did. I left him there—he'll survive—but I made it so it won't be so easy to find him. And then I went looking for you. You left clues everywhere, but you were too drunk to know it. People will see them, but they won't *know* they're clues—for a while. The helm will be a problem, but maybe the Hold-Warden will think Avall took it with him."

"Strynn would know better."

"Aye, but . . . we will leave it here. Even damaged, it's beautiful beyond belief."

Eddyn growled at him, amazed at how quickly sobriety was returning, though with it came a curious lack of will.

Rrath stared at him: no longer the mousy little Priest, but a clever, decisive man. Eddyn wondered if the fawning sycophant had ever really existed.

"More skis are no problem," Rrath informed him. "For the rest, we'll have to share. I wasn't going to take you, but I dare not leave you now. With us, with my clan, you might have a chance. If you help me, they might grant you their protection or patronage. If you stay here, the Hold-Warden will clap you in irons. No matter what you do or say about Avall and his gem, you'll be ruined."

"I'll go," Eddyn managed. "Because I have to."

"Yes, you will," Rrath agreed. "Now, stay here. I have to find you some warmer clothes and get you a pair of skis."

He found them—quickly. Eddyn didn't want to know how or where. He even helped him put them on—leather over fur over leather over leather over wool over sylk over skin. Rrath did the same. Soon enough they'd increased their bulk by half again and Rrath was steering him through another maze of doors toward a heat gate. He guessed, from symbols here and there, that they were deep in the sacred precincts of Priest-Clan.

"This is The Eight's door," Rrath offered, as he opened a thick wood panel no different from any other. "It's called that so that the God can enter and observe us without us knowing. I'm committing sacrilege by using it."

Eddyn nodded mutely, still more than half-numb. His brain didn't quite seem to be working as he let himself be led out into the depth of night. The cold bit him ruthlessly, but also roused him somewhat. Still, it was Rrath who inserted his feet into his skis, stuck a heavy pack that yet weighed nothing at all onto his back, thrust a pole into his hands, then closed The Eight's door behind him and led them both into another stage of life.

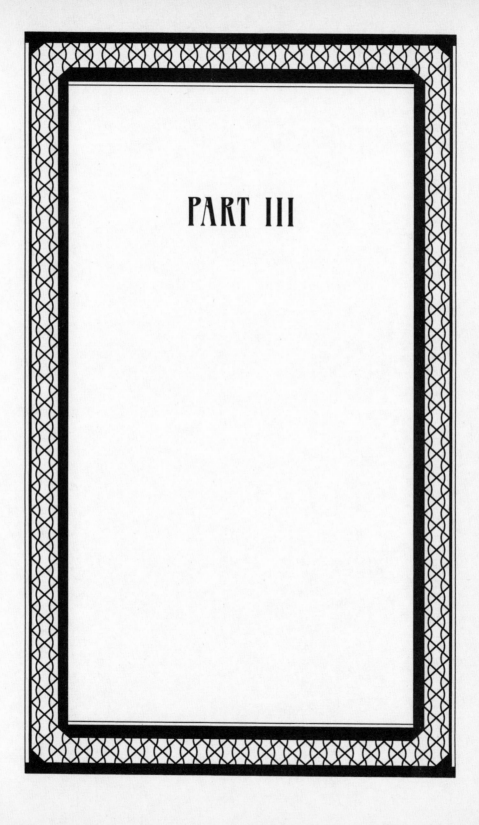

PART III

CHAPTER XXXVII:

SEARCHING

(ERON: ANGEN'S SPINE—DEEP WINTER: DAY XXVI—MORNING)

Merryn was actually shaking when she finally made her way through the last stand of snow-laurel and beheld the Flat before her, gleaming in the morning light.

Some of her agitation was due to simple fatigue, of course. She'd just spent the worst four nights of her life, for a number of very real and apparent reasons—not the least of which being the fact that once she'd fallen into a cycle of traveling by night she'd been unable to break it. First, there'd been the small matter of escaping the scene of her crime as quickly as possible and putting as much distance as she could between War-Hold and herself.

Since then— Well her body had its own ideas about how much sleep it required and when. And those times, regrettably, had coincided first with daylight, then with the worst snowfall she'd seen all winter. She'd sat that one out beneath the eaves of the forest, shivering in her tent, grateful that it was probably worse up at the hold, even if it was also warmer. Unfortunately, when it was finally safe to travel again, the sun was setting—two days later.

The worst had been last night. Never in all her twenty years had she ridden so far under such circumstances: namely cold and dark, with a pall of clouds over the moons that reduced the already sketchy visibility to nothing even in the few open places between War-Hold and the no-man's-land of the Flat. Otherwise, she'd had to rely on the fact that Mud had been trained for this (so Lorvinn said); and was supposed to be preternaturally facile at distinguishing snow from anything else. In any event, she'd proved remarkably surefooted.

But slow. And utterly unconcerned with picking sheltered paths or hastening toward trees (and therefore cover). And the trouble was, there really was only one even halfway-reliable path down from the Hold to the Flat.

Never mind that Krax—Kraxxi, or whoever—had perforce taken another because he'd had to start out somewhere else. He'd have been traveling slow, too, but it would've taken her even longer to commence where he'd begun. She hoped, by taking the main trail, to shave the head start he'd managed. Almost half a day.

Into his territory and away from hers.

She shivered again, this time for another reason.

This was crazy. She'd betrayed the hold, her craft, her clan, her rank, and who-knew-how-many friends, for no clearer reason than that she wanted Kraxxi back in War-Hold and safe.

And full of explanations, now that she knew who he was.

Explanations for leaving, on the one hand, and for abandoning her, in particular, on the other.

The last—she didn't want to think about. What they'd shared had certainly *seemed* real, and growing in intensity daily. But was it? Or had it all been a sham contrived for some more sinister purpose? That was one thing she *would* know, if it killed her.

The other . . .

Kraxxi obviously had *some* reason for leaving so precipitously. But two days of forced introspection brought on by the storm had produced nothing he could've learned in War-Hold that would be in any way crucial to whatever nefarious plans Barrax might have. And still hadn't.

She fumbled absently at her gloves, revealing the ring she'd had from Toz as surety to his sisters. Red opal, or so it appeared. She'd worn it since starting out but not truly marked it until now—mostly because she'd worn gloves the bulk of the time and, frankly, had other things on her mind—like escape and survival. Still, as Toz had also noted, it was not simply a piece of jewelry. Not if it could guide her toward his friend.

Just as another odd red stone had guided Avall's mind to hers.

On a night Kraxxi had shared her bed.

But he hadn't *acted* any different after that.

Or had he?

All at once she was shaking.

Suppose— Suppose Kraxxi had found out about that. He already knew that some red opals had . . . powers.

But she'd never *said* it was a red opal. Never said *anything*, in fact.

Had she?

Another set of chills nearly shook her from the saddle. Her heart froze.

Suppose Kraxxi had witnessed everything? He'd know that at least some people in Eron could communicate mind to mind across vast distances. That would be a useful thing for a king contemplating war to know.

Barrax wanted war. That was a fact.

And if Kraxxi was in exile, information like that could be a significant bargaining tool.

Except that the entire edifice was based on the rankest speculation.

Which in turn raised another anxiety: namely, why Avall hadn't tried to contact her again. There were innumerable possible reasons, but the one that made most sense was that she'd simply not been asleep at the appointed time. And sleep, she assumed, was requisite.

And now—she was moving even farther away from him, which would be unlikely to make resumption of contact easier. Which might be a problem and might not.

In any event, she was about to test Toz's assertion because she'd that moment reached the end of the trail: the place where the rough mass of Angen's Spine terminated in the vast white nothing of the Flat.

There was snow out there, but hopefully not a lot and not deep. Snow was all but unknown in Ixti, and somewhere between here and there must come a place where its pervasive influence faded. Too, it *couldn't* snow much in the Flat, else it would be prairie, not desert. Supposedly the sand was too salty for most plants, and the porous grains drank snowmelt like a lifelong sot, to pour out again in the series of waterfalls along the rim of the Pit.

She suspected she'd find out soon enough.

She yawned, blinked—and realized that she'd been staring at emptiness long enough for Mud to become anxious at inactivity. She named the demon. Fatigue.

She'd barely eaten since leaving—which meant that her body was consuming itself. There was way-bread and -meat in her pack, of course, but she had no appetite for them. On the other hand, Mud needed rest, and who knew when there'd be even minimal forage for her? Sighing, Merryn slid out of the saddle, walked the mare to the edge of the woods where grass might best survive beneath the snow, and tethered her there, still saddled, but minus the saddlebags. Fortunately, Merryn's mount had carried the bulk of the camping gear, so that she had a tent and blankets, as well as other supplies. She unrolled a blanket, coaxed up a tiny fire, and forced herself to make brandied cauf and to set a pot of water to heat with a strip of way-meat inside. The sun was only a finger above the horizon even now, and she thought she might be able to risk a nap while the water boiled. To be sure she didn't oversleep, however, she prowled through her gear and produced a small greenish nut which she set in the flames. *A hand nut,* such things were called, because when placed in a fire they would almost always explode—in exactly a hand. Which was as long as she dared sleep.

And sleep she did.

The nut woke her right on cue, dragging her up from a drowsiness that was truly epic in its depth and quality. She yawned, sniffed at the stench of a cookpot grown too hot and fished it off the fire at once. The way-stew was nothing to brag about, but the vapors did wonders to clear her head, so that she felt reasonably alert when she helped herself to the last of the cauf and began to repack her hasty camp.

Mud seemed happy, too, and Merryn decided to let her forage a little longer while she put one of the numerous ridiculous notions that were assailing her to the test.

Frowning against the glare of sunlight on endless snow, she squatted at the juncture of mountain and plain and removed Toz's ring. A bit of searching produced a length of thread as long as her arm, which she slid through the silver loop beneath the crimson gem.

So what now? Did she simply let it drop and see if it tended a certain way? Or—

She tried that—to no discernible effect, though she went to extremes to hold the string absolutely still, relying on her trained muscles to prevent accidental twitches.

No good—after a pause that tried her nerves.

What next?

Well, she'd heard of a form of divination Common-Clan girls sometimes practiced, in which they'd hang a pearl soaked in tears from a few strands of their own hair and slowly spin it in a circle within a ring of the names of young men they fancied. It was supposed to display a degree of accuracy somewhat above what the cypherers in Lore expected, especially if the tears were augmented by water from Fortune's Well.

And while there was little in common here to there save the concept and basic method, still, as she'd told herself too many times already, she had nothing to lose by trying.

Stilling the thread, she composed herself; willing her mind to go blank, lest that also have an effect. And tried to picture Kraxxi as she'd last seen him; better, as she'd last seen him when she *trusted* him. When he was happy. When his dark face was split by that silly smile and his eyes sparkled like sunlight on water. While she did that, she slowly spun the ring in as perfect a circle as generations of artisan ancestors could achieve, courtesy of instinctive hand-to-eye coordination.

Again, nothing happened.

She closed her eyes, tried harder; tried to imagine Kraxxi out there with a ring like this on his hand, and then *this* ring, with an invisible but real linkage spanning the two, rather like that she'd unconsciously visualized when she'd communicated with Avall.

A third time nothing—

But then that phantom thread began to glow. At the same moment, she felt something shift in her fingers and finally dared open her eyes—to see the ellipse described by the ring gradually narrowing.

Her eyes widened as it grew thinner yet. The stone seemed to be glowing, too. And there was an odd sensation in her head that, while utterly unlike what she'd felt when she'd spoken to Avall, nevertheless seemed to be in that same category, provoking the same senses.

A pause for a breath she didn't know if she dared, so ephemeral was the effect she was experiencing, and she looked down again.

It was true! The ring was swinging in a well-defined arc almost due southeast. And the air around it— There was no good way to describe it, save that it seemed to be trembling.

She tried to alter the direction of swing—and felt resistance. Alarmed, she released the string.

The ring hit the snow and skidded across the light crust—in precisely the direction it had been tending.

Well enough! If not entirely convinced, she at least had something to go on and some rationale for choosing among the otherwise random directions she might travel. She'd stop in midmorning and try again. In the meantime, daylight was wasting, Kraxxi was getting no nearer, and pursuit had surely been mounted three days ago if not sooner.

With a brief prayer to Fate, she remounted and urged poor unsuspecting Mud out into the vast, cold danger of the Flat.

CHAPTER XXXVIII:

COLD SURPRISE

(WESTERN ERON—DEEP WINTER: DAY XXIX—MORNING)

~~~~~~~

You're mad!" Eddyn managed to grit, though he continued to slog along, sliding his skis across the snow with the mindless mechanical aplomb of one of those intricate machines the folks at Iron made for the purpose of rendering endlessly repeated tasks endurable.

But steam powered those machines, or water pressure, or the force of rivers. He had no idea what compelled *him* to persevere save that he had no choice—though his muscles ached; his stomach growled; his very bones seemed to have turned to ice; and his fingers, toes, and face had no feeling at all, nor had had any for days.

At least he could see—enough to know that they'd long since left the trek and ventured into untrodden ways.

First in pursuit of Avall and Rann, who'd also veered that way—they'd found the place where they'd camped beneath the snow—but now, Eddyn feared, in search of something else Rrath wouldn't identify.

Rrath . . .

Something had changed in the shy, fawning young Priest who'd made friends with him an eighth ago, as though that person no longer existed or had been a shell which had subsequently been abandoned to let some darker, more ruthless shape wriggle free.

But what *was* that shape? And why could he, Eddyn syn Argen-yr, not muster gumption enough to challenge it with more than a grunted "you're mad"? Except even that phrase had taken all the will he possessed to utter, and the notion was already expiring beneath a sea of prohibitions, compulsions—he didn't know what to call them—that appeared out of nowhere to subvert his *self*, leaving him only a mindless machine with no more agenda than to move steadily onward and tell Rrath everything Rrath wanted to know.

"Mad—"

That had simply slipped out, like some foulness hacked up from diseased lungs to be spat upon the ground.

Rrath slid to a stop on the crest of a long downhill slope framed with birches and glared at him, expression an odd mix of exasperation, wariness, and genuine concern; as though he knew his duty and would do it, but nevertheless found that task distasteful.

"We'll rest here," Rrath said, kicking off his skis before flopping down on a half-buried stump. His face was pink, almost red; his eyes feverishly bright. He reached to the hot-jar at his waist, unscrewed the cap, drank deeply, then emptied it of cauf grounds and set about refilling it with snow. "Make a fire," he commanded. "A small one."

Eddyn nodded woodenly and did as told. It took a while to find suitable kindling, and he resorted to breaking limbs from the overhanging trees. In spite of that, he soon had an acceptable blaze. The heat warmed his face and hands, warmed some place in his soul that told him something wasn't right, that no one had a hangover that lasted four days, and certainly not on what he'd imbibed. Rrath was cooking, too: a stew of dried meat and vegetables liberally seasoned with butter. He melted water for cauf as well, and added the ground pods along with another ingredient Eddyn didn't recognize, but that probably didn't belong. In spite of those misgivings, however—and his intention not to inhale—those pungent odors found their way into his lungs and stayed, impossibly intoxicating.

Fighting himself all the while, he breathed deeply—and saw Rrath smile, even as he placed a strip of something that might've been bark in his teeth and raised his mouth-mask far up over his nose.

The vapors trickled through Eddyn, first his nostrils, then into his sinuses and thence to his eyes and brain. At the same time, they spread downward through his lungs into the rest of his body, awakening his muscles, filling them with new strength, setting his nerves aflame with anxious energy that had him fidgeting before the stew was done. And all the while the part of Eddyn that was still Eddyn fought and protested and railed—silently. Something lay between thought and word, between desire and deed. Between responding to what he'd been told and initiating independent action.

And that barrier was certainly in effect when Rrath finally finished the stew, gave him a steaming bowlful, and claimed another for himself. Cauf went with it, and brandy, which, with that stuff already dancing through his blood, made his head feel as though it held only the most tenuous connection to his body.

And then Rrath was kicking out the fire and locating his skis, and they were on the move once more.

The first part of the journey—the long perilous descent down the steepest slope they'd yet encountered—was something Eddyn would've enjoyed had he been in command of himself. As it was, it terrified him—but not in the way of normal terror. *This* ignored his emotions but let his strength, his reflexes, even the urge to scream aloud his fear have free rein.

While his body went right on describing graceful, flowing arcs as they fairly flew down the hill into an open meadow surrounded by pines. Rrath was peering around carefully, as though in quest of some specific landmark. Eddyn saw nothing out of the ordinary, save that the landscape was a good bit more rugged than in some places. Here and there eruptions of raw stone rose sheer above the treetops, their harsh facets and broken outlines softened only by tenuous snow. It was as if an army of giants had broken free of Angen's Spine and died here, but not before they'd dragged the ground with frozen fingers into those long, sharp-edged ridges.

But what could Rrath be seeking here? And what was that map he was consulting, that didn't look like any of the standard maps of this desolate region? Eddyn tried a surreptitious check, but Rrath caught him and fixed him with a glare that could've lit a fire. Then, as though censoring his own reaction, he dared a tired smile. "I don't like this either," he said flatly. "But some things—"

He didn't finish. Smoke had begun to issue from the woods—or mist to arise. Certainly there was no flame to produce so many of these white, billowy clouds of diffuse vapor that were wending their way toward him and Rrath from all quarters. He glimpsed movement among the trunks—human shapes. "What?" he began, tensing as though to bolt.

Rrath stopped him with a hand on his arm. "No harm will come to you if you behave appropriately, but be very, very wary."

No harm? What did Rrath mean by that? Something was occurring that ought not to be. It was as though Rrath had sought this place and waited for the smoke—for so it was, now that he'd caught the first whiff of those oddly acrid vapors—to appear in response to his presence. Almost as though this were an assignation.

But no one ventured outside in Deep Winter. And this was nowhere.

A nowhere that apparently contained more than it seemed.

The smoke had reached him and Rrath now, twining about them with delicate, exploratory fingers. "Sit," Rrath hissed. "Or fall."

Eddyn did, oblivious to the way the cold seared his legs and buttocks while he crouched shivering in the snow. The smoke was closer, too, and thicker, blurring the outlines of the trees, rising higher, coiling more densely about them. He tried not to breathe those vapors but couldn't help it. Rrath, however— The Priest seemed to be doing exactly the opposite: inhaling as much as he could. His face was peaceful, serene. Eddyn blinked. He'd been staring at Rrath's face for what seemed an eternity, save that he'd suddenly realized he'd not been thinking at all during that time. He wanted to rise, to flee these fumes that—even more than what Rrath had given him—were prisoning both his body and his mind.

But when he made to leap up, he couldn't. His muscles were suddenly heavy as lead and wouldn't respond beyond a clumsy twitch. Even that unbalanced him, so that he fell backward into the snow, gazing up at the blue, blue sky. At least he could still breathe; at least his heart still beat; at least he could still blink his eyes against that smoke-screened light.

And he could think enough to know that this was wrong.

Then he could only think about how good it would be to sleep.

And then he did.

Eddyn awoke to a sky of richer blue that hinted of afternoon. But also one in which snow clouds were starting to appear, and from which the odd, crystalline flake was drifting down. He still lay flat on his back, but was now moving in a smooth, undulating manner, punctuated by the swish of skis, from which he determined that he lay on some type of litter. Being pulled through open country, at the moment, then through woods as branches blocked the sky.

"Halt!" someone snapped, the words distant as speech heard through stone walls. The movement beneath him slowed. "What?" someone called back. Male, but no more than that was discernible.

"He wakes! He sees!"

"He can't!"

"His eyes moved. We must blindhood him."

"The other?"

"As he was. This one . . . perhaps it is his size . . ."

"Perhaps."

Eddyn tried to twitch his fingers—and managed the merest tremor. Encouraged, he called up all the will he possessed to lunge upright. And failed utterly. Whereupon a dark man-shape swung into view from behind him, and a cloth was drawn over his face that smelled of that strange, thick smoke. He tried not to breathe, but his body had other plans and made him inhale ever more deeply, so that suddenly he wanted only to sleep again. Someone was beside him, too, fumbling a hood over his head, and with that, his one link to the world—to life itself, he feared—was blocked.

Who were these people? What did they want with him and Rrath? And what did Rrath know of them, and how much?

Reality shifted. He was moving again, and that jolt alone was sufficient to send him back to the Dark for a very long time indeed.

At some point reality returned—or light. He could move his head a little, and a fuzzy brightness annoyed his eyes—from a hole in the hood that had shifted into his line of sight. A small joy, true; still, it was enough to grant a glimpse of one of those rock outcrops close enough for its shadow to fall upon them.

He held his breath, then decided that might be noticed, and released it. Clearly he'd been drugged, but the drug didn't work well on someone his size, or there were other factors involved—like fear and anger—that tended to burn off such effects.

In any event, he was sufficiently aware to know that whoever had captured him wouldn't like it if they discovered either his return to consciousness or his modicum of sight. And so he kept his eyes closed, but was still aware of entering a shadow beside one of those outcrops—and of a clicking, scraping sound, and then a rush of heat across him that was surely the most wonderful sensation he'd ever known—whereupon he was moving again. This time, however, whatever supported him was carried, not dragged, and there was more darkness, and then the sense of being inside (perhaps it was the warmth and the lack of wind and the absence of soughing pines). Firelight flickered, and the harsher light of glow-globes, and then came more grating and he was lifted bodily onto the softest bed he'd ever lain upon.

There was light, too, if dim, and he caught a few words before those who'd carried him departed. "It would be best for him to become himself before the meeting. One can be gone too long."

"And the other?"

"He should be back soon. He came to us. He will need to be addressed."

He came to us, Eddyn noted. And then comfort claimed him, and true sleep, and Eddyn knew no more.

Eddyn woke to what seemed an unbelievable splendor of comfort, though, in fact, the chamber was perilously close to bare. He was in a windowless room two spans to a side and the same high. Floor, walls, ceiling: All were seamless stone, and all but the first whitewashed. A plain brown rug covered the floor, while heat flowed in from a grate to one side to exit through vents in the ceiling. By the sulfur smell, he suspected it was born of a hot spring. This was no way station, though; the size and architecture were wrong. He sat up abruptly, noted that he was still clothed, and found that he'd lain atop a bed pad spread across a stone platform along one side of the room. A table and a chair were the only other furniture; light came from candles in iron-wood sconces.

The door was thick oak, hinged on the outside, and—when he tried it—locked. Someone had left food, however: bread, cold meat, tart cheese, and water. More water stood on a platform opposite, with a towel beside it, along with a plain long-tunic of midnight-blue, obviously either brand-new or expertly cleaned. An alcove proved to be a welcome garderobe.

He was a prisoner then, though decently accommodated.

But a prisoner of whom?

He tried to think, found it impossible, and sat down in a nauseous muddle as thoughts of the past turned to thoughts of smoke and days of drug-induced lethargy. But why?

His mind whirled. He had to close his eyes, to bend over with his head between his knees, to retain consciousness. It helped enough for him to recall one thing. Rrath had been with him. Rrath had drugged him. Rrath had contrived it so that they had come here.

Rrath was Priest-Clan.

Which explained much and would explain more if only he could think.

Maybe food would help. He staggered to the table, sank down in the chair, and feasted, finding the fare filling and juicy, if underspiced. He drank a great deal of water, then stripped to his underbreeches, wincing at the smell of sweaty cloth and smoky, much-used leather.

The water and towel made him feel better, and he succumbed to the lure of the robe and put it on, then lay back down with the wet towel across his somewhat feverish brow, wondering why he would ever in the world desire anything to be cool.

He slept—maybe. In any event, he woke to find nothing changed, but himself feeling much improved. His mind felt clearer, too, but along with that came two disturbing realizations.

One was that he'd heard off and on of secret sects within Priest-Clan that formed a kind of shadow government not always in tune with the King or the crafts and clans. A government that had as its only goal assuring Priest-Clan's continued primacy.

It wasn't as easy as it might seem. Every generation, learning increased in Eron. Every generation, people became more secular and fewer believed in The Eight, though enough of High Clan saw the King manifest them to know *something* untoward occurred. And the King—this King, anyway—was certainly no Priest-Clan dupe.

Still, they might feel threatened. And if that gem of Avall's did what he suspected, and what Rrath seemed to think it could, it made sense for Rrath to contact those among his own kind to whom that information would be most useful.

But was Rrath himself a member of this cabal or did he merely know of its existence? He knew how to contact them, but he'd also had to wait for them, which in turn implied the existence of at least one contact inside Gem-Hold.

Reality, it seemed, was not what it appeared.

Eddyn sat up abruptly, poured himself another mug of water—and froze, staring.

Was it safe to do *this*? To eat? To drink? Maybe even to bathe in the water his captors had provided? He'd been dragged at least twice already—more, if what he suspected about the drunk that had precipitated his departure in the first place was true. His captors were masters of fumes and potions. Was there therefore any reason to assume that he wouldn't be poisoned again? Plied with other herbs to other ends?

He *felt* normal enough; his thoughts ran as clearly as they had since starting out. But would he one day reach for a reflex, skill, or piece of knowledge and find it gone?

As if in answer, the door opened to admit a pair of tall, robed men with white-gauze masks over their faces and plain, cross-hilted swords at their sides. Eddyn tried to peer beyond them to whatever lay without, but glimpsed only dimly lit whitewashed walls.

"You've found what we left," the one to the right murmured, his accent flattened in a way Eddyn couldn't identify until he realized that the man had probably been trained to disguise his voice lest he be recognized. "About now you should be wondering if it is safe—or if you've put yourself at risk again."

Eddyn's mouth dropped open, though he stifled the response with an awkward cough and tried to appear calm.

"It is for you to decide," the man went on. "This only we will tell you. You will soon meet the Warden of this place. You would be wise to heed the Warden."

Before he could reply, the men turned on their heels and departed. Eddyn sat back down (when had he stood?), got up and paced, then lay down again. Eventually the door opened once more and the same two men entered, accompanied by a third, bearing a pile of what proved to be more substantial clothing. They watched impassively while Eddyn donned the thick, dark blue house-hose, matching boots, and long-tunic of dull gray edged with royal blue, all beneath a hooded tabard.

The new man studied him briefly, muttered a terse, "You'll do," then motioned him toward the door. Eddyn hesitated, wishing he had the strength to rebel—at least knock these lads around a bit. But there would still be a whole mountain full of these strange men to fight through in order to escape. In the end, he went docilely, slipping into line between the armed men, with the third bringing up the rear.

They turned right down a corridor that was featureless save for doors exactly like his at precise intervals to either side, then turned right again to ascend a tight spiral stair that spat them out midway along a wider hall. That, in turn, terminated in a set of low, but very wide, doors. Not once during that journey did he see another person beyond their company. As they paused before the doors, his captors fell back to either side—all save the newest one, who stepped forward, rapped a certain cadence on the dense, dark wood, then returned to stand behind Eddyn.

Both portals swung outward—noiselessly, and with no one to manipulate them. Eddyn stepped back—directly into the guard, who gently thrust him forward with a muttered, "Go now. And whatever you do, don't lie!"

He resisted—then found that he couldn't, which he chalked up to equal parts of whatever drug he'd been given and his own innate curiosity. Before he knew it, he was walking into a wide, stone-walled hall, empty save for a runner of sapphire carpet down the center and a thronelike chair on a dais at the end. A number of irregularly shaped windows to either side of that seat showed jagged contours, suggesting that they conformed to fissures outside.

The throne was occupied—a figure robed in blue and gray, with a hood hanging far over the face, and both mouth- and eye-veils further masking his identity. Or hers—for the robes were so thick Eddyn couldn't determine gender. Even the hands—thin and frail, but strong-looking—gave no firm indication.

"Eddyn syn Argen-yr," that figure intoned in one of those odd-cadenced voices, which was also pitched so as to obscure the owner's sex.

Eddyn didn't reply. No question had been asked, and he saw no point in quarter given.

"That *is* you?" the figure continued.

"It is, O Warden, if that is your title."

"It serves. But come, sit down. The floor at my feet will do admirably. I will have drinks brought."

"That . . . won't be necessary. I'll stand—and I'm not hungry or thirsty," Eddyn dared.

"You'll drink anyway," the Warden informed him mildly. "So will I, though the . . . spicing may not be the same, which I doubt will surprise you."

Eddyn felt a knot of anger coil with the knot of fear already in his stomach, at the notion of losing control again. "Is that truly *necessary*? It's always possible I might tell you what you want to know without . . . intervention."

"Possible," the Warden conceded, "but not likely. I know who your teachers are."

Eddyn digested this.

"You'd like a name, wouldn't you?" the Warden continued. "You'd like to know who we are and where we are and what we are about. None of these will we tell you."

He paused, glaring irritably at the door, then relaxed as another robed figure entered, bearing a small tray on which two elegant blue-glass bottles stood poised beside delicate, almost transparent, white cups. The Warden took the nearest, motioning the servant—if that's what he or she was—to take the other to Eddyn. Eddyn retrieved the bottle and cup numbly, wondering if he had any chance of bolting—or better yet, taking this man hostage.

"You would never get out," the Warden chuckled. "Having said that, I will also tell you that you *will* get out—if you agree to help us recover a certain object about which you have particular information."

Eddyn tried not to react; but even as he stood there, he felt his plan to salve the honor of Argen-yr by announcing this brilliant new discovery eroding in the face of men far more knowledgeable, competent, and ruthless than he.

"Drink," the Warden urged again. "I won't ask a third time."

Eddyn took a deep breath and poured the contents of the bottle into the cup. The liquid was crystal clear but had an evergreen scent and a thick texture, like a very dense liquor. He sniffed it suspiciously, wincing at the obvious potency. The Warden's gaze pressed upon him, almost palpable. He met it squarely, saw the man raise his cup to his lips, then pause, encouraging Eddyn to do the same.

"If you break it, there are more. You achieve nothing but pain for yourself if you refuse. You will therefore drink."

Eddyn tried to mask all emotion as he slowly raised the cup and, in one swift motion, drained it to the dregs. It tasted good, but the fumes surged through him like fire through brandy. For the briefest of breaths, he was sure his brain had exploded; as though for that instant he knew everything he'd ever thought or seen or done in perfect clarity—simultaneously. And then the effect subsided, leaving him utterly empty.

The Warden smiled. "I've felt that, too," he murmured. "Just so you'll know. We all have. There are no secrets among those who wear these robes."

Eddyn didn't reply.

"You, however, would seem party to a great many secrets indeed."

Again, Eddyn remained silent, attention locked into recapturing certain images from his childhood he'd all but forgotten, which the potion had conjured back with an intensity that made him weak. That was, he realized, the last time he'd been truly happy. The last time he'd been free to be his own man, not what Tyrill or anyone else expected him to be, or what Law made him. Or what duty, pride, and anger forced him to be against his will.

"Now," said the Warden, glancing toward the windows, "two hands remain until sunset. You will spend that time telling me everything you know about Avall syn Argen-a, Strynn san Ferr-ok Avall, and a certain gem one of them is reported to have discovered."

Eddyn's blood went cold. He'd suspected all along that the gem was the reason he and Rrath had been brought (or summoned?) here. But now that he heard as much stated, the fact of it filled him with cold revulsion. *How dare they ask him to betray his clan!* Argen-a and Argen-yr might be rivals, but they were still septs of one whole. Priest-Clan had no right to demand what was Argen's by Law! No right at all.

But while Eddyn knew that in his head, his tongue had overruled him. And while part of him sat back and listened, heartsick, the rest told this terrible robed stranger everything he knew.

When it was over, the only thing he remembered clearly was one final phrase.

"In gratitude for what you have told us, Eddyn, we will let you live. But your soul, young sir, is ours!"

Another drink sealed the discussion, and for once Eddyn was grateful to find himself drugged to oblivion.

Zeff watched impassively as Eddyn was escorted from the room—if being half-dragged, half-carried could be honored by that term. The main doors had barely closed, however, before he was striding with grim determination toward the door by which he'd entered. That opened on a vestibule paneled with intricately carved colored marble, with archways in the three remaining walls. The one to the right gave on a stair, which he descended.

For a very long time. Marble gave way to plain stone, and that, after a locked doorway was opened, to raw rock. Along with that descent into austerity, heat and humidity rose, so that by the time he'd reached his destination, Zeff was sweating.

He ignored it, as he ignored all things unpleasant or distracting. But he did not ignore the urgency of his mission. Still, his legs were tiring as he navigated the stair's last few turns. He vented a relieved sigh as he confronted the final door—to which he alone held the key.

It opened without resistance, revealing a low, sprawling cavern so thick with steam he could barely breathe, never mind the excruciating heat which could cook flesh if exposed too long.

His mission should only require a finger—but one never knew. An incautiously deep breath all but seared his lungs, but he strode with a confidence at odds with the irregular contours of the floor to the only man-touched objects in the place save the door.

A chair of stone was the main thing, positioned precisely by a small Well no more than a half span across barely visible in the rocky floor. A pair of glow-globes lit it, which were also the cavern's sole illumination, so that the whole place had the feel of a fog-filled forest lit by a waning moon.

He found the chair unerringly and sat down, loosening his collar with one hand, even as the other found the silver chalice in its customary place beside the Well. Wasting no time, Zeff scooped a cupful of water, raised it to face level, closed his eyes, uttered a short prayer to The Eight—and drank.

It was utterly flat, like drinking air, yet a semblance of taste hid there, harsh and metallic. And something else he could already feel manifesting. Something that wanted to close out the cavern entirely, to drive him deep into the center of his brain where only instinct lived. Where the God who guarded this Well sometimes manifested.

He didn't need the God now, only His power, and so Zeff fought it, dragged his eyes open, and did one more thing.

The brash young neophyte, Rrath, had brought the key without knowing what it was. Probably their agent inside Gem-Hold hadn't known much either, save that like often called to like. Still, it was she who'd suggested Rrath secure a phial of earth from the vein where this mysterious gem had been found, just in case.

Zeff had that sample now. Moving like a man asleep, he refilled the chalice and held it one-handed, while the other freed the cork stopper from the phial and emptied half its contents into the water.

This, too, Zeff drank.

And had barely time to return the chalice to its place before the reaction.

It was not an elegant rite. Not a thing he would have anyone else observe, even among his own cabal.

He threw up—not a great deal, but with painful conviction. The contents of his stomach fouled the waters of the pool. Heat beat at him: the heat of exertion and tortured flesh and agonized internals. Still, he waited—until the water began to clear. And then, very calmly, he dipped the phial once again into the pool, resealed it, and departed.

A hand later, he passed it to the neophyte, Rrath, with one line of instruction. "You know something of weather-witchery. What you know of that and a sip of this a day will point you to the gem. Do not use it more often."

Rrath's eyes went wide as a child's as he took it. Zeff hoped he wasn't placing power in the hands of fools.

CHAPTER XXXIX:

DEATH ON THE FLAT

(THE FLAT—DEEP WINTER: DAY XXX—MORNING)

~~~~~~~~~~~~~~~~

Kraxxi crested the rise and felt despair rise and clump in his throat. He'd been *sure* this was the right route; sure that when he crossed this last long snow-sheeted ridge and gazed beyond he'd see . . .

What?

An indication of the road, perhaps?

Better, some sign of an actual station. There were supposed to be some along here, and surely, with so much of the world visible—utterly flat horizons in three directions, and not much more on the fourth—he'd have sighted a shattered wall or ruined dome by now.

He was wrong. Nothing relieved the cold white blankness save where Angen's Spine still showed at his back, too close for comfort, for all he'd seen no evidence of the pursuit that would surely have been mounted as soon as Merryn had been able to move.

He'd timed that carefully, so that she'd be under no real threat of exposure, but would still be unable to follow him without, at minimum, returning to the hold for supplies and, optimally, for Ingot, whom he'd released at sunset that first day out. That had been a sign of good faith: proof that he'd fled—escaped, rather—only because he had to, because he followed a higher calling than what he increasingly had no choice but to call love.

His father's approval? His forgiveness? He'd never gain the former or recover the latter, and wasn't sure how he'd manage if either were conferred; whether or not he'd ever really trust them. It didn't matter anyway, when his chances of survival had just taken a turn for the worse, now that there was no chance of finding shelter for the night save the far-too-flimsy tent.

That the snow was diminishing in depth and frequency the farther south he traveled was encouraging, but not enough. His one security was that here, in the desert of all places, he'd be unlikely to run out of water. Feeding himself and the gelding, Balmor, was another matter.

And then he had another problem.

Snow.

Again.

Not much, but sufficient to make him anxious even at the few tiny flakes that drifted down to spot his gloves and the gelding's glossy coat.

A backward glance made him start, for in the hand since he'd last checked, clouds had rolled in from the northwest to blanket a third of the sky. Flat white clouds that could only carry snow. *More* snow.

Fortunately, there was a wind from the north—straight off the ocean— and that might hold the worst of this new storm back. *If* he could stay ahead of it. Exposed as he was, even a minor blizzard could be deadly. Certainly it would do Balmor no good.

As if to emphasize that threat, the wind shifted, sent chill gusts snapping at him like invisible hounds made of ice. Reluctantly—*grimly*—he set his heels to Balmor's sides and urged him to a quicker gait. Not too fast, however; the snow was still calf deep, and overlay less sand than rock-strewn plain. At least whatever hit him would be worse back in the hold. Maybe he should look at it that way: However much the weather inconvenienced him, it would work more delay upon his enemies.

Enemies . . .

He hated thinking of the folks at War-Hold like that.

The snow chased him until close to noon, when it subsided into steady flurries, though the wind couldn't make up its mind whether to join the storm or harry it. Still, he'd let Balmor slow to a relaxed amble when, with no warning whatever, his mount stumbled and pitched forward to the right, screaming as only a badly injured horse could do.

Kraxxi had sense enough to drop the reins and kick free of the stirrups, and to tuck his head and roll when he hit the ground. The snow wasn't much of a cushion, and he did something unpleasant to his shoulder upon impact. His breath whooshed out of him, and he could do nothing but lie there winded and half-stunned while Balmor kept on screaming. The sound made Kraxxi's stomach twitch and his gorge rise, recalling in its endless shrill agony the horses' hideous deaths during the geen attack, which now seemed so long ago.

What had happened? Had Balmor stepped into a hole and lamed himself? Or, worse, broken his leg? If so, he'd have to—

Panic washed over him, threatening to unseat his sanity. He closed his eyes, forced discipline upon himself, and rose. His hip hurt, but not so badly he couldn't stagger back to his stricken mount.

The gelding was thrashing about with a frantic recklessness that hurt to look upon: trying to rise, but unable. His eyes were wide with pain and panic. Kraxxi quickly saw why: a bulge that shouldn't exist in his pastern, that even as he watched erupted into blood and bone.

The screaming intensified.

Kraxxi couldn't stand it.

Lacking more merciful alternatives, he skirted around behind the flailing beast so that he could come at him from above. A pause while he steeled himself; then a quick dash, a stab in the throat, a slash, and a hasty retreat. Blood went everywhere, staining the snow with crimson that drank more snow as it continued to drift down.

Then silence.

What did he do now?

If anything?

Suicide remained an option; in one sense, the only honorable alternative if he intended to salvage his disgrace. Double disgrace now: his murder of his brother and his abandonment of the woman he loved and who likewise, it seemed, loved him.

But his death would accomplish nothing. The last time he'd considered it would've been easier. No one would've mourned him overmuch in Ixti. Certainly not his father, and probably not his mother after a while, because Barrax had seen to it that they had drifted. The triplets wouldn't have been happy, but they were young and resilient. And that was all.

Merryn, however . . .

He dared not think about her, yet could think of no one else. And so, to keep his mind occupied, he set about salvaging as much as possible from the dead horse: tent, blankets, cooking gear, a book on outdoor survival he'd stolen from the hold's Lore hall. Food.

Part of the horse itself. He'd be a fool to leave so much meat to the Flat's invisible scavengers when he might soon be in need himself.

The wind hurried his work, and the snow returned, drifting against Balmor's shattered leg, even as Kraxxi worked to cut the best meat from the accessible haunch and a good strip from the loin. It was sticky, bloody work, and his hands were numb when he finished.

A pause for breath and a drink from his slim store of brandy, and he rose deliberately, turned his back on death, cold, and wind, and started off afoot.

Southeast. A day of that, and if he didn't find the road again, he'd turn more truly south, toward the Pit, where it might, at least, be warmer.

Balmor, had been dead less than a day, but to Kraxxi's feet it seemed an eternity. Not from walking itself, but from constant encounters with innumerable sharp-angled stones that both abraded his soles and upset his balance. Far more than once he'd come perilously close to twisting an ankle, and many times more than that he'd staggered and fallen. What he would do if he actually managed to lame himself, he had no idea. He had a staff of sorts, cut from a tree before entering this evil, blasted place, and that would do for a crutch—or a weapon. But that was small comfort when he pondered the pitiless emptiness of the Flat.

The sky soared above in arrogant blue splendor: a bowl of perfection the poets of his land were fond of lauding. The Flat stretched away in all directions: white and pure and featureless as ever, save where Angen's Spine still showed as a saw-toothed eruption on the horizon. How many days back now? He didn't want to know. Two merely descending that range: both rendered agonizingly slow because of the snow, and excruciatingly nerve-wracking because that was when he most feared pursuit.

Now he'd almost welcome it, because pursuit would inevitably mean capture, which would free him from further decisions.

Except, he discovered, he *liked* being free.

Though even as a prisoner in Eron he'd felt a thousand times more independent than in the palace in Ixtianos.

Or—

He paused, squinting into the gloom of the southern horizons. Something showed there: nothing he could see clearly save that it was a darker displacement amid the gray and white, but nevertheless encouraging. A declivity in the Flat, perhaps, that might mark a dry streambed. An active watercourse that wore a modicum of foliage beside it. Maybe even an intact stretch of road.

Whatever it was, it was a goad.

But distances were deceiving where there were few landmarks and no color (for the sky had gone stark white in a way he didn't like), and he found his legs almost too tired to move before he'd brought the dark line noticeably nearer.

He'd slowed by evening, and had been forced to temper his hope with an infusion of necessity. He'd need to make camp soon or risk being caught out on this desolate place at night. And the cold, even this far south, would be appalling.

But then the line suddenly grew much sharper, because part of it had been masked by a rise so subtle as to be almost undetectable.

And then he saw in truth.

Not the road he'd hoped for or expected; he'd evidently steered too far south for that, which meant he'd crossed it unawares. But this might actually be better, for he seemed to have come upon the rim of the Pit.

And there was life down there, and the air would be marginally warmer.

The sun was setting as he came to the abrupt cutoff at the top of the vast depression. And there, where rocks made an edge that hoarded light and heat, the snow was actually melting.

It still took time he didn't want to spare to find a place out of the wind where he could camp without risking a fatal fall (death was suddenly not so attractive as it had been at noon), but eventually he managed. Not much: a bare cleft in the rocks behind a ledge no wider than his shoulders, but it filled nicely with blankets, and there'd been a lone scrubby bush nearby that made for fire enough to warm his hands and sear a few gobbets of horse.

Warmer than he'd been in days, Kraxxi slept well that night. And when he awoke next morning and dared look down from the ledge, not only did he see the white of spotty snow at the base of that escarpment, but the brown of bare earth—and, here and there, true, living green.

CHAPTER XL:

DIV

It was good to hear Rann laugh.

The high, clear peals all but rang off the transparent bowl of the endless sky, bright as the sun, natural as the muted contours of the snow-draped landscape around them.

Skis swished a counterpoint, while Avall's breath kept rhythm as their pace quickened recklessly on the long, gradual, downhill slope. Finally free of the forest that had slowed them for most of the morning, in summer this was a wide, grass-filled valley. A river glittered in its center. Frozen, surely, and still to be approached with caution.

But not yet.

How long had it been, anyway, Avall wondered, as he poled harder to keep up with his friend, who was skimming along the crests of the banks so fast he barely disrupted the crust. How long since he'd heard Rann laugh like that? Careless, and free, and with complete abandon.

He laughed himself, caught up by his friend's joy, and poled harder yet. A ski tip touched the trailing edge of one of Rann's. Avall slowed, serious again. Even in fun, they were fools to risk accident here.

Then again, most folks would say they were fools anyway.

But maybe not so much as he'd feared.

The first day out had begun well enough. They'd followed the trek road, as they intended to do all the way, and after the troublesome uphill climb at the start, they'd made good time for all they were embraced by nighted for-est. But that close to Gem-Hold, the road was used fairly often and decently maintained; it had looked easy enough to make Bend Station before dark.

They hadn't counted on the unseasonable heat (barely above freezing), which, when the sun rose, made the snow slushy, which slowed them. The upshot was that they'd reached their destination well after nightfall, and then only because the snow refroze with sunset. No one was in residence, but they'd expected no one. A fire, travelers' bread from the stores, with a lit-tle cheese and dried fish, and they'd managed a passable stew without touch-ing their own supplies. Then, tired beyond belief, they'd tumbled into bed and slept far too late the next day.

Unfortunately, the cold had returned, and with it, wind, but they were in serious woods by then, and the trees blocked the keen edge of the winter. They hadn't reached the next station by dark, but had found a fortuitous tree fall and pitched their tent there, out of the wind, with cold food and no real fire, and a determination to continue at first light. Body warmth in a shared bedroll had kept them reasonably comfortable. They'd found the sta-tion midmorning, renewed supplies there, enjoyed a brief fire, then pressed into more open country, through which they'd made good time. Avall had been amazed at how well his legs accommodated the constant motion, but was less pleased with the soreness in his arms and back. Rann complained, too, and they both wished they could find a station with a hot spring, so as to soak the pain away. Brief massages helped, but only a little. Their clothes were too bulky for most tired muscles to be easily accessed.

Snow had caught them the next four nights, the second in the open, leav-ing them no choice but to burrow into it, raise the tent, and pray. It hadn't leaked, but they'd spent the entire night keeping their airhole clear, to wake entombed in eerie light but no more falling snow.

They'd also awakened to a problem. The trek roads were marked by red poles two spans high at sight-distance intervals. They'd been easy enough to spot upon starting out, but the snow had been so bad, the visibility so poor before they'd made their previous camp, that they'd either missed one, it was buried, or was down. In any event, finding a place to sleep out of the wind had seemed more important at the time.

Rann thought he recognized the territory, though, and so they'd pushed on, ever east and south, because sooner or later they'd be bound to reach the Ri-Eron even if they became otherwise lost. Far enough east, they'd come upon the plains, and could also navigate from there. And make good time— if they didn't freeze. They were, they reckoned, less than fourteen days from Tir-Eron.

Which meant that, though technically lost, they still knew where they were going, and thought they were roughly a third of the way to their destination.

It could've been much worse.

They'd reached the bottom of the slope by then, and Rann dug in, twisting his skis around to stop closer than Avall liked to the bank above the stream, which was roughly five spans wide and frozen at least a hand thick. Enough to support their weight.

Avall halted beside him, easing around so that his back was to the wind, before pulling his mouth-mask down, the better to speak.

"Having fun are you?" he drawled. "Never a thought that you might be wearing out your brother?"

"Fun's where you make it," Rann replied breathlessly. His face was flushed—or snow-burned—bright red, but his eyes were sparkling: bluer than the sky. He was panting heavily. Breath made clouds in the air.

"Never mind that we're lost."

"South and east," Rann snorted irritably. "We're bound to cross a trek again—or hit the river. We should be out on the plains in a few more days. Should be clearer then where we are."

"The plains won't forgive us, though. No shelter from the wind. Not much wood for fires. They'll be the hard part. We'll have to rely on stations."

"Food may be the worst—if we don't find any. We'll have to make do with our own rations—and we'll be burning a lot of energy then—more than here, in some ways."

Avall scanned the landscape, started, then scanned it again, squinting into the glare to the east. "Too bad we can't take one of those!" He pointed southeast, toward the fringe of the forest that crowned the rise ahead, where a stain of dark shapes was spreading down the hill. Ice oxen. Among the few animals that could survive outside during the Deep. Mostly they stayed in the woods this season and traveled in large enough herds that their body heat, along with their thick mats of hair, protected them. That and the fact that even at rest, they moved constantly in a slow spiral dance that shifted them from inside to outside and back again, so that no one herd member was exposed to the naked cold too long.

They were also good eating, but to attack one was to attack the herd. Too, it made no sense to kill one when they were courting time, already had food, and hoped to get themselves unlost before dark.

All of which they both knew without saying, and so they pressed on, passing the herd on the opposite bank of the river.

Eventually, the valley narrowed, its eastern terminus rising slowly toward a gap between two forested mountains—which Rann did *not* recall. The river cut deep between them with no space beside, but *that* was on the map and showed that they were maybe twenty shots north of where they ought to be. Which meant they'd do best to cross where they could, then cut through the woods and go overland. Which would not be fun, since the slope there looked particularly onerous. Probably, they'd be better served to assay it without skis.

But backtracking made no sense, for the herd had spread down to the river's edge and were digging through drifts of snow twice as deep as they were tall to get at the buried grass. And several hundred ice oxen ranged along a shot were not to be annoyed. They therefore gritted their teeth, roped themselves together just in case, and forded the stream one at a time. Rann went first, looped to Avall on the north bank, and then, when he was safely on the other side, Avall followed. The ice cracked ominously during the second passage, but by then Rann was extending a hand to him and they were scrambling up the bank, ridiculously clumsy with their skis.

Another shot and they reached the forest and paused on its fringe to re-connoiter. The slope was so steep, and the growth so dense, that bare ground showed here and there. It was also a false comfort, requiring almost three hands of hard scrambling to make the ridge, and by then the sun had passed the zenith and they still had over twenty shots to go by Rann's very uncertain guess to what looked, on the map, to be an abandoned station.

The ridge was mostly open, too, and the wind was fierce. Avall felt it bit-ing at him and tugged his mouth-mask higher. He sat down to put on his skis, for the slope beyond was sparsely treed and not so steep as to preclude that form of locomotion.

But then he got a good look at the horizon and noted two things that dis-turbed him.

One was that the ridge two shots across another, much narrower, valley was much steeper than that they'd just assayed and was mostly sheer escarp-ments and bare rocks in the bargain, with another beyond, even higher. Which almost certainly meant two more hard climbs, equally perilous de-scents, and another night in the wild.

Worse was the smoke.

Though the forests hereabout supported many stands of resin-bearing trees, and forest fires were certainly not unknown, there was almost nothing to start a fire in the winter except man.

But this didn't look like smoke from a campfire. Rather, it was thick and black—oily, in fact—and coming from almost due south, which was also where they assumed the abandoned way station lay.

Rann saw him watching, "You think . . . ?"

"I'd rather not. But we should expect the worst."

"There'll still be shelter," Rann grunted. "But we'll be sleeping out again tonight."

Avall indicated the ridges. "Might be a cave in there."

"Just hope if there is, it's empty."

Avall didn't need to answer. He knew what Rann was thinking. And more and more he really *did* know what Rann was thinking—in his surface mind—or what he was thinking hard about. Thanks to the gem, which, suspended by a chain, lay in a silver cage on his chest. He touched it often; he liked that. And had found that even without priming it with blood it in some odd way heightened his senses. One night, too, the coldest, he and Rann had huddled together with Rann pressed close behind him, and his friend had snaked his hand through all those layers of clothing and found Avall's bare skin and with it the gem, and wrapped his hand around it. And for a long sleepy while, he and Rann had almost been one being.

Too much so. They'd overslept for the second night on the trip, but had also awakened strangely refreshed, if scared to try the like again.

"Damn!" Rann spat beside him, rousing him from his reverie.

"What?" But Avall already knew the answer. It was snowing.

"Better down there than up here," Rann sighed, slipping on his other ski. A moment later, through thick-flying flakes that had reduced visibility by half almost instantly, they started off downhill.

Rann hoped Avall never found out how much their overland trek cost him. He'd thought he was in good shape. Like everyone else in the hold, he'd done his duty in the mines—and had been at it an eighth longer than Avall. Already firm and sleek like most young men of his land and station, his leg muscles had hardened from pedaling, his already trim waist had lost the remnants of its fat, and his torso and arms had filled out from slinging picks and working shovels two hands every other day. But now he missed that surplus, which he could've burned to keep warm.

He didn't know how Avall kept going, though he had some unpleasant suspicions. Anything that could alter your perception and metabolism like the gem did might have other manifestations. He knew for a fact that when Avall slept with the gem on, it was almost as if he were dead. He barely breathed. His heart beat but seldom. And he was far, far cooler than a shivering Rann had ever let on.

None of which he dared tell his friend. And whether or not Rann continued, Avall would proceed regardless. But he also knew that life without his bond-brother would be like daytime without the sun. And so he persevered, panting hard but never complaining, as they made their way across snow that grew ever deeper; through flurries of larger flakes flung harder and more densely every breath by a wind that was like a frigid bellows.

They'd made it down the first valley, though, and up the steep northern side, thanks to a game trail they hadn't seen until they'd literally stumbled onto it. The snow had been sparser there: barely calf deep, which had made it relatively easy to follow it to the ridge. Somewhere along the way it occurred to them that if they continued on that ridge to the right, they'd come upon the ice oxen's backtrail, which should be all but clear of snow.

So they'd bent their way right, down the more gradual slope and into another valley. Maybe a third of the way to where they reckoned the station was.

Or a third of the way to the smoke that still stained the sky, but now, two hands later, finally seemed to be abating. Which meant it had been an impressive blaze indeed. And localized, which didn't bode well for the station.

"I hope you know what you're doing," Avall muttered, though he was in the lead, plodding steadily along now that the land had opened.

"No more than you," Rann breathed. "But that many oxen have to have crossed here somewhere. If we'd had any sense, we'd have looped around behind them when we first saw them. They're surefooted, but they can't cross sheer cliffs in that number. They'd have found the easy way."

"They're not afraid of the cold, either," Avall advised. "They're free to haunt the ridges, we're not. They also weigh ten times what we do, and are lower down. They can stand where we can't."

"Good point."

Avall nodded but slowed anyway. He fished in his pouch for a length of sweet-stick, broke off half, and extended the other to Rann. "Need the energy," he muttered, thrusting one end into his mouth. Rann took the offering without comment, glad he hadn't had to dip into his own store of the energy-rich concoction he'd plundered overmuch already—though Avall, he hoped, didn't know.

Sweetness oozed from the broken end. Rann savored it, sucking at the juice as it slowly melted free and exploded on his tongue. Energy burned through him like the most potent liquor fumes. Not a thing to do in the long run, but for now it sufficed.

"Shouldn't be far," Avall said, and moved on.

It wasn't. They made their way up a long slope lightly covered with birches, then across another ridge—on the other side of which the land was bare save where, thirty spans off, the smooth glaze of snow was broken into a muddy jumble that marked the upper bank of the path the herd had plowed with pure brute strength on their never-ending graze. Grass showed there in spots, but already the ground was refrozen and lightly dusted again. They'd rested here, too; Rann could see the rough, oblong ovals where they'd lain. The place reeked of dung, but it was almost a pleasant smell simply because it spoke of the wild world; not tanned leather, smoke, half-cooked food, and his and Avall's ever-more-rank body odors.

"Looks like the way to travel," Avall noted, as he scrambled down the head-high snowbank.

Rann followed more carefully, pausing at the bottom to remove his skis again, this time for storage across his shoulders. For a while, it looked as though they'd have to travel on foot. It would be slower, but Rann found the notion insanely appealing.

The snow was less troublesome down there, too, for the wind was blowing crossways to the bank and almost horizontally, so that the worst of the near blizzard went above them if they hunched over and stayed near the windward side.

It was like traveling in a canyon, Rann decided, as they bent their way toward the diminishing plume of smoke.

Up another rise, then down, and the route was almost straight. Up *another*, and just on the other side, they saw the hunter.

He was standing maybe twenty spans downslope, close to the snowbank; bow raised, arrow nocked, squinting down the length. He jerked it down at once, as both Rann and Avall uttered startled yips and dived to the side instinctively. Rann thought he saw a scowl, though it was hard to tell through a sudden blast of snow. Avall raised his hands to signal nonaggression. Rann did likewise and followed his friend down the trail, which was half frozen mud and half new snow, with a good bit of dung thrown in.

Not until they were within speaking distance did the man lower his weapon entirely, and only then did Rann determine that what he'd assumed by circumstances was a man was in fact a woman. Fairly tall, granted, and somewhat weathered, but definitely female. She looked wary but not threatening.

"We're not good to eat," Avall called as they approached.

"You'd be a bitch to clean, anyway," the woman gave back carefully. Grinning, but her eyes still looked hard.

Avall nodded toward the smoky horizon. "Looks like the cook fire's already lit."

The woman snorted derisively.

"Herd's not far ahead," Rann added helpfully. "We saw them."

The woman shrugged. "Got mine a while ago. One of the stragglers. You're welcome to some." She pointed back down the curve of the slope with her bow. The trail bent out of sight. Likely that was where the quarry lay.

"Old bull," she continued. "Probably tough. I wounded a calf, but not good enough. I was hoping it had fallen by the way when you two showed."

"Sorry," Avall grunted. "We can help you look."

"Doesn't matter," the woman sighed. "I'm tired. Right now, I'd rather have company."

No names had been exchanged, Rann noted, though that wasn't uncommon. But what was a woman doing out here? Women hunted, but this one didn't have the look of someone on a foraging mission from a station. Which meant she was either Common Clan or unclanned. There were a few out here in the wild, going their own way with their own resources.

"I suspect," Avall said carefully, "that we both have questions."

The woman grimaced. "I'd as soon wait until I've got back to my kill to get acquainted. We can talk while we butcher. The blood would do us all good." Rann's stomach twitched at that, though he'd tasted raw blood before—in small amounts, at the ritual autumn slaughter. He grimaced sourly.

She saw him. Her lips quirked in a wicked, but not unkind, smile. She was younger than she looked, he realized; probably not much older than he, if used to a harder life. "What's the matter, lad? Don't fancy hot, sweet-salty blood, fresh from the vein?"

"I've tried it," Rann acknowledged. "It's part of Harvest, sometimes."

"I know," the woman replied icily. "I'm not unclanned. It's probably congealed by now anyway. In any event, we ought to get back to it. I'm Div, by the way."

Rann started at that: a name so casually offered to a pair of strangers. They'd have to be careful. Share food, maybe. Share names and share a night and they'd be bound by bonds of friendship. Which might be the woman's idea, meeting two men out here alone. If she was alone.

Rann was suddenly wary.

"Avall," Avall volunteered, stopping short of naming clan or craft.

"Rann," Rann mumbled.

No one spoke further as they navigated the trampled ground back to where the herd's path curved right out of sight. Barely had they made the turn, however, when Rann saw the woman's kill. It was a big bull, sure enough. And by the arrow lodged neatly in the juncture of spine and neck, the woman was either an exceedingly good shot or extremely lucky. "Crippled in one leg," she supplied, as if that explained it.

Rann studied the body. It was still warm, almost steaming. The thick, matted hair held heat very well indeed. He was wondering when the woman was going to go for the neck to slice a vein when she knelt beside the haunch instead. "Either of you lads got knives, you can help. Make it go faster. I don't trust the weather."

When Avall divested himself of his gear, Rann reluctantly did the same. "How much of this are you planning to retrieve?" Avall asked casually, but it was a question rife with implication—which she obviously knew.

"Both haunches, now that I've got you lads, if you're willing to tote in exchange for food. The tenderloin if possible." She eyed Rann dubiously, but with a twinkle in her eye. "You might want to start on that," she added in his direction. "Strip the hide off either side of the spine, cut through the fat, and by then we should be finished here."

Rann applied himself to the work. Not as bloody as he'd expected, though his tenure at Tanning hadn't been his favorite eighth. Avall was stone-faced, though his task seemed mostly to be maneuvering the leg while the woman first cut through the bony joint at the hock, then turned to the hip. "Some folks eat the tongue and the balls," she said, to nobody.

"I've done both," Avall informed her. "Didn't care for either."

"One question free," she offered. "You're wondering what I'm doing here. And as soon as I tell you, you'll wonder why I trusted you when I've no reason to except that you're young and out where you've no excuse to be, except that you don't look like you're out on a pleasure hike. Thing is, nobody can afford to turn down friends in the Deep—or trust anybody."

"Not in Deep Winter," Avall agreed, too quickly.

A curt nod. "Like I said, my name's Div. Common Clan, but my husband was Tanner out of Half Gorge, from a minor subsept of that crew. For reasons I refuse to discuss, he managed to get himself unclanned. Fortunately, his family had been decimated during the plague and he knew of some small holds they'd abandoned. One was near here—about a day and a quarter west. We moved there, being handy with living on our own. He died last year. Wound went bad in the Deep and I couldn't get him anywhere. I liked it out here and stayed."

Rann had managed to open the first big flap of skin, revealing a thick layer of fat. It smelled like . . . raw meat. He yawned, stretched. And could be asleep in no time. A snowflake tickled his nose. He scowled. A few more frothed through the air, but the squall had dissipated.

"Question time, now," Div went on, sawing with a vengeance. "What're two obviously High Clan lads doing out here this time of year?"

Avall exchanged glances with Rann. "We're on a mission from Gem-Hold-Winter," he said truthfully. "Something's come up there that I'm not empowered to reveal save to my clan and the King, but which really won't wait until spring because of what it could effect. I can't say more. Anyway, when the thaw hit, we thought it might be safe to try it."

"It?"

"Tir-Eron."

"Not as bad as everyone thinks," Div muttered. "That's as much as you're going to tell me, right?"

Avall shook his head. "As much as I *can* tell you—except that we're in a hurry. We tried to plan this, but . . . it's hard to plan what no one ever does."

"You better thank The Eight for the herd then, and for this warm spell," Div laughed harshly. "It's usually cold enough to freeze piss out here."

"Only goes to slush, now," Avall chuckled back. "Right, Rann?"

She smiled at him, looking younger all the time.

Avall cleared his throat. "My turn for a question." He paused. "What about the fire? Or do you know anything?"

She sighed, looked unhappy. "That was what used to be called Wood-stock Station. There's not much stone around there, so it was made of wood, thus the name. It's also one of the oldest, and not in the best repair, even before it was abandoned. In any event, I stay there some when I'm out hunting. This time of year you have to range pretty far to find anything. Anyway, I arrived down there late yesterday, hunted a bit, got dirty but did no good otherwise. Same this morning. Took a bath in the spring there. Nothing special, but it'll do. Meanwhile, I built up a cook fire in the plaza for some cauf—outside, because at that time it seemed a right fine day. Stockade gate came off in my hand, and I left it, because who's going to come on me in the Deep, anyway?"

Avall raised a brow.

She rolled her eyes in turn. "Not someone, as it turns out; some*thing*. About half that herd, apparently. They ambled in, saw the fire, panicked, ran—and kicked the fire in the process. I had a choice of saving myself and my gear or trying to save a very old and run-down station. I could also find dinner—for an eighth. I salvaged what I could and got the Cold out of there. Unfortunately, the herd had decided to run for a while, so they got pretty far ahead of me. The rest you know."

The leg came free abruptly. Avall sprawled backward but avoided landing in anything too noisome. Div rose, wiped her hands on her leather leggings, and eased around to where Rann had finished with the back fat. "Not a bad job for High Clan," she informed him. "And yes, I know some of you work as hard as anyone—or harder. I've not been there, but . . . almost. You lads don't look lazy. Foolish, maybe, but not lazy."

Avall studied the smoky horizon. "So the station's—"

"Probably gone. It was old wood and there were a lot of flammable stores still around. Tallow, for one thing—apparently this trail was used fairly frequently once upon a time, and was harvested for fat. Which was then stored and forgotten."

"Thus the oily smoke."

"And the duration: shed after shed catching one after another, because of the way the thing's built." She looked up sharply. "You lads weren't planning to stay there tonight were you?"

"We were," Rann acknowledged sourly. "Now— Who knows?"

"You're welcome to stay with me *tomorrow* night," Div offered, starting to slice on the loin. "Tonight— Maybe there's something left at the station, but I doubt it."

"Where'd you say your place is?" Avall wondered.

"West."

Avall frowned. "Out of the way. I'd like to . . . but we can't. We don't dare."

She straightened, looked him straight in the eye. "Your friend will die if he doesn't get some rest," she said flatly. "I can't believe you don't see, and for some reason he's not protesting, but I've seen men—a few—who were out in the Deep too long. It just sort of gnaws them away. You burn more trying to stay warm than you ever imagine, and moving takes twice what it would. But it's so cold you don't notice it at first. And then one day you don't wake up."

Rann froze in place. She'd described him perfectly. Avall was looking at him, too, as though he'd never truly looked at him for days. "Is she right?" he demanded.

"I can go on," Rann muttered, wondering why he bothered with the lie. "I can make it to Tir-Eron—as long as I can rest then."

"Maybe another *day,*" Div snorted. "Maybe enough to get to my hold. Not trying to scare you; just being honest."

"Tonight—" Avall began.

The tenderloin slipped through Rann's hands and tumbled to the ground. Div swore, secured it, wiped it down, and wrapped it expertly in leather she'd brought for that purpose. And studied the sky, which had gone white-gray again. More snowflakes were drifting down. "I don't think we've time to bother with that other haunch," she grumbled. "This is going to be a bad one. Maybe if we can get to the station there'll be enough left for decent shelter. But you lads really need a fire." She sniffed the frigid air. "A fire and a bath."

Rann rose from where he'd been sitting, not truly aware of when he'd decided to do that, and hating himself for suddenly being so tired. Div gave him a hand up and helped him shoulder his gear, but when he reached for the loin, she slapped his hand away. "You're carrying too much now, but there's not much you can drop and not starve or freeze. But come on. Wherever we wind up tonight, three should be warmer than two."

Avall had his own gear shouldered by then—including the heavy haunch. "We can take turnabout on that, if you want," she told him. And started walking.

The skis were awkward when not being worn, but to Rann's relief, Div soon made for a low place in the snowbank, where, it evolved, she'd left her own pair. Before long they were skimming through open woods, dotted with clumps of half-buried laurel, and with more than a few rock outcrops—but not good stone for building. For his part, Rann focused wholly on maintaining the pace—and tried *not* to think about dying.

The snow was getting worse. But worse than that, for Avall, was worrying about Rann. *Why hadn't he said something, dammit?* Sure, he'd been quiet of late, content most days to slog doggedly along. But what was there to talk about? Being cold and hungry and tired? One needed no verbal reminders of what the body experienced firsthand.

Strynn? He dared not even *think* about her, much less talk. And the gem scared him to talk about, though they'd spent a fair bit of time discussing the repercussions of their discoveries, including one they'd avoided before: that it could actually be a very *minor* matter, and they'd turn up at Argen-Hall half-dead, whereupon Eellon would roll his eyes and send them off to bed. (And probably spend the rest of *his* night in deep conference with the King and Nyll of Gem.)

In any event, that wouldn't matter if they didn't get somewhere warm soon. And though trees and head-high boulders took the edge off snow and wind, they also made continuing on skis problematic, so that it was looking extremely unlikely they'd get anywhere before dark—though Div seemed determined to.

"Div," he began—

An impossibly heavy weight hurled itself onto his back, toppling him forward into the nearest bank of snow. Something buried there caught him smartly in the side with a force that made him grateful for the many layers of leather between him and it. He gasped and tried to rise, but couldn't for the weight of whatever was tearing at his back.

At the haunch *on* his back, rather. He caught glimpses of enormous, black-clawed feet, of Div likewise involved with something large and furry, while Rann just stood there between them, looking stunned.

"Birkits!" Div yelled. "Going for the meat, cut it free if you c—"

Her exhortation broke off, but Avall couldn't see why because he was struggling to access his knife, which had wound up under him. He heaved upward, tried to rise, to find the cords that bound the haunch to his back, for that *was* clearly the beast's primary quarry. Unfortunately, that effort allowed a claw to slash his shoulder across the big muscle that ran to his neck. Pain flooded him. He felt a wash of wet, sticky heat as blood flowed across his body under his clothes. Darkness swelled up around him. Receded. And all the while the beast clawed and tore at the haunch.

Avall's world dissolved into pain. Surely he was dying. Why else would reality be shifting so, and perceptions slowing down, so that everything took impossibly long, and he had more than ample time to notice everything? Notice and *analyze*.

Like the fact that even if it got the haunch off, the birkit might quickly realize it had collared not one kind of prey, but two.

Like the fact that Div was evidently unconscious, and that Rann was finally starting to move, his hands shifting languorously toward his belt knife.

And all the while the birkit ripped and tore. *If you'll wait, you can have it!* he thought savagely. And for that instant, that was the whole of his desire.

To his amazement, the tearing ceased. Something hot, wet, and confused darted into his mind. *You speak! You are—not Us. But not—food. Yet you are food.*

Avall's mind reeled. Who was that in his head? Certainly not Rann. *Certainly* not Div. Which only left someone far off. Or—impossibly—

Birkit?

We are We. But what I see in your head when you speak—that is also We.

Avall gulped. This couldn't be happening! Birkits were dumb beasts. They didn't speak. Yet even as he argued that, he realized that he hadn't so much received actual sentences as impressions he'd sorted into words. Along with that, a more desperate part thought frantically along another line and— Well, he only prayed it would work.

Call the other You *off my companion. I know where is more meat.*

More meat? You are meat, but you are Us, because you think with Us. We cannot eat Us.

Avall heard—with his actual ears—a low yowl with an odd inflection to it. An instant later, the weight lifted enough for him to see the birkit that had attacked Div likewise ease off her. She wasn't moving. Rann was, but slowly, oh so slowly.

"Stop, Rann!" Avall called, trying to say the words slowly enough to be comprehensible, since he'd finally figured out—maybe—what was going on. His blood, and maybe some of the birkit's blood, had touched the gem. Its magic had kicked in. Why if he wanted, he could *be* the birkit!

He reached out, then recoiled from the alienness he found. But there was also intelligence of a kind, along with the urge to hunt—not for the kill, but to feed half-grown cubs who were awake and shouldn't be.

Avall tried to picture Div's kill clearly in his mind. The trail. The dead ox. The route they'd taken away from there; some sense of the distance, by the position of the sun.

We will go. We will feed. Better meat than you, and blood meat. By which, Avall determined from the accompanying images, it meant organs.

If You *will free us, we will get more meat for* You.

You are too cold to hunt. You *will die.*

If You *free us,* You *can have some of this meat—only leave us enough to feed ourselves. We must reach shelter. Or we will die.*

You are Us, and Us should not die.

Shelter . . . ?

Shelter is here. And with that came an image of a rock outcrop halfway up the slope ahead, a clear space before an opening, a cave deep enough to keep out the chill, and two birkit cubs hungry and desperate when they should've been asleep.

Shelter for you, maybe.

Shelter is shelter. You hunt for food. You We should not kill. Not Us, but not meat.

Avall tried not to think about the last time he'd been party to a birkit attack, though even then it'd gone after his horse, and only—again—from a dire need to feed cubs. He doubted, however, that it would be good to let this one know his kind had killed birkit-kind.

Abruptly, Avall realized that a great deal was going on of which no one was aware but him, and that he was the only one who could do anything to rectify that situation. Ignoring the pain in his shoulder, he managed to twist into an awkward half sprawl (the skis and backpack made anything else impossible). "They . . . can . . . think . . ." he said slowly, to Rann. "I've . . . been . . . talking . . . to . . . this . . . one. I . . . think . . . the . . . gem . . . lets . . . me . . ."

Rann squinted, then nodded uncertainly and sank down where he was—slowly, oh so slowly.

It was snowing again. Hard. Ground that had been disturbed by their altercation was already dusted with white.

The birkits rose as one, green eyes glowing in the half-light. No thoughts buzzed in Avall's brain, but there was a clear command to leave, and images of the cave.

He hesitated, then rose. Time was shifting again, and the thoughts were fading. Rann moved more naturally. Div, however, didn't look good, though he could see her torso slowly rise and fall with the ghostlike wisps of her breath.

You shelter. We will find this meat. You feed the cubs.

We require fire. Will that trouble You?

Nothing will burn there. There are holes for the fire dung.

Fire dung? Smoke—maybe?

The reply was fading. *Go. You will find it.*

And then the thoughts—and the birkit—were gone.

The other followed, leaving Avall more than half-stunned, as he stood alone in the trail. Rann reached him before he could move.

"What The Eight was *that?*" Rann gasped. "I didn't understand half of it, but there was something about the gem."

Avall shrugged helplessly. "I think I convinced them they'd rather eat Div's dead ox than us. They've got cubs nearby—the warm spell woke them. I . . . promised to feed the cubs. I *think* . . . they'll let us stay in their den. It's not far. We could do worse."

Rann stared at him for a long, confused moment, then knelt beside Div. Avall joined him. She was still unconscious but looked to be intact. "Take off your gear," he told Rann. "I'll get Div's off, and mine, and try to get her up there, then come back for the rest. If you've got it in you, I could use some help with her. She weighs as much as I do, I bet."

Rann squinted through the snow, barely visible in the twilight. It was already a half finger deeper in just that little while. Colder, too. Cold enough to freeze piss before long. A hand, and Div would be covered.

"You're bleeding."

"Div may be dying! Now help me. Or not."

Rann had removed his gear by then. Somehow he and Avall got Div to the lair the birkit had indicated. Got her inside and out of the wind. Got the meat and gear there as well, though Avall made all three trips. By the end of the second, Rann had managed a fire: just where the cave—which was almost large enough to stand in—made the first of several kinks. The ground inside was dry, clean stone; birkits were notoriously neat. Nor was there much smell beyond a musky animal rankness. Avall dropped the last bundle and sank down beside it, situating himself so that he could watch the entrance for the return of the birkits while keeping an eye on the inner reaches of the cave, from which the cat-sized cubs had ventured, snared the bulk of the tenderloin (he'd managed to save a little), and disappeared again. And though he knew he should be tending Rann and Div, he barely had energy to grill a few gobbets of meat over the fire, and to boil some of the rest into a stew of which he made Rann drink the bulk, before weariness ambushed him in what he thought was a restful pause, and carried him off to slumber.

CHAPTER XLI:

THE BEAST WITHIN

(WESTERN ERON–DEEP WINTER: DAY XXXI–EVENING)

~~~~~~~~~~

Avall awoke to flickering flame, uneven heat, and a sense of hungry darkness lurking just beyond the firelight. Cold was out there, too—waiting.

He also woke to pain: the soreness that had been with him so long it had become part of him. The numb ache of body parts exposed to snow too long. Impact bruises. A final burning throb that felt as though someone had laid fire on his shoulder and left the embers there, banked but eager to rage at need.

He blinked into the uncertain gloom. Saw stone, a pair of sprawling shapes wrapped in furs, and assorted piles of gear. Blinked again, and the stone became cave walls: pale tan-gray, irregular but worn smooth by the passage of birkit hide over countless ages. The floor was smooth, too—and level, for what it was.

But the cold—! It was razoring in from outside with a force that made him reluctant to consider what its full impact might be. Which meant, much as he hated to move, that he'd have to: for the sake of the fire which was all that was keeping them alive.

But first he had to see to his companions. Rann lay next to him: asleep, but the look of soft abandon on his features was encouraging. Div was harder to read, but the cursory assessment they'd been able to make of her was that she'd sustained neither broken bones nor life-threatening wounds. Probably she was merely weary—she'd said as much—and her body was responding to that. He hoped. And hoped, more to the point, that she remained asleep a while longer because he had no idea how he was going to explain to her that the birkits who had first rights on this conveniently located shelter had told him it was *permitted* for them to sit out the blizzard there. Div was smart. She'd been in the wild. She surely knew birkit habits better than he. But birkits that talked to humans mind to mind— *That* asked a lot. Too much, perhaps; for by Rrath's logic, that meant they had souls.

In any event, it wouldn't matter if he didn't see to their safety soon. A stick from the fire made a torch, but he gasped at even that simple movement as agony ripped through the shoulder the birkit had savaged during the attack. He bit back a whimper. Tears stung his eyes, mixing with blood and dirt on his cheeks. He hesitated, fearing to inspect his own body yet knowing that sooner or later someone would have to. But not now. For now he could stand it. Meanwhile, other things needed tending. Gritting his teeth against the pain, he scrambled off to explore the cave's recesses in search of a less exposed campsite.

Just at the edge of the firelight, the walls kinked right. Sounds of movement filtered up from there—likely the cubs he'd barely glimpsed before they'd fled with chunks of very fresh, very bloody meat. Scarcely daring to breathe, he followed that route down a short, low-ceilinged tunnel until he came upon a dome-shaped chamber the size of a caravan, in which pale shapes tumbled, pounced, and played as only young carnivores could. The meat was gone.

A smaller tunnel to one side of the den's entrance effused an odor he didn't need to investigate, proof that birkits were particular about where they left their stool—for which he was more grateful than he wanted to admit.

As for accommodations for a trio of humans—the good one seemed to be taken.

A retreat to the main tunnel showed nothing encouraging, either—until a slit in the wall proved, upon investigation, to be a cleft narrow enough to be a squeeze across hips and chest, but which gave onto an empty chamber roughly the size of the birkits' den, with a strong upward draft that sucked at the flame and its smoke alike. It wasn't quite big enough to stand in, but that was the least of their worries, especially as a low ceiling would conserve heat. Indeed, the chamber was reasonably warm already. Further prowling at the opposite end revealed the reason: another slit that, in a twist of truly amazing luck, opened, after three spans or so, onto an underground pool half a span wide, whose waters were actually steaming.

To Avall, deprived of comforts as he'd been and now confronted with warmth and bathing water, it was almost more than he could stand. Assuming the birkits didn't have plans for it.

At which point the torch began to flicker and he was forced to make his way back to his companions. The fire was waning again, but Div was stirring. He poked up the coals, added one of the three remaining sticks of firewood to hand, took a deep breath, and shook her. She groaned softly—then came awake abruptly, reaching for her knife.

"*What!*" she began. Then: "Where—?" Then: "What am I doing alive?"

Avall guffawed—couldn't help it. Whether from nerves, fear, or absurdity, didn't matter. "The same thing I am," he replied to the last. "The rest— I don't want to get into details now because we need to move the fire and tend to Rann. And besides, I doubt you're going to believe it, but—"

"Stop," she barked, sniffing the air. "Birkits. So that's my choice? Be eaten alive or freeze?"

"They think we're them," Avall sighed. "They don't hunt hunters—so they said."

Div's eyes went big as oranges. "They *said*?"

Avall puffed his cheeks. "I know you're going to think I'm mad, but . . . yes. They told me. In their thoughts. I thought at them when they attacked, which is why they stopped."

"They stopped?"

"You're here, aren't you? And alive."

"Where are they now?"

"Hunting, if they haven't died of exposure. I told them about your kill."

You . . . *told* them . . ."

Avall rolled his eyes. Too much was happening too fast, and all he could do now was confront the problem closest to hand and damn the repercussions. "You remember that mission I told you about?" he asked desperately. "Well— Oh, Cold, here, I'll show you." And with that, he thrust his fingers down the collar of his tunic, fumbling for the chain. An instant later, the gem lay in his hand. "It's trust you now, or spend the next who-knows-how-long arguing and hiding and lying, and I don't have energy for that when my bond-brother may be—" He couldn't finish.

Div nodded. "I *understand* friendship. And I'm not sure you're wrong about birkits. I've watched them some. They seem to have . . . respect for other hunters."

Much as he'd have liked to continue that discussion, Avall flourished the stone. "I can tell you about what this does, or would you rather have proof?"

"Proof, if you don't mind."

"It'll take blood. I'm still bleeding a little, but you—"

"How much?"

"A scratch. Access to your bloodstream's all that's needed, so it seems."

She nodded in turn, reached for her knife, and neatly reopened a shallow cut on the heel of her palm, which she'd acquired while butchering the ice ox. It oozed rather than trickled, but that, as far as Avall could tell, was enough. That accomplished, he loosened his top three tunics and laid her hand on the wound in his shoulder with the gem between. There was little contact—less than he'd braced for, in fact: a mere brush against his consciousness. It was evidently sufficient.

Div jerked her hand away. "I've no right to go there!" she gasped. "But I saw enough to know that if you're not telling the truth, you believe you are. And I . . . saw what you remember about the birkits, and in that you did *not* lie."

Avall didn't respond, but he quickly returned the gem whence it came.

"This is important," Div stated flatly.

"But right now two things are more important: moving that fire and tending Rann."

"I'll do the fire," she volunteered. "That way I won't have to think about . . . that other. And then I'm going to have a look at that shoulder!"

Shortly after Avall and Div transferred their gear to the inner cave, Deep Winter returned in truth. The wind howled so loudly it was like the land dying of slow torture, and the cold, even at fair remove, never stopped setting warning blasts against the fire. Even so, they'd had to dare the outdoors to lay in a supply of wood. Fortunately, there was a fresh windfall nearby, and a wealth of kindling no more than a dozen spans from the entrance to the cave.

That accomplished, Div and he rigged a flap over the cleft that blocked the bulk of the wind. With that, the fire, and the steam from the pool, they were soon warm enough to shed their top layer of clothing. Around that time, the birkits returned, but when Avall made his presence known, they rebuffed him, their thoughts filled entirely with relief at no longer being outdoors, coupled with concern for the cubs. Tolerance was the main reaction they projected—like another pack suffered to use the den, or poor relations come to call. Without using the gem, there was no communication beyond that. As best Avall could figure, bonding of any kind left some residual effect, but he still had no idea of its strengths or limitations. Emotional closeness was a factor. So was physical contact. Distance might make a difference, but there'd been no time to test that. And what about material barriers? Was it easier inside than out? Maybe now he'd have time to find out, because with the weather as it was, mission or no mission, he, Div, and Rann were going nowhere for a while. Already they were husbanding their food.

And then there was Rann.

Avall couldn't believe how blind he'd been, to ignore his friend's condition. Though slighter of build, Rann had always been the stronger of the two, and he'd always taken that for granted—seen what he expected to see, he assumed. But Rann had worked himself almost to nothing trying to keep pace—often as not, to *set* the pace—laughing, joking, generally being himself.

Sacrificing himself to . . .

The mission?

Or to Avall?

He'd never dare ask. The important thing was keeping him from slipping from sleep into unconsciousness (so Div said), and in getting food into him. In the end, he slept without their being able to revive him, with Avall and Div taking turns keeping watch.

At some point, they took time to address their own wounds. Avall went first, when Div pointed out that he seemed unable to raise his arm beyond a certain level. In fact, he needed help removing clothing. At least the chamber was warm enough to render that viable, and one of his miner's candles provided sufficient light for Div to inspect the lacerations in his shoulder. They were crusted with blood and bled more when she cleaned them with water from the pool. Lacking any more appropriate binding, Avall tore strips from the hem of his undertunic.

And then it was Div's turn. She wore one less layer than he, and proved surprisingly unconcerned when an assessment of her wounds required she bare her torso, though she did blush.

Avall hadn't the energy for more than a cursory inspection of what proved to be very nice breasts on as hard a frame as he'd ever seen on a woman. What skin didn't sport claw marks was smooth, and very white. White as Strynn's, in fact, which he found himself missing more than expected.

"Legs, too," she confessed, as he snugged the final bandage and helped her slide her tunic back on. "Got me on the thighs with the hind feet." Without further comment, she loosened the ties to her leggings and rolled over on her stomach. Three layers later, leaving only her underdrawers, her flesh was exposed, and along with it, long gashes in the backs of her thighs, one of which looked as though it might be infected. Water cleaned them. A salve from Div's travel kit covered them, while more of Avall's tunic made bandages. Rann was stirring by then, enough that they directed their attention to him. He was not so much delirious as simply not quite awake, but they managed to get some broth down him, helped him attend to a necessary function, and took that opportunity to remove a few layers of his clothes. Avall's nose wrinkled. They really were getting rank.

Maybe a bath in that nice hot spring . . . ?

But he had no energy for that, and without really deciding, he curled up as close to Rann as possible, and before he knew it, slept.

Rann was awake when he roused again, but Avall's bladder required a trip outside, Deep Winter or no. It was early in the day, and he concluded his business quickly, not bothering to check the freezing factor, then returned to find Rann sitting up drinking stew. His hands were shaky and he was pale, but he looked like he might survive if they sheltered there a few days longer.

Not that delay mattered much at this point. It would've been a day or more before they were missed from Gem, to start with; and any pursuit would've encountered the same blizzard they had and been as long delayed, if they survived at all. Div thought another day in the cave at least. Another day of close quarters and the uneasy company of the birkits next door, who, Avall feared, might change their mind anytime about the palatability of humans. They slept a lot—napped a lot, anyway—and during those periods of relaxed awareness, Avall worked with the gem. Which is to say he curved his hand around it and tried to do the various things he'd done before—link with Merryn. Link with Eellon. Link with Strynn. All of which failed. Sometimes he tried, cautiously, to link with Rann without his bond-brother knowing, but all he could manage was to sense whether he was awake or asleep, and get a general read of his emotions—which mostly registered exhaustion.

The birkits were another matter. This time of year was their hibernation season, but any warm spell apparently triggered an awakening that took maximum advantage of the likelihood of available game. They were merely asleep now, and Avall wasn't so sure that wasn't why *he* was sleepy so often. There did seem to be a tenuous connection; certainly more than once he'd awakened hungry and anxious as to where his cub was, only to realize that he *wasn't* a birkit queen. A few times, too, he'd suppressed an urge to lick Rann or Div. As best he could tell, the creatures were strong . . . *thinkers,* he supposed. With reality reduced to primal needs, one would perforce feel those needs intensely.

He wondered if human emotions were experienced that way in turn.

"I'm going to take a bath," Div announced, sometime after noon.

Avall raised a brow. "You do that. We'll go next."

"No peeking," she admonished, though Avall wasn't so certain she didn't mean the opposite. By now she knew he was married, along with the gist of the business between him, Eddyn, and Strynn. She also knew Rann wasn't. His friend had been looking at her, too, with more than casual interest. And she really wasn't much older than either Avall or his bond-brother. Twenty-five, she'd volunteered. What he'd seen of her body gave proof of that.

"Call if you need us," Avall sighed, as Div snared what little spare clothing she possessed, added a healthy torch, and scooted through the opening that led to the spring.

"I'm also going to wash clothes," she advised. "I'd suggest you two lads do the same."

"Fine-looking woman," Rann opined when the two of them were once more alone.

"Interesting, too," Avall agreed. "We could learn a lot from her."

"You planning on taking her with us?"

"We could do worse. She knows the Deep, we don't. We'd have to re-ward her, but I don't have any trouble with that. Maybe Eellon could find her a place with the clan. Assuming she wants one."

"I don't think she will," Rann replied. "She seems happy . . . like this."

Avall nodded. "She likes you, too. I think— Well, if you want to . . . I'll afford you what privacy I can."

Rann cuffed him, surprising him by blushing. "You're overlooking one thing."

"What?"

"What if I get her with child? Or you do?"

Avall chuckled again. "She can't have children. She miscarried her first and it damaged her inside."

"She told you this?"

"She's very forthright. I like that about her."

"So you trust her?"

"Having been in her head a bit, yes I do. Most people are basically good, Rann. Bad things are usually done for a reason—selfishness, or whatever. Even all that with Eddyn was because of the way he was brought up. He wants the same thing we do, as far as his life's concerned."

"You're mighty charitable about someone who raped your wife."

"I didn't say I approved!"

Rann closed his eyes and leaned back, then reached out and patted his hand. "Thanks," he murmured, "before I forget it. Thanks for saving my life."

"After I almost cost it!" Avall retorted with unexpected heat. "I ought to thank you—nonstop for about an eighth!"

"It was important. So are you." He leaned his head on Avall's shoulder.

Avall stroked his hair. "I am a lucky man," he whispered. "I—"

"That was wonderful!" Div crowed, as she crawled out of the passage-way. She thrust the torch back into the fire and returned to her customary place to the right of the tent-skin door. Her hair was wet and, now that it was clean, showed red highlights. She looked paler, too. And hadn't both-ered to re-don the full achievement of furs, choosing instead, a thick under-tunic of unbleached white wool and footed hose of roughly the same color. The soft fabric draped her body in a way Avall found most attractive, especially the way her breasts moved beneath it as she spread her other garments across the floor. He had to remind himself that he was married to the most beautiful woman in the world, that both Strynn and Div trusted him, and that, in any event, Div seemed more interested in Rann—though that could simply be because Avall was unavailable.

Rann slapped his leg. "Our turn, brother."

"Take your time," Div urged, punching up the fire before passing Avall a torch, which he took in his left hand, the other shoulder still being stiff enough to cause trouble with such things.

Avall shot her what he hoped was a cryptic grin, then led the way into the tunnel. He'd been there in quest of water several times, but Rann hadn't. His friend therefore gasped when he entered, though the place wasn't very large: essentially a stony shelf a span wide and two long, fronting a pool of black water the same length but no more than half a span across. The opposite wall was sheer, wet stone, but cracks in the ceiling vented the bulk of the steam.

It wasn't always the same temperature, either, he'd discovered. Some-times it was decidedly cool; once it had been unbearable. Now, it seemed ex-actly right: hot enough to steam, and for that steam to heat the room like a sweat chamber, but not so hot as to put them at risk of scalding.

Securing the torch in a cleft he'd found earlier, Avall claimed a place to the right of the entrance and began working off his clothes. The top two lay-ers of leather he'd left in the main room. They were fairly clean, and little blood had got into them, though perhaps he'd wash them later. The inner layers were something else entirely. Blood had dried on both tunics and the bottom leather, and Rann had to help him with them. His friend whistled when he saw the wounds on his shoulder. "One of these may need to be opened," he observed. "Soak it first, and we'll see."

Avall tried to look but couldn't, so turned his attention to his lower half. As the layers peeled away, he felt increasingly better: freer, lighter. He was already sweating, but it felt good.

He paused with his underhose remaining to watch Rann. With no stiff shoulder, his friend was making quick work of stripping. And though Rann was never unpleasant to look at, Avall's interest was not aesthetic. Rather, he wanted to know exactly how far his friend had pushed himself.

He saw soon enough. Rann wasn't quite skin and bones, but he'd lost easily a tenth of his already sparse weight. Ribs showed where before there'd been sleek muscle, and much of the rest of him looked hard and knotted where it ought to have been smooth and pliable. The muscles of his chest and belly showed more as lines than masses. Rann saw him looking, raised a brow, and—finally naked—slid into the water. Only then did Avall realize he had no idea how deep it was.

Deep enough to lounge in comfortably, he discovered a moment later, as he shed his hose and followed his friend's example.

"This is . . . wonderful," Rann sighed, lying back to float, arms outstretched, hair a dark tangle around his head.

"Indeed!" Avall agreed, and let his head slide under, holding his breath, so that the heat could access as much as possible. It was like a balm: loosening stiff, tired muscles, easing its way into cramps he didn't know he had, probing at his wound in a way that, though excruciating, at the same time bordered on ecstasy. He wished he had soap to attack the grime and wash the oil from his hair, but had to content himself with tearing another strip off his ragged tunic and using that as a washcloth. Rann helped him with his shoulder and the places he couldn't reach, and Avall returned the favor. Perhaps it was the eeriness of the situation: the close quarters, the flickering light (they'd have to get out soon or exhaust their torch), but Avall began to feel an impossible closeness to Rann, as though the mountain was some enormous womb and they a pair of twins waiting to be born. It was sensual but not sexual—or closer, perhaps, than either.

Unfortunately, Avall had a rather less pleasant task to undertake, and with that in mind, hauled himself back on dry land and bent himself to laundering their clothes. He hated to sully the water with all that dirt and blood, but it was wash it off or live in it, and the notion of filth against his newly cleaned skin was appalling. That accomplished, they donned clean hose but decided that anything else was superfluous, and made their way back to the main den. Avall needed three trips to retrieve all the laundry, and by the time he'd concluded the last, was hungry and sleepy again. Happily, Div had concocted another pot of stew, adding the last of the way-meat. From somewhere, too, she produced a flask of brandy.

"I've been saving this," she informed them, offering it first to Rann, then to Avall, before taking a healthy swig herself. Avall folded a blanket into a pad, stuffed it against the wall, and flopped against it. Rann was rolling his head from side to side and rubbing at it as though he had a cramp.

"Rann," Avall called softly. "Come here. Let me take care of that."

"I thought you'd never ask," Rann smiled, and scooted back to sit between Avall's outstretched legs, hands folded loosely in his lap. Avall shook his wet hair out of his face and applied himself to massaging Rann's shoulder. Mostly he felt bones, though there was still muscle, if not the firmness he knew from memory. In spite of the pain from his wound, he kneaded Rann's neck and shoulders for a fair while, then his back, all the way down below the band of his hose. But when he shifted his attention to his head, Avall's shoulder protested vehemently. He grimaced but tried to persevere.

Div looked up at a grunt he hoped Rann hadn't heard, and scowled. "Let me take over. I'm sore, but you're worse."

Avall paused. "She's got a point," he murmured into Rann's hair.

Rann patted his hand and eased around to where Div indicated. She began to work his shoulders much as Avall had . . . his back . . . his head. Rann's rapt expression attested to the quality of her efforts. "My husband worked hard," she explained. "This was something I could do for him."

"The trouble is," Avall replied, relaxing into the bedroll, "once you work on an area, you find that the area next to it feels bad by contrast, and you have to keep going."

"I'm strong," Div shrugged. Then, to Rann: "Lean back."

Rann did, pillowing his head against Div's breast. He looked uncomfortable at first, then seemed to relax. She shifted her attentions to his face.

Avall watched from his corner. Though he was trying hard not to feel jealous, he couldn't deny that emotion. Rann had lain with women, of course: a few more than Avall's two because he wasn't so idealistic, therefore wasn't above an occasional unclanned courtesan. Still, he and Avall had shared with each other more times than either could count during their teens. Even now, with Strynn's knowledge and consent, they sometimes pleasured each other. But Avall had never had to share Rann with someone else so overtly—not even in this minimal manner. Yet if *this* disturbed him so much, how had his bond-brother coped with the knowledge of what he frequently shared with Strynn? Once again, he realized, he'd taken Rann for granted.

Div *wasn't* taking Rann for granted, however. Both her eyes and Rann's were closed as she continued to work his chest, not so much massaging now as caressing. Avall watched her fingers slide farther and farther down each time—finally easing into the top of his hose along the sides. Rann tensed at that, then shifted—and let his hands move onto Div's calves, which he began to stroke. Her deep, shuddering breaths prompted Avall to shift to a less obvious line of sight, though he couldn't turn away entirely—nor wanted to, beyond reasonable discretion. They both knew he was there, for Eight's sake. One of them was a near-total stranger, the other his closest friend; it was for them to say if casual observation was unwelcome.

Apparently neither cared, as Div had given up all pretext of performing a massage and was blatantly teasing Rann's nipples. He was enjoying it, too, and trying his best to reciprocate with what little of her he could reach.

In spite of himself, Avall felt himself becoming aroused and drew his legs up to his chest to obscure that fact. Suddenly in desperate need of a distraction, he closed his eyes and felt for the gem, not bothering to prime it with blood.

He tried to focus solely on the smoothness of the surface, but that only reminded him of other smoothnesses on Rann and Strynn, and so he peered up again—exactly as Div's hand reached Rann's waistband. This time, Rann captured those probing fingers and slid them farther downward and in. An instant later, he'd pushed off his hose, and a moment after that, the inevitable began.

Avall watched through a fall of still-damp hair as Rann shifted around to face Div, drew her tunic over her head, and bent his face to her breasts, then slowly kissed his way down the length of her body until he came to her underhose. These, too, he removed with a certain grim intensity, and then all Avall could see was the full length of Rann's naked back, buttocks, and legs as they lay facing each other—not yet coupling, but with hands and lips and tongues growing ever more venturesome.

Avall closed his eyes—then opened them very wide indeed when a bestial roar echoed through the cavern. *You've woken the birkits,* he thought, only then realizing that Rann and Div were actually all but silent, though Rann was atop her now, his face even more intense, as though his efforts required total concentration. Div's eyes were slitted, as though she'd hungered for what Rann was now providing for a very long time indeed.

Again, Avall lowered his lids, trying not to think of his friends, but of the birkits in the other den, sleeping there, or enjoying a drowsy winter version of their family life, comfortable with each other even in the Deep.

Thinking . . .

Thinking . . .

One moment he was *thinking* about them, and then he *was* one: the male. And he was awake and desperate to mate. He bit at the queen and nudged her with his nose. She growled, batted at him with sheathed claws. Part of him knew she was in heat and ready to breed more cubs, and that the meat of their rare, midwinter feast had awakened that in her, while another part simply wanted to crawl atop her right now and pump a season's worth of hoarded seed into her womb, with slow, methodical thrusts that seemed to last forever.

She fought him, but without conviction—and then he was atop her and *in* her, and Avall was distantly aware of his human body groaning, and of two pairs of eyes gazing at him with pity, and then of arms reaching out, and hands on him—*all* of him—and of his own skin, completely bare now, being stroked and kneaded and caressed. He sprawled across Rann's back, hands thrust between them, rubbing his friend's chest and belly—lower when he could, though Rann and Div had coupled again. He licked the skin between Rann's shoulders, at the nape of his neck; his manhood rose and sought to do something he'd never done with either man or woman, but he recoiled from that and slid off his friend to the ground beside. But he had to mate, *had* to, though he managed to restrain himself until the glaze of ecstasy on Rann's face tightened into grimaces and grunts, then relaxed abruptly—whereupon Avall eased his friend aside and fell atop the woman—what was her name?

Div? No, she was the *queen* and he must have her and sire his cubs. He clutched her breasts desperately, tasted them, as she raked his chest. The gem lay between them as he slid inside her; he grasped it, and she did, and Rann was lying atop him, spent, but becoming aroused again, and he was biting Avall's neck and fumbling for the gem as well, so that each of their hands was upon it. And then reality vanished entirely, replaced by the ecstasy of three minds colliding and three bodies intertwined. Avall's mouth was on Div's and his manhood inside her. She had one hand on his buttocks, one . . . somewhere else. Rann lay athwart him, teasing his free nipple with one hand and one of Div's with the other.

But they were also birkits, and all at once Avall was not merely the male, but the female; and not only himself, but Div being thrust full of himself, and Rann touching everything he could find, and starting to need again. And then Avall climaxed magnificently, and they all rolled over, and it was Avall on the bottom with Rann atop him, and he had a breast in his mouth, and then the birkit climaxed, and the female roared, and they all shifted again, and a mouth closed on his manhood and he didn't know whose, nor cared.

Because somewhere in all that sensation, in all that love, and energy, and pent-up lust, and animal desire, parts of his brain were collapsing. He was Rann. He was Div. He was even, for an instant, Strynn. And then he was himself again, and twice as . . . powerful, because Rann was in his head, too, sharing his strength; and so was he in Rann's, and thus united, in mind and soul as well as body. Every thought, every desire, was twice as potent. Another presence joined them as well: alien, but welcome all the same, and that strengthened him even more, so that Avall knew that the three of them had bonded. And that bonding had awakened parts of himself that heretofore had slept, proving beyond remainder of doubt that he was only, in very small part, his body.

He could go *anywhere*—and did. For an instant, he saw the tangle of bare bodies that was himself, Rann, and Div, and knew that he was going somewhere they couldn't, though it was their strength that supported him. It was a dark place, yet full of light; a place of power, full of peace. Of silence that rang with sounds. He saw something there: a stone in a place that had no ground or sky. He picked it up, clutched it to him, though it twitched in his grasp like a thing alive.

Avall! he heard someone cry! *Come back to us!*

He didn't want to—but had no choice. It was their strength that had raised him here to what had to be the Overworld: the realm of The Eight, where the King and the Priests found them when they cast auguries or prophesied. Perhaps he *should* go back—but he'd bring one thing as surety. *This stone.*

He clutched it desperately. Closed eyes that didn't exist there, folded into himself—and fell back into his own body. The stone rolled from his hand—

A flare of light blazed around the chamber like captive lightning. His heart froze. His blood turned to fire, then to ice. His body twisted in an ecstasy of orgasm, and he shot seed across his belly. And then darkness claimed him, broken only by the birkits' ecstatic howling.

CHAPTER XLII:

SURPRISES IN THE SNOW

(THE FLAT–DEEP WINTER: DAY XXXII–MIDDAY)

~~~~~~~~~~

Merryn had seen the body—or the lump in the snow that masked it—for nearly a hand before she reached it in truth. The trouble was, this part of the Flat was sufficiently level that anything larger than the increasingly troublesome rocks made a discontinuity in the featureless white. Which could build hope *or* dread.

Normally she'd have welcomed either—any change, in fact. This many days out, she was beginning to ache for actual landscape, as she never did on the plains north of Eron Gorge. Then again, those vast fields of quick-grass were never entirely level, and there was always a wood on the horizon, or the sea, or maybe a hold—ruined or otherwise. Never this ongoing *nothing*. For the first time she could understand why trade had never flourished between her land and Ixti. It wasn't so much the physical barrier as the emotional one: this vast emptiness where, unless one were careful, one might go mad from boredom—or die.

As someone evidently had.

Someone she feared she knew. Someone she feared she would hate forever for deserting her, and someone she half hoped she *would* find, because that would require no more decisions beyond what to say when she returned to War-Hold empty-handed. If she were very lucky indeed, War-Hold would say nothing beyond what it would ever have said about missed duty rosters and failed sentryship—unless Lorvinn wanted to say more. But report would go to Tir-Eron as soon as might (and could well be going there even now, given how the break in the weather had made far too many people optimistic and reckless who ought to have better sense). And sooner or later she'd have to return to Tir-Eron, too (unless she wanted to risk outlawry, which she didn't). Never mind that once she arrived, she'd have to face her craft, then her clan, and finally her King. Too vividly she recalled the executions she'd witnessed in the Court of Rites. And too vaguely she recalled the acts that could precipitate a charge of treason.

Still, she might be able to weather it; Eellon would do everything he could, and Preedor and Tryffon of War might assist, once they understood the circumstances. The question would hinge on her rationale for taking this action. And that was something she didn't know herself.

But if that *was* Kraxxi up there, and he was dead, she'd be able to extract proof that she'd simply left to fulfill her duty. A prisoner had escaped while under her care. She'd pursued him. Border violations only mattered if there was a border to violate. Or in this case, if the violation were observed. Besides which, no one really knew where the border was. She certainly didn't, or much care.

The wind shifted abruptly, as it tended to out here, and with it came more cold, and a flurry of snow that could've been swept up off the ground as easily as fallen from the sky. She raised her head, glaring at the heavens, as though daring Weather to make her task more difficult, lest she seek Him/Them out and slay all Eight in His/Their lair.

Still, the squall slowed her, and she moved cautiously, gaze fixed firmly on the lump ahead as the wind stiffened, the clouds lowered, and Deep Winter breathed ever more closely down her neck as though it were some vast predator stalking her farther from its den—and growing hungrier.

It could suck her dry, she knew. If she were not attentive every instant, it would draw all the warmth from her body and carry it howling away to be wasted among winds that would always and forever be chill. And with the warmth would go her life. Not quickly like a candle, but slowly, a little at a time, from the skin out, as her body tried harder and harder to keep her alive. Eventually she'd sleep.

Then? Who knew? Would she even know when she crossed that final threshold? Would she dream, and then the dream wink out? Or would there be one final moment of primal panic when she *knew* she was dying and every part of her protested to no avail—as all those countless souls, including her own father, had surely protested when the plague consumed them from within?

At least she'd go in peace—if she froze.

In another quarter hand, she'd know.

That hand passed at a stone's pace, but she dared not quicken Mud's gait for fear of the uncertain footing.

She knew before she leapt down, however, that the body wasn't Kraxxi.

It was a horse, facing toward her (which was odd) and buried so that only the triple mounds of its shoulders, barrel, and haunches showed above the snow. It had been a chestnut.

Like Balmor, whom Kraxxi had ridden. One of her favorites, too; but Balmor wasn't the only chestnut gelding in the world. Only the most likely.

Steeling herself to an outward air of icy calm, she slid off Mud's sturdy back and slogged through the knee-deep snow toward the head. That brought her face into the wind and the wind brought tears to her eyes. With wet cheeks above the mouth-mask, she knelt by the head and brushed the accumulated snow away—a day's worth at least, to judge by the texture. Soon enough she found what she sought: the white blaze on the forehead, with the skewed tuft of hair that identified Balmor.

Setting her mouth, she worked methodically down the body, checking for clues to what might have occurred. She found the knife slash soon enough, and the frozen blood pooled on the coat and the ground. But Kraxxi wouldn't have done that capriciously. Therefore—

The reason confronted her as soon as she shifted to Balmor's lower side.

Broken leg. He'd stepped in a hole—which meant he'd been ridden too fast to compensate. It hadn't killed him; it wouldn't. But Kraxxi had known he would die and had done the humane thing.

Damn him!

It was well enough to be humane, but better to prevent such things entirely.

Unless—just possibly—he'd been trying to outrun the storm. That could make anyone reckless. The Eight knew she'd quaked in fear—and she'd been mostly behind it, hiding in a tent that threatened more than once to blow away and leave her exposed to Fate.

But this was not the time for such musings, not when Balmor might still have a story to tell. And so she continued to examine the body. A quick check confirmed that he still wore his saddle, though the blanket pad beneath it was gone, as was the rest of his equipment. *Their* equipment—some of it *her* equipment.

But the check revealed something else that almost made her sick, even as she recognized the wisdom. Two good-sized portions had been cut from Balmor's flesh, which could only mean Kraxxi had continued on, probably desperate, but not planning to return to Eron.

With that realization, she rose and cast her gaze about, as though she might see through the latest film of snow to whatever tracks Kraxxi had made as he departed.

She saw nothing.

Not on the ground. But the sky was darkening in the vanguard of another blow. And she was caught in the middle of nowhere with only Mud and the finding stone for company.

At least in Balmor she had a modicum of windbreak—if she could persuade Mud to bed down with her, as she sometimes could. She hated the idea of camping so close to the dead horse, but sense was sense, and it was some shelter and a good supply of meat, and those couldn't be ignored.

Scowling like a demon from the Not-World, she made her way back to Mud, secured the tent and other gear, and began to make hasty camp, keeping one eye on the sky, and one on the ground lest there be other holes. There were none, and she finally pitched the tent at Balmor's back, which put his bulk between her and the prevailing wind. Tent pegs went into frozen ground with difficulty, but they went in—the ground wasn't frozen *too* deep—and there were plenty of rocks to secure the edges. It took time to dust the area free of snow, and more time to move the rocks from the sleeping area, and by then it was close to dark. She had enough slow-stone to make a tiny fire that gave light and a little warmth, and which could heat, but not boil, a bit of brandied cauf, and then it was true night. Mud found space outside the tent, which put Merryn neatly between the live horse and the dead, and she in turn covered the mare with what spare bedding she had before crawling into the tent to sleep.

Blessedly it stopped spitting snow somewhere around midnight, and more blessedly, the wind stilled, though the sky remained overcast, which kept the temperature from falling further. Yet when she awoke the next morning, it was to see the sun shining with all its splendid glare on shots upon shots of unbroken white.

Except where it had already melted the snow off Balmor's back.

She cursed herself even as she yawned and stretched. It was almost noon, and she didn't know whether to be relieved at the unanticipated sleep, which had refreshed her beyond belief, or angry at herself for losing so much of the day.

In any event, Mud was up and needed feeding, which she attended to first, and then broke camp, by which time it was even warmer.

There only remained one thing to do. Much as she hated the notion, so much meat should not be abandoned, and since it was unlikely to spoil before sunset, she cut as much as she could from the remaining loin, then moved on to the shoulder. The squatting made her stiff, however, and she reached over Balmor's barrel to pull herself upright—

Pain such as she'd never experienced lanced into her hand.

She screamed, full and unabashed, and almost yanked it to her mouth be-fore good sense overruled and set her staring at the hole that had penetrated even her glove, which she tugged off. Already her hand was beginning to swell and numbness to seep toward her wrist. Inspection showed a single an-gry wound like a thorn prick in the middle of her palm. What could've made it she had no idea, but whatever it was, she had a feeling it was bad, and more to the point, that she might not last long if she didn't respond immediately.

Suddenly light-headed, she staggered to her feet and eased around Bal-mor's barrel—to see, calmly nibbling away at the edge of the wound in the gelding's neck, a small but very potent-looking black scorpion such as Kraxxi had said made that virulent poison.

But it *was* small (if she was thinking right, which no longer seemed cer-tain), and he'd said that potency was a function of size, which was also a function of age. This one must've been wintering in the hole until disturbed, and only ventured out now because warmth and food promised survival.

It didn't survive long. Anger made her stab it with her dagger. Then, re-membering what Kraxxi had said about *that*, she cleaned the weapon thor-oughly in the snow.

By which time her arm was aflame to the elbow.

What would happen now, or how fast, she had no idea. Something told her that this reaction was both different and more severe than that which she'd experienced from the blowgun dart—which had to do with the *age* of the venom. In any event, she wouldn't get far if she ignored the situation.

But no way was she going to remain here lest others of similar ilk lurk nearby.

Somehow she made it to Mud, but discovered she hadn't the strength in her arm to climb on, and couldn't manage to mount one-handed. And so she had to content herself with leading the mare southwest, toward the brightest light—which made as much sense as anything just then. She managed maybe two hundred paces, then unloaded the tent again. She'd just unrolled it when the first wave of numbness hit her.

The second came as she fumbled her blanket roll down atop the flapping pile of canvas.

The third—which made her vomit—caught her as she tried to squirm into the skimpy shelter.

And the fourth—which emptied her stomach—ambushed her just as she decided that all she wanted in the world was to get out of the wind and be warm, and the only way to do that was to close the tent flap (if she could find it) and let her arm—which was surely glowing red-hot now—heat the place from within.

The fifth made her vision go blurry, from which it never recovered. But that didn't really matter, did it? Because it was night now, and she was going to bed and Avall was going to read her to sleep.

Avall . . .

Avall . . .

Where was her fool of a brother, anyway?

And where was Strynn? She wanted to get a nap, and then play with Strynn.

Where, more to the point, was that tall shadow-shape that was her father?

The sixth spasm wracked her when she lay unconscious in the flaccid tent, with Mud standing placidly by, licking snow.

She was still dreaming, though: of curling around Avall in some warm, red, wet place where there was no pain at all, and one didn't need to bother breathing.

CHAPTER XLIII:

THE BEAST WITHOUT

(WESTERN ERON—DEEP WINTER: DAY XXXIII—MORNING)

~~~~~~~~~

Avall woke to sunlight in his face—which suggested several things at once, some of them contradictory.

One was that *whatever* that had been . . . yesterday (or whenever it had occurred) had in fact killed him and he was now experiencing the bliss Priest-Clan advised one enjoyed in the Overworld before incarnating in Angen again. Except surely if that were the case, his head wouldn't ache so. Or perhaps not *ache* so much as simply feel . . . cracked open, as though all the walls between knowledge, thoughts, and feelings that lay inside it had been ruptured and those things run together like the yolks of so many broken eggs. He certainly seemed to *think* faster now, much more clearly, more like he did when he used the gem. So much so that it frightened him.

The second possibility, as he blinked, made to roll over, and felt smooth bare skin warm against him, was that the several-days' nightmare he'd just endured had all been a preposterous dream, and that this was Strynn beside him awakening to morning in Gem-Hold. Until another blink showed bare stone and a face too angular, a jaw too stubbly, to be his wife's. Rann's, then.

The third, when he looked up, was that it really was the sun.

It was daytime, and someone—it had to be Div—had taken down the tent flap to admit light into the cave. But that wasn't sufficient to account for what he felt on his face. Curious beyond endurance, he scrambled the rest of the way up and peered through the cleft to see his newest companion dressed in half her cold-clothes carefully arranging an array of Avall's signal mirrors to carry sunshine into the recesses of their den.

It was all a joke. A tease.

And because of that, Avall laughed. She saw him, grinned—grinned more when she noted what he wasn't wearing, which occurred at the same time Rann awakened and ran a questing hand up his leg as far as it would go. Avall slapped at him absently, adding a friendly kick for good measure. "Are we alive?" he blurted.

Div regarded him seriously. "I wondered the same thing when I woke up—very happy, by the way, and very . . . satisfied. But yes, I think so. It's—I'm not sure what day, but the sun's out and it's warm again—warm enough to travel, anyway."

Avall yawned, wrinkled his nose, and sniffed appreciatively. She'd cooked while he slept and the fragrance was divine. He wondered what the birkits thought of it—and knew as suddenly. Not much.

All at once he was blushing, as the events of the previous—night? Day? Whenever it had been, and however long ago—came flooding back to him. He slumped against the wall and sat down abruptly. Rann tossed him a pile of fur and fabric, which he began to sort into clothes while Rann also dressed. Like Div, he looked very happy, if more than a little confused. "Food, then talk," Avall told him. Then called the same to Div. "If that's agreeable to you."

Her reply was to join them. "We have to, and I don't mean about what we all did to help each other. I've no regrets about that. And no worries. Nor any guilt. But"—her gaze probed Avall, not accusing, but confused and curious—"that gem of yours—What did it *do?*"

Avall shook his head, impossibly perplexed himself. His mind felt as clear as it ever had, yet at the same time clogged with competing notions. "I'm not sure. I was trying to distract myself from you two, so I tried to think of the birkits next door: all that peace and comfort. I thought it would put me to sleep; hoped that, anyway. Instead, I suddenly *was* the male—or he was me—and we were both incredibly . . . needy. Maybe the birkits picked up what you were doing—you're thinking strong thoughts—instincts, or whatever—when you're doing that. And then I picked it up from them, and the whole thing started . . . piling up back and forth."

Rann frowned as he dared a cup of stew. "But that . . . at the end. I was you, and that's happened before, but there was something . . . different. Not only did I feel like you, but like me, only a more . . . *powerful* me—like everything I experienced was clearer and stronger. To give a crude example, I could feel every part of my body at the same time, with the same intensity, *and* almost the same for you at the same time. It was like you were pouring into me, and I into you, and could feel every point of that contact."

Avall nodded. "What about you, Div?"

She shrugged. "I felt myself—expand. I don't think it was as intense as what you two felt, though I *did* sense the birkits—the queen, anyway. I was certainly there for a moment, with her mate on top of me, biting me, and then *in* me. But I didn't quite feel the same bond, I don't think. Of course I don't know; I wasn't in your heads, as you lads apparently were. Not at any deep level."

Rann gnawed his lip. "Well, Avall and I *are* bond-brothers. We've always been close, so we don't *have* many barriers. Even if what happened to you was the same thing that happened to us, you'd have had to . . . to go farther to reach the same place because you don't know us as well."

Div looked doubtful. "It was wonderful," she conceded at last. "But I'm not sure I ever want to do it again. It scared me beyond anything I've ever done, to come so close to losing my *self*. It was also sharing, granted, but the potential for loss was definitely present."

"I agree," Avall admitted. "But what scares you most? Not being *only* yourself, or having your self laid open like that? Or the . . . power, I guess you could call it, that seems to come with it? Or—"

She shook her head again. "None of those things. What scares me is what came after. At the end, when we broke apart, but were still all there together. That other place, that wasn't this place. That wasn't real, but was *too* real."

"Can that have been . . . the Overworld the Priests are always talking about?" Rann wondered. "The place the King goes when he wears the Masks?"

"Or that comes to him, some might say," Avall countered. "I have no idea."

"We're still avoiding something," Div sighed, setting another stick on the fire. *"What happened at the end? What was that you did?"*

Avall gaped helplessly. "I truly don't know. What was it like for you?"

She closed her eyes as though the memory were too painful—or too sweet. "I was in another place: wild land, and it was warm, but beyond that I don't recall. I wasn't so much *in* you then as watching you, or kind of . . . hanging off you. I know I couldn't control your actions. Anyway, I saw you pick up that stone, and then you wanted to go back—or you felt like you'd lost your balance or something, and you fell back here—and the stone . . . exploded."

"Not so much exploded," Rann corrected, "as simply dissolved into raw power. That place scared me, too," he added. "I wanted us—you, since you were the leader—to come back. I think I called out as much."

"I wonder," Avall mused thoughtfully, "if it could've killed us."

"I don't know," Rann retorted. "It knocked us out, that's for sure! But maybe . . . at the time we were so full of . . . magic, anyway, that it couldn't hurt us. We were partly what it was, or something."

Avall pounded the rock behind him and would've stood up to pace if the ceiling had permitted. "This is impossible!" he spat. "There aren't words to describe what we've just seen and done. What we . . . know. How—"

"That's why we're going to Tir-Eron," Rann reminded him. "It's more important now than ever. Forget clan politics and all that. Someone there needs to *know*!"

Avall grimaced. "I agree. But that's not a *we*, brother. It's an *I*—unless you're feeling better than you were two days ago."

Rann stared him straight in the eye. "I feel fine. I'm with you in this whatever happens. If I die . . . I've just had the most pleasant however-long in my life, and I'll never feel closer to you than I did then. I also know that some things are more important than me. And most important, I know absolutely that there's more to me than this body. I don't know if I'd be me again, but I know that 'I' won't be gone. Death has lost its power over me."

Avall took a deep breath. "But I wouldn't have you anymore and I don't know if I could stand that. But if we do go, promise me one thing: Promise me you'll tell me how you are. Promise me you won't let me push you. Don't be afraid to ask to rest. If I have to, I'll sit you down once a hand and ask you flatly how every part of you is one by one. And you know—now—that I'd know if you're lying."

Div cleared her throat. "I have something to say, too. First, where you go, I go. I . . . have to. You need all the help you can get in the Deep and I can give it to you. But you're right: This is too important to risk on this threadbare trek. You've still got days of woods to cross, never mind the plains. My place is a *day* from here. We could rest there, which we could all use—but in spite of that, my advice to you also is to go on. The weather's favoring us right now. We could make a lot of progress."

"And if we die out there in the cold?"

Avall patted Rann's leg. "If it looks like that's going to happen— Well, for one thing, I think . . . I think the gem would help us. I think it may awaken things in us that'll keep us alive. But I also think it'd make it so that if we—I, anyway—were dying, I could let Strynn know, or Merryn, so that they could find the bodies and carry on . . ."

"What about Eddyn?"

"I'm not sure Eddyn's important anymore."

Div shook her head as if to clear it. "That makes perfect sense and none."

Rann shrugged. "No, he's right: This is bigger than Eddyn and Rrath together. Maybe bigger than anything we know—or, again, maybe nothing.

The fact is, that we can't risk waiting. There are still only a handful of us who know about this thing; three are here, four are back at the hold."

"Where at least two of them may be in serious danger."

"There's no way we could've brought them along," Rann reminded him. "Not a blind man and a pregnant woman. Scary to think about, actually—and I'm not married to one of them."

Div grunted, turned on her heel, and strode back to the mouth of the cave. "We could get a long way before dark," she observed. "We might even make White Bank Station, which is on the main trek from Tir-Eron. If nothing else, we can check what's left of Woodstock and see if any supplies survived there.

"Good idea," Avall agreed, scowling toward the wall between them and the birkits' den.

Something had tickled his mind. A sense of curiosity, of mild disapproval, of . . .

What is it?" Rann asked, eyes narrowed with concern.

Avall shook his head. "I don't know— No, I can't lie about this. I think— *think*—the birkits—one of them—somehow got a sense of what I was thinking just then. Like . . . the weight of clothes on your body when you move. They're there, but you don't notice them unless they're too tight . . ."

It was Div's turn to stare at him. "Were they in your head? Or were you in theirs?"

Avall shrugged again. "Doesn't matter. What matters is that there still seems to be some connection, even without . . . activating the gem." He froze, realizing he'd been moving toward the entrance to their den even as he spoke. "I . . . think I'd better go visit them. I think . . . they want to, or one of them wants to, say . . . good-bye."

Div said nothing as she eased aside for Avall to pass through. A moment later, he'd made his way to the birkits' den. It was only the second time he'd been there. They were curled up in the far corner, dozing—all but the big male, who looked up from where he lolled half-athwart the female, yawned, then fixed Avall with a gaze that showed entirely too much intelligence.

You go?

Avall nodded, started to think *yes*, and realized he'd already done so. Along with it went a confused jumble of images that some passive part of his intellect noted was a combination explanation and excuse, though not rendered in language. Apparently he'd learned—or was learning—to bypass that. The notion appalled him. Without words to rein in thoughts, and thoughts to keep tab on instinct and emotion, it was far too easy to imagine what had happened yesterday recurring.

But that had been good, too, because it had opened the way to that last . . .

event. The thing that had finally decided them that this was bigger than all of them.

He closed his eyes as a tide of thought rolled into him, slipping into his mind through those places where the barriers no longer were, and lodging there.

Den with Us! it demanded. *Hunt with Us! We hunt well together. We can all feed. We can all sleep. We can all mate. We can wait out the cold and welcome the warmth again.*

Avall tried to think a polite refusal. And to think thanks, and found he couldn't without real words. And without intending to think it at all, he also thought, *Never will we hunt birkits again. Not me nor my clan.*

Nor We hunt those of Your den.

And with that, the contact trickled away. Avall blinked, not realizing that he'd gone onto all fours and crawled to within fingers of the big predator's muzzle. He met that green gaze calmly and touched noses with the beast. Its breath was strong but not unpleasant. He reached out and ruffled the fur between its eyes, scratched behind one ear.

Pleasure thrummed through Avall that was almost sexual. The female stirred. A green eye slitted open. Avall felt instincts stir he didn't want awakened, and broke that contact as gently but firmly as he could, then departed.

Rann threw a bundle of gear at him as he reentered their den. And for the next hand he turned his mind to packing, but all that while, a subtle, warm regret rode with him.

As best Avall could tell, it was noon when they finally started out—afoot, for the nonce, the terrain being too rocky and uneven to make skis worthwhile, even on the ice oxen's trail. Still, there was sufficient cover that the snowpack was rarely more than knee deep, save at the entrance to the cave itself, where it came up to Div's waist. The air was cold enough to freeze breath, but it was also very very still, so that what sun made its way through all those tight-woven branches was actually quite warm. Limbs glittered with icicles, where light melted snow and shadows refroze it. The air sang with the soft tinkle of older icicles breaking. For cold, it was quite beautiful. Indeed, Avall almost forgot what they were about, so caught up was he in the glory of the day. Except that he could never forget their agenda entirely, because every time he looked forward he saw Rann.

Div led, to set a pace a normal person could match, not someone with subtly altered perceptions and metabolism such as had driven Avall to exhaust his bond-brother. Rann walked second file ahead of Avall, who went last, keeping a keen eye on Rann lest he show sign of faltering. For himself, it was little work at all, though he still had no idea how he was managing this, save perhaps that the gem was somehow shutting down parts of him he didn't need, or making him process food more efficiently.

In any event, he felt completely tireless, almost warm, in fact, but said nothing about either. As for Rann—he sometimes let his mind drift toward his friend, which was hard to do if there were any distractions. And while once or twice he did get a sense of contact, (at least his breathing wanted to grow more labored), it was so little different from his ordinary perception as not to matter.

And so they passed the midpoint of the afternoon. Once it grew overcast, and snow trickled down, but that did no more than replenish what the sun evaporated. Roughly one hand out, they'd been able to put on their skis and travel that way, following the now-snow-filled valley between higher banks that had once been the trail.

They moved south, toward where Woodstock Station had stood, and once on the even snow of the trail they made good time, skimming along almost without effort, but with mouth-masks raised to shut out the chill air moving around their faces.

The sun was two hands above the horizon when they came in sight of the station.

Raised on a stone embankment at the foot of a hill almost steep enough to be called a mountain, in a curve of a fair-sized river that ought to be tributary to the Ri-Eron, it was easy to see, even in its burned-out state, that the place had already been abandoned. Small pines dotted the buckled pavement of the courtyard, and drifts of leaves and brush lay against what little of the surrounding palisade remained intact—which wasn't much.

Two days of time and half that of snow had quenched the smoke so that not even a thread remained, but a drift of steam still managed to escape the charred remnants of the bathhouse. Avall stared at it in dismay. The spring in the den had been fine, but this would've been even better. At that, it was the best-preserved structure. The rest were reduced to mere stubs of uprights and charred joists; to cracked stone foundations that were testament of extreme heat, and to chimneys that had collapsed on themselves, rendering even their hearths unusable. Trapdoors gaped, showing snow on steps hewn into the rock of the land.

Div studied the sky. "We've a little time. I'd say make a sweep of what you can find belowground. If we find anything to eat, we eat it. The same with anything to drink. But we don't spend much time. We *might* still make White Bank by second moon."

Rann looked at Avall and grinned. "I'll check the spirits cellar," he volunteered. "They like to keep the good stuff surrounded by solid rock."

Avall merely sighed and shook his head.

. . .

Div poured another mug of the truly excellent almond/apple brandy Rann had, against all luck, found exactly where he expected, and licked her lips in anticipation of another long savor of the mellow richness only age could impart. Or age and the subtle scent of woodsmoke that still hung about the place: prisoned odors seasoned with fresh.

She leaned back against the pile of stones that once had marked the well-head and took another healthy swallow, feeling the warmth spread through her. Watching the others. Wondering if she was mad to throw in her lot with them—as though men hadn't driven her to desperate acts before.

Avall was fey: That was clear. But it was a madness that had an origin—beyond a genius he so utterly failed to hide, and a heartbreaking naïveté. That origin was the gem, and she somehow knew her fate was tied up with it as well. Or her escape from this, the third life she'd owned. With that in mind, and a half smile upon her lips, she drained the brandy.

Rann was skulking around the cellars again, feeling lucky after his previous discoveries, which included three more flasks of brandy and two moldy but intact smoked hams, one of which they'd already cut into portions and distributed among themselves. Avall was over at the point, where the palisade bent sharply back above the kink in the river. Rapids frothed below it even now; moving too fast for the snow to ensnare them, especially as a cousin of the spring added its own heat. There'd been a mill of some kind, too; the wheel and bits of machinery still showed. Avall, ever the smith, was plundering those. Looking for brass fittings, he said. Or copper. Or, she supposed, given what he was, silver or gold.

She wished he wouldn't walk so close to the edge. One false move and he'd . . .

She didn't want to think.

It would be her luck, though: hope presented and capriciously yanked away.

She sighed again, took another swig of brandy, and let her eyes drift closed, perplexed at how Rann had managed to get behind her without seeing him emerge. Maybe he'd found a connection between one cellar and another.

A yawn, and she slumped down farther, tugged the fur cloak closer around her face, and licked brandy from her upper lip, wondering why The Eight hadn't seen fit to grant women mustaches.

Rann's tread sounded again—whereupon the light that filtered through closed lids shifted to a darker red, she heard footfalls approaching at a run, and someone was atop her, dragging a knife across her throat.

A knife that caught in a double fold of thick leather and bought her time to shove her attacker away, pile into him, and smash his face with a fist.

Which unshielded her back. Dull agony roared through her as something that had to be an arrow thumped home just above her right hipbone. The impact sprawled her forward, catching her head on a fragment of stone foundation as she fell. Arms and legs went numb. Darkness hovered near. All she could think of was Avall and Rann and the gem, and the future that really was a future that had lain so close and was now, every breath, receding.

Rann emerged blinking from his third journey into the cellar to see someone who was not Avall skirting around the scorched stone behind Div—and then, unbelievably, launch himself atop her. He saw the flash of a knife in that one's hand, but no answering gush of blood, and then the two of them were engaged. But before Div could do more than slam a fist into the man's face, an arrow lodged in her back and she toppled.

Rann froze.

This wasn't happening. It was too . . . remote. There was too much silence, not even grunts, not even breathing. Or else the cold swallowed them all.

Reality asserted. They were under attack! By someone he couldn't see. Who lurked in the bushes. Who fired arrows at . . .

"Avall!" he screamed, lunging up the stairs. Where *was* Avall, anyway? He'd been out on the point . . .

Oh, yes, there he was. No wait, that wasn't him; that was another man. A man with a bow. A man who was about to shoot his best friend!

"Attack!" Rann yelled desperately, pounding across the snow-crusted stones at a dead run made awkward by the spotty ice, the cumbersome furs, and the charred detritus underfoot. On some level he realized that with Div down and Avall under attack, he was vulnerable as well, but the same fey energy that had snared his friend had caught him as securely.

Why wasn't Avall turning? Why was he simply standing there at the apex of the point, ignoring his shouts, letting men draw a bead on him with bows. Two of them now, at least.

"Avall!" he screamed again, louder, running as hard as ever he had in his life. An arrow swished by his head. Another snared the hem of his tunic and lodged there awkwardly. A third speared his sleeve, ripping pain along his arm, but even that didn't matter.

"Avall!"

His friend was heeding him now, was turning . . .

He saw his brother's eyes go wide as he finally found the man drawing a bead on him, then widen farther as they shifted toward Rann, expression shading to concern as Rann stumbled and slid to within three spans of him.

The bowman was distracted, too. "Shoot, damn it!" someone yelled.

Arrows flew in truth.

At Avall.

One missed . . .

One didn't, though neither did it strike flesh.

It caught Avall as he was turning to duck or flee and utterly unbalanced him.

Rann's last image was of Avall poised on that brink, five spans above the river, clamping his hands to his chest and falling . . .

There was no scream.

But there *was* a splash.

And then a blow caught the back of Rann's head, and he was likewise falling.

The world was washed in red, where it ran into Div's eyes. But red was also the color of the pain spreading through her back like melting metal, and the color of the rage bursting through her like that stream below the point. And then she discovered she wasn't dead—quite—and probably ought to move, until spared further decision by a pair of hands that snatched her roughly and rolled her over, jarring the arrow in her back so that agony became the world and only a distant part of her was aware of dark figures looming over her, and rough hands pawing her, oblivious to whether she lived so long as she didn't resist. Nausea pulsed through her at every movement. She thought she groaned. Or retched. One man cowered back, but another cuffed him, and then they were tearing at the lacings of her tunic and exposing her breast—not to rape her, so it appeared, but in search of something . . .

"Not here!" the braver spat.

A movement jostled her head, blurring vision, then clarifying it again. And in that moment, she saw Rann fall as a man leapt from the ruins of the mill and smashed the back of his head with a stick of blackened wood. He collapsed onto himself, and she had no idea what had become of Avall, because the men were at her again, ripping off her clothes as two others seemed to be ripping at Rann's.

Four men, she tallied dully: two on her and two others.

But then one of her assailants was jerked away as though wind had snared a leaf and sent it tumbling. She had the barest sense of great weight thrust upon her, then caught a blur of movement as something large with gray-white fur piled into the man atop her and hurled him to the ground. He screamed, then gurgled, then fell silent, all sound erased by low bestial growls and the hiss of claws ripping cold air.

Div closed her eyes—and suddenly was aflame with anger not her own. She had claws and fangs and there was a dead man beneath her with his throat torn out, and another man running away, snatching at his belt for a dagger he couldn't find, while the other hand clutched a useless bow. He was yelling, but her fury drowned that emotion, and then the two spans between them became one became none, and she was upon him. Part of her—the part that was Div alone—resisted when claws pinned that man down and jaws folded neatly across his neck, jerked once, then deftly turned him over to worry at the juncture of throat and jaw where a gush of liquid red filled the air with a salt-sweet stench that, at this moment, was the sweetest scent in the world, because it was the smell of revenge.

This was revenge, too, wasn't it? *Kin of Our kin; den of Our den; hunter of Our food*—so those unvoiced words seemed to chorus.

The birkits had come. She wondered if she'd be alive to thank them.

And then she *was* them again—one of them—and joining her mate in savaging the other two men who'd instants before looked up from methodically stripping Rann.

A face vanished in a swipe of claws. The other man got up and tried to run, but tripped and winded himself on a piece of equipment from the ruined mill, which flipped him onto his back. He raised his hands to defend himself, but the male landed full upon him, forcing him across the mass of metal. Div heard his spine crack. The man's face went white. He was still alive—from the waist up, though unable to move—when the male ripped all that leather open and began feasting on his liver.

Div was fascinated and repulsed. She was with him, and with the female, and back in herself, while at the same time feeling something of Rann's pain—and a cold blankness that she prayed wasn't Avall.

And then it became too much and darkness cast its cloak upon her.

CHAPTER XLIV:

FORCED TO FLEE

(WESTERN ERON–DEEP WINTER: DAY XXXIII–NEAR SUNSET)

~~~~~~~~

Eddyn was still running.

Uphill. Through the woods. Through knee-deep snow that was impossible going without the skis he'd abandoned before the attack. And *away* from the ruined station where everything was supposed to have been resolved and had instead devolved first into noisy, bloody chaos, then into utter rout.

He hated himself for that running. Running was cowardice and he was no coward. But neither was he a fool, and a half dozen birkits appearing from nowhere in the middle of their attack were not the kinds of odds he'd been conditioned to consider viable when there were no rules save survival and he had no more weapon than a cooking knife. Because they'd not trusted him enough to give him one, and had said they were doing him a favor by not leaving him trussed up in camp.

Which was not what he ought to be thinking when his duty was to ensure his own survival and not wind up some birkit's midwinter feast.

Did anyone else survive? He had no idea. He'd seen a man go down. Seen the birkit that had slain that man turn, look at him, and bound straight toward him.

Which was when he'd started running.

It was still back there; he could hear its steady progress through the snow.

At least Eddyn's longer legs gave him advantage against a creature who, though stronger and heavier than he, was also lower slung.

His goal? Return to camp. Find a weapon. In lieu of that? Find a branch to use as a club—a sharp stick, even—then put a tree at his back and make some kind of stand.

Not be overmassed and die with fangs in a torn throat and his own blood staining the snow.

There *was* a barrier ahead: a piled-stone wall that might once have had some connection to the station. It was a dozen paces away, and higher than his head. If he could get that at his back, he could turn and use main force—

He made it—

Almost.

Just as he reached it, another gray-white shape leapt down from the wall's ragged crest to block further progress.

He glanced back in panic, saw no sign of his pursuer, and tried to puzzle out whether this was the same beast somehow come ahead of him or another that had joined its mate to trap him for a leisurely kill.

That notion did something odd to his brain, and for the briefest moment, he felt remarkably light-headed. A blink, and he found himself staring at the new birkit, wondering how he'd let it get so close, for those green eyes were no more than a span away, and the beast was circling, moving around him in the direction from which he'd come, perhaps to join its fellow.

Its gaze never left him, however; and though he knew such things were unlikely, he thought he could read emotion there. Anger? Perhaps—for the teeth drew back in a snarl. But the beast was backing away as well, as though it had less desire to attack him than to tender a warning.

The other?

There *was* no other. It had fled . . . or left; he could see it ambling down the mountainside toward the station.

Where fresh meat waited.

Its fellow remained, looking at him; not advancing, but not departing either, as though to give its comrade time to secure its escape.

For his part, Eddyn had spotted a broken limb that might make a useful club and was edging that way: right and back. But with every step he took, the beast's lips curled back from those fabled fangs.

And then the air thrummed with a blessedly familiar twang, and an arrow buried itself in the snow fingers to the left of the birkit's nearest foot. The beast snarled and danced away, by which time another bolt had grazed its back close enough to bring blood.

Not the blue bolts the ghost priests used, either; the common brown ones he'd seen over and over in Rrath's stash. A third shaft would've impaled the birkit had the beast not granted him one final snarl and leapt away as the arrow thumped into its shadow.

Eddyn watched it go.

And saw a grim-faced Rrath emerge from behind a clump of laurel upslope and half run, half slide down the grade toward him. Snow clung to every part of his body, which was clad not in the bone-white cloak of the ghost priests, but in the serviceable outdoor furs and leathers he'd worn away from Gem-Hold. His face was flushed, his breath labored, his eyes wide with so many emotions Eddyn couldn't sort them.

What *Eddyn* felt was anger.

He flung himself at Rrath, tumbling him to the ground with his full weight atop the little Priest. A twist of his arms wrenched the bow from his grip and brought it down upon Rrath's neck—not to kill, but to warn.

"You dung!" Eddyn raged. "You could've got us killed! Is it worth it to further your crazy plot? Is *anything* worth dying like this: cold and alone in the snow? This isn't your fight, Eight damn it! It's mine and Avall's, and you don't need to be mucking around in it—you and your friends, who don't care whether either of us survive so long as some Eight-cursed arm of Priest-Clan remains ascendant!"

Rrath tried to buck him off but couldn't. Eddyn saw the failure in his eyes. He saw tears, too: pain, fear, maybe hurt. He didn't know, nor care. All the fury that had simmered inside him since leaving Gem-Hold, that had never been expressed—that whatever drugs Rrath and the rest were forever slipping him kept numbed—had reawakened. And like a fire in oil, it was burning bright indeed.

"I'm not your enemy," Rrath gasped.

"Well, you're sure as Cold not my friend! You've used me to your own ends all the way through this."

"Not anymore."

"What do you mean by that?"

"They're all dead," Rrath breathed, trying with both hands to force the bow away from his throat. "Our only hope of survival is to keep each other alive."

The words took a moment to sink past Eddyn's rage. *"All dead?"* he panted, aghast. "Your . . . friends—*and* the rest? I saw Avall . . ."

Rrath nodded through his fear. "I watched, as they told me to. I saw. The birkits took every . . . attacker. The others were claimed by our . . . allies. I presume they're dead as well."

"And not you?"

"The birkits didn't see me. You ran and they saw you. You shouldn't have done that."

"How do you know so much?"

"Because I've watched them in the clan menagerie and made notes. That's all I can say."

"Bad thing *to* say," Eddyn snapped back, pressing down the bow again. "You have no choice, Rrath. You saved me, and that makes us even. But I'm angry enough to want someone to die, and you've lied to me and used me and—"

"I had no choice," Rrath wailed. "I have oaths I can't break."

"Dung!"

"I'm bending them right now! I should've let the birkit kill you—but for some Eight-cursed reason, I like you. I didn't want that, and not just because you might be useful."

"Prove it."

"What?"

"Anything. Who you are. Who these men are you've delivered us to. How you managed to lead us here through all this empty country."

"I can't say."

"You *will* say!"

"No, I can't! The same . . . the same things that let them control you controls me. I submitted voluntarily, but they did things to me. If I tried to tell you, my brain would stop. If you tried to force me, it might break utterly. I know everything and can tell you nothing. *Nothing*."

"Not even a name?"

"Especially not that. What you call them—ghost priests—that does well enough."

"Then they *are* Priests?"

"I can't say."

"Even silence gives answers."

"Let me up, Eddyn. Please? This accomplishes nothing. Me dead does you no good—especially if others of that kind come around."

"Not *your* kind? *That* kind?"

Rrath gently pushed the bow away and this time Eddyn didn't stop him.

"I don't understand," Eddyn sighed bitterly, as he slumped back on his haunches. "Why didn't those things kill me when they knew they could?"

"Or me," Rrath agreed. "They had to have known I was there, yet they ignored me."

"Because—why?"

Rrath regarded him levelly. "What's the main difference between you and me and our companions?"

Eddyn shook his head. "We're relatively sane, for one thing."

"Are we? We're out here in the middle of nowhere in Deep Winter."

"You know what I mean."

"Think, Eddyn!"

He did—tried to—though the answers he gave himself were increasingly preposterous. Finally he settled on one that seemed safe. "Because we actually know Avall and his group?"

Rrath shook his head. "Not the woman. No one was expecting her."

Another thoughtful pause. "Because we didn't threaten Avall?"

"Didn't *actively* threaten. There's a difference."

Eddyn regarded him warily. "I know you believe they're intelligent, but that sounds like you think they've chosen sides. That's ridiculous!"

"*Is it?* The first shouldn't surprise you. I've mentioned that before, in relation to both birkits and geens. The second—even I have trouble with that because—" He broke off. "This conversation would go better back in camp. At least there's fire there."

"Aren't you concerned about your allies?"

"They won't get any deader. We might."

"And Avall?"

"You saw what happened to him. He won't get any deader either. But anything we do, we have to rearm. Which means the camp."

"You'd give me arms?"

"Your survival increases the odds of mine. Arms increase the odds of both."

Eddyn considered that and gave him a hand up. Together they trudged uphill toward the camp they'd made that afternoon. "You were talking about birkits choosing sides," he prompted.

Rrath nodded glumly. "Which makes no sense. Even if they're intelligent, there's no way they could access enough information about us to decide which side to choose."

Eddyn's gut twitched, as an idea so absurd he knew he was a fool to mention it awoke in his brain and wouldn't stop yelling to be released. "How do *we* know such things?" he dared.

Rrath studied him out of the corner of his eyes. "We're born with some loyalties, or have them ingrained so early we might as well be born with them: loyalty to clan, to craft—"

"Which, with birkits, could translate as loyalty to kind."

"I suppose it could."

"Are we their kind? Any more than Avall is?"

A long thoughtful pause. "We're all hunters. But that didn't stop them before, never mind just now."

"And there's no way we can be the same . . . clan."

"Right."

"So, how else do we form opinions? Or choose sides?"

"From loyalty later on—like the debt I owe you for saving me from the birkit."

"Could Avall and his crew have somehow put these beasts in their debt?"

"You mean so that they . . . killed his killers? That's absurd!"

"Is it?"

Rrath started to shake his head. "If you want to get technical, he spared the one that cornered me. But you're assuming concepts like justice and so on."

"Which would imply they're intelligent, which you already think."

"It would also imply that they can relay events one to another. And you killed the one that attacked me, which was hunting solo—unless it somehow got word to its mate. We know they sometimes hunt together, but how do they communicate? By language, or by . . . something else?"

Eddyn's heart skipped a beat. "You're not saying—"

"I am: There's one form of communication you're overlooking because it's something we'd all overlook, because we don't think of it as real."

Eddyn scowled. And then he knew. "The gem. Surely he didn't . . . summon them through the gem. There'd be no time for them to *get* here, for one thing."

"Not the way we think of time. But something's changed in Avall, we both know that. I don't think we can accept any givens about him now."

"I know he's *dead*! I saw him fall. Over the cliff. It's a sheer drop to ice-cold water. If the fall didn't kill him, the cold will."

"Are you sure?"

"As sure as logic makes me," Eddyn replied carefully. "In any event, close as we are to all that, I'd feel a lot better prowling around down there if I was armed."

Rrath sighed but nodded. They made short work of pillaging their camp for weapons—and healing supplies, lest any of their erstwhile comrades survive. Though what they'd do if they encountered Rann or that stranger-woman who'd been with them, he had no idea—if they weren't dead, too.

"Would they come after us, do you suppose?" Rrath asked Eddyn.

Eddyn shrugged. "I don't know the woman, so she's a wild factor. Rann's not aggressive by nature; but he's very smart, very loyal, and entirely devoted to Avall. So he might. But he didn't see me, and unless you were careless, he didn't see you; and besides, from what you said, he's dead with the rest."

"Another reason we need to go back down there. If they're dead, they're dead; if not—they won't think to look for us if they don't know we're here."

Eddyn nodded.

"We still ought to take medical supplies." Rrath paused, once more surveying the sky. "I don't like the looks of that," he grumbled, pointing to the massive dark cloud banks to the east. "That's coming straight in over the sea and it's cold as the Not-World. It'll pick up a lot of water and be full of snow. We need to be in shelter when it hits."

"Then we need to hurry. I'd say we should give the station a cursory ex-
amination at best, since it's on the way, but spend most of our time looking
for Avall, who's almost certain to be the one with the gem."

"Which means I ought to be able to find him eventually," Rrath broke in.
"But judging by that sky, I'd say that if there're any delays at all, we shelter
in the station cellars, since they're bound to be sturdier than these tents we've
been sleeping in. If you don't mind sleeping with dead men."

"Bodies are shells," Eddyn grunted and rose, armed now with a solid-
looking staff, a bow and quiver, and a good longsword at his hip. Not to
mention the dagger at his belt, for close fighting. With whom or what, he
didn't want to ponder.

Rrath spared another apprehensive glance at the sky. The sun was half a
hand from setting. "We have to hurry," he said. "It's going to be dark soon."

As if in answer, wind howled through the pines. Old snow blew free; new
snow joined it. Eddyn shivered.

"Bodies are shells," Rrath repeated, and started down the hill.

Eddyn followed grimly, wondering, not for the first time, if he was going
to spend his whole life having decisions made for him by people who didn't
know they were doing that. When had Rrath become the dominant person-
ality, anyway?

He shook his head to clear it, but hadn't gone far—the station was not yet
in sight; maybe one shot off—when leaves stirred in a nearby laurel thicket.
Rrath instantly raised his bow, while Eddyn's sword was in his hand before
he thought, but by then, there'd been movement from a second bush as well.
Eddyn froze in his tracks.

By which time he saw a flash of gray-white fur in a third location. "At
least three of them," he whispered. "All between here and there. If we kill
one, the others—"

"I know," Rrath muttered under his breath. "But this doesn't make any
sense. They *should've* let us blunder into ambush, then torn us to shreds."

"You're seeing what you want to see," Eddyn replied, easing forward.

The instant he took his second step, a birkit sauntered out of the laurel,
followed immediately by another, then a third, and a fourth Eddyn had in
nowise detected. The beasts fanned out on the route Eddyn and Rrath
planned to take, but showed no other sign of hostility. It was as though the
creatures were blocking their way. "Go left," he advised, "toward the river,
but not toward the station. See what they do then."

Rrath paused, then nodded, but waited for Eddyn to make the first move.
At deep breath, and he sidled left, which was slightly downhill. Which was
also toward the part of the river they'd need to check in any case, it being
where Avall's body would've washed.

The birkits didn't move.

Another step—

Still no response, though green eyes swiveled to follow their movements.

Another— *Two* more.

Eyes followed.

Three more—and heads turned.

Ten, and the nearest birkit rose lazily and began to pace them, maintaining distance.

A deep breath, and Eddyn dared a step toward that beast.

Lips curled back from fangs; a low rumble issued from the throat. Warning.

He backed up hastily.

The lips fell back into place.

"They really are blocking us!" Eddyn hissed.

"So it would seem," Rrath agreed. "The question now becomes . . . why? Why would they want to protect a half dozen corpses?"

"Guarding prey?"

"Possibly, but they don't really *like* to eat people."

Eddyn swallowed hard. "Maybe they're not all corpses."

"Either answer's as absurd as the other."

Eddyn checked the sky again. The sun was two fingers above the horizon.

"We have to hurry," Rrath reminded him, nodding in that direction.

Eddyn's response was to continue downhill, skirting the knoll that held the station, aiming for the river that kinked around its precipitous flanks.

The birkits shadowed them, not threatening, but maintaining a steady distance, which was all the proof they needed that *something* up in the ruins was worthy of protection.

Not that they could get at it.

"One more try," Eddyn suggested, as they arrived beneath the escarpment's northeast face. Without waiting for Rrath's reply, he darted forward again—and found himself facing at least a dozen birkits. He backed away as quickly, grateful to be alive.

"It won't work," Rrath grumbled. "Not now."

"Then when?"

"They can't stay here forever. And intelligent or not, birkits know enough to get out of weather like we're about to have." A shiver punctuated his remark as a swirl of wind found them—cousin to that already howling through the tops of the surrounding pines. Rrath's eyes were troubled. "We really don't have much time—less than I thought. Wind like this will chill you to death before you know it."

"How *much* time?"

"Maybe a finger—if we're to get back to camp and don't mind fumbling around in the dark."

"What about the station?"

Rrath regarded him levelly. "Do you really think those things are going to let us anywhere near there? I don't know about you, but the idea of fighting for my bed in the middle of a blizzard doesn't appeal to me."

Eddyn suppressed an urge to glare at him. Instead, he started down the final embankment above the riverside. With less cover, the snow was deeper there—waist deep, in places—and he lost his footing once and disappeared beneath it, to reappear on the frozen beach beside it. Another dozen strides put him where he could look out at the river itself, as well as up at the escarpment. A bit of millwork showed there, but that was all.

He could also see the cataract that was the reason it had been built there in the first place. It was mostly frozen now, save close to the nearer bank, where it still flowed freely in a riot of foaming water—possibly because the hot spring at the station kept it clear. In any event, there was a narrow open channel by the nearer bank—

In fact, now he looked, it was exactly where Avall would've fallen. A glance left showed it continuing out of sight around a bend. Which would be the place to look for Avall's body if it had washed up nearby. Eddyn said as much.

Rrath looked at the sky, and sighed. "We're taking a risk," he muttered. "But . . . maybe we'd better know."

Eddyn simply turned and strode toward that outthrust spit of land. Without skis, the going was treacherous, the pace preposterously slow. At least the snow insulated their lower parts against the wind, which truly was bitter in the relatively open gorge.

They didn't find Avall.

But they found something that, to Eddyn's frozen face and fingers, was almost better.

A boathouse, at the point where the current changed. Not large—basically a storage building and rain shelter for boating parties from the station. A few decaying hulls were still about: drawn up during the plague, probably, and never relaunched. Too rotten to use, which was a shame, but a good source of firewood.

The door was locked, but a sturdy shoulder applied twice overcame it. Eddyn and Rrath all but tumbled over each other to get inside. Which revealed a common room three spans square, with a fireplace at the opposite end, and a changing room to either side, each with a garderobe. There were also shutters on the windows, and a fair bit of intact furniture.

Which was good, because the wind was beginning to wail more fiercely.

Rrath lifted a brow in query.

Eddyn snorted. "What? Stay here and be warm but hungry, or return for more supplies?"

It was foolish, but Eddyn was tired of being cold and hungry and under other people's command. He was also strong and brave.

And so he made the necessary trek back to the campsite on the ridge (paced by birkits all the way), retrieved his and Rrath's bedrolls, skis, and all the food he could scrounge, and, by virtue of the extra speed the skis entailed made it back to the shelter just before it was assailed by a wind he doubted he could've faced and continued to advance.

The building shook and rattled. A few shingles tore noisily from the roof, revealing a hole in one corner. But Rrath, bless him, had a fire going by then.

The place was exposed, though—with snow already half up the walls and getting higher. With nothing to do except wait out the storm, Eddyn resigned himself to wondering what in the world to do about the gem and the clan, and how in the world even Rrath could ever find Avall's body.

CHAPTER XLV:

WAKING INTO DEATH

(WESTERN ERON—DEEP WINTER: DAY XXXIII—SUNSET)

~~~~~~~~~~~~

Rann regained consciousness into the worst pain he'd ever experienced, every last grain of it centered in the back of his head. Every movement set stars exploding behind his eyes; every thought brought a new summons to the Dark. A blink was like thunder; a breath like having his brain smote flat upon a forge. He moved anyway—and the pain redoubled. He folded over himself, retched out the contents of his stomach, then moved and retched again. Over and over.

And then another pain found him.

"Avall," he croaked, lunging forward still on hands and knees to where his friend had stood before—

Before . . .

He couldn't face it.

Thought vanished. He looked anyway, let the wash of agony through his skull and down his neck, and the probing of cold on his bare face and torso have their way with him while he thrust his head beyond the precipice down which his friend had fallen, hands resting unnoticed in Avall's footprints.

Nothing . . .

Only the river showed down there; only an endlessly varied froth of cold water framed in ice that had swallowed his friend as surely as winter swallowed summer.

But summer would return. Avall would not.

He didn't have to *think* the word. The whole world *was* the word.
Dead.
His friend of all friends was dead.
Wounded. Bled dry. Killed by the fall. Drowned.
Avall was no more.
Nor was their mission.

Numbly he made his way to his feet, feeling the pain slide down into his spine, then explode into his head again. He reeled. Cold slapped his chest. Somehow he fumbled his garments closed, clumsily, one-handed, wondering dumbly what had happened, and answering his own question.

Someone had ambushed them. Someone who had wanted something they didn't know how to find. And—

He blinked.

Blood was everywhere, and birkit spoor, but no sign of those predators remained. As for their assailants—two bodies he could see, sprawling in pools of gore, white fabric, and twilight—they could've been anyone. Fighting dizziness, he knelt by the nearest, though the man lacked most of his face. He tried not to look there, as he bared the shoulder. But where the clan tattoo should have been was only scar tissue: an ugly red welt as though fire had burned out what had once been imprinted. There was no other insignia, though the fellow was youngish—thirty, maybe—and fit. The heavy winter clothing was of good material and well made. He was also, by the way his face and hands were weathered, a man used to living outdoors and away from civilization.

Rann couldn't bring himself to check the disemboweled one.

All of which investigation lasted maybe a dozen breaths before he recalled that they'd been three, not two and staggered off in search of Div.

The headache—concussion, likely—ambushed him twice in that short distance, threatening him with darkness, so that by the time he found her he'd been reduced to a slow crawl on hands and knees.

Div was sitting up, but staring into space as if dazed, entranced, or drunk. "Div!" he called weakly, then hesitated, having no proof that it was safe to expose himself so blatantly, or that the attack was anywise concluded, despite evidence to the contrary.

She blinked at him, scowled, then fumbled for the closure of her coat. He saw the flash of white skin, proof they'd been treated alike. He started to rise, but the agony in his skull dropped him to his knees as blackness washed over him. When he looked up again, it was to feel her hands on his shoulders drawing him toward her.

"Avall," he groaned without thinking. "These bastards killed Avall!"

Div simply held him. He hugged her back, fiercely, letting go of everything he'd feared to release, giving himself over to endless sobs. "I wish they'd shoot me now," he managed into the fur-fringed leather. "It would hurt less."

"So would freezing," she murmured. "It's getting dark, lad. We have to get a fire going. We have to have food. I . . . have a wound—"

Rann heard the words and yet he didn't. "I won't stay here."

"We must—tonight. We've no choice."

"Avall."

"He *is* gone then?"

Rann nodded bleakly—then stopped as the throb in his skull grew too great. "I saw him fall. The water's wild there. Who knows where he is?"

"Water that's cold enough can keep you alive sometimes," Div cautioned. "I've seen it. When I was with the birkit, I didn't feel him . . . dead."

The words made no sense. Birkits had been here, but—

"We'll search. Tomorrow. It's sunset and a storm's coming on. We'd have maybe half a hand of twilight. We need to spend that making sure *we* survive. Are you aware that the back of your head is bleeding?"

As if it mattered. Nor did he reply to the rest, for to reply was to hope, and hope was not a thing he could rely on. Avall was dead. To think otherwise and be disappointed was more than he could contemplate.

She slapped him. Not hard, but enough to get his attention. The impact sent his head reeling. He retched again. Doubled over, heaving.

"You're hurt," she repeated. "So am I." She shook him. "I've got an arrow in my back, Rann! I can't get it out, not what's left."

"I've never—"

"Neither have I! We'll both learn something. But you have to do it. Without it, I'll die—and you have to have me whichever course we take."

"Whichever?"

"We'll talk about it later! For now, we have to get to shelter, get a fire going. You may need attention yourself. If you go to sleep with a knot like that on your head, you might never wake up! Get hold of yourself."

Rann grunted dumbly and sat up. For the first time he actually looked at Div. Blood soaked her from the hips down, from where a stump of arrow protruded from her lower back. He reached for her, but she shook her head. "Crawl," she mumbled, sounding much wearier than when he'd found her. In the end, he dragged her toward the cellar stairs.

On the way they passed two more bodies. "No clan," he told her, as though mere conversation might keep her alive. "I don't know who they are."

"People who know who *we* are and what we carry," she managed. "Not bandits. The birkits killed them," she added. "I was with one. I— Stop!"

He did, squinting through a haze of pain into the increasing gloom beyond the palisade, as he too sensed a presence. He saw nothing.

Then movement in a shadow. The big male—maybe.

Thoughts rubbed against his own. Less words than . . . impressions, and weak for all that, like a voice heard far away. *You are kin. We will protect You. The other two have gone.*

Other two?

More images flashed into Rann's mind. Faces filtered through the memories of beasts but which he nevertheless recognized. Eddyn and Rrath.

They seek your littermate.

Avall?

He-who-speaks-loud.

Avall.

Div groaned. Tugged at his sleeve. "Did you catch any of that?" he whispered.

"Enough to know they're after Avall. Do you know those men?"

A deep breath. "One's the infamous Eddyn you've heard so much about."

"And . . . the other?"

Rann scowled through double vision. "Rrath. He's a Priest. Innocuous little lad, so we thought. Apparently not. He and Eddyn certainly knew each other, but this would imply that more folks knew."

"*Outside* folk," Div added.

"Maybe so. I—"

He broke off abruptly. Warmth had pulsed through the knot in the back of his head. An odd sensation, too: one he'd never felt before. As though that brief contact with the birkits had broken some dam that had held in his pain, and that slow wash of heat was healing. He reaching back to touch the sticky knot. Pain coursing through him in waves. He closed his eyes—had to.

He had no time for this! No time to be sick, to hurt, to fight to keep himself conscious. He had things that must be done or he'd die. And he didn't want to die. He'd pushed himself to the limit to keep pace with Avall—and past that limit without knowing, as though his body were one thing and his mind another.

Because he'd wanted something badly enough to ignore his body to a higher end.

He had a higher end now, and nothing was different, except there was no Avall.

He had to get hold of himself.

So he could help Div, so he could survive. And most of all, so he could do right for Avall.

The warmth returned, pulsing through his head like fire through straw, and in its wake came a sort of mumbling buzz somewhere between his physical body and his thoughts. The pain abated.

Not vanished. But definitely lessened. He could think more clearly now. He prayed the . . . effect continued.

"Rann?"

Div was watching him through pain-slitted eyes.

"Nothing. I just— All at once I felt better."

Div didn't reply because, quite suddenly, she was unconscious.

Panic froze Rann for an instant, but then he felt the wind shift and blow colder. Snow trickled down: windfall at first, then new flakes from a sky grown leaden all in a finger's time. Somehow he got her down the stairs into the cellar. Wine casks lined two sides, a third was the stairs, but the fourth contained a tiny fireplace built into the foundations of one of the upper ones. Maybe he could find wood; if not, the casks would burn. In any event, he needed light, but there was a cache of candles by the hearth that hadn't entirely melted. Working quickly lest the darkness return, he lit four, arranging them around Div at the foot of the stairs where the light was best. Wind slapped at him and made the candles flicker, but vision was tolerable— barely. As carefully as he could, he stretched her facedown on the floor. More carefully, he cut away her coat, then both layers beneath, and finally her undertunic. Each revealed more sticky red than the one before, and more of the arrow shaft that protruded from the big muscle above her hip. The wound was ragged where they'd moved her carelessly while searching her, but wasn't bleeding as freely as it might. A further check showed the arrowhead near the crest of her hipbone, not quite breaking the skin. Which meant it would hurt like hell to free it—but was doable if he pushed from the back, then pulled from the other side.

Steeling himself, he did that, feeling his gorge rise yet again, grateful he had nothing left to bring up. Grateful, too, that he had something to distract him from thinking about Avall.

He didn't remember the particulars, but suddenly he was holding half an arrow, and blood was flowing freely but in quantities he could manage. He bound the wound with part of a dead man's tunic, then covered her with all the spare bedding they possessed—including Avall's, which he'd shucked upon arriving. That accomplished, he got a fire going with odd lots of wood scavenged from above, where the wind was now howling fiercely and the air was as much white as black, even in the dark. He got a stew warming, too, then checked on Div again. Still unconscious, but she was breathing steadily enough that he risked leaving her to make three more trips topside. The wind was like steel ice, and he had to move hunched over, and at that was blown down once. Still, he managed to drag the three most intact bodies down, closing what remained of the cellar door (charred on one side only), when he'd finished.

And had to sit down abruptly, as dizziness washed over him and the headache threatened to roar to life from its embers. He fought it. It fought back, and for a time darkness claimed him, but eventually he woke into a comfortable gloom, with the pain once more in abeyance.

Taking advantage of that, he made short work of stripping the bodies of their clothing, as much for the warmth that gear could provide as for any mysteries that might be revealed. All three were male, older than he, and fit—as he'd noted earlier—with plenty of signs on their faces and bodies of rigorous outdoor life. None wore jewelry, nor insignia of any kind save identical white cloaks above their furs, and the obliterated clan tattoos. Except one, where, faint but clear, part of what could only be the sigil of Priest-Clan showed.

By the time he'd finished with that one and was sorting through their pouches for food and medicine, the stew was steaming and Div was stirring again.

She woke abruptly, then grimaced with pain as she tried to roll over. Another grimace. A groan. Then: "Help me sit up."

Rann hesitated, then complied, pillowing her against the barrel nearest the fire, with one of their attackers' rolled-up cloaks behind her and another covering everything below the chin. He dipped stew for her, helped her drink.

"Back, or forward?" she demanded.

Rann started, unprepared for such a query when half a hand before she'd been confronting life and death. He closed his eyes, sank against the wall beside her, nursing his stew, wondering whether his headache would stay vanquished, and along with that whether he dared sleep. He was too tired to think, yet dared not avoid it. "With Avall dead, I have to get to Tir-Eron," he said finally. "I have no choice, and I owe it to him. But—"

"What?"

He stared at the bloodstained flagstones. Snow was trickling in through the rents in the trapdoor. "But I owe it to Strynn to tell her what's happened."

"And there're people out here who will kill you."

He nodded again.

"Which way will *they* go?"

"On to Tir-Eron, probably. Their information still exists. The question is, who are these men with whom Eddyn and Rrath allied themselves? Where do they come from, and how many more are there?"

"Wherever they're from," Div replied, "it *has* to be between here and Gem-Hold, or the two you know couldn't have hooked up with them—or survived the blizzard, for that matter. Trouble is, we don't know where this place is or how many of them there are. I—"

"What you're saying," Rann broke in, "is that the risks of going back could be worse than those of continuing on, if we factor out the weather."

"I guess," Div sighed, as she sipped her broth again.

Rann snorted. "You don't look convinced."

She nodded weakly. "That storm out there: I know its type. It'll be worse toward the coast, worse on the plains. If we're lucky, it'll take care of your two enemies if they've gone on, though sense says they'd try to get back here tonight."

We will not let them came a thought unbidden. *They have gone to ground. We will not let them near this place until You are safe away. But We will not kill them unless they force Us.*

Again Rann started, but chose to say nothing—yet.

"You need help," he mumbled. "Rest, at the very least. We'd have to go back for those."

Another shrug. "If things go as they might, we could get back to the birkits' den tomorrow, assuming the storm slacks off a bit. Another day to my hold, and we could go on to Gem from there. It could easily take seven days, but with that storm, we could wait here that long anyway, and the farther away from it we both are, the better. Even if I can't go on, you could send a healer from the hold, or bring one."

"But what about Avall's mission?"

"Sometimes," Div whispered, "you have to think of what is, not what might be."

"Maybe," Rann yawned, snuggling down farther in his cloak.

"Most would say the living should take precedence over the dead."

"Maybe," Rann repeated.

Div didn't reply, because Div was asleep—or unconscious. Rann waited as long as he dared and punched up the fire again, feeding it everything to hand until it was hot as a forge. He was actually sweating when he rolled into his blankets.

The cellar was still warm when he awoke to the distant sounds of birkits yowling warning.

And into life without Avall.

CHAPTER XLVI:

IN THE PIT

(THE PIT—DEEP WINTER: DAY XXXIV—MIDDAY)

~~~~~~~~~~

Kraxxi had lost himself.

—Nearly.

It wasn't difficult, actually, not when the entire world had collapsed around him, the whole of reality narrowed to guilt and cold and snow and ice.

And now to be relatively warm again! Enough to shed the top two layers of clothing, in any event. And to see colors that really *were* colors, not the eternal white of the snow-covered Flat. More than once on that trek across the Flat he'd wanted to cut his own flesh simply to see the hot, red gush of blood.

And then Balmor had died and he'd had enough red and more.

But here, at least, there was green. Not much, and only a little of it held the brightness of new growth, but it was enough to lift his spirits, especially when, now and then, he caught glimpses of tiny red flowers.

Not that winter was gone in any sense—they hadn't even reached the solstice yet. But here at the base of the escarpment that walled the Pit from the Flat, there was less wind and more sunlight. And water that wasn't frozen issuing from the tawny sandstone walls in a thousand variations, from mere trickles that refroze to an icy sheen to massive cataracts three spans wide that poured into basins that became rivers before the sand drank them down once more. There should be a river along the base of the escarpment, but there wasn't. Rather, there was a series, but none lasted more than a shot.

Long enough to drown some forms of life and support a narrow strip of others.

Like here, where the cliffs to his left rose particularly tall (fifty spans, at a guess), and the river at their feet was easily four spans wide. There was grass, too—a belt of it maybe half a shot across. But he could see where the desert began again beyond, to the south. And this time there was no snow, only sun-dried sand.

It was false spring, but it was *like* spring, and that was all that mattered.

Indeed, so light was Kraxxi's heart that for a time he dared remove his boots, and the two pairs of footed leggings beneath them, and stalk along in just his hose. He wished he could remove those as well, but the complex layerings of garments higher up made that inexpedient.

In any event, his toes quickly grew cold, and he sat down on a moss-covered rock and tugged on his boots once more—but compensated by re-moving another layer from his torso. Not too much, and he still had to carry it, which was no relief to legs already protesting mightily, though they were far stronger now than they'd ever been. How many shots had he walked? He had no idea. Too many. Enough to bring him full into the Pit, but not so far as to put him anywhere near its southern rim. That following the escarp-ment also meant he was going out of his way didn't concern him. It would give his father's anger—his hurt, or whatever—longer to cool. It would give him more time in which to become rational.

But it would never give Barrax time enough to love him.

Sighing, Kraxxi stuffed the remnants of the horsemeat he'd roasted over last night's fire between two hunks of the coarse bread he'd con-trived from what was left of Balmor's now-useless oats, and munched it absently. He also studied the sky—clear blue, save at the northwest, where the inevitable thin white clouds reminded him of the ever-present threat of snow. The sun was high—just past noon. And the days *would* be getting longer soon, the sun warmer, as the year moved on toward spring.

Which would bring what?

Not an end to chaos, perhaps, as much as a beginning of another kind. It all depended on what Barrax did with the information Kraxxi intended to relay. And the gods knew he'd pondered that enough already. He would pass on word about the jewel to his father. If Barrax had any sense, he'd real-ize that war with Eron was foolish, and more so now that they had means of instant communication. Maybe only two practitioners, granted. But two could easily become more. Someone had made the first bronze spear after all, or flaked the first arrowhead.

Yes, his mission had clarified since he left War-Hold, and was now less one of reconciliation between two men than one to prevent war between two lands.

Another bite finished the meal. He rose, hoisted his assorted packs, filled his water bag at the nearby stream, and started off again. But now he turned his steps more truly east. Time to forget the Pit and return to the Flat (the escarpment was lowering anyway). Time to start toward Ixti.

In spite of his intentions, it still took Kraxxi a day to find a likely way up to the Flat. Either the snowmelt streams were too deep and wide, or else the rocks were too high or steep for a completely inexperienced climber such as him to assail. He knew the theory of rock climbing, of course—as he knew the theory of many things. But that didn't mean he'd trust himself on what were, in effect, sheer surfaces with minimal handholds at best. Not with *his* head for heights, never mind what a climb would require in the way of physical strength he wasn't sure he possessed. There were no trails up or down, either (not even game trails, which told him something), and he'd almost begun to despair when, a hand after noon, he noted a notch on the rim above him, where the Flat proved not so flat after all. The cliff wall angled there, too: still steep, but such that if he fell he wouldn't necessarily continue straight down to his death. Slipping, sliding, and abrasions were another matter, but ones he was prepared to risk if it meant getting out. If nothing else, he could get his bearings—assuming he could catch sight of the tail end of the Winter Wall, which had been visible, to some degree, almost a third of the way across the Flat.

Before he dared anything, however, Kraxxi replenished his supplies—water, cress, cat-rush roots, and what little horsemeat remained. Hunting hadn't been good in the Pit, and he'd found almost no meat to swell his stores save a few repulsive-looking fish that seemed to have revived with the coming of water into their sun-dried beds.

It was still winter, he reminded himself for the thousandth time, and in fact, snow had drifted down upon him as recently as that morning. It hadn't stuck, however; and now the air, though still crisply chill, was certainly well above freezing.

In spite of that, he wore gloves, as much to save his hands from stone cuts and the odd scorpion as for any other reason. And was soon glad of them, for he fell immediately upon assailing the slope and abraded one knee badly—in spite of four layers of fabric and leather.

That sobered him, so that he decided then and there to take as much time as safety dictated. In any event, if he got no satisfaction up top, he could always come down again.

But not yet.

Slowly, slowly, he progressed up the slope. It was harder going than expected, and he had to scoot sideways more than planned in order to avoid places where the rock face was either too sheer or there were simply no viable rests for hands or feet. The wind was picking up, too, and it wasn't a warm one. By the time he was halfway up, snowflakes were falling. It had grown colder as well, and a few of them were sticking.

But curiosity—and stubbornness—now had him in thrall, and so he continued upward.

Two thirds of the way, he reckoned, then three fourths, and the slope was becoming steeper when he hadn't expected. He was also getting tired, though he had no urge whatever to go back down. Four spans remained at best, but the cliff went almost straight up here, though there were numerous, if precarious, handholds.

There was also a narrow chimney, and it was into this he finally inserted himself, relishing the security of having something at his back to support him as he clawed his way up its opposite face. The wind was less there, too, and he found himself sweating.

He completed the first span before he knew it.

Another—harder—and he'd made halfway, and then, finally, was within an arm's reach of the top.

He misjudged a hold, however (the missing finger joint didn't help) and slid most of the way back down, tearing his knees and shoulders in the process. Almost he cried at that, and not from pain.

But he knew he could do it now: knew the chimney's tricks, and so he tried once more.

One moment his hands tugged at stone, the next, his right was silhouetted against open air, then clamping down on a surface that truly was horizontal. The other followed. He kicked at the stone savagely, pushing with his back as well, and suddenly he was struggling over, to lie winded and drained on the bare, compacted sand of the Flat. Snow tickled his nose, but the ground beneath him was dry, save where spots of crystal ice touched it, darkened it, then evaporated once more.

It felt good just to lie there, and so he did. And slept, though he'd not intended to.

When he awoke, the sun was westering, but a good chunk of daylight remained. The air was clear, too, as was the sky: perfect for what he'd intended, which was to try to locate the Winter Wall.

Slowly he rose and eased away from the cliff, which suddenly made him giddy. Only when he was a full two spans from that edge did he finally turn and assess his surroundings.

He did indeed see mountains—much closer than expected: dark triangular shapes cut out against the eastern sky.

Only . . . those shapes were too regular, weren't they? And what were those odd flapping shapes above them? Surely not hovering birds.

And did he maybe smell smoke? And perhaps, just possibly, hear voices?

Reality shifted, tumbling him to his knees from pure shock. He'd expected one thing and found another and his brain had been slow adapting.

Tents.

He'd stumbled upon a sea of tents!

Still a shot or more away, but tents.

Before he knew it, before reason had a chance to protest, he'd risen to his feet and started toward them.

Soon enough, they gained clarity and color—tan predominated, but brighter hues also showed, especially upon the flags. And he'd recognized some of those flags now: the ensigns of his father's pet cavalry. He *did* smell smoke, too. And could hear voices and the occasional whinny of a horse, or the clang of metal against metal, that could be either sparring or a portable forge.

And then he saw people—in the high-peaked helms his father's army affected. Which also meant they saw him—whereupon a pair of them sheathed the swords they'd been sharpening and rushed toward him.

Their words were odd, however, and it took him a moment to realize it was only Ixtian spoken loud and in a hurry—which shamed him. Surely he hadn't been away that long, and he'd had Tozri to talk to, after all. Or maybe it was simply that he'd heard no voices at all for longer than he dared think.

"Who are you?" the first soldier to reach him demanded.

"Prisoner," he replied shakily, unwilling to give his name.

"From where?"

"From Eron. Escaped from Eron. From War-Hold."

"No one escapes from War-Hold."

"I did."

The soldier looked at him keenly. He had a narrow face, dark eyes. A scar on one cheek that disappeared into a neatly trimmed line of mustache. "Who are you?" he rasped again.

The other man joined him, stared at Kraxxi intently, then grinned a wicked grin. "You don't know who this is?" he laughed.

"I do not," the narrow-faced man replied haughtily.

"Why, what you've got there," the newcomer told him, "is the king's lost son himself: Kraxxi the traitor."

Kraxxi didn't reply.

Nor did he speak when they fed him, let him bathe, and then clapped him in irons.

And even then, he only said one thing: "I will say nothing until I have seen my father."

CHAPTER XLVII:

BACKTRACKING

(WESTERN ERON–DEEP WINTER: DAY XXXV–AFTERNOON)

~~~~~~~~~~~~~

Rann was grateful for shock, he decided—somewhere between Woodstock Station and a certain birkits' den—because it kept him from thinking when his main business was to stay alive. Certainly it had been a blessing that first day after the attack, when he'd awakened to a less-pounding head and a Div who seemed nowhere near as feverish as she ought to be, and whose wounds looked less severe than he recalled. Maybe it was the gem. But she didn't *have* the gem and had only touched it once with her naked blood. But perhaps it left some residue. Or maybe there was something inside it that entered your body when you fed it blood, and that somehow kept you alive because that's what the gem desired. Which meant it might keep Avall alive, too. Div thought he could have survived. Rann didn't see how. And then he'd stopped thinking about it, because if he thought Avall was dead and he turned up alive—well, he could deal with that. But the opposite—he'd forbidden his mind to go there. In any event they had more imminent concerns.

Div slept most of that day, while the storm raged. They argued alternative actions that night, agreed at last on returning to Gem by way of Div's hold as representing both the safest alternative and the greatest good for the greatest number—and emerged the next morning to see blue sky to the west and storm clouds still veiling the east. Whereupon Div decided they might make the birkits' den by nightfall.

The birkits thought so, too—they'd evidently waited out the storm nearby—and in fact acted as both escorts and guides when Rann or Div lost their landmarks and threatened to go awry, for the storm had utterly obliterated the ice oxen's trail. They saw them rarely, but they saw them. And just past dusk they arrived at the den in which they'd sheltered before. Div shared out some of the ham from the station and made the best stew Rann had ever tasted (or maybe he was just hungry), and he changed her bandages and noted steady improvement. And when he found himself sobbing into sleep, she comforted him with her body as much as her wound allowed. Her skin was smoother than Avall's, her flesh as strong and firm. And for all she offered, he was grateful. She was a good woman, was Div. He had no idea how she fit into the life he'd had—before—but he suddenly loathed the notion of existence without her.

And now that Avall was gone— Well, he really was alone, except, maybe, for Merryn and Strynn. Of his own line, none remained, save his rather distant mother, an aunt, and his cousin Lykkon.

The next morning, he bathed in the pool, gave the birkits half the remaining ham, and with the sun still only a third of the way up the sky, he and Div departed.

The wind was in their face, waging war with the water-storm that ravaged the coast, blocking all the western horizon with a wall of gray so deep it was almost black. It stung, and slowed their progress, and put trees down in their path, but they soldiered on. To their surprise, around noon, the big male birkit joined them. Rann felt his thoughts tickling the edges of his mind, and tried to open himself to them.

You go?

Yes.

Not wise!

No.

Why?

No choice.

We will go with You.

You need not. You owe us nothing.

You made a vow. Someone who knows that vow should live.

Which means that Avall's dead?

There is no way to tell—and now We are too far.

Rann pondered this.

Show Us where You would go.

Rann tried to picture Gem-Hold, and with it, what he knew of Div's hold from her descriptions.

There are dens between here and there. We will go with You, show You, help You. We will hunt for each other when We can.

We will, Rann agreed at last. *But if you can—if you have the strength and it will not put you at risk— Could you—one of you—seek . . . my friend?*

When We can, We will.

And that was all. Rann told Div about the conversation but she had little to add, save that she'd heard only ghosts and whispers of their dialogue, and that it would be hard for her to break her wary ways. She didn't want to slay birkits, she conceded. But neither did she have any way of knowing if any she might meet ten years or tenscore shots from here would know of their pledge with these. She didn't want to die presuming on friendship that didn't exist.

Rann agreed, in theory. And decided to raise the topic next time he had the opportunity.

A hand before sunset, they reached Div's hold.

Before the plague, it had been a summer hunting lodge for one of the septs of Div's husband's much-depleted clan. It still had its waist-high stone palisade, its sturdy rough-log walls, and its roof of split-board shingles. Most of the windows were intact, but many had been replaced with oiled leather, and in any case, all were shuttered against the winter. There was also an indoor well, a smokehouse, and an empty stable connected to the main structure.

The interior was somewhat gloomy, courtesy of dark wood walls, but still warm and comfortable, with a weather gate, a large common hall complete with fireplace, and a kitchen behind it. Wings to either side led to four suites, one of which had been rendered unusable by a tree that had fallen atop it. Only one garderobe was functional (Div admitted to being inept at keeping such things in repair), but there was an intact bath—except that one had to heat water on the fire unless one wanted to freeze.

Div mostly lived in the common room, even cooking there. She'd also moved a shut-bed near the fireplace, which he was certain kept her plenty warm at night. Otherwise, there was a wealth of furniture but most of it was run-down and some was moldy. Some had even been used for firewood. The walls were plastered with cured skins of all kinds (including not a few birkits') where they weren't covered with long skeins of drying herbs. These—skins and herbs—Div explained, were how she made her living: trading with assorted treks for whatever she might need, then melting into the woods once more.

Barely had they unloaded their gear in the vestibule, however, when the wind shifted, bringing the storm up from the coast, so that it wasn't safe to go out. Nor did they spend the evening alone, for a pair of unfamiliar birkits showed up a hand after they did (on the vanguard of the storm, in fact), and they had little choice but to admit them. If the beasts had any opinions regarding the hides of their kin scattered about, no comments were forthcoming, and Rann only hoped (when he dared think on those lines at all), that they smelled the smoke with which they were cured instead of their own scent.

Hoped, perhaps, but an unguarded thought evidently reached one.

We die. That one informed him. *Better to die thus, quickly, than of sickness or weakness.*

Quick death, or slow one, the other chimed in. *That is the choice. We choose quick when We choose at all.*

Rann started to reply, but those comments reminded him of Avall: standing on the edge of that cliff, then falling. Freezing was supposed to be painless, drowning an agony. If Avall had been lucky, perhaps he'd been unconscious and it wouldn't have mattered.

Perhaps.

In any event, he and Div ate well that night, went to bed early, slept securely knowing their premises were guarded, and woke before dawn the next day. The sky had cleared to the west, whence the chill wind came. But that way also lay Gem-Hold. There were caves along the way, the birkits said. Rann hoped they were right. Over breakfast, Div surprised him by announcing that she could conclude what little healing she still required in her own hold and would therefore not be accompanying him. He protested, citing the availability of trained healers at Gem-Hold, but in the end had no choice but to accede to her wishes.

With no more excuses for delay, he left shortly after sunrise, entering a world of dark green firs and snow stained pink by light. Rann was full, he was clean, he was strong again. He had trustworthy companions and a goal. But his soul, as he swept doggedly along on his painted skis, was as empty as the cloudless sky.

CHAPTER XLVIII:

IN LYNNZ'S TENT

(THE FLAT—DEEP WINTER: DAY XXXVII—AFTERNOON)

All Kraxxi wanted was sleep.

Which was the one thing they denied him.

The climb had wasted him more than he knew. The food (hot, rich, and endless) had sated him; the bath had relaxed his tired limbs. Clean clothes were a blessed balm, as were soft carpets underfoot and the warmth of countless fires. Relief that he was among people again, and that death in the wild was no longer probable was a salve to his mind.

And to his mission.

If not truly back in Ixti, he was *among* Ixtians now. And his options, formerly infinite, had narrowed to two. Meet his father. Or not. And the likeliest stimulus to *not* was the demon that always haunted him: the red-wristed monster called suicide.

Barrax wasn't in the camp—no surprise. He was back in Ixtianos planning . . . something Kraxxi was reasonably sure he wouldn't like. This was an expeditionary force sent into the Flat for two reasons: to seek a certain renegade prince, and perhaps to extend the tiniest of curious probes into the southern reaches of Eron while it was in effect closed down for the winter. They were slightly less than halfway across the Flat, as far as he could tell, having *finally* glimpsed the Winter Wall on his way to the bathing tent. That was as far as it was safe to go, in this place and season.

Which would've been even more interesting—possibly even alarming—

had he had any sleep. His mind, however, was muddled, where he sprawled at ease in a crimson tent carpeted in green and littered with low chairs and cushions. He occupied the centermost, as comfortable in body as could be. But every time he nodded, one of the four guards stationed at arm's length around him poked him with a padded staff. Or beat a drum loudly for a quarter hand. Or laid ice across his brow. Or made him drink ever-more-potent draughts of distilled kaf.

His body was barely present, certainly no longer anything of which he was much aware. His mind worked on two levels at once: the tense, anxious expectancy wrought by the kaf, and the veil of mental fatigue that wrapped it. He wanted the latter to win, but the kaf high wouldn't let it.

They had to be keeping him awake for a reason.

Part of him knew why, too. The rest increasingly didn't care.

Which *was* the reason.

They were keeping him comfortable because he was who he was, and because they feared Barrax's wrath if they didn't.

They were keeping him awake to break his mind, so that he'd tell them everything they wanted to know about why he, of all people, had returned to a place where he was under sentence of death.

"I want to see my father," he'd demanded. And that was all, though he'd said it—*thought* he had—easily a hundred times. "I will not speak save to him."

There'd been no reply, and no one had raised a hand against him save one man who'd made to cuff him—and been laid flat on the sand for his trouble.

Perhaps he *should* speak. Tell them what he knew. Then maybe they'd let him sleep.

Neither occurred, though they fed him more food and more kaf, and tried not to laugh when trips to the officers' latrine became once-per-hand occasions. Those kept him awake too, but by midafternoon two days after his arrival, he was starting to stagger.

But he didn't talk either, though someone finally arrived with padded manacles they placed on his wrists and ankles, not so tight as to preclude normal ambulation, but rendering it impossible to run or ride.

At dusk, the tent flap opened and a pair of unfamiliar guards strode in: hard-faced young men, and rather tired-looking—a bit dusty around the soles of their elegant, curl-tipped boots, and showing a few smudges here and there. They wore expensive armor, though: mail above padded velvet and leather. Gold-chased helms glittered, and golden studs gleamed on their gauntlets. Sylk cloaks showed colors Kraxxi knew, but he couldn't make out the insignia for the plethora of rippling folds. Their swords sported golden hilts; their waists showed geen-claw daggers. And they carried gold-washed ceremonial spears permitted only to those under royal warrant.

"You are summoned," the one on the right intoned.

Sensing the need for ritual response as much as consciously thinking it, Kraxxi rose—surprised to find that his legs had gone shaky. He paused for breath and composed himself. Let reflex wrap the clamoring kaf-fiend inside him so that, while he moved, it was as though he did so in a fog—as though it was not truly him who walked across the carpet to stand between those two glowering men, then paused as they eased the door-drapes aside and followed him out to where two more men in identical livery waited. They said nothing, merely turned and began marching in a slow, solemn step he had no trouble matching, even in chains. The movement made their cloaks billow, and he finally saw their insignia.

Lord Lynnz. His father's favorite brother-in-law and also his war commander. And maybe the second most powerful man in the kingdom.

Not someone he had any cause to love, for it had been Lynnz who'd found the woman who'd become first the royal concubine and then Azzli's mother. What Lynnz was doing here, Kraxxi didn't want to know—but already did.

He was also in charge of Barrax's torturers.

The trip to Lynnz's tent seemed to take forever, and in fact it was on the opposite side of the camp from where Kraxxi had been lodged. Men stared at him. A few women, too, though Lynnz had never cared for women with martial inclinations. Torches flared in woven-metal cages contrived to keep flame away from fabric. Wind from the north made the banner and pennants snap like whips. Snowflakes danced here and there like frantic stars gone mad before finally dying.

And then they made their way around the impressive curve of the food tent, and found themselves facing Lynnz's portable sanctum.

A veritable palace of fabric it was: a high central section flanked on all four sides by four more, with the corners filled by slightly lower, thinner segments lit from within so that they glowed like melting amber. There was music, too: drum and soft-flute.

Kraxxi stood straighter, trying to remember who he was, why he was here, and what he would and would not say.

Soldiers flanked the entrance. One looked at the fore-rank of his escort and promptly ducked inside to return a moment later. A nod prompted a grunt from Kraxxi's senior guard, who then twisted around as though to grasp his arms, one to a side. Someone nudged him from behind, but he flinched away and started forward on his own free will. The guards fell back. He didn't have to duck to enter the vestibule of his half uncle's tent. Nor did he perform any sort of obeisance upon reaching the inner chamber.

He barely noted the richness—carpets, yellow-sylk hangings disguising the tent's serviceable canvas. Four braziers in shielded holders that warmed the room. Candles for light.

And his half uncle sitting like a king amid a plethora of embroidered cushions upon a makeshift dais. He looked less king than soldier, though. His face was tanned and lined; his fine clothing showed stains of dirt, sand, and wind, and darker spots that could be melting snow. To judge by the piles of armor and outdoor clothing strewn about, he'd clearly just arrived. Kraxxi could smell the hot cider he was drinking as soon as he inhaled.

"Leave us," Lynnz snapped, motioning to the guards. "Four of you shall remain in each outer chamber. None of you have ears," he added, "or I will have them added to my collection."

The guards departed at once. Lynnz looked Kraxxi up and down. "You've grown," he said matter-of-factly. "Not in height as much as in presence. Exile seems to have favored you. Last I saw you, you were clearly a boy. I'm not so certain now."

Kraxxi did not reply.

"Speaking is not a crime."

"I will speak only to my father."

"I am his voice here. I came here from . . . more important things . . . expressly to see you. I won't have that effort wasted."

"I will speak only to my father. Anyone else— He might construe that as treason."

Lynnz glared at him. "You're a fine one to speak of treason!"

"You know only shadows of the truth."

"I know enough! I know you killed your brother. I know you know what that means, both to you and to your father."

Lynnz hadn't offered him a seat, Kraxxi noted. Which was certainly no oversight.

"You don't know why I've returned."

The glare intensified. "I *could* know easily enough. It would be best if you simply told me."

"Suppose I did," Kraxxi challenged, "and Barrax found out what I had told you, and it was something he wouldn't have you know."

"You've learned wordcraft as well, I see," Lynnz snorted. "Perhaps all my men should endure exile in Eron."

"I've never said I was in Eron."

"Indeed, you did. You told the men who found you."

Kraxxi's mind went blank. *Surely he hadn't revealed that! Certainly he'd not intended to.* Or maybe he had. Maybe he'd been more crazed than he thought. He did remember speaking to the men who'd found him—but could no longer recall what he'd told them. Or rather, what he *had* said, had *intended* to say, and *should've* said were jumbled together in his brain, leaving him dangerously numb.

He wavered where he stood. His vision went out of focus. All eloquence fled.

"You've not slept."

"They wouldn't let me."

"That was their order, should you be found and I within a day's ride."

"I'm glad it wasn't a day."

"Ah, my lad, but it was! And more."

Kraxxi's brain spun again. He tried to count meals, drinks, trips to the latrine. Nothing would sit still in his head long enough to be tallied. He hated it, too, and more because, bare moments earlier, he thought he'd been remarkably lucid: at least Lynnz's match in verbal sparring.

"You waste my time, boy!" Lynnz thundered.

"I save your life," Kraxxi retorted, fighting his way back to coherence, "if my father learns you forced knowledge from me that by rights belongs only to him."

"You play dangerous games."

Kraxxi laughed—he couldn't help it. "I seem to have become good at that."

"We're ten days from Ixtianos. Can you go without sleep that long?"

"Can you go without your head a thousandth part that long?" Kraxxi countered. "I can't prove what I have to say is important, but you can't prove it's not."

"I don't play bluffing games with boys!"

"Nor do I," Kraxxi gave back smugly, even as part of him gaped at his own audacity. "I prefer playing them with kings."

"You're a fool!"

"Perhaps," Kraxxi said—and said no more, because blackness suddenly claimed him and he collapsed.

He returned to himself to find something hard beneath him, which proved to be a length of the chain that bound his hands. The light had shifted, too, so that he assumed it was now full dark. He was neither hungry nor thirsty, however, so couldn't have been unconscious long. And his bladder was under control, which was more proof. A brazier smoked near his head, its pungent fumes wafting toward his face. Fumes that had called him back from that darkness he most desired, where there was no pain, no worry, nothing but blessed peace.

The fumes grew thicker, found their way into his sinuses and thence to his brain. Tiny explosions he could almost see ripped away the fog there. He coughed, choked, opened his eyes, and made to prop himself up on his elbow.

The chain wouldn't let him, and the light hurt his eyes, like looking full into the sun. A young woman stood near him, fanning the smoke into his face with a long-handled fan. Her expression was blank—carefully so.

"I know you're awake," Lynnz drawled from the dais, now with a platter of food before him and a steaming pitcher ready to hand. He'd shed another layer of clothing, for the room was hot—else Kraxxi was running a fever.

"I . . . want to see my father . . ." It was all he could think to say. All other sense had vanished—or was cut off from his tongue by the same odd, intense distancing the fumes evoked.

Lynnz stared at Kraxxi a long, cold moment. Kraxxi wasn't sure he didn't see death in those brown eyes. Was there any real reason Lynnz *couldn't* slay him here? He had a death sentence on him, maybe even a price his own half uncle might be willing to claim. Both those things were possible. Or— He'd hinted at things that might upset the balance of power between Ixti and Eron. Might Lynnz himself be after that information? Certainly, he was one step closer to the throne.

And why could part of him think such things through, another not think at all, while a third simply went on repeating endlessly, "I want to see my father . . ."?

Lynnz was clearly losing patience with that, however, and had just called for a guard, when Kraxxi heard a commotion without, followed by low voices and the scuff of boots, the rattle of chains—and a voice, hesitant, but clear, calling out, "Lord Lynnz! Forgive the interruption, but there is something here that may be of interest to you *now*."

Lynnz's glare could've melted metal. "Bring it in!" he growled.

More noise, and the curtain to the outer tent parted. Two more guards strode in, with a third figure held upright between them. Middle height, clad in travel-stained snow gear.

Kraxxi squinted. Something about the proportions. Not a man . . .

And the face: He'd seen it too—

But not this tired, gaunt-eyed, and hollow.

Merryn.

Almost, he called her name, but good sense silenced him.

Nothing stopped her seeing him, however. Nor could anything disguise the blaze of recognition that flashed through her eyes before she managed to suppress it.

It was enough, for Lynnz. "You know this man?" he asked casually.

Merryn didn't answer.

"She knows him," one of the guards supplied. "She was found in the Flat five days north of here, almost dead of scorpion poison. But," he added with a smirking flourish, "she was also wearing this." With that he stepped forward and dropped something into Lynnz's hand. Something that flashed silver and red.

"Well," Lynnz chuckled, when he'd inspected it. "I believe I know someone who has a twin to this ring."

His gaze slid to Kraxxi and stayed there, seemingly forever, unmoving.

Tired as she was—and that was tired indeed—Merryn assessed the situation instantly. These men had found Kraxxi, or Kraxxi had found them, and his homecoming hadn't been to his liking. He was tired—that much was obvious. The rest—

It was amazing what one could pick up when one feigned unconsciousness—and ignorance of the Ixtian language. From what she'd overheard from the men who'd found her all but dead in the snow, she had the dubious pleasure of the company of Lord Lynnz, whom she'd also divined was not only Barrax's war-leader, but also his chief of torturers, the effects of which she suspected she was witnessing.

She also doubted he'd give her and Kraxxi any time in which to speak alone. She wouldn't either, in his position.

But his attention was on Kraxxi now. Calling his bluff. Waiting for him to make the first move.

She moved instead. Her hands were chained, but they'd kept her feet free for riding, on the theory that even should she escape on horseback, a woman with chained hands in the Flat would soon be dead.

Those feet acted now. A kick to the left knocked over a badly placed brazier, spilling coals on the rug and the thin sylk hangings alike. Fire roared up at once, clawing for the ceiling in half a breath. The spinning followthrough took the guard to her right at knee level, knocking him into his fellow behind her, as Merryn twisted back around and rolled forward—which put her in the center of the room.

Lynnz rose at once, reaching for the geen-claw dagger at his hip. Merryn tucked in her arms and head and rolled into his legs as he dived toward her, his face a mask of red-gold fury in the waxing flames. "Fire!" someone yelled. Another cursed in Ixtian. Armor rattled as her erstwhile guards sought to untangle themselves and beat at the fire at once.

Caught off-balance, Lynnz tripped over her and went sprawling, which gave her time to reach Kraxxi, who was looking at her as though she'd grown two heads.

Abruptly they were face-to-face.

"Tell them who I am," she hissed in frantic Eronese. "You they might believe."

"But—"

"They know we know each other. There's no sense in lying about that."

Kraxxi started to reply, but his gaze shifted in response to movement she couldn't see. "I love you," he said frankly. Then yelled at the top of his lungs, "She's cousin to the King of Eron."

Lynnz froze in the act of turning, as Merryn twisted round to watch his face. "You've bought her life," he spat. "You've also bought her a lifetime of pain."

And with that he strode forward, dagger upraised.

But instead of dispatching either of them, as Merryn knew he desired to do, he marched past, stabbed the tent wall on that side, and ripped down.

"Bring them or face the fire," he called over his shoulder. "There's no way to save the tent."

Merryn thought briefly of ending it all right there, simply because she was too tired to consider any alternative. But even as her guards hauled her to her feet, with others hard on their heels intent on Kraxxi, she saw his face again.

"I love you," he mouthed once more, wild-eyed. And then they were herded outside, and for the next hand fire ruled the night.

Lynnz's tent burned to the sand, but no others. Yet in Merryn's heart, and maybe in Kraxxi's—though they separated them at once—hope burned a tiny bit brighter.

CHAPTER XLIX:

SEEING IN THE NIGHT

(ERON: GEM-HOLD-WINTER—DEEP WINTER: DAY XLII—LATE AFTERNOON)

~~~~~~~~~~~~~~~~~

Rann's thighs were burning with fatigue as he made the last long push up the slope toward the notch in the horizon he'd been keyed on for most of the day. He was alone now; the last of his birkit escorts had abandoned him at dawn. Strange that—preposterous, even—yet he'd had no choice but to trust them; not after they'd shown him enough dens to tide him through five days in the wild. True, one of those stony bolt-holes had been impossibly cramped, and he'd had to share it with four alarmingly distrustful beasts (for the bonding was fading quickly and barely existed with any save those he'd first encountered). Still, it was better than the alternative. Once, too, he'd been compelled to push himself to absolute exhaustion—so much so that he'd decided to collapse there in the snow and let the cold take him rather than exert himself so much as another half hand. Whereupon they'd convinced him—with images, urgings, and a threat or two—that salvation lay over the hill. And it had.

So he'd survived, and now Gem-Hold, with all its warmth and security and the friends he had there, beckoned: beyond this final rise.

He hoped.

He wasn't approaching by the trek. The birkits knew other ways: straighter ways. Ways that proved surprisingly easy to navigate on skis— when the weather cooperated. He was certain there were parts of him deep in the bones of his fingers, feet, and cheeks that would never be warm again.

Just as there were places in his heart and soul and mind that would never be the same as they'd been half an eighth ago—or however long it had been since he'd learned about Avall and the gem. Life had been simple then: the routine of the hold, the duties of his craft, the mines, frequent contact with his best friend, getting reacquainted with Strynn. The occasional forays outdoors.

But the things the gem had shown him . . . ! About Avall, whom he now knew ten times better than heretofore. Or Strynn, who was effectively a whole other person. And of course he hadn't known Div, either—or shared minds with what he'd always regarded as dangerous predators.

He still hadn't pondered the full repercussions of any of that, never mind the other things he'd learned: closeness beyond hope with people he loved; communication of a kind with them when they weren't present; communication over longer distances, perhaps, with all the social—and, he hated to say it—martial possibilities that entailed. Reasonable proof that the soul survived the body and could exist independent of it. The fact that birkits had intelligence, which implied that they had souls. The urge to see if a similar bond could be had with other creatures. The need to explore the limits of the bond in general.

And, of course, the negative elements as well. Like the complicating of already complex clan politics, especially as regarded Argen-a and Argen-yr. Like the trouble with Eddyn and whether he still lived, and what would happen if he recovered the gem. Like the enigma of Rrath and the larger puzzle of Priest-Clan, and who those strange men who'd attacked them had been.

That last disturbed him. Priest-Clan must indeed be in shambles to countenance such a thing—assuming it *was* countenanced. On the other hand, their power rested in interceding with The Eight—and if the gem had made that possible on an individual level, then that effectively negated a large reason for a powerful clan's existence. And then there was the smaller matter of whatever had happened back in the cave, when they'd brought back part of the Overworld—and it had somehow changed into Power upon its arrival. That was almost impossible to comprehend, and was surely a matter for Lore to ponder.

With Smith's grace, of course.

Never mind the fact that a great deal more occurred outside during the Deep than most folks imagined; that there *was* human activity out there, some of it rather suspect. And the fact that he had himself faced the Deep and with extraordinary assistance, under extraordinary circumstances, survived.

All at once the enormity of it crashed down on him and sent his mind reeling—or perhaps that was a blast of colder wind that might be The Eight's way of reminding him that in Deep Winter it was never wise to tarry.

Sighing, he moved on, feeling his muscles relax into their familiar, weary routine, only to halt again at the top of the slope, as relief beyond all knowing welled up in him. Flushed and breathless, he slumped against a fir tree, savoring the view.

He'd made it! Had emerged on the southern rim of the vale that embraced Gem-Hold. He could see that enormous structure now; more importantly he could see *people*! Fur-clad men and women clearing the side court one last time before sunset, when the night wind would freeze stray water solid. Others scurried over porches, sweeping snow from floors and seats and railings; or chipped away at the worst of the icicles; or oversaw the roof mirrors that kept the weight of snow from crushing even those well-engineered panes.

It wasn't home, but he felt insanely glad to see it. And so he lingered, glorying in the vista. Blue sky (no clouds at the moment); the black glower of the mountain. The white of the hold. The red banners that flew here and there, and the long, multicolored pennant atop that was the hold's official heraldry. Green trees daring to show needles even in winter, and the dark spikes of trunks.

Absently, he sought the other roads that met there. The trek, over to the right, was kept open half a shot. North Trail was cleared to some degree once every eight days, since it was their primary hunting route and led to a small emergency hold half a day farther north. South Trail opened up— he had to stand again to check—maybe a hundred strides to the left. The birkits' route was one no one had ever used.

The birkits . . .

They'd long since gone—or *it* had. He was never certain how many accompanied him, though he'd never seen more than one at any given time since leaving Div's hold. Males, all—expendable, he assumed, like himself, save for the siring of offspring.

Which, he reflected, was both the joy and sorrow of Div. She'd never conceive, so he had no need to worry about fatherhood taking him unawares. But suppose he *wanted* a child by her? That could never happen. And what of the Law, that said he must be named father of three?

All of which, he conceded, was premature, given that he had no idea how he truly felt about her save that he was comfortable in her presence. But some of that, he suspected, was because his mother had been in service most of his adolescence, so that Div, in some sense, filled that function. And partner. Confidante. Maybe even sister.

Lover.

It was something he had to discuss with Strynn, because there was no one else to whom he dared reveal such personal things. No one living.

And Strynn was in Gem-Hold—and Gem-Hold was less than a finger away. He'd already started downslope when a realization struck him he wished he'd considered earlier.

Did Strynn know that Avall was dead? They had a link of some kind. It lessened with distance, but emotions strengthened it in turn. Would she have known when that link dissolved?

He hadn't. And he and Avall had been closer than Avall and Strynn.

All at once Rann was skiing as fast as he ever had in his life. And even as he skimmed across the snow, some mysterious store of strength that had sustained him through days uncounted drained away, so that for one brief awful instant he truly did think he was dying.

Strynn was in her common room working on the inscription for the new sword of state, with Kylin playing softly on his lap harp, when a knock sounded on the door. She always kept it locked now, not only to ensure the privacy of her crafting, but also from an unsourced fear that had come upon her shortly after word of Avall's disappearance had become common knowledge. Avall's and Rann's, she amended, whose departure had initially gone unnoticed in the minor, if localized, furor over Eddyn and Rrath's defection. She'd had a bit of time then. No one wanted to be around two grown men with raging flux, when the pox had spread from South Wing to Middle and even apprentice healers looked harried. The upshot was that she'd managed to keep matters vague until several days had elapsed.

But Eddyn and Rrath had contrived no such cover; they'd simply vanished, leaving an angry, confused, injured Kylin in their wake—and a Strynn who'd found herself answering questions to which she had no good replies, because it was known that neither she nor Avall had any love for Eddyn. The local Sub–Clan-Chief had questioned her first—the one from Argen-yr—then the Subchief from Smithcraft, then the one from her own Clan Ferr. Between them, she'd managed to account thrice over for every instant of her time since anyone recalled having seen Eddyn to the date his absence was finally noted. Therefore she couldn't have murdered him.

All of which worked fine—until the Subchief of Priest-Clan made a polite call and asked rather more probing questions that hinted that she *might* also know something about the gem. And finally the Hold-Warden herself, who, it evolved, cared less than nothing about clan politics, and more than she reasonably ought about why four men had thought they had a wraith's chance of surviving the Deep.

No one was saying anything, but there were mutterings.

And now this knock . . .

And another on its heels, this one rather more frantic.

She flung a polishing cloth across the sword, inverted her drawing pad, and rose, smoothing her robe across her bulging stomach. "Who is it?" she called carefully.

"Messenger," a muffled voice replied.

"From whom?"

Something brushed her mind: a terrible urgency that might have been her own or might not, but that carried with it a distinct sense of familiarity along with a fervent desperation so fierce she recoiled from it instinctively.

"Please—"

She threw the bolt, stepping back to admit a cloaked and hooded figure whose bulk hinted of layer upon layer of undergear. He stumbled as he entered, perhaps from weariness, possibly from relief at seeing her—or maybe in simple urgency to close the door behind him and lock it.

"Sorry," he began, as he stood dripping on the vestibule. "I'm not thinking very well today . . ."

Relief washed over her: her own, and— *Rann's.*

"Rann?" she breathed, as though that confirmed his existence. But it *was* Rann, his face burned dark by cold and wind, and with a wash of stubble on cheeks that had grown gaunt since last she'd seen him. His eyes were feverishly bright, and he moved like someone who had no idea what his next act would be but knew there had to be one.

"Sit," she commanded, dragging him toward the chair that faced hers, only then realizing how hot the room must feel to someone so thickly arrayed. She propped him against the wall instead, and divested him of an odd white cloak, the top two layers of fur tunics, and one pair of leather leggings. He looked fairly normal once she acquired some sense of his shape—except that he still wore more clothes than most folks did indoors, which meant he was thin indeed.

"Strynn . . ." he began more than once, but she shushed him each time with a terse, "Not yet."

Only when he was seated, with his boots off and his feet nestled in the thick carpet, a mug of steaming cider in one hand, and the cold meats that were her untouched lunch at the other, did she finally address her flood of queries.

"What's happened?" she dared, giving vent to what she'd been trying *not* to think since Rann's arrival; what she would never know if he didn't speak, what would change everything if he did. And through it all, Kylin continued playing.

.   .   .

Words tumbled over themselves in Rann's brain, so many none made sense—just as it made no sense the way all strength had drained from him as he'd made his way here. Which had left a feral alertness that had suggested stealth might be in order, that reminded him, as he'd reminded himself countless times, that his presence had surely been marked by now, and the ruse of illness no longer mattered.

Still, he'd veered off at the last possible moment and made his way to the door by which he and Avall had departed, and so come at Argen's chambers that way, minus his skis and pack, but too tired and numb of mind to remove the rest of his gear. At that, he'd had to wait trembling in a little-used garderobe-vestibule while Argen's common hall cleared. Almost he'd gone to sleep there, but finally old man Morzin had ambled off on whatever nameless errand consumed men his age who actually preferred to remain at winter holds, and he'd managed to make that final dash to Avall's suite, hoping against hope Strynn was in residence.

And here he was, with too much to say, and so much of it wonderful and so much of it impossibly dire, that he could do nothing but sit and stare while hot metal warmed his hands and the fumes of potent spiced cider spun through his nostrils like the headiest wine.

And music. There was music, which meant—

"Kylin," he sighed, as his gaze finally found the unobtrusive figure. "Does—"

"He knows what we know," Strynn finished. "He's suffered because of all this. He's— You could say he's under my protection."

The harper cleared his throat. "Lady, if you would rather—"

"You can stay," Rann broke in wearily. "Don't think I don't like you. It's just that—right now—"

"I can hold my tongue," Kylin rasped. "I've learned such things the hard way."

The bitterness startled Rann. Clearly he was not the only one with a story in need of telling. He took a long draught of cider, watching the vapors curl as though entranced. "Strynn," he began—and then lost himself in contemplation of that name and of the woman herself. *Avall's wife. His friend. The most beautiful woman of her time,* who now sat before him looking tired and drained when she should glow with health and anticipation. But there were hard lines on her mouth and brow where she'd clinched them in concentration if not outright worry.

And the feelings that poured off her like heat from a forge: excitement and concern and naked fear. All masked by a patient silence he could neither have conjured nor endured.

"Avall's not here," he heard himself say. "That is, he . . . couldn't come. I returned because I had a choice: forward or back, and back made more sense. I didn't abandon him, if that's what you're thinking, but he— Well, he just couldn't come."

Strynn laid a hand on his. "I've waited this long, I can wait longer. But tell me everything!" The grip strengthened. "Start where you will, Rann— but *tell* me!"

He did. In what order he could, sparing nothing: not himself, not Avall, not Div. When he came to the coupling in the cave, he hesitated, then related that as well, stressing that it wasn't Avall's fault but his and Div's; and that the gem had played a significant part.

"I've shared him before," Strynn murmured. "Sometimes comfort means more than convention."

Rann nodded sagely, wondering if that wasn't guilt that had washed against his mind just then; if perhaps her gaze had drifted ever so slightly toward Kylin.

And still he hesitated. He was coming up on *that* part now, and didn't know how to tell her what he feared, or if he could name it himself. Still, the dam was breached; the words would take him there.

And then he *was* there, letting the words have their way, supply their own detail in ever-increasing clarity.

"*. . . and then he fell.*"

He'd said it now. Possibility had become fact, as dread had become pain for poor Strynn, who sat there as if she'd taken some impossibly forceful blow on the tourney field and been completely winded.

"Dead?" Kylin dared at last what they would not.

Rann shrugged helplessly. "I don't know. He fell into very cold water. Sometimes that can save you, but the cold would've claimed him, surely."

Strynn's eyes narrowed. "But *you* believe he's alive? Yet you're here—and you'd wouldn't be if you thought—"

Another shrug. "I don't *know*! I don't see how he could be, but . . . with the closeness we'd had since sharing through the gem . . . I think I'd have known. I think it would be as though part of my brain . . . fell off, or was walled closed, or something."

Strynn gnawed her lip.

"I have another reason to hope," Rann choked, fearing to say even that, lest she counter with some objection that might dash it.

"What?"

"That— Oh, I don't *know*, Strynn!" he burst out. "This is all so strange, so impossible, so completely unbelievable."

"What?" she repeated more urgently. And for the first time, Rann heard a hard edge in her voice.

"It's just that—I think the gem has something in it, or to it, or around it—some magic—that . . . takes care of those who own it. It gave Avall extra stamina. It either sustained me while I tried to keep up with him, or else it drained off me and made me keep going to keep Avall alive. I heal better; I can endure more. I—" He broke off, groping for words.

She puffed her cheeks. "Rann," she began carefully. "I've got something to tell you that could have a major bearing on all this."

A brow quirked up. "Yes?"

Wordlessly, she reached to her collar and drew a length of fine silver chain from within her bosom. It glittered in the waning sunlight, but what glittered more brightly was that which was set in a silver frame at one end.

A gem exactly like the one Avall had found, only smaller.

Rann's breath caught as she slipped it over her head and extended it to him. He touched it tentatively, felt . . . something he couldn't identify, except perhaps a vague sense of familiarity. He looked up at Strynn. She was—almost—grinning.

"The night after you left I couldn't sleep, which I'm sure doesn't surprise you. I went wandering: one of the advantages of being pregnant, you know. Anyway, to cut to the heart, I found myself down in the mines—not the place where I sort rocks with the other women, I mean the actual mines: Argen's vein. I'd never been there since the day Avall first showed it to me, but nobody questioned my presence, though I'm sure someone with this"—she patted her distended abdomen—"would be *somewhat* rare down there. In any event, I wasn't wearing anything particularly fancy, and it was . . . it was as though something actually made me crawl into that vein where Avall found the gem. Again, I had the right, but—I don't know, Rann, it was as though something was compelling me—maybe just the fact that I wanted a gem like that for the sword, so as to match what Avall was putting on the helm. It doesn't really matter. The point is, I managed to get my very awkward self in there—with no one noticing. And I just wriggled farther and farther in—I'd told myself I'd stop if it looked like I was getting stuck. I didn't. Eventually, I made it to the end of the tunnel. And found this stone: just stuck there in the end wall, behind some loose earth I scraped away."

Rann's eyes were huge. "Does anyone know?"

Strynn shook her head. "Not that I'm aware of, though I've been very anxious. Still, the Mine-Master was more concerned with my clothes and condition than anything I'd found."

"Thank The Eight," Rann breathed. He paused for a sip of cider, then went on. "I take it you've worked with it?"

She nodded. "I've primed it with blood mostly to help me work—but—"

"Did you ever use it to try to contact anyone?" Rann broke in urgently. "Avall, in particular?"

Another nod. "I tried. I tried a lot, but . . . nothing. No, that's not really true. But this stone's smaller. And I could never relax. Maybe it was just that I never really believed, even though he told me it worked."

Rann shook his head, full at once with hope and despair. "Eight damn it!" he spat finally. "There's just so much we don't know about all this. There have to be rules, Strynn, there *have* to be! But I'm damned if I can figure any of them out. I—"

"Which is the point I was aiming toward when I first mentioned it," Strynn broke in. "Since I primed the stone with blood, I've had almost no trouble with any of the problems pregnant women have. No sickness, no swelling. And I'm more aware of the child, or it is of me, but I try not to use it too much because I don't know what its effect on the baby might be."

Rann's heart flip-flopped. "So you think," he began hopefully, "that the gem might *be* having an effect on your health?"

"I think so."

Rann masked concern with another drink of cider. "It's one thing to heal a wound quickly or soothe a woman's stomach. It's another to save a man who's drowning—or freezing—or both."

"You did look for the body, didn't you?" Kylin inquired softly, though his fingers never stopped moving on the harp strings.

"Not as much as I'd like," Rann admitted. "There was no easy way down to the river from where we were. I hurt like the Not-God; Div was injured; and we didn't know who'd attacked us, how many there were, or if they'd return. And when we did know, it was night and a storm was upon us. I'm sorry, Strynn," he went on. "But I was almost certain—then—that he was dead. I *wasn't* dead, and neither was Div. Returning was the only realistic choice if anyone was going to learn the truth about any of this. And the river was frozen over farther down."

"These attackers," Kylin queried again. "They were—"

"Priest-Clan, I suspect: some kind of radical sect—which is one more thing the clan and the King need to know about. But it's worse than that, Strynn, it wasn't just Priest-Clan, it was them plus—"

"—Rrath and Eddyn," Kylin finished for him. "It had to be. They left not long after you did. They had to have had the same goal."

"The gem," Strynn breathed. "That's what Kylin and I suspect. And I thank The Eight every day that they don't know I have another."

"I want Eddyn dead," Kylin said abruptly, but with as much iron anger in his voice as Rann had ever heard.

"But you think he went on?" Strynn persisted, ignoring the musician.

"That's what the birkits said. Which means they might've been caught in the storm."

"Which means they might also have the gem and be in Tir-Eron by now."

"Somehow I don't think so."

Strynn—almost—glared at him. "How can you know that, Rann? There's too much here we don't know, too much being taken as truth that rests on the shakiest speculation."

Rann wouldn't look at her. She was going where he'd feared she would. Undermining his hope. She didn't know it, but she was. He couldn't let her. A deep breath. Then: "Strynn, I'm not sure I should ask this, or suggest this, or even *think* this, but . . . if you're willing, you and I could try to link through your gem and . . . use it to look for Avall."

Strynn closed her eyes. For a moment Rann thought she'd had some kind of attack. He started to rise, but a warning "No" from Kylin stopped him. He wondered how the harper knew he'd moved, if he was blind. "Air tells me things," Kylin murmured, as though Rann had asked it aloud—which maybe he effectively had, since his mind seemed to send forth his stronger thoughts fairly clearly.

He'd started to query that when Strynn opened her eyes again. "I don't want to do it because it scares me as itself, and it scares me because of what I might find. But not knowing, maybe forever: That scares me even more."

"Now?"

She shook her head. "You have to rest. I have to think. At midnight. He should be asleep then, if he lives. There should be less distracting him."

"I defer to you in this," Rann sighed through a yawn.

Strynn rose decisively. "You bathe. You need it. Help yourself to what you want of Avall's clothes, since it's better no one knows you're here. I'll order more food—I'm a pregnant woman, remember? And then you'll sleep, and at midnight I'll wake you."

Rann suddenly realized that whatever residual strength had sustained him through his conversation was ebbing away. He rose uneasily and staggered toward the bath. Kylin watched him go with sightless eyes that seemed to see more than his own.

Midnight found Strynn in the bed she and her husband had shared, lying beside his best friend. Rann had managed to bathe himself, and she'd managed to get a good hunk of red meat and cheese down him, with bread and oranges. And cider but no wine, because wine made one dull. She offered cauf, but he refused, fearing the effect any stimulant might have on his confused metabolism.

And then they could delay no longer. A brief discussion had concluded with an agreement that Kylin should not only stay with them "just in case," but that he should also play for them, because his music would help them relax.

So it was that Strynn retrieved her day-knife from the bedside table and laid it between her and Rann, who'd changed into a long night robe. She wore one as well, though day clothes would've sufficed—but again, it helped them relax.

Finally, Strynn reached into the neck of her robe and drew out the second gem—*her* gem—as uniquely hers as anything of that ilk could be. It was smaller than Avall's, and Rann wondered if that might affect its strength or other properties. Still, there was no way to know without trying, and so he held his breath while Strynn sliced her palm and laid it on the gem, then passed the blade to him.

He had to force himself to reciprocate, for all he was inured to pain. But this really was the final threshold. A finger from now he might know in truth whether Avall lived. And if he did, there was cause to continue living himself. If not—there was still—maybe—Div.

Except that she could never be solace for the loss of his bond-brother.

Closing his eyes, he drew the knife along his palm. It took three passes before he felt the trickle of blood and opened his eyes. Red showed there. Sparing an anxious smile for Strynn, he closed his eyes again and twined his fingers with hers.

A deep breath, and he let go.

It was the same as before, yet not the same, as lime tastes like lemon yet different. He sensed Strynn's mind like an open room he was welcome to enter, while at the same time felt the walls of his own mind dissolving. Neither crossed into the other's space; rather, they united in the not-place between, and of one unspoken—or sensed—accord, built an image of Avall in the place where their two selves met and mingled but never entirely joined.

Except in their love for him, their desire for him, their concern for him, and their insatiable need to know what had become of her husband, their lover, and his best friend.

And then reality twitched and vanished, save for Kylin's music that supported them as they rode into the nothingness of the Overworld sky.

Avall? they chorused together.

Avall! Avall! Avall!

There was no direction to define them, but memory supplied a surrogate, a template for the real places that lay beneath the not-place of the Overworld. They went that way, thought-of-one-thought, and found . . .

Nothing.

Nothing at all, save a great cold emptiness.

Nothing at all of Avall.

Almost they retreated in despair, but that disappointment woke anger in Rann, and he fed that anger to Strynn all unknowing. It woke another, more primal anger, too: that of Strynn's unborn child. And suddenly they were all three stronger.

Avall, Rann shouted in the not-place.

Avall, Avall, Avall.

And this time . . .

No words, no names, no memory; not even dreams. But a sense of a *self* that answered to that name. And a sense of incredible, bone-chilling cold, that went beyond anything Rann had experienced, even in the worst of the Deep.

But it *was* a feeling. Not an emptiness. Not . . . death.

"He lives!" Rann gasped under his breath.

"Yes," Strynn choked through a rising tide of sobs, "and wherever he is, he's cold beyond all knowing."

Rann's reply was an uncontrolled shiver.

The gem forgotten, they reached toward each other in an embrace that held nothing of sex but everything of closeness, relief, and comfort.

Kylin sensed it, too, and left off harping to join them, curled up in a green-velvet knot on Strynn's free side, with his head pillowed against her shoulder and one hand stroking her hair.

And locked in that knot of hope, they talked and wept until morning.

Epilogue: Flotsam

(Eron: the Ri-Eron—Day XLIII—evening)

~~~~~~~~~~

He was dead.

Or was he?

His blood still flowed—at some primal, minimal level.

His heart still beat—a few dozen times a hand.

He didn't breathe, yet air still found his blood to keep his brain alive.

That brain still conjured images, though slow as the birth of stars. His soul still tethered there, suspended, yet primed to flee.

Sometimes that soul hovered near—assuring itself he lived. Other times it looked down with bodiless eyes to where his corporeal aspect swept along underwater. Under *ice*, often enough, in the middle current of the Ri-Eron, that never, even in the heart of Deep Winter, froze solid.

Why did he not die? That which should've been beyond wondering wondered.

Because part of him was warm: a point of heat that was not heat as the Craft-Chief of Lore would have described it. A point that lay fixed by soaked clothing hard against his chest, where it warmed him enough for life.

Heat from that place he'd visited but once.

Heat from the Overworld.

From The Eight, perhaps—if they existed.

How long he had drifted, he had no idea. If he numbered time, he would think. If he thought, he would worry. About the cold. About the great fish that haunted the Ri-Eron, from which even The Eight might not protect him if they chose to feed. About the quest unfinished. About Strynn and Rann and Merryn—

But he was dead, and therefore free.

Or was he?

The cold had grown more insidious, was passing beyond numbness to pain.

Water lapped insistently at the gates of his nose.

His lungs hurt.

The warmth receded.

He tried to follow and could not. Yet in that following he learned one thing. There was something *in* him that was not *of* him, that maintained the link between life and body.

But it was breaking now . . .

Breaking . . . .

Splintering . . .

Fraying away . . .

Gone!

He was cold as he had never been cold.

He was drowning.

He, who had thought himself dead, was dying in truth.

Desperate, he flailed upward. Motion launched fires into limbs that hadn't moved in time uncounted.

He also *wished*.

No focused thought, simply an all-encompassing desire to be able to breathe again—and be warm again.

And then he simply *was not*.

When he *was* again, he was lying, wet and gasping, by a fire.